AGENTS, AGREEMENTS AND AGGRAVATIONS

AGENTS, AGREEMENTS AND AGGRAVATIONS

IN HER PARANORMAL MAJESTY'S SECRET SERVICE™
BOOK THREE

MICHAEL ANDERLE

DISRUPTIVE IMAGINATION

AGENTS, AGREEMENTS, & AGGRAVATIONS
TEAM

Thanks to the JIT Readers

Deb Mader
Debi Sateren
Diane L. Smith
Dorothy Lloyd
Jackey Hankard-Brodie
Kathleen Fettig
Kerry Mortimer
Larry Omans
Micky Cocker
Veronica Stephan-Miller

If I've missed anyone, please let me know!

Editor
The Skyhunter Editing Team

LMBPN Publishing
PMB 196, 2540 South Maryland Pkwy
Las Vegas, NV 89109

First US Edition, May 2020
Version 1.02, December 2020
ebook ISBN: 978-1-64202-936-9
Print ISBN: 978-1-64202-937-6

DEDICATION

To Family, Friends and
Those Who Love
to Read.
May We All Enjoy Grace
to Live the Life We Are
Called.

— Michael

GENEVIEVE KING'S UK TO US TRAVEL GUIDE

An insight into how the Americans butcher the queen's English

UK (Correct) — *US (Wrong)*

- **Aluminium (*ah-luh-min-ee-um*)** — Aluminum (*ah-loo-min-uhm*…WHAT?)
- **American Football** — *Football*
- **Bathroom / Toilet / Loo** — *Restroom*
- **Biscuit** — *Cookie*
- **Bonnet (Car)** — *Hood*
- **Broadsheet** — *Newspaper*
- **Car Park** — *Parking Lot*
- **Chips** — *French Fries*
- **Crisps** — *Potato Chips*
- **Dual carriageway** — *Highway, freeway*
- **Dummy** — *Pacifier*
- **Duvet** — *Blanket (yes there are duvets, but not in this story)*
- **Extension lead** — *Extension cord*
- **Flat** — *Apartment*
- **Football** — *Soccer*
- **Garden** — *Yard*
- **Holiday** — *Vacation*
- **Ice lolly** — *Popsicle*
- **Jumper** — *Sweater*
- **Knickers** — *Panties*
- **Lift** — *Elevator*
- **Lorry** — *Truck*
- **Mad** — *Insane / Crazy*
- **Motorway** — *Highway*
- **Mummy** — *Mommy*
- **Nappy** — *Diaper*
- **Number Plate** — *License Plate*

- **Oregano (*or-i-gah-no*)** — *Oregano (or-eh-ga-no...I mean, come on!)*
- **Pants** — *Underwear*
- **Pavement** — *Sidewalk*
- **Peckish** — *Hungry*
- **Police / Bobbies / Pigs / Boys in Blue** — *Cops / Police*
- **Potato (*poh-tah-to*)** — *Potato (pah-tay-to)*
- **Rubbish** — *Trash*
- **Shop** — *Store*
- **Sofa** — *Couch*
- **Sweets** — *Candy*
- **Torch** — *Flashlight*
- **Tomato (*toh-mah-to*)** — *Tomato (tah-may-to)*
- **Trainers** — *Sneakers*
- **Trollied** — *Drunk/plastered*
- **Trousers** — *Pants*
- **Tube** — *Subway*
- **Waistcoat** — *Vest*
- **Wardrobe** — *Closet*
- **Windscreen** — *Windshield*

CHAPTER ONE

<u>Richmond, Virginia, USA</u>

Wind whispered through the waist-high weeds as Jennie stared up at the old manor.

It had been a thing of beauty once. A mansion that could have befitted a lord or duke of some kind but had been lost and forgotten in the tangles of time. For almost two centuries, the house had stood solitary, only ever violated by brave teenagers who sought to find an answer to the ages-old ghost stories that circulated the schoolyard quads.

The front section of the house protruded like a giant's tongue. The east wing and the west wing fanned out like ears and stretched to the reaches of their peripheral vision. It was no wonder the kids in the local neighborhood called this the "monster's manor."

Windows were smashed, wooden beams creaked and moaned in the midnight winds, and somewhere inside was the presence they were seeking. A darkness that had yet to be given a name.

Jennie King clicked her tongue and placed her hands on her hips. She wore a short-sleeved white shirt with decorative cuffs, the pale flesh of her arms exposed. She felt no chill, despite the hungry wind nipping at her skin. Cool confidence masked her face, and a pair of round vintage sunglasses hid her eyes from view.

"The monster's manor, my arse," she muttered to herself. "Didn't their parents ever tell them that monsters aren't real?"

Baxter Scampton chuckled beside her. He was larger than Jennie by a good measure. His biceps were as wide as her face, and he rested the head of a large wrench on his shoulder. If someone were to walk past them both, they might be forgiven for believing that two moon-bathed ghosts stood on the lawn.

Only, they would never be able to see Baxter, would they? Because Baxter was, indeed, a specter.

"Monsters aren't real?" Baxter gave Jennie the side-eye. "Have you met *you*?"

Jennie pursed her lips. "Ouch, that's cold. It's not my fault I'm a little…different."

"A little different? Milky Ways and Butterfingers are a little different. You're like comparing Jell-O to steak."

"I'm unique."

Baxter nodded. "That's one word for it. Unique. Probably sums it up, considering I'm yet to meet *anyone* like you on this strange giant marble we call planet Earth."

Jennie laughed softly and kept her gaze up at the house.

Baxter followed her line of sight, cross-examining each of the windows and performing a mental calculation of how many rooms this place must have. "Are you serious about this, Jennie? I'm sure there are a thousand vacant properties scattered along the coast. There are easier ways to get what it is that you want. Cheaper, too."

"I want this one. I've already put the payment down."

Baxter puffed a mist of air from his nose and muttered, "Of course you have." His voice returned to its usual volume. "Wouldn't this have been easier with the others? I mean, not that I don't appreciate spending some alone time with you, but we could be in and out in a jiffy; monsters or no monsters."

"You know why we had to keep quiet," Jennie replied. "We would have had to fight through the bureaucracy of SIA politics, we would have had to request permission and wait for the administrative belt to begin turning. By the time we would have gotten the okay—if we would at all, considering the health and safety violations that no doubt plague this building—I'd be closer to dead than I would be to living."

It was difficult to tell what was going on inside her head. With her eyes masked by her glasses, he couldn't get a read on her. Baxter only knew that what Jennie wanted, Jennie often got.

Baxter gave her an incredulous look. "You're a hundred years old, and you look as though you just turned twenty-five. How much deader can you look?"

Jennie gave an appreciative grin. "I'm a little bit older than that. But thanks, you know how to boost a girl's confidence."

Baxter fixed her with a firm look. "I wasn't talking about the SIA. I know your feelings toward them: friends, sure, but wrapped in politics and red tape. I meant the others. You know, our guys."

"I wanted it to be a surprise. So, sue me." She patted Baxter on the shoulder before striding toward the front door.

The front door didn't need encouragement to open. The thick stench of dust and decay filled the air as it creaked its hello on rusted hinges.

Jennie closed her eyes while Baxter closed the door behind them. She took a deep breath and listened to the deep quiet of the house. The moans and groans of the boards they'd heard outside had stilled, as though the house was holding its breath. The skin on the nape of her neck broke out in gooseflesh as she sensed what she was after.

A small grin broke out on her face. "It's definitely here."

Baxter looked around the empty hallway, with its crooked portraits and layers of mud, dust, and grime that slicked the floor. There were trails of footprints around the hall, but even those suggested that it had been some time since anyone had entered the house.

Baxter grumbled, a hint of sarcasm in his voice. "Good. I was worried that we'd arrive at an empty house, free from spirits."

Jennie spoke as if soothing a child. "Not scared, are we, Bax? A big brave specter like you? It doesn't seem like all that long ago we were down in Virginia, fighting off an army of possessed vagrants and Queen Victoria. And here you are, afraid over an itty-bitty specter?"

Baxter followed in Jennie's steps as she grinned and roamed around the downstairs, taking a left into an ancient drawing room. "Okay, two things here. The first thing you've got to remember is that we had backup—a whole army, in fact. *You* could draw from a number of specters and help in keeping us alive, whereas, right now, I'm your sole source of spectral energy. That's a lot of pressure for one specter to have."

Jennie traced a clean line over the top of a mahogany fireplace with one finger. "Okay, I'll give you that one. Next?"

"The second point, in case you've forgotten, I've never been inside a haunted house. I've heard stories, of course. Tales of rooms warping and furniture coming alive and being tossed around the place. People disappearing into portals and never returning. Instant death, sudden suffocation, blood dripping from the walls," Baxter grew breathless as he continued, "Little children appearing at the end of the corridor, sudden blackouts…"

"Baxter!" Jennie hissed, an amused look on her face.

Baxter stopped abruptly and met Jennie's eyes.

Jennie shook her head. "I can't believe it. A specter, spooked by the ghost stories of mortals? Don't you think that you and I might be more frightening than all the things that could exist in this house?"

Baxter considered this. "I suppose since you put it that way."

"Don't let the stories spook you. The worst that could be in this house is some poor human or creature who died years ago and has found themselves trapped inside. This will be a straight in and out job. Clear the house, and the house will be ours. Simple as that, all right?"

They continued through the bottom floor of the manor and found nothing more than a few broken items and a couple of scurrying rats. Rotten food festered in the kitchen, and they passed through there with fingers pinching their nostrils until they returned to the hallway once more.

Jennie swept her hands wide. "See? Nothing to fear. How about we speed up this process? You take the basement, and I'll take the upstairs?"

"Why do I have to take the basement?" Baxter protested.

Jennie cocked an eyebrow. "What's your issue with the basement?"

Baxter looked at her as though it was the most obvious thing in the world. "The basement? You know, where they keep the bodies? Where the traps are set? Where Dracula sleeps during the daytime?"

Jennie frowned. "Dude, it's night time. You think that Count Dracula would A, be living in Richmond, and, B, still be asleep in the middle of the night?"

Baxter remained silent.

"Fine! You take the upstairs, and I'll take the basement." Jennie gave Baxter a gentle shove toward the stairs and made her own way toward the door beneath the stairs.

A sudden explosion of noise came from above as the tinkling notes of a grand piano rang through the corridors.

Baxter searched for Jennie, but she had already disappeared into the darkness of the basement.

Jennie's voice trailed behind her, "No swapsies!"

Baxter called out when she didn't reappear. "Wait! You're not serious?"

Jennie chuckled to herself as she descended the stairs into the impenetrable darkness.

She couldn't blame Baxter at all. His fear of the twisted creations that death could bring was well-founded considering the monsters he had seen while journeying alongside Jennie. But she knew that he would be okay. She had already detected what resided in this house, and there was nothing there that could kill them. With a little confidence, Baxter would be able to hold his own.

The air turned cold as she approached the bottom. She switched on her flashlight and was met with a conical beam of light that illuminated the strange array of objects in the room.

It was cavernous, easily almost the entire size of one of the wings. Occasionally the flashlight beam hit a concrete pillar that supported the room. There were hundreds of piles of objects, some covered in dust sheets, others decaying and rotting atop one another. There seemed to be no order or care to what lay beneath, it was almost as though a museum had kicked out its contents and left them in the room to fade with time.

Jennie's skin tingled. She was getting close. She focused her attention on channeling the tingling sensation that ran in the very marrow of her bones and acted as her own unique radar and honed in.

Midway through the room, Jennie noticed the first tell-tale signs of another presence in there with her when she came to a mountainous pile of magazines, newspapers, and books that reached almost to the ceiling.

Jennie took a step back and studied the pile. The pages were yellow and somehow damp. There was a faint white glow leaking from the center.

"It's funny. When you think of poltergeists, you don't think of studious specters." Jennie's voice echoed loudly around the basement. "You must have absorbed quite the store of information in that tidy little bed of yours."

For a moment, there was no response. Then, with a sudden monstrous ferocity, three poltergeists burst out from the books, exploding the pages around them into a sudden storm.

A deafening cackle followed them as they flew around the basement, whipping up trails of debris and mess wherever they soared.

"Or not…" Jennie studied their movements. She lowered the arms she had raised in defense against the papers that floated to the ground like fallen leaves and narrowed her eyes at the glowing specters.

They simultaneously sped back toward her, coming at Jennie from different angles. Jennie ducked at the last moment and they all collided, bashing their heads and crashing to the floor.

Jennie winked. "Oops."

Their expressions of anger and pain were replaced with mischief. The poltergeists exchanged a look, then spun rapidly around Jennie, closing her into a tight circle as more and more debris was drawn into their tornado.

Jennie stood placidly in the center, biding her time, and when the poltergeists stopped, and the debris eventually stopped, too, they were gone. Far from sight.

But not from sound, Jennie thought as she heard the fading cackles of one of the poltergeists.

Jennie massaged one of her temples with her thumb and forefinger and sighed. *I forget how much poltergeists like playing games. Maybe Baxter's having more luck than me?* She glanced at the ceiling, hoping to hear something, but no sound came back.

CHAPTER TWO

<u>Richmond, Virginia, USA</u>

Baxter recalibrated himself on the way up the stairs. He wasn't sure where the initial fear had come from. He had been a specter for almost a century, and he had come across ghosts and specters of all types along the way.

He supposed some of it had come from the world that Jennie opened his eyes to. He'd always thought he knew enough about the spectral world that nothing would surprise him, yet along the way he had encountered wraiths, *sturmgeists*, the Obake, and a whole host of things he had never dreamed would be able to exist in the world.

Not to mention Jennie, of course. She was a breed all of her own.

Baxter drew his pistol and readied his wrench—that helped steel his nerves. The piano had fallen silent, but that did nothing to settle his imagination. The only saving grace he had was that the stairs made no noise under the feather-weight of his spectral feet.

The upstairs might once have been beautiful. Gold-framed portraits lined the walls, vases stood on pedestals. A faded blood-red carpet lined the upstairs hallway. Baxter was able to see in each direction for a hundred feet or so before the hallway came to an abrupt end. A multitude of doors led off the hallway, and that was only the second story. The stairs lapped back on themselves and made their way to the third story, too.

No wonder Jennie seemed so interested in this place. It's huge! *The potential here is amazing...*

He padded carefully along the hall toward where instinct told him the piano had been playing. A doorway with a golden plaque reading, Music Room, confirmed his suspicions.

He melted through the door and came into a room filled with musical instruments. The walls were lined with guitars, and a grand piano took center stage, hidden beneath a large gray sheet. The curtains flapped gently in a breeze that seemed impossible, given that the windows had been closed when Baxter had looked up at the second-story from outside.

A childish giggle sent a chill down Baxter's spine. Something white flashed behind the piano.

"Hello?" Baxter offered to the room. "Who's there?"

He skirted the piano and looked underneath, but there was no one there. A blast of music caused him to jump, and he would have bashed his head against the underside of the piano had he been mortal.

He rose to his full height and narrowed his eyes. He couldn't quite see the keys playing, but the music was actually rather pretty, a melody he had heard before, but had never bothered to learn the name of the song or composer.

"Impressive," he called out. "But can you play something a bit more contemporary? *Take Me to Church* by Hozier, perhaps?"

Surprisingly, the piano obeyed, immediately playing the melancholy steps among minor chords.

Baxter scratched his chin. "Not bad, not bad. What about some Beatles?"

The piano switched effortlessly into an enchanting rendition of the Beatles' *Let It Be.*

Baxter grinned as he skirted the piano, half-expecting to find someone in the seat. When he reached the front, he could see no sign of anyone there. The keys were moving by themselves.

While Baxter knew that there were some specters blessed with the ability to turn wholly invisible, among them were the terrifying wraiths, something told him that he was missing something. When he had encountered wraiths before, he had felt the air cool and had been met with a soul-filling chill.

Baxter sat on the piano stool and placed his fingers on the keys. He had never played the piano before but had always imagined that one day he might learn. He hit the keys spasmodically, thumping his fingers down and sending a chorus of dissonance into the room. The sound was awful, notes clashing, highs and lows overlapping, but after a few seconds, something interesting happened.

Grunts and cries of protest came from inside the piano. Baxter raised an eyebrow and lifted the lid. Inside were two creatures he could only describe as spectral imps, clutching the still-vibrating strings and curling their bodies away from the hammers.

Baxter jumped back, letting the lid slam back down on the imps.

"Ow!" one of them complained.

"Stupid giant," the other reprimanded.

Baxter suddenly felt sorry for the pair. He imagined them inside the piano, having to avoid the hammers as they slammed on the strings and made their music. He opened the lid again, but they were both gone.

White-hot pain seared his ankles.

"Son of a—" Baxter kicked at the two creatures whose teeth were locked onto his flesh. They clung tightly, not dissuaded from their mission as he kicked and kicked. When that didn't work, Baxter reached down and plucked them off by the scruffs of their necks.

He held them up in front of his face as they grunted and lashed out with their hands. They had short, sharp claws and their teeth ended in needle-like points. Their eyes were narrowed, and they gnashed their teeth as though their lives depended on it.

"What the hell are you two?" He shook them violently, and they calmed themselves. "You've got a hell of a chomp."

"You hurt us," the one on the left growled. Her hair was shoulder-length, and she wore a dress that was in near-tatters. Pale skin poked out between the holes showing flesh covered in scars. "You're mean."

The other imp, a male with thick eyebrows and a ruined shirt, agreed. "What was that for? We played your music, didn't we?"

Baxter's face softened. "You're both specters. The hammers couldn't hurt you. They just pass straight through you, don't they?"

The female imp began cackling, revealing her impressive display of razor-like teeth. She vibrated in his hands, the laughter wracking her whole body. "You're not stupid like the others. You're not stupid at all! Those mortal children, they're easy to fool, but you're a tough one."

The boy imp joined in her laughter, creating an orchestra that was painful to Baxter's ears. He had been tempted to join them, but the harsh squeals of their mirth gnawed at his eardrums.

"Will you two stop it?"

The pair looked at each other, then repeated in mockery, "*Will you two stop it!*"

Their laughter only grew louder. As they jiggled in his hands, Baxter noticed that more music was joining in. The piano began to play of its own volition, strings joined the chorus, and a trumpet began to blow from somewhere.

Baxter scanned the room but could find no sign of the brass section. When he looked back at his hands, the imps were gone, their laughter dissipating into the strange symphony.

What the hell is going on?

"Where'd ya go?" he called through cupped hands that soon clapped to his ears in an effort to drown out the din.

The imps melted into view on the piano top, their legs swinging off the edge above the keys. Baxter became aware of movement all around him, and the next thing he knew, there were dozens of the little creatures appearing from behind all the instruments.

They leered at him with hungry, entertained eyes.

"Shit," Baxter muttered, turning to the door, only to find more blocking his path. He glanced at his wrench and sighed.

Jennie heard the faintest thumps of the action occurring above her, but she was too far away to help. The poltergeists were playing hide and seek, and if there's one thing that Jennie excelled at, it was finding specters.

She closed her eyes and latched onto their spectral frequencies. In the dark space behind her eyelids, she could see them as though she were an infrared camera, and their heat signatures betrayed them. She homed in on the one closest to her and advanced on him.

"Poltergeists…" she crooned, stepping carefully over the detritus that littered the floor. "Come out, come out, wherever you are…"

She approached a stack of broken chairs and could see his eyes staring directly at her. She didn't blame him for assuming he was safe. He didn't know the full extent of her gifts, after all.

When she was within ten feet, the chairs barreled toward her. The poltergeist leapt out with a jolly cackle and grabbed anything that came to his hands, hurling pieces of furniture violently at Jennie.

Jennie blocked a chair with her arms, then sidestepped so she had a clear line of sight. She narrowed her eyes and muttered, "Bingo," before extending her arms and latching onto the poltergeist.

A tendril of spectral energy wormed its way from the poltergeist toward her body, and she felt the satisfying connection the moment it joined. Through the tendril, she felt the poltergeist's energy. She understood his emotions and the limits of his powers.

The poltergeist was too busy with attacking Jennie. He only felt the bond when it was too late. He held a chair leg in his hand and tried to beat at the tendril, but the leg passed right through it. In a sudden burst of panic, he tossed the leg at Jennie and tried to speed away.

He only made it five feet before Jennie stilled him, using the tendril to hold him back. The poltergeist's power filtered through her and she felt herself begin to rise, floating above the ground with her arms out like a religious effigy of old.

The poltergeist continued wriggling, his instincts telling him to find some way—any way—to wreak as much havoc and destruction as possible. It was in their natures, they were chaotic, mischievous things who cared not for the people they hurt.

And this one was scared.

Jennie dragged the poltergeist toward her. The closer he got, the harder he fought, his face twisted into a mask of anger. His teeth sharpened to points, and his ears were elongated, giving him an elf-like appearance.

Jennie pulled the poltergeist until he was just out of arm's reach. She wasn't stupid enough to bring him within range of damaging her, after all. She locked eyes with the poltergeist and grinned. "One down, three to go."

The poltergeist responded with a blood-curdling yowl. He opened his mouth, unhinging his jaw to create the horrendous cry.

The other two poltergeists responded to the call, emerging from their hiding places and streaming toward Jennie and her captive.

Jennie used the poltergeist's power to fuel her flight. She locked her arms to her side and sped like a bullet around the basement, narrowly avoiding the pair who gave chase, the poltergeist she had captured looking like a passenger stuck in a motorcycle's sidecar.

She slalomed around pillars, avoiding the projectiles the other poltergeists picked up and tossed as they flew after her. She wanted to outrun them, to circle behind them and get into a position where she could take them both down together, but that option appeared to be off the table. Those suckers were damn fast.

Jennie darted toward the basement stairs and abruptly stopped. Caught off-guard, the pair struggled to stop their own momentum, and as they almost crashed into Jennie, she threw out her arms and sent two additional tendrils to latch onto the pair.

Jennie struggled for breath. "That's two, and that's three." She lowered herself to her feet, thankful to feel the sturdiness of the floor beneath her, and left the other three hovering around her like moons around a planet.

"You've got some kick to your power," Jennie admired. "But I don't think much of your hiding skills. You've got this whole house to yourself, and you hang out among the shit that has been discarded, used, and forgotten. Why is that?"

The poltergeists growled, none of them wishing to say a word. Jennie brought them closer to the ground and played with her powers, holding them tightly under her control.

Jennie smiled coldly when they didn't reply. "It's probably best you tell me willingly. In case you haven't noticed, I've got a particular set of skills that could make your world a living nightmare."

The poltergeist on her right opened his mouth, then closed it when the others narrowed their eyes at him. He had a dark sweep of hair that remained impossibly combed back and glued to his skull. He wore a crimson dressing robe that floated as lazily as he did.

Jennie pointed in his direction. "You were going to say something. What was it?"

The poltergeist glanced at the others, then lowered his eyes.

"Tell me!" Jennie shouted, making a conscious effort to drain his powers from him. The tendril binding the pair flashed a bright white and thickened while the glow that had been coming from the poltergeist began to dull. His eyes widened in alarm, and a series of guttural utterances came from his throat.

Jennie pushed some of his powers back toward him. "Ready to talk?

The poltergeist furrowed his brow. "You talk to us of nightmares, yet you have no idea, *human*." His voice was like that of an eighty-year-smoker, every syllable was an effort.

The others shook their heads in an effort to shut him up. The first one Jennie had captured opened his mouth and gave that ear-shattering squeal again, only stopping when Jennie barked at him and drained his powers enough to silence him. She could feel the fury in the energy running through her, the anger warming her insides.

"Keep talking," Jennie barked at the poltergeist.

The poltergeist growled. "Once we were great lords residing in this home, free to roam the hallways and grounds without care. Now, we are nothing more than slaves in the confines of this place. There is an unspeakable darkness here, *human*. A being for whom there is no name. We cower in the shadows, emerging only to play with the intruders who break into our residence. When the mortals run in fear, we dive back to our safe dwellings, knowing that if we don't, soon enough, *she* will come and do it for us."

Jennie looked deeply into the poltergeist's eyes, trying to detect the lies and mischief she was almost certain were coming from his lips. Instead, she found only fear. "You're telling the truth, aren't you? There really is something here that you fear? Something that has you trapped in this concrete prison?"

"No!" the first poltergeist squealed, forcing the words to leave his lips.

He shut up at Jennie's glance. She returned to the poltergeist who seemed willing to talk.

"The house is *alive*," he managed. "She communicates through the fabric of this building. Her minions are all around, defending, deflecting, trapping those who wander into her lair."

The poltergeist who had been quiet the longest now spoke. "She speaks of torment. She barricades us in and tears at our existence. For what little we know of poltergeists, this should not be possible. We should be able to play to the very borders of our property, but alas, we cannot."

The third poltergeist choked the words, "Shut up! Shut up! Shut up!"

Jennie drew all three before her, hanging them in the air, shoulder-to-shoulder so she could look at them all at once. "I sensed no being when I entered this house."

"Why would you, *mortal?*" the first poltergeist barked.

"In case you're *that* slow that you can't work out what is going on here, I am more than just a mortal. Exhibit A: you are all bound under my power." She scratched her chin and deliberated for a moment. "If there really is a presence in this house that needs vanquishing, then you may just be in luck. You've stumbled across someone who makes a living out of fixing nuisances. The only downside of this is that when I'm done, I'll likely have to evict you guys, too."

"Ha! We'd like to see you try—" The poltergeist's words were lost under Jennie's strangling hold.

Jennie narrowed her eyes. "Understand that there are some significant changes coming to this house. *Your* future, however, is as of yet undetermined." She unlatched them all at once, and they all collapsed to the floor. "Now, tell me everything that it is you think you know. It's unlike a spectral force to be undetectable by me."

"What are you?" one of the poltergeists croaked.

"Jennie King. But you can call me, 'Rogue.'"

CHAPTER THREE

<u>Richmond, Virginia, USA</u>

They closed in on Baxter, encircling him. He was an island, and they were the sea threatening to drown him.

Baxter realized that this was the first time he'd been in this kind of situation alone. Sure, he had had scrapes and the occasional fight throughout the years, but those had been with your run-of-the-mill specters. New York had its turf wars, and remaining unaligned had always been a gamble, but it was rare he encountered specters like this.

They laughed at him and pointed, their little eyebrows knitted together. Some of them leered, many of them laughed, a few clapped hands to their mouth, reprimanding Baxter for "using a naughty word."

Shit.

Baxter squared his feet and readied his wrench. He didn't want to fight unless he had to, and this looked like one of those times.

Remember, just because they look like children, doesn't mean that they are. They're imps. Little creatures of the dead. They want to hurt you, cripple you...

"Just know that once I'm forced to fight, there's no going back."

Baxter aimed his words at the two imps he had originally met, but could not find them among the crowd. All of the boys looked the same, and all of the girls, too. There were minor differences, but mostly they all blurred into one mass.

"Ooo, the big giant is *scaaared.*"

"He doesn't want us to get *huuurt.*"

"I don't think he understands who he's dealing with."

Something hit his shoulder. Baxter spun around, and a searing pain throbbed from the site of impact. He clawed at his back only to find an imp had somehow jumped six feet off the ground and was now biting him.

He plucked the imp off and tossed him back into his brethren.

The others didn't like that.

They swarmed toward him like insects. Baxter spun and swung his wrench in a tidy arc, bowling dozens of imps aside. His wrench vibrated as it hit the imps, and many were sent sprawling back into the walls where they disappeared.

While Baxter had to crouch slightly to hit them with his wrench, he provided a platform for others to leap onto him. They scratched at him and dug their tiny teeth into his spectral flesh, pulling and ripping hungrily through his clothes.

Baxter stood up straight and swatted at the parts he could reach with his hand and the wrench. He hooked his weapon over his shoulder and swished it like a windshield wiper, relieving some of the pain as the tiny creatures were batted to the floor.

Anger began to fuel him. They had seemed so innocent at first. *That's what happens when you let your guard down.*

Baxter fired half a dozen shots with his pistol, each shot clearing three to four of the imps and incapacitating them. With every gunshot, they grew more ravenous, and more of them appeared from the walls.

Baxter tried to fight through the pain as more of them crawled over him like scarabs. He eyed the exit. It was only twenty feet away, but it seemed a greater distance than that. He trudged toward the door, clearing any imps that got in his way, gritting his teeth against the pain burning along his back and the backs of his legs.

He reached the door and placed a hand in front of him. He intended to melt through the door and find a way to Jennie. She'd know what to do, surely? These little cretins must be in her bestiary of specters? Only, his hand didn't pass right through, as expected. The door was solid.

He tried again, walking straight at the door, but he was rebuffed. He punched at the door but only succeeded in hurting his fist.

What the hell? The only walls or doors I know that can do this are imbued with spectral energy. Only the SIA and the SIS have that technology. Why would it be here?

Baxter didn't have time to question any further, for as he bashed his fist repeatedly against the door, a strange noise caught his attention from behind. The gnawing bites of the imps retreated as suddenly as they had started, and by the time the last of the gnawing had stopped, Baxter's blood ran cold.

A rolling roar growled from the center of the room. Baxter closed his eyes and prepared himself for what he was about to see. In his mind he saw a giant tiger or a predatory wolf. He pictured the maw of a giant beast waiting for him, dribbling with saliva, a being created from the collected mass of the imps that had oh so recently attacked him.

When he finally turned around, he was not disappointed.

———

Jennie felt their presence the moment she arrived on the upstairs landing. She dashed toward the music room and tried to open the door, but it was stuck fast. She banged with her fist and heard only a faint reply from Baxter, lost almost entirely over the growling of some creature.

Jennie crouched and peeped through the keyhole. She could only make out Baxter in front of her, and some large dark shape beyond him. She focused her attention on filtering her power through the keyhole in order to latch onto Baxter.

When the connection was forged, Jennie activated herself and turned spectral. She made an attempt to walk through the door but found that she was blocked.

"What the…"

Jennie tried again, confusion spreading across her features. The door was perfectly ordinary, if a little outdated in design, so why could she not make it through?

A cacophonous howl erupted from the room, and at that moment, Jennie's patience was lost. "Ah, well. Who needs keys and locks when you've got a Big Bitch?"

She drew the ancient pistol from her holster, the unique firearm that somehow looked like it belonged in a time far beyond this one, and blasted the door handle. The wood yielded, leaving a large splintered crater that allowed her to boot the door open.

"Freeze, shit-bags!" Jennie yelled, announcing herself to the room.

Her jaw nearly dropped when she saw what was in front of her.

A monstrous dog, large enough to occupy almost the entirety of the room. Although she wasn't familiar with dog breeds, she could easily say that it was closer to a Rottweiler than it was a chihuahua. Its fur shone with spectral light, and its eyes were dilated into pure whiteness. It reared on its haunches and snapped its massive jaws at Baxter.

Jennie smirked. "I see you've found a new pet."

"I don't want one!" Baxter protested. "I'm not even sure it's a dog. A few seconds ago, it was dozens of tiny people."

"People?"

"Imps."

"Oh," Jennie replied, readying both her guns and eyeing the creature. "You really should say things clearly the first time around. It saves a load of time in re-explaining."

"I'm sorry, but in case you haven't noticed, Cerberus is keeping us company, and he looks hungry—"

Baxter dived sideways as the dog snapped at him, missing his form by mere inches. The dog frowned and howled at the ceiling once more.

"Not Cerberus," Jennie clarified. "Cerberus has three heads and guards the entrance to the Underworld."

Baxter gave an incredulous laugh. "You talk as though Cerberus is real."

"You talk as though he isn't." Jennie's arms fell by her sides as her head tilted. "What *are* you, creature? I've never come across a specter that can avoid detection *and* shift forms like this, too. Usually one, not the other."

She snapped from her thoughts when the dog whirled on her and bared its teeth. She shot at the ceiling and the specter flinched, recoiling and letting out a booming bark. Parts of the creature's form separated and rejoined, as though it was about to shed its skin, then thought better of it.

"Not used to firearms, no?" Jennie slowly holstered her weapons. "There. See? We're no threat."

Baxter was backed against the wall, his pistol at the ready if he needed it. "Jennie? I'd highly advise against un-arming yourself."

Jennie looked out from over the top of her glasses. "Really? You're going to preach to me about how to deal with specters?"

She spread her arms wide and matched the dog's gaze. It was a fearsome thing, looming fifteen-feet tall. Its maw could swallow her whole, and that's what she was counting on.

"Hey, bitch. How about you sort yourself out, eh?" She clapped her hands. "Dinner time!"

The dog appeared to grin, before rearing back and then springing on top of her. Jennie disconnected from Baxter and allowed her mortal form to take the brunt of the chomp as the dog's mouth enveloped her whole.

The dog couldn't feel a thing. A confused growl rumbled from its throat.

"Sorry about this, pooch. It's just the way it has to be." Jennie quickly latched onto the dog, returning to her spectral self. Now that they were ghost on ghost, Jennie felt the cramping confines of the dog's throat. She pressed her hands and feet to the sides and trapped herself in its gullet, causing the dog to choke.

The dog reared up, then retreated back into the corner of the room, as if by shrinking, it might free the blockage. It coughed, it spluttered, it wheezed, and still Jennie held firm.

The strangest part of it all, as Jennie held on for the strangest rodeo ride she had ever experienced, was the flood of memories and emotions that pulsed through the great creature. They came to her in camera flashes, causing her blood to boil as she focused her energy on keeping the dog in check.

A woman in a cream frock, her hair slick from the rain, standing before a house that looked like this one, but where the grounds were neatly kept and the interior maintained. Another flash as the woman looked out from the nest of her four-poster bed at a man and a gaggle of small children.

A crazed woman, dressed like a priestess, but seen through fading eyes. She chanted an incomprehensible incantation before everything went black.

Children crying.

The pain of a grieving mother.

Jennie narrowed her eyes. They had been the first accidents in this house, the first ghosts to have accommodated the halls. But what about the rest? She saw a montage of three brothers laughing and sharing drinks. Blood splattering the walls. A slow-motion video reel of the house falling to ruin.

It was no wonder the people of the neighborhood called this place the monster manor when enough people had died here to create such an amalgamation of spirits. Specters who could...

What? Conjoin? Become one? This gives a whole new meaning to a workplace union.

The creature began to sputter and flicker like the static of an old TV. The dog's limbs weakened, and from its skin came the shape of dozens of individuals, children, or things that may once have been children, breaking free of the host.

"Baxter, help them along, would you?" Jennie called from the depths of the throat.

Baxter readied his wrench in his hand and hacked at the dog's leg as though he were felling a tree. The leg shook and flickered, and after the third hit, exploded into a dozen imps who tumbled out and rolled on the floor, momentarily dazed.

That was the first building block. Baxter went for the back leg, and it caved faster than the first. Jennie felt the dog lower to the ground, and the firm channel of its throat became soft and fragmented as the dog weakened and became what it had originally been from the start.

Soon enough, Jennie was standing on solid ground. The floor was littered in dozens of tiny impish creatures, but that wasn't what caught Jennie's attention the most. In the center of where the dog had been, were a man and a woman, holding hands.

Their faces were contorted with anger. Dark hair hung lankly over their faces. Though there was clearly a power within them that was impressive, Jennie couldn't *feel* them at all. There was no spectral reading whatsoever. Not even a hint.

They stared at each other for a moment before Jennie broke the silence. "I'm sorry we had to do that. We only attack when we ourselves are attacked."

The couple remained silent, staring at Jennie with dark eyes.

Baxter took a few tentative steps toward Jennie's side. His hand adjusted on his pistol and the woman's eyes flicked toward the firearm, then back to Jennie.

Jennie spread her arms out to her side. "This house has been inhabited by darkness for far too long. I know that pain can make the darkness in death alluring, but there is more to life than scaring children and living in solitude, believe me, I've seen worse situations turn into brighter futures."

The man's arm flexed. His jaw clenched as though he was biting back a thought. The woman simply leered.

"Your residency in this property has caused quite a stir over the years," Jennie continued, a shadow of a smile on her face. "Your time here has been tortured. Surely you are tired of the anger? Surely you long to be free of this…this…pain?"

A sudden explosion of atrocious sound came as the woman let out a pained scream. The man closed his eyes, waited out the cry, then calmly spoke.

"You know nothing of torture, spectral stranger. This house is all that we have. It's all that we've ever wanted. We will not surrender it for death, nor honor. You are trespassers, and you will leave, never to return, as have so many over the years. Leave us to rest in peace, or you will face your own undoing."

Jennie frowned. "We can't do that, I'm afraid. I can't stand to see specters suffering, so…"

"*And what will you do?*" the man hissed. "Heal us of our wounds? Strike us into the abyss? Exorcize us from all that we have ever known?" His face twisted into something that didn't resemble humanity anymore. The imps around them began to scatter as dark energy leaked from the couple. "If you shall not listen to reason, then we have no option but to impart the wrath of all that we know!"

They rose from the floor, the woman's eyes wide and her mouth agape. Her hair floated around her as if she were now trapped underwater. A dark cloud seeped and grew around them, filtering into the room like ashen cigarette smoke.

"*This house and all within it belong to us! There is nothing beyond our control. You do not understand the extent that we and the house are one, and you come here with the audacity to eject us from our nest? To coo us from our residence? You are a new breed of stupid,* human…"

Jennie raised her eyebrows, only slightly unsettled by the sudden swell of energy, more so because she still had trouble sensing it within the reaches of her power. Baxter had a signature she could feel a mile off, this couple had nothing.

"Now, let's not resort to name-calling," Jennie quipped.

The man erupted in a sudden fury of black smoke, his and his partner's eyes were shining white beacons, guiding them through the fog. "*Begone!*"

And then something happened that Jennie had never experienced before. The doors behind her flew open, and a flurry of wind attacked her and Baxter. She braced an arm against the sudden onslaught, but it was too much. The wind dragged them both, pulling them out of the room with monstrous force.

"Hold on, Bax!" Jennie shouted over the wind, but it stole her words. He whipped out of sight, a blur of spectral energy, and disappeared from the room. Jennie's feet slipped, and she scrambled to clutch the door jamb and hang on.

The shadowy couple was a thunderous cloud and the imps had vanished, disappearing to Lord-knew-where. Jennie squinted through eyelids assaulted with winds and tried to latch onto the pair, to grip them and form some kind of anchor that would keep her in the room.

Her fingers slipped, and she was taken. The wind was unnatural, carrying her on gusting currents which trailed toward the front door. The door was already open and waiting to expel her, and just a few seconds later, her ass hit the soft, damp grass of the lawn. The house coughed her out, then the door slammed shut.

A groan came from the tangles of weeds beside her. Jennie looked across to find Baxter in an uncomfortable knot on the lawn.

He rolled over and straightened himself up, hand massaging his head. "Well, that could have gone better."

Jennie glanced up at the music room window, dismayed to find that the room now stood in solitary darkness. She huffed. "That's certainly one way to put it."

Somewhere from the depths of the house, they could hear the cackling of the poltergeists.

CHAPTER FOUR

Route 95, Virginia, USA

Jennie white-knuckled the Mustang on the ride back to Washington.

The highway was almost entirely clear, with only a few semi-trucks and eager businessmen returning from their late-night meetings with their concubines. Clouds drifted lazily overhead, catching the moonlight and turning them a ghostly silver.

They hadn't spoken for thirty minutes. Baxter watched the world whizz by outside the window, sensing that Jennie needed time to think.

That was one thing she loved about Baxter, he could read a room. She thought back to all the sidekicks Queen Victoria had given her over the years, remembering their endless chatter and their grating admonishments of her actions.

Jennie chewed her tongue. She couldn't make heads nor tails of it at all. It should have been an easy job, a walk in the park, but the specters had taken her by surprise.

When was the last time that had happened?

She had read a stack of books and newspaper articles on the monster manor, or, to give it its proper name, Mendleson Manor, and every glimpse of spectral activity had correlated to some kind of presence living there.

She had expected poltergeists and little more. Perhaps a ghoul or a run-of-the-mill specter who hadn't been inducted into the possibilities of what the spectral world could offer, but whatever that thing was...

It wasn't entirely natural.

Is any of this natural?

The worst part of it all was that Jennie had allowed herself to get excited. To have cleared Mendleson Manor would have been the icing on the top of the cake, the best way to conclude a job well done in Virginia's capital.

It seemed that her investment was not going to pan out—at least for now.

"Seems a shame to go home empty-handed," Jennie announced at last, declaring an end to their silence. Not that it had been complete silence, what with the roaring of the Mustang's engine and the faint crooning of Billie Eilish playing on Jennie's phone.

"Empty-handed?" Baxter scoffed. "Rogue, we've just spent a week in Richmond dealing with sensitive spectral issues. On your own, you exorcized a two-hundred-year-old poltergeist from Richmond City Hall. Together we gave a warning to the group of cocky specters haunting the Boy Scouts of America. We made connections with a four-hundred-year-old army general who now has your cell phone number and promised to guard the McGuire Veterans Hospital and guide specters into their new life, and *still* you're unsatisfied?"

Jennie shrugged. "I wanted to clear the house."

Baxter laughed and unclipped his seatbelt. He mumbled, "I don't even know why I have this on," before turning in his seat to get a better look at Jennie.

Despite the lack of sleep she'd had over the past few days, she looked as awake and healthy as anyone he had ever met. Her eyebrows were knitted together in thought, and her eyes locked on the road. "It was a pretty cool house."

"That's what I'm saying!" Jennie declared. "Can you imagine what we could do from there as a base of operations? There are enough rooms to accommodate both the mortals and the specters on our team, the basement would make a great storage facility. We could add more lights—of course, we'd have to sort out the electricity and get some wi-fi running through there. No point being an intelligence organization without sufficient network and data entry points—and the location?" Jennie gave a heaving sigh. "Located on a hilltop above the city, overlooking everything, yet overlooked by none. It's perfect."

"There'll be other properties."

Jennie signaled right and abruptly swung the Mustang into a rest area. She slammed on the brakes, and Baxter had to cling on to stop himself flying through the front of the car. "I want *that* house."

Baxter ran a hand down his face. "It belongs to someone else. Why do you want it so badly?"

Jennie rested her head against the leather seat and ignored the fading honks of an angry vehicle she had cut off in her sudden, erratic maneuver. "Because the souls inside are broken." Her words were soft, contemplative. "I'd want the house with or without the specters, but after seeing that display of power, I can't stop thinking about the spectral couple."

"You know you can just say 'couple,' right? It's me, remember?"

Jennie laughed, the sound cutting through the tension of the car. "Sorry, I default to speaking to mortals, still. A habit it'll take a while to break from." Her face straightened. "That house is more than just a potential property investment. It's a place that has captured tortured souls. They're hurting, Bax. They don't even realize that they are hurting, but they are. Specters can only begin to absorb the presence of those within the house after hundreds of painful years. To make a house yield and obey like they did, that's the work of dark power. Pain and hate and anger can contort a specter's abilities and create something..."

"Bad?" Baxter suggested.

Jennie wrinkled her nose. "Is that the best you could come up with?"

"I'm not a wordsmith."

"But…'bad?' Even Sandra could come up with a better synonym than that."

Baxter rolled his eyes. "Well, what were you going to say, then?"

Jennie searched her brain. "Dark?"

"You've already used 'dark.' You can't repeat it."

"When did I use dark?"

"You said, 'that's the work of dark power.'"

Jennie laughed and bounced her fists on her thighs. "Fine. How about 'twisted?' It creates something twisted?"

Baxter pinched his chin. "Better, I guess. What was your point, anyway?"

Jennie shook her head and laughed. "My point is that the house needs healing, and I like to consider myself something of a spectral physician."

It was Baxter's turn to laugh. "Of all the things I've heard you be called, or thought of calling you myself, I've never once considered you as a physician."

Jennie mimed putting on latex gloves and winked. "Well, then. Prepare to be impressed. That house is wounded, and the doctor is going to find a way to heal it."

She eased the car into drive and left the rest area, quickly accelerating back to her steady ninety miles per hour. As she slalomed past the sparse traffic and caught up with the cars that had overtaken her in their pause, she chewed her lip and mused.

Baxter sighed, a knowing smile on his face. "You've already bought the house, haven't you?"

Washington DC, USA

The SIA had expanded noticeably in the weeks following the showdown in Alexandria. Agents scurried through the halls with iPads in hand, barely lifting their heads to nod at their colleagues. The headquarters had seemed an adequate size to conduct their affairs before, now it felt cramped with so many agents roaming the halls and meeting rooms. Issues were coming in thick and fast from the surrounding states as the net of their intelligence was cast wider, and resources were poured into monitoring spectral activity.

The President had put some urgency on the growth of the department after he had been debriefed. His primary concern had shifted from the realm of mortal terrorism as the reality of the spectral world came to light.

Many of the President's closest advisors didn't understand the sudden shift in resources and the secrecy behind it all, but their elected leader understood that secrecy was the only way that this should operate. The fewer people who knew, the better. The world wasn't ready for this kind of revelation.

Jennie pulled into the SIA parking lot in the early hours of the morning. She glanced around the lot at the near-identical black saloon cars that filled every available space.

Every available space but one.

Jennie had been smart enough to negotiate her own parking space at the SIA HQ. Having seen the kind of growth successful government departments could undertake in short time periods, she had accounted for every eventuality.

Only on one occasion did she have to track down an SIA agent who thought he could park in her spot. He wasn't difficult to find, either. His "Wave Hello for Joe," tag hung from his wing mirror, with the word "Perkins," scribbled beneath it. Jennie narrowed her eyes and found Joe Perkins in the break room. With a little "gentle" convincing, he moved his car, and never again returned to that spot.

Jennie had actually not seen him since. Maybe it was the threat of sending specters to his bedside to ensure he never slept a wink again…

She slipped her car into her space, thumbed off the ignition, and headed inside.

One of the main upgrades the SIA had installed in recent weeks was the introduction of the Rec Room. This was located in a walled-off section of the basement that had previously been nothing more than a space set aside for large gatherings. The room had since been fitted with table tennis and pool tables, dartboards, a video game corner, and a matted section for agents to utilize for meditation and yoga.

This was where Jennie found her compadres.

Tanya was the first to spot Jennie across the room. She rushed her with a hug, leaving Sandra and Lupe sitting on the couch playing their video game.

"You're back!" Tanya exclaimed excitedly.

"Looks that way." Jennie nodded at the others. "Lupe getting any better yet?"

Tanya laughed. "Nope. You'd think a man who was raised during the technological revolution would have a better grasp on NBA 2K19 than a girl who had been trapped in rock for centuries, but apparently not."

Baxter squinted at the TV screen. "What's the score?"

"One-nineteen to seventeen."

Jennie crossed the room. "That doesn't sound too bad." She examined the score. "Oh, I thought you meant one-nineteen to one-seventeen. Not one-nineteen to literally seventeen."

Lupe strained his neck but kept his eyes on the screen. "Don't mock! Kids are just better at video games, okay? They pick things up more easily."

"Maybe millennials." Baxter chuckled. "I'm sorry, this is ridiculous."

Lupe slammed his controller down on the couch. "Fine! You try and do better, see how that goes."

A handful of agents who were playing table tennis nearby stopped and stared their way, sensing the brewing competition. Their SI goggles had recently had a makeover, thanks to Hendrick and his new team. Instead of the dark-lensed swimming goggles with green LEDs, around the rims, they were now sleek black sunglasses, with the LEDs set along the bridge.

Baxter hopped over the back of the couch and took the controller. "Okay, let's see what we're working with here. Three minutes to go. This button does...okay! That's good. Yep. Pass it over. Woah! Nice. Final pass, then. What's shoot— Oh! Okay, that's a *dunk!*"

Sandra giggled and looked over her shoulder at Lupe. "Beginner's luck?"

Lupe grumbled as the rest of them laughed.

The final score was 127–39, Baxter had closed the gap impressively, but it would never have been enough in the time left. When they were done, Jennie invited them back to her quarters where it would be a little quieter and they could discuss the events of the last few days.

Jennie made quick work of preparing Tanya and Lupe's drinks, surprising them with cocktails of their favorite blends. Tanya had shown an affinity to gins, and so Jennie had cycled through the classics—Tom Collins, Perfect Spritz, French 75, and Gin Fizz, and had been forced to stretch her creations with some lesser-known concoctions like the Gin Sours, the Fitzgerald, an Aviation, and a Casino. This time, she served Tanya a...

"Gimlet."

Tanya looked at Jennie as though she were mad. "Excuse me?"

"It's a Gimlet. Super simple to make, but rarely ever concocted these days. Try it. Let me know what you think."

Tanya took a sip and raised her eyebrows in delight. "Sweet."

"And for my dear Lupe..." She carefully took a tall glass filled near the brim with a deep yellow liquid. "A Canelazo. One of the greatest Latin cocktails I've had the fortune to try."

Lupe furrowed his brow. "Which Latin country did you source this from?"

Jennie coughed into her hand and muttered something indistinguishable.

"Excuse me?" Lupe asked.

"Ecuador," Jennie answered.

Lupe tsked. "It's not Mexican, though, is it?"

Baxter rolled his eyes. "Neither are you anymore, hombre. You live in the U-S-of-A, now. Get used to it. She's doing you a solid."

"It's an insult to my Latin heritage," Lupe protested.

Jennie picked up her own tumbler, half-filled with a cocktail the color of cloudy mahogany—the Sazerac—and gestured at Lupe. "I'm sorry, okay. Outside of the Mexican Sunset, Mexico's hardly known for its copious wealth of cocktail recipes. I've had to source from the Latin cousins, so sue me."

"I may just do that." Lupe begrudgingly sipped from his glass, doing his best to hide his surprise at the sweetness of his drink. He sighed. "It's not that bad."

"What a compliment!" Tanya called.

Jennie waved a hand. "That's the closest I'll ever get to a thanks." She raised her glass. "You're welcome, Lupe."

When Jennie finally took a seat on her couch, Tanya rested her elbow on the back and leaned closer to Jennie. "Well?"

"Well, what?" Jennie asked, looking up at her.

Tanya sighed in exasperation. "Are you going to tell us about your big adventure? Come on, we were all curious why you and Baxter had to disappear on a secret mission, just the two of you. It felt a little bit like being the witness to a parent's divorce. Lupe was weeping every second that you were gone."

Lupe spluttered. "*I was not!*"

Jennie, Baxter, Tanya, and Sandra exploded in laughter. When they were finished, Tanya added, "Well?"

Baxter half-shrugged. "You said it yourself, it was a secret mission."

"Yeah, but..." Tanya bounced her eyebrows. "Nothing's secret between us, right? We know everything that's going on here. Right down to Jennie's ongoing plans to emancipate from the SIA and establish her own thing."

Jennie raised her eyebrows.

"What?" Tanya protested. "Like it's some big secret? Dude, the Summer Court has been a work in progress for ages. When are we going to get the goddamn show on the road?"

Jennie turned to Baxter. "Since when has she been this vocal? I thought she was all about protecting the little ones and living a quiet life."

Tanya rolled her eyes. "Oh, come on. These last few weeks have been boring as hell for me and Sandra. The agents are getting all the missions, and there's nothing to do when you're off gallivanting with

Baxter. Come on, Jennie, tell us we're heading off on a grand adventure soon and you need the whole party by your side? *Please?*"

Lupe chuckled, then slurped the rest of his drink. It was gone in seconds, and his straw gurgled the final dregs loudly.

Jennie sipped her drink, then crossed her legs. "If things are so boring around here, then where's Carolyn and Feng Mian? They're off on a mission of their own, *helping* the agents. You know that you could be doing that, too, if you didn't have such a resistance to instruction."

Jennie looked out from over her glasses, a mischievous grin on her face.

"I don't have a problem with instruction, I have a problem with authority." Tanya returned the grin and looped an arm around Sandra's shoulders. The young specter stared at the floor, clearly bored by the conversation. "I pledged my life to you, Jennie. I'll follow you to the end. I won't follow some obnoxious twenty-something agent who acts like he's Bill Murray on the hunt for ghosts just because he's been inducted into the SIA. I won't do it. I'm better than that."

Baxter and Jennie exchanged a glance.

"What?" Tanya asked.

"Nothing," Jennie replied. "That was a lot of pent up pressure just let out through a tiny hole right there."

"Innuendo," Baxter quipped.

"*Anyway,*" Jennie segued back to the subject at hand. "I hate to tell you you're right, but there is something I need your help with. I won't go into it until we've got all the gang here. You know how much I hate repeating myself."

"What?" Baxter asked.

"I said, you know how much I hate…" Jennie sighed. "Very funny. Point is, you'll have to wait until Feng Mian and Carolyn are back. I'm not doing this without them."

"You might be waiting a while." Lupe was slumped in his chair, trying to get the last few drops of his drink from the glass. "Feng Mian's gone out with the SIA to deal with a rising situation in Chinatown, New York. Apparently, the Dragon is back, and this time he's got backup."

"Shit," Jennie muttered. "I thought he died?"

Lupe shrugged. "I didn't see a specter rise from his body. He must have survived somehow."

Jennie considered this, then asked, "Where are Feng Mian's parents? Are they with him?"

Tanya answered. "They left! The pair of them just disappeared one day. When Feng Mian went looking for them, they'd left him a note saying they were going to reconnect by traveling across the world, something they'd been meaning to do for years but had never gotten around to."

Baxter's mouth fell open. "You're kidding. How did Feng Mian take it?"

Tanya looked at Baxter as though he should already know the answer. "How do you think? He's in Chinatown with the *SIA*, for God's sake."

"Who have they sent out with him?" Jennie asked.

"Not sure of their names. A group of the new recruits," Tanya replied. "To be honest, I'm not privy to that much stuff anymore. They're keeping me out of the loop on a lot of things. I think they see me as a glorified babysitter to Sandra."

Jennie's face turned serious as she straightened in her chair. "This was my exact worry when we took to embedding ourselves in the SIA. If we're to be the representatives of King's Court, we need to be treated as such. We need a top-level overview of what's going on in the organization, not to be used as pawns to achieve whatever it is they're after."

Baxter raised an eyebrow. "What are you saying?"

"I'm saying I think I need to have a word with the Special Agent in Charge. Re-establish our agreement."

Lupe toasted his empty glass. "Good luck, Rogue. You'll need it."

CHAPTER FIVE

Washington DC, USA

The corridor leading to Agent Kurt Rogers' office was one of the quietest areas of the HQ. Agents and analysts talked as they passed each other at the intersection of the corridor some fifty feet back, but they quieted in the presence of the head of the SIA.

Jennie, however, was unperturbed.

Her footsteps echoed loudly in the hall. She knocked three times on the door and announced herself. After a second's pause, the entry pad flashed green, and the door unlocked.

Jennie marched in. "Rogers, we need to talk."

"You might want to check who exactly you're talking to before you storm into a room," a voice that wasn't Kurt Rogers' replied.

Tom Hopkins was sitting behind the desk, illuminated only by a desk lamp as he struggled to process a heaping pile of paperwork. The computer screen was almost buried, and the table contained a slew of stained coffee mugs. He looked at Jennie as though he had forgotten she even existed.

"You're not Kurt," Jennie observed.

Tom nodded, reclining in his chair and resting an elbow over the back. He looked exhausted. The light accentuated the heavy bags that hung from his eyes, and he sported a healthy measure of unshaven stubble on his cheeks.

Tom gave a half-assed grin. "You're correct. Can't beat you for your observational abilities."

Jennie cocked an eyebrow and scanned him. He wore the same black fatigues that he had worn during the battle in Alexandria, although in his death, they had turned strangely opalescent.

"What is it you need, Jennie? In case you haven't noticed, things are a little hectic around here."

Jennie hesitated, then took the seat on the other side of the desk. She moved a stack of papers as well as Rogers' coat to make room for herself. "I need to talk to Rogers."

"He's not here," Hopkins told her.

"I can see that," Jennie replied acidly. "When will he be back?"

Tom exploded with laughter. "That's the million-dollar question!" He slammed both hands on the desk, but his spectral form made no noise. "In case you haven't noticed, things have ramped up around here. We've got recruiting drives coming out of the wazoo. We've got cases coming in left, right, and center, and we've got a Special Agent in Charge who is stuck in so many meetings that he's been forced to take on an assistant in the absence of him and his own assistant so that the wheels can keep turning around here."

"An assistant?" Jennie's head tilted to the left. "You mean, you're..."

Tom extended a hand across the desk, his manner frantic. "Pleased to meet you! Tom Hopkins, PA to the SAiC. Is there anything I can get for you today? Coffee? Tea? A mint? A hot chocolate? Oh, you'd like a meeting with Rogers? Let me have a look at his calendar. Sure thing, he'll be free in...thirteen months."

Jennie shook her head in disbelief. "I had no idea things would change so much."

Tom sat back and exhaled, taking a moment to calm himself. "I'm sorry, Ms. King. It's just a real fall from grace to go from commanding a team to operating as Rogers' secretary. Don't get me wrong, it has its perks, but things really have snowballed here. The scale that we're growing at, we're still trying to find ways to make things work."

"But why are you filling a PA role?" Jennie couldn't get her head around it. "Why couldn't you continue your old position? Your team respected you. They would have died for you, and many did."

Tom nodded solemnly. "I know, I know. I thought things would be okay, too. I had a good few weeks rebuilding my team and getting things in order under the pressures of the growing department. However, they needed someone experienced enough to look at the allocation of agency resources, and it just so happens I'm the best man for the job."

"And you're okay with that?" Jennie asked.

"I do what I'm needed to do. That's the way it goes," Hopkins replied.

The phone rang, the sound filling the silence that followed Hopkins' words. He frowned at the phone before finally picking up the receiver. After a series of "Yes," and "Umms," he placed the receiver back down.

"Lucky us, one of our agents has blocked in two other cars," he grumbled. "The best of the best, my ass." He glanced at Jennie as if suddenly remembering she was there. "I'm sorry, you came in here for something. What problems could possibly befall the incredible Genevieve King?" His tone was sarcastic, but she sensed no malice in them, only a kind of sore jealousy.

"I need my men back, Hopkins," Jennie commanded. "They're off in the field with the other agents, when I need them for my own endeavors. I was promised that we'd be kept abreast of changes and my team would be left alone, and I'm now finding that issues are cropping up that have involved us in the past, and that my people have been *ordered* by the SIA to accompany your units."

Tom shrugged, sadness in his eyes. "Join the club. Do you know who they got to replace me?"

Jennie remained tight-lipped.

"Daggro." Hopkins laughed and shook his head. "Fucking Daggro, the ambitious bitch. A great field operative, but she'd been coming for my role for years. I tried to persuade Rogers to take on Rhone, but she'd already got her claws into him. As I say, Ms. King, times change. Better get used to it."

Jennie shook her head, a sly grin on her face. "Is that your final answer?"

Hopkins looked at her apologetically. "It's the only answer I've got." He leaned forward and rifled through the paperwork again. "Look, I'll speak to Rogers when I get him alone, but I don't know what more I can do from my position. The department is going through a huge shift in the wake of recent events. The President is on our back—the goddamn *President*. He has the final say. No arguments."

Jennie rose to her feet and gave a resolute nod. "Well, thank you for your time, Agent Hopkins. It's been truly worthwhile."

Tom couldn't help but laugh. "Off the record, I like you, Jennie. I always have. Whatever you've got planned—and don't think I'm stupid enough to know you haven't got an ace up your sleeve—just be careful, okay? You may have struck a deal with the Queen and the President, but that doesn't mean that your journey will be easy. There's still everything to play for here."

Jennie smiled. "Oh, don't I know it."

She turned to leave. As she opened the door, Hopkins added, "My money's on you, Ms. King." He turned his attention to Rogers' computer as the door closed behind her.

———

Jennie was deep in thought when she took a left at the cross-junction and made her way toward Hendrick's lab.

There was no denying that it was Hendrick's lab anymore. Proctor had yielded defeat to the man who outmatched his knowledge of the chemicals and substances that blurred the barrier between life and death. After weeks of fighting for the top spot, Proctor happily took second and obeyed Hendrick's orders and commands.

Jennie heard the chatter in the hallway before she'd made it to the next corner. The sounds were familiar, the jostling and banter of high school jocks. There was laughter, play fighting, and the unmistakable chatter of what one jock had done with a female agent the night before.

A boisterous voice laughed. "She'll have a tough time walking straight today, I assure you."

"I thought she wasn't that into you?"

"Funny what happens when alcohol gets involved," the first voice retorted.

Jennie rounded the corner and saw the five of them, dressed in their SIA fatigues. They were young, in their early twenties, and they were handsome for the most part.

A shitty attitude can sour a pretty man.

Jennie kept her focus on her way ahead but could feel the hungry eyes on her as she strode on past. It was a hazard of her pain, she supposed. Sure, wearing a leather corset wasn't always comfortable, but that was what kept her sharp. If she was constantly in some sort of pain, she'd always be prepared and on edge. Who could really hurt her that badly when she was already hurting herself?

A long whistle came out of one of the guys' mouths. Jennie closed her eyes and sighed.

The leery agent muttered loudly enough to be heard. "Of course, if I had known steak was on the table, I wouldn't have gone for a cheap-ass burger last night."

A couple of the other guys laughed but hissed at him to shut up. Another whispered, "Dude, don't you know who that is?"

"Who cares? Women are women. All it takes is a little alcohol and a measure of charm and they all go weak at the knees." He raised his voice. "Ain't that right, darling?"

Jennie stopped in her tracks. She had been more than happy to carry on while they kept their ridiculous chauvinism to themselves. She'd had enough of her fair share of men lusting after her tight form, drawn by her glow of fiery hair. There was little to surprise her anymore. But, since these men were a part of the SIA—the SIA she had helped get to where it was today—she figured a lesson was in order.

Jennie composed herself and spun on the spot. She used her most sickly sweet voice. "I'm sorry, gentlemen. What was that?"

There was a rumble of awkward laughter. The instigator of the group, a young man with his hair quiffed up at the front, gave a cocky smile. He broke from the group and took a few brave steps toward her. "I said you're pretty hot, darling. You don't seem half as scary as people say."

Jennie knew he knew who she was. "Are you sure about that?

The agent bit his lip. "I know what you're capable of. Must be lonely at the top. Bet you need a strong, handsome guy at your side just to get through the cold nights. What do you think?"

Jennie closed the gap between them, and his eyes flickered for just a second. She bit her lip and leaned toward him, then at the last minute, nodded toward his group. "I'll take your mate on the right."

The other lad, a guy with a crop of blond hair, choked.

Quiff frowned. "I thought you'd be better than that." He closed the gap entirely and wrapped a hand around her waist. A moment later, he was sliding it toward her ass.

Jennie waited for her moment. When he finally slapped her ass, she knew it was time.

Jennie grabbed the guy's wrist and held it firm. She spun and twisted his arm at the same time, using her weight as the fulcrum to throw him into a messy barrel roll.

He landed on his back on the laminate floor and struggled to get to his feet, but Jennie held her grip on his wrist, shifting her grip to apply pressure to his wrist and his knuckles. As she did this, she placed a boot against his throat to discourage further chat.

One of his group made a step forward to help him but froze the instant he met Jennie's icy glare. A single popping sound came from one of his fingers before he yielded and cried out his surrender.

Jennie bent closer to the complaining guy on the floor. His jaw was clenched against the pain as he attempted to hold in his anguish. "You're brave, I'll give you that. But if you so much as look at my ass again, let alone think about slapping it, I'll make sure you're never able to use your hands again. Can't fire a weapon without a trigger finger, can we?"

"You can't do this." The guy was still wriggling, despite Jennie's warnings. "We're SIA personnel. We'll have HR on your ass so fast that you'll be out the door before you can regret not taking me up on my offer. I'm a good time, baby."

Jennie snorted in disbelief. She had to give it to him; even under duress, he was confident. Annoyingly, that'd get him far in this business.

"You may be personnel, but I'm not." Jennie applied extra pressure to his thumb and gave a measured twist. She felt the thumb come free from its socket as it became looser than the rest of his fingers. "The SIA is really in trouble if you're the standard of agent they're turning out. It was shockingly easy to incapacitate you."

The guy howled in pain, letting it all out into the corridor. A few agents had joined to watch by the others, more amused than worried.

Jennie released his hand and pushed it back toward him with a smile. "Might I suggest you apply for a refresher course in hand-to-hand? When your reminder to show some respect heals, of course."

His thumb smacked on the ground, and he yelled again. "I'll get you for this, bitch. I'll get you!"

Jennie strode away, making extra effort to shake her hips. She glanced over her shoulder. "Baby, you'll never have anyone like me."

She placed her middle finger behind her head and headed onto Hendrick's lab. The others waited until Jennie was out of sight before running to help him up off the floor.

"How long was I away for?"

Jennie marveled at the changes to the laboratory. What had previously been a single room crammed with all the equipment needed to make a science lab function had been expanded through both the east and west walls.

Construction was still underway on the east wall extension, but through a large archway on the west wall, Jennie could make out additional tables, as well as a stack of cardboard boxes, all labeled "Caution: Fragile."

"Eight days, thirteen hours, and two minutes," Hendrick replied without irony.

"Eight days?" Jennie retorted. "I was away for a week."

Hendrick nodded. "But you haven't visited the lab in eight days."

Jennie laughed and inspected the changes. A team of three workers was drilling and hammering the east wall, kicking up clouds of dust into the lab. "They work fast, don't they?"

Hendrick, who looked like a naked mole rat turned human, removed his glasses and cleaned off a fresh layer of fine dust. "It's all about speed at the moment. No one in here cares about the finer parts of the work that needs to be conducted in order to advance our progress." He traced a finger across a table and left a clean smudge behind. "Look at this. Non-stop dust. We can't work in these conditions."

"Then why are you?" Jennie motioned to the workers. "Why not wait until they're gone?"

"Because the alternative means fraternizing with an ever-expanding group of agents," Hendrick replied. "I'm not sure if you've met the new wave, but they're not my type of people. Besides, I'm happiest when I'm occupied and focused on a job at hand. Dust or no dust, I'll find a way to make this work. In fact, I already have. Come, see."

Jennie followed Hendrick toward a cubicle that had been created in the far corner of the room from a white PVC shower curtain. The cubicle had no air leaks, or any gaps among the folds of the fabric, and was large enough to house two people, maybe even three at a push.

Inside was one of their smaller desks, filled with the instruments Hendrick had been busy working with.

"What is this?" Jennie picked up an object the size of a board game die. She twisted it in her hands before Hendrick realized what she was doing and quickly snatched it from her.

"Be careful with that!" Hendrick tutted and placed the object delicately back on the table. "As our means of imbuing objects is advancing, we're working on new devices that expand the limitations of what we've previously known can be accomplished in the spectral plane. We've imbued firearms, handcuffs, goggles, you name it, we've mostly found ways to make them effective in spectral combat."

"So, this is a way to play Monopoly with ghosts?" Jennie chuckled.

Hendrick was not impressed. "This might be the most important device I've created yet. It's a prototype, mind, but it has yielded positive results so far."

"What does it do?"

Hendrick studied Jennie for a few moments with scrutinous eyes. She began to wonder if she was going to be live bait for his experiment when he shouldered past her and into the lab.

Jennie followed Hendrick out of the curtain.

He spotted a nearby specter. The ghost was resting against a table and trying to scroll on the screen of an iPad.

"Hey, Ashleigh!"

The specter hunted for the source of the call and found Hendrick. "You know this sucks, right? Can't you change the hardware on these things so they recognize spectral touch? All I want to do is read the goddamn news—"

Hendrick tossed the tiny cube at him before he could finish. The minute the cube made contact with his spectral flesh, it erupted in a brilliant white. Threads of light exploded from every angle, shooting out like the webs of a spider. They blanketed him and wrapped around his body, and he fell to the floor.

Jennie's mouth fell agape.

Ashleigh sighed. "Should I expect that every time I ask you a question?"

The trace of a laugh came across Hendrick's face. "Good work, soldier. I'm indebted for your service. As before, wait ten minutes, and you'll be free."

Hendrick disappeared back into the curtained area without a word. Jennie stared at the specter in amused shock.

"Oh, I don't mind this," Ashleigh explained without a hint of annoyance. "I'm literally employed to be the guinea pig for the R&D lab. It's not too bad. Pays well, but then…" He nodded at the bonds holding him still. "Shit like this happens."

Jennie left the bemused Ashleigh on the floor and followed Hendrick back into the cubicle. She burst out laughing. "Is this really your job now? Torturing specters with new inventions?"

"Part of it," Hendrick replied without mirth. "Every job has its perks, I suppose. The real thrill comes from the invention. Pretty slick, don't you think?"

"I'll say," Jennie admired.

Hendrick picked up a pencil sketch he had drawn and laid it flat on the table. "Imagine a dozen of those contraptions firing from a single shot. You'd have half your enemies down and bound before you'd even started the fight."

Jennie gave Hendrick a look. He didn't have to face her to see it; he had always been instinctual that way. "What?"

"Remember your days in London, producing perfumes and concoctions for the Paranormal Court and me? Who'd have thought you'd have such an affinity for firearms and combat?"

Hendrick nodded. "After decades working in one medium, it's nice to put that knowledge to use in a world where it matters. With you fronting the SIA's progress, I feel like I'm making a real contribution to spectral science."

A sadness came over Jennie. Although Hendrick believed in her, she knew the progress wasn't entirely for her. As long as she was a cog in the SIA's machine, all the progress would be in the name of the SIA. She needed to break free, establish her own organization before she got swept up in this rapid pace of progress from the SIA.

"Speaking of," Jennie started. "I may have something that I need you to look at. It's going to take a bit of work, but the reward will be massive."

"What do you have in mind?"

Jennie tapped her lip, thinking about the best way to explain what it is she wanted. "How would you feel about creating a power source that amplifies spectral activity and detects that which cannot be detected?"

Hendrick raised his eyebrows. She could almost see the whites of his eyes through the squinting behind his glasses. "Go on..."

CHAPTER SIX

Washington DC, USA

Two days later, Jennie stood with her hands on her hips, looking more like a superhero than a regular mortal. "I'm going back to Richmond, and I'm taking a team with me."

She had always stood out among the SIA, with her selection of vintage clothing a stark contrast to their fatigues, and now more so than ever as the numbers of black-clad agents increased in volume through the halls.

Daggro glanced up from her desk, a smug expression on her face. "On what grounds?"

Jennie looked around the old office that had once belonged to Hopkins. Daggro had wasted no time in making it her own, removing all traces of his personal items and replacing them with…well, nothing. The office was as cold and barren as she had learned Daggro to be.

"My reasons are my own," came Jennie's tight-lipped reply.

Daggro leaned back and let out a dramatic exhalation. She rested her hands on her stomach, just inches from her SIA regulation pistols, and chewed her lip. "I'm not sure I can allow you to do that without proper authorization."

It was Jennie's turn to give a smug grin. "I wasn't asking you. I was telling you. Consider it a courtesy so that no one worries where I am while I'm gone."

Daggro held her stare. The tension in the air was palpable. "Which team did you have in mind?"

Jennie told her.

Daggro chuckled, happy to have the upper hand. "*You* may be able to gallivant wherever you like but know that SIA agents are contracted to remain within the orders and confines of the SIA." She leaned across the desk. "I knew this day would come. Already looking to emancipate yourself from us, aren't you? You've just gotten over one war, and now you're looking to start a second?"

Jennie remained silent. She didn't need to clarify that this would be the third battle she'd been involved in since arriving on US soil, nor did she want to give Daggro any satisfaction in showing that she was getting to her. Daggro fed off misery. Jennie would not submit to show any of her own.

"I'm not looking for emancipation," Jennie replied flatly. "I'm merely continuing with my initial objective. Speak to your superior, he knows the nature of my business. I'm not sure he'd likely have shared it with those within the lower ranks. He's still a good agent, you know Agent Hopkins."

Daggro's cheeks flushed red as her satisfied smirk faded.

Jennie grinned. "I appreciate you taking time from your busy schedule to see me."

Jennie made to leave, but Daggro called after her. "No SIA agents. No SIA equipment. You want to abandon the agency for your own self-interests, then fine. Just know that not only will you be on your own out there, your absence will drag the morale of the whole team down."

Jennie turned, surprised. "Have you just given me your first ever compliment?"

Daggro growled.

Jennie threw a lock of hair over her shoulder. "I always knew you needed me, Daggro. You'd just never admit it, would you? I've survived through longer and worse with nothing but these two pistols by my side. Don't worry, though. I won't be on my own out there. I'm recalling everyone I supplied to the agency as a consultant. Get my people back here; we're leaving."

And then she was gone, leaving an unsettled Daggro in her wake.

<hr />

Jennie emerged into the bright Washington sunshine a little after midday.

It had been some time since she had seen the sun in its full glory. For the last week or so, she had operated only by night—*carpe noctem!*—and she was thankful that the lenses of her glasses were tinted. Even with them on, she had to shield her face from its rays.

"That's the problem with vampires." Agent Rhone laughed, appearing behind Jennie. "They can't stay in the sun all that long. It does things to their skin."

Jennie was surprisingly glad to see Rhone. After all the changes that had happened at the SIA over the last few weeks, it was good to see that nothing had changed with him. She embraced him and smiled. "I think you'll find that vampires immediately burst into flame in the sun. Or at least the ones that I've met do."

Rhone's face fell. "Please don't tell me we've got vampires to worry about, too?"

Jennie chuckled. "I'm only kidding. I've never encountered any vampires. Although, that's not to say they don't exist. Maybe they're just less attention-hungry than specters are?"

Baxter strode over from where he had been waiting inside the Mustang, melting out of the car door to cross to the pair. "We're not that bad, are we?"

"Not all of you," Jennie replied with a grin. "There are some good specters among you."

They stood in the middle of the SIA parking lot, the smell of warm asphalt all around them. It was the kind of heat where the roads in the distance warbled, and the traffic moved at a lazy pace. All around them were rows and rows of black SUVs, sedans, cruisers, and other sundry government vehicles. Jennie's Mustang, although a sleek black like the rest of the vehicles, stood out like a sore thumb. It was a horse among mules, and even now the sight of it made Jennie's heart leap.

Jennie wandered over to the Mustang and rested against the hood. The others followed. "So, Rhone, I assume this is just a flying visit? I was made to understand that I'm not allowed to take any agents. The SIA is very precious about protecting their own."

Rhone gave a knowing nod. "Daggro is letting the power get to her head. It won't last forever. As soon as Rogers is back, things will recalibrate. He's on your side, Rogue. We all are. Just know that."

Jennie studied his eyes, sensing the honesty within. She wanted to believe him, she really did. But her experience with large government-led organizations over the last century or so had left her with a few scars that were difficult to heal. She had only just got into the position where she was trusting others to join *her* team, and already the SIA—the organization she had helped induct into the spectral world—was cracking at the edges. Maybe the organization would rebalance, but Jennie had witnessed enough to know what the pressure of such a large operation could do to mortals.

"It's a shame you can't join us," Jennie replied, deciding to side-step Rhone's statement. "You're one of the good ones."

Rhone nodded to where a group of men and women were emerging from the SIA HQ. "You'll be fine out there, I'm sure. Your team will carry you far. The only problem is going to be fitting them all in your car."

They were a strange group. Leading the front of the charge, and surprising Jennie since as far as she knew the government had the right to recall them to active service, were the three conduits Jennie had helped to rescue the specters from their hideaway beneath the Lincoln Memorial. Ula Huntington, Triton Ward, and Roman Long looked a fierce team as they took confident strides toward them.

At least the SIA hadn't stolen them yet. Jennie smiled. Good old Hopkins, he had her back.

Behind them, Carolyn, Tanya, Sandra, and Lupe wandered across the parking lot, struggling to keep up with the leading three. Tanya was presently in spectral form, thanks to her connection with Sandra, and they held hands as they walked. Lupe had his hood shadowing his face, while Carolyn just looked pleased to see Jennie and Baxter ahead.

Carolyn ran ahead, shoving past the others to get to Jennie, earning herself unimpressed looks from the conduits.

"Jennie!" Carolyn embraced Jennie and beamed. "Good to see you."

Baxter coughed.

Carolyn chuckled. "And you, of course, Bax."

Jennie made a strange noise as Carolyn unwrapped herself from their hug. "Careful. You'll give people the impression that I'm a nice person and not the badass I truly am."

Ula scoffed, a smirk on her face. "I see you're still as modest as always."

Jennie shrugged. "It's just a part of my charm." She turned her attention back to Carolyn and stuck out her tongue. "I'm glad we waited for you, how was your *top-secret* mission?"

Carolyn rolled her eyes. "Boring as shit. There were reports from the east side of the city that a gang of specters was terrorizing a small farming family. Groans, things moving at night in the barn, things like that. Turns out that the father was running his own secret brothel and hiding the women in the basement beneath the barn in the daytime. There was no need for a specter to help at all."

Jennie turned up her lip. "The SIA really need to focus on sorting out their intelligence ahead of time. Just because there's a mention of spectral activity, doesn't mean they immediately have to muscle their way in and show them who's boss. The guys in the UK learned that one pretty quickly. If it's a real spectral issue, they'll *know*."

Rhone cleared his throat and raised a hand. "I mean, I'm right here, Jennie."

Jennie winked. "Am I wrong?"

Rhone half-shrugged. "The guys are just excited because the department is growing. As we spread out more into the neighboring states and set up our reconnaissance teams there'll be a few of these.

Every wave of growth eventually settles down in the end. I've seen it enough times, working for the government."

Jennie wrapped an arm around Rhone's shoulder. "Ever the optimist, aren't you? It's a shame you can't come with us, you know. I'd love to have you on my team."

Rhone raised his eyebrows. "We're all the same team, remember?"

"And what team is that?" Baxter questioned.

"Justice," Jennie and Rhone stated in unison, before laughing and setting off after the others. Even Ula had a smirk on her face. Triton and Roman, however, did not.

Tanya had already climbed into the back of Jennie's car and was letting out some of the heat that had accumulated inside. She poked her head out of the door. "Are we getting on the road, or not? I'd appreciate some air-con blasting out this heatwave."

Triton did a cursory headcount. "We're not all going to fit in there. How are we supposed to all journey together?"

Rhone held out a set of keys. "Take my car. You'll need it more than I will."

Jennie looked up in surprise. "Daggro made it perfectly clear. This is my mission, no SIA equipment. You don't want to get reprimanded by that spiteful bitch."

Rhone's eyes flicked toward a CCTV camera stationed on the wall nearby.

Jennie nodded in understanding, raising her voice. "Although, she is wonderful," she announced, "and amazing, and I don't know what we would do without her."

Rhone chuckled, muttering quietly enough so that only Jennie could hear, "Take it. Seriously, I can handle her. You go do what you need to do."

Jennie moved so that the camera couldn't catch the exchange, then pocketed the keys and hugged him again. "Thank you."

"You're welcome. Go get 'em."

They divided among the two cars, with the three conduits taking Rhone's black Chevrolet Equinox. Jennie, Baxter, Carolyn, Tanya, and

Sandra took the Mustang. Jennie thumbed the ignition and got the car purring.

They all looked set to get going when Hendrick burst out of the front doors of the SIA HQ and began half-shuffling, half-running toward them. His eyes were narrowed so tightly that it looked as if he was running totally blind. A large black satchel swung from the crook of his arm.

"What's Hendrick doing?" Carolyn asked with her nose pressed to the glass so tightly it was a wonder that she didn't melt out.

"He's joining us," Jennie replied. "The old mole has been holed up for so long I figured he might want to wander outside and get some sun on his skin." Hendrick grimaced, holding the bag over his head to block the sun. "Maybe there's a reason moles stay underground…"

Much to Ula's discomfort, Jennie assigned Hendrick to the Chevrolet. He clambered up into the high base of the SUV, made himself comfortable beside a disgruntled Roman, and soon they were ready to go.

"All set, chaps?" Jennie asked, turning around to face her passengers.

After a unanimous thumbs-up, she hit play on her phone and filled the car with the aggressive bumping bass of an urban UK rap artist.

Tanya covered Sandra's ears. "What the hell is this?"

"Stormzy," Jennie replied, craning her neck to look through the rearview. "Downloaded his album after our trip to London. Forgot all about it. Catchy, don't you think?"

"Yeah, about as catchy as herpes," Baxter mumbled.

"What?" Jennie shouted over the music.

"I said it rocks!" Baxter lied, exchanging a look with the others as they hid their laughs behind their hands.

CHAPTER SEVEN

Route 95, Virginia, USA

The road trip to Richmond may just have been one of the happiest times of Jennie's life.

After a rocky start, the group began to get in the groove of Stormzy. They learned the choruses of a number of his popular hits—*Own It* was a particular favorite—and as the sun shone above them they sailed the highway, reminiscing, laughing, joking, and imagining what the atmosphere must have been like with the three conduits and Hendrick in the Chevrolet.

It felt like years since Jennie had felt this unburdened and, in a way, she supposed it had been. The last time she had been truly happy would have been those final days when her parents were still around at the turn of the twentieth century, before her induction into the Paranormal Court. Life had changed forever when she had taken her place as Rogue.

They stopped for food at a Denny's on the outskirts of the city. The hostess questioned their motives when Jennie insisted on seating for ten, but her pointed headcount of the seven mortals she could see fell on deaf ears, so she let it drop and took them to the open booths by the window at the back.

They drank milkshakes and devoured burgers, watching out the wide glass windows as the sun painted the sky in licorice colors. When they were sufficiently fed and watered, they hopped back in their vehicles and drove the final stretch to the place Jennie was ready to face once again.

Mendleson Manor.

They waited around the corner, biding their time until night had fallen and they were truly alone. The manor lay at the top of a hill a short drive from the city, and many dog walkers and young lovers migrated to the heights to take advantage of the vantage point of the city.

"So...it's a house?" Carolyn asked, unimpressed. "What's so great about that?"

Jennie leaned against the cold metal of her car, one foot resting against the car door as she monitored a teen couple who laughed, kissed, then hurried their pace as they caught notice of the odd group waiting nearby.

"A couple of things, really. Baxter and I stumbled across it during our mission and found signs of spectral activity. We tried to clear it by ourselves but failed."

Sandra's mouth fell open. "*You* failed? I thought you were a superhero?"

Tanya laughed and rolled her eyes.

"I wish," Jennie cooed. "But even superheroes have their weak points. We came across something I've never encountered before inside that house. A type of specter that didn't show up on my radar." She turned to the conduits. "I'm wondering if you guys will be able to sense it at all. The fact that it escaped my radar has greatly alarmed me. I've never come across something that felt truly undetectable before."

Ula, Roman, and Triton stared at the building in the distance.

Ula answered, "Some faint spectral activity, perhaps. Though it's likely just being in close proximity to these guys." She thumbed toward Baxter, Sandra, and Carolyn.

"You've got me worried," Carolyn declared. "Something that beat the great Rogue? Are we strong enough to defeat it ourselves?"

Jennie shrugged. "We'll find out soon enough. When the church bells chime midnight, we'll take to the building and try once again."

Carolyn lowered her head. "Man, I wish Feng Mian was here. His shields might come in handy. Where did you guys say he was, anyway?"

"Out fighting the Dragon," Jennie grumbled with a hint of bitterness.

Carolyn gasped. *"The Dragon?"*

Baxter nodded. "Apparently so. Seems he's back and causing a ruckus in NYC."

Carolyn arched an eyebrow. "But isn't he with us? Y'know, a member of the Spectral Plane?"

Baxter grinned. "I think we're going for the Summer Court now."

Lupe raised a finger. "Actually, it's the King's Court."

Jennie laughed, deciding not to engage in that debate. "He's where he's needed. We can do this without him. We're going to have to. We need to clear this house."

Roman spoke up, breaking his reverent silence. "There's a motive here that you're not telling us."

Jennie stared at him for a moment. "I'm sorry, was there a question there, somewhere?"

Before he could reply, the church bells tolled midnight. Jennie checked the coast was clear.

It was.

Jennie clapped her hands. "Enough of that business, it's showtime."

Richmond, Virginia, USA

Jennie got a feeling of déjà vu as she looked at the manor. Although she was standing in the exact same spot, and the house looked exactly the same as it had before, something *felt* different.

Maybe the house has awakened, and I can finally sense the spectral power? Perhaps it's on edge, knowing that we'd come back?

"It's big," Carolyn declared, stating the obvious.

"Huge," Lupe agreed.

Hendrick squinted up at the building. "It's hungry."

They all turned to him, but if anyone else had something to say, they kept it to themselves.

Jennie led them up the overgrown path and toward the front door. This time, when she tried to open the door, she was alarmed to find that it was locked. Last time it had yielded like butter to a hot knife, but now entry was barred.

Baxter stepped forward. "I'll try to open it from the inside."

Even Baxter could not get through, no matter how he had pushed against the frame.

"They've done it again," Baxter complained.

"Done what?" Carolyn looked between them both with curiosity. "What are you not telling us?"

Jennie addressed the group. "There's a conjoined spirit inside, a specter who has become one with the house. During our last visit, I found only a few poltergeists in the basement, but Baxter encountered the main spectral mass."

"There were hundreds of tiny spectral imps," Baxter explained. "They attacked me all at once, and then when I tried to leave, they somehow merged together and became a part of this... this...*creature.*"

Lupe had lowered his hood, beads of sweat peppering his brow, his face contorted in worry. "Creature?"

"A huge white dog," Baxter continued. "It filled the entire music room, all the imps joining to become one with the motherlode. When we attacked it, we managed to separate the darkness, but we only revealed the ancient couple who were the puppeteers of the whole situation."

Roman clamped a cigar between his teeth and lit the end. "Now, we're talking."

Jennie chuckled. "The truth is, we don't know what we're dealing with here. Only that there is a dark power involved. We must first expel the lynchpins before the house will yield to us. Find the couple and deal with them together. Once they're gone, this will be a piece of cake."

Tanya nodded resolutely. "That all sounds good, Jennie. But how do we get in if they're blocking the doors?"

The shriveled, ancient man that was Hendrick reached into his satchel and drew out several metallic vials with LED lights striping the sides.

He passed them to Jennie. She placed them into the many loops and pockets she had on her pants and belt. When she was finished, there were around a dozen decorating her body, the lights glowing like small fireflies.

"What's that?" Baxter asked.

Jennie motioned to Hendrick. "Care to explain?"

"Spectral power cells," Hendrick replied in an unimpressed tone. "A way for Jennie to draw additional power if ever needed. While she can rely on specters to provide the energy for her powers, these cells will capture energy as she expends it, and increase the boosts associated with her skills."

Carolyn struggled to follow. "In layman's terms?"

This time, Jennie answered. "Imagine it this way: if specters are the batteries that fuel my powers, this removes some of the reliance on nearby specters. I could journey alone and power myself for a short period of time—provided I'd topped up from a specter to begin with. What is incredible about Hendrick's latest effort, is that as I latch onto specters, these capsules charge, and in doing so, the technology embedded within will create double the power against the initial input. Essentially, they're power boosters for me."

Lupe shook his head in awe. "How the hell do you invent this stuff?"

Hendrick pushed his glasses up his nose. "Science."

Tanya laughed. "Glad we cleared that up."

"Care to give us a demonstration?" Baxter asked.

Jennie faced the door and closed her eyes. She latched onto Baxter, and as the spectral connection joined the pair, a humming started.

The cells along her waist grew brighter, and soon the LED lights were shining with white beams.

Jennie unlatched from Baxter and turned her attention to the door. She lifted her hands and felt for the spectral force hidden within the door reacting to her. A beam of energy shot from her hands and wrestled with dark shadows holding the door shut.

White light and black shadow tousled. Jennie grimaced and could feel the power fighting back. After a few seconds of this tug-of-war, the cells depleted, and Jennie was knocked three steps back.

Jennie chewed her lip. "It's still going to need all of us. Sandra, do you mind giving me a hand here? Ula, Roman, Triton, stand at the ready, we're not sure what may happen next."

Sandra took position next to Jennie. Jennie latched onto Baxter, and Carolyn and soon, her cells were charged again. She focused on the door with Sandra and resumed her effort to break the block. The door erupted in a rectangle of white light as a girder-bending shriek filled the night air.

The shadows danced with the light, but they were no match. The darkness receded in a perfect arc around the door, and Jennie called to the conduits to open it while they had the chance.

Roman, Ula, and Triton needed no encouragement. They sprinted up the stairs and gave the door a generous application of boot leather. On the second attempt, the door yielded to their kicks and they were inside.

Jennie and Sandra held the darkness at bay as they ushered the others inside. When everyone else was inside, they crossed the threshold and released their power.

The darkness rushed in as the doors slammed shut, barricading them all inside. Triton tried the handle. "It's stuck fast. I hope you have an escape plan at the ready."

Jennie stared at the manor, on edge by how different the entire house felt compared to last time. Before, it had been an ancient ruin, ready for exploration and discovery. This time it was in defensive mode. The moonlight hardly touched the interior through the glass, the shadows moved as if they were alive, and the very air had turned frigid enough to frost their breath.

"There is no escape plan," Jennie replied quietly, already preparing for a coming attack. "We succeed, or we die trying."

"My preference is we succeed." Carolyn grinned, trying to add some levity to the situation.

Hendrick didn't pick up on this. "*Obviously*. Who would want to die trying?"

Carolyn looked to the others for help.

Jennie smiled, the expression slipping away as she took her first steps toward the staircase. She wanted to make her way to the music room, the place where it had begun.

She had no idea that the attack would come long before she made it to the top of the stairs.

CHAPTER EIGHT

Richmond, Virginia, USA

The stairs creaked, bowing slightly as though the boards were rotten, which was strange considering the last time she'd had no issue climbing them.

"Take it easy," Jennie instructed. "Things are different this time. We need to expect the unexpected."

Tanya screamed. Her foot fell through one of the boards, forcing her to cling onto Lupe for support. He held her tight, his other hand holding onto the banister.

Tanya dragged her foot out of the hole and stared into the darkness. Cackling glee echoed up from out of the pit as the poltergeists wheeled excitedly around the basement.

"Come on!" Jennie shouted, exploding into a run.

The others followed her lead. Baxter was at her side. She was only a few steps from safety when something strange happened. She had counted the five steps she needed to ascend to make it to the landing, but somehow they began to stretch on before her, casting themselves into an infinite treadmill. Jennie was sure she was moving, but there they were, five steps in front of her, again, and again.

And again.

And again.

"Jennie? What's going on?" Carolyn cried.

Jennie glanced over her shoulder. The stairs were gone. Only the bodies of her comrades were visible, floating on a bed of darkness as they all ran after her, suspended above an eternal abyss.

"The manor is playing with our minds," Jennie declared. "Don't let it in. If we do, we'll… *Shit—*"

Jennie's stomach jumped to her throat. The floor opened and the landing slipped away. She became aware of splintered wood and a sudden drop before her feet found concrete and she was jarred by the abrupt stop.

She bent her knees, positioning into a roll to absorb the shock.

Jennie stood and looked around the dark basement for the others. She could hear their groans but couldn't see them. She drew her cell phone and activated the flashlight app, sending its conical beam of light into the darkness.

She didn't like what she saw.

The specters were fine and on their feet already. Jennie was relieved to see that Sandra had turned Tanya spectral and she had been cushioned from the blow.

Ula, Roman, and Triton had each landed in an uneasy pile, but due to their military training had braced themselves for the fall. A strange lump moved across Triton's back, and Jennie almost laughed when Hendrick turned and came into view.

She counted the fallen, discovering one person missing. "Where's Lupe?"

A pained grunt came from the middle of one of the piles of trashy antiques. "Over here!"

Jennie ran over the debris and found Lupe holding his shin in a pile of vintage appliances. Sewing machines and an old gas oven were stacked near the top of the pile. A large shard of wood was protruding from Lupe's skin.

"It's deep!" Lupe complained. "It's deep! I'm going to die! I'm going to die!"

"Hendrick! We need you."

The mole-like man shuffled across the junk at surprising speed, settling in beside Lupe. "It is merely a flesh wound. We can fix this up in an instant."

He grabbed the wood, and Lupe reacted by slapping away his hand. "What are you doing, you psychopath? It hurts!"

Hendrick showed no sympathy at all. Instead, he motioned for Jennie to hold Lupe down while he got to work. She obliged and gripped Lupe's shoulders with surprising strength. Hendrick clasped the wood and ripped it out in one swift move. A moment later, amidst Lupe's cries of anguish, he had applied a gelatinous ointment and wrapped the wound in gauze.

"There," Hendrick declared.

Lupe screwed his eyes shut, then noticed that the pain had instantly vanished. He tentatively glanced at his shin and gave it a small wriggle. "What did you do to me?"

Hendrick shrugged and pushed his glasses up on his nose with a finger. "Fixed you."

Lupe looked at Jennie. She shook her head. "Just let it go. He doesn't share his secrets, but they work. Trust me."

Lupe examined his leg, expecting to see a glob of blood collecting on the gauze, but the damn thing was clean. "Impossible."

"Nothing is impossible," Hendrick croaked, nodding at the three shining specters flying toward them.

"Right on cue," Jennie sighed.

The poltergeists cackled, circling above them at an impressive speed. The conduits stood ready with their weapons and aimed them at the specters, but Jennie quelled their eagerness. "Don't shoot. They're as much victims of the house as we are."

The specters soared overhead again, this time sucking up furniture and bric-a-brac around them in the mini-gale they created.

The team shielded against the barrage with their arms before Jennie called out to them, "Enough! Do I need to give you another demonstration of my powers?"

The poltergeist in the robe hesitated and floated above Jennie. "You have returned? Are you stupid as well as dumb?"

The second specter paused beside him. He elbowed the first poltergeist hard in the ribs. "Stupid and dumb are the same thing."

"You would know," the first specter retorted.

They squared up and stared at each other with anger in their faces, only breaking apart when the third poltergeist swept between them and hurled a stack of books at Jennie.

He pivoted with a triumphant laugh, and tried to escape in a flurry of movement, but Jennie latched on and held him back. His mirth melted into instant concern as he struggled against her bond. "Release me! Brothers, assist me, won't you?"

The other poltergeists folded their arms and grinned. "Your mess. You get out of it."

Jennie exchanged a look with the pair. "And you thought *you* were the dumb ones."

They cackled enthusiastically, watching their brother squirm. The specter Jennie had control of tried everything he could to free himself as she dragged him closer toward her, but nothing worked.

Eventually, he gave up and glared at her, folding his arms. "It's no fun if you cheat."

"It's no fun if you forget what I'm capable of," Jennie retorted, holding the poltergeist an arm's length away. "Have we not already been through all of this with you?"

"It's in our nature," the first brother declared. "Don't blame us for what we've become. Mischief is our business, darkness is our friend."

Baxter looked at him curiously. "I thought it was the darkness that was keeping you lot holed up in this squalid little basement?"

The first brother gasped. "Squalid?"

The second brother placed a hand on his chest. "Little?"

The third brother chuckled darkly. "This basement is a palace." His laughter faded as his thoughts took over. "Although it's not the same as roaming the upstairs halls and haunting the brave little children."

"You met them, didn't you?" the first brother asked. "You saw them together?" He knitted his fingers as though sharing a dirty secret.

"How was it? Did she scare you? Oh, I bet she did, didn't she? Terrorized you and flung you from the house. Poor little mortal."

Jennie glared at the specter, and he instantly shut up. "You three know this house better than anyone else we know. How long has the darkness lived in the house? How did this all come to be?"

The poltergeists exchanged glances with each other and asked for the third to be released from Jennie's grip. She obliged, and they entered a huddle in which all that could be heard was their furious whispering.

They eventually broke apart. The second poltergeist took a slight move toward the group. "We will tell you. Though, we wish for something in return."

Jennie curled her lip. "Name it."

In unison, they replied, "We wish for our freedom."

Carolyn pulled up beside Jennie. "I thought poltergeists couldn't be freed from the locations in which they haunt? Are you asking to be exorcized?"

At once, all three poltergeists' eyes widened in fear. They waved their hands.

The first poltergeist nearly choked. "No! No, no, no! Not that. Not that at all!"

The third poltergeist clarified, "We mean that we know there are skills within you beyond our understanding, and you are clearly on the warpath to expunge the evil from this house. What we ask is that you do not include us in your fruitful bounty."

The first brother pulled a face. "Fruitful bounty?"

The third brother groaned. "*Excuse* me for getting decorative with language."

The second brother exploded in laughter.

The third brother continued. "What I mean to say is, leave us be. We like this house. We mean no harm to those who intrude within the borders of our property. We just wish to have some fun."

"At others' expense," Baxter grumbled.

The first brother grinned. "Usually."

"Often," added the second brother, his smile stretching across his face.

"Fine." Jennie offered a hand. "You help us, we'll help you."

Baxter leaned toward Jennie. "Are you sure about this? What about the plan?"

Jennie spoke out the side of her mouth, "Don't worry. We got this."

The second brother clapped his hands. "Well, thanks for whispering for our benefit, there was *no* way we heard that." He floated toward Jennie and grabbed her hand. "Either way, a deal's a deal. No taking it back now that it's been made. An agreement among gentlemen."

"Gentlemen?" Carolyn scoffed. "I'm surprised you have any morals at all."

Jennie interjected before the poltergeists could reply. "A deal is a deal. Tell us what you know."

The three floated down to sit on the piles of trash on the ground. As the house creaked and groaned above them, they told them everything.

The house hadn't always been haunted, most houses don't begin their life cycle tormented by the specters. Built atop the hill for a wealthy couple who had traveled over from Britain, the house had once been a shining beacon of what could be achieved by those who pursued the American dream.

Life was simple, to begin with. The Mendlesons did what every young couple did and built a home to become their nest. Annabel Mendleson was a fertile woman and bore many children in her lifetime, delivering children for her husband until she was well into her forties. By the time her final breath was counted, there would be no less than twenty-six of her offspring roaming around the house, including many sets of twins and even one of triplets.

As the years went on, Annabel grew concerned about the darkness that had begun to creep into her life. Age had darkened her vision, and soon enough, she realized that her eyesight was failing her. A few months later her vision failed entirely, leaving her to stumble around the house and chase the children while her husband Theodor continued to make the money and run the business.

One night, a storm hit Richmond. The rains yelled, and the winds shouted back. The house rocked on its foundations, and lightning broke the darkness in camera flashes. It was on this night that Annabel summoned a priestess to her bedside who promised to return her eyesight.

The priestess could be heard calling and declaring her chants from across the city. Her voice, unnaturally loud, carried into the ears of the children. They hid in their beds as flashes of white exploded from the Mendlesons' windows.

When Annabel's husband returned home, fighting the elements to reach his manor, his wife was nowhere to be seen.

Not much is known about what happened that night, only that Annabel disappeared. The children knew nothing of what occurred in that room, yet they sensed that their mother was still near. Often, they would dream of her standing and watching by their bedsides, but when they woke up, they'd see nothing but the shadows crawling around the room.

Until one day, they too began to disappear.

It is said that Annabel took the children, one by one, dragging them into her bosom and holding them within the confines of their house. Theodor receded from the community, concerned for his children's safety, and soon abandoned his business altogether. Six months after Annabel went missing, he had but one child remaining.

He clung to that boy for dear life, yet refused to abandon the house, hoping he could bring back the other children. Late one night, his wish was granted, although it was not in the way he had expected.

Annabel came to him at midnight, in the middle of Richmond's next great storm. She looked peaceful, glowing in white light and surrounded by her children. She invited Theodor and their youngest son to join them, claiming that they would forever be united, immortal and able to live their lives together. Theodor, so weary worn and desperate, said yes almost instantly.

It was two weeks later that the postman discovered that the house was all but empty, realizing that his deliveries had stacked up against the door and were blocking the mailbox.

There was an investigation, and then the house was put on the market. It remained empty until three months after the disappearance of the Mendlesons, when the house was purchased by…

"By three brothers?" Baxter was enraptured by the story, his head resting on the cradle of his hands. "That was when you bought the house?"

The brothers nodded.

The first brother broke out of his reverie. He always left the story-telling to the third, knowing how much better he was at speaking. "We didn't know what we were getting into. It happened almost at once. Two weeks into living in the house, and we were taken, offered the choice of immortality, and we took it."

Carolyn frowned. "Just like that? Two weeks? Seems unlikely."

"They have power," the second brother insisted. "It's almost hypnotic. We were promised immortality, a doorway into the spectral realm, and instead, we were twisted by their power and turned into… into *this*."

Sadness washed over the trio. For the first time since Jennie had met them, they had lost the edge of their elfish appearance and looked almost normal, a blurry reflection of who they once might have been.

"So, how do we destroy the darkness?" Lupe asked. "This sounds like some powerful stuff."

Jennie turned back to him. "We give them what they've always wanted. We unite them forever in eternity."

"An exorcism?" Carolyn sat up eagerly.

"The largest one I may ever have performed," Jennie replied, her face resolute. "But first, I need to know a little bit more about this priestess. Tell me, brothers, what do you know of her and her spells?"

The brothers exchanged a grim look before telling Jennie what they knew.

Jennie turned to Hendrick. "Think you can lend a hand?"

Hendrick unzipped his satchel. "I always like a challenge."

CHAPTER NINE

<u>Richmond, Virginia, USA</u>

They prepared themselves at the bottom of the basement staircase. Above them, the house lay in wait, the boards creaking as though it was talking to itself.

"This isn't going to be pretty, folks." Jennie's eyes narrowed. The door above them was ajar. That seemed strange to her. The house was tempting them, playing with them after its triumph on the stairs.

"On my count," Jennie instructed. "Three. Two. One…"

She made a break for it, speeding up the stairs two at a time. When she reached the door, it tried to slam shut, but she jammed her fingers in its way. Pain throbbed in each digit, but she held fast.

Ula, Roman, and Triton came to her aid, the four of them managing to peel the door open and enter into the house.

Jennie hadn't been expecting what was in front of her.

The house had morphed entirely, its layout changing while they had been down in the basement. The walls appeared warped and uneven, and the floor was tilted. There were no windows and only a few doors that were half the size of the ones she had seen before.

"It's a trick." Jennie tried to remember the layout of the house in her head, while the three conduits took positions with their weapons.

Ula went ahead and crashed into something she couldn't see. According to the projection, she should be in the middle of the room, but the sound of a vase breaking came to them, and Ula was left nursing her arm. "The house is projecting what it wants us to see. Proceed with caution and follow me."

They poured out of the basement and moved quickly, hugging the wall to the staircase. Although the rest of the house was a false projection, Jennie didn't want to chance going up the stairs. She would have to find another way.

"Breakout!" Jennie instructed, sending the team into action.

Baxter, Tanya, and Sandra peeled away and fumbled for the doorway that had led through to the kitchen. Baxter had been one of the few to see the downstairs layout, so he put his knowledge to the test.

Lupe, Carolyn, and Roman went next, racing ahead and disappearing through a door that shouldn't have been there, accompanied by the third of the poltergeist brothers. Ula and Triton were paired with the other two. They took their position, disappearing into the east wing as their spectral guides showed them the way.

Jennie and Baxter were accompanied by Hendrick, who, despite his years mostly spent in quiet labs and dark places by himself, appeared to be enjoying the experience immensely. The imminent danger they found themselves in seemed to be no bother.

"*This* is what it's like to be Rogue, huh?" he mused, the corners of his mouth upturned into a strange smile. "Exciting."

Jennie couldn't help but let out a small laugh before waving the pair onwards and taking her position in the west wing.

They ran through corridors that seemed too small to fit them. The shadows danced around them and created illusions made to confuse and guide them out of the house. On one occasion, Jennie opened a door and found that she was staring at the front lawn, the house tricking her into navigating toward the front door.

"Son of a bitch!" She screwed her fists in anger and fought against the immense pressure that was determined to drive her out of the house.

At least the house is getting confused. Trying to eject this many parties can't be an easy feat, right?

On a couple of occasions, they could hear cries of alarm from the others, although they disappeared almost as quickly as they had come. By the time Jennie found what she was almost certain to be the room directly below the music room, she felt as though she had been fighting for hours.

Jennie pulled her cell from her pocket. The screen flickered with static. She hoped that was just another trick. She tapped a few areas on the screen and heard the whooshing sound of a message sent. All that was left to do was hope that the others could *receive* her text.

"Ready to dive back in?" Jennie shouted, her voice straining to be heard above the increasing gale that was whipping their coats and clothes.

Baxter shrugged. "I guess there's only one answer, right?"

Hendrick beamed, the wrinkles in his forehead deepening into trenches. "Oh, boy."

Jennie latched onto Baxter and turned spectral. Immediately the cells around her waist began charging, lighting up one by one as the power magnified. Baxter doubled over and offered a cradle with his hands. Jennie placed a foot in. She gripped his shoulders and looked into his eyes, her hair whipping frantically about her face.

"On your count," she instructed.

Baxter counted to three, then launched Jennie into the air. At the same time, she jumped, disappearing through the ceiling above.

The music room was the only room that hadn't been altered by the Mendlesons. Although the walls were darkened and it looked as though she were viewing the room in an old polaroid, the layout and the furniture remained untouched.

She concentrated on her connection with Baxter and pulled him up toward her. His head appeared through the floorboards, then his arms, and he clambered to his feet.

He smirked. "Ready for your violin lesson?"

Jennie gave him a look that suggested that now was not the time to be kidding.

She turned her attention to the floor and lined up the Big Bitch. She set off three quick shots and created a hole large enough to fit a man through. Taking a coil of rope she had found among the debris in the basement, she tied a loop and lowered it to Hendrick. He placed his foot in the loop and held on tight as Jennie struggled to haul him up, surprised by just how dense and heavy he was.

She grunted. "Jesus, maybe you should create a potion to lose a few pounds."

Meanwhile, the darkness around the room began to grow. As she focused on hauling Hendrick up, small flashes appeared at the corners of the room as the imps returned.

Baxter scanned the increasing number of imps. "Jennie…I don't mean to be *that* guy, but maybe you should hurry."

Hendrick was almost up.

"I'm doing all that I can right now." She grimaced. "Where are the others?"

As if summoned by the question, the door to the music room exploded into a thousand wooden shards. Ula, Roman, and Triton appeared through a dense fog, accompanied by the others.

"Remind us never to follow you into a haunted house ever again," Ula declared, looking disheveled and breathing heavily.

Jennie laughed, but the sound was quickly snatched by the growing presence in the room. "They're back, folks. Hold onto your hats, things are about to get dicey in here!"

They assembled in a semi-circle as the shadows became caught in the wind and whipped into a frenzy in the center of the room. The piano deconstructed before their eyes and became a part of the whirlwind that slowly began to coalesce into the great hound Baxter had witnessed before.

"I'm guessing that saying 'heel, boy,' won't work," Carolyn cried out.

They aimed their weapons. Sandra glowed with her power, ready to act on Jennie's command. Between them all, Jennie hoped they'd have enough power to overcome the damn beast.

The imps flew into the hound and became a part of its body. It reared on its haunches and released an angry bark.

Jennie kicked the plan into action. "Conduits, now!"

Ula, Roman, Triton, and even Lupe, sprinted at the beast. They ducked and dived to avoid its massive jaws and leaped onto its body, crawling over its back and sides. It snapped its jaws toward them but could not reach. The poltergeists jumped in, flying around the dog's face at breakneck speeds and confusing its line of focus.

With the distraction in place, Jennie commanded Baxter and Carolyn to attack. Baxter readied his wrench, then leaped forward and bashed the great metal head against the dog's muzzle. It cried out in pain, and its eyes flashed an angry white. Carolyn borrowed Baxter's pistol and sent five shots at the dog's feet, causing it to dance in pain.

Hendrick glanced up at Jennie, seemingly unaffected at all by the whole ordeal. He had a monk-like calm that Jennie respected, but couldn't understand completely. "Now?" he asked.

Jennie shook her head, eyes fixed on the beast. "Not yet. Soon."

The dog thrashed around the room, doing whatever it could to try and escape the sudden onslaught. Soon enough, the imps were freed from the dog's form and it began to shrink, until all that was left was the shadow-infested couple, floating ten feet above the ground and staring angrily at the intruders.

Theodor Mendleson opened his mouth to speak, but Annabel spoke first. A banshee-shriek filled the room, causing everyone to cup their hands over their ears. When she was done, she launched herself at Jennie, dragging Theodor with her.

Jennie squared her feet but couldn't entirely resist the force of the blow. She was thrown backward as the weight of the couple threw her into the wall. Her head cracked against the plaster, but the adrenaline surging through her kept the edge off.

She grasped the woman's arms. Annabel's face was inches from hers, a contorted mass of rage spitting in her direction. Jennie could feel the anger within the darkness that surrounded her, decades and centuries of torment. She hated that pain, and wanted to remove it from her and help her. No one should have to endure that much misery.

"We're here to help," she managed, fighting against Annabel. Theodor was less inclined to fight, limply holding on and bracing himself against his wife's torment. "Let us help you!"

"No!" Annabel screamed.

Over Annabel's shoulder, Jennie saw the others engaged in a fight with the imps. Shots were fired as they did what they could to control the pest problem. Everyone was tied up in some kind of combat.

Despite Annabel's furious efforts to attack her, Jennie did her best to focus on the job at hand. She looked internally and felt for a connection with Annabel and Theodore. Her spectral tendril connected with the darkness, fighting through the shadow until she found the heart within. She wasn't surprised to find that at the woman's center was immense fear.

Fear leads to anger.

Anger leads to hate.

Hate leads to suffering.

Great, we're back at Star Wars again...

"You don't have to live like this," Jennie managed. "You don't have to experience pain like this. We can help you. Let us help you."

Annabel responded with an incomprehensible shriek.

"Fine. Have it your way."

Jennie pushed back, her spectral cells fighting to recharge as she expended the energy against Annabel and got to her feet. Annabel's eyes widened in alarm, and she furiously tried to hold onto Jennie.

Jennie managed to work a bit of distance between them. She rocked on her heels as Annabel's power matched hers. Theodor responded to Jennie's sudden threat and helped his wife, adding to the struggle.

"Sandra. Time!" Jennie shouted.

Sandra gave a steeled nod and broke free from her cohort of imps. She closed the distance between them, looking so out of place as the small girl that she was, yet her power was strong. She stretched her arms out toward Annabel and Theodor, and a beam of light connected them together. The others worked around her to keep her clear from the path of the ever-frantic imps.

Annabel froze, only for a moment. She twisted her attention away from Jennie to look at this new threat and flailed her limbs in an effort to break the connection. Shadows danced off of her and tried to make for the girl who was glowing a bright white, her features disappearing behind the light.

"Good girl," Jennie encouraged. "Hendrick, it's over to you, boy. Show them how it's done."

Hendrick, who had been silently marveling at the action, ignored by all imps, waddled over and reached into his bag. He drew out three vials that were filled with a substance not too dissimilar from the silver liquid they had collected from the Shadow's base of operations.

"What is that?" Theodor asked, terror present on his face.

Jennie grinned. "A little bit of what put you where you were in the first place, combined with some modern technology that we've been working on. We'd tell you the specifics, but it's patent-pending." She glanced at Hendrick. "Also, I have no idea what kind of magic that man works."

Annabel kicked into her final rage, tugging against Jennie and Sandra's hold. Even the imps cowered in fear at the sight of her.

"Let them have it," Jennie instructed.

Hendrick nodded and walked beneath the pair. He uncorked the vials and held them above his head. The liquid snaked out like a sentient worm and immediately combined with the couple.

The darkness broke. A blinding flash spiked as the substance worked its magic and tore into the couple. There came a crash as they fell limply to the floor, then all that had been projected in darkness and shadow receded.

Jennie lowered her hand from her eyes and peered down at the couple on the floor. Their mortal bodies had finally been released, and now they lay side-by-side. Theodor blinked and opened his eyes. Startled, he pushed into a sitting position and glanced around the room.

"Where are we?"

All around him, the imps had collapsed, too. In their places were the bodies of the children, teens, and young adults who had gone missing all those years ago. They blinked and sat up, dazed by the whole experience.

"You are home," Jennie replied, kneeling by Theodor's side. "You are safe, though this will not last for long. You owe a debt to death, and it will soon come to claim you."

Theodor turned to Annabel and grabbed her shoulders. He shook her and then kissed her on the lips. "Annie? Annie, wake up."

Annabel's eyelids fluttered, her features twisted in confusion. "Theo? Is that you? What happened? I had the craziest dream."

Theodor laughed, tears making his eyes sparkle. He embraced her and wiped his nose on his sleeve. "I think we all shared that dream. But," he glanced around the room, "We're together, at long last."

Jennie smiled. "It's been some time. Over two hundred years, to be exact. You wanted immortality, but you didn't know what price it would cost you. I think you both found your answer in the end."

Annabel screwed her face up, trying to remember. She touched Theodor's face, and it was at that moment that he remembered her former visual impairment. "It's me, my love. I'm here, so don't worry about your vision. Life beyond the veil might fix it."

The children gathered around her now, all piling into a large hug. Theodor and Annabel laughed, some of the children cried. Jennie watched from the side-lines with a smile on her face.

Beyond pain, there is love. Love springs eternal.

As they grouped around each other, their light began to fade.

"It's time," Hendrick stated. "Death waits for no one."

"It's waited years for us," Theodor replied, a warble of worry in his voice. He looked around at his wife and children. "Do not be afraid. Whatever comes next, we will conquer this together."

Annabel silently cried, the largest smile on her face. "Thank you, whoever you are. Thank you, a thousand times, over. You do not understand how long we have lived in this prison."

Jennie gave a nod that Annabel didn't see. "Everyone deserves love and freedom. Now, go. Enjoy yours."

And with that, the family faded from view, disappearing into the realm that man was yet to understand.

The room was silent for a long while as Jennie and the others paid their respects to the Mendlesons. Even the poltergeists remained quiet, their faces downcast. It wasn't until Jennie finally stood up and spoke into the emptiness where they had been that the silence was broken. "Whatever the veil brings, may you all rest in peace."

Baxter stood beside her. She rested her head on his shoulder and allowed herself a moment to breathe.

Soon she would get to work on fixing up the manor. But first, it was time to let the others in on her masterplan.

CHAPTER TEN

<u>Washington DC, USA</u>

Rhone didn't like this at all. Everything about the situation was wrong.

Daggro stared at Rhone from across her desk—*Hopkins'* desk—with the faintest trace of a smile on her face. In front of her was an iPad and a sheaf of paper documents. Her computer screen was already half twisted toward Rhone. "I think you know why you're here."

"Because you've missed my dashing good looks and you're finally ready to meet me in the supply closet for a quickie?" Rhone winked.

Daggro's face curdled. "Do you really think you should be talking that way to your superior?"

Rhone chuckled. "C'mon, it wasn't that long ago we shared a damn office. We've worked side-by-side, you and me. Ever since this department was founded, we've climbed the ladder together, don't tell me you've already let the power go to your head."

Daggro continued to stare, her expression hard to read. She bridged her fingers together and rested her chin on top of them, leaning closer to Rhone. "You of all people should be aware that this department is growing more rapidly than anything the government has ever known. Since our little outing to Alexandria, and the new contract with the Paranormal Court, we've grown our workforce by five hundred percent. Our reach, in regard to spectral control and operations, has widened to as far as New York in the east, and West Virginia in the west.

"As one of the fastest-growing federal agencies, there are opportunities to expand across the board. Opportunities for promotions, raises, to gain new skill sets. I have seized such an opportunity and I am now *your* superior, so you would do well to remember that, Agent Rhone."

Rhone saluted. "Yes, ma'am." He felt displeasure at the sick joy that brought Daggro.

"The point is," Daggro continued, "that in this time of growth, we need to be working together. Agents need to be working on the same side. Orders must be obeyed. United we stand, divided we fall, it's on our damn currency for fuck's sake."

Daggro slammed a handful of copper coins on the desk, causing Rhone to flinch.

"Work together," Rhone responded. "Got it. Anything else...*boss?*"

Daggro leaned back in her chair and twisted the monitor the remainder of the distance so that it faced Rhone. She tapped a button on the keyboard, and CCTV footage filled the screen. The footage showed Rhone and Jennie in the parking lot. It captured the moment of their "hug" as Rhone handed her the keys to his Chevrolet. A moment later, it skipped forward to the conduits and Hendrick climbing inside and driving away.

"The same side?" Daggro asked. "Does that look like the same side to you?"

Rhone did his best to look innocent, sticking out his bottom lip and shaking his head. "I don't know what you're asking, Holly. I was saying goodbye to some friends."

"It's *Special Agent Daggro,* to you, Rhone. And you know the command, if that spoilt bitch wants to run off and play in her own sandbox, then she's more than permitted to do so. However, she goes without our resources or our aid."

"Seems a lonely life."

"It should be," Daggro growled. "You provided that woman with a vehicle to assist in her endeavors. That car is SIA property and you willingly handed it over to Rogue, contrary to clear instructions from your superiors not to."

Despite himself, Rhone smiled. "Oops."

Daggro flushed red. Rhone had seen this type of behavior before, a childish brat who thought that authority brought her respect. Rhone had no problem respecting his superiors when they showed they had the agency's best interest at heart. But Daggro was using her position to abuse and bully, and that was something he wouldn't be subjected to.

Daggro unconsciously grabbed a piece of paper and screwed it into a ball in her fist. She slammed a hand on the table and shouted, "I will not take that kind of insubordination in my department. I have a line of agents training to be in a position to take your spot. I'd expect better from you."

Rhone, looking unfazed, waved a hand. "Please, Daggro, you know as well as I do that it'll be months before anyone is trained to be in a position to do what I do. Take a breather, we can figure this out. It was one vehicle, what harm could it do?"

Daggro exhaled loudly through her nostrils and sat back in her chair. She took a few steadying breaths and closed her eyes. When she opened them, there was a strange smile on her face. "You think you're indispensable, don't you?"

"Hopkins certainly thought so," Rhone replied. "He thought we both were. We were a team, remember?"

Daggro nodded her head slowly. She reached into her lower drawer and presented a piece of paper to Rhone. "That's right, Rhone. We *were* a team. Things are changing around here, and I'm not sure you quite fit the cut anymore."

Rhone chuckled, though there was a nervousness there. "What are you talking about?"

It was Daggro's turn to chuckle. "Agent Rhone, I hereby dismiss you from the Spectral Intelligence Agency, on account of misconduct, disobeying a direct instruction, and refusing to cooperate with a superior's requests."

Rhone's mouth fell open. "Hold on a minute, I..."

Daggro interjected. "This dismissal is effective immediately, please take your things and leave the premises as fast. Two guards are waiting outside to assist you in this. An investigation will be opened imminently to further explore the charges. However, with the evidence I have, your outlook is bleak. Please feel free to appeal, although I don't like your chances should you explore that route."

Daggro pressed a button and a small buzzer went off. The door opened and two agents who Rhone had never seen before, but looked half his age, stood either side of his chair.

"If there's anything else?" Daggro asked, smug satisfaction on her face.

Rhone shook his head and narrowed his eyes. "What the hell happened to you?"

Daggro laced her hands behind her head. "Success, my friend... Success..."

Without another word, Rhone was guided out of the room.

Richmond, Virginia, USA

The manor already felt like a different place as the sun came up over the horizon and sent golden shafts of light filtering through the grimy windows.

Jennie roamed around the manor, familiarizing herself with its layout. There were three floors, and each of them offered fresh insights into the house's past and filled her with ideas of how she could repurpose the place.

The others had also taken to exploring the house. She could hear them downstairs, laughing and calling to one another as they discovered new treasures and found pieces of interest. Carolyn had even come across a few hidden rooms that might turn out handy in the future.

Baxter stood by her side as Jennie leaned against the door jamb and studied the master bedroom. A grand four-poster bed took one side of the room, yet there was easily enough floor space to fit a dozen more beds in there if she wanted.

The specter smiled. "It's a great find."

Jennie nodded. "I told you. The old library had blueprints of this place, and I saw the potential instantly. Far enough away from the SIA that we won't have to worry about constantly butting heads, but close enough that we can find a way to work together…and keep an eye on them, of course."

Baxter chuckled, then his face grew somber.

"What is it?" Jennie asked.

"It's just…the Mendlesons. There was so much misery there. How did you know you could heal them? What if all they wanted was to reside here forever? How did you know what to do?"

A far-off look came over Jennie, and she strode into the room. She crossed to the thick moth-bitten curtains that blocked the sunlight from breathing life into the room and pinched the material between her fingers. "No one wants to live in pain forever, Bax. It was obvious that they needed help crossing over to the other side. Darkness and hatred communicate one major message, and that's pain and suffering. Annabel wanted to be with her family, and she got all that she ever wanted, she just didn't know the price it would cost."

"But to see through all of that and…and know that they were going to be okay." He paused. "You *do* know that they're okay, don't you?"

Jennie wrinkled her brow. "No. Nothing is certain when you cross over beyond the veil, you should know that. What I do know is that every story must have an ending, so that others may have a beginning." She drew open the curtain in one sweep and blinked in the morning light.

Baxter moved to the center of the room and looked around. "You realize that your motives could be misconstrued for selfishness?" He glanced at her but didn't move his head, gauging her response as he played Devil's advocate. "Some might say you're justifying this all to yourself so you could use this house."

Jennie laced her fingers behind her back and stared out over the city. Richmond truly was a beautiful place, viewed from up high. Morning traffic was steady, and she could see the market coming alive far off in the depths of the town.

"My priority is and has always been spectral survival. I know my role with the Queen was often to mute problems, but it's only ever been for the greater good. The Mendlesons were suffering. I relieved their pain. Even if this manor hadn't been a motivation for me, I would still have acted the same. The manor is a fortunate by-product of healing, and I swear on the Mendlesons' name that this house will be put to good use." She turned over her shoulder with a mischievous smile. "Besides, you should know I don't give a shit what people think of me. I do the job, and that's that. Let others think what they may."

Baxter offered a slow round of applause. "All hail the King's Court."

Jennie gathered her group to assemble in the drawing room. There were enough couches to seat them all, and the borders of the room were decorated with vintage wooden sideboards filled with glasses full of liquor that had aged to the point of extinction. A large chandelier hovered overhead, spiderwebs and dust turning the light into something that more closely resembled gray cotton candy.

Jennie spread her arms wide and presented the manor. "Well? What do you all think?"

Carolyn was the first to answer. "This place is *amazing*. I must have counted at least eighteen bedrooms. There are also two kitchens and a bunch of hidden rooms filled with children's toys and, well, one of them may have contained something that could either be interpreted as a mini-prison or..."

"Bondage gear," Triton finished. He patted Carolyn's thigh. "I understand it's difficult for someone of your age to speak about such things."

Tanya placed her hands over Sandra's ears.

Carolyn shrugged. "Yeah, bondage gear."

Jennie and the others started laughing.

Lupe spoke over the laughter. "Hopefully it was the former, not the latter. The last thing we need to think about is the Mendlesons getting involved in BDSM." This elicited more laughs from the group.

"Anyway..." Jennie managed, trying to pull them back on track. "It's a great place, right? Big, roomy, a great view."

"Yeah, it's lovely," Ula chipped in. "Probably one of the biggest private houses I've seen. It's a trove of treasures, though it certainly needs some looking after. I don't even have asthma, but I'm pretty sure I've inhaled enough dust to trigger an asthma attack."

Carolyn crossed her legs and gave Jennie an inquisitive look. "Why are you talking about this place like a real estate agent? You looking to buy this plot?" She sat forward with sudden excitement. "Oh. My. God. You are, aren't you? That's *so* Jennie!"

Jennie exchanged a glance with Baxter and found him smiling. Though he remained quiet, his eyes seemed to say, "Go on..."

Jennie drew her cell from her pocket and held out a screen to the rest of the group. "The property is already in my name. Bax and I met the agent and made the payment a few days ago. Mendleson Manor is now officially King Manor."

There was an audible gasp from some of the people in the room. Even Roman, who traditionally held a permanent poker face, raised his eyebrows.

"How?" Tanya scoffed. "How is this possible? This place must sell for, like...I don't know...millions?"

Jennie pocketed her cell and shrugged. "Several million, yeah. We don't need to go into the minutia of my finances, but suffice to say that years of investing, saving, and working under the Queen creates a nice little nest egg to occasionally splash on things like this."

Lupe glared at Jennie.

"What?" she asked.

"You're hiding away millions, and you let me pay for your meal at the diner?" Lupe grumbled.

Jennie chuckled. "One good turn deserves another. You can have priority pick on your new bedroom."

The others gave Jennie confused looks.

"You want us to live here?" Sandra asked, mouth wide open. Jennie couldn't imagine what this would mean to Sandra, a girl from a time when only the aristocracy lived in extravagance.

"I do," Jennie confirmed. "This purchase is an investment on my part as we strive to become what we set out to become. I've emancipated myself from the Paranormal Court, I have contracts in place to secure our exploration of the United States and its surrounding regions, this is where we make our stand and truly bring the King's Court into life."

"The King's Court?" Triton scoffed derisively. "Who came up with that name?"

Jennie looked out over the top of her glasses. "You don't like it?"

Triton laughed, looking around at the others for reassurance. Everyone remained quiet, not used to someone questioning Jennie's wisdom. "The King's Court? Seriously?"

"What did you have in mind?" Jennie asked, curious to see where his train of thought was going.

Triton shrugged. "I'd have thought you'd want to get away from all that stuff. Kings and Queens. Royalty. Y'know…Start afresh?"

Jennie and the others chuckled. "I appreciate your honesty, we need more of that around here. But I'm happy to embrace my long life and the names and lessons it has bound me with. King is my surname, we're separating from the Queen, so King it shall be. All in favor, say 'aye.'"

The chorus of "ayes" was more resounding than the raising of hands.

"Well, that settles it. Ladies and gentlemen, welcome to the King's Court. Now, shall we set about making this dust-ridden hovel of a manor a home?"

CHAPTER ELEVEN

<u>Chinatown, New York, USA</u>

The streets were all but empty, and rain slicked the sidewalk. Neon signs lit Feng Mian and the agents' ways through the passageways as they sneaked under vibrant red roofs upturned like artichoke leaves, and continued onwards toward their destination.

They had already encountered a few of his minions. The Dragon was a fat, balding man who would much rather let others do his dirty work as he allowed an endless stream of beautiful women to attend to his every need.

Feng Mian had encountered him before. In fact, it was thanks to the Dragon that he had been reunited with his parents after many long years. His mother had been held hostage by the Dragon, who, although he was a mere mortal, had taken a particular interest in the spectral world, and seemed determined to leak the secrets of their existence to the wider world.

Feng Mian had believed him dead. Their last encounter had given Feng Mian the very real idea that the man had died, choking on his own phlegm. But somehow that had turned out not to be the case, and Feng Mian wanted to know how and why. It was the only reason he had accepted this mission.

The agent leading the troop raised a fist in the air, and the group halted behind him. He went by the name of Agent Christian, although his demeanor was unlike anything of a religious nature. Feng Mian had overheard the nicknames the other agents and specters had given the square-jawed veteran, the most common of which loosely translated to "Berserker." Christian was a no holds barred renegade who would stop at nothing to count a mission complete.

Christian paused in the darkness. A group of civilians crossed the road, just up ahead. Judging by the way they walked, they'd had a few to drink and were on their way back from the festivities.

When they were out of sight, Christian waved the team on, running with a slight hunch in order to lead through the sight of his rifle.

They had already run into a number of rogue groups of the Dragon's followers. It seemed that the Dragon had been putting in work to increase his defenses since the incident where Feng Mian, Jennie, and the others had stormed the apartment building and caught him off-guard. Now he had clusters of guards patrolling the streets who were no match for Feng Mian and the SIA when taken by surprise.

However, when even slightly alerted to imminent danger, they defended themselves well. The last scuffle had seen one agent shot in the leg with a silenced pistol, and a specter damaged to the point that his recovery would take a week.

Their destination came into view just a few blocks farther on. They knew they were onto something when they paused and Christian indicated the roofs overhead. Patrolmen strolled along the roofs with rifles readied in their hands. Their silhouettes were stark in the moonlight.

Feng Mian's nostrils flared. He had been out with this troop for close to a week already, tracking down their target, and he was longing to get back to his family. Not even just his parents, who had rejected the SIA's offer of acting as field agents and taking their own way out in order to pursue their travels of the world, but his makeshift family, too. Jennie, Baxter, Carolyn, Lupe, even little

Sandra, they all sprang into his mind as he was summoned forward to take his position at the head of the group.

The problem with dealing with mortals was a simple one: it was almost impossible to tell who had been gifted with the sight of the conduits, and who hadn't. Given that the specters had the capacity of regenerative healing, it was their job to take point and tease out the conduits among the enemy.

Feng Mian broke away from the shadows, his hands ready to cast his protective barrier should he need it.

Three specters followed behind him, closely huddled as they examined their surroundings. They had been a good crew so far, one of the only reasons Feng Mian felt able to stay with them for so long. Although Feng Mian remained relatively quiet, he enjoyed their mirthful banter and their shared history when they sat up talking late into the night and took lookout for the agents. Specters needed less sleep than mortals, and so while the young new recruits snoozed on Christian's schedule, Feng Mian had become familiar with the others.

"Up top. Look," Tina whispered, pointing over Feng Mian's shoulder at a darkened apartment window above the tiny storefront.

Out of the sixteen or so apartments they could see from the street, only one had a window slightly ajar. Although the lookout did their best to stay hidden, Feng Mian spotted the glint of the muzzle of a gun as it arced and looked for a target.

Feng Mian nodded and activated his shield. For a conduit, the white-blue light that sparked into life would be an active target. The barrier enveloped all four specters as they hesitated and waited for the barrage of gunshots.

Nothing came. The street remained silent, only the sheeting rain whispered on the cobbled streets.

Feng Mian glanced back at Christian, who ushered them forward with a simple gesture.

They walked to the tiny textile store, the window display filled wall-to-wall with the latest fabrics and threads, and even a few home-made woolen Chinese dragons. Inside, all was dark. They peered inside looking for movement but found nothing.

Feng Mian and his team passed through the glass and entered the store.

The whispering rain vanished instantly, and all that was left was a thick quiet. Feng Mian knew that quiet. It meant trouble. When the world held its breath, it could only do so for so long before it had to exhale.

"Nice place," Bruno, a former tenth-dan karate tournament fighter who had fallen victim to a nasty heart attack in the summer of '86, muttered. He had short, dark hair and a square jaw, and glanced around the room with a grim expression on his face. "Smells like my nana's house in here."

"Piss and dust?" Tina replied.

"You got it," Bruno replied.

They broke out of their formation and checked the room. On the surface, there was no sign that something was amiss here, but then again, that was how criminals operated. They didn't place flashy neon signs above their business stating, "Come in the back, we have guns and drugs and *prisoners*!"

Maisy, the third of their company, ran her finger along the top of a shelf and tsked. A clean white streak was left behind from the dust. "Ew, gross. I think we're clear, though, folks."

"That's something, at least," Tina confirmed. "If you don't count the two dozen armed men scattered about the roofs."

Bruno grinned and bumped his fists together. "You know what that means, though? Time for the party to begin. Right, Feng Mian?"

Feng Mian nodded. He had made it to a side door that opened onto a set of stairs leading both up and down. He ushered them through and sent them running up the stairs, and was about to follow them when he heard footsteps from below.

He lingered behind and melted into the shadows, waiting to see who it was.

Bruno outpaced the others with ease. Within a matter of seconds, he had sprinted up three flights of stairs.

He waited for the others when he reached the fourth. "You two head up and get to work."

"What are you going to be doing?" Tina asked, a suspicious eyebrow raised.

"Taking out the scout, of course," Bruno replied.

Tina looked at Maisy and scoffed. "Always have to play the macho man, don't you?"

He nodded. "I *am* the man."

Maisy shook her head. "A pig-headed man."

Bruno winked. "Don't pretend you don't love it. Now, come on, the Berserker's waiting."

Bruno waited until the other two were out of sight before he melted into the apartment and got to work.

The apartment was covered in darkness. The smell of spices and incense filled the air. He snuck along the hallway, through to the living room, and gunned for the window, hoping that if he got his math right, he'd find the scout ready and waiting.

There was no one there.

Bruno moved to the window to get a better sense of where he was. From somewhere above, he heard the tell-tale pop of a pistol. A moment later, a body fell past his window, crashing to the pavement with a heavy thud.

Great work, girls. But where is the scout?

It didn't matter at that point. Drawn by their fallen comrade, the rest of the gunmen were alerted and rushed to the corners of their respective buildings to get a better line of sight on their attackers. Another burst of fire and another body fell.

Son of a bitch. I'm missing all the action.

Bruno spun on his heels and instantly froze as he came face-to-face with a man aiming a rifle at his chest. He wore a mask over his mouth, and his body was shrouded in dark fatigues. The only splash of color on his person was his red hand wraps, which had been embossed with the emblem of a golden dragon. "You thought you could slip past us unnoticed?"

Bruno shrugged. "I had hoped."

The man examined him. Another round of gunfire came from above, though this didn't appear to faze the man. "You are putting yourself in a dangerous position, specter. Tell me. What would it be like to die twice?"

Bruno squared his feet and readied his stance. He cleared his mind and honed in on his years of training. "I think just the once is fine for me. Why didn't you raise the alarm when you could see us?"

"An enemy caught off-guard is an easy enemy to defeat."

Bruno nodded. "Funny. That was our plan, too." His eyes flicked down to the rifle as he batted the muzzle of the gun to the side and shouted, "Surprise!"

Instinctively, the man pulled the trigger, and his bullets sent the window into an explosion of shards.

Bruno knocked the weapon out of the man's hands with a swift follow-up punch and disarmed him. The man was ready, managing to block Bruno's kick by crossing his arms over his body and planting his feet.

The man gritted his teeth and shouted at the top of his voice. "Now, men! *Now!*"

Bruno didn't have the chance to look outside where the scouts on the rooftop began firing into the street where the SIA agents were hiding. They knew they were there, they had known the entire time and were just waiting to catch them off-guard.

Bruno raised his guard and waited to see what the man would do. The man threw two quick jabs, followed by a right hook. Bruno swept the hook aside and used the opening the man had left to return with his own jab. The man stumbled back, and Bruno took advantage of him being off-balance by delivering a kick to his knee.

The man avoided the kick and took a step back, moving closer to the wall. Bruno charged at the man, switching from defense to offense in a split second. He rushed the man, and the back of his knees caught on a sideboard, then buckled, and he hit the wall. Bruno took the opportunity to appropriate a large oil painting and smash it over his opponent's head.

The canvas yielded, and the picture caught around his neck like ruffles on a Tudor collar. The man growled and raised both legs at once to kick at Bruno.

Bruno stumbled backward, and his foot hit something on the floor.

The gun.

Bruno picked up the weapon and aimed it at the man.

The man sneered. "Go ahead. See what good it'll do you. The Dragon has many heads. Defeat one, another three will grow back."

Bruno chuckled. "I think you'll find that's a hydra."

The man raised an eyebrow in confusion. It was the last thing he ever did before his head exploded into a thousand tiny fragments.

Feng Mian held his breath and pressed himself against the wall.

It was a woman. Her footsteps were soft and her hair was long. It swept in a cascading ponytail down her back and paused just at the top of her thighs. She was beautiful, with pale skin, a small frame, and green eyes that seemed to penetrate the gloomy light of the stairwell. She wore a red kimono decorated with a large golden dragon.

She hummed to herself, a song that Feng Mian hadn't heard in years, and he wondered where something so delicate could fit into all of this chaos. He knew a rose could grow through concrete, but this latest development caught him off-guard.

The woman passed him, her head stuck in her own thoughts. It was only when she reached the door to the textile shop that she flinched and snapped from her reverie.

Bullets were flying. The unmistakable pop of gunfire rattled from outside.

Her eyes widened, giving Feng Mian a detailed momentary

glimpse at those emerald eyes before she sprinted hurriedly downstairs with her kimono sweeping behind her.

Feng Mian followed her.

CHAPTER TWELVE

<u>Chinatown, New York, USA</u>

The stairs went farther down than Feng Mian had anticipated.

How many underground bunkers and apartments are there in this city? he wondered.

The woman showed no sign that she knew she was being followed, and soon the sounds of gunfire were left far behind. He followed the trail of her perfume, feeling the stirrings of lust within him for the first time in years.

The impossibility of such a thing drew Feng Mian onward.

The woman moved fast, and he moved with her until she reached the bottom of a final set of stairs where her progress was stalled by a thick steel door with a keypad by the handle.

Feng Mian stood next to her, his heart beating faster than he'd like. She tapped in a six-digit combination that made the lock click and ran inside.

Feng Mian paused and allowed her to leave. Things were eerily silent above him and he wasn't sure if it was the distance or the boding of bad news for his team. He had a choice to make. Follow through the door, or turn back and help his team. He found himself wondering what Jennie would do in that situation.

He found that he had no answer to that question. Jennie truly was a mixed bag of tricks, and she had proven herself to be unpredictable in every situation. She had always yielded results, but if there was a method to her madness, he failed to see it.

Heart or head? Heart or head?

In the absence of the woman's presence, Feng Mian found he was able to think clearly. He knew the way to the underground lair, and he knew the code. With his team to help him, they'd stand a better chance at getting inside.

Feng Mian headed up the stairs and back to the front of the store.

The din of gunfire shouldn't have reassured him, but at least it told him that his people were still alive and fighting. He dashed out into the street and found himself standing next to the still body of one of the fallen scouts. He muttered a silent prayer of respect for the soon-to-be-spectral soul of his comrade. Knowing he needed to move fast, he picked up the imbued pistol, then aimed at the roofs and joined Christian and his team's battle.

There were only a few of them left. On the roof, he could see the spectral glow of Tina, Maisy, and Bruno engaging in combat and bringing the enemy down. Christian and his team were scattered and ducked behind cars, hydrants, mailboxes, and anything that could shield them from the striking bullets. To Feng Mian's dismay, he noted a couple of SIA agents face-down on the street corner.

Feng Mian fired off several shots and waited near the body of the fallen enemy. Soon his spectral form would rise, and that was when they'd need their control most of all.

"All clear!" Christian called as the final enemy dropped. "Into position!"

The agents worked fast, some scaling the fire escapes and others covering the bodies at street level. Within a matter of moments, specters began to rise from the fallen bodies and the SIA agents slapped their spectral handcuffs on their wrists, eliminating any further threat.

Feng Mian watched the specter rise beside him with a cold stare.

The specter looked confused, at first, then became aware of what had happened. He turned to Feng Mian and his eyes flickered to the gun in Feng Mian's hand. "That's mine—"

Feng Mian smashed him in the face with the butt of the gun, then caught his wrist in a deadlock.

Christian strode over to Feng Mian with a satisfied smile on his face. There was a graze on his forehead, but little other sign of injury. "Good work, Feng."

Feng Mian nodded.

"Thought we lost you for a while there. Your spectral buddies were actively helping up on the roofs, and you were... Where were you exactly?"

Feng Mian told Christian about the steel door and the combination lock. He failed to include the part about the pretty woman.

Christian's mistrustful glare melted a few degrees. "Good work. Maybe there is some hope for you, after all."

Feng Mian's jaw clenched.

Christian called out to the remaining SIA agents and specters, "Fall in, folks! Time to head underground and flush out the sewage. Ricky, Jarvis, you keep an eye on these pieces of trash and wait until the cleanup crew rolls in. The local authorities are likely going to get a call about this, and we need to be prepared to make this all disappear."

A man and woman who looked as though they'd make a mean power couple in a *Die Hard* movie nodded and got to work.

Christian gathered the others to him and then addressed Feng Mian. "Okay, hound dog. Show us the way."

Feng Mian lingered on Christian's shit-eating grin, annoyance bubbling in his veins. He remained silent and melted into the store.

At least with Jennie, she made me feel like part of the team, not just some tool to be exploited for their own personal gain.

Feng Mian shook his head, reminding himself to remain cool and focus on his breathing.

We're all on the same team here. It's all about the end goal. Justice for mortals and specters alike.

The steel door clicked open and kicked the emergency lighting into action.

Another set of steps led them down into the dark. As they neared the bottom the light grew fainter, and by the time they turned a corner, the stairwell was in near-total darkness. Only a faint pink hue appeared from around another corner, and by the time they peeked around the bend, they saw where the light was coming from.

There was no door into another room. There was no secret wall or key code or anything traditional here. Instead, a beaded curtain hung limply from the top of an arch as the smell of incense burning filled their nostrils.

Christian stood beside Feng Mian, his SI goggles struggling to adjust to the dim light, yet a smile grew on his face. "Well, this I was not expecting."

Beyond the beads was a large, plush lounge filled almost wall to wall with bean bags and couches of varying shapes, sizes, and colors. The walls were lit by red-filtered lights, and along the entirety of one wall was a long, narrow trough lit with fire. Men and women wandered around the lounge, some engaged in conversation, others lying seductively on the couches, nearly all with drinks in their hands and masks on their faces.

They were animal masks, mostly made of leather. They covered the entirety of their features, which was in stark contrast to the fact that they were all naked from the waist up. Servers wandered around with trays of hors d'oeuvres, and a strange, almost hypnotic music was playing from somewhere they could not see.

"In all my long history of defending the people, I can't say I've ever had to barge into an orgy," Christian mumbled. He winked at his comrade, standing behind. "Perks of the job, eh?"

The man gave a faint chuckle, yet the moment Christian turned away, the laughter faded.

Christian tucked back against the wall and held up three fingers to his crew, the pre-arranged sign for specters to investigate ahead of the mortals.

Feng Mian caught the other specters' glances and gave an internal sigh. He nodded and they moved to explore the room, Bruno looking much more eager than Maisy, although Tina appeared to be more enthusiastic than them both.

Feng Mian didn't know what to call what he was seeing. It wasn't exactly an orgy, as the only romance involved appeared in the form of a strange trio in the corner who were taking it in turns to share kisses. Yet, there was definitely a tension in the room that many could have called erotic.

They slalomed through people and around the odd assortment of chairs, taking note of the stitched golden dragons on the pillows, the trays, the tapestries on the wall, and pretty much everywhere they looked.

In the far corner, the room narrowed into a corridor and opened into a secondary lounge. Feng Mian and the specters wandered through and were surprised to see that this room was just as full.

A server with a tray of sliders passed Bruno. He looked longingly at the tray and licked his lips. "Man, those look good."

Maisy turned up her nose. "They're green. The buns are green."

"Probably just infused with wasabi." Bruno sighed. "Man, I miss food."

"Look," Tina hissed, drawing their attention to a door at the far side of the room guarded by two men who could not have looked more out of place at the party. Two bouncers, both of them goliaths in suits, wearing shades and earpieces. "Suspicious, much?"

Feng Mian nodded.

Maisy rubbed her hands together. "We'll never know for sure unless we go in and have a peek. Shall we do some investigating?"

They sneaked closer to the door and stopped when the bouncers' heads turned toward them.

Conduits.

They faced off, neither party doing anything other than staring. Feng Mian wondered what they were guarding inside, hoping that it would be as simple as them opening the door and finding the Dragon, but knowing that that wouldn't likely be the case.

"Get the others," Feng Mian muttered. "We're going to need them."

They backed away slowly, the bouncers' eyes following them until they were out of sight.

Christian listened as they shared the details of what they'd discovered. "Okay. If we're going to do this, we need to be swift. Most of them don't know we're here, correct?"

"No other conduits detected," Tina confirmed.

Christian nodded. "Good. So time to raise the roof, really kick off this party, and then break into that room."

Without hesitation, Christian strode into the lounge and fired a volley of shots at the ceiling. The noise was deafening and all eyes turned to him, although he didn't get the reaction he thought he'd get.

He expected the room to fall into chaos, for the people to duck and hide and scream, but instead, he was met with silence as they all stared at him through the eyeholes in their leather masks.

"Interesting," Christian commented before raising his voice and barking his commands. "Everyone remain still and calm. We are with the government, and we do not wish to harm you. Make no sudden movements, and everything will be over soon."

Again that heavy silence. Christian looked perturbed.

Led by Feng Mian, he wove through the crowd and entered the second room. Feng Mian warned him about the bouncers, but when they reached the door, neither of them was in sight.

The civilians were unsettling, watching them with unblinking eyes as they approached the door and pressed an ear to the wood. There was no keypad, no lock, no security. By all appearances, the door may as well have just been the entrance to a utility closet.

Christian leaned toward Feng Mian. "You know what to do."

Feng Mian raised his shields and led the other specters inside. They had two more in their company since the agents who had died had joined them.

The moment they entered the room, gunshots exploded in their ears. Muzzle flashes erupted like mini fireworks as bullet after bullet was fired at the specters. Feng Mian's shield flashed as the bullets ricocheted off and many scattered across the floor. A few of the shots bounced back to their senders and injured those aiming their weapons.

Feng Mian strained to hold up his defenses as he peered through narrowed eyes at the number of gunmen in the room. By his count there were six, but there could easily have been more beyond the flashes of light.

"Shoot them," Feng Mian cried out to the others who had been so taken aback by the volley that they had frozen.

Tina and Maisy snapped into action and shot blindly around them. One by one the men and women fell, until they were at last left in silence.

The afterburn of the muzzle flashes painted their vision. Feng Mian tried to blink it away but could only see stars for a few moments. When finally he was able to see into the room, his eyes locked onto a fat man with greasy skin and a rotund stomach.

The Dragon.

The Dragon looked to be in a dire state. He held an oxygen mask to his mouth and took heavy breaths. Feng Mian recognized the woman in the red kimono kneeling beside him.

"Well met." The Dragon chuckled, the sound more like a car engine backfiring. "Always nice to see you again."

The other specters looked at Feng Mian. He paid no attention.

The Dragon spluttered into the mask. Flecks of blood painted the inside of the clear apparatus. "You may as well send in your cronies. This looks like the end of my line, after all."

Bruno told Maisy to fetch Christian and the others. When they entered the doorway, their weapons were raised, poised for any eventuality.

Christian stepped ahead of the group and aimed his gun at the Dragon. "I see we found you at last. The Dragon, I assume?"

The Dragon nodded, the movement slow and labored. "Your organization has been causing quite a stir among my men. I thought that we'd be meeting eventually, though I was almost certain that I'd be dead before I had the privilege."

"Men like you don't die," Christian growled. "Even if you did, your legacy would live on. I'm sure a smart man like you will have measures in place to continue your tyranny across the city."

"Tyranny?" The Dragon smirked. "Why, whatever do you mean?"

Christian shook his head. "Human trafficking. Spectral and mortal abduction. Your currency is in people, and that is something that we cannot allow to continue. You may think that you're invincible as long as you spread your reach far and wide, but I can say with certainty that this is the end of the line."

The Dragon nodded, his eyebrows knitting together. He removed the mask and placed it on his sweating chest. "In ancient China, warlords would place the heads of their enemies on pikes and display them on the walls of the city. The severed heads would send a message to all who dared rise up against them that punishment would be severe, and retribution swift. The heads would be left to rot as a warning to all."

"Sounds like a grand idea," Christian agreed. "Where would you like your head to be placed?"

The Dragon placed his mask back to his mouth and took several deep breaths. Their patience was being tested.

"That's exactly my point. There is nowhere to place my head. You may kill me in cold blood, but I have been living beyond death for decades. My condition should have killed me twenty years ago, yet here I am. You're right to think I've got aces up my sleeve, for my legacy *will* go on. There's nowhere you can parade my corpse to prevent the spread of my dominion. It's too late. As usual, you are too late."

A burst of coughs exploded from the Dragon, and a glob of blood flew from his lips. The blood stained his pale face, and he laid his head back as if he were in tremendous pain.

"Do we help him?" an agent asked.

Christian ignored him.

After a few painful moments, the Dragon leaned across to the woman and gave a nod. She gracefully raised herself from her kneeling position and crossed to Christian. She presented him with a black box that he opened to reveal a golden brooch. The brooch was in the shape of a dragon eating its own tail, curled around in a perfect circle.

"What is this supposed to mean?" Christian asked.

The Dragon wheezed and choked, finally managing to speak as a dribble of blood fell onto his stomach. "The Dragon is eternal, Agent. Chop off one head and three more grow back."

Bruno threw his hands in the air. "That's a *hydra!*"

Christian weighed the brooch in his hand. It was heavy, definitely not a fake. Something like this would cost a small fortune.

The woman bowed and returned to her position as the Dragon fell into his most dire fit of coughs yet. He doubled over, face pained as he spat and spluttered until finally, he collapsed and his head hit the floor. He flopped to the side and lay still.

A silence fell over the room.

Christian stared levelly at the body before inspecting the brooch once more. "That saves us a job. A job well done and a free piece of jewelry. Guess this'll fetch a pretty price in the pawnshop."

Feng Mian muttered, "You can't sell it."

"Relax, I'm just joking. HQ will be pleased with what we've accomplished here today, gents. Let's scout the room, pick up any last detail we might be able to pluck from this clusterfuck of an orgy, and roll out before the zombies decide to attack us."

The agents divided and searched the room. Their mission had been to bring in the Dragon, *alive*, and on that front, they had failed. However, if they could find the links to close down all of the Dragon's operations in that room, then they'd be able to call this a job well done.

Feng Mian didn't join in the search, instead opting to approach the woman. He knelt in front of her and studied the delicate features of her face.

Her eyes locked onto his. Feng Mian flinched. She could see him.

She spoke in perfect Mandarin, which only Feng Mian was able to interpret, her lips barely moving, her voice hardly audible. "You saved me."

Feng Mian glanced around the room, but the others were too preoccupied to notice. "You were a slave?"

The woman gave a slight nod. Again, barely perceptible to the naked eye. "The Dragon has his hostages. There is no escape until the Dragon dies. Thank you."

Feng Mian was confused. He asked the woman why she had ignored him on the stairwell. He wondered where she had been heading to.

"I was seeking succor. I grew weary of this work and found a moment to escape. When I heard the gunfire, I ran back. I didn't know what else to do." Her eyes shimmered. "Thank you, kind stranger."

"Feng Mian."

"Jiao."

Christian called out when they discovered a room out back with a computer set up and linked to a server. Nearby, one of the other agents declared his discovery of a stack of weapons, paper documents, and drugs.

Feng Mian offered Jiao a hand. "Come. You are safe now. We will keep you away from harm."

Jiao gave the faintest trace of a smile. "Safety is not an option. You and your men must hurry. More danger will come."

Feng Mian marveled at her porcelain skin. There was an innocence etched into every inch of her. His heart fluttered, and if he had been capable of it, his cheeks would have bloomed with red.

Feng Mian relayed Jiao's message, and they sped up their search. When the Dragon's spectral spirit stirred from his bloated corpse, the agents were ready and bound him in cuffs. All the while, the civilians in the other rooms remained motionless.

CHAPTER THIRTEEN

<u>**Richmond, Virginia, USA**</u>

The doorbell rang for the twentieth time that morning.

Carolyn opened the door and waved at a mailman who could neither see nor hear her, leaving him with a concerned look as he stared up at the dilapidated manor. "Jennie! Package for you!"

Jennie rushed down the stairs, two at a time. "Hey! Thanks for that." She signed for the package, taking note of the pale color of the mailman's face. "Oh, don't worry about that. Automatic door. We're gutting the house and turning it into a twenty-second-century techno-palace."

"Right," the postman managed, still freaked out by the door opening by itself. "Okay. Techno-palace."

He was halfway down the overgrown path when he turned back and called, "It's the twenty-first century, though."

Jennie rolled her eyes and shut the door. Faintly she heard the cackling of the poltergeist brothers as they hurled trash at the mailman and chased him off the premises.

Should've chosen a rottweiler, instead. Dogs make much better guards than poltergeists. Poor, poor mailman.

The manor was coming along nicely. A full two days since they had cleared out the darkness that had possessed the house, and already it was beginning to look like a whole new building.

Priority number one had been to clear the dust and stink from decades of neglect out of each room. Windows had been opened, except for a few stubborn exceptions whose handles had rusted shut, and the curtains had been pulled wide open. Sunlight shone proudly through the glass and bathed the manor in a golden light as motes of dust were disturbed and sent into wild tornadoes that soon filtered out of the windows and back into the Richmond air.

The conduits made use of themselves by removing any furniture that was beyond repair and needed to be destroyed. Lupe and Tanya busied themselves with coming up with ideas for the layout of the manor and deciding which rooms would do what, and the specters set about mapping out all of the hidden rooms within its walls.

Jennie, meanwhile, spent her time shopping online and ordering everything that she would need to establish the first and most important room out of the brand-new King's Court HQ. The package that had just been delivered would be the final piece in the whole equation to make the room operational, and as she unwrapped the cardboard box and placed the golden bell on top of the walnut bar, she smiled and nodded with approval. "There. We are open for business."

Baxter laughed, appearing in the archway behind her. "Certainly got your priorities straight, haven't you?"

The makeshift bar was set into the corner of the reception room, just off the main entranceway. Earlier that day, Jennie had driven into town and bought the waist-high refrigerators and put them in place, ready for when electricity would be installed in the house.

The bar she had found in an upstairs room, and she had dusted off its surface and applied a careful layer of varnish to bring the wood back to life. She'd also found a number of matching cupboards nearby that she placed along the back wall to store her full collection of spirits, juices, and equipment when she got around to ordering them in.

Jennie smirked. "There's no party without cocktails. Just think, Bax, when this is all finished, we're finally going to have a place we can all call home." She placed her hands on her hips and examined the room, taking a deep breath. "I can't remember the last place that felt like home to me."

Baxter hopped onto one of the cupboards and swung his legs. "What about your place in London? The one beneath the theatre? Weren't you there for decades?"

Jennie shook her head. "No. I mean, yes, but I was hardly ever there. That place was nice, a retreat from the erratic pace the life I lived, but it never felt like home. Every day was some kind of journey or adventure, so it became more like a bunker to sleep and rest and recover. I tried to make it a home, but I never realized what was truly missing."

Baxter smiled. "Friends?"

"Family," Jennie corrected. She met Baxter's eyes and her cheeks reddened. "Still, now that the bar is set, and the house is almost clear of all its junk, it's really starting to feel like something, isn't it?"

Baxter hopped off the counter and joined Jennie in the middle of the room. It was easily forty-foot wide and fifty-foot long. The bar looked almost lost in the corner, but he knew that once they added some fresh couches and items of furniture, the room would soon fill out.

"Yeah, it is." Baxter glanced up at the glass chandelier with its holders containing ancient half-melted candles. They hadn't quite gotten around to looking at the ceiling fixtures. "When is the electricity getting installed?"

"It was supposed to be this morning," Jennie replied. "But the McFarlene brothers chased the contractors away."

Baxter cocked an eyebrow. "The McFarlene brothers?"

"The poltergeists," Jennie clarified. At Baxter's confused glance, she added, "Yeah, they're an interesting bunch. I managed to pull some more info from them earlier. Want to know their first names?"

Baxter half-shrugged. "Sure. Seeing as they live here."

"Don, Jerry, and Graham." Jennie glanced out of the window when one of the brothers whizzed by. "They were supposed to be keeping away nosy onlookers, but instead they scared the crap out of our installation guy. I called the company, and they're sending someone out this afternoon. Hopefully this one'll have more balls than the last wimp."

It turned out that she did. When the installation lady came around in the mid-afternoon, she paused at the end of the pathway and looked up at the building. After a deep, steadying breath, she walked up the path, doing her best to ignore the legends and tales she had heard about the manor as she knocked on the door and awaited the answer.

Jennie opened the door with a reassuring grin, just as one of the brothers appeared over the woman's shoulder. He held the broken legs of chairs in each hand and froze under Jennie's stare. The woman turned over her shoulder but saw nothing there, little realizing how close she had been to her first experience of a haunting.

Jennie liked the woman. She was receptive to Jennie's requests, no matter how odd they seemed. What Jennie was asking for would require a large chunk of additional power to be directed from the city's power grid, but that was okay since she had the cash to pay for it.

At one point, the woman joked about needing additional power generators. When Jennie told her how much she was willing to invest, she almost choked. By the time she left, Jennie was feeling optimistic. A promise had been made that her requests would be granted, and power provided within the next forty-eight hours.

Jennie closed the door and turned to Baxter. "Just in time. The internet guys are coming in two days. No power equals no wi-fi."

Baxter laughed.

Carolyn had joined them in the hallway, a notepad in her hand.

"Two days?" Carolyn gave Jennie an incredulous look. "Whenever I wanted wi-fi installed, it was always a three-week process."

Jennie nodded her head sagely. "Money talks. Add enough zeroes and the world bows to you. How goes the planning?"

They grouped in the reception lounge. Jennie cast a longing glance at the bar, then took a seat on the moth-bitten couches they had dragged into the room temporarily until the new furniture was delivered.

Carolyn showed them her ideas, having added impressively detailed drawings to her notepad. With the help of Sandra, they had passed through every wall and mapped every single room in the house, including thirteen secret places.

By the time Carolyn had shown her all she had done, Jennie knew she had chosen the right woman for the job. The upper two floors had been converted into a residential complex. Most were individual rooms. However, in a pinch, up to fourteen people could comfortably share one of the manor's luxuriously large bedrooms.

The third floor was to be made into a base of operations, with rooms assigned for computer rooms, offices, training facilities, and a laboratory for Hendrick.

"Speaking of, where is the old guy?" Baxter asked.

Jennie nearly snorted as she remembered Hendrick's wrinkled face, deep in slumber. "He's hibernating. Turns out, all the action of clearing out the house exhausted his frail body. He tucked himself up in the master bedroom almost immediately after our group meeting, and he's been sleeping there ever since."

Carolyn raised her eyebrows. "Someone might want to check that he's not dead."

Jennie shook her head. "Not that old mole. I don't think that guy will ever die. Something in his constitution keeps him going. What's this room here?"

An eager look came over Carolyn's face as she listed the rooms on the first floor, that included the reception room they were sitting in, as well as a rec room that doubled as a private theater for the manor.

Jennie's eyes grew glossy behind her glasses. That was just one of the reasons she wore the dark lenses: to hide the emotion that might betray her in a fight. She removed them and cleaned the lenses, glancing at Carolyn with a strange expression.

"Why a theater?" Jennie couldn't keep the warble from her voice. "We don't need one in the King's Court."

Carolyn tilted her head and smiled. "Every Court needs a place to enjoy a show. Even Henry VIII had his jesters. And, besides, I've seen your place in London. It's below a *theater*. Don't tell me that the arts don't have a place in your heart." She placed a hand on Jennie's shoulder and looked deep into her eyes. "This isn't just a place to operate and fight corrupt specters and mortals. This is to be your *home*, remember?"

Jennie did something that neither Baxter nor Carolyn expected. She wrapped her arms around Carolyn's neck and cried with happiness.

CHAPTER FOURTEEN

Special Agent Holly Daggro was the first one to spot the Mustang pulling up in the parking lot. With the tinted windows, she couldn't see who had accompanied Jennie on her return to HQ, but she knew for certain that the pompous bitch would be driving.

Sure enough, Jennie exited the vehicle looking more like a steampunk princess than the agent she was supposed to be. It was a waste, Daggro thought. All that ability and power, and she still refused to cooperate. It was all about her, the selfish bitch. All about Rogue, and no one else.

Still, Daggro had power now, and that meant something. Rogers had left her standing as acting Special Agent in Charge while he was off doing whatever it was he had to do for the President, and so the SIA was hers to operate.

Daggro called two passing agents into her office and instructed them to summon Rogue to her office. When they left, she paced around the neatly kept space and poured herself a glass of water. A series of CCTV feeds tracked their progress, and smug satisfaction came over her face when she saw Rogue's immediate resistance to instruction.

Oh, but we have an agreement, don't we? Let's all work together nicely, shall we? You may be independent on paper, but we're growing faster than you can imagine. Soon you'll have to yield to our superiority. It's only a matter of time. And you won't like that, will you? The girl who has spent so many years at the top of the food chain, reduced to nothing more than a cog in the machine. Sure, your resistance is strong now, but even the sharpest knives grow dull over time.

Rogue didn't even bother knocking on her door, choosing instead to barge in and place her hands on her hips. "What is it, Daggro? I'm not here for you."

Daggro eyed her levelly and took her time in her reply. "I was getting worried about you, Rogue. Gone for four days now and not even a word to check in with the SIA? You're our greatest asset, and you're off, well… Where *did* you go?"

Rogue's nostrils flared, but she kept her cool. "That's my business. I only returned here because I heard that the mission in Chinatown had been a success. Feng Mian is a good friend of mine, and I wanted to be sure he was okay."

Daggro laughed, the sound unnatural from her thin lips. "Please, Rogue. I wasn't born yesterday. You're up to something, and I want to know what it is."

Rogue shrugged. "Can't a friend visit a friend and check that friend is okay after they haven't seen that friend for a long time?"

They stared at each other for a moment, before Rogue added, "Are we done?"

Daggro nodded. "For now. Don't forget, I have eyes and ears to the ground here. Camera feeds capture everything that goes on in the SIA, and Rogers will be interested to know the insubordination you've already inspired in one of your former colleagues. Interesting, that, too. You brought back your Mustang but didn't return the Chevrolet. Rhone will be most displeased."

Rogue rolled her eyes. "That's what this is about? A *car*? Don't worry, Rhone can have his car back the next time I swing it by. I'll let him know when I pass him in the halls—unless he's out on some mission, that is?"

Daggro leered, revealing a row of pristine white teeth. "Oh, you don't know?" She told Rogue about her encounter with Rhone and his dismissal.

The color drained from Rogue's face. It was satisfying to watch. Daggro was almost positive that people rarely got the upper hand on this woman, and here she was reveling in the rewards. Rebellion was fueled by the resisters, and the more resistance Daggro could remove, the easier it would be to push the SIA in the right direction and turn the organization into the spectral powerhouse it should be.

Rogue crossed over to Daggro's desk, a thundercloud brewing behind her. She removed her glasses and gave Daggro the first real look at her eyes she had ever seen. A world of memory and knowledge swirled in the depths of her pupils as her eyes narrowed and fixed on the agent.

"You're playing with fire," Jennie growled in a low voice, aware of the guards behind her. "I hope you know what you're doing here."

Daggro feigned innocence. "Me? I don't know what you mean, Rogue. We're all on the same side, aren't we?"

Rogue stood to her full height and placed her glasses back on. "Just wait until Rogers is back. He and I will be having words."

"Oh, didn't you hear?" Daggro cooed. "Rogers won't be back for at least a few weeks. Life at the top is busy, particular when you're at the President's beck and call. They want to make sure that the strategy for the SIA is perfect and the department becomes the main authority nationwide. I'm sure they wouldn't want anything to get in their way." She fixed her eyes on Rogue. "Anything. At. All."

Rogue held her gaze for a few moments before sweeping out of the room without another word. Daggro followed her on the cameras as she strutted through the corridors and toward her old room.

Not that it's your room anymore, is it, Rogue? Things can change in a heartbeat around here. I hope you like your new roommates.

Jennie met Baxter in the corridor, and he fell into step immediately.

She was silent, and he didn't need to ask why. Something had happened in there and considering that it was Daggro Jennie had been speaking to, he could throw a few guesses around and come pretty close to the mark.

Jennie strode past agents without meeting their eyes, although many of them certainly took a good hard stare at the fabled Rogue. When her quarters came into view, she felt a strange relief that she couldn't quite believe. Only a few days ago, this had been a temporary home for her, but now she felt like she was being ousted.

And I'm fine with that. Wait until they see my new place. They'll be laughing on the other side of their faces, then.

She paused with her hand hovering over the thumb scanner, hearing voices inside. Jennie gritted her teeth and scanned herself in, and the door opened to reveal a cohort of agents sitting and talking in *her* living room.

"Woohoo!" one of the agents cried with excitement. Jennie saw it was the jock whose finger she had dislocated. "They said to keep an eye out for our new roommate, but I never thought I'd be so lucky. Me and you together again, babe. It's like fate. =This is the start of our love story."

The other agents grew quiet, yet the smiles stayed on their faces. Without a word, Jennie crossed the living room and entered her bedroom. Luckily for the new agents, they hadn't touched her stuff. Jennie retrieved a small bag of trinkets that she had come to collect before heading back to Richmond.

The agent grinned as she appeared in the living space again. They were now throwing around a football, taking turns catching it. Drinks bottles and litter were scattered over the coffee table. "You know you can't fight it, babe. Me and you. Come on, give it a go, won't you?"

Jennie's face hardened. "Wasn't my last warning enough for you, kid?"

The agent stuck out his tongue. "Foreplay, baby. It's all foreplay. I like a woman who can take control."

Jennie turned to Baxter. None of the agents wore their SI glasses, so none of them could see the specter. She gave a subtle nod.

Jennie folded her arms. "Believe me, one night with me would kill you."

The agent smirked. "I bet it'd be worth it." His eyes shifted to the bedroom. "Come on. It's right there. Why don't you show me what you're working with—"

He cut off as his pants suddenly dropped to his ankles. To everyone's surprise, the jock was wearing a greying pair of tighty-whiteys with a number of holes around the crotch. His eyes widened as he hurried to pull them back up. When he was standing once more, Baxter picked up a bottle of beer and poured it over his head.

The agent's face grew dark. "What the hell?"

"What?" Jennie fluttered her eyelashes. "You asked me to show you what I'm working with. Here you go; I'm working with specters." She crossed to the door and looked over her shoulder. "If you suggest I sleep with you again, I'll make sure my specters haunt you every night until your dying day. Got it?"

She didn't wait for a response.

Baxter didn't stop laughing until they were outside the room that had been assigned to Feng Mian. Jennie had heard that he was back from gossiping agents in the corridors discussing the capture of the elusive Dragon.

"This'll be a nice surprise for him." Jennie grinned as she knocked on the door.

It opened almost instantly, and Feng Mian gave a slight nod by way of a greeting.

Such a laconic, Jennie thought as she hugged him and welcomed him back. "I hear you've been up to quite a lot. Single-handedly catching the Dragon, eh?"

"Not single-handedly. We had a team," Feng Mian corrected dryly.

Jennie rolled her eyes. "I'm kidding. Damn, you still haven't found that sense of humor you've been looking for so long."

Baxter laughed. The sound of pots clattering came from the other room.

Jennie raised an eyebrow. "Someone else is here?"

Feng Mian's eyes lowered a fraction. Her curiosity piqued, Jennie moved to the kitchen where she found a petite woman wearing a red kimono readying a meal on the stove. A large wok was filled with noodles, veggies, and the smell that came off the food was tantalizing.

Jennie smirked. "Hello."

"*Nǐ hǎo,*" the woman replied in Mandarin, looking abashedly back to her wok.

Jennie waved Baxter over, and he joined her with an open mouth. They both turned back to Feng Mian and re-joined him on the couch. Jennie playfully punched his shoulder. "You *dog!*"

Feng Mian simply stared back.

"Look at you, I didn't know you had it in you." Jennie chuckled. "A specter and a mortal. It's like an extreme version of Romeo and Juliet."

Baxter leaned forward, resting his elbows on his knees as an eager expression came over him. "You hitting that, Feng Mian? Are you?"

Feng Mian sighed at the crudity. "No. I am *not* 'hitting that.' Jiao was a servant of the Dragon, and we rescued her from his clutches. I am providing a safe space for her to recover and rest from the dire situation she found herself in. To suggest that I am in some way taking advantage or romancing the poor woman is offensive to both myself and Jiao."

Jennie looked over the top of her glasses, scrutinizing Feng Mian as he spoke. "Hmm… I'm not convinced. But, fine. If you want to keep your secrets, then go ahead. We'll not say another word about you and your lover."

Feng Mian gave a stern nod. Jiao appeared at the doorway, holding a plate out in front of her as though ready to present it to her master.

Baxter winked. "She is cute, though."

Feng Mian waved Jiao inside and scooted over to allow her to sit nearby. She knelt in front of the coffee table and placed her dinner on top. She attacked it with chopsticks, not uttering a single word as

Feng Mian filled Jennie and Baxter in on the situation with the Dragon.

"He's really back?" Jennie asked. "I could have sworn he died during the raid in the Dragon's Den."

"So did many," Feng Mian agreed. "However, intelligence reached the SIA of disturbances in New York City. Emblems with the dragon on were found at a number of raid sites and other situations, which when connected and pieced together created a picture of a deep-rooted underground criminal ring. The Dragon was sick, that much was clear from the beginning, although that didn't slow down his operation at all. It was only after we saw his spirit exit his body that we were certain that this time he had died. According to Jiao, the Dragon often faked death to escape unwanted situations, and there were many who didn't bother to check for the truth, wanting nothing more than for him to actually die in the first place. Lupe, Tanya, and I should have been more thorough. I can only apologize for us all."

Jennie shook her head. "Forget about it. You got him this time, and that's all that matters. He's in custody, and that's the first step in unraveling the web that binds this all together. You've done well. We can't ask for more than that."

Feng Mian looked longingly at Jiao's food as she finished up the last pieces on her plate. When she was done, she silently took the plate into the kitchen. A moment later, they could hear the taps running and Jiao scrubbing the dishes.

"She's quiet, isn't she?" Baxter commented.

"She's traumatized by the whole ordeal," Feng Mian clarified. "She was promised a new life here, and the Dragon made her his latest plaything."

Jennie's hand moved to her mouth. "That's awful."

Feng Mian glanced toward the kitchen. "It could have been worse. In the days before his illness took over, he was agile and fit and would take advantage of his servants. By the time Jiao joined his ranks, he was too far gone. She planned her escape, and as fate would have it, we intervened and aided her efforts."

Jennie gave Jiao a sympathetic smile as she returned back into the room and knelt like a faithful dog beside Feng Mian. There was an awkward silence until Baxter broke it. "You're a conduit?"

The woman turned with glossy eyes. "I am."

"Is that why the Dragon kept you?" he asked.

Jiao considered this a moment, her face surprisingly neutral. "I don't know. Perhaps."

Baxter waited as if she was going to say more, but nothing else came. "Wow. You're talkative."

Jennie glared at Bax. "Play nice. Jiao, you must have seen some things at the Dragon's side. Why is it that the SIA hasn't questioned you further? You must have been privy to all kinds of information."

Jiao gently shook her head. "I am afraid that is not true. I was called upon when needed and sent out when private matters arose."

"Besides," Feng Mian continued, "The Dragon is in custody. They have a team interrogating him right now. They'll get their answers eventually."

Jennie remembered her interrogation with the stooges from the Shadows from weeks ago. Daggro and Rhone had failed in getting any information from the man until Jennie had stepped in and taken charge.

"Not likely," she muttered. "One last question from me, Jiao. How deeply rooted is the Dragon's grip on NYC? Is this something we should be concerning ourselves with? Or has the situation handled itself now?"

Jiao reached for green tea in a china cup, her hands shaking ever so slightly. She took a sip, then answered. "The Dragon spreads deep. The golden beast is a virus that needs containing. I don't know when, but something else will arise. Legacy is key in our culture, and the Dragon will live on."

Interesting, Jennie thought as she studied Jiao closely. Although there was no threat in her words, there was definitely fear. She knew something that she wasn't letting on, but perhaps this wasn't the best situation to try and extract the information from her.

"I think I'd like to have a word with this Dragon," Jennie announced.

Baxter exchanged a look with Feng. "Are you sure that's wise? We're already treading on eggshells just being here at the moment. Do you really want to stir up the pot even more, especially with Rogers and Rhone gone?"

Jennie nodded resolutely. "Bax, I've been stirring the pot and treading on eggshells since before you died. The only way to make an omelet is to smash a few eggs, and we need to get to the yolk of it all."

Baxter grimaced. "Please stop."

CHAPTER FIFTEEN

<u>Richmond, Virginia, USA</u>

Lupe stared open-mouthed at the mound of boxes in the entrance-way. Stacks of cardboard boxes littered the space and created a hazardous environment to work around. Even the stairs, which had to be at least twelve-feet wide, had been narrowed to a mere sliver that those remaining at the manor had to navigate to get to the upper floors.

Tanya watched Lupe with a smug expression on her face. "What's the problem? Never put together flat-pack furniture before?"

Lupe glared at Tanya. Sandra appeared at the doorway beside her, her gaze fixed on a brand-new Roomba that made its way around the house, collecting dust and dirt from the hardwood floor. She had taken a strange fascination to the device, and stumbled behind it like a zombie, a permanent amused smile on her sweet face.

"I have," Lupe growled. "Just not this many at once. I put together a TV stand in my old apartment in Brooklyn. Took me three hours. There's enough stuff here to last a week."

Tanya laughed. "That's why we have help. Where are the conduits?"

Lupe nodded toward the end of the path where Ula, Triton, and

Roman were helping a deliveryman unload the back of his truck. "Unloading the furniture. Couches, lamps, kitchen appliances, everything needed to finally make this house a home."

"What about the Nutribullet?" Tanya asked eagerly. "Is that coming today?"

Lupe sighed and studied the boxes, looking for something small enough to contain the juicer. "Your guess is as good as mine."

Tanya nodded. Her stomach rumbled and she stared longingly in the direction of the kitchen. "I hope it is. It would be nice to have oven-cooked food. As much as living off fresh fruit, baked beans, and take-out has been delightful, my body is hungry for a proper meal."

She leaned against the wall and accidentally flicked the light switch with her shoulder. Intense light flooded their vision from the ornate chandelier that had replaced the old candle-dependent version.

She quickly switched the light off as the others came through the door and looked for a place to pop the couch down.

"At least the electricity is working." Tanya chuckled.

Sandra clapped her hands as the Roomba bumped into the wall and corrected course.

Washington DC, USA

The holding cells were in the lower levels of the HQ. Jennie had come across them a few times before and was glad to see that this was one of the main areas that had been unaffected by so much change.

The walls were different, however, imbued with the spectral defense barriers they had incorporated in the early days of Jennie's arrival. This was both positive and negative, considering that captives could no longer escape, but Jennie also couldn't worm her way in, either.

Jennie was halfway down the hallway when three agents blocked her path.

"I'm sorry, ma'am, no further. Direct instructions from the SAiC," a woman with a thick neck and a stern face declared. "Authorized personnel only."

Jennie gave an empathetic nod. "Of course. We only wish to see a friend of ours for a brief moment, then we'll be out of your way."

She latched onto Baxter and turned spectral before walking straight through the agents.

They pivoted, and Jennie heard the unmistakable sound of firearms being readied.

She paused and spoke with cool confidence. "You're not going to shoot me. I'm the greatest ally you guys have."

The tinny sound of someone talking into the agent's earpiece reached Jennie's ears. She had no doubt of who was on the other side of that line.

"Give it up, Daggro," Jennie called, voice raised. "This is happening. I don't want to cause trouble. If anything, I want to assist your cause. Your agents aren't made for spectral interrogation. I made a living out of it. You've seen me work, so let this one go, and I'll be out of your hair before the first seeds of a conscience begin to grow within your stone-cold heart."

There was a moment's silence. Daggro spoke in a hushed tone, undetectable by the others. The woman pressed a finger to her ear and nodded. "Follow me."

Jennie let out an internal sigh of relief. She wasn't sure that Daggro would have let that one slide, but it seemed that even she knew when to draw the line and concede. It was a small win, but at least it was something.

Jennie wasn't sure what she had been expecting, but the Dragon was nothing like she had envisioned.

He was an obese spectral blob, veiled only in a small scrap of material that covered his private area. It was like what she imagined would happen if sumo wrestlers ever crossed with the fashionistas working on the catwalk. A long sash wrapped several times around him, and for that, she was thankful.

The Dragon sat cross-legged and stared straight ahead when they were allowed into his holding cell.

"He has bigger boobs than any woman I've ever seen," Baxter muttered out the side of this mouth.

Jennie had to work to keep herself from laughing.

"The Dragon, I presume?" Jennie asked.

The Dragon's eyes flicked toward her. There was a serenity in that stare, a calm she could feel on the surface. "You'd be right. And who might you be?"

Jennie introduced the others. When she called Feng Mian's name, the Dragon smirked. "Good to see you again."

Feng Mian remained silent, though Jennie noticed his hands were poised with a slight glow, ready to kick into action if it indeed came to that.

"You look well," Jennie told the Dragon. "Nothing at all like I was told you looked in your final moments of mortality."

The Dragon puffed out his huge chest and smiled.

A sucker for compliments? That could come in useful...

"Spectrality becomes me, does it not?" The Dragon took a deep breath in and stretched his stomach even further than Jennie thought possible. "For years I clung onto life, afraid to cross into the spectral realm, although I knew the benefits that would come my way. Call me old-fashioned, but there's something about death that remains ingrained in the human condition that makes us go to extreme lengths to avoid it.

"Our primal instinct is to protect ourselves. To cling to life and take advantage of every last breath. Had I known just what a liberating experience death would be, I wouldn't have waited so long. I would have hung myself from the rafters and operated my little project from the spectral side of life. Oh, well. You live and learn—or die and learn, in this case."

He laughed, though at first, it wasn't apparent that that was what he was doing. Jennie waited until he was silent once more.

"But I suppose that's not the true reason you're here, is it?" the Dragon continued. "I'm assuming you want answers from me, the same answers those puny agents outside tried to extract. I'm sorry to tell you that I'm a closed book. You may have me trapped, but I have my own secrets trapped within, too."

Jennie grinned. "There we have it. The first admission. There's more to your puzzle. You're hiding secrets."

The Dragon shrugged. "So what if I am? Maybe I'm not. Who knows? The point is, what are a bunch of mortals going to do about it?"

Feng Mian uncharacteristically broke ahead of the group and stood before the Dragon. "You make a big mistake. Before you is no mere mortal. Rogue is leagues above what those damn mortals could ever hope to be. I'd watch your mouth in front of her, for some things are more fearsome in life than the Dragon." He nodded at the long dragon tattoo that snaked up the man's arm. "It's apt that you name your legacy after a creature of myth. Soon enough, all that will be left of you are the stories we tell of your demise."

Jennie felt a strange sense of pride at Feng Mian's words.

The Dragon, however, was unmoved. "Very well. If this is to be your next interrogation attempt, come at me. I'm curious to see what this mythological beast can bring to the equation."

Feng Mian stepped aside, and Jennie took his place. "Are you sure you don't want to do this the easy way? Honestly, once you get my engine revving, there's no going back. Not even the SIA will be able to save you once I get going."

The Dragon narrowed his eyes and looked darkly at her. "Bring it on."

Jennie sighed. "Okay, then. Feng Mian, hit it."

Feng Mian clapped his hands, and a blast of spectral energy pulsed from between his palms. The lights blew as the circuits shorted, and even the electric keypad that operated the door to the cell stopped working.

The live feed to the camera shorted, and the only source of light left came from Jennie.

She sent out tendrils of spectral energy to connect with the Dragon and latched onto his power.

The Dragon jittered nervously, unsure what this strange sorcery was and at that moment Jennie felt his panic and confusion running through her as she experienced his emotional state through their connection

Jennie locked eyes with the Dragon. "Strange, isn't it? I can't explain it either, yet here we are. Are you ready to talk yet?"

The Dragon glared.

Jennie continued. "You know, back in 1923, I encountered someone as stubborn as you." She curled her arms in front of her in a mime of a large person. "I was still relatively young, barely into my career at that point. I believed that the larger the specter, the less control I had on them.

She tilted her head, her eyes boring into the Dragon's. "Turned out that was all crap. This guy was *huge*. At least double your size, if you can believe it. He had been one of the henchmen for a notorious mobster somewhere in Eastern Europe—I can hardly remember where anymore —and we needed answers. I latched onto that bad boy and wrung him out like a sponge, draining his power and manipulating his gifts until he was nothing more than a ball of spectral blubber crying on the floor."

People moved behind the door. There were raised voices and people banging their fists against its frame. The lock didn't budge.

The Dragon grimaced. "What answers do you seek? You have me bound and captured, what more can I do?"

Jennie smirked. "Good boy, now we're playing ball. I want you to tell me who your successor is. You were sick; there's no way you left the game without introducing somebody else to the field. Tell us who the new Dragon is."

The Dragon looked impressed. "I have to admit, you're not as stupid as the other ones. But, alas, you'll have to kill me first."

He cried out in pain as Jennie drained the energy from his body. His glow faded to nothing more than a dull pulsing light as he struggled for release. Jennie was glad to detect no real curveballs in regards to his powers—at least, none yet. Time would tell what powers the Dragon would inherit.

"A name," Jennie instructed.

The banging on the door grew louder. Voices cried over the top of one another. Through it all, Jennie heard Daggro calling a muffled command.

The Dragon grinned. "Your time is short."

"So's my patience," Jennie shot back. "A name."

The Dragon was stubborn, she had to give him that. She drained him further, not believing he was going to yield, but with a final pulse of power from Jennie, he squealed.

"Ren." He panted as though he'd ran a mile. "Ren-Min-Bi."

Jennie retained her connection to his emotions for a moment, wanting to make sure there was no falsehood in his information. Satisfied, she cut off her connection and plunged them all back into darkness.

Just in time, too. The lights flickered back into action, and the door swung open so suddenly that half a dozen agents fell into the room. Behind them stood Daggro, her face a picture of anger.

Jennie and Daggro stared at each other silently for a few seconds, before Jennie spoke. "We have a name."

If Daggro was pleased, she didn't show it.

CHAPTER SIXTEEN

Washington DC, USA

Former Special Agent Alan Rhone sat on the couch of his one-bed apartment and watched his sixth consecutive episode of *Game of Thrones.*

He had fallen in love with the show. So much so, that in the few days since he had been fired from his position in the SIA, he had worked his way through four seasons of the damned thing, and was already anticipating the excitement of the show's climax.

He scooped a spoonful of sodden Fruit Loops into his mouth and scratched his face. A healthy rash of beard had taken over where the smooth skin had been, and his usually perfect hair had remained untouched and now stood at strange angles.

Still, it's nice to have a break, isn't it?

He had been serving the government for over a decade without a rest. In that time, he had never requested a day off, had never taken any annual leave, and had bound himself to the service of the United States of America. Never would he have been able to foresee that the woman he had risen through the ranks with at the SIA would have the power to cut him loose.

When the episode finished and the credits rolled, Rhone rose from the couch and placed the bowl next to the stack of unwashed dishes by the sink. He stretched and looked out of the window at the rose gold of the sunset falling beyond the Washington hills, feeling a strange sense of calm.

When was the last time he had been this calm? He couldn't remember. Years ago, perhaps.

He raised an arm, and a strange smell caught his attention. He sniffed his pits and discovered that it was him. With heavy feet, he trudged to the bathroom and took a shower, feeling rejuvenated by the steaming water raining down on him.

He didn't bother with soap or gels or any other cosmetics. Instead, he switched off the water, wrapped a towel around himself, and made his way back through the living room with the intention of going to the bedroom, falling into bed and closing his eyes.

"What in Sam Hill happened to you?" Jennie smiled at him from the couch. She held his discarded shirt in her hand and wrinkled her nose. "Been busy, have we?"

Rhone finished getting himself dressed in the cleanest clothes he could find and returned to the living room, still tugging down the hem of his t-shirt. "It's rude to enter without knocking."

Jennie shrugged. "You make it so easy. This apartment doesn't have any alarms, no security whatsoever. It's like you're inviting people to rob you. Did you even work for the government?" She glanced around the apartment. "Not that there's much to steal. This place is a shithole, Rhone."

Rhone nodded in agreement. "Sure is. Just a quick stop until I get back on my feet."

Jennie raised an eyebrow. "Don't they pay you better than this in the SIA? Special agents must have some benefits."

"I do okay." He planted himself on the arm of the couch and looked around. "It's a government salary so we do it for love and labor over glory. Besides, I just wanted a roof over my head before I start looking for other apartments and other work. Coffee?"

Jennie craned her head to see the mound of dishes and crockery piled by the sink. "Sure. But, first, let's clean up this swamp and get to talking. I've got a proposition for you."

They made swift work of the dishes, standing side-by-side as they conquered the tower and left behind a smooth, clean surface. Jennie and Rhone laughed almost the entire time. For years Jennie had been in a privileged position of never needing to worry about doing things by hand, but something about returning to the basics and experiencing a glimpse of what she considered to be "normal life" was rejuvenating.

As they chatted and laughed, Jennie glanced out of the window at the nearby houses with their manicured lawns and the rising apartment blocks nearby. For a brief moment, she wondered what life would be like if it were all simpler.

Finally, Rhone threw the towel over his shoulder and they high-fived. Jennie switched on the kettle, and as the water began to boil, she told Rhone her proposition.

"I want you to work with me." There was a sincerity in her face, readable even behind the dark lenses of her glasses. "Fulltime."

A smile crept onto Rhone's face. "I thought you'd ask me that eventually, although I figured it would be a little longer than four days. Are you really serious about establishing your own organization?"

The kettle boiled. Jennie looked uncertain as she picked up a jar of instant coffee and looked for a spoon. Rhone helped her and took over as she continued. "I've been serious about this ever since I learned of the Queen's betrayal. She promised me she'd leave the United States alone, and my plan has always been to build something here. The only thing I'm lacking is a team of agents who are willing to stand by my side and help me build it all."

Rhone handed Jennie a steaming mug, and he was shocked to see her sipping the scalding liquid. He blew on his and tested the temperature, instantly regretting it as his lip went numb.

"You're going to hit a lot of resistance," Rhone mused. "The SIA wants to work *with* you, but if you start stealing their agents, they're going to get hostile. With Daggro temporarily taking the helm and Rogers in the President's pocket, it's all in her hands. She already doesn't like you. I wouldn't do anything too brash that might upset her even more."

Jennie glanced at the floor, a playful grin on her face.

Rhone sighed. "What did you do?"

Jennie explained the situation with the Dragon and the interrogation in his cell.

"Come on, Jennie. You're just giving them more reasons to hate you." Rhone led Jennie back to the couch and took a seat. He had to move another soiled shirt off the back of the couch to sit comfortably.

"I speak only one language, and that language is progress." Jennie placed her empty mug on the table. "I got the answers they were too stupid to get. Can you blame me for wanting to get to the bottom of a real issue in NYC?"

Rhone shook his head. "I suppose not. But there are other methods. Other channels…"

"Channels that are hidden under layers of bureaucracy," Jennie retorted. "Spectraldom is different from mortality, Rhone. Things move fast. We can't be afraid to take action when trouble arises. Specters wait for nothing. And, if we *do* make a wrong decision, we live and we learn. We move on. That's the way of the King's Court."

Rhone grinned. "Catchy name."

Jennie smiled. "Thanks."

Rhone managed to take his first proper mouthful of coffee. "How did you leave it with Daggro, anyway?"

Jennie sat back and chewed her lip. "She was fuming, of course, but she couldn't argue with me in front of her people. I got what they failed to retrieve. There's now a name in the mix. With that, they can actually start looking at intelligence in the city and seeing if they can track down this Ren-Min-Bi. It's a win for her, although she was certainly happy to see me leave."

"You've got her in a difficult position," Rhone told her. "The agency needs you."

"To be honest, I think she's likely going to change the locks so I can't return." Jennie placed a hand on Rhone's knee. "Now we're both exiled! How does that feel?"

Rhone laughed. "She won't change the locks. She doesn't have the power to. You have an agreement in place with the President, and that's something that she can't override. She may be able to make you uncomfortable there, but I'm guessing that's not an issue for you?"

Jennie shook her head. "Not one bit. Speaking of, are you going to give me an answer, or not? The others are waiting for you in the car. I kind of want to get moving and find out how the house is shaping up."

Rhone raised an eyebrow. "What house? You left who in the car?"

Jennie stood and held out a hand, her smile stretched from ear to ear. "Come on, Special Agent Rhone. This is a one-time offer. Are you in, or are you out?"

Rhone took her hand and gripped it tightly. "I'm offended you even need to ask."

Jennie sniffed the air. "You might want to clean yourself up first."

***

Twenty minutes later, they hit the road at full throttle.

Jennie was glad to be leaving Washington behind. She had never been one to submit to hostility, but it was clear that things were changing at a rapid pace and she was losing her welcome. While she needed the SIA on her side as her organization grew, she wasn't sad to be heading toward her brand-new base of operations.

She drove faster than she should have, using Feng Mian to anticipate speed cameras and short them out before they could detect her speed. When they reached Richmond, Rhone fixed his gaze out the window and marveled at the town.

"It's beautiful." He was sitting beside Feng Mian and Jiao in the back. Night had fallen, and the lights of the city twinkled like stars as they climbed the hill to King Manor. "What a view."

"Wait until you see it from the top of the hill." Jennie pointed toward the manor where light spilled out the large glass windows. "That's where we're headed."

Rhone shook his head incredulously. "You have got to be kidding me."

Baxter turned in his seat. "Does Jennie ever kid?"

"Poorly," Rhone replied. "That must have cost you a fortune."

Jennie considered this. "Somewhat. You can't put a price on justice, though."

Jennie was pleased to see that the front lawn had finally been taken care of as they entered through the wrought-iron gates that bordered the property and trod down the stone path. Rhone, now wearing a pair of SI glasses Jennie had smuggled from the SIA on his face, stared in wonder at the green blurs that sped around the house, engaged in some kind of spectral race.

"Poltergeists," Jennie explained. "The McFarlene brothers. Former tenants and collateral of the specters that had inhabited this house for centuries. They're something akin to guard dogs, now. They've been scaring away the nosy kids, neighbors, and press as we've been doing up the house. Handy to have, really. You wouldn't believe the number of people who try to spy on this house at night."

"I thought you said poltergeists were evil and needed to be expunged?" Rhone questioned.

Jennie half-shrugged. "They can be. It's on rare occasions that you can keep them somewhat under control. Usually, they need a good enough incentive to obey. The fact that they are allowed to remain mischievous on our behalf, as well as the fact that I'm promising not to exorcise them is likely enough to keep them on a tight leash."

A blur of green appeared around the corner of the house. It sped toward Jennie and darted through her, leaving behind a high-pitched cackle as it worked to catch up with its brothers.

"For the most part," Jennie added. "Come on, let me show you what we're working with here."

Jennie, Baxter, Rhone, and even Feng Mian gasped as they walked into the entryway. Jiao remained silent behind them all.

Lupe, Tanya, and the conduits had worked hard to clear the boxes and everything was now in order. The chandelier glowed like a halo above them, and as Jennie gave Feng Mian, Jiao, and Rhone the guided tour, she could not have been more overjoyed.

The manor was a totally different place. Couches and furniture decorated the downstairs rooms and provided places to lounge in comfort. Appliances had been installed, and the electricity and water were running. She practically skipped around the place as she took her cellphone and tapped on the screen to cast the music to a set of smart speakers she had asked to be installed around the bottom floor.

A thought suddenly occurred to her. She broke free of the group and sprinted toward the reception room with its square of white leather couches, and beelined for the bar—*her* bar.

"They're here! They're here!" She practically squealed with excitement as she tore open the cupboard doors and found the shelves inside filled with ingredients, tools, cups, and glasses she had ordered. They were in no particular order, so she would have to sort them out later, but she was ecstatic to find that the fridge was also full, and there was even a jar of maraschino cherries on the countertop.

She glanced up and found Lupe, Tanya, Carolyn, and the others standing in the archway. "It's all here. You guys rock."

Lupe and Tanya filled her in as she busied herself making her first cocktail in King Manor—a White Russian. Classic. Rhone was taken upstairs by Carolyn and told to choose a room for himself to occupy, and at one point, Sandra wandered through the room behind the Roomba and followed it with a giggle.

"She's been doing that for hours." There was fondness on Tanya's face, an expression that only a mother could wear. "She loves it. Fascinates her. At one point, I saw her standing on it and swirling around the kitchen, laughing as though there was nothing better in the world."

When Rhone returned with Carolyn, Jennie finished making drinks for everyone. They laughed and talked and listened to music. Baxter started dancing as a song that he hadn't heard since his childhood played over the speakers.

Jennie's eyes were watery with tears. "This all looks fantastic, guys. There's still some work to do, but we're almost at the point where we'll be able to operate. The phones and computers should all be here tomorrow, as well as Hendrick's gear, and then we can really get this show on the road." She looked around the room, confused. "Where is Hendrick, anyway?"

Carolyn laughed. "He's upstairs, playing with his gear."

Jennie gave her a look.

Carolyn beamed. "It came a day early, Jennie. It all did. Come on, let me show you."

Jennie, Baxter, Feng Mian, Jiao, and Rhone followed Carolyn upstairs. She opened the door to what had once been the music room, and in its place were long rows of desks with more computers than Jennie could count at a glance. Phones were on each desk, and cables were neatly bundled in rows.

"Imagine this space filled with agents," Jennie marveled. "All working together to detect spectral issues and relaying them to our field agents." Her cheeks hurt from smiling.

Carolyn laughed. "But wait, there's more!"

She showed them Hendrick's lab, a space triple the size of his old room in which the old mole looked lost. He hardly raised his head as he busied himself with organizing stacks of flasks, beakers, and burners, along with the rest of his equipment. Carolyn also showed them meeting rooms, an on-site training facility, a storage room for weapons and other spectrally-imbued equipment, and an interrogation room, as well as several holding cells.

Jennie placed her hands on her hips, imagining the situation with the Dragon, but in a house of her own. "It's all coming together. The walls are going to be spectrally-imbued, aren't they?"

Carolyn nodded. "That's Hendrick's first priority."

Jennie looked impressed. "There might be a position for you as the project manager. Or maybe we can change the title to something more modern."

"People pointer!" Carolyn exclaimed.

Baxter scoffed. "Maybe not."

"Let's keep working on it." Jennie scanned the room one more time. "It's perfect."

Carolyn shook her head. "There's still more!"

Jennie raised an eyebrow.

"Just follow me," she instructed.

Carolyn took Jennie back down the wide staircase and toward a room at the back of the manor that she had sped past on her first tour of the lower floor. She opened the door, and Jennie's mouth fell open.

It wasn't finished yet, but the pieces were all in construction. Timber beams mapped out the shape of the stage, and velvet curtains lay on the floor, ready to be attached to a proscenium arch. There were boxes stacked on either side of the room with illustrations of rowed seating on the brown packaging.

"We weren't going to show it to you until it was finished," Carolyn explained. "But I just couldn't wait. What do you think?"

Jennie searched through over a hundred years of memory and experience for the right words to say at that moment. Yet, even then, nothing sprang to mind.

So this is what true happiness feels like...

Jennie hugged Carolyn so tightly that she almost choked, then, aided by the others, got to work in piecing the makeshift theatre together.

CHAPTER SEVENTEEN

<u>Washington DC, USA</u>

The Dragon sat in the quiet of his cell and meditated.

It was something that had always kept him calm. Even in his dying days, when the pain in his chest and throat had become all too painful, he had meditated.

There was something almost magical in the art, a sense of being able to bend and warp your own reality as you tricked your mind into believing that all was well. True masters could slow their heartbeats to a third of their original pace with nothing more than thought. Stress could be alleviated, and pain could be numbed. Meditation was a superpower, and it was to this art that the Dragon attributed a lot of his success.

The voices floated around in his head. They were faint and muddled, as though he were driving through a loud tunnel and the radio was too low in volume. He could hear how many there were, he just couldn't hone in on their frequencies.

He steadied his breathing. Somewhere inside him, he still felt the ghostly beating of a heart. It wasn't truly there, he knew. However, decades of living in a biological body were enough to trick him into feeling the heart's phantom beats.

The voices grew in volume. They had been there since he had taken his final breath and fallen still on the apartment floor, laying in a pool of his own blood. The moment he had resurrected as a specter they had gnawed at him, talking in a whisper, but finally they were growing more vocal.

Who are you? He wondered after the voices. They hadn't been there in life, so what were they in death? Sometimes he fancied he could pick out a selection of voices that he knew, specters who had accompanied his devilish schemes as he ruled the roost as the feared Dragon.

That had been who he once was, although he knew that that was no longer his title. In truth, he had forgotten who he was long ago, and in passing over the mantle to his next in line, he had foregone any identity he'd once had. Did that make him a ghost?

Maybe.

Did that make him an enigma?

Possibly.

Did that make him invincible?

Definitely not.

He was *the* Dragon, but he wasn't the only dragon. A family can only survive by breeding, and he had been very selective in that process.

He opened his eyes and for a half-moment saw the ghost of the woman who had visited his cell. She still played on his mind, as much as he tried to clear it. She was powerful and had bound him in bonds that he couldn't understand. Putting her Hollywood face and those killer breasts aside, beneath it all was a killer. He had surrounded himself in enough of the like to know one when he saw one, and this woman was exactly that.

In fact, part of the Dragon's anxiety had been because of this woman and the threat that she posed. He hadn't come across her before, but he was glad she had made herself known. Imagine if he had gone ahead with his plan without knowing about the powerful enemy who waited beyond these prison walls.

He shook away the thoughts from his mind and concentrated on the voices. Somewhere inside the jumble of individual voices, he would find what he was looking for eventually. It was all he had left to do as he waited for the first stage of his plan to kick into action.

Soon they would come. Soon he would be free. Soon the reign of the dragons would come to the world, and all who stood in his way would be burned in the process.

It was late, not that Daggro could tell in her windowless office. Her vision had gone blurry, and she knew that she needed a good night's sleep.

But who has the time? With things around here moving one hundred miles per hour, eight hours of sleep was the equivalent of three working days.

Still, her hands trembled, and there was only so much caffeine her body could take. She had found Hendrick's store of energizers in the laboratory last week and had made her way through the entire supply. When she had run out, she had ordered Proctor to make some more.

Proctor had been less than helpful, informing Daggro that the formula was something that Hendrick had refused to share, and the best he could do was *try* to replicate it.

Try?

TRY?

Daggro had instructed him to get to work, but so far, nothing had come to fruition.

An hour later and she finally gave in. If she didn't find her quarters now, she'd likely fall asleep on her desk, and that was no way for a leader to go. This was her shot. With Rogers absent and Hopkins removed from his post, this was her chance to shine, and that was something she wasn't going to waste.

The hallways were nearly all empty, which was a strange contrast to the last few weeks. Agents were all either in their quarters catching up on sleep, or out in the field and bringing justice to the world. She grunted at the brave specters and agents who acknowledged her in the halls, then turned a final bend toward her quarters.

An agent walked past her and gave a sly nod. Daggro nodded back. She didn't recognize the agent, but then they had been growing so quickly, how was she ever going to know every member of staff employed by the SIA?

Her bed felt like a cloud, the room deftly silent. She drank a glass of water and didn't even bother kicking off her SIA fatigues. Within minutes, she was asleep.

It was in the land of dreams that the realization of what she had seen came to her, not that it would wake her up. Nothing could wake her up from her slumber, not even an agent in her hallways with a dragon tattoo creeping out from under his collar and painting his neck.

⸺

Darius Chu placed a finger to the receiver in his ear. "I'm in."

It had been trickier than he had anticipated, but he had finally done it. The SIA HQ hadn't been hard to find, but gaining entry had been a colossal pain in the ass. Almost a week of tailing the movements of the unsuspecting agent who chose not to sleep at the HQ and instead retire to his home with his wife outside of work hours had paid off.

He'd return the uniform to him eventually. He'd unbind them both and give them back their freedom once he was done with his uniform and keycards. For now, he had a job to do.

"Go ahead. Keep low." The voice in his ear was encouraging, feminine—a soft voice that reminded him of his mother. "Take it easy."

Darius knew that the key to conquering any break-in was confidence. People won't question you if you looked like you belonged. He strode through the entryway, scanned himself in—or, rather, scanned Ian Dryscall in—and made his way toward where he imagined the stairwell to be.

Their informant had laid quite the map in his head, and as he walked along the halls, he felt as though he had been here before.

Which was useful, considering that speed made the job all the easier to accomplish.

After turning left at a junction in the corridors, Darius' heart stopped. Daggro was walking straight toward him. She looked awful, her hair a thatched bird's nest, and her eyelids dark and heavy. He knew her from the pictures he had been shown ahead of the mission. She should have been off duty by now.

She floated past him like a ghost, barely registering his existence when he acknowledged her. He heard her disappear into a nearby room and breathed a sigh of relief.

Thank your lucky stars, Darius. Now it's showtime.

He passed down the stairs and found the holding cells. This was where things had the highest chance of getting messy. One wrong move and the whole plan could be foiled. It was a lot of pressure to put on one man, but Darius wasn't just any man. He had trained for this moment for years. From the first time the Dragon had introduced him into his inner ring and imparted his wisdom of the spectral realm, he had been prepared.

Two guards blocked the door. "Hey. No unauthorized personnel."

Darius drew his two pistols faster than the guards could blink. He shot them simultaneously, and the darts silently flew from the barrels and into their necks. Their eyes widened for just a moment before they slipped down the walls and were soon snoring.

He grabbed one of the guard's keycards and swiped himself into the cells. He didn't spare a glance back at the CCTV cameras, knowing that every second wasted was a second he could lose the Dragon and fail him.

That was something he could not allow.

He peered into the cells through the letterbox windows, a grin spreading on his face when he found the Dragon sitting cross-legged and in a world of his own. The glasses he had taken from the agent worked perfectly, and it was crazy to think that he could now see specters, just because of a piece of technology.

The Dragon glowed like a holy effigy. Darius set to work installing the tiny metal device that had been created purely for this moment—a device that would hack into the lock and replicate the last code used to open it.

Is there anything technology can't do?

The lock clicked. He checked through the window. The Dragon didn't bat an eyelid.

The door creaked as it opened. Darius stepped inside. He paused in front of the Dragon and waited. The world was silent.

Out of nowhere, Darius' head was filled with a chaotic din. It sounded like a thousand voices all screaming at once, and he clapped his hands to his ears. He fell to his knees and grunted against the pain that filled his head, wondering what the hell was going on and if maybe this was some kind of new alarm the SIA had installed to prevent intruders.

Then, as suddenly as it started, it stopped. Darius was left breathless, surprised to find himself on all fours. He glanced up at the Dragon, expecting him to be in a similar position from the assault of noise, but instead found him grinning, his eyes boring into Darius.

The Dragon chuckled. "You have done well, my child."

CHAPTER EIGHTEEN

Richmond, Virginia, USA

Jennie sat by the window of her bedroom and stared out across the city. She had bought a plush armchair for the occasion and was thankful she could take full advantage.

Sunset was her favorite time of day. The time when the world went to sleep and became her playground. The sky was a collage of oranges, pinks, and purples, and she reclined in her chair and soaked it all in.

Baxter was sitting in a chair across from her, squinting against the sun's rays. "How can you stare at it for so long? Isn't it supposed to make you blind?"

Jennie tapped her glasses.

"Oh," Baxter muttered as he realized his mistake. "Smart."

"I'm not just a pretty face." She crossed her legs, then sipped her martini. The others would awaken soon, and they would once again get to work assembling their group. Jennie had already made a rudimentary list of the people she wanted in her squad, but obtaining them would be a whole other matter entirely.

Baxter turned away from the sunset and watched Jennie closely.

She was still, looking more like a statue of a goddess than a living being.

"It's rude to stare." She grinned. "Not that I blame you, of course."

Baxter rolled his eyes. "Narcissism is unbecoming on you."

Jennie raised her eyebrows.

"Don't be filthy," Baxter reprimanded. "Ha, ha. 'Coming.' I get it. What I mean is that you're not that person. Don't pretend to be."

"I know," Jennie replied. She took a deep breath, her mind weighed with thought. "This is the calm before the storm, Bax. I've been resisting it all while we've been putting legs into this place, but I know it to be true. Nothing ever stays quiet for long, and sooner or later, the call will come that'll kickstart us into the rest of our lives as part of King's Court. Beginnings don't last forever. Although you can sometimes stretch them like taffy, eventually it'll reach a point where it snaps. Everything breaks in the end."

Baxter nodded thoughtfully. "I hope this isn't one of your motivational speeches. Because if it is, it stinks."

Jennie laughed and turned to Baxter. "All I mean is that we should appreciate every last moment of this. This calm, it's an illusion. Swans may look graceful on the surface of a pond, but below the water, their feet are frantically kicking. That's our life now and forever."

"Do you regret your choices?" Baxter asked, genuine curiosity in his voice.

Jennie didn't hesitate in her reply. "Not one bit. Would I have made a few changes along the way? Sure. Hindsight is twenty-twenty, and if I did it all over again, I might have taken some different turns. But, without those turns, I wouldn't be here. With you. Watching this." She stared back out to the city. "It's beautiful, isn't it?"

Baxter tried once again to look but couldn't hold his gaze. "It's offensive. It's attacking my eyes."

Jennie laughed, a real full-belly laugh. "I'm glad you're with me, Baxter. I really am."

"I'm glad I'm with you, too." Baxter put a hand on Jennie's knee. There was no romance there, just the affection of two friends staring out at the world and thankful for each other's company.

A gentle knock came on the door. Jennie finished her martini and placed the glass down on a nearby table. "Come in."

Carolyn melted halfway through the door, then stopped and disappeared. She returned a moment later, opening the door with a sheet of paper in her free hand. She looked abashed when she saw Baxter's hand on Jennie's leg. "I'm sorry, am I interrupting something?"

Baxter and Jennie laughed.

"Not at all." Jennie waved her over. "I've just realized, I'm going to have to get that door spectrally imbued. Soon enough, we'll have people trying to break into our HQ and take us out while we sleep. That I can't allow."

A strange expression came over Carolyn. "It's funny you should mention that."

Baxter's face straightened. "What is it?"

Carolyn handed over the paper. "It's the SIA. They've had an incident."

Jennie's eyes danced over the page, her eyebrows lifting slowly as she went. "You've got to be kidding me." She handed the paper to Baxter.

Baxter read it and looked up at Carolyn. "The Dragon is gone? Taken? Man, Daggro is going to be in *trouble*."

Jennie took the paper from Baxter and re-read the words. "Remember what I was saying before about the calm before the storm, Bax? Well, here it is. The pin that'll make the balloon pop."

Carolyn waved her hands. "Too many analogies. What do you want us to do?"

Jennie's face grew resolute. "We established the King's Court to serve and protect the people. I think it's about time we introduce our little organization to the world and give them a sample of what we're capable of."

"But we haven't hired our full team, yet," Baxter complained. "We've got more agents to recruit. How are a dozen members of King's Court going to work with the SIA without them swallowing up our operation entirely? They're too big already."

Carolyn pointed to the document. "If they were *that* big, why would they ask for help? They may have the numbers, but we've got the secret weapon. Genevieve Penelope King."

Jennie cocked her head. "That's not my middle name."

Carolyn bashed her fist into her open palm. "Dammit. I don't know why I thought it would be."

"Why do you want to know her middle name?" Baxter asked.

Carolyn shrugged. "She's an enigma, wrapped in a mystery, shaped like a question mark. I want to unravel the secret and find out as much as possible." She tapped her chin thoughtfully. "Who knows, maybe there'll be a book in it someday."

"The point is," Jennie laughed, bringing them back to the topic, "Carolyn is right. They need us, and we're going to help them. Justice is objective, and our objective is justice. Besides, a return visit to the SIA could be just what we need to recruit the other members of our team."

Carolyn laughed incredulously. "Snatching them from right under their noses? I like it."

Jennie grinned. "Maybe not as brazen as that, but we can certainly do some work while we're there. They'll already be on edge with Rhone on our team, so this could get tricky."

Baxter took a final glance out the window, glad to see the sun had now all but disappeared beyond the horizon. "*Carpe noctem?*"

Jennie smirked. "*Carpe noctem.*"

"But why can't we come?" Tanya complained as Jennie delivered the news of their departure.

"Why?" Jennie folded her arms. "Because I've just invested a crap-ton of money into this manor, and we're going to need more than a trio of poltergeists to act as security."

She knew this was going to be a tricky situation. The reality was that she didn't need all of her team to drive down to the SIA. A select few would be able to handle it.

"And besides," Jennie continued, "I need people here monitoring the phone lines and checking that nothing else crops up while we're gone. If we need backup, we'll call for you. You'll be in safe hands, too. Ula, Roman, Triton, you're acting as security for King Manor, okay?"

Although they didn't look pleased, they nodded obediently. It was one of the things Jennie loved about them. Their military training was so ingrained in their natures that they played ball and were reliable operatives.

Tanya wasn't convinced. "Who's going to call us? The only people that are able to contact you right now are the SIA. We haven't exactly advertised the King's Court's services in the Yelp directories, have we?"

Jennie took Tanya's shoulders in her hands and looked straight into her eyes. "I have a job for you, okay? Something that requires you stay locally. In my research notes of this town, there's information about a group that concerns themselves with paranormal phenomena. They meet once a month in a bar near City Hall. I want you to ingratiate yourself with them and see if there's anyone in the group with powers to give their suspicions validity. They could be useful allies to bring to our side."

Tanya's features softened. "Fine."

They waved goodbye to the others, with even Hendrick making the time to exit the lab where he'd been holed up for over twenty-four hours, and soon they were in Jennie's Mustang and back on the straight asphalt of Route 295.

"You don't think they took it too hard, do you?" Jennie asked Baxter, turning down Ariana Grande so he could hear her talk.

"Forget about it," Carolyn answered, cutting in before Baxter could answer. "They get it. When you and Baxter disappeared to Washington to go and find the SIA, we understood. This whole game is bigger than all of us. We can't stick together the entire time. They get that, even if they are a little disappointed."

"We'll need all hands on deck," Jennie assured herself. "Everyone plays a part. When this thing explodes, it's likely we're hardly going to see each other for days, maybe even weeks at a time."

Feng Mian remained tight-lipped and lost in thought. Rhone nodded solemnly in the back. He looked strange, dressed in a black shirt and dark blue jeans. He had handed in his SIA uniform when he had received his expulsion, and though his clothes made him appear more handsome than before, he certainly looked strange.

"They're not going to let me in," Rhone muttered.

Jennie craned her head to look in the rearview. "They will. You're with me. They have no jurisdiction over my team and who I choose to affiliate with."

Rhone didn't look convinced.

The highway blurred by them as they raced on to Washington. Night had fully fallen, and the stars were out. There were hardly any cars to slow their progress, and they soon pulled into the SIA parking lot.

"Bastards!" Jennie exclaimed.

Her space had been taken. Well, not just taken, removed. The sign that had reserved her space was gone, and in its place was yet another pristine black SUV with a parking permit on the dashboard.

"Still think they're going to let us in?" Rhone asked.

Jennie didn't answer. Instead, she scanned the parking lot until she found a narrow space between two operative vehicles.

Jennie examined the tiny gap between her car and the cars on either side. "If they so much as ding my car, I'm going to be pissed."

They met only a little resistance as they entered the facility. Jennie's passcodes, fingerprints, and keycards still worked, and the few agents they did encounter didn't bat an eyelid as Rhone walked in with her.

"Guess news travels slowly to those out of the loop," Rhone mused.

Daggro wasn't difficult to find. Jennie knocked on her office door, and Daggro buzzed them in. A number of fierce-looking agents and one analyst were sitting in a circle around her desk.

Daggro's face fell when her eyes locked with Rhone's. "What is *he* doing here? I thought you'd been disgraced and thrown out into the streets."

"You should know me better than that." Rhone grinned. "I'm like herpes. Every time you think I'm gone, I come right on back."

Daggro stood, resting her knuckles on her desk. "Thompson, Gregor, remove him."

Two meat-head agents rose and made to move toward Rhone, but Jennie stood in their way. "He's with me, Daggro. Stand your men down if you want assistance with this case. You may not be as high and mighty as you thought you were if you've just allowed the damn *Dragon* to walk out of here unimpeded." Her eyes bored into Daggro's. "What the hell kind of operation are you running here if one of the highest-ranking threats to the spectral world on the east coast is able to just walk out of your facility? Does Rogers know about this yet?"

Daggro bit her tongue. Her hands trembled. She clearly had something to say but decided not to say it. She took a breath and replied, "No. No, he does not. And he doesn't need to be bothered with this information when he's already busy with a thousand other things."

Sure. And because you're trying to protect your ass from getting reprimanded by the man.

The other agents in the room shuffled awkwardly. Jennie stared down the meat-heads until they returned to their chairs. "Good boys," she praised.

One of Daggro's agents filled them in on the situation. It seemed a ghost—a term they used for an undetected mortal, not a specter—had made his way into the facility and released the Dragon from his cage.

"Undetected?" Jennie questioned. "How?"

Daggro's face grew red. "If we knew that, we would have been able to stop him, wouldn't we?"

Jennie asked the room a multitude of questions, trying to decipher how all of this was possible. At one point, the analyst, a man with unkempt hair and a thick pair of glasses filled them in on the science behind their security, explaining that even he couldn't understand it. He retrieved a device from his bag and showed it to the group.

"This is an advanced piece of equipment," he informed the group. "The coding and hardware installations in this are exquisite. To be able to fit so much technology into something of this size is almost unheard of, let alone the capacity of what it was able to do."

The device collected traces of every interaction with a biological scanner and filtered through an advanced database of information that had been sourced through methods they couldn't fathom.

"It works like a hyper-advanced jigsaw puzzle fixer," he explained, admiration in his eyes. "Astounding…"

"We were hoping that there might be something that you can do with your powers," Daggro reluctantly seethed at last. "Whoever this was left no other clues, and while we have a team analyzing the origin of this piece of hardware, I really need to get some legs moving on this case."

Jennie beamed and placed her hand on her chest. "Me? You'd like help, from…*me*? Oh, Daggro, I don't know. I mean, I'm not half as good as you or your agents, am I?"

Daggro's nostrils flared. Her jaw clenched. "Don't piss me off, King."

Jennie leaned forward, her eyes narrowing. "Say please."

Daggro stared at Jennie for a long moment. All agents in the room were silent, wondering when the tug-of-war was going to end.

Finally, Daggro spoke, her lips hardly moving. "Please."

CHAPTER NINETEEN

<u>Washington DC, USA</u>

The cell seemed a whole lot larger without the whale of a specter taking up half the space.

The holding cells were quiet. White powder chalked the door handles and every surface where fingerprints might have been left during the escape effort. However, no forensics team would be able to trace the spectral clues that alerted themselves to Jennie as she walked into the cell.

"I hope this isn't a trap," Baxter declared. "Lure Jennie into a cell and shut the door. It wouldn't be a smart way to go."

Jennie raised an eyebrow. "You really think I'd be dumb enough to fall for that?"

Although, with the seed of the idea placed in her head, she turned to the door and checked it was still open. Carolyn, Feng Mian, and Rhone waited in the hallway, keeping the SIA agents engaged while Jennie worked.

A tingle chilled the nape of Jennie's neck. She filtered through the spectral energy and removed the traces of Baxter that, by now, had become like a second skin to her. There was a frequency in the room, a ghost of something that had been here before, and she wanted to know what it was.

"You picking up anything?" Baxter asked. Outside they heard Rhone and the SIA agents laughing about something they couldn't hear.

That's something, at least. Nice to know that Rhone has still kept his personality upbeat throughout the entire upheaval.

"There's definitely something here." Jennie scratched her head and slowly moved around the room. She felt like a divining rod as she maneuvered around and dialed in on what she was feeling.

When she reached the spot where the Dragon had been sitting, she mimicked his position, taking a seat on the cold steel bench and folding her legs. She rested her hands on her knees, closed her eyes, and took a meditative breath. Instantly she was overwhelmed with the memory of the time she had spent in India, learning the techniques of pure meditation from the gurus of the fatherland of modern Buddhist practices.

She saw herself on the outcrop of a steep mountain, the forest laid out before her. A golden sun warmed her body as she let go of the anger and anguish of her past life, knowing that if she could only control her emotions, her life would be simpler.

And it had worked. Life had been simpler.

Simpler, but never easy.

She soaked herself in the remnants of the spectral energy that lingered in the cell. It was rare she had come across this phenomenon. Often, only the powerful among the specters left traces of their abilities, but she could hear them now, drawn into her head as she gathered the pieces together and solved her own puzzle.

One voice. Two voices. A dozen voices. It was as though Jennie were sitting in a park and listening to the surrounding civilians as they went about their daily life. She could almost see them as they spoke to her, their voices growing aggressively louder by the second.

The crowd grew in mass, the noise grew in volume, and soon Jennie's head was filled with the raucous shouting of the group. Although she kept her exterior calm and serene, inside they were waging war, and suddenly the group exploded into a thousand screams. The noise was an assault on her senses. Jennie grimaced and screwed her eyes shut. Somewhere beyond the screams, she could faintly hear Baxter calling for her, asking if she was okay.

Jennie's head lifted to the ceiling, and her eyes snapped open as a diorama of what had occurred before came to her. She could see him clearly, the Dragon, forcing his power onto the unknown intruder who bowed low on his knees.

And then the silence came. Everything cut off as though someone had unplugged it from the mains. Baxter appeared before her as the final whisperings of the Dragon's mind came into her head.

Jennie saw Baxter, as though she was seeing him for the first time.

Baxter waved his hand in front of her face. "Jennie? Jennie, are you okay? What did you see?"

The truth was that she wasn't quite sure of what she saw. What she did know was that this whole thing went much deeper than they had originally anticipated.

Richmond, Virginia, USA

Tanya watched Jiao roaming around the massive house like a ghost. Her pale skin was almost translucent, her beauty iridescent. Her dark hair was neatly groomed and fell over her slight shoulders.

"She creeps me out," Sandra whispered to Tanya, looking up at her from her side. Connected to Tanya, they were both spectral and, as far as they were aware, invisible.

Tanya laughed internally. It was the first time Sandra had stopped chasing the Roomba in days, and that was only because the thing needed charging. She was glad to have Sandra, Lupe, and the three conduits with her, but that didn't stop her discomfort at being left with a complete stranger.

"What is she doing?" Sandra asked.

Jiao was kneeling in the center of the kitchen. She smoothed down the front of her red kimono, then bowed low and placed her hands on the floor. When she was finished, she stood up and rooted through the cupboards. She pulled out a saucepan, then began boiling some water.

Intrigued, Tanya made herself known by asking Sandra to disconnect from her and taking a stand beside the cupboards. She folded her arms. Outside the manor, a group of children screamed as the poltergeists did their work in chasing them away.

"What are you making?" Tanya asked.

Jiao gave a small shrug. "I'm still working that out. This kitchen is huge, but it's not stocked to feed many people." She took a packet of dried ramen from one of the cupboards and placed the contents into the boiling pan. "Where I came from, our kitchen stock offered an abundance of flavors. Food spilled out when you opened the doors, and each meal was a discovery for the senses."

Tanya opened a few of the cupboards and felt a slight wave of shame. "Yeah, we really need to think about getting some proper food in. I'll be honest, I'm not complaining about a week's worth of pizza, but it's high time my body got some nutrients."

Jiao turned silent once more as she busied herself with finding anything she could make a meal with. She seemed unabashed by Tanya's presence and continued focusing on her own thing, soon producing three plates full of something that, despite the lack of ingredients, smelled absolutely delicious.

Tanya laughed. "You've got a large stomach."

Jiao slid the plate toward Tanya. "The second one is for you. Come, sit. In my culture, it's an honor to share food with guests."

Tanya took a seat, and Sandra sat beside her. "In the US, it's compulsory to eat everything yourself. Did you know we have one of the highest obesity rates in the world?"

"I did," Jiao replied. "Because I too am from the United States."

Tanya blushed, realizing the snap judgment she had made. "I'm sorry, I didn't mean…"

Jiao shook her head, expertly wielding a set of chopsticks as she extracted noodles from the plate. "Not at all. My family is from mainland China, but I was born and raised in New York City. The differences in culture are huge, but I'm thankful for the opportunity to experience both sides of the coin and learn the customs of each country."

Jiao popped the bite on her chopsticks into her mouth and quietly chewed. Everything she did seemed dainty and quaint. Tanya found herself envying how some people seemed to be born with a quiet grace that you just couldn't emulate.

"Can I ask you a question?" Tanya asked as her stomach grew full. "Well, two questions, really."

"Of course," Jiao replied.

Tanya nodded to the counter. "Who's that plate for?"

Jiao didn't even raise her eyes toward Sandra. "Your friend."

"You're a conduit?" Tanya asked, surprised.

Jiao considered this. "I suppose so. If that's the word you have for it. I don't believe I'm able to perceive specters to the level of your friend, Jennie, but I am certainly able to detect their relative shape. Your friend must be hungry, no?"

Tanya requested that Sandra latch onto her, and a moment later she was spectral again. Sandra seemed unfazed by Jiao's revelation and was happy to sit quietly and bear witness to the conversation.

"I think she's okay," Tanya answered at last. "Specters aren't really able to digest food."

"The gesture can mean more than the matter," Jiao replied sagely.

A small smirk found its way onto Tanya's lips. This woman was fascinating. "My other question. How did you end up entangled in service to the Dragon? When last I encountered him, I didn't see you there, and it seemed as though he had died. What's your story?"

Jiao finished her meal, eating every last morsel. She took her time answering, so much so that at one point, Tanya wondered if she needed to repeat herself.

Finally, she answered. "It's a long, complicated story, but it's no doubt one that you will have heard before. I do not wish to detail it right now, as I'm simply glad to be free from his clutches. I am eternally grateful to you and your friends for your hospitality and will do everything in my power to aid you as best I can. No amount of service will be a just repayment for my freedom."

Tanya cocked her head empathetically. "Is everything in your life about service?"

"What do you mean?" Jiao asked, taking the final plate and placing it before Sandra. Although the girl was a specter, even Tanya could see her mouth was watering.

"We're all free here," Tanya explained. "We work under one umbrella, but we're all living in the land of the free. You don't *owe* us anything. If you're here, you're here of your own free will. You don't need to *serve* us, but you can always help us."

Jiao looked confused.

"What I'm saying," Tanya continued, "Is that if you're going to remain here with us, you need to loosen up! The Dragon clearly found something valuable in you, so I'm sure you can assist us in our work. As a matter of fact… Yeah, you can accompany us to our meeting this afternoon. We've made contact with the group calling themselves the Paranormanimals—a most ridiculous name if I've ever heard one—and we're going to ask them a few questions. What do you say?"

Jiao considered this a moment, then gave a gentle nod. "Okay. Sounds fun."

Sandra tugged Tanya's sleeve and nodded toward Jiao.

"Oh, yeah," Tanya added. "If we're going to initiate you into this gang of ours, you're going to have to switch your wardrobe. You know you're still sporting the emblem of the Dragon, right?"

Jiao's pale cheeks colored red. "I have nothing else to wear."

Sandra beamed. "Don't worry, we've got you covered. Tanya's wardrobe is *ridiculously* overstocked."

Tanya shot Sandra with a stern look.

"What? Your wardrobe is *packed*." She turned her attention back to Jiao. "Honestly, you'll be fine. I bet you'd look killer in a nice pair of slacks and a loose sweater."

Tanya laughed, not quite believing this sudden explosion from Sandra. "Since when did you become a hard-core fashionista?"

Sandra stuck out her tongue.

CHAPTER TWENTY

<u>Washington DC, USA</u>

When Daggro brought everyone back together into a private meeting room, all eyes were on Jennie.

Jennie's voice was level, but her heart rate was elevated. "The Dragon is up to something, and it's not going to be pretty. He's ingrained himself with a number of figureheads of local criminal organizations, and he's working to get them all banded together."

Daggro narrowed her eyes. "How do you know this? You got all of this from sniffing the spot where he sat?"

"I saw it," Jennie explained, choosing not to elaborate on her methods. Over the years, she had learned that the more she tried to explain, the more questions were asked. "Their faces came to me, one by one. A roundtable of some of the most influential criminal heads in the city. We have to shut this down."

"Who are we talking about here?" one of the other agents asked. "Do you have names?"

"No," Jennie replied. "I have a location. Beneath the Rockefeller Center. There's a chamber there. That's all I know."

She sat back and waited for the admonishment, for the barrage of accusations that she didn't know what she was talking about, and how could the SIA—an agency based solely on *intelligence* and data—trust the words coming from her mouth?

She was surprised to find that no one said a thing. Daggro frowned and shook her head. "We'll assemble you a team, Rogue. I want you out there with our men and women hunting this bastard down. And believe me when I say that if you've got a card up your sleeve, or you do anything to betray us, it won't be me you'll have to deal with. This will go all the way to the top."

Jennie rolled her eyes. "The only reason I'm getting involved now is to stop this going all the way to the top and to protect *your* arses."

The agents exchanged looks that Daggro clearly did not appreciate.

Jennie rose to her feet and clapped her hands. "Well, no time like the present, eh? There's a maniacal spectral drug lord on the warpath, and he's about to magnify his inner circle. We best get to it." She reached the door, then turned and added, "Oh, and just so you know, *I'm* choosing my team. If you want me to help you, we do this my way." She pulled out her phone and tapped the screen. A moment later, Daggro's cell lit up. "That's my list of requests. If you have any questions, let me know. In the meantime, I'm going to round up the troops."

Daggro seethed but nodded silent acquiescence. Even she wasn't dumb enough to argue in this situation.

Rhone waved smugly as he left.

To give her due credit, Daggro left Jennie well enough alone as she collected her team together.

Not that she didn't have spies, of course. Jennie clocked the familiar faces trailing them around as they navigated the halls and tracked down the agents she required to get things done. Her team was already assembled in her head; it was just a case of finding them all and hoping that many weren't out on a mission.

"Put out a call to the conduits," Jennie instructed, tossing her phone to Rhone. "We'll need their skills, plus we can return your car and bulk up our transport for the return journey."

Rhone looked uneasily over his shoulder. "Return to here?"

Jennie smirked and lowered her voice. "Return to Richmond, dude. Come on, keep up with me. This is just a trial mission for our new recruits." She glanced at the agent at the end of the corridor, nonchalantly tapping his iPad and waved. "Yoohoo!"

The agent frowned and disappeared around the corner, only to reappear a few moments later.

Their first point of call was the one that Jennie was most excited about. She found Ruby in the shooting range, honing her accuracy with the SIA's standard-issue weapons.

"Getting good," Jennie admired, unfazed by the bursts from the Glock.

Ruby removed her headphones and a look of surprise washed over her features. "Jennie! Well, if you aren't a sight for sore eyes."

Ruby ran over and hugged Jennie. She returned the affection awkwardly, patting Ruby's shoulder. "How goes the training?"

Ruby's smile slipped. "Boring. Ever since the showdown in Virginia I figured I'd proven I can handle myself. I was out there with real agents, doing real work instead of just being locked inside this oversized kindergarten. But since we got back, they don't want to know. Apparently, it was a risk putting an under-aged agent in the field, and I'm to spend the next year of my life under the SIA's tutelage."

She sighed. "I never thought I'd be cut out for this. But I held my own out there, Jennie—you saw! I'm wasted here. I come down to the shooting range twice a day just to kill time. I'm the only agent in this damn place who isn't old enough to drink liquor, and they treat me like a kid."

Jennie examined the target at the end of the range. Bullet holes riddled the middle of the forehead, with only a couple straying an inch or two from the others.

"You're quite the dead shot," Jennie approved. "How about we put your skills to greater use? How's your hand-to-hand combat?"

Ruby told them that it was improving. That on a couple of occasions, she had managed to wrestle and take down an agent larger than her in the dojo.

Jennie turned to Baxter and Rhone and exchanged a look. They shrugged as if to say, "Your decision, boss." Jennie extended a hand and declared, "Welcome to the team."

Ruby's eyes lit up as she lunged for another hug with Jennie.

The next few agents were more difficult to track down, and at first, Jennie thought that she may have missed the boat on them both. Agent Jack Hansen and Agent Clive Bannon had been the whole reason Jennie had come across the SIA, and she was more than keen to bring them into the fold. With their reputations now preceding them, however, she was almost certain that they would be out somewhere in the field.

After the fourth circuit of the facility, Baxter placed a hand on Jennie's shoulder. "I think we're going to have to leave them a note or something. If what you've said is true, time is short and we need to head out."

Jennie raised her eyebrows. "If what I've said is true?"

Baxter laughed. "You know what I mean."

Just then a group of agents rounded the corner, clearly returning from a stint in the field. Jennie examined the half-dozen agents, who, due to their uniforms and SI glasses, were easily all interchangeable with each other. As they passed, she stepped aside.

It was only when they were a few feet away that one of the agents removed his glasses and broke free from the rest. "Jennie? Is that you?"

Jack waved the others on and told Jennie about the mission they had just returned from. It seemed that since the media had decided to allude to some kind of paranormal investigation after the incident with the Queen—although where they had received that information, Jennie had no idea—paranormal groups were growing restless in the neighboring states and doing everything they believed possible to raise spirits and summon the occult.

Jack explained, "Most of the groups have been unsuccessful, but we've detected a few academics who have gotten involved and actually have access to ancient scriptures that have risen a few polter-geists and, in one case, a decrepit specter who had chosen to lie inside his body in the grave and wither over time. Man, was that guy ugly. Anyway, things are getting crazy out there. Who knew there were so many spectral issues happening in the everyday world around us?"

Jennie gave an understanding nod. "Welcome to my world."

When Jack asked what Jennie and the others were doing back, Jennie explained the situation with the Dragon.

"The Dragon is back?" Jack frowned. "Damn. That's big." He beamed and offered a hand. "I'm in."

Baxter laughed. "We haven't even asked yet."

"Come on," Jack replied. "I know you guys. Whatever it is, I want in. Color me interested."

Jennie asked where they might find Clive.

Jack shrugged. "That I can't tell you. We've been sort of scattered across the SIA since the Virginian showdown. Not sure if it's one of Daggro's latest schemes to dispel the infamous group associated with you—obviously *that* worked." He laughed. "I've not seen him for days."

"Damn," Jennie muttered. "We'll have to go on without him, poten-tially recruit him retrospectively. It's a shame. I could've used his talents."

Their final stop was a place that no one had been expecting. Even the agents Daggro had tailing them looked confused as they entered the SIA's scholarly quarters. Jennie had never had any use for this room but found that stepping inside took her back half a century. The intoxicating scent of old books overwhelmed her senses as she looked upon the walls that were lined from end to end with shelves stocked with ancient texts.

"Man, Tanya would love this. Did she ever visit here?" Jennie asked.

Baxter chewed the inside of his cheek. "Not sure. It would be a shame if she didn't. Remember her collection back in NYC?"

Jennie did, as though it were yesterday. Back then, things had been simpler.

The memory of Worthington sitting on Tanya's couch came to mind and Jennie shuddered.

Rhone scratched his chin. The whole way over to the library, Jack had been questioning him about his state of dress. Rhone had avoided the questions, clearly not over his state of dismissal, but like an excitable puppy, Jack would not let it go.

Rhone used the library as an excuse to divert Jack's attention. "What are we doing here, anyway? Are you reading up about NYC's mobsters? Or maybe there's a spell somewhere that'll help you kill the Dragon?"

Jennie shook her head, a sly smile appearing on her lips. She pointed toward a darkened corner where a woman was sitting by the light of a lamp, lost in reading a large book.

Jennie took a seat behind Julia and watched her for a few moments. The woman showed no sign of noticing her. Jennie leaned over her shoulder and read some of the page. "Necromancers have notoriously been portrayed as evil over the realms of history, with a distinction being made between users of magic to align them with a particular faction. Those who brace their magic for good have embraced the name of 'wizard,' while those who have been shunned for the intention behind their magic being tarnished with the 'necromancer' title…Interesting."

Julia's ears pricked up as she was broken from her reverie. She looked over her shoulder and found Jennie beaming at her. "Hey, pal."

Julia looked between the book and Jennie, suddenly defensive. "It's not what you think. Honestly, I know how this could look, but I was curious as to what the core differences are between the two. I'm not looking at dark magic again. I promise, Jennie. It was a one-time thing—"

Jack chuckled. "Sounds like a recovering crack addict, doesn't she?"

Julia glared at the agent.

"Relax," Jennie soothed. "I don't really care what gets you off when you're on your own. Work through this entire library and uncover secrets of raising bodies from the crypt and turning them into an uncontrollable army of zombies, whatever, I just wanted to ask if you'd be interested in a little day trip?"

"Her?" Carolyn questioned. "Why?"

"She's knowledgeable," Jennie replied, taking the book from Julia's hands and chuckling as she flicked through the pages. "Who else do you know would have read through two hundred pages of *The Mysteries of the Magic Beyond*?" She leaned forward conspiratorially. "Besides, I'm fairly certain that you haven't chosen an alliance yet, have you?"

Julia looked at Jennie blankly.

Jennie laughed. "That's what I thought. How about it, doll face? Fancy getting out of this fetid dusty room and into the big wide world?"

Julia was hesitant. "Okay…but this isn't going to be for long, is it? I was kind of hoping to make my way through that middle shelf before the weekend."

CHAPTER TWENTY-ONE

<u>Richmond, Virginia, USA</u>

After the number of paranormal adventures they had been on that had taken place during the middle of the night, it felt strange for Tanya to finally be attending a meeting while the sun was at its zenith.

The city of Richmond was picturesque and reminded her of postcards and pictures she had seen on the front of magazines for housewives. It was a stark contrast to the concrete jungle she had grown up in.

The only thing to ruin the beautiful vista was the distant sound of drilling and machinery.

"What is that?" Sandra asked, tipping her head to listen to the noise.

"It's the quarry," Tanya replied. She had seen news of the disturbances in the local newspaper. The city's Mayor had undertaken a sudden interest in a site just off from the town's main perimeter in which something—although the paper had not stated what—was abundant in the soil and could provide a good source of income for the town's architectural societies.

"Why is it so noisy?" Sandra complained.

Tanya thought how best to explain, settling with a brief explanation of the types of machinery that can be used, and touching only slightly on the internal combustion engine, and how noise can be generated and heard, even from miles away.

Sandra looked dissatisfied by the answers but said no more. Tanya didn't know how else to explain it. She hardly knew herself.

Soon enough, they arrived at their venue next to City Hall. The bar was called the Golden Dragon. *Nothing ominous about that,* Tanya thought. It was a quaint little mock-Tudor with white-painted walls and rich dark beams. A swinging sign showed a mythical dragon—more akin to the types found in tales of legend, as opposed to the Chinese variety, Tanya was glad to see. They entered and found a sign leading them to the room upstairs where the Paranormanimals met once a month.

They were exactly as Tanya expected. A collection of mostly women sat around in gothic clothing, eyes thick with dark makeup. The curtains were drawn, although they did little to block the sun, and a variety of tarot cards, crystal balls, and even a Ouija board took the center of the table.

"Welcome, sisters," a sultry voice declared. "Please, take a seat and join our company."

"Most certainly," Tanya replied, not sure what else to say. Sandra sat on her lap, and Jiao silently took a seat beside them.

They waited for the last of the stragglers to enter before the woman spoke again. She wore a dark purple cloak that shadowed her face, but even in the dark, Tanya could tell that she was in her fifties, at least. She was a plump woman, and strands of greying hair betrayed her as they snuck out from the folds of her hood.

She introduced herself as Madam Celestine. Tanya fought hard not to roll her eyes, having encountered many of these hacks before, women who could speak well enough of the paranormal phenomena to trick the gullible into believing that they had the gift of sight.

"I trust that everyone has brought with them their talisman?" Madame Celestine asked the room. "For those who are joining us for the first time, the talisman is often a trinket or item of some kind of sentimental value that can sometimes act as a vessel through which one can communicate with the deceased." She held up a saltshaker, thick and domed at the top with three holes for the salt to pour. "This, for example, was my late husband's. He was a huge fan of salt. Sprinkled it on everything, he did. Unfortunately, that was what led to his early demise." Madame Celestine brought the shaker to her nose and took a deep sniff. "I can still smell his fingers. I can still feel his presence in the print marks on the glass."

Tanya stared at the woman. She couldn't remember the last time she'd taken such an intimate examination of a seemingly ordinary object.

When they were all settled in and had described their talismans, Madame Celestine set about creating a group seance in which they each tried to tap into their loved ones. Out of eight attendees—excluding Tanya, Sandra, and Jiao—only two were able to manage some kind of connection.

Tanya remained unconvinced. Surely, if someone had actually appeared, Sandra would have alerted her. Although she could not see the girl sitting on her lap, she was faintly aware of her presence.

They performed a few more exercises as the hours passed, and eventually finished with Madame Celestine presenting a Ouija board to contact the spirits. They stared at the board for five minutes after she asked the spirits to speak to them, then the spiritualist's hands began to move as they were guided around the letters on the board.

This had been something that clearly even Madame Celestine wasn't expecting. She called excitedly for someone to note down the letters as the planchette moved seemingly of its own accord.

They finally ended up with the word Bogus written on a napkin.

"Bogus?" the madame asked, scratching her chin. "What does it mean, 'bogus?'"

Tanya had to hold in her laugh as she imagined Sandra guiding the woman's hand and helping her to her conclusion. "Well, you know. It could mean any number of things."

"Perhaps it's a code," one woman suggested.

"Was it a secret word of yours?" another woman asked. "A cutesy name or something that was meaningful?"

Madame Celestine shook her head and closed the seance with a final word spoken in what Tanya recognized as an amateur attempt at faking Latin.

"Thank you for coming, everyone," Madame Celestine finished. "For our next meeting, I'd like you to find a passage from an ancient text that talks about the communion of the dead. Remember, Holly will be running the session next month since I won't be here. Was that all, Holly?"

Holly nodded.

Tanya took her opportunity to speak privately with Madame Celestine as the others filed out the room. "May I speak with you a moment?"

The spiritualist didn't glance up from packing her items away in her bag. "Sure, how can I help?"

Tanya didn't know what to ask. She had been sent here to establish a connection for Jennie, but she wasn't sure of what to do. She ran with, "Your experiences over the years with spirits...have you ever seen them or made a connection with any in this town?"

The sunlight faded as a dark cloud covered it up outside.

Madame Celestine looked offended. "Of course. Are you just another reporter trying to hack into my works and discredit me in the Richmond Gazette?"

"No, no. Of course not," Tanya soothed. "I'm just asking because I'm interested in specters and the paranormal."

Madame Celestine's eyebrow raised. "Have you ever encountered a spirit yourself?"

Boy, where do I even begin? Tanya thought, her hand unconsciously looking for Sandra's even though she wouldn't be able to hold it in her mortal form. "Something like that. Can you tell me a little bit about Richmond's spectral hotspots? I'm new in town, see, and this stuff I find endlessly fascinating."

Madame Celestine examined her for a moment then defrosted. "I'd love nothing more, dear. How about you buy me a drink and I'll chew your ear off for free?"

Tanya threw a glance at Jiao. "Sounds perfect."

. . .

Washington DC, USA

The conduits were ready and waiting in the car by the time Jennie and the others emerged from the SIA HQ. They split themselves into groups and were soon roaring down the highway toward NYC.

"Feels like ages since I've been back," Baxter mused. "You know, at one point, New York was the only city I'd ever known. It was home."

"Same here," Carolyn agreed. "This time last year I would never have imagined that this is where I'd be. I had it all planned out—my life, my lover, my career. Now look where I am."

Jennie grinned and pulled down her glasses an inch. "I know. Pretty awesome, right?"

They sped along the black roads guided only by their headlights and the odd street lamp as they passed through cities. Soon enough, the skyline of New York came into view, its towering buildings illuminated in a ghostly silver glow under the light of a near-full moon.

"I wonder what the Spectral Plane people are up to," Carolyn muttered. "They were all so useful before, and now."

"They've just gone back to their old lives," Jennie replied. "Think of them as civilian reserves, they don't need to constantly be prepared for battle. They'll be there when we need them. Otherwise, there's no need to pull them from their lives. After all, what are we fighting for if not peaceful lives? We can summon our allies if we need to—and who knows, we may well need to yet. But, for now, I'm confident that we've got a team that can at least crack this walnut open and get to the meat inside."

Baxter laughed.

"Who is the Spectral Plane?" Julia asked. She had swapped cars with Rhone so that those with official military or federal experience could share a ride. Ruby was sitting beside her in the back, with Carolyn and Feng Mian awkwardly sharing their seats.

Baxter turned around in his seat. "It's kind of a long story."

"*I'd* love to hear it," Ruby insisted. "Please, go on."

Baxter smiled and informed them as briefly as he could about the former battle in Times Square and the spectral supporters they had amassed along the way.

"Your life is amazing," Ruby breathed when Baxter was done. "I wish I was dead."

Jennie looked pitifully into the rearview mirror. "Don't wish your life away too soon. You've got a lot to offer, kid. Look at me, if death was all it was cracked up to be, don't you think I'd have taken it a long time ago?"

Jennie parked on East Fifty-First Street, pulling the car up beside Baxter's old haunt.

"Radio City Music Hall," he announced. "Man, that takes me back. I could tell you stories about every single nook and cranny of that place. I could draw a blueprint on the back of my hand with my eyes closed. And the tech they had… Oh, man, if you ever want to experience the latest technological advances in sound systems for auditoriums, you've just *got* to check out what they've got in-house. Crisp, clean, music and sound fills your every pore—"

"Baxter?" Jennie interrupted.

He hadn't realized he'd closed his eyes as he was lost in his train of thought. He cleared his throat and sat upright. "Right. Yeah, sorry. I just miss it, I guess."

"I'm hoping that your enthusiasm for the Music Hall will yield us a certain advantage," Jennie explained. "Did you ever go to Rockefeller Center? You can't just have stuck within the auditorium."

Baxter raised his eyebrows.

Jennie laughed. "I mean, of course *you* could have. But are there any routes that we could use to get from one into the other? Maybe a secret passageway or something?"

"The world isn't all underground tunnels and intricate labyrinthian systems," Baxter answered. "New York is different from London in many ways."

She looked at him expectantly.

He grinned. "But, yeah. Yeah, there is. Come on, I'll show you."

CHAPTER TWENTY-TWO

New York City, New York, USA

They had once been labeled "the Infamous Seven." Decades ago, before technology had advanced the power of the NYPD and data could be hacked, there had been seven criminal overlords.

They each had their own turf. Splitting New York into seven territories and establishing their boundaries hadn't been an easy negotiation. It had, in fact, taken seven years to come to a solution that everyone had been happy with, but they had managed it in the end.

Their names were feared among the underground. To step across your boundaries or to double-cross one of the infamous seven would result in torture or death. Of course, at the time, nobody had known about the spectral realm, and the seven profited on the fear that death was the final end.

Little did they realize how wrong they were.

They were restless and aged. Five of the original seven were present, and each man was in their late seventies. The only non-original sitting at the table was a woman by the name of Cassie Ferriss, who sat in her father's place as the matriarch of the order. It was clear from looking at her that she could handle her own.

Darius Chu entered the room, and the chatter immediately

stopped. Each head had a representative who stood behind their chair, though Darius had none. That confused the others. They wondered what the deal was, why Darius would be so stupid as to leave behind his protection when the stakes were so high. One stray bullet and the Dragon would be short a nephew.

"Thank you for agreeing to meet at such short notice." Darius swept his gaze around the table. "I realize that my calling this meeting is slightly unorthodox, and although we could quip and establish that this is something of a reunion, I know that you're all wondering what the truth is behind my assembling the group."

Darius remained standing beside his chair. Tommy Vincenzo knitted his brows together and addressed the room. He spoke with the ghost of an Italian lilt. "I can't work out if you're stupid or just dumb."

Darius didn't rise to the bait. He waited patiently, knowing that each word was sacred in this room.

Vincenzo scoffed and looked at the others for help. "He summons us as though he's the fucking kingpin of New York and wants to bring us back for our greatest hits, and he stands by his chair like a mug, not even doing us the courtesy of sitting down and facing us as a man. What is this, Chu? Your uncle's dead and his will asked for one more laugh at his old buddy's expense?"

"It's been sixteen years," Bobby Dalton added. He had once been fat, but now age had taken some of the weight away, leaving him with large folds of flesh that wobbled as he spoke. His forehead was liver-spotted, and one of his eyes remained half-closed as he spoke. "Our stings ain't what they used to be. There was a reason that we disbanded all those years ago, and that was to not get caught. The cops wanted us all, and each one of us was a domino that, when knocked, would link to the other one. We've been working alone for years, and it works just fine for us. It may not bring in the money we once had, but it's a living."

Cassie Ferriss remained silent, her gaze locked on Darius, who did not wither at their remarks.

"It's true that things have changed," Darius agreed. "The world has moved on. Life is different. Crime has changed. I wouldn't be here today if it wasn't for a change in circumstance that has brought a fortuitous opportunity our way."

He reached beneath the chair and pulled out a sports bag. Inside the bag were six envelopes and six packages. He walked around the room and handed one to each person sitting around the table. "My uncle, may he rest in peace, came across a revolutionary piece of information. For almost a year, he has worked within something truly extraordinary, and he would like to share it with you."

Craig Cowley, a prolific serial killer who in his heyday had evaded all attempts at discovery by the NYPD, scowled and threw his letter and package into the center of the table. "Fuck this, Junior. Either get to the point or count me out. I'm supposed to be in a penthouse getting sponge-bathed by Portuguese nurses right now. Hurry the fuck up."

There was a chorus of agreement.

Darius nodded, his face betraying no emotion whatsoever. "Very well." His voice rose in volume as his arms swept wide. "The game is changing, gentlemen...and lady. For years criminals have sought a method to evade detection entirely and steal some of the city's greatest treasures. Well, I'm here to tell you today that my uncle left me instructions for a secret weapon. A way for you all to go back to your glory days, a time when the world trembled before your feet, and we have discovered a way to remain unaccountable and free from any possibility of jail time."

That grabbed their attention.

He swept a hand toward their envelopes. "Please, if you'd like to open your letters."

Each letter was a replica of the others, and each held a simple message.

This gift is for you, for when we once again meet in the afterlife.

A wave of confusion swept across the room. A few accusations of some kind of traitorous trick were thrown. Vincenzo and Doltan joined Cowley in throwing their packages.

Darius laughed. "I assure you, the only thing that could kill you in this room is the shock of what you are about to discover."

Cassie Ferriss was the first to take her package and tear the brown parcel wrapping. She tore off the end, and a pair of high-tech sunglasses slipped onto the table.

She scoffed, showing the glasses to her second behind her. "New from Ray-Ban? This is hardly revolutionary."

Ruben McAffey and Sammy Garcia, two ex-cons with track records in smuggling drugs into the city, examined their glasses and placed them on their faces. They instantly gasped.

Cassie followed suit and nearly fell off her chair. Their reaction was enough to make the other heads of houses command their number twos to retrieve their packages.

Darius stepped behind his chair and placed his hands on the back-rest. Sitting smugly on the chair was the ghostly visage of the Dragon, known affectionately to his former comrades as Peter Zhao.

Vincenzo removed the glasses. There was a green LED strip along the top of the frame that pulsed with a strange kind of energy. He placed them back on, not quite understanding what he was seeing. "Is this some kind of trick? Some sort of VR or AR, or whatever it is they're calling it, these days?"

Zhao shook his head, a smug grin stretching ear to ear. "This is no trick, friends. There is no illusion here. Everything you need to know, I will tell you, but first, you have to believe it is me, talking to you from beyond the grave."

"Bullshit!" Doltan cried, hurling his glasses at the wall. The lenses shattered. "What trickery is this?"

To those who could see him, Zhao closed his eyes, and in the next second, every person in the room except Darius, who had been prepared for such an event, clasped their hands to their ears. A shrill, glass-shattering scream filled their heads and made their eyes throb. They grimaced, and Sammy Garcia's nose began to bleed.

The screaming stopped.

"What was that?" Vincenzo asked.

Zhao opened his eyes and gave the group his warmest smile.

"That's the whistle, gentlemen. It signifies that life is about to change in New York. A new race has started, and I want you all to join me as we see just how far we can bend this city before it breaks."

It was strange being back inside the Radio City Music Hall.

Jennie remembered the first time she had been here. Her first encounter with Baxter felt like a lifetime ago. Although, in truth, most of her life felt that way.

It must have been a dead night for the Music Hall. The place was absolutely deserted. Baxter kept getting distracted by his old haunt as he showed them the way to the basement, and it took a lot longer than Jennie had hoped.

Ruby kept in step with Jennie, occasionally throwing an admiring glance her way. "How are you so confident about your hunches? What real evidence is there that we're going to find them?" It wasn't an accusation, merely a comment.

"Experience," Jennie replied. "I've been doing this for long enough now that I know what is right and what isn't. Specters can leave clues in the wake of tremendous power, and that is often their downfall, especially those who choose to use their gifts for evil."

Ruby considered this. "But a room you've never visited under the Rockefeller Center? How did you know *that?*"

Jennie tapped a finger to her nose. "Even architecture leaves its clues. Once you've lived as long as I have, you begin to pick up on the grain of the wood, the grading of the glass, the intricacies of the marble, and the metal."

Even Baxter looked impressed. "Wow, really?"

"No." Jennie laughed. "The Dragon held the location in his head. There was even a flash of an invitation written in calligraphy that mentioned the meeting location."

Ruby chuckled.

The basement was nothing more than a cold stone space free from clutter and as cold as the grave. Baxter stood by a crack in the floor and shouted, "Geronimo!" He took a small hop and then sunk through the floor and into the tunnels below.

The mortals among them raised their eyebrows. Rhone scratched his head. "I'm not being difficult, but most of us can't do that. How are we supposed to follow you?"

Jennie latched onto Baxter and jumped where he had jumped, her body disappearing through the floor. A moment later, a tile that had formerly been all but invisible popped free and scraped across the floor.

"Here you go, sirs." She beamed and turned to Julia and Ruby. "And ladies."

They piled in one by one. Only Julia hesitated before the gaping darkness in the floor.

Jennie waited for her. "Problem?"

"I don't know if I'm cut out for this," Julia complained. Worry lines marked her brow. "You're telling me that on the other side of this tunnel we're going to contain a bunch of mob bosses before they have a chance to react? What if they're armed?"

Jennie pushed herself back up and sat on the lip of the hole. She patted the floor beside her and Julia took a seat. "I wouldn't have brought you along here if I didn't think you could handle yourself. The truth is, I don't want you front and center for this. I want you to observe what goes down from afar. You're a scholar at heart, and out of everyone here, you're the most informed on spectral histories and archetypes. Second only to myself." She nodded to Julia's hip. "You have a pistol, but that's only a backup. We'll handle it in there, but all you have to do is monitor the situation, okay?"

Julia nodded and carefully lowered herself down. Roman supported her, easing her down to her feet on the tunnel's uneven floor.

Jack and Rhone engaged their flashlights and illuminated the way ahead. They walked in relative silence toward the Rockefeller Center, not knowing what was going to happen when they arrived.

CHAPTER TWENTY-THREE

<u>Richmond, Virginia, USA</u>

Lupe awoke from his nap, dazed and confused.

His sleep schedule was all over the place, and his body had taken its time to adjust to the change of scenery now that he had taken full residence at King's Court. The sun was still pouring through the curtains, although at a guess he figured it was nearer to evening than it was to morning.

He stretched and headed out of his room.

It was a long way from his bedroom to the ground floor. A number of staircases stood in his way, and it was almost five minutes later that he walked into the living area and paused in the doorway.

The house was all but silent. Usually he could hear Sandra giggling and playing with new technologies Jennie had ordered in, but there was nothing now. The only sign of life that Lupe could see was the shriveled old man sitting cross-legged on the couch with a bowl of cereal cradled in his lap.

He gave an awkward wave. "Hi."

Hendrick froze with his spoon in his mouth.

Lupe looked over his shoulder as if hoping that someone else would appear would actually make it happen. He couldn't recall a time he'd ever been left alone with Hendrick, and actually any particular time in which they had spoken more than a few words together.

Hendrick finished his mouthful and placed the spoon back in the bowl. He stared at Lupe with studious eyes, his gaze fixing on his leg. "How is it?"

Lupe had no idea what Hendrick was talking about. "How's what?"

"Your leg," Hendrick clarified. "It was hurt. I fixed it."

Realization dawned on Lupe, the memory of the wooden splinter in his leg coming back in a painful wave. "Oh, right. Yeah. It's good." He wiggled the leg in the air. "Thanks."

Another beat of silence passed between them, made heavier by the enormity of the house. Lupe once more looked around him for the others. It seemed strange that they were alone, and he wondered if he were still in the throes of some dream.

"Where's Tanya?" he asked at last.

Hendrick's attention had returned to his cereal. The awkwardness that was clear in Lupe's body language had clearly not crossed over to Hendrick, who seemed more than comfortable enjoying his food.

Hendrick shrugged his shoulders. "They went out. Something about some group in the city. I'm surprised you're not with them."

Lupe clapped a hand to his forehead. "*The Paranormanimals*. I was supposed to go with them, why didn't they wait for me?" Annoyance crossed over his features. "They really left without me?"

"I guess," Hendrick replied passively.

Lupe sighed and took a seat on the couch across from Hendrick. He racked his brain for an answer. "Why wouldn't they wake me up? We're supposed to be in this together. I could've been some help."

Hendrick placed his bowl down and reached for a cup of something sweet-smelling but that Lupe couldn't identify. "Jennie asked for people to watch the house. With Ula, Roman, and Triton gone, the reins fall to you and me." He slurped loudly, gasped, then placed the drink down. He brought the bowl back to his lap. "We're a team now."

Lupe wasn't sure whether to laugh at this or not. "The conduits are gone, too? Where?"

Hendrick shrugged again, the repetitiveness of the action beginning to grate on Lupe. "Not my concern."

Lupe stewed in a swamp of abandonment. His blood boiled, and he wasn't sure how to handle it. What made things worse was the Zen exterior of the little man across from him, and how unmarred he was by everything.

Hendrick finished his bowl and tilted his head, his keen eyes boring into Lupe's. "Look at it this way, you're trusted by Jennie to keep the house safe. Everyone plays a part, but not everyone can play an *active* part. Do you think I'd ever been out in the field before we purged this house of its darkness? No. My life has been spent in laboratories examining the mysteries of science and the spectral realm. I have no bad feelings. Combat is not my forte, and I've learned over the years to accept that."

Lupe thought back to all of his involvement in the spectral realm since he had first encountered specters in New York and had accidentally formed the Spectral Plane. He had loved the attention that had come with being needed as head of the group, but combat was not his strong point. Sure, he had provided support on a number of missions, but with Jennie's skills, and now the conduits and agents, too, there seemed to be little room left for him to fight the bad guys first-hand.

Without saying a word, Hendrick seemed to understand what Lupe was thinking. He rose to his feet, although it didn't give him anything extra in height compared to his position on the couch, and placed his hands in his pockets. "You know, with this new setup in King's Court, I'm likely going to be in the market for a new assistant soon. If this thing explodes the way Jennie is hoping—and knowing her, I'm more than confident it will—I'm going to need more hands on deck."

Lupe let out a derisive laugh. "Me? Come on, I don't know the first thing about any of that mumbo jumbo science. I'll hold you back rather than help you."

Hendrick shrugged once more. "Son, in case you haven't noticed, I'm really old, and no amount of elixirs or concoctions are going to keep me living forever. I've already evaded natural death by a number of years, and I continue to keep trying as long as I live."

"How old *are* you?" Lupe asked.

"Don't interrupt," Hendrick snapped. "Point is, I need to pass on my knowledge so that others may learn and keep my legacy alive, the same way my mentor did before me. It's the only true path to immortality, at least that I've found so far."

Lupe chewed his lip. "What about Proctor? Didn't he—"

"Proctor was a bone head with his ego so far up his ass that he couldn't see the woods through the trees. Helpful, yes, but with his own motives. A guy with a blackened heart. I need courage and earnestness and honesty and someone who has fought for good and is willing to learn. Is that you?"

Lupe wasn't sure of the answer. After a moment's silence, Hendrick turned and shuffled away, calling, "Decision's in your hands, Sanchez."

Lupe sat alone in that room for a long while, trying his best to figure his place in all of this. Perhaps it was about time that he looked at things differently and learned a new craft that could really contribute to the success of King's Court.

New York City, New York, USA

The tunnels led them into a series of underground corridors that looked to have been all but abandoned over time. The walls were covered in cobwebs, sconces held dead torches, and the smell of mildew and earth was rife in the air.

Jennie followed her gut, already sensing the spectral power around her. They were nearby, but Jennie had no idea what to expect. From what she could sense, there was only one of them. Hopefully that would work in her favor.

All was painfully silent. She turned to the others and held a finger to her lips, approaching a door that had been handled recently by others. The rusted brass handles were free from dust, and handprints littered the door.

Jennie waited until they were all gathered near, ensuring Julia was far back and out of reach. She held up three fingers and began her countdown. The others readied their weapons, unsure what to expect, relying on the element of surprise to aid them.

She reached zero and shouldered the door.

It swung open readily, slamming into the wall. They stormed in shouting and aimed their weapons, tracking everyone in the room, ready to lock the place down and stop whatever the hell was going on in this place.

Jennie's stomach fell. The wind was knocked out of their sails as they fixed their gazes on the only two people in the room.

The Dragon sat placidly at the far end of a long table. He grinned, looking healthier than they had ever seen him—minus the spectral glow. Offset behind him, was a man in all black fatigues with a dark crop of hair, his arms laced behind his back as he stood to attention.

"Jennie!" The Dragon swept his arms wide as if greeting an old friend. "I wondered how long it would be until you showed up. Call me crazy, but something told me that you'd be the smart one to figure your way here."

Jennie stared levelly at him. "How did you know?"

The Dragon shrugged. "Same way you did, I suppose." He rose to his feet, stretching his legs and experimenting with his newfound mobility. "This spectral plane is something incredible, isn't it? To think I was terrified of plunging myself into this dimension for years. *Years!* The possibilities that exist, the powers that can be wielded, it's no wonder you'd rather play with specters than mortals."

Jennie turned to the agents and shook her head. "Don't listen to him."

The Dragon continued, not even looking at his guests, but instead his eyes wide with hungry fascination as he lost himself in his thoughts. "Little did I know the powers they would bring. Specters have a wonderful array of gifts to be utilized, but this…" He glanced at Jennie. "*We're* connected, you know?"

Jennie folded her arms. "I highly doubt that."

The Dragon moved toward her. Ula, Roman, and Triton raised

their weapons to their eye line, and for the first time, the Dragon paused, the smile not fading from his face. "But we are. I saw you. You tapped into something inside me, and I saw you looking inside my head. You saw this place. You saw my intentions. Somehow you bonded yourself to me, and now I can see you."

Baxter frowned and stepped forward protectively. "Bullshit."

The Dragon's eyes bore into Jennie's, his smile growing wider. "Not at all. I can see you, Jennie. Shadows of your thoughts come to me. There are voices in my head, thousands of them, they drove me crazy at first, had me wondering whether I'd made the right decision in choosing this existence. But the moment you connected with me, you made yourself known. You filtered yourself out of the others, and if I really try, I can hear you."

His eyes grew dark. "I know all your darkest secrets, Genevieve. Everything that hides in your heart, I can hear. All I have to do is root around a little, and I can find it."

Jennie's skin prickled. "You heard Bax. Bullshit."

The Dragon took a step forward, raising his hands instantly as the conduits flinched and threatened to fire at him. He pursed his lips and lowered his voice to little more than a whisper. "I know about Annabelle Lyons."

Jennie's upper lip curled and she snarled. It wasn't possible; how could he know? No one but Jennie knew about the little girl who had been the first demonstration of her hold on specters. Annabelle, the little spectral girl at the Savoy who had been Jennie's first encounter.

Jennie's stare grew cold. "I don't know what you're talking about."

"Ah…" The Dragon chuckled. "But you do, don't you?"

Was he somewhere in her head right now? Could the Dragon hear the thoughts as they spun inside her mind? By the look in his eyes, she bet he could, and that made her beyond uncomfortable.

"What is all this?" Baxter asked, breaking the tension between the pair. "Where are the others that Jennie saw?"

The Dragon broke his fix on Jennie and returned to his seat. The man stood statuesque behind him. "They're gone, already working on their part of the bargain. Not all of them, unfortunately—though that doesn't surprise me, a long time has come and gone since we were all in partnership with each other. Poor old Bobby didn't want to take the plunge and become a part of the plan, so I killed him."

"And turned him into a specter?" Baxter asked.

The look the Dragon returned suggested that that wasn't the case.

All Baxter could say was, "Oh."

The Dragon placed his spectral hands on the table and looked at them each in turn. "Well, I'm sorry to say this, but you're all too late. As it stands. I currently have five of the original seven crime lords of New York reinstating their power and demonstrating to the world that they're back on form. There'll be some healthy cash involved, of course, but that's not why they're doing this. They have all the cash they could ever need."

Julia's voice came out as an uncertain squeak. She knew the ways maniacal psychopaths thought, but she had never encountered those of the spectral kind. "What have you promised them, then?"

"Immunity," the Dragon replied simply. "And a glimpse behind the curtain. They're old, you see. All not too far from their own death beds. They're having a play with some spectral friends of mine who are able to avoid the mortal police. We call it a 'hands-off sting.' They seemed to like that expression."

The Dragon turned over his shoulder. "What's the time?"

The silent man checked his watch and leaned forward. "22:58, sir."

The grin returned to the Dragon's mouth. He snapped his fingers, and the man handed him a manilla envelope. The Dragon took it and slid it across the table toward Jennie. "You may not think I know you that well, but I know you like a challenge. So, here's yours: every hour on the hour until dawn, a bomb is going to explode in New York City."

Jennie tore open the envelope and pulled out the contents.

The Dragon continued, "Inside, you'll find your first clues. Think of this as a magnified Easter egg hunt, only with far direr consequences. This chase will test your limits, test your knowledge, and most of all, show me what you're capable of."

"What if we choose just to kill you now?" Carolyn growled.

The Dragon laughed. "Bomb number six."

Jennie scanned to number six and read the clue aloud. "Once you have completed the other five tasks, the Dragon shall deliver your final clue personally."

Her party grumbled and broke into uneasy chatter. The Dragon reveled in their discomfort. "Better get going, King. The first bomb strikes at midnight, and I know that you'd hate to see an entire section of the city explode."

Jennie's heart raced, hatred burning through her as she looked into the Dragon's cold, dead eyes. More than anything, she wanted to exorcise him there and then. To pull out the Saber of Holy Divinity and send him into the abyss.

But her hands were tied. Lives hung in the balance.

"We'll be back," Jennie warned, making no reservations in hiding her fury.

"Oh, that's the other thing," he replied. "The Dragon title gets passed along when the monarch dies. You can simply call me Peter."

He laughed loudly as they raced out of the chamber and headed to the surface.

CHAPTER TWENTY-FOUR

<u>Richmond, Virginia, USA</u>

Jiao remained silent, for the most part. Madame Celestine took great interest in the petite woman, but she gave nothing back.

"Tell me about your spectral experiences," she asked.

Tanya told the spiritualist about her position in New York and the studies she had been involved in. She talked about her library and got all the way up to her first encounter with Sandra when she started ducking the truth. She wasn't ready to reveal to Madame Celestine that she had a spectral companion—who she hoped was sitting somewhere nearby right now.

Madame Celestine looked impressed. "Wow, so you're pretty clued up on this stuff."

"I guess," Tanya replied. "Maybe not so much in the practical side of things like yourself. I never went too deeply down the rabbit hole of summoning spirits and looking for vehicles to help them communicate with us. I'm fascinated by your methods. Tell me about your greatest spectral experience."

Madame Celestine gladly regaled the tale of her visit to the local cemetery when she was fifteen years old. The story was littered in clichés about ghouls rising from the grave, but now that Tanya knew about the spectral world, she understood that there was likely a grain of truth in there.

To tell the truth, the more the Madame spoke, the more Tanya saw herself in the woman. Is this how Tanya could have ended up if Jennie hadn't found her and introduced her to the truth?

"They chased us from the gravestones, but I never forgot that day," Madame Celestine finished. "The same fear that struck my friends was not found in me. I made it my mission to discover the truth about specters, and here I am. I've communicated with them since, of course, just never seen the physical manifestation of one the same way I did so many moons ago."

It had grown dark outside. The drilling and growling of the machines still hadn't stopped, and Tanya wondered why. With the hour growing late, surely their operators should be ready to shut them down and call it a night?

"Maybe it'll happen someday," Tanya suggested. "It's only a matter of time."

The Madame nodded and finished her gin, unconvinced. "Still, as long as I can breed faith into my followers, that's all I really care about. I may not discover the truth in my lifetime, but that doesn't mean I can't inspire future generations." She stared out of the window at the moon and sighed. "Someday. Maybe."

Tanya raised her drink to her lips when the sound of an explosion came from afar. They looked out the window toward the horizon where the sky had grown light, if only for a moment. A deep rumbling ran through the city in soft shockwaves, as though a grade 1 earthquake had been detected on the Richter scale.

"What was that?" Tanya asked.

Madame Celestine shook her head. "Damn quarry. They've been threatening to use explosives to speed up their dig for months, but the city council has been pushing back. Guess they finally got permission." She checked her watch. "Little late in the day to be—"

Tanya couldn't explain what happened next. She tracked the dark shadow speeding through the streets outside even as it leaped up toward them and broke through the window. Glass scattered over the table and the shape pounced on Madame Celestine.

Her head was thrown back, hitting the wall so hard it left a hole. Madame Celestine screamed, but even that was interrupted. For a moment it looked as though she had died, until her head resumed to its usual position on her neck, her eyes now white.

"Freedom..." Her voice had changed and become a deep baritone. There were edges to her voice, as though it had been modulated through a computer. She spoke slowly, calmly. "Finally. At long last, I am free."

The eyes fixed on Tanya, who hadn't realized Sandra had turned her spectral. Several nearby patrons got up in a hurry and left.

Madame Celestine grinned. "A human with spectral abilities? What a treat. Perhaps you can become my plaything. Perhaps this whole city will become my plaything. When my army rises, and the dead walk again, this city will know the great injustice it poured upon its people all those years ago."

Tanya's throat was dry, but she found her voice.

"Who...Who are you? What injustice are you talking about?"

Madame Celestine grinned, showing a row of yellowed teeth. "Oh, dear conduit, all will become clear soon enough. This vessel is mine now."

Something strange followed, something Tanya would later struggle to relay to Jennie, Lupe, and Baxter. Madame Celestine rose from her seat and flew out the broken window. Bits of skin caught on the glass, but if she felt any pain, she didn't show it.

Tanya watched in stunned awe as Madame Celestine flew above the rooftops, disappearing somewhere into the streets beyond. Only when she was out of sight did she speak again.

She turned to Jiao, surprise on both their faces. "What the *fuck* just happened?"

New York City, New York, USA
"What the hell do we do?" Carolyn asked, working her hair

nervously with her hands as they crowded around Jennie and studied the sheet of paper.

The instructions were simple. On the paper was a listing of six titles in bold. Underneath each title was a written clue that, when answered, would reveal the location of the next detonation site. Jennie was lost in thought as they waited for some kind of answer from them.

"Jennie?" Carolyn nudged. "Hello? Time is precious."

Jennie nodded slowly as she came out of her reverie. "He's playing us, relying on panic. That's what a man who comes from his kind of background would do. If we panic, we fail, that's the key to him succeeding with this." She scanned the clues again, her brain not quite switching into gear in order to work them out. She handed the paper to Rhone. "Here, you're experienced in running field ops with groups of agents. Divide and conquer, you should set the field."

Rhone looked at her incredulously. "Jennie…I was just fired from the SIA. I can't…"

"You can, and you will," Jennie interjected. "You weren't terminated because you're shit at your job. You were dismissed because you were wronged out of the job you deserve. I trust you, and I need you to do this."

Baxter moved closer to Jennie. "Why do I sense we're about to split off and go on a solo mission?"

Jennie smiled. "Because you can read me like a book. The only difference is that *I'm* going solo. You're going to join the others, Bax."

The rest of the group were surprised by this revelation.

"The math adds up," Jennie continued. "There are eleven of us and six clues. Split into pairs and seek each detonation device. I'll go alone to solve my riddle."

"Are you sure?" Baxter gave Jennie a longing look.

Jennie shot him a reassuring grin. "I've been doing this for years, Bax. I haven't failed yet. Go ahead, seek the clues. Call upon the Spectral Plane to help out if you need to, Lord knows they could be useful. I've got my own path to tread."

Baxter raised an eyebrow. "You're going to pull the information out of him now, aren't you?"

Jennie's face hardened. "Even if it kills me."

Jennie nudged open the door to the hidden chamber. She had a hunch that she would find him there, and as usual, her hunch was right.

"Genevieve," Peter stated, that smug smile on his face.

Jennie closed the door quietly behind her. The air was cast in a pregnant tension. "I had hoped I wouldn't be right. I had hoped that you wouldn't be here."

Peter nodded. "I know."

Jennie took a seat at the opposite end of the table. "You say you can hear the voices in my head. What are they telling you now?"

Peter chuckled. "I won't repeat such profanity."

Jennie nodded. "Nice."

Peter leaned forward, elbows resting on the table. Jennie noticed his protege was absent. "So, what'll it take for you to extract this clue from me, Genevieve? Are you planning on using your full strength to make me squeal? You've done it before, why not try it again? Or is that too cliché for you?"

Jennie reclined and kicked her feet onto the table. "I'm not sure yet. I normally like to assess the mettle of specters before I cast my powers and bleed them like a stuck pig. You could just give me the clue now. Save us both some time."

Peter laughed, the sound ringing around the room. "Please. Why would I cut to the chase and waste an opportunity for some fun? Besides, I need to give my brethren a chance to get into position. After all, I know you'll be like a greyhound to a rabbit. One sniff of a direction, and this will all be over without any fireworks."

Jennie picked a piece of lint off her top casually. "Will there be fireworks? Even you wouldn't set afire the city you love."

The smile faltered on Peter's face. A note of recognition followed. "You can see straight through me, can't you?"

Jennie nodded. "Of course. You're a specter."

"You know that's not what I mean," Peter replied, a cold note in his voice. "The link…it's two-way. Since when?"

Jennie grinned. "Since the moment we first bonded, I suppose. Since you screeched inside my head in a jail cell in the SIA HQ, I've felt a connection with you." She leaned forward, eyes growing dark. "You think you have the upper hand, but if you can see inside my mind, I can see inside yours, and I know the game you're trying to play. Keep my people and me busy while your men go off and scour the neighboring states, putting themselves in positions of power where they might grow their little enterprise."

Peter saw no point in denying it. "They're all already halfway to their destinations. I've got one heading to Pennsylvania, another to New Jersey, someone heading to Connecticut, and one going to Massachusetts."

"Smart," Jennie nodded.

"Thanks." Peter sat back and adjusted his shirt collar. "This game is about to blow wide open. I hope you're ready for the next stage. For years I've grown my own underground empire and built a band of loyal followers, and now, partnering with the crime lords of old, we'll spread across the country and blow this bitch wide open."

Jennie clapped slowly. "Impressive. But why are you telling me all this, when I already know? I can read it in your head."

Peter considered this. "I guess it's just to show you. To demonstrate that even you don't have access to everything."

Peter clapped his hands, and a group of mortals Jennie had never seen before came out from traps set into the stone walls. They had dark expressions on their faces and were large, even by Baxter's standards.

"How?" Jennie asked, rising to her feet and moving her hands to her guns.

"Selective memory recall," Peter crooned. "You have access to the memories and thoughts I allow you to have. Meditation has always aided in helping me control my thoughts, and in hiding the truth about what was hidden in this room, you were none-the-wiser."

They pointed their pistols at Jennie. She scowled and moved her hands away from her own.

"That's a dirty trick," Jennie growled.

Peter seemed to take this as a compliment. "Thanks. And now, if you'd like to follow us, we'll happily escort you—"

Jennie drew her pistols in a flash and let off two shots, immediately taking out two men on either side. She shot their arms, incapacitating them, but tried to avoid killing them where she could.

She pivoted, expecting a barrage of shots in retaliation, but nothing came. Instead, the horrendous screeching filled her head, sounding like metal scraping on metal at a volume that shook her brain cells. She clapped her hands to her ears and was horrified to see that she was the only one affected in the room. Peter simply stared at her with a satisfied look.

When he was done, Jennie was on the floor. The mortals rushed to her and bound her in cuffs, and soon she was being marched toward the doors.

Peter smiled and waved her away, pausing his men only long enough to say, "Oh, and one more thing, Genevieve. Those fireworks we discussed? They were real. I hope your friends enjoy them."

Jennie tried to latch onto Peter and turn spectral so she could melt through the handcuffs. Her head hung when she realized that that wasn't an option. The son-of-bitches had stolen SIA technology when they had broken Peter free.

Think, Jennie. Think.

A voice returned to her. *Don't think too hard. Remember, I can hear everything.*

Somewhere on the surface above, Jennie felt and heard the unmistakable sound of explosions.

CHAPTER TWENTY-FIVE

<u>**New York City, New York, USA**</u>

The shockwaves were felt across most of the city of New York.

An explosion, creating a mushroom cloud over fifty feet high, sent civilians running and screaming. The bomb set off just over a kilometer away from where Rhone, Carolyn, Feng Mian, Ula, Triton, Roman, Julia, Ruby, Jack, and Baxter were standing, discussing the finer points of their separation.

They had been in a deadlock, with Rhone figuring out who should pair with who to act upon the clues the Dragon—Peter Zhao—had given to them to stop the bombs.

A part of them had believed that he was bluffing. No one could set up a treasure hunt this extreme so fast, but they had clearly underestimated the guy.

Throwing caution to the wind, Rhone urged everyone to join them as he led the charge. As the mortal with the most experience in handling situations like this, no one argued. Even Baxter, who had ridden by Jennie's side through more than he ever thought would be possible, nodded and let Rhone take them onward.

They reached the coast of the city and found the site of the bomb. Smoke poured from the southernmost tip of Roosevelt Island, and

Four Freedoms State Park was now in tatters. Raging fires burned along the ground, and the black cotton smoke billowed angrily into the atmosphere. Despite the inherent danger, civilians gathered en masse across the water and took pictures on their cell phones and updated their social media feeds with the excitement.

"I hate mortals," Baxter grunted.

Even the conduits, Ula, Triton, and Roman, nodded in silent agreement. Ruby abashedly lowered her own cell and cast a sheepish look at the floor.

Rhone examined the paper in his hand, reading through the six clues. "Which one would this have been? I can't figure it out. The riddles are too obtuse."

"Does it matter?" Carolyn asked. "We've already failed. The son of a bitch tricked us. He said we had time."

Baxter stared over the water as the sirens of fire engines and cop cars began arriving on the scene. "Of course, it matters. This proves the psychopath isn't true to his word. If one bomb has already exploded, that means five more will soon. We can't rely on the luxury of time in this case."

"Fuck," Rhone growled as he scratched his head. "What do we know about the Dragon and his friends?"

"His name is Peter," Ruby corrected.

Rhone shot her a look.

"What?" she added. "I thought it was relevant."

Julia, who had been staring at her cell phone and scrolling through information pages, tapped the phone excitedly. "Here it is. I knew I'd heard the names before. The Dragon was part of a group known as the Infamous Seven. They were a crime syndicate who worked together in the eighties, splitting the city into seven separate bases of operation. Although their crimes were known to law enforcement, NYPD was never successfully able to lock down the kingpins of each operation and prevent the crimes." She scrolled further down. "Looks like they came close on a few occasions. They've even got names listed here of the syndicate bosses, although the report says that this information was never confirmed."

"What were their names?" Rhone asked, coming behind Julia and narrowing his eyes on the screen.

Julia listed the names. "Tommy Vincenzo, Ruben McAffey, Bobby Doltan, Dominic Ferriss, Craig Cowley, Sammie Garcia and… Oh. That's interesting."

"What?" Carolyn asked, taking a sudden interest. "Who is it?"

Rhone nodded solemnly. "As Ruby said, Peter Zhao."

"Well, that seems like too much of a coincidence," Baxter pointed out.

Julia tapped an image and excitedly flashed it around the group. "They've even got a map marking the boundaries between their territories. All speculative, of course, but it might be something useful to shut this shit down. Lower Manhattan, Midtown Manhattan, Upper East Side, Harlem, Upper Manhattan, Washington Heights, and Inwood."

Carolyn's eyes were drawn to the fire and smoke. "That's seven territories, but we only have six clues. Does that mean that one of them is a dud?"

"I don't know." Rhone passed the paper to Julia, inspired by her quick thinking and research. He pointed to the flames. "All I do know is that I don't want to see more of that happen in this city. Julia, you're on riddle duty. Where to next?"

Julia grinned, excited by the challenge, and peered over the top of the paper. She pointed to clue number two. "Really? You didn't get that almost instantly?"

Julia re-read the riddle out loud, frowning in concentration. "It happened during the July 4th celebration; Sammy walked several miles from Thirty-Second Street all the way to Sixty-Third without seeing anyone or being seen by anyone. It was a clear sunny day, and he could see where he was going. He did not use any disguise or unusual method of transportation. Even though Manhattan was swarming with people, not one person saw him. How could this be possible?"

They had split into two teams in order to cover the distance faster. Baxter had led his own team, while Julia had partnered with Rhone, Triton, Roman, and Ula. None of them had an answer for her.

"Trust me to get the non-New Yorkers." Julia sighed. "Those streets are in Manhattan. Well, Midtown Manhattan, to be exact. That's where we'll find our next location."

They hailed a cab and sped off in the direction of Midtown Manhattan. Traffic was dense, the city already panicking after the explosion on Roosevelt Island. After twenty minutes of exhaust-choked congestion, they hopped out of the car and ran.

When they reached Thirty-Second Street, they all looked around, half-expecting to see something obvious that would lead them to what they were searching for—not that they had any real idea. Julia re-read the clue, her lips moving silently as she racked her brains and tried to figure it out.

Rhone encouraged the conduits to get involved. "Any ideas?"

"None," Ula replied. "We're not overly familiar with this city. This wild goose chase is as foreign to me as navigating through the wilds of the Congo."

"You served in the Congo?" Rhone asked, surprised.

Ula's face straightened. "That's classified."

Triton grinned. When Rhone looked at him for an answer, he added, "Same as Ula, sir. Unfortunately, without sufficient intel to navigate this landscape, I have little to offer. Thinking in riddles is not my forte. You give me a target to eradicate, I'll find it. Guns speak louder than words."

Rhone raised an eyebrow. "You really believe that?"

Triton, Ula, and Roman all nodded. Triton replied, "Yes, sir. We do."

Not for the first time in his life, Rhone was pleased that he hadn't gone into the military. At least you got to keep some semblance of self in the federal government. All he knew of ex-military officers was the stone-cold stares of killers.

Still, you do what you've got to do to survive. I don't blame them at all. The environment is different. I switch from suit to uniform, but the hostilities of modern living are nothing compared to warzones.

Julia laughed, staring at the sky. The sudden explosion of mirth was manic and had Rhone flinching. "Of course! Of course! It's so simple." She slapped the paper with her hand, a triumphant look on her face. "It's the sewers. The only way you can travel without meeting anyone in broad daylight is the sewers. Well, that, or flying on a private jet." She paused and examined the sky. "My money's on the sewers."

Rhone placed his hands on his hips. "Are you sure?"

"Is calzone the best food ever created?" Julia replied.

Rhone looked back at the conduits who all stared blankly.

Julia sighed. "Yes. Yes, it is. Damn, you guys really need to try out some of that Italian food when this is all said and done."

"I've had a calzone before," Roman commented, his voice deep and baritone. "It's a broken pizza. Big whoop."

Julia laughed off his words. "You've clearly never tried one in NYC. I know a great place. I'll take you sometime." She glanced around and found a nearby manhole cover. "Ah! Someone help me with this."

As Rhone strolled over to help Julia raise the heavy metal lid, Ula leaned closer to Roman. "I see someone has got themselves a date with a pretty little thing."

Roman frowned. His jaw clenched.

Triton chuckled, patted Roman's chest. "She's all yours, big guy."

They left Roman grumbling as they followed Julia and Rhone down the ladder and into the sewers of Midtown Manhattan.

Baxter waited until the others were out of sight before he set off toward his true destination.

Carolyn and Feng Mian followed dutifully, with Ruby and Jack at the back of the pack. They half-ran back toward the Rockefeller

Center, none of them questioning Baxter's motives as he took them through the Radio City Music Hall.

Baxter was worried about Jennie. With the explosion acting as proof that some serious shit was going on here, there was a knot in his stomach that only grew tighter the closer they got toward the hidden chambers. The silence beneath the world was uncanny and in stark contrast to the mayhem taking place above.

The journey back was faster than Baxter had been expecting, and soon they stood outside the thick chamber doors. He paused and pressed his ear to the door.

More silence.

He held up his fingers and counted down. Jack's face hardened, and even Ruby had an impressively determined look in her eyes as she aimed her gun at the door, ready to boot the damn thing down.

"Feng Mian..." was the only thing that Baxter offered as Feng Mian took his position at the front and cast his barrier.

Baxter reached zero. Jack roared and booted the door, sending it flying back on its hinges. They stormed the chamber with Feng Mian in the lead, prepared for whatever assault may come their way. They were half-expecting the room to be choked with enemies firing shots at them, criminals and thugs and scum launching a volley of bullets their way.

They deflated as they entered the empty room. The only sign that people had been here was Peter's chair and the crooked angle it sat at, indicating that someone had risen from the table and not bothered to tuck it back in.

Baxter's stomach fell.

Carolyn breathed heavily. "Where is she? Baxter? Where the fuck is she?"

Baxter frowned, that knot in his stomach growing ever tighter. "I honestly don't know."

CHAPTER TWENTY-SIX

New York City, New York, USA

Jennie came out of her daze in phases. Each attempt to open her eyes brought on a fresh wave of pain as her headache set in, beating the inside of her skull like a bass drum. Even through her narrowed eyelids, she was aware of the intense light coming from somewhere nearby, and perhaps it was that that hurt her the most.

She swallowed, but it was a struggle. Her mouth was dry.

"For Queen and country," she muttered, not entirely sure what she was talking about. Every time she closed her eyes, she was transported back to Buckingham Palace, to the days when she had been a resident within its walls. A time when aristocrats and people of note would give her a wide berth in the hallways and mutter behind her back.

She had only been a weapon back then. Nothing more than a tool for the Queen to snuff out her enemies and keep hold of her power.

Power...

That was always what the fight was for. It was never about balance or happiness or the moral high ground. It was always some egotistical shark gunning for a bigger portion of the world. As though notoriety and infamy were the only steps on the ladder toward immortality.

She supposed, in a way, that was the case. History remembered the victors and the downright nasty. Jack the Ripper's legacy was still alive today, and what did he contribute to the world? Enigma and mystery. A portfolio of crimes that involved taking the lives of London prostitutes in brutal ways. Should he be remembered? Maybe that was a question for someone else to answer.

Peter was just one example of those maniacs. Every now and then, a runt slips through the net, and the world underestimates them. If they had squashed him when he was small, things would have been a little easier. Now he was a bear…No, he was a dragon, and that made things trickier.

Still, you don't always know which bugs are going to metamorphose into monsters. Sometimes you've just got to roll the dice and hope, and in this case, we lost.

Jennie peeled her eyes open and saw nothing but blue sky ahead. She tried to shield her eyes but found her hands bound to the arms of a chair. She rested a moment, closing her eyes to assuage the pounding headache, then tried again. There was glass in front of her, a huge pane of it. The city unfolded below her as though it was made of Lego. She was high up, and she already had an inkling of where she was.

She had seen Worthington exorcized here.

How original, she thought. *The bad guys sitting up in their ivory tower. The only ivory tower with a killer view and enough rep to please a sociopath.*

Jennie tugged against her bonds, but her muscles ached. She had no memory of being beaten, but she also had no memory of being transported. Had they drugged her? Maybe. Very likely. She tried once more to free herself but made no progress. Eventually, she rested her head back and closed her eyes. The sun, magnified through the glass, was burning hot. She was sweating, though it wasn't so much from the heat. It was from the columns of smoke rising from the tip of Roosevelt Island.

Goddamn it, Peter. You've really picked the wrong girl to piss off.

Footsteps broke the silence behind her. A chuckle followed. "Morning, sleepyhead. Are you ready to witness your destruction?"

They searched the chamber, inspected every nook and cranny, but turned up empty. Even as they left the underground, they poked their heads into any side room and scoured the floor for some kind of trail. There was nothing to find, no clues left behind.

Ruby pulled up the photo of the page of riddles she had taken on her phone. "I guess there's only one way forward. We're trapped in this game, and we have to take it in turns around the board before we can reach the end."

Baxter let out an angry shout. It was so uncharacteristic that Carolyn and Feng Mian stared at him warily. His hands were balled into fists, and his arms shook. "She's a good person. She's a damn good person, and she's been taken. What is it about this shitty excuse for a world that has the good guys placed in such dire straits? Why can't evil relent for long enough that people can enjoy a day in peace?"

Jack strode over to Baxter and tried to place his hands on his shoulders. He could see him through his SI glasses, but without the powers of the conduits, he passed straight through. "Dude, you need to relax. You can't stop the evil. The most we can do is hold it at bay. I'm with you, I'd love the world to be all sunshine and rainbows, but until that day comes, I'm happy to fight on the side of good. We'll get her back. We'll stop this. We always do."

Baxter sighed and nodded his head. "I'm sorry. You're right."

Jack chuckled. "Besides, it's *Jennie*. They've kidnapped a ticking time bomb. They shouldn't be worrying about the rest of the city, they should worry about the person they've just captured. The Dragon… sorry, *Peter*, has no idea what he's done."

"Aside from spreading the danger across the entirety of New York?" Carolyn replied. "Why is it always in the city that I love that the greatest tragedies happen?"

Feng Mian raised an eyebrow.

"What?" Carolyn asked.

"Attila the Hun?" Feng Mian replied.

Ruby added, "Hitler."

"The Black Plague," Jack stated.

Carolyn waved her arms. "Fine, fine. You know what I meant, okay?"

When they came out topside, things hadn't improved all that much. Helicopters flew overhead toward the site of the explosion, the authorities little knowing that more incidents were likely to occur.

Jack followed the bird and frowned. "We've got to let them know. This is bigger than just us. The city needs to be aware of the danger."

"What about SIA protocol?" Ruby asked.

Baxter was quick to reply. "Fuck protocol! He's right. The city needs to know. This isn't a case of mortals versus specters. This is a case of preventing as many casualties as possible."

Ruby sheepishly cleared her throat. "Erm...I meant that the SIA *needs* to know. As the overarching dominant force in Spectral Relations in the United States, it's vital that the agency is aware of what's going on."

"Oh," Baxter replied.

Jack dialed in the call. They could hear the tinny voice of Daggro on the other side of the line. Jack was minimal in his responses, but it was clear that Daggro wasn't pleased with what was going on. A few minutes later, Jack hit the red button to hang up and filled them in. "Daggro is sending agents to accompany us. She feels that the SIA needs to have a heavier hand in this, particularly with Jennie out of the picture for now. We're to expect their arrival shortly, and they'll send in a call when they're here."

"And the local authorities?" Ruby nudged.

Jack nodded. "HQ is calling them in. We're to proceed with the treasure hunt and do what we can to progress in the meantime. Daggro has also requested you forward the clues to her, Ruby."

Ruby held her phone up proudly. "Already on it!"

Carolyn leaned closer to Baxter. "Does Jennie really believe they're going to leave the SIA for the King's Court?"

Baxter shrugged. "Not my call to make. Though, there is something that we *can* do in the meantime. Hey, Ruby, can I borrow your phone?"

Ruby raised an eyebrow but agreed. "What are you doing?"

"You've got your guys, I've got mine." Baxter grinned. "I think it's about time we phoned in for our reinforcements. Let's have a reunion of the Spectral Plane."

Washington DC, USA

Acting Special Agent in Charge Holly Daggro ran a hand down her tired face.

She had hardly slept over the last week. Life in the driver's seat of the SIA had been exhausting as call after call came in, detailing spectral disturbances in the surrounding states. Her team had grown vastly, and her superior was nowhere to be seen. This had really become a one-woman operation, and there were almost too many moving points to keep track of.

"I need an assistant," Daggro muttered, not for the first time that day. The problem was, in order to get clearance for official assistance, she would need the backing of her superior. However, Special Agent in Charge Kurt Rogers was buried deep in the throes of strategizing and communicating with the President of the United States. That left little in the way of methods to communicate with him.

Daggro's hair was untidy. She'd been unable to find time to comb the tangles out. With the absence of Hendrick and his magical formulas—*where the hell was that guy*—she had resorted to copious amounts of coffee, but even that didn't feel like enough these days.

Her door opened, and a young agent stood there. "You asked to see me?"

He was objectively attractive. Slim, muscular build, a square jaw, eyes that sparkled even in the dark. By all appearances, he was the very definition of a jock.

Still, that didn't mean he could barge in without her instruction.

"You're supposed to knock and wait," Daggro muttered.

He looked at the door, then shrugged. "I thought this would be quicker. Wasn't this an urgent meeting?"

Daggro thought of arguing. After all, it wouldn't serve to have juniors testing her authority while she was serving in this state but instead chose to look past it. She liked the guy's spunk. He had all the hallmarks of an agent willing to prove himself and get the job done.

She motioned to a spare chair. "Sit, Agent Lionus."

He stood by the chair, looking uncertainly at the stacks of papers on the chair.

Daggro grinned. "Just knock them on the floor."

He obeyed, taking a seat across from her. "You should probably get a cleaner in here at some point. I thought we were messy down in the dorms."

Daggro couldn't help but smile. She had placed Agent Lionus and his comrades in Jennie's room, partly to capitalize on space to fit every new recruit into the HQ, partly to piss the bitch off.

Daggro sat back in her chair and steepled her fingers together. "Agent Lionus, I believe that you are aware of the expansion currently undergoing within the SIA. We're growing at an alarming rate, and it's nigh on impossible to try and keep on track with every single mission we have going, here."

Lionus nodded but remained silent. Even he knew better than to stop the flow of his superior.

Daggro continued. "I've been watching you. Reports show that you get shit done and you don't mess around. I need an agent to help me, act as a kind of…assistant, if you will. I think you're that agent."

His eyebrows lifted. Daggro got a better look at those killer eyes. Bright enough to stun a woman so he could drag her back to his lair. "I appreciate the offer, but are you sure there aren't better qualified agents ?"

Yes. Yes, there are. But I don't need experience. I need a mind I can mold to my way of thinking. A yes boy who will obey without question and do my bidding.

"What better way to qualify yourself than by grasping opportunities?" Daggro crooned. She sighed and shrugged. "Maybe you're not the agent I thought you could be."

Agent Lionus sat up straight and quickly changed his tune. "Of course, I can do that, boss. Whatever you need. I'm your guy. Just say the word and it's done."

That's better.

"There's a situation that needs attending to in New York," Daggro started, explaining the call that had come in and the explosions that had shaken the city. "I need you to arrange and send a team out there. You have my full confidence and backing to take what you need and get to the bottom of it."

His eyes lit up. "Can we take the jets?"

Daggro grinned. "No. Choppers will do. Anything else you need, sure. Just keep me abreast of what's going on, and ensure that I'm in the loop on everything. I don't want an agent to fart without me knowing about it, got that?"

He nodded. "I do."

"Good." Daggro tapped a few buttons on her iPad. "The brief is now in your inbox. Get to work and don't let me down. I can't stress to you how important it is that this goes right, and what a step up this could be for you."

Agent Lionus nodded eagerly and headed for the door. He paused with his hand on the handle and turned over his shoulder. "Why me? Surely you're better experienced to handle something like this?"

Daggro's face hardened. "In case you haven't noticed, I'm snowed under right now. I've got the oversight of the entire SIA. You think I have time to get in the field and get shit done? No. That's why I need you, an ambitious guy gunning for great prospects. Don't think I haven't read your reports."

Agent Lionus returned a crooked grin. "You got it."

When he closed the door, the smile slid off Daggro's face. She wondered whether she had done the right thing, but what choice did she have?

Maybe Rogers would praise her when he returned. Maybe not. All she knew was that she needed sleep, and in order for that to happen, things had to change around here.

CHAPTER TWENTY-SEVEN

<u>Richmond, Virginia, USA</u>

Tanya and Jiao scoured the city until it grew dark.

They had hired a vehicle on Jennie's credit card, a run-around that could be used in the city. The purple VW Beetle had little get up and go, but it was enough to get them around the streets.

Traffic was quiet, as was the city. In the wake of the strange explosion from the quarry, it was as though the world had fallen asleep already. That might have made it easier for searching, but the darkness certainly didn't aid them.

"What the hell was that?" Tanya muttered for the fourth time that evening. "I've never seen anything like it in my life."

Jiao remained silent in the passenger seat, eyes narrowed to the streets, which were quaintly lit by the arc sodiums.

"She flew. She *flew*. Out the window." Tanya shook her head. "I've seen strange things happen, Jiao. Hell, I've seen a house try and fight me back. But nothing like that. It was like she's a vampire, or Professor Snape or Voldemort or something. Stuff like that shouldn't happen in real life."

Jiao's pale face was stoic as she replied. "Lots of stuff shouldn't happen in real life. If life were as we wanted it to be, I certainly wouldn't have spent so much time as the Dragon's little sidepiece."

Tanya's ears warmed. "You guys never… I mean… He didn't…?"

Jiao looked at her expectantly.

Tanya sighed. "You never slept together, did you?"

"Yes," Jiao replied.

"I'm sorry," Tanya offered.

Jiao waved a hand. "Not in the way you believe. Yes, we slept in the same beds on some nights, but if you're talking about the colloquial term of 'sleep' and are suggesting that we engaged in coital relations, then no, we didn't."

Tanya breathed a sigh of relief. "Oh, thank God."

Jiao looked out the window as they passed a launderette and an antique store. "The Dragon was too fat and ill to engage in such activities. Although he appreciated the company of women, he could not perform in that way. His health was in such decline in the end that the most he could do was pant. I guess I was one of the lucky ones, to be the last of his line of concubines."

New York City, New York, USA

A knock on the door woke Jennie from her slumber.

It was dark outside. From her perch at the top of the Empire State Building, she could see a few stars dotted around. A full moon lit the sky. Jennie suddenly missed Richmond. There was far less in the way of light pollution, which let the stars come out in their full glory. She hadn't seen a sky like that since she'd left England.

Jennie sighed. "I'd say you can't come in, but I'm guessing that's not going to stop you?"

The door creaked open. Light footsteps padded toward her. A thin man with a creased face kept a cautious distance as he came into view. He held a bowl and a spoon in his hands.

"Zhao wishes for you to eat." His hands trembled. A look of concern was on his face, as though he had been asked to approach a tiger while covered in a meat suit. "You're hungry, aren't you?"

"No," Jennie shot back, no sooner realizing as she said it that she was actually starving. Her stomach audibly rumbled, and she growled in annoyance. Peter was in her head, still. She could feel him there like a parasite, monitoring her every thought. She glanced at the bowl and resigned herself to the situation. "Fine. Yes."

He sat in front of her and spoon-fed the slop in the bowl. Some kind of thick oatmeal which had the consistency of glue. Jennie had eaten worse in her lifetime, but that didn't mean she enjoyed any of this.

When it was finished, he dabbed at her chin with a cloth, keeping his body at arm's length away. He offered her water, which she greedily drank.

He silently gathered his things and made to leave.

"What's your part in this?" Jennie asked. The man froze. "What does Zhao have on you that turns you into a glorified babysitter? You must have dreams? Hopes? Goals? Why are you here?"

The man looked into her eyes for a long time. She thought he might answer her, but after a beat, he shuffled to the door and closed it softly behind him.

"Damn," Jennie muttered. "I thought I had something there." She screwed her eyes shut and looked inside of herself. *Why are you doing this, Zhao? Why inflict pain and torture on this world?*

And then, a faint voice returned, speaking in such a way that Jennie was almost certain Peter Zhao was standing right behind her. "Because the world wronged me. Now I can finally turn the tables."

Not for long, Jennie thought with a grin. *Not once I'm free.*

She realized that she had thought her words in the chamber where Zhao could access. It was violating, having someone inside her head. Instead, she changed her thoughts and began to engage the practices she had learned years ago. Her headache was gone, which made the process all the easier.

Don't think what you don't want him to hear...

Shit.

Peter Zhao is the Emperor of the World. He is my one true love. Only Peter can give me the things the world has deprived me of.

She grinned, remembering what Zhao had said to her before taking her hostage. *"You have access to the memories and thoughts I allow you to have."*

Two can play that game, Jennie thought.

Oh. Shit! This is going to take some practice.

"I wonder if we're going to run into humanoid turtles," Rhone muttered, the long tunnels of the sewers carrying his voice in bouncing echoes.

Ula looked at him blankly.

Rhone emphasized. "You know, Teenage Mutant Ninja Turtles? Heroes in a half-shell?"

Ula shook her head.

Rhone gave an incredulous look. "Donatello? Raphael? Michelangelo? And… Oh, crap. I can never remember the fourth."

"Leonardo," Julia supplied.

"Thank you! Leonardo!" Rhone smirked. "He was my favorite, too. Not sure how I keep forgetting that one."

Roman scoffed. "I'm sorry, Agent Rhone. While you were watching children's cartoons, we were off protecting the country from invaders, terrorists, and scum."

Rhone raised an eyebrow. The conduits didn't look much older than he was. *How is it they've never even heard of the Turtles?*

"You've never watched television?" he asked.

Triton adjusted the grip on his rifle, making a conscious effort to keep his voice quiet. "We were each born into military serving families. Television was a precious luxury, one that we weren't afforded. From a young age, we were taught to hone our skills, build our strength, and understand the strategies which can make the difference between life or death while fighting the unpredictable forces which spring up across the world."

"Wow," Rhone replied. "Maybe *you* should be leading this expedition."

"It had crossed our mind," Roman grumbled.

Ula slapped Roman on his stomach. "No. We were taught to obey orders, and Jennie has assigned you as the lead, here. Besides, New York is much closer to your wheelhouse of knowledge than it is to our own. We're with you, Captain."

Rhone exchanged a look with Julia and narrowed down his focus on the tunnel ahead, only breaking his focus to briefly mutter to Julia, "Hey, at least we don't have any pizza. That'd draw them straight to us."

Julia bit her lips to hide her laughter. "Aaand we're back to Italian food."

The tunnels stank. A thin channel of sludge and sewage ran alongside them. Rhone did his best to avoid staring at the items floating in the thick liquid. They pulled their collars up to cover their noses as they walked ever further into the sewer system.

They reached a cross-section, and Julia pointed them onward. They looked forlornly at her, realizing that they'd either have to jump clear over the gap or risk wading through the muck.

"You first," Rhone encouraged.

Julia frowned. Her eyes lingered on the sludge. "Throw me."

Rhone couldn't catch his laugh in time. "Throw you? I thought that nobody tosses a dwarf?"

He turned to the others for approval, a smirk on his face. His smile faded. "Oh, right. I forgot you guys are oblivious to all pop culture references. Lord of the Rings? No?"

They returned a blank stare.

Rhone sighed. "Lucky me, stuck with you lot. Okay, Julia, how do you propose we do this?"

Julia, who had, at one point, been a flyer for her high school cheerleading team, talked Rhone through a technique which would see her launching from a cradle Rhone would make with his hands, jumping at the same moment that he raised his hands in order to maximize the distance.

She steadied herself by holding his shoulders. They did a few test bounces. Julia cast a cautious glance at the ceiling. "Not too high, okay?"

"You'll be lucky if any of this works," Rhone replied dryly.

Ula bumped Roman's hip. "Are you going to take that? He's hitting on your girl."

Roman grumbled. Triton laughed. Julia rolled her eyes.

They counted to three and Julia leaped. The maneuver worked surprisingly well, giving her enough distance to cross over the sewage and land safely on the other side. She flew slightly higher than planned but managed to steady herself on the landing by throwing one foot down and running to a stop at the damp wall.

"Eww!" She rubbed her hands down her top.

"Would you rather the moss, or the sludge?" Ula asked.

Julia lowered her head. "The moss."

Rhone let out a long breath and steadied himself for the next toss. "Okay, who's next?"

No sooner had he crouched into position than Ula, Roman, and Triton took a running start and jumped across the gap in one swift bound. They landed with quiet grace, coming to a stop before they reached Julia.

"Real classy, guys," Rhone complained. He glanced doubtfully at the viscous liquid pouring out fumes of stink. "Here goes nothing."

He took a few steps back, then followed the others. As he took off from the stone floor, one of his feet slipped. He managed to still get a good distance on the launch, although his face twisted in fear as the sludge streamed under him. He reached out his arms and landed awkwardly on the stone. One foot trailed behind and dipped into the sludge. His toes grew cold, and he could feel the slime seeping into the holes where he laced his shoes.

Triton grabbed his wrists, pulling him quickly out of the sewage. He winked. "Classy."

"Hey, we all have bad days." Rhone picked himself up and shook his foot. "Shit."

Ula grinned. "Probably."

Although Rhone's cheeks colored, they all laughed at that.

A knocking came from farther along the sewer. They all stopped at once and fell silent. Julia's eyes were unblinking, while the others readied their weapons.

"I'm so not prepared for this kind of fight," Julia whispered.

Without looking at her, Rhone handed her a pistol, its side laden with the same green lights that rimmed the SI glasses. "You better get ready and quickly. Shit is about to go down."

They sneaked onward toward the source of the sound. Although they strained to hear anything further, all had fallen silent ahead. Cut into the walls of the sewers were shallow recesses, which they used as cover as they advanced as quickly as they dared, ready for any eventuality ahead.

Julia trailed behind the group, doubtfully holding the pistol. When she had been working for the Umbra, things had been different. They had been surrounded by people who would die to protect her. But now that the group was a literal handful, she felt exposed and nervous.

What if people started shooting? What if they were overrun? She knew she was attractive, relatively speaking, and worried what their enemies would do if she was held captive. Men could become monsters when given ultimate power over a woman.

The only thing keeping her hopeful was the experienced vets pacing ahead of her. These three ex-forces, and the federal agent who dealt with this kind of situation daily. Who better to walk behind than these?

Still, that didn't stop her from glancing longingly down the tunnel behind her.

A few minutes later, Rhone raised a fist to halt them. The conduits obeyed instantly. Julia almost ran into the back of the others. There were noises ahead, gentle footsteps pacing.

Rhone lowered his fist and raised his rifle to his eye line. They curved around a bend and found the first lot of their enemy.

Finally, Julia thought. *I was beginning to think we'd been led on a wild goose chase.*

Two men and one woman in ninja-yoroi, dark material wraps that clothed their entire bodies but left room for flexibility. The only part of their bodies exposed were dark eyes through slits in their face masks.

They were pacing in front of an entrance to their right. If Rhone and the others hugged their wall, they would be able to get them. But there was almost no way to catch them off-guard.

"Ninjas?" Julia mouthed to Rhone.

Ula caught this and shook her head. "Of course not," she replied in the same near-whisper. "Why would real ninjas be standing guard in a goddamn sewer? It has to all be for show."

Rhone took a steady step forward, but Roman halted him with a hand on his shoulder. He waved him aside as he reached into his pocket without looking and drew out something that looked like a collapsible metal straw.

Julia watched with fascination as the other conduits followed suit. They each then took something else from their pockets and held it to the mouth of the straw. Standing side-by-side, they narrowed their eyes, selected their targets, and exhaled sharply.

Their cheeks puffed as three tiny darts sped through the air. Julia lost sight of the projectiles but knew they'd hit their mark when they immediately clutched their necks and fell to the ground.

Rhone nodded, impressed. Ula held up the straw and gave a grin, whispering, "You learn a lot out there in the jungle."

She said no more, leaving Julia in awe as they nudged forward and approached the opening the guards had been protecting.

They had gotten lucky. There were more guards stationed inside the tunnel. The conduits quickly dragged the bodies out of sight of the main entrance and peeked around the corners.

There were two more sets of guards spaced fifty meters apart along the tunnel. At the farthest point they could see, a shaft of light was beaming down from the surface above. It was milky and white. Julia wondered if it was sunlight or moonlight.

How long have we been down here?

Where the light touched, was a podium with a device strapped to its center.

The bomb!

Julia motioned to Rhone, but he had already clocked the device. He turned to the conduits and muttered in a barely audible whisper, "We approach slowly. One wrong move could set them all off."

"Are they kamikazes?" Julia asked.

Triton chewed his lip. "Not likely. Either way, this is a delicate play. We alarm the troops, we risk triggering it all. Whether they're kamikazes or not, they've been sent to do a job. We stop them with stealth. That's all we have here."

Roman grunted his agreement.

"But how?" Julia asked. "They're everywhere."

Rhone glanced down at the guards they'd taken out. He raised his eyebrows at the conduits.

"Finally," Roman grumbled, a grin appearing on his face. "A chance to get our hands dirty."

Julia suddenly connected what Rhone was suggesting. "You can't be serious?"

Rhone shrugged. "It's all we've got." His eyes found the conduits. "Stealth, baby. Stealth."

CHAPTER TWENTY-EIGHT

<u>Red Hook, Brooklyn, USA</u>

The warehouse in the abandoned industrial district of Red Hook was simple to find. When the large building came back into sight, Baxter, Carolyn, and Feng Mian were overwhelmed with nostalgia at the place that had been their gathering and training ground for the battle that had taken place in Times Square.

Carolyn sighed. "Back at the warehouse, and we're gearing up for another battle. I really wish we could say that the situation was different now. At some point, the world has got to be safe, right? This is exhausting."

Baxter chuckled. "You'd think so. Unfortunately, evil never sleeps. Ask Jennie, she's been fighting this shit for over a hundred years. Without the villains, there would be no need for heroes."

"Not necessarily," Feng Mian countered. "There are many kinds of heroism, many small acts people are capable of that bring light to the world."

Ruby and Jack were sitting uncomfortably in the back of the cab. The specters had squeezed in around them, and they found it almost impossible not to join in on the conversation. If they did, they were almost certain the cabbie would kick them out for acting crazy and speaking to themselves. Native New Yorkers had little tolerance for the insane.

They pulled up about a hundred meters from the warehouse. Although the cabbie couldn't see anything amiss as he asked for their fee, Ruby and Jack were taken aback by the amount of activity taking place outside the warehouse.

There were dozens of specters, if not hundreds. They roamed the outside of the warehouse, talking to each other in groups, some in the midst of scraps as they tested their fighting skills. A few kicked their legs over the edge of the concrete dock, watching the sunset over the waters around New York City.

From the upper floors of the warehouse, where a number of balconies were littered along its edge, specters stood and watched out over the others, heads and eyes turning their way as the yellow cab waited.

"I said, twenty bucks," the cabbie grunted. "If I have to ask again, I won't be so kind."

Jack snapped out of his distraction and slapped an even twenty in the cabbie's waiting palm. They stepped out of the car and wandered toward the specters.

The closer they got, the more heads turned to examine the strangers. After a moment, a dozen or so specters who had shielded their eyes from the sunset beamed and tore over to the group. They greeted Baxter, Carolyn, and Feng Mian with eager handshakes, treating them like bona fide celebrities. Soon enough, dozens more specters surrounded them. There were some familiar faces from the fight against Worthington and the rogue group of rebels from the Paranormal Court, as well as a number of fresh-faced specters who must have been recruited in the length of time between then and now.

Questions were hurled at them. Many asked where Rogue was, and if she'd be joining them at all. Baxter and Carolyn did their best to field questions as they were all guided into the warehouse toward the makeshift bar that Jennie had left in her wake all those weeks ago.

Jack and Ruby couldn't stop smiling. The inside of the warehouse was even busier than the outside, and it seemed strange to them both to be lost in this world that was far from their own. They'd both experienced specters in small doses, but this warehouse and its surrounding neglected buildings had become something of a shanty town for specters.

Eventually, they all found seats in what had once been the foreman's office in the warehouse. Specters waited outside as a portly specter ushered the crowd out and allowed them all some breathing space.

Baxter laughed. "Thanks, Jimmy."

Jimmy Dean, who had once acted as a spectral refrigerator for Jennie to store drinks as they prepared for battle, beamed at Baxter. His demeanor had changed almost entirely since that day, and it appeared as though he had become something of a leader for the Spectral Plane in New York.

Jimmy gave a hearty chuckle. "I can honestly say that I haven't seen a reaction like that in weeks. People have really taken to this little corner of the city, but nothing gets the group more riled up than the appearance of celebrities. If Rogue had been here, too, I don't know what they would have done!"

A woman with a tight ringlet of curls and a dark mark across her neck laughed. "They probably would have shat their pants. It takes a lot to excite a specter, but that would've done it."

Jimmy rolled his eyes. "Do you have to be so crass?"

"Tell me I'm wrong," the woman replied.

Jimmy waved a hand, his smile unfaltering. "You'll have to excuse Amy. She lived a sheltered life and now makes it her mission to roam the city and pick up any curses and insults she comes across."

Amy smiled, clearly pleased by this introduction. "I'm making a scrapbook."

Ruby and Jack exchanged a look and laughed.

Amy crossed over to Jack and took a seat beside him, her face inches from his. She examined his SI glasses with interest. "Oooh! What are those?"

Jack took off his SI glasses to allow Amy to get a better look, momentarily forgetting that he'd lose his access to the specters. The glasses floated in front of him, and it was unsettling to suddenly realize that he was technically sitting in an empty office with only Ruby beside him. He looked through the glass window and the warehouse was bare, containing nothing more than dust and concrete and steel.

The feeling made him nauseous, reminding him of the feeling of slipping out of a VR experience without taking the necessary steps to readjust.

He snatched the glasses back.

"Hey!" Amy exclaimed, her voice snapping back into focus as the arms of the glasses connected with his ears. "What was that for?"

"Nothing personal," Jack explained. "These allow me to see you guys. Without them, it feels like it's just me and Ruby on some weird-ass date in the middle of nowhere." He turned to Ruby. "I'm sorry, but you're far too young for me."

"*Ewww!*" Ruby exclaimed as the others fell about laughing.

Baxter came to their rescue as Amy obnoxiously floated in front of Jack's face, eyes narrowing on the technological components of the glasses. "They're both mortals, but they're with us. They're part of the SIA."

"Of course." Jimmy nodded knowingly since a faction of the Spectral Plane had peeled off and played a part in helping Jennie against the Queen in Virginia.

Baxter went on to explain what had happened in the interim after the Spectral Plane was sent back to New York. He described Jennie's plan to create her own organization, momentarily forgetting that Jack and Ruby had been clueless about this.

"That's why Jennie wanted us involved in this mission?" Jack gasped.

Baxter shook his head. "Not now." He then went on to describe the situation with the Dragon and how they managed to find their way back to NYC.

Jimmy pinched his chin, eyes deep in thought. "There's always trouble wherever you guys come in. I've ordered a group of our guys to investigate the explosion. I should've known it had something to do with you guys."

"*We* didn't do it," Ruby clarified. "A psychopathic specter did it. We're just here to pick up the pieces."

Baxter nodded. "I hate to ask again, but we need you guys. We've been given a list of clues to the bombs' locations and little time to solve them. All we know is that the bomb that went off is going to be the first of many. We really need all hands on deck to find the others and stop further destruction. Do you think you can help us?"

Jimmy considered this, staring out of the window at the specters speculating openly and pointing at Baxter, Carolyn, and Feng Mian. A wry smile crept up his mouth. "Baxter? I'm surprised you had to ask. Tell us what we need to know, and we'll get our asses in gear. You say this is time-sensitive. How time-sensitive are we talking?"

Carolyn leaned forward, resting her elbows on her knees. "The Dragon's people have set five more bombs in less than five hours."

Jimmy's smile faded. Amy turned to him, mortified. "Is now a good time to curse?"

Jimmy nodded. "Yes, Amy. I think it is."

"Give it your best," Jack agreed with amusement.

Amy's eyes flicked away while she thought. "Motherfucking dripping piss-flap of a zombie-teabagger," she spat. "We *have* to stop those bombs."

Ruby's and Carolyn's eyes widened as they caught each other's stare.

Jack couldn't hold back his grin. "Impressive."

***

Roman was too big to fit inside the guard's clothing, so he handed over the bundle of wrappings to Rhone.

Rhone dressed quickly, and soon enough, it was almost impossible to discern him, Ula, and Triton from the three guards who they'd hit with the blow darts.

What the hell was in those darts? Rhone wondered.

The only difference between them and the originals was that they wore their firearm harnesses over the soft, black fabric. They concealed their weapons behind their backs, covering the harness straps in the many folds of the outfits before they were ready.

Rhone took the lead and gave the thumbs up.

Ula glanced over her shoulder at the grimacing Roman. "Hands off each other, okay, ladies?"

Roman and Julia flushed hot pink and took a step away from each other.

Ula chuckled quietly as they entered the tunnel.

They stalked along the tunnel in single file, clinging to the shadows. The dark clothing they wore acted as excellent camouflage, but they couldn't stifle their steps completely. They walked slowly and quietly until they reached the first pair of guards stationed, where Rhone and Triton split to address one each while Ula waited. Their plan was to create a fictional reason why they had to step back from the view of the other guards, then take them out of the equation.

Ula stood guard in the position where one of the guards had been, acting normally to avoid triggering suspicion in the other guards. If they saw that she was standing sentinel without a worry, the muted scuffling sounds might be ignored.

With a quick glance farther down the tunnel, Rhone and Triton shoved the pair into a recess on the opposite side of the tunnel. Rhone applied a sleeper hold to one guard while Triton took care of the other. The guards panicked and choked out the air from their lungs, and a moment later, they were unconscious and lying on the floor.

Jack stepped behind Ula, keeping out of sight. "Two more uniforms," he muttered. "Think we should dress the others?"

"Nah," Ula replied without turning. "They're probably up against the wall right now, caught in the throes of passion." She thanked God that the mask was hiding her smile.

There were two more guards stationed down the tunnel before they'd reach their final destination. These ones weren't stupid and had clocked that something was amiss. They turned and waited for Triton and Rhone as Ula waited a safe distance back, eyeing the situation to ensure that she could jump in if needed.

"You were ordered to remain at your station," one of the guards spat. "What are you doing?"

The other guard shifted uneasily, reaching for something at his side.

Rhone had to think fast. He couldn't fake the other guard's voices, he didn't know how they sounded. Instead, he nodded at Triton and they both drew their weapons, causing both guards to freeze.

A quick glance at the guards by the bomb showed that they weren't looking at that moment. Rhone took this as a blessing and guided his guard into the closest recess, while Triton did the same.

"Who are you?" the guard hissed.

"Your worst nightmare," Rhone replied, masking his voice by lowering it an octave.

Dude, you sound like Batman. He flushed beneath the material of his mask, thinking how stupid he sounded. Still, best to remain consistent.

He shoved the barrel of the rifle into the guard's stomach. There was something hard there.

Kevlar?

"How do we defuse the bomb?" Rhone asked urgently.

The man's eyes narrowed. "How the hell should I know? You think I'm a bomb technician?"

His voice grew dangerously loud.

Rhone pressed the barrel even harder. "Keep your voice down. How long until the bomb detonates?"

The man's eyes rolled. "Again, you think I'm given that information? Soon? All I know is that the minute boss man gives the order, we're sprinting for safety. You think I want to be caught under a massive pile of rubble?"

Rhone studied the man. "You're not kamikazes?"

The man scoffed. "Because of the ninja gear? Come on. That's racist. Not all oriental warrior types are suicide bombers."

A scuffle behind made Rhone turn and look over his shoulder to find Triton with one arm hooked around the guard's neck, and the other desperately holding his wrist as he fought to keep a six-inch blade from stabbing into him.

That moment of distraction was all the guard needed.

Rhone was shoved back, away from the recess. He appeared in the tunnel and caught the eye of those near the bomb. The guard he had been aiming his rifle at jumped out and shouted, "Intruders! Intruders!"

The guard instantly drew a pistol and was halfway to aiming it at Rhone when Rhone pulled the trigger and shot him in the shoulder. Another bullet found his shin, and he was certain the guard was incapacitated.

Footsteps came from both sides of the tunnel as Ula ran toward them, and the guards kicked into gear to work against the intruders.

Triton choked out the guard and lay him on the floor, taking his knife and patting him down for weapons. He found a pistol and put it to work.

Rhone and Triton ducked back into the recess. Rhone peeked around and drew back quickly as stone chipped away from the bullets hitting the corner.

Shit. We need to get to the bomb. Now.

The only saving grace he could think of was that the guard laying in pain beside him had told them they weren't suicide bombers.

Maybe he *isn't. But are the others?*

Turning back the way he had come, he saw Ula out in the open. He wondered what she was doing as she aimed her weapon above Rhone's head and shot at the wall. In her madness, she almost looked like...

Like one of them.

Rhone couldn't help but appreciate the woman's smarts at that moment. By looking like she was gunning for the intruders, the others would think she was on their side. That would give her a chance to get close enough to help out.

She zeroed in on them, moving across to Rhone. When she was a mere foot away from ducking out of sight, she turned her weapon on the enemy and sent a spray of bullets their way. Rhone heard the cries of pain and anguish as the enemy fell to the floor.

Ula stopped beside him, breathless but determined. "You okay?" she panted.

Rhone pulled down his mask and grinned. "Much better now you've stopped pointing a gun at me. That was some smart thinking."

Ula winked.

Triton's voice carried across to them. "When you two love birds are finished sucking each other's dicks, can you help out, here?"

Rhone's eyes widened as he spotted a grenade in Triton's hand. He pulled the pin and tossed it toward the enemy.

What is he doing? There's already one bomb to worry about!

The bomb detonated. Rhone waited for the ceiling to crumble and the tunnels to collapse, then realized what had happened as smoke billowed their way and clouded the tunnels in fog.

Julia held her hands to her ears. She had watched the action from afar, but the minute the bullets started flying, Roman had pulled her back.

His body was huge compared to hers. It was like being blocked in by a cement pillar. He wore a musky aftershave that she found oddly pleasant and her cheeks flushed as she…

No. What are you doing? All that talk of flirting has gotten into your head, girl.

She looked up into Roman's eyes. His cheeks had a three-day rash of stubble and his grim face was set in a determined stare as he leaned across and examined the tunnel entrance.

"Aren't you going down there to help them?" Julia asked, her voice a mouse's whisper.

Roman grunted. "No clear path." He touched a finger to his ear. Julia wasn't sure why since she could see nothing there. "Triton. Operation Nimbus."

Julia raised an eyebrow. Roman caught her look. "Micro-receivers. Flesh-colored and as small as the head of a pin. A remnant from the army."

Julia had no idea what any of that meant, but she knew that she felt safe cocooned by Roman's body.

She flinched when a louder explosion came. The next thing she knew, Roman was pulling her behind him and standing in the entrance of the tunnel. "Stay close behind me. No matter where I go, use me as a shield. Got it?"

Why could Julia not stop staring at his lips at that moment? She nodded.

Roman took off at a steady pace into the smoke. Even just a few paces away, the smoke was dense enough to cause him to fade like a dark specter. She saw him draw something from his pocket and place them on his face. Whatever it was, he navigated the smoke with a certainty that she definitely didn't feel.

Julia screamed when a bullet ricocheted above her. Rocks rained down. She side-stepped, then re-aligned herself to remain behind Roman.

He turned over his shoulder. "Every scream draws them to us. Shut up."

Julia blushed, then fell in step.

They charged onward. Roman let off a number of shots with his rifle, joining the cacophony of what she hoped was gunfire coming from the other conduits and Rhone. Figures joined her and Roman and they continued toward the center of the tunnel, praying that a sudden explosion wouldn't send them flying backward.

The gunfire stopped. The conduits checked in with Rhone. He gave a nod, squinting through the smoke. They gathered around the bomb, and the conduits stood guard while Rhone investigated the device. Julia could just make out the faint shapes of fallen enemies on the floor, their legs the only part visible before their bodies disappeared into the fog.

"Fuck," Rhone muttered, despair in his voice. "You've got to be kidding me."

Ula, Roman, and Triton looked over their shoulder at him. Rhone held up a scrap of paper that had been taped to the side of the device. Written in thick black marker were the words, "Gotcha!"

"It was a trick?" Ula gasped.

Rhone's lips grew thin as the paper shook in his fists.

CHAPTER TWENTY-NINE

<u>Richmond, Virginia, USA</u>

The manor was silent when Tanya, Sandra, and Jiao returned.

It was creepy, reminding Tanya of how it had felt when they had first arrived and taken down the Mendlesons. There was a chill in the rooms, the lights were off, and there was no one home that they could see.

"How could a couple live here by themselves for so long?" Tanya asked the room.

Jiao answered. "Perhaps that was why they had so many children?"

Tanya supposed she was right. "Still, it's creepy when it's quiet. At least when the others were here, there was some kind of atmosphere. It felt more like a home with more people." Her mind turned to Jennie and the others. "I hope they're okay." She checked her phone. "Nothing from them at the minute. How long did they say they'd be gone for?"

"A day or two," Sandra replied, already searching for the Roomba. A moment later, the droning hum appeared from the device and Sandra clapped her hands.

Tanya and Jiao worked their way around the lower floor and found no one. They headed upstairs, taking their time as they examined each room in turn. A mixture of relief and concern came when they heard activity in the laboratory. Two voices were muffled through the door.

Jiao reached for the handle. Tanya stopped her.

"What if they're dangerous?" Tanya asked.

Jiao shook her head and opened the door, Tanya close behind. She let out a relieved laugh when she clocked Hendrick and Lupe working around the various benches and work surfaces.

Lupe looked at the door, then looked away.

"Hey guys," Tanya cried cheerily. "Thought everyone here had gone out and left! This house gets quiet when there's hardly anyone here."

Lupe busied himself unpacking a cardboard box. Foam peanuts sprinkled over the floor as he carefully lifted glassware and placed them on the side.

"Funny that, isn't it?" Lupe grumbled. "Imagine being the only two left in the house."

The penny dropped on Tanya's face. She moved her hand to her mouth. "Lupe! I'm so sorry, I got carried away and forgot that you would want to come, too! I should've checked, but these last few days have been crazy and I—"

"I heard you," Lupe interjected, his face sullen. "You forgot. It's fine."

A beat of silence passed between them. Lupe carried on unpacking while Hendrick organized the cupboards and started setting out a load of equipment to add to the already confusing assortment of objects scattered around the large makeshift lab.

Tanya sensed the annoyance in Lupe and moved closer. "Lupe...I..."

Lupe raised a hand, his brow furrowed. Although he was clearly annoyed, his voice was soft. "Forget it, Tanya. You've actually done me a favor. All this time, I've been following around the agents and the specters and thinking that I can play an active part in the battle against injustice. I thought I could do it from the frontlines, but I'm not a fighter. I'm... Well, I don't know what I am exactly. I can't shoot,

I don't do well in combat, so Hendrick has offered me an alternative. He's going to teach me his way. I'm going to become his new apprentice and help in a way that doesn't put my life at risk and gives me more use."

Tanya's head tilted to the side. "Are you sure?"

A reassuring smile appeared on Lupe's face. "Yeah. Yeah, I am. Was I pissed when I found out you abandoned me? Sure. Of course. But it actually might be the biggest favor you've done for me. At least here I can have an impact." His features softened, and he hugged Tanya. Jiao stood silently beside them. Tanya was certain Lupe wiped a tear from the corner of one eye. "But enough about me. What happened out there? Did you find the Paranormanimals?"

Tanya and Jiao exchanged a look.

"Something like that," Tanya explained. "We may have a slight problem on our hands."

Lupe's smile widened. "When don't we have problems? Please. Tell me. It's about time we saw some action since the others are away and hogging it all."

Jennie fought sleep with a determination that only she could muster. Eventually, as the night sky wheeled above her, someone familiar came to her side.

She could feel his signature, like a bloodhound trained to the scent of a fox. The moment he entered the room, her mind felt foggy, and she could feel him like fingers rooting around inside it.

"Genevieve." Peter Zhao's words were smug. He stepped into view and took a seat on the ledge by the glass, just a few feet from Jennie. "Pleasant evening, isn't it?"

Jennie growled but declined to speak. She couldn't move. The bonds were spectrally imbued, so even slipping into specterdom wouldn't work on the former Dragon.

Zhao stared out over the city. "Amazing, isn't it? The first settlers came to this area in 1624. Just under four hundred years later, here we are. A veritable metropolis. A thousand buildings. A million places to hide."

Jennie stared at the back of his head, imagined puncturing the skull with a sharp object. Peter swiveled and grinned. "I wouldn't be thinking that way if I were you. You want your freedom, right? Best start behaving."

Jennie allowed the thoughts to dissipate. "I didn't have you down as such a sentimental type. Considering how willing you were to blow up a portion of the neighboring islands."

"Of course," Zhao replied. "I wouldn't dare risk damaging the core of my own city, would I? Four hundred years to build, and a minute to destroy it all. It would be easy, but how would that benefit me at all?"

Jennie raised an eyebrow. She connected to Zhao and filtered through *his* mind, scanning for something which made sense. Suddenly, as if revealing itself from behind a veil, Jennie saw the truth clearly. "There were never any other bombs, were there?"

Zhao grinned. "Of course, not. You've been slipping in and out of consciousness for hours, you'd have seen the bombs if they had been set the way I had told you."

Jennie's blood boiled. The part of her thoughts she was trying to keep locked away was threatening to spill. She had to control it. Had to regulate her breathing and focus only on what she wanted Zhao to see.

"Your friends are alive and well," Zhao continued. "In fact, they destroyed some of my people not too long ago. You may be wondering how I know. My followers are loyal—even more so now— and if they haven't returned my calls, I can only assume that they're dead. If not now, then they will be soon. Still, an eye for an eye, I think. Your friends damage my people, I'll damage theirs. Fair trade, don't you think?"

He advanced on Jennie with a greedy look on his face. His eyes were dark. He grabbed her wrists over the cuffs and stared into her eyes. "I've heard that whatever scars you in mortal life will follow you through to specterdom. I wonder how the great Genevieve King would react to having her eyeballs scooped from her face, one by one. Death wouldn't be salvation from your blindness, would it?"

Jennie's nostrils flared. She readied herself.

Zhao cocked his head. "Nothing to reply? Ah, well. I gave you a chance to protest."

He picked up a Stanley knife and brought it to her face. One hand pinned her neck and kept her head still. She patiently waited, eyes fixing on the point where the blade narrowed to its keen edge.

Zhao started laughing, his hand shaking with each movement. The knife was an inch away when Jennie narrowed her eyes, allowed her conscious thought to register what she'd been hiding. Zhao saw it too late, his attention focused on the blade. She latched onto him and pushed forward with her full force, summoning the energy she had been honing since she was a child.

Peter's hand slipped from her neck. He flew through the glass without resistance and hovered thirty feet outside the building. A severe drop was below him, and although Jennie knew it was likely he wouldn't permanently fade from existence, the fall would be enough to send a simple message.

Don't fuck with me.

Jennie locked eyes with Peter. He tried to wriggle and react, but it was useless. Jennie raised the fingers of one hand as much as she could and gave a simple wave.

Then she let him drop.

The specters were already riled.

Those who were willing and able to help were outside the warehouse. The plan was simple, to divide and search New York. They'd each been assigned districts and territories, and it would be their role to search in any location where they believed the clues might be leading.

Baxter hoped it would be enough. Already they'd wasted enough time and night had fallen. Soon the bombs would start rolling.

Why hadn't they already?

He raised Jack's cell to the sky and angled it for a signal.

"You know that does nothing anymore?" Ruby smirked. "We're in New York, not the ass-end of Pittsburgh. It's only rural areas you struggle for signal."

Baxter grimaced. "Then why aren't they picking up?"

It was then that the phone started vibrating. He tapped the answer button and put it on speakerphone. "Julia? Rhone? That you?"

Julia's voice came through. "Erm. Of course. Didn't it say so on the phone's screen?"

Baxter had been in such a hurry to answer that he hadn't even checked.

"No?" he replied.

Carolyn snatched the phone. "Where are you guys? What's going on? Have you found anything?"

"The whole thing's a setup," Julia replied, her voice breathy. "We encountered some of the Dragon's—sorry, Zhao's—goons, and we discovered a bomb, too."

"That's great!" Baxter called out. "Did you defuse it?"

Julia paused. "Kind of. It's bad news, guys. The bombs are fake. They're leading us down a dead end."

Julia explained the note they'd found and the useless fake bomb which had been sat in the sewer.

"So, what does that mean?" Jimmy asked, turning to each of the group in turn. "It can't be fake. Roosevelt exploded."

Rhone's voice came on the line. "We don't know. Something's fishy, here, and it's not just the run-off waste from the fish markets in the sewer. Where are you guys? We need to reconvene and work this shit out."

Baxter gave them an address, and they promised they'd be there as quickly as they could. Rhone hung up.

Jimmy's face was wrinkled in confusion. "What the hell is going on here, guys? Are there bombs, or not?"

Baxter scratched his chin. "I don't know. Zhao's either a super genius, or an idiot, but whatever's going on, he's already one step ahead of us. He has Jennie, and he has explosives. Whether he's choosing to blow up more of New York or not, I don't know, but what we do know is that he's dangerous."

"What motivation has he got to destroy the city?" Ruby asked. "Or us for that matter!"

Jack turned to Baxter. "Didn't you say that Zhao mentioned a name when you interrogated him in his cell? Something about Ray-Man?"

"Ren-Min-Bi is the next Dragon," Baxter muttered, deep in thought. "What was that?"

Ruby held up her phone screen. "It's the Chinese currency. Renminbi is the official currency of China."

Carolyn balked. "What has that got to do with anything going on here?"

Baxter considered this, then let out a frustrated sigh. "Riddles! What is it with this guy and riddles?"

"Maybe there's something to do with the stock market?" Jack suggested. "Or the travel bureaus. Maybe there's some kind of link there?"

None of them had any better ideas.

"We'll wait for the others to get here then work out our next move," Baxter instructed. "The good news is that we have numbers to move and utilize. The bad news is we're down one Rogue, and we have no clue where to go next."

"There's more bad news," Carolyn declared, pointing her finger to the sky where a series of black helicopters was flying toward them. It was only when they landed in the open area outside the warehouse that they saw the SIA logo painted on the externals.

Baxter sighed. "Oh, shit."

CHAPTER THIRTY

It couldn't have looked any more like a cheesy FBI flick on the silver screen. The helicopters landed, one by one, and the door opened on the chopper closest to Jack and Ruby.

The propellers whirled overhead, tousling their hair, and an agent jumped out onto the ground with neat precision. His groomed, blond hair was gelled into perfect spikes, and he wore a pair of over-the-top aviator shades.

"Sup, bitches." He advanced on Jack with a crooked grin. "What a set of circumstances, huh? Turn our back for five minutes and the city falls to shit. What have you been doing out here?"

Jack looked at the man confusedly. "Lionus? What are you doing here?"

Lionus peeled his glasses off and pocketed them with fanfare. "You're lucky I like you, Hanson. If you were anyone else, I might have detected a tone of derision, there. Maybe a little disrespect. I wouldn't advise that you speak that way to a superior."

Jack scoffed. "*You're* my superior? Says who? You're nothing but a junior who's just graduated. I've got milk in my fridge that's older than you."

Lionus maintained his grin. Behind him, two more agents, roughly his age, stood menacingly and crossed their arms in front of them.

"Says Daggro," Lionus informed them. "The acting Special Agent in Charge needs someone she can trust to operate the outreach since she's currently office-bound. Guess who she chose to take the reins."

Ruby burst out laughing, then wilted once Lionus fixed her with an intense glare. "You can't be serious?"

Baxter tried to place where he knew the man from. He was young and traditionally handsome, but his arrogance sharpened his features. There was a bruise slightly above his eye, and Baxter wondered if he could just be...

Yes. The dude who came onto Jennie. How the hell did he get put in charge, here?

Clearly, Jack had the same thoughts. "I could spend the day listing agents better-qualified than you are to take that role. Why you?"

Lionus shrugged. "It's not my place to question the decisions of the higher management, just to perform the duties as required. Think of it this way. You're all my bitches, and this is my operation to handle. With that in mind, give me the skinny on what's been going down. They said something about additional bombs?"

Jack remained silent, unsure whether to answer him or not. Lionus waited expectantly, and after a moment Jack relented, filling him in on what they knew so far.

"Sounds like a real shitshow." Lionus drew his SI glasses from a separate pocket and placed them once again on his face. He immediately flinched when he noticed the number of specters currently surrounding them. "What the hell? You didn't warn me we were surrounded by *them*."

"Them?" Baxter snorted. "You might want to be careful how you phrase that, pal. Isn't the SIA meant to be an organization that brings mortals and specters together?"

Lionus' mouth twisted into a snarl. He tried to remain cool. "Yes. Just took me by surprise, is all." He half-heartedly waved at everyone. "Henson, Ruby, follow me onto the chopper. We've got some business to attend to."

Before Baxter and the other specters could complain at this clear division between specters and mortals, another cab pulled up curbside. The cabbie stared open-mouthed at the helicopters in the clearing, as Rhone, Julia, and the conduits stepped out of the car.

Rhone shook his head and sighed. "When did the shit-brigade get here?"

Lionus snarled. "Agent Rhone, I'd suggest you be careful with how you attend to a senior-ranked member of the SIA."

Rhone strode over to Lionus while Ula tossed a couple of notes into the cabbie's hand. As the car slowly drifted away, he stormed up to Lionus and stopped just a foot in front of him. He was taller than the lad, wearing his age and experience on his features like a mask.

Lionus held his ground, but even Baxter could see that there was a hesitation in his demeanor.

"In case you haven't been given the memo," Rhone started, "I no longer work for the SIA and therefore have no part to play in any dutiful lines or loyalty to the organization."

Lionus' snarl morphed into a sick grin. "That's right. Disgraced and fired from the SIA. Must be a lonely boat to be floating in."

Rhone returned the grin. "Actually, it was the best thing that ever happened to me. I've found a new employer. Someone who actually gives a shit about her employees and has the faculties to do something about the situations we keep finding ourselves in."

Lionus held Rhone's eyes. "Yeah? And where is she now?"

Rhone's confident facade flickered. He closed the gap between himself and Lionus and grabbed the punk by his collar, his face a hair's width from the kid. "Listen, you little shit. I've encountered fuckboys like you before. I know how your mind works and what you're trying to achieve here. Seniority doesn't give you experience, kid. Jennie has single-handedly pulled together every operation over the last few months that has had a significant impact on the SIA. Any operation you've been involved in has been walking the dogs compared to the dragons we've fought along the way—pun intended. If you think you can stand there and try to give *me* or these specters any orders because Daggro has finally lost it and assigned you to the big leagues, you've got another think coming. This is *our* operation. The SIA will play nicely, or they will not play at all. Got it?"

Baxter and Carolyn nodded, impressed. There came an uncertain round of applause from the specters gathered around. Lionus' cool didn't slip as he brought his hand up to Rhone's wrist and eased it away. He brushed down the front of his shirt and walked toward the helicopter, shouting, "Henson. Kepnes. Follow me, please."

Jack and Ruby gave the others a longing look and followed Lionus and his two agents onto the chopper.

"Sorry, guys," Jack whined. "They're still paying our checks."

When the helicopter doors closed, the others were left staring at the tinted windows.

Julia scoffed. "Who the hell is that guy? He's like shit you've stepped in, only personified."

Baxter sighed. "Just when you think things can't get any worse…" He spun to the others. "Leave it, for now. Fill us in, what the hell happened down there?"

Zhao returned in a fit of fury, although he had learned at least one thing from his lesson.

Jennie didn't have the satisfaction of seeing Zhao hit the ground, but she knew the moment that he had thanks to the ear-splitting squeal that erupted in her head.

She tried to cover her ears, but her hands were bound. She grimaced and writhed as the sound threatened to explode her eardrums and drive her crazy. She had been smug for a few moments, waiting for any sign that Zhao had completed his descent, but now she regretted her complacency.

The squealing was like fingernails scraped on a chalkboard and pumped through a megaphone. She wondered when it would stop and, just when she thought she could take no more, her relief finally came.

A voice appeared in her head. *Well played, King. Don't forget, I have access to you.* Inside *you. You mess with the Dragon's fire, expect to get burned.*

Jennie panted and thought, *You said you weren't the dragon anymore.*

A brief beat of silence before a soft chuckle echoed inside her.

Jennie soaked in the silence, glad for the relief from the squeal. She had only been a prisoner for one night, and already she was sick of this situation. There had to be a way out of here. There had to be something she could do to force her escape.

Her eyes widened, and she rocked her head back as she remembered that Zhao had access to her thoughts.

How do you free yourself from a prison when the warden knows your every thought?

Jennie tried to empty her mind and simply listen to the world. True yogis could erase their thoughts and exist purely in the present, at one with the sights, smells, and sounds of the world around them.

It had been something she had struggled to do for years. While she had come a long way in meditative practices, she had never quite achieved complete Zen. But she tried it now.

She stared out of the window at the city around her. Lights blinked and traffic ran lazily through the streets as dawn showed its head. Inside the room was the smell of her own sweat, mixed with a faint note of dusty carpet, and the remnant of a buffet that had been served in the room at some point over the previous few days.

There was a faint chill in the air, enough to cause her skin to prickle. She could make out the footsteps of Zhao's men in the rooms behind her, slow and measured. Car engines met her ears and somewhere far off a plane hummed through the clouds.

And there…Somewhere below, the faint bass-line thud of music.

Music…

Jennie gasped and immediately tried to shut the thought away in a private lockbox, holding onto the thought while focusing on other things. It was like trying to hold onto a fish underwater, the thought doing its best to vanish while she desperately tried to keep enough of a hold to claim it as her own.

Music. That was the answer. Or, at least, it was worth a try.

Jennie closed her eyes and pictured her Spotify playlist. She ran an imaginary finger down the list until she found what she was looking for.

An oldie, but a goodie.

She imagined selecting the track, and Queen's *Don't Stop Me Now*, began playing in her head. She had loved Queen from the first moment she had seen them live in concert. She hadn't bought a ticket, hadn't even meant to attend, but specters can choose some funny places to arise. Incidentally, the jolly feud that was triggered by Jennie on that fateful day may just be the first-ever recorded example of what has since commonly been labeled as a "mosh pit."

A grin crept onto Jennie's face. Somewhere far off she fancied she could hear Zhao's confused words, but she blocked it all out, losing herself in the music. When the first full verse kicked in, she opened her eyes and scanned the room, looking for anything that could be of use to her.

It was the clearest she'd been able to see for hours, and as she eyed the FM radio in the corner and the large potted plant, she allowed herself brief moments to imagine what use they could be to her. As fast as the thoughts came, they went again.

Don't stop me now.

Jennie twisted her neck over her shoulder, and her grin morphed into a wide beam. In the corner of the room, piled untidily next to a trolley with stale glasses of water and coffee-stained cups, was her utility belt, complete with Hendrick's power cells.

Why would Zhao not have taken them?

Jennie focused on the music and interrupted her thoughts. The song was reaching its conclusion, and she already knew which tune she'd artfully fade into next: *Somebody to Love.*

The spectral power cells had been left when Zhao realized that he understood nothing of the equipment that Jennie carried. The guns he had snatched and hidden somewhere, but the belt, and even Jennie's watch and glasses he had thrown carelessly into the corner.

However, the spectral power must have been picked up by the batteries at the moment that Jennie latched onto Zhao to hurl him from the roof. For, as she was excited to see, the cells showed a quarter charge across their LED panels each.

Everything was a theory at this point, and Jennie couldn't allow herself to overthink. It was one of the hardest things she'd ever done to allow her instincts to take over while she consciously focused on singing in her own head. She closed her eyes, felt for the cells, and tried something that she thought wouldn't work.

In for a penny, in for a pound. A phrase her mother used to say to her. Even to this day, she never quite understood its origins, though its meaning was clear.

The belt slid off the table. Jennie's heart pounded with excitement. She hoped to the heavens that Zhao couldn't see through her then, that all he could see in the lenses of her eyes were the mullets and fros of four rock stars entertaining the crowds.

With a final push of will, the belt flew onto Jennie's lap. She looked away from the belt, adjusting her knees to lever the pockets to her fingertips. She found something and hooked a finger inside a glass vial. Perfect. But which one was it?

Killer Queen. Killer Queen next. I love that song. Never quite got the lyrics, but...

Jennie's eyes flickered to the vial. It wasn't the one she wanted. She shifted the belt further along and tried the next pocket.

Why would Mary Antoinette eat cake? Did she have a weird way she ate?

She held another vial in her hand. Another flicker of her eyes. Perfect.

Jennie had been in enough scrapes to have mastered the art of undoing the vial's cap with one hand. Only, with the angle her hand was at, she was certain that this wasn't going to be a clean break.

Her heart pounded even faster. *Don't focus on that, Jennie.*

Zhao's voice in the back of her mind. *Huh?*

Jennie sang at the top of her lungs. *"Dynamite with a laser beam! Guaranteed to blow your mind!"*

She tilted the vial into the cuffs. The liquid spilled down the metal and began to eat its bonds. Whatever concoction Hendrick had put together flashed as it battled with the spectral imbuement.

The liquid finished eating through the cuff and trickled onto her hand. Her skin raged with fire, and she smelled her flesh burning. She tore her hand from the cuff, careful not to look directly at it, instead focusing on the world outside. She blindly fumbled a second vial and freed the other hand. Splashes of the acid found her arms and left angry red burns that she'd have to get Hendrick's help to heal much later.

She fumbled with the straps around her feet and untied herself. The burning was all-encompassing. Jennie ran to the buffet table and threw the water on herself. Dashes of water wet her white top and caused segments of it to go almost translucent.

Jennie sighed with relief as the burns stopped, barely aware that she had stopped all thought of singing. She turned at the sound of the door opening and found herself staring into the eyes of a confused guard.

His eyes lingered on her chest. Her eyes lingered on his pistol.

Jennie smirked. "That's right, kid. I'm the Killer Queen."

She moved so quickly that the man didn't stand a chance.

CHAPTER THIRTY-ONE

New York City, New York, USA

Maybe luck was on Jennie's side, or maybe it was some higher being, but the disturbance with the man at the door did little to raise attention.

More fortuitous than that, Jennie found her phone amongst the pile of her items that had been stripped, and while the guard snoozed soundly on the floor, she placed her glasses back on her face. She switched on her phone and was disappointed to find there was only a small amount of charge left. She forced herself not to dwell on what she found, still doing her best to shut Zhao out of her mind.

She blindly patted the guard down and found the pistol. She relieved him of the firearm and stumbled across a set of earphones, too.

Perfect.

Jennie instinctively found her Spotify app and opened her Get Pumped playlist. Music blared in her ears and removed some of the cognitive focus she had been forced to put on. She felt drained, and the music playing in her ears was like stepping into a refreshing bath.

It was all instinct. She was certain that, if Zhao didn't already know she was coming, he would soon. She stepped to the door, adjusted her belt, then placed her hand on the handle.

Pistol at the ready, she stepped into the room. Her instincts worked for her, honed to a keen edge over decades of work. She shot three guards before they could so much as register her appearance. Only when the room was clear did she have a proper look at what was in front of her.

Adrenaline coursing through her body, Jennie took another pistol from a fallen guard and balanced them both in her hands. She'd done well so far, but she'd need to focus to make it out of this place alive. Perhaps the music would help silence some of her thoughts to Zhao, but it was time to throw caution to the wind and storm her way out of the building.

She checked each room on the upper floor for enemies and found only one. This guard had hidden behind the door as she entered. She sensed him before she saw him and whirled. She knocked his wrist and sent the gun he had been holding—*Jennie's pistol*—from his hand. She knocked the Big Bitch into the air before tossing her borrowed pistol aside and grabbing it as it fell.

It felt good to be back in control.

The man cowered before her. She held the gun to his face. A tear rolled down his cheek.

Jennie sighed, speaking slightly louder than she meant to with the music playing in her ears. "You're one of the lucky ones. Don't forget my mercy."

She freed a vial from its pouch and blew the silver sleep powder into the man's face. He was unconscious before he hit the floor.

Jennie examined the Big Bitch and was alarmed to see a scratch down its usually pristine metal exterior. "Son of a bitch!" She kissed the barrel. "Still, it's nice that you're back with me."

Somewhere far off, she was aware of a specter yelling in rage. Zhao? More than likely.

She made a break for it, unsurprised to find a half dozen guards storming the upper floors from the elevator. Jennie sent off two shots, then ducked behind a table. She waited until they paused to reload, then leaned around and shot two guards in the ankles. The glance gave her an overview of the men and their positions. Without looking, she angled the Big Bitch over the top of the desk and fired twice more.

Return fire halted. A few groans broke the silence that followed.

Jennie rose to her full height and studied the men. They all wore dark fatigues that she would associate with ninjas. *Why wouldn't Zhao's men have proper armor?*

There was no time to answer her own question.

The elevator pinged as she pressed the button. She went inside, jabbed the "G" button, and exited before the doors closed. She took to the stairwell and removed her boots. She used the laces to tie them around her belt as she softly padded down the stairs.

Darius Chu received the demanding call from Zhao as he shouted into his earpiece and informed him of the situation.

King had escaped. Somehow. It didn't seem possible.

Yet, when Zhao crawled into the lobby, all of Darius' doubts faded away.

The man was a mess, which made no sense to Darius. He was certain that Zhao had been upstairs with the rest of his comrades when last he checked. After the effort of taking over the Empire State Building at night, passing off the operation as Federal with fake FBI badges and convincing the management the case be left well enough alone until morning, Zhao had been immensely thorough in ensuring that nothing should happen to King and she'd be held captive until the rest of the plan had unfolded.

So how had Zhao ended up outside?

Only one answer came to him. He must have fallen from above. But, if that was the case, surely a specter could turn immaterial and land safely?

Zhao used arms that appeared broken in various places to crawl along the floor. His legs were dead weight. His body twisted into unnatural contortions. He couldn't see guts or the white of bone, but he knew enough to know that Zhao was in pain.

He didn't even have to ask before Zhao answered. "Teething problems. I'm still learning to control my powers. I tried to turn immaterial, but apparently falling over a hundred floors is enough to take your mind away from any focus it may have."

Who was Darius to argue?

"She's really escaped?" Darius asked.

Zhao nodded. The movement appeared painful. The surrounding guards tried not to look at the sickening sight of Zhao for too long. "Yes. She's on her way down. Get her before the whole thing falls apart."

Darius was about to send a group of guards upstairs when he noticed the light on the elevator. "Wait. She's coming down in the main elevator."

His spider senses tingled. Something wasn't right. Why would King go straight down the main access route when she knew that the lobby would likely be guarded?

Darius grinned. He instructed a handful of guards to monitor the stairs for the first two floors, while the rest waited in the lobby, each guard's eye fixed down the scope of their weapon.

"She's up to something," Zhao gurgled.

Darius forced himself to look at the mess on the floor. "Sir. You need to get out of here."

"Tell me something I don't know," Zhao managed.

Darius snapped his fingers toward a specter who had been waiting patiently for instructions. "You. Get Zhao out of here."

"Where shall I take him?" the specter replied.

Zhao answered. "The safe house. Take me to the safe house."

She knelt beside Zhao and scooped him up. At least in spectral form, his weight wasn't as much of an issue, though thanks to the awkward angles his body was twisted in, he wasn't easy to carry.

He grimaced as she cradled him across her arms. The elevator closed in on the ground floor.

"Go," Zhao instructed. "Now."

Darius turned his attention to the elevator doors and waited. Maybe he had outsmarted Jennie. Yet, knowing what he knew about her, maybe they hadn't. The only thing they could trust was that they needed to expect the unexpected.

———

Jennie heard their footsteps far below.

She couldn't count them, but she knew they were there. Booted footsteps carried far in an empty stairwell.

Which is why I took mine off.

The earphones hung limply around her neck. She had removed them, knowing that she would need to hear as she journeyed ahead. All she could hope was that she wasn't completely transparent and that Zhao wouldn't anticipate her next move.

Which was what, exactly?

Jennie didn't know. As always, she knew that plans only held so much weight in these situations. Things never turned out the way you planned, so it was useful to learn how to react to the unexpected. Maybe Zhao had sent them up the stairs. All she knew was that she needed to find a way past them.

Having the Big Bitch back in her life gave her some assurance. She sneaked onward, slowing down as the footsteps echoed around her. She chanced a look down below and saw dark shapes moving, though they stopped when they reached the second floor.

Interesting...

Jennie continued in silence, steadying her breath. Her socks padded without a murmur on the stairs, and soon she was only one floor above the others.

Although they tried to remain quiet, she could hear a cornucopia of sounds. Fatigues rustling as the guards adjusted their positions. Guns clacking as they checked their ammo and readied their fire. Breathing and murmuring from the group.

Jennie could take them, of that she was sure. But what then? These wouldn't be the only guards waiting for her, so how many were armed and ready on the next floor, and the ground floor, too?

Time for some out of the box thinking, Jennie thought, then tried to close off the conscious part of her mind again. An idea had come, but it would be dangerous if Zhao caught hold of it.

It was then that she realized that Zhao had fallen silent. There wasn't even a trace of him in her mind.

Not that that could count for much. There was so much of his power that she was yet to understand.

Jennie closed her eyes and found her center. She tapped into the spectral power cells, knowing she only had limited juice and this would be a risky maneuver.

She stepped toward the wall and turned spectral. With a leveled hop, she threw herself sideways and out into the street below.

Her stomach flew into her throat as she dropped like a pin toward the concrete. The cells were fast depleting, and Jennie only hoped she had enough power to stick the landing.

The ground met her. She absorbed the shock and sunk a foot below the surface. She speedily climbed out and freed herself right at the moment that the cells depleted.

A woman passed, still dolled up from a night at the clubs. Jennie recognized that look as the infamous "walk of shame," and the woman blinked in surprise when Jennie appeared in the air before her.

Jennie landed and regained her balance. She stared at the woman for a moment, the stranger's mouth open in a perfect O. Jennie scrambled for something to explain what had happened, but instead settled with, "Amazing what kinds of illusions alcohol can induce." She placed a hand on the woman's shoulder. "I hope he was worth it. Most guys aren't."

With that, she walked away.

The elevator dinged as the cabin reached the ground floor. The guards shuffled and readied for fire. The doors opened...

…to nothingness.

"Fuck," Darius growled. "Everyone up the stairwell. She must still be here!"

The guards kicked into action, the message carrying up the stairs. Guards flooded their way upstairs, kicking down doors on each floor and scouring the building for Jennie.

A few minutes later, the search was over. It was clear that she was gone.

Darius growled, eyes furrowing at the chair where Jennie had previously been tied. He picked up the remnants of the cuffs then let out a yelp of pain as the residual acid burned his palm.

Not for the first time, he wondered just exactly who this woman was and how she was able to accomplish the impossible.

"Send out a search party," he instructed a nearby guard. "She may still be close. Search every street and building within a three-block radius."

The guard nodded and left.

Darius tapped the receiver in his ear and dialed Zhao. "I'm sorry, boss. She's gone."

He wasn't expecting the answer he received. "I know."

CHAPTER THIRTY-TWO

New York City, New York, USA

"Renminbi?" Rhone cleaned the lenses of his goggles between pinched fingers. "What has Chinese currency got to do with any of this?"

Julia chewed her lip. "Just another drop in the ocean, it seems. All we're finding are scraps of clues that we're trying to piece together. None of it makes any sense yet, but it will. I'm sure of it."

They had informed the others of all that had happened down in the sewers, and Baxter had, likewise, filled them in on the situation with the Spectral Plane. All specters and mortals looked set to mobilize into the streets, yet the SIA still hadn't emerged from their choppers.

Roman growled. "We need to get moving. This is why I don't concern myself with bureaucracy anymore. Sometimes things just need to happen."

Carolyn nodded. "What's taking them so long?"

As if they had heard the others, the doors to the helicopters opened and the agents stepped out. The propellers had stopped whirring some time ago. Jack and Ruby's faces were difficult to read.

Lionus approached them, leaving his agents in his wake. The

cocky smile had faded, and it looked as though what he wanted to say would be painful. "You have the numbers. Let's mobilize the units. Here's the plan…" He unfolded a map covered in thick pen lines and circles and presented it to Rhone.

Rhone snatched it from him and studied it. He threw it back at Lionus. "No. That's not what we had in mind. We've just spent our own precious time arranging the groups in a way that they understand, and now you want us to confuse everyone further by reassigning everyone? The first rule of leadership is communication, son. You can't lock yourself in a flying cabin and make up your own shit while we're left waiting."

Lionus' brow furrowed. "Look, Rhone. I've been ordered to handle this situation, and we'll do it my way, or—"

Ruby growled in frustration and stepped between the men. "Enough of this bullshit! While you two are comparing dicks, there are dangerous criminals out there armed with explosives. Whether or not they're *going* to use them isn't the question. The real question is, can you both put your goddamn egos aside and just get on with saving people already? We're wasting time!"

There was a beat of silence before Carolyn started clapping. A dozen or so specters joined in, impressed.

Lionus' face flushed. He whirled on Ruby and grabbed her collar. "I will not stand for this insubordination. Get your ass in the chopper. You, too, Agent Hansen."

Jack brushed past Lionus as Ruby slipped his grip and knocked him with her shoulder. Lionus grabbed Jack's wrist, but Jack easily pulled himself free.

Jack raised an eyebrow. "Just try it, buddy."

Lionus' face flushed an angry crimson. His hands shook. "This is ridiculous! I am in charge here! You *will* obey my orders."

Baxter sighed and looked pitifully at the man. "Respect isn't earned by barking orders, kid. It's earned by mutual respect, understanding your friends and enemies, and knowing when to let the more experienced step in. But, hey. If you want to try and command these specters, then go for it." He raised his voice. "Spectral Plane. Agent

Lionus is your new commander. He says you're to listen to him from now on."

Carolyn hid her laugh behind her hand. The specters all turned to Lionus at once, before a chorus of laughter rippled across them in waves.

Lionus ground his teeth and stared in fury at Baxter, who just shrugged. "As I said. Respect is earned, not taken."

Rhone struggled to hide his own grin. "Face it, Lionus. This is our arena. We could use your help, but leave the real work to the experts." Without waiting for an answer, Rhone called, "Spectral Plane, roll out!"

Jimmy Dean repeated Rhone's words at the back and kicked the specters into action.

Although they had learned that the second bomb had been a decoy, there was still no guarantee that the others were not active. A large portion of the specters was sent to solve the riddles and scour the city for any sign of mischief, while a smaller portion was designated to checking any and all foreign currency bureaus for something that might make the renminbi clue make any kind of sense.

As the specters deployed, Rhone addressed Lionus once more. "All jokes aside, your choppers would provide a great view from the sky. We need you up there."

Lionus held his stare for a long minute before huffing and whirling on the spot. He marched back to the helicopter, shouted at the pilot, and the blades kicked into gear.

Baxter sighed. "He's going to be trouble, isn't he?"

Rhone nodded. "He already is."

Like Jennie's spectral power cells, her cell phone had died.

She roamed the streets, keeping close to the long shadows cast by the early morning sun, and watching for the enemy. She was already five blocks away, unaware of the limitations of their hunt but knowing that she couldn't risk being found right now.

Despite her best efforts to blend in, the city's early-risers turned their heads at the disheveled woman with two pistols holstered around her hips. She moved fast, taking each block one at a time, wondering how best to get after the one thing she so needed.

A charger.

Without GPS on her phone, she had no idea how to get back to her car. The city was nothing more than an urban jungle, each block looking eerily similar to the next. The only saving grace was that the streets were numbered, and there was some kind of order, but even then, she only knew she was parked on Forty-Eighth. She could find that street by tracing northerly up the city, but the rest was a mystery. She had at least two miles width-wise in which she'd have to hunt for the place she'd parked the Mustang.

A cop spotted her from across the street. He called out to her and raised a hand. Jennie made a dash for it and disappeared down an alleyway, keeping her feelers out for any sign of nearby specters. There had to be something, surely. The last time she had spent considerable time in New York, it felt like all she ever ran into were…

Specters.

There were two mid-way down the alley. They sat on top of a dumpster, deep in conversation. They appeared harmless enough—not that that would have been a problem—and they turned at the sound of Jennie's feet echoing around the narrow walls.

"Where's she off to in such a hurry?" the elderly woman chortled.

The second woman, at least twenty years her junior, clutched a spectral handbag with one hand and adjusted her glasses with another. "Always trouble in this city, isn't there?"

They showed no alarm until Jennie was in front of them. The cop's voice could be heard behind them. A whistle blew. A number of civilians poked their heads around the alleyway.

"Uh-oh," the elder woman crooned.

Jennie met their eyes, and they both flinched.

"Do you think she can see us?" the elder woman asked.

"Clear as day," Jennie answered. "Hold still. This might feel a little strange to you."

Jennie latched onto the pair and turned spectral just as the cop appeared around the corner. A couple of civilians gasped and pointed down the alley, telling him they saw her disappear into the dumpster.

"No, you don't get it," one of them said. "She *disappeared* into the dumpster."

The cop shook his head, clearly used to bullshit stories in a city rife with crackheads and heroin junkies.

The two women froze as they surveyed the tendril that connected them to Jennie. She felt their powers surge through her and was pleased to see that her spectral power cells were slowly filling up as she maintained her connection and remained out of sight of the cop.

The officer searched the alley, opening the dumpster when he eventually reached it. His confident facade slipped when he saw that the woman wasn't there—not realizing that Jennie and two other women were hanging onto the angled dumpster lid—and let it fall shut.

He clasped his radio and muttered an order. A moment later, he wandered down the alley and out of sight.

Jennie thanked the ladies and hopped off the dumpster.

"Don't mention it?" the younger woman replied uncertainly.

Jennie teased her way to the end of the alley and searched for the cop. She spotted him at a crossing to her left so ducked out and turned right. She slalomed her way through blocks until she felt she was back on track, and within twenty minutes, relief flooded her as she found the Rockefeller Center looking ahead.

The Mustang was exactly where she had left it. However, after she was done patting the hood and allowing herself to revel in the fact she had located the car again, she patted her pockets, and her blood ran cold.

The keys! Shit. Where are the keys?

In her mind's eye, she thought back to the Empire State Building and pictured the table with her items on. Had the key fallen out as she picked up her gear? Was it even there to start with? Surely no one had stolen her...

A satisfying jangle came as she thumbed one of the pouches on her utility belt. She wasn't sure how, but the keys must have worked their way into the pouch through the last manic hour.

The leather felt like a hug. The car thrummed to her touch. She dug out the cable for her phone and set the cell on charge, cradling the device in its dock.

After a few seconds, the cell switched itself on. She was bombarded with notifications as the phone connected to the satellites and synchronized itself.

Missed calls, text messages, WhatsApp messages. The guys had really tried to get a hold of her.

But why? If any more bombs had gone off, Jennie would have known it, right? She had a near-perfect view across the majority of New York from that window. She would have seen the chaos and disruption.

Jennie dialed in Rhone's number and hit call. Rhone answered on the second ring.

It was strange to be back at the Plaza. Jennie had thrown enough cash at the receptionist to secure the room she had booked upon her first visit to New York.

The view was just as she remembered it. Central Park unfolded before her like a welcome mat. The others sat on the couches and were quiet, each one unable to anticipate how Jennie would lead them.

"The specters are already out there?" Jennie asked without turning.

Rhone answered. "They set off not too long ago. They've been instructed to check in with us regularly, dialing into the spectral frequencies Baxter has assigned for them. We should know more soon."

"And the SIA?" Jennie didn't need to ask the question. She could see their half a dozen black helicopters hovering over the city like flies around a carcass.

Rhone had already relayed to her the disruption that had come with Lionus. Although the SIA had already taken to the air by the time they had reunited with Jennie, she had a bad feeling in her stomach. Something was amiss. The guys were holding back on telling her something, but she had no idea what.

"They're keeping abreast of the situation," Baxter informed her. "It's likely that Daggro will send more agents out as things progress, but since everything has fallen quiet for the past eight hours, there's little to bring them here."

Carolyn leaned forward, eyes wide and sparkling. "What's our next step, Jennie?"

Jennie sighed. She knew the question was coming, but the truth was that she had no idea. They were in the thick of it, unable to see a way out. Zhao had escaped and left his game of riddles hanging in the air like loose stalactites in a cave. One loud noise and the whole thing might crash down on them.

"The riddles are false," Jennie replied at last, diverting from the question somewhat. "Zhao is not going to destroy New York. He loves this city too much to be the reason it gets destroyed. He said so himself. I don't think we have that to fear."

"Then where are the seven?" Carolyn asked. "You mentioned the others, but we've yet to come close to even finding them."

Jennie finally turned around. "I don't know."

Julia piped up. "And renminbi? What was that? Why was that what you drew from the Dragon?"

"Peter," Carolyn corrected.

"I don't know," Jennie repeated. She hated this. The others were all looking at her expectantly, as though she were the answer to all the problems. Most of the time that was true, but they were at a dead end. Only one possibility remained, and Jennie wasn't sure that she had the power to complete what was on her mind.

Jennie crossed over to the bar and opened the cupboard while the others waited in silence. Julia began to ask what Jennie was doing, but Baxter silenced her.

She took out a bottle of vodka and a cocktail shaker. She held the shaker in her hand, looked at it indecisively, then finally placed it back in the cupboard. She unscrewed the vodka and drained a third of the bottle nonstop.

Baxter watched without blinking. He knew how serious things would have to be for Jennie to be drinking straight from the bottle.

When she was done, she wiped her mouth on her forearm. She gasped and rested both hands on the counter. She looked out from over the top of her glasses at the others, and let out a heavy breath. "I have an idea. But it might be dangerous. If this goes wrong, it could cost us everything. Zhao will be onto us. We might kickstart whatever process is in waiting. I don't know if it'll work, and the repercussions could be enormous."

A pregnant silence followed. After a few moments, Carolyn clapped her hands and stood up. "No change there, then. Let's do it."

CHAPTER THIRTY-THREE

New York City, New York, USA

Jennie took the center in the living room, sitting cross-legged on the coffee table with her eyes closed. The only audible sounds were hums of traffic and the whirring of helicopter propellers in the distance.

Jennie took a steadying breath, unsure how this was even going to work. The seed of the idea was simple, but executing would be a whole other matter.

She reached out to the surrounding specters, latching onto Carolyn, Feng Mian, and Baxter. Would three be enough? That would remain to be seen. She vanished from mortal sight and felt their power flowing through her. All of them had extraordinary talents. Skills which were rare amongst specters, and maybe that would be useful here.

The spectral power filled her up like a well. It cooled her blood and heightened her senses. Her skin broke out in gooseflesh, and her hairs stood on end. Behind her glasses, her eyes flicked rapidly back and forth in their sockets.

Hold on, Jennie. No rush. Take your time.

Ghosts of memories flooded through her, the patterns and forces that lived in the specters. They weren't clear enough to hold onto, but she could feel their emotions and their pasts filling her soul. Around her waist, the power cells throbbed with spectral light. Maybe they would boost her signals. Maybe they wouldn't. All would remain to be seen.

Jennie's spine straightened. Her fingertips rested on her knees. She was flooded with power and zoned in to unlock her mind. The lockbox she had tried to keep safe from Zhao was open and available for him to dive into. She hadn't felt him since he had disappeared from the Empire State building and wondered if his powers relied on proximity. Either way, if he was inside of her somewhere…

Maybe I could get to him.

Jennie filtered through the multitude of things occurring behind her closed eyelids. Everything was cast in a bright array of holy light. She tried to drill down to the last thing she had felt of Zhao, the faint echo in her mind as she descended the stairs. She found something, a crumb at best, but maybe it was enough.

She honed all of her concentration on the crumb. It grew larger, emitting a strange sound she couldn't make out. It sounded unintelligible, as though an alien had broken into a radio station and lowered its volume to near nothing. Jennie focused and forced it toward her, and the voices grew louder. She zoomed in and found herself peeking through a tiny window of someone's mind. Two pairs of eyes, narrowed and piercing, staring at a poor female specter who looked as though she couldn't care whether she was present or not.

"How long will it take to fix me?" Zhao's voice was loud enough to discern now. She could feel his anger inside of her, a bubbling pit of rage in her gut. "I cannot continue like this."

The woman spared him a passive glance and shrugged. "A few days. Maybe a week."

Zhao picked up a vase and hurled it at the woman. She showed no indication that she was bothered as the vase passed right through her. "That's not good enough!" A surge of white-hot pain passed up Jennie's arm, as though she could feel his pain. In her periphery, she could make out the mangled shape of his body.

The woman shrugged. "Not much I can do about it. There's no spectral healing acceleration. Well, except in some rare cases. Looks like you're not gifted with it." She gave a derisive chuckle and took a seat across from him.

Zhao pinched at his eyes. For a moment, Jennie's view was blocked by fat, spectral thumbs. She tried to decipher where they were, but the room they were in had no recognizable features. It could have been a disused utility closet for all she knew.

"My associates won't be pleased," Zhao growled. "They're waiting on my command, and I can't give it to them in this state. What will they think of me?"

Again, the woman shrugged. "I'd think it was pretty badass."

"What do you mean?" Zhao asked.

The woman may as well have been filing her spectral nails. Jennie couldn't understand the relationship here. Was this specter hired to help Zhao navigate his new life? Was she someone that he'd known previously? Why was she helping him?

"Think about it," the woman continued. "You call up your guys and give them the okay looking like this, and you're showing them that you can't be killed. Even when specters are mangled and broken, they can continue—with the exception of holy light, that is. Here..." She handed him a handled mirror.

Jennie audibly gasped as she saw Zhao's reflection. Whatever bones were left in Zhao's head had been broken and set apart. He looked like an egg that had been dropped while inside a balloon. Bits of shell poked out where it shouldn't, and his eyes and mouth were twisted into the likes of a Picasso painting.

At Jennie's gasp, Zhao narrowed his eyes and studied himself in the mirror. He leaned closer, examining his pupils.

Jennie had a sudden, worrying thought. *Can he see me?*

Out of nowhere, Jennie's body throbbed with heat. Zhao's anger transferred into her, and she was overwhelmed with fury. He stared in the mirror, and his voice came into her head as though he was standing next to her. *Of course I can see you, bitch. Clever girl, working out the two-way part of our intercom. I didn't think you had it in you.*

Sitting in the living room, Jennie grumbled. A moan of pain escaped her lips. Rhone leaned forward, but Ula held him back.

Why are you doing this? Jennie asked. *What's the point of all of this?*

Zhao grinned at his reflection, his mouth contorted and alien in shape. The woman looked at him curiously. *Why does anyone do anything? Power, girl. I may have been unable to dominate in life, but with this gift they call death, I can finally sit on the throne and call myself king. With my mortal minions at my side, there'll be no one left who can stop us.*

You'll never win this, Jennie replied, instilling as much of an authoritative grace as she could while the anger coursed through her. *You don't know what* I'm *capable of.*

No, Zhao admitted. *But thanks to you, I'm learning.* A pause. *You still haven't solved any of my riddles yet, have you? Say hi to Renminbi when you get the chance to meet her.*

Zhao cast one last look at Jennie before a sudden burst of white filled Jennie's mind. She felt the physical sensation of being kicked away before she mentally reappeared in the room. She was knocked back, but Roman and Triton caught her before she could fall off the table.

"What happened?" Carolyn asked. "Did you find him? Do you know where he is?"

Jennie was breathless. She waited a moment before replying. Her mind was still spinning as she tried to process what Zhao had just told her, and what she had just seen.

Two things clung to her mind. The first was the *Taste the Orient* takeout flyer that had been tossed to the floor.

The other was a very interesting factoid about Renminbi. Zhao had called the new Dragon *her.*

That rules out fifty percent of the population. Progress is progress.

Jennie's eyes met Carolyn's as she relayed what had just happened.

Richmond, Virginia, USA

The western face of the manor overlooked the city and offered the best views all around. Lupe, Tanya, and Jiao were sitting at a table across from each other on the second floor, watching the city wake up and come to life.

Traffic was steady. There were no signs of anything being amiss. That seemed strange to Lupe, given what Tanya had told him about Madame Celestine and her possession by the specter.

They ate breakfast in peaceful quiet, only vaguely aware of the poltergeists speeding around the lawn and racing around the outside of the house.

When do they ever rest? Lupe wondered.

For that matter, when would they get some rest? Tanya, the only other mortal present besides Hendrick, looked beat. Her eyes were dark and half-closed. She ate slowly, occasionally throwing a lazy glance out of the window at the city.

"Here." Lupe offered her a vial of one of Hendrick's potions.

Hendrick had stocked him up with a handful so that he could stay awake and learn faster as an apprentice. After all, in Hendrick's words, "Sleep slows the mind."

Which was contrary to everything Lupe had ever been told, but when in Rome…

Tanya took the vial. "Thanks." She hesitated. "Did *you* make this?"

Lupe let out a laugh. "No. I haven't even started brewing yet. You're in safe hands, don't worry. It's not like you're going to turn into a frog if you try it."

Tanya laughed, then drank the formula. Instantly, the weight of her weariness faded. Her eyes grew bright. Her spine straightened, and a look of relief came over her. "You're not going to offer one to Jiao?"

Jiao held up a hand. "I need no chemicals to enhance my mind."

Lupe raised an eyebrow at the petite woman. Sure, she didn't look half as bad as Tanya had, but everyone could use a pickup, surely?

"I've learned a lot through my upbringing, as well as my time with the Dragon," Jiao explained, her voice soft and delicate. "I train my mind and conserve my energy. The trivial things of common life don't affect me in the same way as your everyday folk. Meditation and mindfulness conserve energy and holds off the need for sleep. Stress and panic and the pace of everyday life are enough to drive people into an early grave. That's not the life I want."

Lupe found a vial for himself and held it in the air. "Well, good for you." He drained it in one, feeling its instant effects.

They sat for a while longer, enjoying the morning quiet. They had debated trying to call Jennie and the others but thought better of it. With things quiet once again, there was no need to disturb them while they were clearly busy. Whatever event had occurred the previous evening, they would be able to handle themselves. As of yet, there had been no further disruption.

Lupe's ears pricked up. In the streets below, a handful of cop cars blared their sirens and flashed their lights. An ambulance followed not far behind.

Tanya stood and moved closer to the glass. She pressed her face against its cool surface and shielded her eyes from the morning sun. "That seems ominous."

Lupe joined her at the window. Jiao remained where she was, sipping her green tea.

The cops sped into the heart of the city, traffic shifting to the sides to allow them to pass. A knot tightened in Lupe's stomach. He didn't know how he knew, but somehow this was connected to Tanya's telling of events from last night.

Tanya turned to look at Lupe. "Up for a road trip?"

Lupe considered this. He shook his head. "My position is here now. I can source you some items from Hendrick's stash that may be useful."

Tanya rolled her eyes and grabbed his wrist. Before he knew it, he was being dragged to the door. "Come on, you wet blanket. This is just an investigatory outing. Besides, you don't *know* any chemistry yet."

Jiao drained her tea and followed closely behind.

Lupe half-heartedly protested, drawn forward by his own curiosity. As they passed the laboratory, he dropped his eyes, hoping to avoid Hendrick's stare. What would the man think if he was already heading back out onto a mission when he promised he'd train?

It's not a mission. It's a friend accompanying a friend to bolster numbers and investigate what's going on. A reconnaissance mission.

Damn...It is a mission.

But not a true mission. There are no guns and shots fired and explosions.

I hope...

Tanya dragged Lupe onward and collected Sandra along the way. Soon they were all in the car. She twisted the ignition, pressed the accelerator, and headed out into the city.

Meanwhile, Hendrick peeked through the gap in the laboratory door, with a knowing grin on his face.

It wasn't difficult to find the source of the disruption. Tanya eased off on the speed as they approached the place where the flashing blues lit the surrounding buildings.

They parked nearby, their attention fixed on the glass that lay shattered on the sidewalk around a three-story building with mostly glass covering its front facade, the building had clearly been hit by something that caused all of the windows to shatter.

Witnesses were being interviewed. A woman was wrapped in a blanket, shivering as she addressed the questions of a middle-aged cop. Tanya thumbed through her phone, where she'd typed in the building's address.

"The Second Richmond Community Center," Tanya read its listing on Google. "Apparently, it's used often in the mornings for yoga classes and Pilates. Sometimes they have meetings for the local slimming club to gather and support each other on their weight loss journey. Today, it's the yoga class."

Lupe watched one woman who was standing with her arms folded while sitting in the back of an open police car. "Why is it called the Second Community Center?"

Tanya raised an eyebrow. "Really? That's the part that grabbed your attention? You're right. Maybe this life isn't for you."

Lupe snorted. "Seemed like an apt question."

Tanya ignored him. "What the hell happened here? It looks like nobody is really hurt, but something smashed all of the windows. Kids throwing rocks?"

From behind one of the cop cars, Sandra appeared, strolling back toward them. She walked through the hood of their car and stood in the center console. "Their stories don't all add up, but there is one common theme. The windows smashed of their own accord, and three of their yoga class started acting strangely. That woman over there said that ten minutes into their class, a howling wind came out of nowhere, and three of the women stood up and left without a word. When she called out to find out what was going on… *Crash!*"

She clapped her hands together so sharply that she made Tanya and Lupe jump. Jiao was unaffected in the back.

Tanya recovered. "This *has* to have something to do with last night. How do we get close enough to interrogate those guys? Do you think we can talk to the cops?"

Lupe shook his head. "I doubt it."

"Why don't you ask that woman?" Jiao offered.

The woman in question was walking about two blocks down from where they were parked. She crossed from one side of the street to the other, a dream-like expression on her face. She wore yoga pants and a tube top, and parts of her body were blotted with crimson.

Tanya glanced from the woman to the cops, who appeared not to have noticed, before cranking the car into reverse.

She caught up with the woman and drove alongside her after the woman ignored her requests to stop so they could talk. In fact, she showed no sign of any recognition whatsoever. Her eyes were blank, white marbles, and her footsteps labored as though she were sleep-walking.

"I'm beginning to think we're onto something," Lupe muttered. "This isn't normal."

Sandra leaned through the two front seats and pointed ahead to where another woman was drifting lazily onward, her luminescent orange yoga pants almost impossible to miss. "Look…"

"It's like they're possessed," Jiao commented.

The idea of it made them all shudder.

Tanya's face hardened. "I have a bad feeling about this."

Lupe nodded his agreement. "Let's just follow them. Stay a little way back, just in case anything comes out."

Tanya looked as though she was about to argue back, then realized what Lupe was saying. Their numbers were too small to have any impact if something big were to come out at them. What if they encountered another spirit like the Mendlesons? What if it was another *sturmgeist* like the one that Jennie had so thoroughly described to them? Hell, what if it was nothing more than a simple terrorist plot?

What could the four of them do against something like that? Jennie and the others were off in Washington, for all they knew.

Doing nothing wasn't an option, not while they were aware that *something* was going down. They needed to open the lid of the jar and peek at the horror within.

Hopefully, they'd be looking at nothing more than a fresh batch of marmalade, and nothing like a rotting, festering jar of moldy jelly.

Tanya shook her head to shake away the image. She slowed to a near crawl, and dropped back behind the woman, following her at a snail's pace through the city.

CHAPTER THIRTY-FOUR

<u>New York City, New York, USA</u>

The lights were all off as they approached the front of Taste the Orient.

On the outside, it was nothing more than a simple Chinese restaurant, but Jennie was almost certain they were somewhere inside. She could feel Zhao's power exuding from the building.

Why hadn't he fled?

They had made their trip in impressive time, knowing that time was critical in this operation. As they sped toward the restaurant, specters checked in with them and updated them as Baxter had requested. No one had found anything in the city that in any way linked to Zhao...

Yet.

Jennie latched onto the specters, and melted through the door and unlocked the building. A security alarm blared. Feng Mian took care of the alarm by short-circuiting the device and sent the room back into silence.

They raced up the stairs, Jennie using Zhao's power as a divining rod. By the time she made it to the third floor, she knew he was nearby. She wasted no time in booting open the door and aiming the

Big Bitch at Zhao, but she definitely wasn't prepared for what was in front of her.

Zhao was a mangled mess. He hardly looked human…or specter. Parts of his body were beginning to heal from the fall, but most of him was yet to work his way back into true form.

A small TV played the news in the background. The female specter Jennie had seen in her vision was sitting on a rotting chair beside the TV set.

"Hi." She spoke so nonchalantly that it was disarming.

Jennie turned her attention to Zhao and aimed the Big Bitch at him. "Enough games, Zhao. Consider this my final warning. My team is with me. I'm ending this before it can go any farther. Tell us what you know before I blow you into a thousand pieces."

Zhao chuckled, the sound like mud running down a drain. "What are you going to do to me? Mutilate me more than I already am? Please, girl. Think about what you're saying. I'm already a mess."

Jennie didn't want to look at him, but she had no choice. She had to get to the bottom of his stinking riddles. "Tell us what your plan is, Zhao. My patience is running thin."

Baxter tapped her shoulder. "Er, Jennie?"

Jennie brushed his hand away. "Tell me!" she roared at Zhao.

Zhao grinned and turned toward the TV. A clock on the wall chimed nine AM. The moment the ringing started, a ticker-tape rolled across the news broadcast, detailing the eruption of bombs across New York's neighboring states.

Amateur footage on shaky phone cameras showed explosions billowing black clouds into the sky while people screamed and ran for the hills.

The woman spoke to the camera, pressing a finger to her ear with a look of shock on her face. "Live and exclusive, we are getting reports of devastation in neighboring state capitals. So far, confirmed explosions have occurred in Harrisburg, Pennsylvania, another in Trenton, New Jersey, a third in Hartford, Connecticut, and a fourth in Boston, Massachusetts. It is unclear at this point what the cause of these explosions is, or how many casualties may have been affected, but we will be sure to keep you updated on the situation."

Jennie and her team stared at the screen with morbid fascination. It seemed almost impossible to be seeing the amount of destruction that was occurring as footage showed first-person perspectives of civilians running for the hills. Buildings collapsed and cars were crushed as smoke covered a wide radius of each attack.

Jennie scowled. "You son of a bitch!"

She dived at Zhao, forgetting her gun and going for him with fists. At that moment, pummeling the mangled specter's brains into a pulp would be a thousand times more satisfying than shooting him.

How had he done this? How had he orchestrated this whole plan? Sure, he had mentioned the neighboring states, but it was hard to tell what was truth and what was fiction as it poured out of his hollow of a mouth.

To her surprise, Jennie passed straight through Zhao. She slid across the floor and knocked into a table, sending a lamp crashing to the floor. The woman watched passively. Jennie rose and tried to attack again, once more finding only thin air.

Baxter ran forward. "Jennie! Jennie!"

"You son of a bitch, Zhao!" Jennie shouted, flailing her arms, only stopping when Baxter caught them and held her back. He was surprised by her strength. Even with his thick muscles it was an effort to restrain her.

"Jennie, calm down," Baxter soothed. "There's no one there."

The words cut through Jennie's anger instantly. Confusion filled her face as she spun to face Baxter and looked at him as though nothing in the world could have been crazier than what he had just said.

Yet true enough, when Jennie turned once more to where Zhao had been, there was no sign of him.

"What the..." Jennie muttered, flushing with embarrassment for the first time in years. "How?"

The spectral woman stared at her knowingly. "Look inside you, dear. It's amazing what imagination can do, is it not?"

Jennie caught her breath and heard Zhao inside her head once more.

If you play with my head, I'm going to play with yours. His laughter was abrasive, grating inside her mind. *Amazing what a little cognitive manipulation can do, isn't it? You may think you see me, but can you really trust your eyes now? What's the difference between reality and the images I put inside your head?*

She blinked and Zhao was sitting right in front of her. Jennie reached forward and swiped her hand through nothing.

Baxter let her go, a concerned expression on his face. "Jennie? What's going on? Are you okay?"

Jennie nodded slowly, unsure of how to answer. No, she didn't feel okay. Zhao was well and truly in her head, and she needed to find a way to catch him and expel him from her thoughts.

Also, the world was on fire.

The spectral woman laughed, apparently pleased at the state of things before her. Jennie's eyes locked onto her, and an idea clicked into place. "You're coming with us," she ordered.

The woman's face fell. She pushed backward and tried to fade through the walls, but Jennie latched onto her. "Nice try." She turned to face the others. "This shitshow has officially been upgraded to a clusterfuck. Assemble every available man, woman, and specter, and bring them back to Red Hook." She sighed. "I'm sorry Rhone, you're going to need to update Jack and Ruby so they can inform Lionus. Wait, before that, call Daggro. We need greater SIA intervention, and I don't trust that little weasel as far as we can throw him."

Rhone looked crestfallen but nodded nonetheless. Triton took a step forward. "Even with all of that, are we going to have the numbers we need to stop the spread of this chaos?"

Jennie considered this, still finding it hard to shake off Zhao's thoughts inside her head. She was aware that he would be looking in on her, but that didn't matter. It might do him good to know the forces that he was messing with.

"I've got a contact," Jennie announced at last. "You guys probably aren't going to like this, but we need all hands on deck."

She felt Zhao's curiosity peak in her mind. *That's right, baby specter. You've kicked the wrong hornet nest. You truly have no idea what and who you're messing with here. Level up, baby. It's game time.*

Richmond, Virginia, USA

The expressionless women led them to the outskirts of the city. They stopped for no one, forcing civilians to move out of their path. Their pace didn't falter, and the journey felt like it took forever.

Lupe complained, "Can't we just strap them to the hood and let them point the way? It'd be faster."

Tanya laughed. She had no intention of exiting the car to grab them. For all she knew, that could snap them from their reverie, and her curiosity was raging. Somehow, she knew this was connected to the specter they'd witnessed last night and the explosive sounds of the quarry.

A fact that was confirmed when they passed a road sign reading, "Richmond Quarry Site: 1 mile."

"What the hell is going on over there?" Tanya muttered.

The city dissolved behind them, opening out into the rolling hills surrounding the city. They passed fields and farms, heading ever closer to the quarry and its relentless drilling and humming of machinery. There were more people gathering along the roads and paths and walking toward the quarry, each with that same blank look in their eyes.

Sandra retreated into her chair. "I don't like the look of this."

"Me neither," Tanya agreed.

Jiao watched with fascination.

They decided to park a short distance from the quarry and walk the last few hundred meters. The quarry was easy to find. They simply followed the incessant noise from the machines. Soon they found themselves at the top of a hill, overlooking a large man-made cut that had been dug into the ground.

It stretched for half a kilometer in either direction and was about as deep as it was wide. A sloping haul road wide enough for the machines to pass two abreast connected the upper level to the bottom of the cut, its surface smoothed from the heavy vehicles that passed up and down.

They inched on their stomachs and peered over the edge of the rock face, seeing a smattering of people gathering on the quarry floor almost directly beneath them. The drill on the opposite face of the cut continued working as if the operator hadn't seen the gathering people. The loader/drivers similarly continued to remove the rock as it was cleaved into manageable chunks, seemingly unaware of the danger they posed to the people nearby.

The strangest part of it all was that the possessed—for what other word was there for them?—all looked in the same direction, facing the wall that was directly below Tanya, Lupe, Sandra, and Jiao. They couldn't see the point of fascination from their vantage point, but something in Tanya's gut told her it probably wasn't good.

Lupe squinted, his lips moving silently as he counted the number of individuals. "Twenty-three so far. Twenty-three standing there. And, look, more are coming. What is going on here?"

Jiao answered. "They've found something. Something in the rock."

The possibility had crossed Tanya's mind. Through her years of research and dabbling with the knowledge of the spectral realm, she had come across various pieces of research detailing old relics that had been dug up from the ground. Many linked back several hundred years, some even further than that. Each had some remnant of spectral energy which, until Jennie revealed the spectral realm to her in its entirety, had remained nothing more than a mystery.

"We need to get down there," Tanya urged, her eyes tracking the additional possessed slowly making their way into the quarry. "We need to see what they've found."

"But how are we going to get down there?" Lupe asked. "What if they all turn on us at once? What if whatever's making them do this decides they don't like us meddling? What then? Are we going to leave Hendrick all alone in the manor, locked away in his lab while the city goes insane?"

Tanya smirked. "Don't get ahead of yourself, dude. We don't know that's what's happening."

"Of course that's what's happening," Lupe replied. "Think about it, in the last few months, has anything ever been a case of being simple and easy to solve? No. We're tied in with *Jennie*. Everything we do is fraught with danger. We can't even buy chocolate fro-yo without fear of getting attacked by specters."

Tanya raised an eyebrow. "You really loved that fro-yo, didn't you?"

"It was the best!" Lupe replied, a little loudly.

They ducked their heads for a few minutes. When they thought they were safe again, they peeked back out.

It was strange that the work appeared to be continuing while the possessed gathered. Surely that would increase the chances of accidents down there? Perhaps a rockfall, or a landslide, or a piece of machinery going rogue and turning one of the possessed into pulp?

Lupe narrowed his eyes, then sighed. "We have to call Jennie. This is too big for us to—"

Tanya shushed him with a finger and pointed down below.

Madame Celestine walked out from the rock face below them, appearing before the possessed with her fingers laced behind her back. Her hood was lowered, leaving her silver hair flying gracefully behind her in the wind. She studied each person in turn and, although they couldn't see her face, they were sure that her eyes would also be as blank as the possessed.

"What is she doing?" Sandra muttered.

No one replied. They simply watched as she patiently waited for the others to finish walking down the road. Lupe counted thirty in total before they were all in position, and then a strange thing happened.

The sky darkened, and the world around them appeared to slow for a moment. The sound of the machines was suddenly muted, as though they'd been plunged underwater and could only hear sounds as fuzzy shapes. They turned their heads upon seeing a dark rippling shape speeding down the access road toward the quarry.

The shape looked like a boiling cloud of darkness. An orb with feathers of dark shadows streaking behind it. Where it sped, the air rippled around it like tarmac on a hot summer's day. It traced its way down the access road and found its target by launching into Madame Celestine, much in the same way it had attacked the previous night.

Madame Celestine's body jerked. Her head lowered, then raised to the others. A voice that wasn't her own started to speak.

Just then, their hearing returned to its former clarity, and the sound of the machines kicked back in. Tanya's heart sank. They could only make out the tone of the voice coming from Madame Celestine, but not the words.

The possessed stared obediently at Madame Celestine before she turned on the spot and walked back into the rock face below them. The possessed fell in line, trailing behind Madame Celestine like ducklings following their mother.

Then they were gone.

They waited a long moment before anyone moved. The machines hummed on as if nothing had happened.

Tanya was the first to speak. "We might as well go back to the manor. There's nothing we can do here without Jennie."

Tanya, Lupe, Sandra, and Jiao racked their brains to try and find some kind of plausible explanation as they returned to the car, their silence breaking the minute the doors were closed and they felt safe once again. Tanya kicked the car into action and sped away from that place, knowing that if they stayed any longer, something drastic might happen. Not that anything drastic *hadn't* happened, but how the hell did they approach and handle this?

Lupe stared at the quarry through the rear window. "I have so many questions."

"Join the club," Tanya replied.

"We *have* to tell Jennie," Sandra urged. "She'll know what to do. She always knows what to do."

Tanya looked at the girl in the rear-view mirror. "She's clearly busy, Sandra. We can't trouble her with this, too."

"But this is *huge!*" Sandra complained. "Even if she can't come back, she'll be able to help us out, surely? There's a power we don't understand down there. I felt it. It was unlike anything I've felt before."

Lupe remained tight-lipped, deep in thought.

Tanya knew Sandra was right, but there was a reason for her hesitation to call Jennie. It wasn't just that Jennie was busy, she also hated being a burden on the woman. She'd come to know Jennie as a friend, and she couldn't understand her work ethic. How she had so much energy and resilience to dive into one problem after another. Tanya had only been along for the ride for a few months, and she was already exhausted. She wanted to protect Jennie where she could.

Jennie doesn't need protecting. This is her life.

She knew Sandra was right. Things were evolving fast in Richmond, and action needed to be taken before it was too late. For all they knew, the whole city could be possessed in a matter of days. What then? What would Jennie have to return to?

Tanya sighed and tapped her phone. She put the call on speaker and waited for Jennie to answer.

A part of her hoped she wouldn't. Yet, after a couple of rings, Jennie spoke to the car.

"Hello? Tanya?"

Tanya looked once more into Sandra's eyes before answering. "Hey, Jennie. Er, I think we've got a problem."

Jennie gave a short chuckle. "I was wondering when you'd call."

CHAPTER THIRTY-FIVE

New York City, New York, USA

Jennie hung up the phone and allowed herself a moment to think.

How had it become so messy so quickly? Less than twenty-four hours ago, their worries had been small. Zhao had escaped, but there was little more to it. Now, not only were they being beaten to the finish line in every direction they ran, but parts of the country blazed, and Tanya and Lupe were in trouble down in Richmond.

We have to upscale, Jennie had thought after Tanya had informed her of their situation. *We're too small for this kind of operation. We need people covering every site and working together.*

She had placed another two calls after getting off the line with Tanya. The first had been to Daggro, detailing the information that Jennie had and demanding deployment of more troops. Daggro had been hesitant, even more so when she realized the information hadn't come first-hand from Lionus, but she had agreed to move the agents into action.

The last call was one she hadn't thought she'd be making for a long time. Every time she thought she was free of reliance, she found that that wasn't quite true.

Jennie pushed aside her misgivings. *It's all teething problems. Every organization needs help in the beginning. Besides, they promised. We made a truce. We're all in this together, at the end of the day.*

Jennie had made her requests to the last person she wanted to request from. Surprisingly, the call had been amicable, and help was promised. When she was finished, she strolled back to the others and found Baxter.

He looked at her with something like sympathy. "Is it done?"

Jennie nodded and rested her head on his shoulder for just a moment.

Buckingham Palace, London, England

The last thing Queen Victoria had expected that afternoon as she strode across the lawns of the palace, was to be notified by her valet about a phone call from America.

Things had grown dramatically quieter since the business in London and Virginia with Rogue. The wheels of the world turned and, while there was still trouble across the globe, Victoria found herself able to enjoy a time of relative peace in her own territory.

Victoria hiked up her dress and walked briskly toward the large doors and made her way through the palace. Still catching up with modern times, Victoria preferred to take her calls on the landline in her boudoir. She took a seat by an ornate golden dresser as she pressed the phone to her ear.

She had to admit that she was surprised. Genevieve's words were even and measured, and Victoria knew things must be serious if she was reaching out and asking *her* for help. After the fuss they'd made in Virginia and the paperwork they'd all signed in Washington, she had assumed they would go their separate ways, and that would be that. Genevieve would claim her prize, and all would be well.

For a short while, at least. The idea of one day reclaiming owner-ship of the globe hadn't faded from Victoria's mind, although at that moment, her priorities lay elsewhere.

When she placed the phone down, she thought a long while. Her two meat-head guards flanked her, and she could hear Elizabeth addressing her mortals somewhere in the palace, away from the hidden corridors and chambers that allowed the SIS their access to Victoria without arousing suspicion. It seemed a shame that Victoria's heir to the mortal throne didn't have the powers of conduits, but such things couldn't be rectified, she supposed.

When an agent appeared in the doorway, Victoria spun toward her. She was younger than Clark and Tiptry had been, yet she had earned her reputation as a formidable leader of the SIS in the days and weeks that had followed their deaths. Agent Harrie Sturgeon stood to attention and greeted Victoria with a bow.

That was one thing Victoria liked about the new head of the SIS. She had manners and courtesy. Knowing one's place was something that seemed to have been lost in these modern times.

Victoria let Agent Sturgeon hold the bow a second longer before giving her permission to speak.

"You wanted to see me, Your Majesty?" Sturgeon asked.

Victoria gave a curt nod. "It seems our friends across the Atlantic are in something of a pickle. They have requested our assistance in a matter that is rather pressing."

Sturgeon nodded. "I'm assuming this is to do with the bombings along the East Coast?"

Victoria looked at her, impressed. "How did you know?"

"It's all over the news," Sturgeon replied respectfully. "Covered by every major news channel."

Victoria spun slightly in her chair. "Do we believe it's a spectral issue?"

Sturgeon considered this. "Authorities are reporting no sign of mortal involvement in these cases. I think it's wise to assume specters have been utilized to trigger the bombs and remain out of sight of the mortal eye."

Victoria imagined the scenario all too clearly. She recalled similar occasions where conduits who had discovered that specters could do their bidding had used them as a way to get off scot-free from destructive crimes.

"Do you wish for me to deploy the troops?" Sturgeon asked. "I can have every available unit mobilized in a couple of hours. We could be on US soil before midnight."

Victoria chewed her lip. There was a bubble of anger in her stomach that hadn't faded since she had been forced to pick up the pen and sign the peace treaty with the United States and Genevieve King. She had ignored it and focused primarily on her issues with the Empire, cleaning up minor political scrapes occurring around the East India Trading routes, as well as a territorial scuffle that had briefly broken out in Australia, yet the pang of rejection still hadn't entirely faded.

Part of her wanted to teach Genevieve a lesson. To say, "No, this is your fight to deal with. You wanted freedom, you've got it."

Yet, there was something about the girl she couldn't let go of. At her heart, Victoria was a mother. Her maternal instinct refused to give up. She retained her pity for Genevieve, and it left a morsel of care and consideration for the girl. As much as she wanted to strike out in anger, she had to protect her own.

Victoria let out a long breath. "Deploy the troops. But wait an hour. Let them sweat a bit before we swoop into their rescue."

"Specters *and* mortals?" Sturgeon asked.

Victoria grinned. "Yes. Clark and Tiptry will no doubt enjoy a little bit of fresh air and action. They've been rather inactive since their deaths."

"As you wish, Your Majesty." Sturgeon bowed low and left the room.

Victoria turned to the wall, where a large mirror showed her reflection. Her two guards stood silently behind her. "What do you think, boys? Can Genevieve really find a way to stand on her own two feet?"

Neither guard answered.

Victoria groaned. "What good are you both? Muscles you've got in abundance, but where's the *fun*?"

Red Hook, Brooklyn, USA

Jennie took a steadying breath. "This day is just getting suckier and suckier."

Baxter nodded, both fixing their gaze on the chopper as it lowered to land in the open courtyard by the warehouse. "It's got to be done."

Jennie chuckled. "That should be my next tattoo."

The helicopter landed. The doors opened, and the shit-eating grin of Agent Lionus met them. "Ah, there she is. My humble piece of eye candy. Glad to see you're finally free of Zhao's clutches."

He strode over until he was just a few feet away and looked Jennie up and down, eyes lingering without shame on her breasts and ass. "You're still as good as you've ever looked."

Jennie raised an eyebrow. "Funny, I thought with a promotion you might have at least found a level of professionalism that was suitable. But it seems that a kick in the nuts has done little to simmer your shit down and turn you into a decent human being."

"Enough foreplay." Lionus smirked. "We've got shit going wild and we need to move. I suggest we divide and conquer. Daggro has given me orders to split our present reserve of troops—which includes you guys—and make a decision as to who goes where." He wiggled his eyebrows. "Lucky Jennie, you can ride shotgun with me. There's only one seat so you'll have to sit on my lap, I'm afraid."

Jennie didn't rise to the bait. She did, however, agree in part with his statement. "Nice try, but here's how the grown-ups are going to handle this. I'm going to commandeer your chopper. *You* are going to join your men in another. We need to spread our resources over the affected cities, then feedback on what the hell is going on out there. Once we know what's happening, we can look for any common threads and work together to lock down the faces behind all of this."

"Don't you mean the face?" Baxter asked, confused. "Unless Zhao sprouted another head and you didn't tell us."

Jennie shook her head. "I think we're looking at a hydra here, not a dragon."

Somewhere back in Washington, a specter named Bruno's ears were burning.

Lionus scoffed, interrupting again. "What makes you think I'm surrendering my chopper to you? Do you know who I—"

Jennie had had enough. She grabbed Lionus around the throat and squeezed tightly. His voice was pinched into silence.

A gasp came from the other agents as Jennie raised him two inches off the floor.

Lionus forgot all his training. He grabbed Jennie's wrists and kicked his legs, struggling helplessly.

Jennie stared at Lionus over the top of her glasses, her brow furrowed. "I'm afraid you've got no choice in the matter. I need faster transport, and you've got enough spare spaces on the chopper to accommodate you all." She swept an arm to indicate the city and the agents and specters gathered around, watching in stunned silence. "This whole damn thing is bigger than you, kid. Swing your dick another time, because we've got to move. Unless you want the blood of more civilians on your hands, you need to pipe down and get the fuck over yourself. Got it?"

She waited expectantly. Lionus' face went red.

Jennie repeated. "Got it?"

Lionus managed a choked, "Yes."

Jennie let go, and he crumpled to the ground. He picked himself up and adjusted his collar, his face like thunder. He snapped his fingers and summoned the other agents to another helicopter, mumbling, "Wait until Daggro hears this shit," as he went.

Jennie breezed toward the chopper and knocked on the pilot's door.

The pilot opened his door a mere inch, fear on his face. "I'm afraid I'm not authorized to fly this anywhere other than SIA-assigned business."

Jennie gave a curt nod. "I understand. However, I'm going to present you with two alternative options. Number one, I drag you out onto the tarmac and fly the damn thing myself. Or, number two, you accept a healthy sum of cash to compensate you for your burdens and fly me like an air taxi to where I need to go."

The pilot thought about this. He leaned conspiratorially out the door and whispered. "I never really liked that kid, anyway."

Jennie grinned. "Do you have a bird of your own?"

"I do. Back in Baltimore. A beautiful Airbus HI35. Near mint condition." He smiled.

"Great," Jennie commented with a grin. "Let's go to your place and grab it. Don't want to piss off the SIA any more than we need to."

The pilot looked relieved. Baxter raised an eyebrow.

"What?" she bellowed as the propellers kicked into gear. "Believe it or not, I'm not here to cause trouble. I'm here to get the job done."

Baxter waved a hand. "You misunderstand my confusion. I'm not saying you're wanting to cause trouble, I'm questioning the premise of you being able to pilot a helicopter."

Jennie laughed. "Oh, Bax. Haven't you learned anything about me by now?"

CHAPTER THIRTY-SIX

<u>**Washington DC, USA**</u>

For as long as he could remember, Kurt Rogers had dreamed of gracing the rooms of the White House.

It was the pinnacle of what he viewed as success, the ultimate realization of his dream of serving his country. The White House was where all the major decision veins of the country ran toward America's beating heart. Anyone who had permission to enter the hallowed halls of the White House had reached an unmatched level of political and personal access.

That feeling of elation hadn't lasted for long after he'd completed the paperwork that allowed him to be by the President's side without risking national security.

Rogers was beyond tired. Every day was a whirlwind of state meetings and project briefings. In the aftermath of the showdown in Virginia, the President had taken to Rogers like a blind man to a retriever. Rogers had barely left his side. He had been assigned personal quarters in which to sleep, and was at the President's beck and call twenty-four/seven while the SIA pushed its expansion and metamorphosed into a fully-fledged arm of the federal government without him to steer the ship.

He had been let into all the secrets by proxy. Area 51 was a conspiracy theorist's wet dream. They had evidence of aliens and their technology, although they weren't currently holding any aliens that were living. He was present for discussions pertaining to the economic status of the country, and others on managing international relations with third-world countries whose global status' as dictatorships were only the surface story. Running the country was a goddamn headache, and if he felt tired, he wondered how the hell the President coped with it all.

And then the bombs went off.

His cell went wild, but there was no time to answer. His day had been packed full of business meetings and engagements, but his schedule went out of the window when the President summoned him into the Oval Office and sat him in front of the desk.

Four officials stood solemnly behind him. They may as well have been statues for all that they moved and said.

The President exuded a cool calm, though Rogers wasn't sure how he managed it. His silver hair was neatly parted, and his suit pristine. "Things have escalated."

Was that a statement or a question?

Rogers went with the latter. "Yes, sir. I've just heard the news."

The President hardly blinked. "What is your agency doing to fix this mess? Is it spectrally-related?"

Rogers thought back to the message he'd received from Daggro that morning. Apparently, she already had agents in the field looking into a New York criminal who had been thought to be defeated and returned. It seemed highly unlikely that these attacks weren't somehow connected, but they had to find the correlation before acting.

"That's still to be determined," Rogers replied. "Though I highly suspect that it is. The SIA already has units deployed in New York. My stand-in has ordered them to the scene and they'll be arriving shortly. She is mobilizing the entire agency as we speak and sending units to each attack site."

The President examined Rogers coolly for a few moments, then gave a gentle nod. "Do you have this handled?"

There was a question. *Did* Rogers have this handled? He'd already had to fight for every scrap of federal funding that he could get to expand the SIA's department, but that wasn't the main issue. The real problem was that the rate of growth hadn't been accompanied by the same growth in the agency's leadership structure. They needed leaders at the helm who understood the enemy. The bulk of their new agents had only recently been introduced to the spectral world. How could they battle an enemy they were unprepared for, especially when a growth like this suddenly occurred?

Yet, Rogers knew that wasn't what the President was asking. "Yes. This attack will consume my full attention until we've caught the culprits and can send them rotting into a jail cell."

The President looked at him once more with those studious eyes. Rogers felt vulnerable under that glare, exposed, as though the President could see every thought going on behind his eyes.

At last, the President nodded. "Very well. Screw a lid on this situation. I'm going to have a tough time calming the nation. How do you let your people know that not only are you battling terrorists from foreign lands, you're also fighting an invisible enemy?" He turned to address one of his officials. "Make sure Rogers has everything he needs to stay on top of this. Rogers, I'm giving you whatever funding you need. This is serious. Don't let your country down."

Rogers thanked the President and exited the office. He paused for a moment outside the door and took a deep breath. His phone was still receiving new alerts when he took it out. Somehow he had to filter through them all to digest all available information.

As Rogers processed his messages, one thought remained in the back of his mind. One person who had been in this game longer than anyone, who might in some way become their saving grace.

Come on, Jennie. We need you now more than ever.

He stood by a window and watched as a helicopter soared overhead, wondering who was inside and where they might be heading.

The journey was much faster than expected, and as Jennie flew further from New York, the constantly pervading feeling that Zhao was in her head began to fade.

He's still in New York. That much is clear.

But is he? How can you trust your own thoughts after what happened before?

Baltimore unfolded before her, a place she hadn't visited since her expedition to flush out Brendan Koa and get to the bottom of the situation with the Shadows. It looked different from up high, more like a toy town than the thriving city it was.

The pilot, Ashton Langton, flew them over the city center toward an affluent area just outside of the city. Houses with lush lawns and gated fences were patchworked below them as they came in to land on a large round H.

The Airbus H135 was a thousand times more comfortable than the SIA's chopper. Ashton promised to return the chopper when their mission was complete but was glad to be riding his own as they headed onward and over Washington.

The city fell away behind them, and soon enough, they arrived in Richmond. Jennie directed Ashton to the manor, which could easily be viewed from afar. They landed softly on the back lawn as three poltergeists sped around the corner and started hurling tin cans and other objects at the chopper.

"Stop! It's us," Jennie called as she opened the door.

The poltergeists looked on in horror, upset to see they'd attacked their savior.

"We're so sorry!" Don McFarlene clapped his cheeks with his hands, his face stretching into a warped mask. "We didn't know it was you!"

Jennie laughed. "It's okay, you're just doing your job. Great work, by the way.

Jerry McFarlene gave a keen thumbs-up, and Graham sped toward them to pick the cans up from where they littered the lawn.

"Jennie!" Tanya's voice came from the back door as she sprinted toward them.

"What about us?" Baxter complained. "It's always Jennie, never Baxter, or Carolyn, or Feng Mian."

Tanya smirked. "You know I missed you too, buddy." Sandra shared her power with Tanya so that the woman could grab Baxter in a headlock.

Baxter played along, allowing her to rub her knuckles on the top of his head.

"Okay, okay." He laughed. "Enough of that."

Jennie smiled at them both. "Tell me what's going on, Tanya. We don't have a lot of time right now."

Tanya's face became serious. "I'm going to have to show you. This isn't really a thing I can just explain."

"Why?" Baxter asked.

Lupe appeared at the doorway. "Because we don't know."

Tanya nodded. "There's something fishy going on down at the quarry, and we don't have the numbers or knowledge to do anything about it. We need to go in there and investigate, but we're just three mortals and a specter."

Jennie counted in her head and raised an eyebrow. "Don't you mean *four* mortals and a specter?"

Tanya laughed. "I forgot about Hendrick!"

Lupe smirked. "You're great at forgetting people."

"What does that mean?" Jennie asked.

Tanya sighed. "Nothing."

"I wasn't even talking about Hendrick," Jennie continued. "Where's Jiao?"

Tanya glanced over her shoulder. "Oh. I don't know. Must be inside the manor somewhere. She's been with us all day, maybe she's tired."

"Perhaps." Jennie turned to the others. "Okay, here's the deal. We're going to be working with the SIA, and I don't want any arguments. I haven't got time to massage people's egos or worry about any kind of political bullshit. These guys need numbers, and that's what we're going to give them. You got that?"

The others nodded. Jennie had brought along everyone from her team except Jack and Ruby, who had been ordered to return to the SIA by Agent Lionus.

Jennie hesitated before her announcement, making it clear that she didn't want to do what she was about to do. "Ula, Triton, Roman, you're to stay here and help these guys. Feng Mian. You, too."

Carolyn's eyes widened. "Wait! No. Not Feng Mian. He's been like a father to…"

"He's not dying." Jennie met Carolyn's stare. "You two are just getting separated for a short while, okay? They don't know what they're going to meet down there, and Feng Mian's abilities aren't only unique, but they've gotten us out of a hell of a lot of scrapes. Feng Mian, you got any comment on that?"

Feng Mian shook his head. "Happy to serve."

The conduits stepped away from the chopper and closer to Jennie. "Are you sure about this?" Ula asked. "Won't you need us with you?"

Jennie showed the trace of a smile. "We've got a fresh injection of help coming. You know as well as I do that this is all about priorities, and I'm needed back with the others. Once everything is settled down, we'll be back. Just keep in constant contact and let us know what's going on."

She turned her attention toward Roman. "Roman. I know you're not one for words, and you're a great follower, but I'm putting you in charge of this operation, do you understand?"

Roman's face hardened. He stood up a little straighter. "I do."

"You lead this pack, and you make sure that no one gets hurt. I'm putting my full trust in you, and I believe that you can make this happen. You got that?"

Something flickered behind Roman's dark eyes. The faintest hint of emotion. He saluted. "It is an absolute honor and privilege. I will not let you down."

Jennie smiled. "I know you won't.

She turned on the lawn and looked up at the manor. "Maybe someday we'll really be able to turn this into a base of operations. But for now, we're going to have to say goodbye. Sorry this has been a brief visit, Spirit Mother."

Tanya grinned at the mention of her former title. "Don't mention it, Rogue. Thank you for swinging by. We can take it from here."

Jennie knelt toward Sandra and paused. She tilted her head toward Tanya. "There is just one more thing…"

Tanya's face fell. "No."

Jennie held Sandra's shoulders in her hands and looked into her innocent, spectral face. "I need you, pal. You're my Wi-Fi booster, and I need you to help me hunt a bad guy."

Tanya went to her knees and clutched Sandra.

Jennie bit her lip. "I'm sorry, Tanya. It's only for a short while, and you have a whole cohort of people to back you up now. An even trade. One Sandra, for a bunch of these thugs." She turned to Ula. "Sorry."

Ula waved a hand as if to say, "Don't worry about it."

It took some convincing, but after Sandra disconnected from Tanya, Tanya couldn't argue anymore. Sandra slipped out of her hands, and before Tanya knew where she was, she appeared by the helicopter.

Jennie rose and took Tanya's shoulders in her hands instead. "I'll look after her. I promise. We honestly need her right now, and she'll do more good with me than she will with you."

Tanya's lip wobbled. "You don't know that."

Jennie smiled and tilted her head. "Really?"

Reluctantly, Tanya laughed. She jumped into Jennie's arms and hugged her. "Bring her back in one piece, please, yeah?"

Jennie promised she would. Jennie didn't make promises lightly.

Baxter and Carolyn said their goodbyes, and Julia and Ashton watched with Sandra from the comfort of the chopper. Soon they were back in the air and heading off toward New York.

Jennie spared one last glance toward the manor, finding the tiny figure of Jiao watching from one of the upper windows. As their eyes met, Jennie received a spike of pain in her head. For the most fleeting of moments, she felt Zhao in her head, and an unknown emotion surged through her that was not her own.

Excitement? Had it been excitement?

CHAPTER THIRTY-SEVEN

New York City, New York, USA

Zhao's plans were going swimmingly. There had been some initial teething problems, but that had to be expected. He knew from the first moment of meeting Genevieve—the one the specters called Rogue—that she was going to be his biggest problem. From the first time he had discovered the spectral kingdom, he had delved into research to understand what lay ahead in death.

This operation had been months in the planning. As a newborn specter, he wanted to flex his muscles, test his abilities, and play with what was possible in the spectral realm. Sure, that might mean destruction for the mortals, but if it meant he could show that he meant business to everyone in the spectral realm, then the pain was worth the reward.

Zhao saw his image in the top corner of the large TV screen and grinned. Evidence of his point was in front of him. The little window reflected his vulgar manipulation back at him, the disfigured form of his body as a number of other windows on the screen showed him the dark and stern faces of his partners in crime.

Mere mortals. You have no idea who you're dealing with.

"I see that *most* of you have delivered according to plan," Zhao admonished. His brow was stern and his eyes dark. "I suppose five detonations is good work overall, although I thought we'd agreed that there'd be seven in total."

Each face was level and difficult to read. Over the years, these crime lords had learned to hold their poker face and show no fear.

"Ruben. Craig. You've disappointed me," Zhao continued.

Ruben McAffey and Craig Cowley stared at their cameras. Behind them, Zhao could make out a bunch of their henchmen, standing obediently in wait. They weren't there because they were any threat, but it was a power play Zhao knew well. Make it seem as though you're untouchable, and you're more likely to intimidate the others.

"There were…complications," Craig Cowley replied when it became clear that Ruben wasn't going to be the first to. The glasses he wore masked his emotions even further, but there was a trace of something there. Contempt, perhaps?

Zhao nudged him onward. "What complications? I wanted Baltimore to blow, too."

"Baltimore is already on high alert," Craig replied. "Even with spectral assistance, the feds are roaming this damn city. There must have been some kind of activity here not too long ago because the SIA have their claws into everything. A number of my spectral assistants have been contained and brought in for questioning at a local facility masquerading as a laundromat. Those who have returned have informed me that below-ground is an SIA facility monitoring all spectral activity within a fifty-mile radius. This can't be done."

Zhao took a deep breath. "Anything is possible when you have the balls to *try!*"

None of the men and women on the camera flinched. Zhao colored, a wave of embarrassment hitting him after his outburst. It should be so simple. With specters to aid them, surely wasn't anything possible?

Craig cleared his throat and continued. "It is in no way my fault that you assigned me a city in a state that is already prepared for such measures. You promised us that this would be easy, that we would be able to deliver on these actions without consequence, but *you* lied."

Zhao composed himself. He had jumped the gun. Sure, maybe as a newborn specter, he'd believed that the world wasn't quite prepared for his kind of notoriety, but hadn't Genevieve already proven that maybe there were some systems in place? Perhaps she had already gotten her grubby little mitts into places like Baltimore, Maryland.

"And you?" Zhao crooned, diverting the subject toward Ruben, who had remained silent thus far. "You had the pride of place. Washington. Where are my fireworks?"

Ruben took a long breath. The others waited patiently as his silence lingered. Eventually, he replied with only two words. "I'm out."

Zhao stared unblinkingly at his screen. He sighed. "I've always been told that I've got an accurate gut feeling, that the things I think are going to happen…will. I'm sorry it had to come to this."

Ruben made a choking sound, and his head snapped at an unnatural angle as a pair of invisible hands grabbed his face and twisted violently.

The other crime lords flinched at that one.

Cassie Ferriss kicked her chair back and stood up in shock. "How…"

"What have you done?" Tommy Vincenzo growled.

Zhao remained in his chair, passively watching as Ruben slipped from the desk. His computer followed, and after crashing on the floor, his digital feed flickered in and out.

Zhao addressed their concerns. "I've learned a lot over these past few weeks. Specters come in all shapes and forms. Most specters are gifted only with the barest of skills, but there are some, such as me, who inherit abilities that transcend all understanding. You see, my friend Ruben has been followed ever since he left New York, and I've had constant reports from a new friend of mine who delights in destruction."

The digital feed righted itself as invisible hands placed it back on the desk. In the background, a series of shots fired, and one by one, Ruben's henchmen fell.

Zhao grinned. "It also helps when you meet specters who have a grudge against your enemy."

Once the room fell silent, the chair adjusted itself. A moment later, a specter flickered into view.

"How is this possible?" Cassie asked.

Zhao held his grin. "As I said, there are a thousand unique skills a specter can be blessed with. One of which is pure invisibility, surpassing even that of a specter from the eye of a mortal. These individuals can hide even from specters."

A man in a pinstripe suit appeared before them on the empty chair. His dark hair was combed back neatly, and his Tommy gun was on the desk beside him as he adjusted the screen.

Zhao leaned back in his chair. "Friends, meet Rico."

Rico waved a few fingers at the digital gathering.

"Rico is just one of my new allies," Zhao continued. "Rest assured that I have a number of his friends following each of you. You betray me, stray from the plan, or don't deliver, and I will know."

The others on the camera growled and looked ready to protest but knew better than to risk death at a junction like this.

"Gentlemen, lady, we are moving into the next phase of our plan. We are the virus, and we will soon spread. Listen closely, because things are going to get *real* fun from here on out…"

Rico leered at the camera and chuckled.

Richmond, Virginia, USA

They waited for nightfall before hopping into the rental car and cruising over to the quarry.

It felt strange to Tanya to be without Sandra. The eternal child had been a permanent accompaniment, stuck to her hip ever since they had first discovered her in New York. She had been Sandra's guardian almost from the moment of her spectral birth and brought her up to speed with the modern world.

As they drove in relative silence toward the excavation site, she felt more alone surrounded by mortals than she ever had surrounded by specters. The only positive of the whole experience was Roman had fished out a spare set of SI glasses for her to remain in contact with everyone since Sandra had been her source of access to the specters, and now she was gone.

Lupe and Hendrick had stayed behind, as was expected. The conduits took the back seat, while Jiao took the front, and Feng Mian melted and stood in the trunk.

The city faded into silhouettes behind them as the quarry came into view.

The first thing that struck Tanya was that the machines had stopped their incessant whirring. She supposed she hadn't heard them working at night, so there must be a curfew imposed upon them despite their production schedule.

The group sneaked to the edge of the pit, the place where they had seen the possessed gathering around Madame Celestine as that strange force had darted toward her. The bottom of the cut was empty. Or, at least, they assumed it was. With no lamps or lights lit down there, it was impossible to tell.

"Switch to IR," Roman muttered. Ula and Triton copied and tapped the controls on their glasses. Their heads swept back and forth as they examined the sight.

"Zero bogeys," Roman confirmed.

Tanya's heart rate had doubled. She placed a hand on Roman's shoulder, surprised by how warm he was. "That doesn't mean anything, though, right? Specters don't give off a heat signature."

Roman moved her hand firmly away without looking. "No. But humans do."

Ula turned to look at her. "If they are really possessed humans, they have to have some kind of heat trace. No biological body of a human can survive cold for that long. Organs and functions will just break down."

Feng Mian remained silent beside them, though Tanya was sure she saw his eyes occasionally flick in Jiao's direction. She wondered how she could get them to get over their differences and admit they liked each other.

Roman led the way as they skirted the upper level of the quarry and made their way toward the only entrance down—the haul road.

Out there, they were exposed. The chilly wind bit their exposed skin. Triton kept watch at the rear as the others pressed on, using the downhill momentum to break into a sprint.

They reached the bottom without incident. From down here, the upper level appeared magnified, as though the drop had doubled in size since they'd descended. They stuck close to the wall and made their way toward the rock face where Madame Celestine had disappeared. The reason she'd been able to do so was clear when the tunnel came into sight. The group hurried toward the tunnel's entrance, determined to get to the bottom of the mystery.

The tunnel arch was huge, easily three times the height of Roman, who stood over six-foot tall. The machines were lonely skeletons under the dim starlight. The dark inside the mouth of the cave was oppressive, even from the outside.

Roman tapped his ear. "All clear?"

Triton confirmed it was from his vantage point at the top of the haul road.

"Onward we go," Roman ordered.

They made a direct line for the cave, Roman only pausing once to tap his glasses and ensure that they were alone. When they reached the entrance, they stopped and examined its perfectly smooth edges. There were faint boot imprints from people heading inside, but there was something strange about how they looked.

"Careful," Ula muttered to Roman, pointing at the floor. "Footsteps leading in."

"None leading out," Roman confirmed. "Be prepared, guys. This could get rocky."

Despite their need for caution, the only way to see inside was by using light. Ula switched on a large torch and the cave illuminated, revealing a ceiling of stalactites that looked like fangs and walls wet with moisture. The cave wound deeper ahead of them as though they were walking into the gullet of an enormous worm.

Tanya shuddered and tried to hide it. Jiao walked beside her, fascinated.

At one point, a loud *whoosh* came toward them, and Roman and

Ula flinched and prepared their weapons. A second later, dozens of bats, disturbed by the torch's beam, sped out into the night, squeaking as they went.

There was little more action after that, as they walked ever into the darkness. After what felt like miles, the tunnel narrowed to a point. Tanya believed that she must be somewhere beneath the edges of the city. The rock seemed different here. Somehow more like redbrick than mud and sandstone.

Ula moved to the front with Roman, and they advanced more slowly. The cave shrank to nothing more than the size of a garage door. Tanya was certain she could make out voices in the distance, muffled and nothing more than mutters.

"Turn the light off," Tanya urged in the quietest whisper she could manage.

Ula shook her head. "It's too late."

Ula and Roman broke ahead at a run. The torchlight wobbled all around them and dizzied Tanya as she struggled to keep up with them. Luckily the floor was even, and she only had to worry about keeping up as she chased after the two conduits.

They made it through the door, emerging into a long room with a low roof. Shadowy figures came at them, moving so quickly that the torch could barely catch them at all.

Arms grabbed Tanya around the neck. She doubled over and hurled the attacker off her. She grasped for her own torch at her side and shone it, glad that as Jiao did the same, more light filled the room and illuminated their enemy.

There were only a dozen of them, but they moved quickly. Tanya recognized a handful of them instantly as their yoga pants flashed luminous colors in the light. The possessed came at them, revealing worn crop tops and tight stomachs dirty with the mud from the cave.

When it became obvious that their enemy had no firearms, Ula and Roman switched to suppression mode. They swept roundhouse kicks and threw hammer-fisted punches, sending their enemy sprawling. Tanya ducked and scrapped with a few who came her way, doing her best to shake them off, despite the fact they seemed determined to grab her hair and pull her to the ground.

One woman leapt at Tanya. She instinctively caught her, cradling her like a five-year-old until the woman scratched at her face. Tanya gasped and pushed her away, stumbling back in the process. She fell on her ass and the woman continued her assault, oddly silent as she did.

Tanya covered her face to protect it from the blows. Surprise filled her when the woman's weight suddenly vanished. She scrambled out of the way of Jiao's fighting and observed with wide eyes as her flowing techniques allowed her to take out her enemies while avoiding their blows. Her movements were practiced and calm, effective in much the same way Tanya had observed Feng Mian's battling to be.

Who are you? Tanya wondered, trying to think back to a moment when Jiao might have exhibited these skills. With fighting skills like that, how was she ever captured by the Dragon?

Guns trump fists, girl.

After Jiao was finished, she helped Tanya back to her feet while Ula and Roman finished incapacitating the last of their enemy. Unconscious bodies littered the floor.

"What the hell is all of this about?" Tanya asked, touching her face and hissing as the raw skin from the scratches burned.

"Are you okay?" Ula asked. "You look like my kitten's scratching post."

Tanya waved a hand, her attention caught as Feng Mian appeared from behind an excavator the size of an SUV, which they had failed to see in all the fighting. He motioned them over.

Behind the excavator was a raw, cutout section of the wall that had not yet been smoothed like the rest. It created a shallow chamber that resembled a topside bus shelter. Lying lengthways along the chamber was a decrepit, stone sarcophagus.

An inscription was instilled across the side. The stone box, which must have once been weighted down with a heavy lid to prevent the dead from rising, was askew. A foul stink poured from within.

Roman examined the darkness inside with his torch, not a single care or emotion on his face. A dusty skeleton met his stare, the rest of the tomb seemingly empty.

"What does it mean?" Ula queried.

Jiao raised her cell and took half a dozen images of the inscription. "Hard to say. It's an ancient language, and one that could be difficult to decipher."

Tanya's gaze moved from the sarcophagus to the unconscious bodies and back again. "Whatever it is, I think we can safely say this box is the source of all of our problems."

CHAPTER THIRTY-EIGHT

New York City, New York, USA

The sun was beginning to set as Ashton flew the chopper back into the heart of the Big Apple.

"You ready?" Jennie asked Sandra, smiling at the spectral girl sitting cuddled into her side.

Sandra gave a nod and straightened in her chair. Jennie could already feel the power of the girl flooding through her.

How did one girl amass so much spectral energy?

"Sweep the city, Ashton," Jennie instructed. "Go as low as you dare. We *must* nail it this time."

Ashton complied, the helicopter lurching as he brought it around and closer to the rooftops of the city's skyscrapers. They started at the southern point of the city, slaloming back and forth like a giant with a metal detector looking for loose change.

Sandra closed her eyes. Jennie followed suit. It was incredible how much they could sense of the city. With Sandra's powers magnifying Jennie's ability to see, spectral activity opened up before her. She could make out the frequencies of hundreds of specters on the streets and in buildings below. Not enough to identify each of them, maybe, but enough to know they were there. Jennie had never seen them from this angle before, had never given a thought to how occupied the mortal space was by specters.

They covered Lower Manhattan and found nothing of note. There was a faint trace of the connection Jennie and Zhao shared, but not enough to convince her he was anywhere below them.

Migrating up to Midtown Manhattan and sweeping over Times Square, they looked down upon the thousands of residents making their way to and from work, enjoying shows, and frequenting the restaurants and bars. It didn't matter how much danger the city was in, New Yorkers would always find a way to carry on as though the world would never stop turning.

Zhao's frequency grew infinitesimally stronger. They were on the right track. The helicopter flew over Central Park, Jennie fixing her eyes on the sun-reflected windows of her Plaza apartment with a smile. People walked their dogs below, cars choked the streets, and a cop car blared its sirens somewhere in the distance.

"I'm getting something," Sandra called, her voice almost snatched by the chopper's blades.

Me too, Jennie thought. There was a tingle inside. The fingers of Zhao were clutching inside her head, already trying to mess with her.

"Keep going!" she shouted to Ashton.

He grinned. "I was planning to!"

They passed over the Museum of the City of New York, where they had first come across Sandra in their initial scuffle with the Spectral Plane. It was like taking an aerial tour of Jennie's first weeks in New York. Things hadn't been simple then either.

When will they ever be?

An image flashed into Jennie's head. It came in such vivid color and clarity that, for a moment, it disarmed her and pained her head.

Zhao. He was looking at her in the mirror, a perfect view from atop the Empire State Building. Her gut tugged at her, every part of her wanting to order Ashton to go back to where they'd come from.

Baxter leaned forward, face full of concern. "Jennie, are you okay? What is it?"

Sandra opened her eyes.

"I can see him. He's... It's telling me he's back where we came from. At the Empire State Building. But I didn't feel him there before."

Sandra looked back at the colossal tower, confused. "I don't feel anything that way, Jennie. We're on the right path, can't you feel it?"

Jennie shook her head. "He's inside my thoughts. I can't block it out. He's blinded me to the truth, I'm sure of it. It's down to you, Sandra."

Sandra caught Baxter's eyes. He gave a reassuring smile and nodded. "You're up."

Sandra's face grew resolute. She funneled her gift into the connection that she and Jennie shared and urged Ashton onward, calling directions as they closed in on Zhao's location. They flew north, passing over Washington Heights, Jennie looking more and more pained as she clutched the sides of her heads and grimaced.

"He's a determined fucker, I can tell you that much," Jennie grumbled in reply to Baxter's concern.

Sandra ignored the bad word, focusing instead on directing Ashton. The energy signature was growing stronger. She ordered him toward the west coast, where the George Washington Bridge crossed over the Hudson.

"There!" She pointed at a small, solitary red lighthouse by the water's edge.

Jennie forced her eyes open. It was hard for her to see the world with Zhao covering the truth and injecting her mind with a superimposed image of the Empire State Building. She could see the room she had been detained in and the offices next door. Zhao watched from the window. He was able now to stand, although his limbs hadn't yet recovered entirely from his kiss with concrete. He watched over the city, his hands clasped behind his back to support his crooked spine as though he were an extreme sufferer of scoliosis.

Jennie fought against Zhao, feeling his anger inside of her as they zeroed in on his location. Ashton brought the chopper down on the lawn beside the lighthouse, causing a few nosy civilians to take a few steps back and film on their cell phones.

Baxter looked at the little red lighthouse. The lights were off and the place looked deserted. "Are you sure he's here?"

Sandra's response was simple. "Yes."

Unbidden, Jennie's head filled with the same resounding shriek she had experienced back in Washington. That felt like a lifetime ago, a life that felt very different from this one. "Yes. He's here."

They spilled out of the chopper and onto the lawn. Ashton remained behind, the keen driver of the getaway vehicle. Julia stayed close by, studying her cell phone with a scrutinous eye as she read a series of articles.

Jennie brought Rhone closer to her and leaned in close. "You're going to have to take this one. I can't lead here."

Rhone raised an eyebrow. "Are you sure?"

"He's inside my head," Jennie explained. "Any plan of action I make is going to be spilled to him instantly. I'll stand back while you do your thing. Just let me know the part I need to play when I need to play it, and act fast, okay? Zhao is slippery as hell, and we've got new arrivals coming soon. I want to be there to greet them when they come."

She backed away, turning away from the intrigued looks of her companions. Rhone gave the orders, and soon they assembled out the front of the lighthouse.

Rhone approached the iron fence ringing the building. There was a padlock on the gate that melted easily with some help from one of Jennie's vials. She sighed, unhappy to be handing over her final measure of the solution. Hopefully, Hendrick would have more upon her return.

They passed through the gate and tried the door. Surprisingly it yielded easily to Rhone's touch. He nudged the door open and was instantly confronted by attackers.

They were ready for them. Of course, they had been. Zhao had a hotline directly into Jennie's head and could see through her eyes.

Rhone took the first shot, darting inside the building and forcing Zhao's men up the stairs. They piled up and around the spiral staircase, firing down at him and the others with standard ammunition.

It appeared they hadn't expected so many specters.

Baxter and Carolyn rushed up the stairs. Carolyn exercised her powers, focusing her energy on the pistols in their enemy's hands. She wanted to test her capacity to control the weapons in the same way she had controlled the Bhoots' weapons way back in London.

The pistol shook in the man's hands, then streamed toward her as though pulled on an invisible string. Carolyn caught the weapon and turned it on him, sending a shot into his shin.

The man shouted in pain before collapsing and falling down the stairs. Rhone darted to him and slapped a pair of cuffs on his wrist and a banister spindle before he could do any more damage.

Baxter raced ahead to where a number of specters were joining the fray. They shot at him and sent a few bullets into his shoulder and thigh. He growled and continued toward them, firing at the furthest with his own pistol before swinging his wrench in a wide arc and clobbering the ones in front of him. He drove himself forward, despite his own pain, knowing how vital his mission was. His only purpose was to make room for Jennie so she could finally take care of Zhao once and for all.

Carolyn fired off several more shots with the mortal's pistol and took down three of the black-clad enemy. It was tough going, seeing that they had to navigate the thin staircase to the top of the lighthouse. In the meantime, who knew what waited at the top? Maybe Zhao had already jumped onto the lawn and fled?

Jennie was prepared for this and waited outside the lighthouse, her eyes fixed on the walkway encircling the glass housing that topped the building.

It was torture, listening to her comrades fight her battle. She should be in there, working her way to the top with them, but she wanted to give Zhao as little possible notice of what he was dealing with as she could.

Sandra waited beside her, quiet and still. Jennie had kept her back, wanting to stay true to her promise to Tanya. Sandra would return to the manor in one piece. If there was one person she wanted to keep as safe as possible, it was this girl. The girl with powers that surpassed any she'd seen in other specters. She needed her.

Shots fired inside the lighthouse brought Jennie out of her reverie. Cries of pain rang out. Behind Jennie and Sandra, a few brave civilians watched from the tree line of Fort Washington Park. The commotion was drawing attention, which was the opposite of what Jennie wanted. But what else could she do?

Just when Jennie was getting antsy to join, Rhone poked his head out the door and waved her inside. Jennie didn't hesitate as she sped onward, leaping over fallen bodies and making her way to the top of the spiral staircase. She passed Baxter and Carolyn, who offered encouraging smiles as she passed.

Later, Jennie would admire Rhone and these specters for the part they'd played in this. But for now, she had an ex-Dragon to find.

The stairs spiraled and ended at a door. Jennie kicked the door with her boot heel, and she bounced back. It was tough, but another two kicks swung it wide open.

Zhao stood at the window, his hands laced behind his back in the same way she had seen in the Empire State Building, only this view was less glamorous, offering only a vista of the setting sun rippling on the water.

Jennie raised the Big Bitch to the back of his head. She could feel his presence in her head, as though he were looking at himself through her eyes.

Zhao took a deep breath and held his gaze on the water. "I suppose that this is the end for me, isn't it? Less than a week since my death and already I'm wishing that I crossed over into the abyss and saved myself the heartache of all of this chasing and chaos."

Jennie held still, finger poised on the trigger. Sandra clutched her leg and waited behind her. The others hovered in the doorway.

"What is death?" Zhao continued, lost in his thoughts. "I suppose that death is just the end. In which case, maybe today will see the death of Peter Zhao as my name vanishes and goes with me into the grave. If death is really just about endings, then already I know that I have done my piece to gain immortality. The baton has been passed. That is enough."

Jennie narrowed her eyes, a wave of rolling anger boiling in the pit of her stomach. This man had caused so much damage already, had penetrated her thoughts and found a way to make her vulnerable. He had manipulated her and made her see things that weren't there. Even at this point in time, she wondered if what she was seeing was true.

As if to prove her point, Zhao answered her doubts. "Yes, this is reality, Genevieve. There are no more illusions left to cast. You have found me, and I have no doubt that I will be gone soon. You have methods for that; I've already plucked that knowledge from your mind."

He turned toward her, resting his back against the internal glass of the lantern room. A giant bulb on a rotation platform took the center of the room. "Before I die, I request the answer to one question."

He waited for Jennie to answer. She remained silent.

"Very well." He chuckled. "When will it ever be over for you? I see the struggles you carry. I've explored your darkest secrets and seen the truths you hide. Will you ever be satisfied?"

Jennie growled. "You don't know what you're talking about."

"It's ambitious, I'll admit," Zhao continued, undeterred. "To build what you're trying to would be a monumental achievement. But what then? Injustice will never cease. The world you've promised your mother and father will never come to fruition. Peace is a pipe dream, and injustice is a reality that must be shared in this world. Yin and Yang. It's all about balance. Harmony is an illusion."

Jennie winced at the mention of her parents. For a fleeting moment, Zhao cast Jennie's final moments with her parents in her mind, the pair who had been taken so young. Torn apart by the very world that Jennie spent the rest of her life protecting.

Her jaw clenched. "That's the point, Zhao. Injustice will never cease. Neither will justice. That's why I go on—to ensure that there is balance in the world, and those who dream of a brighter tomorrow may see at least a glimpse of what might be. I'm under no delusion that a perfect utopia will exist, but without people like my team and me, there's more of a chance that the world will burn, and smoke will fill the skies. That's a reality I cannot allow."

Zhao smiled. There was no menace in that grin, just a deep-seated understanding. "You know that even with me gone, this will not be over, don't you? The Dragon lives on. She will find you, and she will continue my legacy. The wheels are already in motion."

Jennie nodded. "That's a sacrifice I'm willing to make. I've spent my life slaying monsters. What's one more to my death count?"

She lowered the Big Bitch and stepped back to allow Sandra before Zhao. He leered down at the girl but froze as she raised a hand in the air and fixed him to the spot.

"Any last words?" Jennie asked.

Zhao contemplated this. "Yes. Just this: you'd better act fast, Genevieve. Old enemies are more difficult to murder than me, and the fireworks you've seen are nothing compared to what will soon come." His face split into a predatory grin. "Remember Renminbi?"

"Now," Jennie instructed.

Sandra began to chant as her power, and her spectral light flooded the room. She shone like the bulb that would soon beam to the waters as Zhao started to scream as the Latin fell from her lips.

Jennie collapsed to her knees, the shrieking enough to fill her head. Baxter and Carolyn dropped, too. Rhone stared at them all, helpless.

The only person holding their focus was Sandra as she summoned her power of exorcism, the same power that had vanquished Worthington not too far from where they stood. The same power that had taught Queen Victoria a valuable lesson in who she was messing with. Light flooded the room until all that was left was white.

Jennie saw them, then. Her parents, in a flickering montage of memory induced by Zhao as his final parting gift to Jennie.

A few moments later, the light was gone.

And so was Zhao.

CHAPTER THIRTY-NINE

Red Hook, Brooklyn, USA

A string of cars came speeding down the lamp-lit street toward the warehouses at Red Hook.

There were easily two dozen vehicles, maybe more. In the sky, a number of helicopters flew toward them, ready to land in the spaces vacated by the remaining specters and Jennie's team.

The first chopper to touch down was a rental, undecorated and unsophisticated in its design. From the open door hopped a woman who looked only a little older than Jennie. Her eyes were shaded by SI glasses and her frame muscular.

She beelined for Jennie and held out her hand. "Rogue."

"Sturgeon," Jennie replied, accepting the handshake. "It's been some time since we last crossed paths. Last I knew, you were in the minor leagues. When did you get this upgrade?"

"When you killed my predecessors," Sturgeon replied flatly. There was little humor in her words. "How's the situation looking?"

"Dire," Jennie answered, explaining that she had taken out Zhao, but there were still more areas to explore. "We're yet to hear back from Lionus at the SIA, and the specters swarming New York have found nothing additional of note, other than a few crack dens and illegal armories in people's basements."

Sturgeon's eyebrow flickered. "You *killed* our prime suspect?"

"Had to," Jennie retorted without regret. "The man was a threat to our entire justice system. If you'd met him, you'd have known."

Sturgeon huffed disbelievingly. "Even you should know better than to kill a key suspect in cold blood. We could have detained him. Interrogated him."

Carolyn scoffed. "That worked so well for the SIA."

Sturgeon turned on her, face like thunder, looking over the specter. "*We* are not the SIA, young specter. *We* are the SIS. We have over a century more experience than your infantile organization, and *we* can make our captives squawk."

Jennie chuckled and drew Sturgeon's attention back to the matter at hand. "Things must have changed a *lot* then since I last sat in on your interrogations. You couldn't get a minister to confess to the truth while dosed up on truth serum."

Sturgeon regained her composure and wiped her glasses. "A lot has changed. If you had left us a suspect, we could have extricated the information we desired. As it is, we're left with… What, exactly?"

Jennie handed over a piece of paper, on one side was printed a map of the east coast with markings of the detonation sites. New York and Hartford, Connecticut, were crossed out. "We've got those sites covered. SIA's Agent Lionus reported that he's covering that site and looking for answers. No response thus far."

Sturgeon studied the map. "We'll split between us and take Pennsylvania and New Jersey."

"Great," Jennie replied. "That leaves us with Boston." She asked for Sturgeon's phone and keyed in her number. "Keep in touch. Contact and update on the hour. We need regular communication to make sure we're covering as much ground as possible."

Sturgeon hesitated.

"What?" Jennie asked. Her shoulders softened as she realized the problem. "I get it. Queeny wants you to take charge, doesn't she? Well, you're going to have to get over your own egos. We're all in this together, and I've got at least a century more experience than you do."

Sturgeon stared at her levelly. "Still."

Jennie moved closer, her voice softer. "Sturgeon. You know me. We've worked together before. This is not a time for a battle of wills, we need to pull in and make this happen. Don't make the same mistake that Clark and Tiptry made. For once, can we all do this as a team? It's already a struggle with the goddam SIA waving their dicks around."

Sturgeon considered this. She looked at the chopper over her shoulder, and for the first time, Jennie saw the specters accompanying her.

She gave a curt nod to Agents Clark and Tiptry, unfortunate casualties of the Alexandrian skirmish. "Don't become like them. You're better than that."

Although Sturgeon didn't give a direct reply to this, Jennie could tell she was considering it. She bid them goodbye and went to address the rest of the SIS agents who were waiting patiently for their commands.

Jennie walked toward the chopper closest to the warehouse, the Airbus' blades already spinning. Baxter caught up to her pace. "Do you really think they're going to play along?"

Jennie debated this in her head. "I hope so. Whatever happens, we've now got agents from both sides, and specters too, covering a wide area of the east coast. With any luck, one of us will find the linchpin of this whole operation and shut the damn thing down before things progress any further."

As they climbed into the chopper, Julia sat waiting, her eyes fixed on and illuminated by her cell phone screen.

"Found a new porn channel?" Carolyn quipped.

Julia shook her head. "No. It's a message from the guys over in Richmond. Jennie, check this out."

Jennie examined the series of images sent over by Jiao. "A sarcophagus? Oh, that's never a good sign." She pinched the screen and enlarged the image. "What language is this?"

"I don't know," Julia replied. "But I'm going to find out."

"Well, get a move on. We'll be up in the air for a couple of hours, but once we're in Boston, we'll need all hands on deck." Jennie watched the world fall away beneath her as they were lifted into the air.

God, spectral trouble is just like waiting for the bus. Nothing for ages, then they all come along at once.

Richmond, Virginia, USA

Lupe met them at the door, confusion on his face as Rhone and Triton walked in, each carrying the body of an unconscious yoga student.

"What the…" he tried to say before Tanya cut over him.

"Not now," she snapped.

Even the poltergeists' attention was caught as they lumbered them upstairs and toward the rooms that would soon become the holding cells. Currently, there was no protection to keep specters from entering the room, but the lock would be enough to deter mortals.

They placed them inside the room and watched them for a few minutes. The girl on the left had shocking red hair, and a cut across her brow. A dark bruise was already forming on her exposed stomach. The woman on the right was younger, petite, with blonde hair. Her lip was cut, and gentle snores came from her lips.

Roman held the others behind him and knelt between the pair. He unscrewed the lid of a bottle of water and threw it on each of their faces in turn.

Immediately the girls awoke, springing onto all fours like feral animals. They leapt at Roman, who managed to grab the red-head and pin her down by the throat to the floor. Triton rushed into the room and grabbed the blonde woman's arms, trapping them behind her back and holding her still.

"Calm down!" Triton growled, his muscles straining to keep her in his grasp. Roman flipped the redhead over and pushed her face to the ground, cursing her for giving him angry scratches on his arm and face to match Tanya's.

Lupe shook his head. "What the hell have you brought into this house? What's wrong with them?"

"We don't know," Tanya replied. "That's what we want to find out. Feng Mian, any ideas?"

Feng Mian crossed over to Roman and his hostage and placed a hand on her forehead. He looked deep into her eyes even as she huffed and tried to chomp at his fingers. "Definitely possessed. I don't know how to dispel the darkness inside, though."

She tried to bite his hand.

"She can see you?" Lupe asked. "Is she a conduit?"

Ula shook her head. "Doubtful. It might just be the spectral power inside her that allows her to see. Whoever this woman is, she's not herself right now. Nor is the other one. Roman, what do you suggest?"

Roman half-turned over his shoulder. "We keep them detained and search for an answer. Drop a line to Julia, perhaps? She's dealt with possessions before. In the meantime, we set up a guard and restrict them to this room. Who knows, perhaps time in isolation will help flush out the darkness."

Tanya touched her cheek, forgetting the scratches for a moment, and winced. "We can't leave them together, surely? They'll kill each other."

"They didn't kill each other in that cave," Roman replied. "They should be okay together. The guards can keep an eye on them. Feng Mian, Ula, you're up first."

They backed out of the room, leaving Roman and Triton with their captives. Once everyone was clear, they shoved the possessed women against the wall and slipped out of the room, locking the door behind them.

Feng Mian and Ula took their stations, standing either side of the door as the women banged and slammed their fists against the solid wood.

"What was this room before?" Triton asked.

Tanya shrugged. "A storage room. No windows, a solid plastered ceiling. Perfect detention for mortals."

"You'll need to upgrade before you capture specters," Roman grunted.

Tanya nodded her agreement.

They switched guard through the night, each playing their part to keep their detainees in check. Lupe and Triton took the next shift on guard, then Roman and Tanya. At some point in the early hours, Hendrick and Jiao switched in, although Hendrick was considerably more reluctant than the others had been.

"I have important work to do," he protested into the empty corridor. "This is a waste of my talents."

Jiao remained silent, back resting against the wall beside the door. The banging had finally stopped, the two women having either grown weary or simply given up. She stared into the gloom and saw shapes moving in the shadows on the wall.

"Jennie would *not* want me wasting time just standing here. I've so much to unpack and arrange. I need help and staff. Do you know how difficult it is to build a laboratory from scratch? The number of things you forget to order that you don't realize until you need them. Thank God for twenty-four-hour delivery."

Jiao ignored the ancient mole man. Her attention was directed at the room behind her. The women intrigued her. She wondered how possession worked and whether they would be able to expunge the power from them. What was the purpose of it all? What had they uncovered?

The others were either fast asleep or preoccupied in their rooms. Despite Hendrick's formula for tiredness, nothing could beat a good night's rest. Jiao rose to her feet and pressed her ear against the door.

"They're asleep," Hendrick stated matter-of-factly.

Jiao raised an eyebrow.

"I may be old, but my hearing is magnificent." Hendrick tapped his ear. "They're snoring beside the door."

Jiao rested her hand on the golden knob and pinched the key with the fingers of her other hand. She twisted the key until it clicked in the lock.

Despite her strange behavior, Hendrick allowed this. "You're making a mistake."

Jiao entered nonetheless, having to lean a little more weight against the door to open it wide enough to squeeze through. Out of everyone in the house, this was a maneuver that only she could manage with her narrow frame.

The women were out cold. Their hair was stressed into nests, and their fingernails were broken and blood caked their fingertips. Jiao knelt beside them and placed a hand on the blonde woman's forehead, remembering the lessons she had been taught by *him* and the rituals and arcane movements she had learned. A sense of cold calm passed from her to the sleeping woman.

Jiao wore three rings on her fingers, and each gave off a golden glow. The girl's eyes remained closed, but a long gasp came from her mouth as though she were trying to steam up a window with her breath. Something snaked out of her throat like the fumes after a smoker's inhalation.

The gaseous cloud, no larger than the size of a tennis ball, hovered above her. Jiao repeated her action with the redhead girl, and another dark orb joined the air in front of her.

She checked that no one was watching behind her and nudged the door closed, leaving only an inch in case she needed to make a quick escape.

She rose to her feet and studied the gaseous orbs. They made their own shapes and pulsed with their own life. They pushed themselves together and became a larger ball, and when Jiao extended a hand and smiled, it hovered above her palm. She could almost feel the weight of it.

A single declaration came from the orb, transferred more so in her mind than in real words. "Thank you."

The next thing she knew, the orb darted for the gap in the door and sped out of the house.

Hendrick thought he saw something streaking past him, but as good as his hearing was, he had learned not to trust his eyes.

CHAPTER FORTY

Boston, Massachusetts, USA

The Airbus touched down in North Street Park, across from the Rose Kennedy Greenway. From the air, it was easy to see where the bomb had detonated, given the surrounding mass of cop cars that encircled the red brick building of the Public Market.

When they had passed over, smoke was still filtering in faint ribbons. Rhone narrowed his eyes, looking down from the air. "It's not like the markets I saw as a kid. They were all outdoor, open-air. Stalls upon stalls of greengrocers, cheeses, toys, and wine."

Boston Public Market sold all of those things yet existed in the comfort of an old corner building, which took up almost the entire block. As they retreated a safe enough distance away to hopefully deflect unwanted attention from themselves, they saw that one side of the building was exposed, the brickwork shoved violently into the streets with the bomb's blast.

Inside was just a mess.

They jumped out of the chopper and onto soft grass. Jennie thanked Ashton and told him to wait in the chopper. He saluted. "Happy to," came his cheery reply.

Julia was less inclined to jump out of the helicopter. Already she had spent a considerable amount of time on her phone, looking for the answers to the riddle of the sarcophagus. A short while ago, she had determined the language to be some lost cousin of Latin, and she had managed to translate half of the words on the side of the stone box.

"Are you coming?" Jennie asked.

Julia waved a hand without looking. "Bomb sites and gunfire are more your thing. I'll keep working on this." Her eyes widened as her screen went black. "Shit! Ashton, don't suppose you have a power cable, do you?"

Ashton fished into a compartment underneath a panel of dials and pulled out a flat black box with a wire sticking out. "Mobile charging unit. Not sure how much juice is left in there. Worth a shot."

Jennie rolled her eyes. "We'll leave you both to it."

"And hands off," Rhone added with a smirk. "Julia's promised to Roman. You don't want to piss that guy off."

Julia glared at Rhone.

They crossed over the Greenway and waited out of sight from the market building. Cop cars encircled the front of the building and the road was closed to pedestrian and vehicular traffic.

Jennie adjusted her earpiece and checked she was tuned in with Rhone. He would act as a guard while the specters explored the site, hopefully undetected.

"Call it in if you see anything suspect," Jennie instructed.

Rhone grinned. "You act like I've never done this before."

Jennie latched onto Baxter, Carolyn, and Sandra and turned spectral. Her spectral power cells activated and filled with power. Jennie still hadn't gotten used to that sensation, it was as though she had been injected with additional adrenaline. Each step was like she was being given assistance. It was effortless, powerful.

They walked through cop cars, passing through a number of cops who shivered but blamed it on the night's chill. They passed through the threshold and took in the extent of the damage.

Stalls had been reduced to tatters of canvas and metal frames. The stairwell no longer supported a passage to the balconies. There was a lingering smell of food items, and the floor was littered with debris everywhere they looked.

Jennie guided the specters onward, using the evidence before them to track the location of the bomb. It wasn't too difficult to find, given that a group of two men and two women were gathered around a section of blackened ground where a crater had been blown into the floor.

The younger woman placed her hands on her hips and shook her head. She wore a dark blue uniform, her hair tied back in a severe ponytail. "A fresh-meat salesman? Why would someone selling meat want to destroy himself and his business, as well as his competitors around him?"

"Why does anyone do anything like this?" one of the men replied. "Could be a number of reasons. We'll have to examine all the possibilities here."

"Like what?" the other woman asked. Jennie instantly recognized her for the trainee she was.

The second man picked up a piece of metallic shrapnel, its edges razor sharp from the explosion. "Mental health issues, relationship worries, competitor envy, possibly even entry into an extremist terrorist organization. With the other cities suffering casualties like this, that's where I'm placing my bet. It seems too coincidental to be a one-off scenario. This shit was planned."

No kidding, Jennie thought.

They stood behind them and listened for a short while but gleaned nothing of note. Jennie passed through them, examining the evidence herself. There was more at stake. Given that Sturgeon and the SIS were already on her for killing their primary suspect, she needed to find something tangible among the debris. Something that would get her back on the track to solving this damn riddle and helping get this over with.

I had to. He was a maniac. If he slipped through our net again, who knew what more he was capable of.

But that wasn't the whole truth, was it? The truth was that he had been inside her head. An invader in the only place where Jennie ever truly felt safe. Attacking her thoughts and rifling through her memories. That kind of damage was worse than anything physical for her.

Besides, he had passed on the baton, hadn't he? He had introduced a new Dragon...somewhere. What use could he have been? Even under interrogation, Jennie doubted he would yield anything useful. A short week in the spectral world, and already he was happy to die.

A claymore mine had been the device used to cause such destruction. There was evidence of three of them set up in different directions to maximize the blast radius. Jennie brushed her finger over the lettering on a shard of metal casing and sighed.

Why are people so determined to cause destruction? That was a question she'd never know the answer to.

"Anything?" Jennie asked.

Carolyn and Baxter were spread out in different directions. Once more they were turning up empty-handed. They could piece together the claymore, perhaps. Gather the serial numbers and track down the purchase history of the device. They could follow the cops and question the family of the owners of the market stall.

But all of that took time, and time was something Jennie knew they didn't have.

Something caught her eye, standing back against the wall of the upper level, a flash of white. Jennie turned to the specter, and he tensed. She stood up slowly, scared to spook him.

But it was too late.

The man took off at a sprint.

"Go!" Jennie shouted, catching the attention of Carolyn, Sandra, and Baxter. They had just enough time to see the specter disappearing around a corner before they kicked into action.

With the stairs blown out, they had to get creative. Jennie called for Carolyn to stay on the lower floor and cover the outside with Sandra, while Baxter caught up with her stride. As they ran, he picked her up with his muscular arms, swung her around, and sent her flying toward the balcony. Her fingertips clutched the guardrail, and she hauled herself over.

The specter was still in sight. She sprinted toward him, knowing that he'd likely have the advantage of knowing the layout of the building. Yet, she still had an ace up her sleeve.

Not yet. Let's do this amicably.

Jennie gained momentum and closed the gap. He made a sharp right, and Jennie countered by running through the walls at a forty-five-degree angle. Her spectral power cells enabled her to keep going, even though her connection to Baxter and Carolyn was waning.

She came out to an empty corridor. The entire left side of the walls was made of glass. Jennie focused her thoughts and felt for the specter, surprised by how strong the spectral signal was up here.

Either he's a really strong specter, or...

She didn't need to finish her thought. From a doorway at the end of the corridor came a group of half a dozen specters. The specter she had been chasing was among them, hidden at the back. Based on the apron that he wore, and the grease and bloodstains on the white of his linens, she gathered that he was the meat vendor who had triggered the explosion.

A woman with wide shoulders and a square jaw stepped out of the group. She had a buzz cut and held a spectral machete in her hand. She readied her stance, a sickening grin on her face.

"The infamous Rogue," the woman crooned, a note of admiration in her words. "I wondered how long it would be until we met. In all honesty, I thought you were nothing more than a fairy tale. A rumor muttered among the specters to scare us into obedience. It's nice to see some truth to the fable."

"You've heard of me?" Jennie asked, genuinely curious as to how far her legend had spread across the US. It had been hit and miss, so far. Those in the populated areas of spectral activity had some kind of inkling, but there were still a great many who hadn't heard of her.

The woman gave a curt nod. "The Paranormal Court told us about your powers when they tried to tame Massachusetts. Their venture didn't go very far, but your name did stick. I'm not sure how much of your legend I believe, though. You know that rumor is more powerful than fiction."

Jennie slowed her breathing and calmed herself. Five against one.

Six, if the butcher got involved. Not the greatest odds, but she had taken worse.

Jennie's hand moved to her guns.

"Oh, no." The woman laughed. "No firearms. That's cheating. I want to see what you're capable of without long-range weapons."

Jennie didn't often play to those who tried to test her ego, but in that situation, she felt charitable. As her first encounter with specters in a strange state, it would pay dividends to provide a show that the specters could tell the tale of to their peers.

Jennie drew both guns, then tossed them lazily aside. "Fine. Have it your way."

The woman grinned. The other specters drew their makeshift weapons. One had a table leg, another a switchblade, and one held what looked like a roughly hewn edge of a tin can attached to a length of copper wire.

Jennie made the first step toward the group. They readied themselves for the attack. As she neared them, she sent out her spectral feelers. Her cells automatically began to fill as Jennie studied their abilities while trying not to raise the alarm.

One of the specters had increased strength. That could be useful.

Another had slightly increased speed. Another bonus.

The woman leered and came at her at a full sprint, raising her machete high for the swing. Jennie easily sidestepped the blow and swung around to the woman's side. She shoved her through the corridor wall and out of sight.

The others took that as their cue to attack. Jennie didn't shy away, throwing herself among the fray and working through the group. The sharpened metal whistled through the air toward her, and she narrowly avoided its blade. A fist knocked her shoulder and sent her off-balance, but she countered by grabbing a fistful of one specter's shirt and pulling herself up. She used the momentum to toss him at the wall where he, too, disappeared.

Jennie blocked a punch and returned with a kick. She ducked the table leg and grabbed the base of the instrument. Freeing the specter of his weapon, she pummeled his head and threw the table leg away.

It skittered across the floor and melted through the window, falling to the street below. Carolyn and Sandra saw this and looked up at the window with curiosity.

The butcher remained behind the group fighting, watching with grim fascination. Jennie would get to him later.

A kick caught her behind the knee. Jennie dropped to one knee and latched onto a specter just before her switchblade reached her. The specter froze, her face a mask of disbelief. Jennie growled and threw her hands out, forcing the specter away from her in the same direction as the table leg.

The specter cried out in frustration, her body unable to move as she disappeared from the window. Sandra and Carolyn finally had someone to work on.

Jennie rose to her feet and blocked a series of punches and kicks. She returned with her own jabs, toying with the specters while they tried to take her down. Their skills were credible, and a few blows caught her off-guard, but after a number of kicks to one of the specter's thighs, she heard the satisfying crunch of a bone breaking.

There was no time to celebrate. The lead woman returned through the wall, face like thunder. "Stand aside," she bellowed as she sprinted at Jennie.

Jennie latched onto the two specters who had shown an increase in their abilities. Their power flowed through her and increased her speed and strength, though only slightly. It was enough to avoid the singing blade as the woman attempted to carve her in two. On the backswing, Jennie was one step ahead. She flung her body back, landing on her hands as the blade passed inches above where her face had been.

Jennie affirmed her grip on the ground and kicked at the woman's knee. It was a good strike, but it wasn't enough. The woman was determined. She struck at the ground, barely missing Jennie as she completed her maneuver and rolled out of the way.

Jennie pushed herself to her feet and ran at the woman.

The butcher stepped out of the way as Jennie leaped and threw the woman out of the window. She held her waist, both of them plummeting toward the tarmac. They landed with a sickening crunch, though Jennie used the woman as a crash mat.

The woman yelled in pain. Carolyn and Sandra, who had already disarmed and disabled the man Jennie had tossed from the window, came inside and helped her restrain the woman. Jennie relieved the woman of her machete and held her down with her boot heel.

"You said no weapons," Jennie reprimanded.

The woman gurgled. "I said no firearms."

Jennie grinned. "Cheeky. I like it. Girls, keep her restrained, I'm going to need to jump back to collect my things."

As she finished speaking, Baxter appeared from the lower floor of the building, eyes wide at the chaos. "What the hell happened? I lost you guys."

"Later," Jennie replied. "Boost me."

Baxter looked up at the window. "Might be a little too late."

The remaining enemies gathered at the ledge. The man who had been thrown through the wall stared at them, Jennie's weapons raised in his hands.

"Let her go," the man commanded. "It's over."

Jennie turned to Carolyn. "Together?"

Carolyn smiled. "Sure."

Before the group knew what was happening, Carolyn extended her arms, and the weapons flew through the air and landed safely in her fingers. The next moment, Jennie latched onto the remaining specters and *pulled* them, sending them crashing to the ground. The only remaining specter was the butcher, who she latched onto and guided him softly out the window and onto the ground.

"Sandra, hold the others," Jennie instructed.

Sandra obeyed, crossing over to the confused specters who froze instantly under her power.

Jennie motioned the butcher over. She released her hold over him, identifying him as someone she needn't worry about. If he was truly dangerous, he would have joined in with the fight.

"Do you know this woman?" she asked as he cautiously approached.

He shook his head. "I've never seen her before today." His brows knitted together. "What is happening to me? What in the name of Sam Hill is going on? Am I dreaming?"

Jennie recognized the confusion of a man freshly born into specterdom. "I'm sorry to say this is no dream. You are dead. My presumption is that you died at the hands of those morons. Am I right?"

The woman on the ground gurgled through her grin.

Jennie kicked her in the face in an attempt to wipe the smile off of it. She turned back to the man. "Your name?"

"Sam," the man replied. "Please tell me you're kidding. This is all some kind of terrible nightmare. I can't be dead. I have a family. Children."

Carolyn huffed. "Join the club."

Baxter raised an eyebrow.

"Okay, maybe not kids," Carolyn clarified. "But I had a fiancé and my dogs, okay?"

Jennie crossed to the man and placed a hand on his arm. "I'm sorry. This is real, and I'll be sure to get someone to explain everything to you so that you can work out your options and be properly inducted into spectral life. For now, we've got bigger fish to fry. These fuckwits blew up your business, destroyed a landmark, and killed a bunch of civilians in the process. I'm going to track down who did this, and we're going to bring the world to rights."

She returned her attention to the woman on the ground. "As for you, I've got a couple of very simple questions for you: who sent you, and what were you promised in return?"

The woman held her gaze and was silent. Jennie was wondering whether she was going to have to force her to speak when she finally replied. "You'll have to kill me first."

Jennie pinched her eyes. "Fine. That can be arranged."

She snapped her fingers and indicated a swap with Sandra. While Jennie held the others pinned down, Sandra knelt by the woman's side. She closed her eyes and placed her hands on the woman's chest.

White light emanated from her center and the woman's eyes grew wide.

She screamed, the heat of the exorcism coursing through her body. "Wait! Wait! I'll talk! Please!"

Sandra retracted her power and the white light disappeared. She swapped once more with Jennie.

Jennie knelt by the woman's side and stroked the hair away from her face. "Ready to talk now, sweetie?"

The woman's chest rose and fell as she panted and caught her breath. "How… Who the hell are you all?"

"We're the King's Court." Baxter grinned.

Carolyn added, "And you're under arrest."

Jennie chuckled. "Time to start squeaking, little mouse. My patience is running thin."

CHAPTER FORTY-ONE

<u>Richmond, Virginia, USA</u>

Tanya scratched her head, holding the door wide open with her other hand. "What do you mean, they just got better?"

She had been on her way downstairs to switch with Roman and Ula, checking the notifications on her cell phone, when she heard the two conduits deep in conversation further down the hallway.

The door was ajar. Roman and Ula stared inside at something she could not see. Tanya broke into a run, all thoughts of reprimanding Lupe for oversleeping when it was his turn to watch pushed from her mind as she arrived at the holding cell and saw what the pair were seeing.

The two women were sitting with knees to their chests against the far wall, not a note of malice in their confused eyes. The two animals that had attacked Roman and Triton the previous night were gone, leaving nothing behind but regular, unpossessed yoga students.

Ula shrugged.

Even Roman couldn't hide his surprise. "We opened the door to check on them both because they had been quiet for so long, and we found them like this."

The redhead woman rubbed her cheek. "What happened to us? Why is my face so sore?"

A flash of the previous night came to Tanya, Roman's hand pressing the woman's face onto the hard floor.

Ula looked to Tanya. "Do you want to take this one?"

Tanya entered the room, keeping a safe distance from the two women. "We were actually hoping you'd be able to help *us* with that." She explained to them what had happened at the yoga center and the journey they had taken to the quarry and the tunnels beneath. "What do you remember?"

The women looked at each other. The blonde shook her head, determined to remain silent.

"It's all a blur," the redhead answered. "One minute I was watching the Toya—that's the yoga instructor—the next thing I know, every-thing went dark. All I could see were shapes and patterns as though I was looking at a TV screen through murky water."

"I remember anger," the blonde woman added. "*I* felt angry. Angrier than I'd ever felt. I can't explain it, but it didn't feel like mine. It was like my body was tapped into someone else's emotions and…I couldn't control it."

"Yeah," the redhead agreed.

Tanya asked for their names, discovering that the redhead was called Lyla, and the blonde was called Krissie. She nudged them for more answers but could glean little more from them than they had already shared. Apparently, their entire experience was a mass of unknowns and anger.

"Are you going to let us out now?" Lyla asked, rubbing her throat. Her voice was cracked and her throat dry. "I just want to go home and see if my cat is okay."

Tanya glanced up at Roman, his face difficult to read. "We can't do that, I'm afraid. Not right now, anyway. You two have been through an ordeal, and we don't yet know that it's completely over. We could set you free, and the same thing could be triggered again. We don't know what's causing this, but we can prevent you from causing harm to others if you agree to stay."

We have some *idea*, Tanya thought, suddenly remembering the message from Julia she had received on her cell.

The women sighed but nodded their understanding.

"Can we at least have something to eat and drink?" Krissie asked. "I'm starving."

Ula fetched them each a couple of bottles of water. They sat with them while they ate their fill of snack bars and fruit. When they were finished, Ula made sure to remove any packaging that could somehow be utilized as a weapon if the tides were to turn again.

Roman folded his arms. "Better?"

The women nodded.

"Good." He turned and made to close the door, leaving them alone in the room once more.

"Wait!" Lyla cried.

Roman paused.

Lyla fixed her gaze on her knees, wilting under his stare. "Can't we at least sit out there with you? You can watch over us. It's just…being kept in this room feels like we're in prison."

Roman considered this. "Not yet. We'll give it twelve hours and monitor your situation. If you like, Ula can keep the door open and watch over you two, so it feels less enclosed. If either of you tries anything stupid, your privileges will be immediately taken away."

Ula, added a softer note to the conversation, added, "We're here to help you. You aren't trapped, okay? You're with the good guys. We want to fix this as much as you do."

Roman and Tanya exited the room and left them to it.

They ended up downstairs in the reception lounge, where they claimed sofas across from each other. Tanya immediately went to her phone while Roman launched into externalizing his thoughts.

"Something must have happened to expel the specters," he muttered. "I've never seen anything like it before, that specters can work their way out of those they possess. Not without some kind of encouragement, anyway. They know more than they're letting on, I'm sure of it. We have to worm out the rest of the information. They're our only key."

"Not the *only* key," Tanya replied, fascination etched on her face. "Julia's translated the sarcophagus. Listen to this: Here lies the Dreadnought Conqueror, Rathbourne Valerius. Gifted, cursed, loved, feared."

Roman raised an eyebrow. "The Dreadnought Conqueror? That's an impressive title if I've ever heard one."

Tanya waved a hand to hush Roman. "A day may come when the forgotten is lost to the past, and the future may know the terrible darkness that once plagued these lands. A scourge, proud and strong, a terrible curse once sealed, never to be broken open, unless darkness is what you seek to govern this land.

"Breaker of the lid, beware. What's done cannot be undone."

Tanya slowly turned to Roman. "That doesn't sound good."

"No," Roman replied. "No, it does not."

Boston, Massachusetts, USA

The lower floor of the skyscraper was a bank. The next few floors were office space, but the remaining twenty floors were given over to apartments.

The entrance to the apartments was through a shaded alley at the side of the building. Jennie, Rhone, Baxter, Carolyn, and Sandra gathered around the door. The woman with the machete, Terri, had been dragged along for the ride, and Sam the butcher had joined them, too.

"Up there?" Jennie asked.

The woman hesitated in her answer. She glanced at Sandra, then sighed. "Yes."

"How far?" Baxter queried.

Terri looked up. "Floor thirteen."

Jennie counted the floors. Thirteen wasn't hard to identify, it was the only floor where all of the windows were closed and dark.

"It looks abandoned," Carolyn noted. "Why would an entire floor of a residency be closed off? Is that where they keep all the vampires?"

Although she was joking, it wasn't met with laughter.

Jennie shaded her eyes. "Some skyscrapers discount the thirteenth floor and pretend it doesn't exist. I've seen it often in hotels, but rarely in apartment blocks."

"Why the thirteenth floor?" Sandra asked.

"Unlucky thirteen," Baxter answered. "For the superstitious among you."

Jennie continued. "It is said that the dead and the cursed inhabit floor thirteen of any building. In holiday destinations, some elevators skip from twelve to fourteen on their button panels. Some hotels have thrown away the keys to the doors on floor thirteen. Others schedule cleaners once a month just to keep away the dust, dirt, and mold, but even then the cleaners are paid a premium. Many are only hired the once, unable to return because of the things they've seen."

"A safe haven for specters, then," Carolyn commented.

"Arguably a self-fulfilling superstition," Jennie offered. "If you build it, they will come. There are still things and forces in this world we don't yet understand. Let's hope that this building is different."

Baxter melted through the door and unlocked it from the inside. They passed through a quiet reception area, barely registering the attention of the concierge, who was reading the latest Grisham novel.

Baxter opened the security door to the stairwell, and they made their way upstairs.

They knew when they had reached the thirteenth floor when they came across the peeling paint on the wooden door. Where the other entryways had been immaculately painted and kept, this door had been neglected. There was no keypad panel like the other doors, either, just a typical handle and key combination.

"You'll have to wait outside," Jennie told Rhone.

"Lookout again?" Rhone protested.

Jennie laughed. "I'm kidding. We wouldn't leave you. Come on, we'll open it from the inside for you."

The door creaked open, and they found themselves in a quiet corridor. The air was cooler here. A series of yellowed doors that might once have been painted white stood quiet and forgotten.

Jennie led the way, tiptoeing quietly along the dusty carpet. At the end of the corridor, they reached a final door, and she heard people talking inside the room.

"Specters or mortals?" Carolyn asked, exaggerating her lip movements to counter for her quiet tone.

Jennie closed her eyes and reached out to feel the spectral energy coming from the room. "Both."

Jennie booted near the handle and sent the door swinging in. There was no delicacy with this entry. Rhone was right behind her, ready to go,

They charged into the room, guns trained and poised on the people within. They were in a large living room, clearly in a space that would once have been imagined to be a luxury suite. Two large sofas filled the center of the room, and a group of specters and mortals jumped to their feet at their approach.

There were over a dozen, at a quick count. Jennie was hyper-aware that the mortals looking would only see Rhone and herself. Two against a dozen gave them the impression they had great odds.

Hopefully, the specters would tell their leader otherwise.

The leader was distinguishable from the others as she was the only one who remained sitting. She wore SI glasses. She calmed her entourage with a gentle word and leaned slightly to the left to get a better view of the specter they had captured.

"Terri?" the woman crooned. "You disappoint me. Betraying your own kind like that, and for what? What did they offer you?"

Terri remained silent.

"How many of them are there?" a small man with a bald head asked. "They have specters?"

"A handful," the woman replied.

"We can take them," another added.

The woman shook her head, eyes fixed on Jennie. "Not if what they say about that woman is true. Genevieve King, I believe?"

"Call me Rogue," Jennie replied. "Only my friends have the right to call me by my true name."

"Maybe we can be friends someday?" the woman replied. She pushed herself free of her chair and approached Jennie. She extended a hand, leaving a six-foot gap between them. "Cassie Ferriss. I've heard a lot about you."

Jennie remained where she was. "I've heard nothing about you. I've heard your father was a big deal, though."

Cassie's composed expression faltered, but only for a moment. "Yes, it's difficult walking in Daddy's footsteps, but my men make it all the easier. He was a bold character, which is something that I've never been." She studied Jennie through narrowed eyes and lowered her hand. "Tell me, is it true you have lived beyond the ages?"

"If you're asking if I'm immortal, I don't know," Jennie replied. "People have tried to test that theory, and every single one of them now lives in the void. If you're asking if I age, the answer is the same. I don't know. What I do know is that I've lived long enough to be able to solve problems like the ones that you've been causing, and I'm growing tired of playing nice."

The woman placed a hand on her chest, eyebrows raised in faux surprise. "You call this playing nice? You barged into our abode without permission, and you've no doubt slain my specters. Well, except for the traitor standing behind you."

Terri shrunk out of sight.

One of the men to Cassie's right made a move toward his waist. Jennie aimed her pistol at him and fired a warning shot that grazed the skin of the top of his hand. "Hands where I can see them, slim."

"Slim?" Carolyn whispered to Baxter. "He's larger than you are."

Baxter elbowed her playfully.

"Semantics aside," Jennie continued, hiding her smile, "are you going to be the one to tell me the master plan behind all this destruction, or are you going to be a footnote in the victory speech I write when this is all done? I'm planning on thanking the dead for their contributions."

Cassie chewed her lip. The men grew restless around her. She lowered her eyes to the floor, then sighed and met Jennie's again. "Very well. Let's see what you're capable of."

She whipped her hand into her pocket and drew a small pistol. In a flash, she fired three shots at Jennie and the others.

Jennie threw herself aside, shoving Rhone out from the line of fire. The bullets passed through the specters, which they were all thankful for, considering they weren't spectrally imbued.

Finding the wall and righting themselves, Jennie put her guns to work. She fired four times before they even managed to draw their weapons, each bullet taking down one of the enemies.

Cassie threw herself behind the men and women guarding her and ran for a door at the back of the room. The TV smashed. Lights went out. The specters engaged in their own battle as Jennie and Rhone focused on the mortals.

Rhone ducked through the door to the hall and used the wall for cover. Jennie dived forward and found a space beneath the kitchenette's countertop. She fired three more bullets and caught three individuals in their shins.

A bullet whizzed by her and smashed the window. Somewhere nearby, Baxter and Carolyn fought with the specters, Baxter's wrench reverberating as the metal met bone. Sandra dragged Terri into the corridor to keep her safe from harm and under control.

Jennie stood up during a brief pause in fire, risking exposure for a glance at the remaining gunmen. Someone was waiting, and they managed to hit just above the side of her waist. Her leg still hurt from the machete wound she'd received previously, but she powered through, eliminating the man who had dared to attack.

Only three mortals were left. Jennie hated killing mercilessly, but she needed to get to Cassie. She couldn't imagine how there would be, but she didn't want the woman to take an escape route to the outside world and run away.

Jennie fired the Big Bitch. The bullets tore through one man's gut and carried on through to the next. Red blood splatted the wall, and a chunk of plaster exploded from the impact.

The final man lined up his shot, aiming straight at Jennie's face. Before he could fire, Rhone shot with his pistol and knocked the gun out of the man's hand. He clutched the bloody mess where his fingers had been and charged at Jennie.

She was ready. She screwed her hands into fists and delivered a right hook to his jaw. The man's eyes rolled back in his head, and he corkscrewed to the floor and lay still.

"Jennie, come on," Rhone called.

They passed through the specters fighting hand-to-hand, heading for the door at the back of the room. It opened into a large master bedroom, complete with a four-poster bed. Large glass windows looked out onto Boston below.

Cassie was sitting cross-legged in the center of the bed. Her face was composed and neutral. Her hands were already bound in handcuffs. She looked at them expectantly.

Rhone turned to Jennie. "What trickery is this?"

"No trickery," Cassie replied. "I knew your skills were unmatchable, but I wanted to see it for myself. The way Zhao described your powers, it seemed unreal. If there was a chance I could escape you, I would have taken it. As it is, I know I stand no chance."

Jennie furrowed her brow. "What are you saying?"

Cassie's eyes dropped to the bed in shame. "My father left a legacy that I could never hope to bear. His name is legend, my name is the footnote you described earlier. Yet, I tried and pushed to become something that I never truly wanted to be." She glanced out the window toward where the collapsed roof of the market could be viewed. "I've done horrible things, I know that. I never felt like I had a choice. It was never an option to do something else."

She turned back to Jennie, eyes watery and pleading. "But you... You are my only chance at redemption. If I had ever gone straight, all of my father's old followers would come for me. But under your protection, maybe I can live to see another day..."

Jennie considered this, eyes deep in thought. They certainly needed help, and having someone who knew as much as Cassie did about the Seven wouldn't be a bad thing.

"Please?" Cassie begged.

Jennie made her decision. She advanced on Cassie and offered the hand that had been neglected before. Cassie took it, both her hands reaching out due to the cuffs. When their hands connected, Jennie pulled Cassie toward her roughly. "Any funny business and I will not hesitate to destroy you. You are on probation. One wrong turn, and I send you out for the wolves to devour, you got that?"

Cassie nodded eagerly. Rhone moved to unlock the cuffs, the key laying neatly on the pillow.

Jennie held him back. "No. Leave those on. This may still be a trap."

Yet, something inside her told her that it wasn't. Jennie had learned to read honesty in people's eyes, and Cassie had meant every word she'd said.

CHAPTER FORTY-TWO

Taylor Bennett sat on her balcony and watched the sunrise.

It was a cloudier morning than they'd had for a while. Tufts of white smattered the skyline, exploding into crayon smudges of pastels as the city was thrown into long shadows.

This view was something that she had earned after nearly four decades of climbing the ranks through the military. She had bought the six-bed estate with a significant portion of her pension, and she spent most of her mornings watching over the city that she had fought so hard to defend.

Her wife was off in Austin, Texas, busying herself with conferences and cramped meeting rooms. It made the house feel empty on occasion, but she was glad for her. At nearly twenty years her junior, Wendy still had a whole life ahead of her. How she kept herself busy was none of Taylor's business.

Taylor enjoyed the quiet. She enjoyed the peace. Over the last few weeks, the stillness of the morning had been disturbed by the growling of machinery and drilling, but for some reason, that wasn't happening today. Birds were singing, the streets were quiet, and all of the disruptions she had read about on her social media feed the day before had died down.

Whatever happened in the community center was a mystery. She had limited ideas on how the glass had been smashed across several floors without anyone witnessing the act. In her experience of planned attacks, she might have attributed the damage to a high-frequency sonar disruptor if this were a terrorist attack. Or perhaps some kids had coordinated their efforts to break all the windows at once. The papers and media outlets were at a loss to find the truth. No projectiles had been found, and no one there had witnessed anyone hurling rocks.

It was a mystery.

Taylor loathed mysteries. She liked cold, hard facts. Getting to the bottom of a mystery was like savoring the final melted droplets of a triple fudge sundae. Delicious, but the brain freeze along the way was painful and discomforting.

In the office behind her, a wall was lined with weaponry she had accumulated over the years. She still cleaned the items regularly, but she hadn't fired a gun in nearly half a decade. She missed the electric thrill of the kickback as she pulled the trigger but had to admit that blowing holes in people for a living grew tiresome after a while. There was no pleasure in destruction, and only the affirmation that justice was its own reward allowed her to sleep at night. It was an exchange, snuff out one life in order to save hundreds more.

Taylor drank from a lukewarm cup of tea, then stretched her arms as the sun winked over the far reaches of the city. Directly above her, the moon refused to make way for its cousin.

Over the far reaches of the city, something shifted. A shadow, it looked like. Unlike the other shadows, this one was moving swiftly, disappearing into long dark stretches and appearing for half a second before vanishing again.

Taylor rubbed her tired eyes. She hadn't slept well last night and worried that her migraines might return. Often an oncoming episode would be signified by dark patterns taking over her sight, swimming like minuscule fish in the liquid of her eyes.

But, no. The shadow was definitely still there, in the streets. She tilted her head and leaned forward, tracking its progress as it broke between shadows and grew larger on its approach.

A disquiet settled in her stomach. She looked at the sky, wondering if some silent machine was passing overhead. Not that that was possible, she knew, with the exception of hot air balloons and paragliders. But this shadow was moving too fast for that, surely.

The shadow reached Neverdon Crescent and that strange feeling grew stronger. Something in Taylor's gut told her to prepare for the foreign invader, the unexplainable shadow streaking toward *her*.

The shadow took shape, becoming a ball of darkness with a smoky tail following in its wake.

What the hell?

Taylor rose from her chair. She turned, sliding the glass doors open to enter her study. She grabbed a pistol from the wall and rooted through the drawers for some ammunition. She was organized, the drawers were divided into neat portions where bullets and magazines were stored. Still, she hadn't expected to reach in on such short notice, and it had been a while since she set the system up.

She could hear the shadow approaching, a faint whoosh as though a jet plane was nearing. She managed to secure a magazine and lock it into the chamber before she cocked the pistol and aimed it at the open balcony door.

The shadow descended upon her, arriving as a smoky orb at least six feet in diameter. It raised itself over the balcony and crashed toward her. Glass shattered. Taylor was able to fire one shot into the belly of the beast before it consumed her.

She was thrown backward. Her body hit the wall. Her grip remained tight on the pistol as she slid to the floor.

She remained there for a few minutes, surprised by how little pain she felt. Warm liquid leaked from her ears, but she was okay. By God, she was okay.

Taylor pushed herself to her feet and cracked her neck. Her eyes roamed the weapons decorating the walls. A sudden desire to take each and every firearm and load them, head out into the streets, and put them all into action overwhelmed her. A primal desire to kill and destroy consumed every fiber of her being.

She felt young. Younger than she'd felt in years. The creaks and aches of her bones and joints had vanished, and the strength…Oh, the strength she felt, as though there were two people inside of her.

Taylor laughed, a deep, throaty, cackling laugh. Somewhere outside, someone shouted up to her balcony, drawn by the shattering of glass. "Hey! Are you okay? Hello?"

Taylor's head spun so suddenly it should have made her dizzy. Her eyes were drawn to the shattered glass doors.

"Hello?" the woman repeated. "Do you need me to come in?"

Taylor paused, that boiling feeling of superiority roiling in her gut. From out of nowhere, a voice spoke in her head.

Well, aren't you going to answer her?

Taylor nodded and strode to the balcony. She rested one hand on the guardrail and stared down, her brow furrowed, her eyes nothing more than milky orbs.

"Oh." The woman sighed. "I'm glad you're okay. Do you need help? What happened—"

Taylor took a single shot, the bullet finding its target dead center in the woman's forehead. The woman fell to the ground. Nearby, faces peered from curtains to look for the source of the disturbance.

Taylor lowered the gun, hiding it from sight. The voice inside her head, a masculine voice filled with years of experience and wonder, chuckled.

Good girl. Come now. There's much work to be done.

Taylor didn't argue. She couldn't. How could she argue with a sentiment that made so much sense?

Lupe followed Hendrick like a shadow, remaining only a couple of steps behind him, wherever he went.

The laboratory was coming together. Only when instructed did

Lupe leave Hendrick's side to collect equipment or to tidy the mess the old man had left behind.

He was entrancing to watch. Each movement, each contribution to a formula was measured and precise. Lupe had imagined that Hendrick would have some kind of recipe book, or at least need to refer to notes to double-check his working on occasion, but not until then had he realized just how much knowledge was held deep inside his brain.

Lupe loved it. He didn't think he would, but he did. He asked questions, he listened closely, making notes on a yellow legal pad as he went until Hendrick reprimanded him for writing down his secrets and told him to hold the information in his head.

"If I wanted to create a public cookbook, I'd be able to write it down myself," Hendrick scolded as he dropped three droplets of silvery solution into a metallic box with thick glass windows and filled with a thin green liquid. "These are *secrets*, Lupe, passed down from generation to generation. You soak it all up in that big brain of yours, or I find a new apprentice. Understand?"

Lupe had no clue what they were working on, but Hendrick certainly did. The moment the silvery solution dropped into the box, rather than gathering at the bottom, or sinking to the top, it took on a life of its own, swimming around the mass of green liquid like a fish. After a few seconds, the silver liquid coalesced, concentrating on the left-hand side of the box.

Hendrick spun the box, but the silver remained in the same location each time.

"Perfect," he exclaimed, his face creasing as he smiled.

"What is it?" Lupe asked.

Hendrick ignored him and handed Lupe the box. "You'll see soon enough."

The liquid acted even more strangely when they met the others in the reception room. Twelve hours had passed since they had discovered that the darkness invading the two women was gone, and they'd joined the rest of the group on the couches as they stuffed their faces and drank greedily from coffee cups.

Heads turned when Lupe and Hendrick entered the room. Lupe did as instructed and placed the box in the center of the table where the silver liquid inside started spinning in slow circles around the edge of the box.

The two women were sitting between Roman and Triton. They were still under guard, but the threat of another possessive episode had clearly passed. Light poured in from the large windows and brought the sun's warmth into the house. Jiao was nowhere to be seen.

Tanya glanced at the others around the room as silence followed the box's placement. "Am I going to have to be the one to ask this?" When no one replied, she added, "What the heck is that?"

Lupe looked to Hendrick expectantly. While there was plenty of space to sit, Hendrick chose to stand, fingers laced behind his back. "Your compass."

The silver liquid spun to the wall nearest the window as the poltergeists continued their never-ending race outside of the house and sped past. The liquid followed their trajectory, slowly moving in circles around the box. Each time the McFarlene brothers appeared at the glass, the fish met them in its box by the closest side.

"A spectral compass?" Feng Mian asked. "How is that possible?"

Once again, Lupe turned to Hendrick for help.

Hendrick cleared his throat. "Simple, really. From the distilled essences of specters remaining from the concentration we took in the Umbra's HQ, I've been able to slowly sift through the solution and separate the parts of the specters' remaining organic matter. I was able to concentrate the silver solution further, giving us access to the abilities the specters once possessed."

He lifted the box. "In this case, this specter who provided this energy once had an affinity of spectral detection. Something both Jennie and Sandra have shown an aptitude in. I know nothing about the specters and their stories, but their essences are biologically different and can be used in different ways."

Ula raised a hand. "Hold on, hold on. Are you saying that specters are organic? I thought only mortals had biological makeups?"

A grin appeared on Hendrick's face. "Astute observation. While you're right, specters cannot be technically labeled as organic matter, they do have an energy signature. There is yet to be a name attributed to the state of matter that composes a specter, but since they exist in this world and since there is a way to physically touch, see, and hear specters—evidenced through conduits and the latest technologies—we cannot rule out the fact that there is something biological and organic in their makeup."

"So, science lesson aside, what are we looking at here?" Tanya asked.

Hendrick scratched the bridge of his nose, then returned his hand behind his back. His gaze fixed on the swimming silver liquid. "I've told you—a compass. The essence of the specter contained within the essence will migrate toward the side of the box that is closest to spectral energy. At the moment, it is tracking the McFarlene brothers, but take it out into the city and..."

"It'll find the Dreadnought," Triton finished for him. "Hendrick, that's genius."

Ula nodded her appreciation. "It's probably a good idea if we have no specters with us when we go. Good timing that Sandra is with Jennie in NYC, eh?"

Tanya's face hardened. "They've moved on to Boston. Jennie updated me this morning."

"Damn, sounds like they're on a trail of their own," Ula replied.

Tanya changed the subject, returning their attention to the compass. "So you're saying we can take this into the city and it'll detect spectral activity? How will we know if we're tracking the..." her eyes found Ula's "Dreadnought? Surely other specters will be detected too? We could be on a wild goose chase for days."

Hendrick opened his mouth to reply, but Lupe cut in first. "If this Dreadnought is powerful enough to take over bodies and create an army of possessed specters, then he must be strong. His spectral signature will be much greater than any of the other riff-raff we find in this town." He turned uncertainly to Hendrick. "Right?"

Hendrick gave a curt nod.

Tanya clapped her hands together. "Okay, then. Detect the enemy, take him down. We can do that, right?"

Ula, Roman, and Triton nodded in agreement, unconsciously moving their hands toward their weapons.

Lyla and Krissie exchanged a glance.

"What was that?" Feng Mian asked, catching the exchange.

Lyla gave a half-hearted shrug. "How are you going to take him down? I mean, I'm still totally confused by what the hell is happening here, but there is clearly something at play that is not of this world. First, we find out that specters are real, and now you're going after some kind of…what? Demon? What is this thing?"

"We don't know," Tanya answered simply. "But what we do know is that if it carries on as it has been, then soon the town could be overrun, possessed like you two were only last night."

"Can you all do that head thing?" Krissie asked, looking around the room at each of them in turn.

Tanya raised an eyebrow. "What head thing?"

Lyla's eyes lit up as a sudden memory came back to her. "That's right! Your friend. That small one with dark hair. She helped us. She did something." She looked at Krissie. "Right?"

Krissie nodded.

Tanya studied the pair. "What do you mean 'did something?' Who?"

"We don't know her name," Lyla replied. "She's short. Asian-looking. I've not seen her since."

Roman's attention had been caught. "Jiao?"

Once again, Lyla shrugged. "Sure?"

"What did she do to you?" Tanya asked.

Krissie put her hand to her forehead. "She just touched us, like this, I think. It's all a blur, but I remember it as if coming out of a dream. She touched our heads, and somehow the darkness was lifted."

Tanya's brow was creased in confused thought. She met Feng Mian's eyes. "How is that even possible?"

Feng Mian stared levelly back. "I don't know."

It was then that they noticed Jiao wasn't sitting with them. "Where is she?" Tanya asked.

"Last I saw her, she was upstairs," Ula replied. "In her bedroom. Haven't seen her since."

Tanya's eyes widened. Without another word, she leapt from the couch and ran up the stairs.

She wasted no time with pleasantries and barged into Jiao's room. While not the largest suite in the manor, there was still plenty of room for Jiao to be swallowed by the size of it. If it hadn't been for Jiao speaking on her cell to someone in the far corner, Tanya wouldn't have noticed her at all.

Jiao's head whipped around. She hung up the phone instantly and pocketed it. "Tanya? Don't you know better than to barge in?"

Tanya crossed the room and sat on the edge of the bed near Jiao's chair. In the doorway, Roman and Ula gathered. "*You* healed those girls?"

Jiao's brows knitted together. "I'm sorry?"

Tanya shook her head. "Don't play dumb with me, those two girls just told us. You drove the specters out of their bodies? How did you do that? Why didn't you tell us?"

Jiao stared down at her feet, her face a mask of innocence. "It was just something I wanted to try. A trick I picked up while working for the Dragon. He tried possession on a few occasions, and I prepared myself, terrified I might be next."

Tanya sat across from Jiao and took her hands. "Jiao, it worries me that you'd hide something like that from us. Particularly now, when we're battling an enemy whose undoing might require it." She gave a reassuring smile. "You freed those women, okay? You saved them. You *helped* us. You're not with the Dragon anymore, so you can let go of any worries or doubts you might have. Be honest with us. We've been honest with you."

Jiao looked up, her eyes covered in a wet sheen. "I'm sorry."

Tanya let out a small laugh. "Don't be. Just show us how you did it, and we can start helping the others we might find. Is it easy to do?"

Jiao shrugged. "Somewhat. It involves some precise drawing and an incantation. I can teach you."

Tanya studied her features. Her lips were impossibly red, her eyes dark amber. It was no wonder Feng Mian was attracted to her. "I mean it, Jiao. You are safe here. The worst is behind you. Just trust us, okay? You don't have to hide anything from us."

Jiao nodded and pawed away a stray tear. "Thank you."

Tanya led Jiao out of the room and down toward the others. They passed Roman and Ula and disappeared down the stairs, and the two conduits waited until they were out of earshot.

Ula let out a deep breath. "I know what you're thinking."

Roman's face was set. "I know."

The question went unsaid between them, but it was something that neither of them would forget as easily as Tanya.

Who was Jiao on the phone to?

CHAPTER FORTY-THREE

Somewhere over Philadelphia, USA

A multitude of information was coming in thick and fast. Updates attacked Jennie's cell phone, detailing the latest from the searches occurring in all the major cities that had been attacked in Zhao's operation.

She had managed to pull information from Hartford, albeit reluctantly. Lionus was being less than cooperative, but a sharply worded reminder regarding the involvement of Kurt Rogers made him spill the beans. Sturgeon, Tiptry, Clark, and their men had yet to find anything of note in Pennsylvania and New Jersey, although they too had stumbled across specters who may be of use in the investigations.

Cassie Ferries was sitting across from Jennie, studying her through narrowed eyes. Jennie still didn't entirely trust Cassie, but she had given them enough information to proceed toward Baltimore. Jennie had already called ahead to Daggro to warn her of their movements and to share the information they'd received from Cassie earlier that day.

"The plan didn't fully go into action," Cassie had told them when they found a room clear of dead bodies and started their line of questioning. "Zhao wanted six other explosions simultaneously. That was the plan."

"But there were only four," Baxter declared.

"Exactly." Cassie adjusted in her seat and wiped sweating palms on her trousers. "Two of them failed. One was supposed to go off in Baltimore, and another in Washington."

"Washington!" Rhone exclaimed. "Not the White House?"

Cassie shook her head. "No, that would have been too high profile, even for specters to break into and plant the device. Zhao knew that there were links in Washington with you, Jennie, and the SIA, given his containment. He looked for something a little less in the public eye, but with enough impact. Y'know, like the Public Market in Boston."

"Where was the target?" Jennie nudged.

Cassie's eyes met hers. "The JFK Performing Arts Center."

"Jesus," Julia muttered. "That's a pretty big deal."

"They're all big deals," Jennie retorted. "So, what happened? Why didn't Washington or Baltimore happen while the other four did?"

Cassie glanced at Terri, the specter she had called a traitor for helping Jennie. Everyone in the Airbus could sense the irony of Cassie's sudden switch in loyalties. "Cowley, who was the guy stationed in Baltimore, got cold feet. He and his spectral assistants came across the SIA's outreach headquarters in Baltimore and worried they'd get found out too easily. They didn't have enough time to get things in place."

"Thank God for that," Rhone murmured. "Makes me thankful we diversified when we could. That's one thing we can thank the Umbra for."

Carolyn nodded in agreement.

"And Washington?" Jennie encouraged. "What about there? I notice that you don't seem so concerned about our nation's capital."

Cassie's eyes glazed over as a memory suddenly came to her. She took a moment before replying. "Ruben McAffey was sent to Washington, but he got more than cold feet. He was plotting to escape, to rebel. He wanted nothing more to do with Zhao or the seven. So, Zhao…"

Cassie went quiet. They waited patiently for her to continue. "Zhao sent a specter to kill him. He broke his neck live on our video feed. We all saw it, the way his head twisted to that unnatural angle. The next thing we knew, he was dead."

Jennie placed a hand on Cassie's knee, feeling compassion for her for the first time. "It's okay. It's over now." She waited a few moments before adding, "Do you know who it was? Surely with SI glasses, they would have seen the specter?"

Cassie shook her head. "The specter was invisible until he wasn't. Totally undetectable, until he *chose* to show himself. If creatures like that exist, how can the rest of us be safe?"

Jennie assured Cassie that as long as she stuck with them, she'd be safe. They had encountered these kinds of specters along their way, and the good news was they had survived each and every encounter.

Baxter shuffled in his chair, leaning closer to Cassie and Jennie. "What happened to Ruben after?"

Cassie raised an eyebrow. "What do you mean?"

"Well, dead things rise," Baxter explained. "What happened to his specter?"

Cassie's eyes widened. "I didn't even think of that!"

Jennie tried to soothe her. "I'm sure it's okay. Just because a man was killed by a specter, I don't believe his loyalties will change. He was a traitor to Zhao, he will remain as such."

"How can you be sure," Carolyn asked.

"Experience," Jennie replied. "Still, just to be safe, we'll alert Daggro and give her a heads up. She can send what agents remain to guard the performing arts center and keep an eye on Washington. From what you're saying, Cassie, Baltimore is our most pressing priority right now. Let's jump in the chopper and hash out the details on the way."

She had called Daggro, unsurprised by her surly replies to her questions. Daggro sounded almost unrecognizable, her voice a harsh scratch down the phone. As they drifted over Philadelphia, they were all deep in thought, wondering what would be awaiting them when they arrived in Baltimore. Hoping they wouldn't be too late.

An hour or so later, and Baltimore came into sight. They touched down in Patterson Park a little after midday, landing far enough away from where Craig was rumored to be that he wouldn't detect their arrival, but close enough that they could easily hail a cab and get to where they needed to go if the SIA didn't come through.

A group of SIA agents was waiting for them when they arrived. Jennie was surprised by this. She hopped out and greeted the lead agent, a man with tight curls of dark hair and a scar running across his chin.

"Agent Erik," the man announced, offering a hand. "It's an honor."

Jennie tried to detect sarcasm in that tone but found none.

"And you, former Agent Rhone," Erik added, shaking Rhone's hand. "I'm sorry to hear about your dismissal from the agency."

Rhone smirked. "It was a mutual agreement, let me assure you. I didn't want to work for a psychotic bitch, and Daggro was determined to be one."

Erik's face remained passive, but there was humor in his eyes. "While I can't speak ill of our superior, it is a damn shame that things ended that way. Some people can wind themselves up so tightly that they don't know how to undo what they've done. Time will achieve that for her, I'm sure."

Jennie decided that she liked this man, who was honest but respectful even in a situation such as this. She had begun to lose hope that anyone else in the SIA could show an ounce of integrity and charisma.

"Erik, what's the situation here?" Jennie asked. "Have you been searching? Anything show up on the radar?"

Erik glanced at the city behind him. "Nothing whatsoever. We've scoured Maryland Science Museum and found nothing of note. A few agents are still there searching the finer crevices, but no sign of anything amiss. Are you certain that was where the attack was due to take place?"

Jennie looked at Cassie.

Cassie nodded. "One hundred percent."

When Jennie saw Erik's expectant gaze, she added, "She's our informant. One of the seven responsible for making all of this shit happen. I'll be honest, five out of seven successful detonations isn't a great success rate, but finding her and bringing her around to our way of thinking is."

One of Erik's agents broke rank. "Do you trust her?"

Erik looked as though he was about to reprimand the agent, but he let it lie. "Well?"

Jennie considered this carefully. She had no other choice in this situation, so she replied. "Yes. Yes, I do."

"Okay, then," Erik replied. "In that case, lead the charge, Rogue. After hearing tales of your exploits, it'll be an honor working alongside you."

Jennie smiled. "I like you, Erik. Do you know why?"

Erik told her he didn't.

"Because you're one of the first agents who has spoken about working *alongside* me." Jennie laughed. "It's amazing how many of you federal types fight for dominance and want to take the lead. Let's make this happen together, okay? Show me what you've done so far."

Maryland Science Museum was much more than a museum. It was an entire complex, complete with an IMAX cinema and a planetarium.

The outside of the building was cordoned off to hold back the public who had gathered to take photos of the building and the agents making their way in and out. Police had been called in by the SIA. They made their presence felt at the cordon and worked at diverting the media so the SIA could search in peace.

Erik parked around the back and allowed himself access through a rear door. A single reporter tried to follow him, shouting questions as they entered. Sandra pushed a pulse of spectral energy and disabled her camera and microphone.

The inside was deserted, their footsteps echoing like thunderclaps in the empty space. Jennie nudged Cassie to the front of them and ordered her to lead the way.

Cassie glanced around the main lobby, indicating the front of the building. It was entirely made from glass, curving around the building to its entire four-story height.

"This is where the bomb should have detonated, if they had made it," Cassie offered. "Behind this reception desk. But there's nothing here."

Jennie thought aloud. "Craig was already worried about getting caught. SIA is much more present here than elsewhere. He wouldn't have gone for something so obvious, knowing that there'd be no easy escape for him."

"Wouldn't it be specters doing the job?" Baxter asked. "In Boston, you made specters perform the duties, didn't you, Cass?"

Cassie's eyes fell to the floor. "Some of the seven are more brazen than others. I'm smart enough to allow specters to do my bidding. Even if they did turn out to be traitors." Her eyes found Terri's again, and the specter shrank back. "Craig was younger than some of the others. He might have wanted the thrill of doing it himself."

Jennie chewed on that. "Do you really believe that?"

"How did you contact him?" Rhone asked. "You said you had a video link to you all, but did you have any other contact with him? A phone number, perhaps?"

Cassie unlocked her cellphone and tapped through to her contacts. She found Craig's number and held it up to Rhone.

Rhone and Erik exchanged a look. Jennie caught the drift of their unspoken message.

"What?" Carolyn asked.

"Call him," Jennie instructed to Cassie. "Call him now. Tell him you're concerned about him and want to help. Keep him on the phone for as long as possible. Erik, you can triangulate the signal, right?"

"Of course," Erik confirmed. "But we can't do this out in the field. We need to hook the phone up to our servers back at HQ."

Jennie glanced around the wide-open lobby and spotted a few agents standing guard at the front doors. Another cluster was roaming upstairs and searching for clues. "Okay, we've got enough coverage here. Let's drop back to base and see what we can dig up."

They left the museum, hopped in a cab, and sped toward the Baltimore HQ. Jennie messaged Ashton to follow.

CHAPTER FORTY-FOUR

<u>Richmond, Virginia, USA</u>

Triton took the wheel while Tanya rode shotgun with Hendrick's spectral compass in her hand.

The silvery substance inside was strange. It moved and flitted like a fish, but it had no defined shape. Watching it reminded her of lying on the grass in Central Park and watching the clouds float ahead as they morphed and twisted into creatures and items.

They hadn't detected anything of note yet. They were slaloming up and down the streets, working their way toward the quarry. Business was going on as usual, the citizens of Richmond strolled along the sidewalk without a care in the world for the hidden horror that had been unleashed underground. There had been little in the papers, too, other than a brief nod at the breaking of the yoga studio windows.

"I still don't get why they're choosing to remain at the manor," Tanya muttered. "I thought they wanted their freedom."

Ula replied from the back seat of the car. Roman was beside her with Feng Mian accommodating the final seat. "They're scared. They should be, too. After what we've let them in on, how are they going to continue their normal everyday lives in the city?"

Triton grumbled in agreement. "Do we think they're more susceptible now? Y'know… Considering they've been possessed once, could it happen again?"

Tanya considered this, staring out of the window at the buildings as they blurred on by. "I don't know. We hardly know everything. I've updated Julia and she's looking into it, but who knows how long that will take?"

They rounded a corner and headed toward the rising slopes on the north side of town. Mansions and luxury condos littered the rises, and the streets were emptier up here.

The box reacted in her hand. Tanya felt the energy give small pulses as the silver liquid coalesced at the far side of the box and pointed toward the hill.

Roman side-eyed the box. "That way?"

"Worth a shot," Tanya replied.

They hadn't been expecting what they found. The box led them to a street where three cop cars were gathered in front of a house with their lights flashing but their engines off. The cops were interviewing well-to-do neighbors who stood with arms folded and disbelieving faces.

They parked nearby, leaving the cube in the car. It was obvious where it was directing them to once they'd noticed the shattered glass winking in the sunlight.

"From out of nowhere," one woman explained, her eyes lit up with excitement. Surely there was little adventure in a neighborhood like this. "I heard it from my place ten doors down."

"Definitely a gunshot?" a portly cop asked.

The woman nodded emphatically. "Oh, yes. I'd know that sound anywhere."

The cop raised an eyebrow.

"Oh, I don't mean I've heard one personally," she continued, her shock causing her to ramble verbally. "My son is big on those video games. Y'know the ones where they're in the army and they play on the front line? Headsets and keyboards and controllers. Isn't technology amazing?"

Tanya glanced at the others and made her way toward a cop

leaning against the hood of his car and scribbling notes. He looked up at their approach, studying the strange array of individuals before him. "Can I help you?"

Tanya opened her mouth to talk, but Roman cut in.

"Yeah, we're former associates of the lady who lived here," he explained, taking on a tone that Tanya had not heard in him before. He sounded friendly and approachable. "Former colleagues, as a matter of fact. We're just wondering what happened here?"

The cop eyed him curiously, then shifted his attention back to his pad. "Sorry, folks. That's classified at this point. Unless you have information to give us on the individual that lived here, then you've got no business, and I recommend you walk on by."

From across the other side of the cop car, the lady mimed a bird flying across the sky. "Straight over our heads, I promise you. I know how it sounds. I saw her."

Tanya drew closer to Roman and the others. She whispered, "Come on, let's find another way around. We've got no jurisdiction here."

They sent Feng Mian to explore the perimeter, but every inch was covered by cops or witnesses. Upon his return, they asked if he'd take a look inside the building.

Feng Mian did as asked, walking straight past the boys in blue and up the steps to the front door. He melted through and disappeared from sight.

***

It was a dream home, something that might have been pulled directly from the *Perfect Homes* catalog. Everything was neat and pristine, light poured into the house, and there was a smell of lemons and pine in the air.

Feng Mian ascended the stairs and searched for the shattered balcony. It wasn't difficult to find. The door had been left open, and glass covered the carpets.

He examined the room, taking note of the myriad weapons

displayed on the wall. On a large oak desk, a lamp, a pot of pens, and a Mac took center stage. The view from the balcony was beautiful.

Feng Mian rifled through the open drawer and saw the neatly collected ammunition. It was clear that something had been taken from the drawer recently, and given the range of weapons missing from the brackets on the wall, Feng Mian had a good guess as to what.

He examined the surrounding rooms, half-expecting to find the guy they were looking for, but there was nothing here. Was the specter strong enough that he left a spectral signature behind, even after he was gone? It was possible. They'd seen that with Zhao.

If only Jennie were around to aid in this capture…

Feng Mian headed into the sunshine and examined the view from the balcony. The quarry was somewhere to the south-east, too far to see from here.

So why would he come all this way to attack one person?

A final glance at the empty brackets on the wall made Feng Mian's heart sink. He glanced down at his comrades, lurking in the shadows by the houses below, and shook his head.

Tanya frowned, her teeth grinding behind closed lips. "Why? Why would this damn compass pick up *residual* spectral frequencies? Is this guy really that strong?"

"We need to be alert," Ula warned. "Not only does he have slaves, but he also has weapons, too. This is getting out of hand. If we don't move fast, we're fucked."

Roman gave a curt nod. "Agreed. I think it's time that we call in reinforcements. Our reconnaissance can only go so far. If they're recruiting more people to their cause who come with their own weapons, then we're soon going to be vastly outnumbered. Tanya, hit up Jennie and see what she can offer, would you? Tell her it's of vital importance."

Tanya sighed. She had wanted to try and wrap this one up without Jennie's help, but it seemed there was no other choice.

Ula seemed to read her mind. "It's not a failure to ask for help. It's a failure to not accept help when the time calls for it. We've done what we can alone, but now we need to bolster our numbers and fast. There's no room for hubris in war."

Tanya sent the message, deciding not to call Jennie considering her team was already wrapped up in their own problems. On her lap, the silver liquid swam around its tank, hunting for specters.

They had scanned the vast majority of the city, finding nothing more after the visit to the house, and now they were heading back to the manor. They drove through the center of a town, and through a local market. Traffic was thick and slowed their progress home. Tanya wound down her window to let the fresh air soothe her skin. It was refreshing.

Outside the window, market stalls displayed their wares under candy cane striped awnings. Vendors offered fresh veggies, locally sourced meats, cheeses, and more. Dozens of customers crowded around the stalls as the vendors shouted their deals and drew in more custom.

"The world keeps turning," Tanya muttered, resting her chin on her hand. "How is it possible? These people have *no* idea what's coming."

"What's already here," Triton added.

Tanya turned over her shoulder, confused. Triton nodded toward her lap, where the fish had started circling in a crazy whirlpool of excitement. At last, it settled toward the far side of the market square.

Tanya glanced over the canopies, already sensing a change in the air around them. A second later, they heard the first scream.

Taylor stared out from eyes bordered with shadow.

This felt good. The market was packed, which would make gathering more victims to her purpose simple. That's how she thought of it—*her* purpose. She had yet to discover that she was nothing more than the puppet, and someone was pulling her strings.

In her left hand was her trusty Glock. In her right hand was her faithful Kalashnikov rifle from her days serving out in Iraq. The market warped before her, turning into a scene from the sandbox. The cobbles and paving were replaced with sand and sun-bleached stone, the air warping from the heat.

These would do just fine—if they knelt before her, that was. She spoke with words that didn't sound like her own, but that was okay. She sounded more powerful, terrifying, even. These people would have no choice but to bow to her power.

"On the floor," she declared, making no attempt to hide her weapons.

A woman screamed and threw herself to the floor. Her forehead pressed to the ground, she made her obeisance.

Taylor smiled. *Good. One down...*

Eyes were drawn to the screaming woman. The realization of what was happening pulsed out from Taylor in ripples. Some stared with disbelief, others with fear, a strange few stared with mild amusement, as if the bullets in those firearms were nothing more than marshmallows.

"On. The. Floor," Taylor repeated, her voice rising with each word. "*Now.*"

Chaos erupted. People sprinted in all directions. The stallholders abandoned their stock and fled into the stampeding crowd away from the woman. The unfortunate hundred nearest to Taylor froze, not daring to move a muscle.

Someone in the crowd fired at Taylor, missing her right shoulder by inches.

Taylor fired back with the accuracy she had honed over decades of service. The bullet found its mark, catching her assailant on the cheek as he moved toward the bullet's trajectory by accident.

More screams broke out. Those who had frozen worked their way to the floor, hands spread out before them and lips kissing the floor. A select few of the older population struggled, but even they managed a crooked curtsy.

In the distance, the sirens blared.

Good, Taylor thought. *My first victims.* She examined the herd fleeing from her and strafed them with bullets, reveling as her targets collapsed and fell to the floor.

Taylor laughed. The sound of it was more masculine than she had ever been, but she paid it no mind. She took a step toward the cowering shoppers and raised her voice for all to hear. "Faithful subjects, you have been selected to bear witness to the great and powerful glory of old. You are the second wave of my army, and you shall cower before the terrible wrath of the Dreadnought Conqueror."

She dropped her weapons and swept a hand over the crowd. As she did, dark shadows flitted from her fingertips, snaking their way toward the bowing citizens. "Loyalty will be rewarded. Betrayal will end in death. You are now bound to me, and I to you, and together we shall join together on our noble quest to make Him rise."

"Who?" a brave man shouted from the back, his eyes fixed to the asphalt. "What the fuck are you talking about?"

Taylor struggled to suppress a grin. She aimed the Glock and fired at his head. He flopped sideways and lay still. "Answers will be given in time. Faith will take you a long way toward victory, my brothers and sisters in arms."

The shadows from her fingers grew thick, and a haze of dark smoke settled around those on the floor. They held their breath, but soon could hold them no longer. Their eyes turned white when they were forced to inhale, and one by one, they got back to their feet and stood obediently awaiting their orders.

Good, the Dreadnought's voice said in Taylor's head. *And so it begins.*

At the sound of gunfire, Roman, Ula, and Triton leaped out of the car.

Tanya stayed behind, staring in wonder at the flood of people running her way. Those in the vehicles in front and behind were fleeing, but Tanya knew they had to help out.

Feng Mian waited outside the car. "Are you coming?"

Tanya looked uncertainly at the pistol at her waist. What could she do with that? She wasn't trained. She wasn't as adept with a weapon as the conduits, and the person shooting the gun seemed ready and willing to fire at anyone who stood in their way.

Tanya closed her eyes and steadied her breathing. The conduits had gone from sight. She thought back to the battle at Alexandria, a time when she had played a part in protecting the city and much of the United States by helping take down Koa. "I'm nothing without Sandra."

Feng Mian poked his head through the door. "You don't need Sandra to be great. All you need is to find the strength within your heart."

Tanya raised an eyebrow. "You're going to make me puke." When Feng Mian said no more, she opened her door and joined him. "Fine. But if I die today, I'm coming back to haunt you."

Feng Mian smirked as they ran against the tide of people.

It was almost impossible to gain any momentum. Not only did they need to swerve around the market stalls to gain any progress, but people ran into them, blocked them, scurrying toward them in their desperate bids to run away from the crazed shooter.

At one point, blood splattered near Tanya as a man went down to her right. She only saw him for a half-second before he was down, and more screams erupted around her.

A man's voice rose above the din. It was authoritative and commanding. Tanya saw the light at the end of the tunnel as she passed the last few civilians but was pulled back suddenly as a pair of hands clutched her waist and dragged her behind a stand selling handcrafted wooden toys.

She was about to protest when she saw Ula's face beside hers, a finger to her lips. The stampede was clearing, and in their wake, they left behind a bowing crowd covered in a thin layer of dark smoke.

"What the…" Tanya muttered.

Roman was on the other side of Ula, lining up his shot. He waited, clearly curious to see what was going to happen next. Tanya stared at the woman to whom the rest were bowing, wondering where the man's voice had come from. When she opened her mouth and spoke, Tanya discovered the answer.

"Take the shot," Tanya urged.

Roman hesitated. "She's innocent. It's the beast inside that needs expunging."

"Take it," Ula echoed.

Roman rose slowly, about to bellow out his commands for the woman to surrender when the rest of the crowd began to rise. His shot was blocked by rows of heads, and he appeared reluctant to step into the smoke surrounding them.

"Shit," he growled.

Tanya whipped her head to Feng Mian. "I've got an idea. It's risky as shit, and I need you for it. You in?"

Feng Mian nodded.

Before the conduits could pull her back again, Tanya ran out toward the back of the crowd. She couldn't get a visual on the woman, but judging by the direction the others were staring, she could find her way there.

She waited by the edge of the smoke. Feng Mian joined her and activated his shield, surrounding her in a bubble of white light. She pushed her way forward, alarmed by the vacant stares on the faces of the crowd. Only the whites of their eyes showed.

Just like Krissie and Lyla…

She had to use some muscle to nudge people out of her way, but soon she neared the front. She broke free of the final possessed and caught the attention of the woman standing before them.

Her eyes flickered to the weapons at the woman's feet. "Let me guess. You live in the northern quarter of the city? High balcony? Smashed glass? Are those the missing weapons?"

Alarm came over the woman's face, as though some memory was triggered inside her. A second later it was gone, replaced by a dark grin. A man's voice leaked from her feminine lips. "You are unaffected by my magic?"

"I have my methods," Tanya replied, wondering if she could see Feng Mian and his barrier around her. Without her SI glasses, she knew she wouldn't be able to. "What is it you want, Rathbourne? What is the purpose of all of this?"

The woman's face contorted into a twisted set of features. For a moment, another face became visible, staring at her with eyes larger than they should have been. "What I was promised so long ago. Dominion. Rule. The world to bow at my feet."

Tanya shook her head and muttered. "It's always the same with you ancient guys." She addressed Rathbourne. "Times have changed. You are no longer the dominant just because you can fight and force people to your will. We have methods and means to contain you, and we will use whatever is necessary to do so. If sending you back into that stone tomb is the only way to make it so, we will ensure it happens. Give up now before this gets messy."

Rathbourne's laugh came unnaturally from the woman's mouth. The face twisted back into her true presence. The woman blinked confusedly. She made a move to bend down and grab her weapons, when a powerful voice shouted, "Freeze! Hands in the air, now!"

To her right, Roman aimed his gun at the woman. To her left, Triton covered the side. Ula stood on top of one of the stalls and locked her rifle on the woman.

"Surrender," Roman commanded. "Come along quietly or take the consequences."

The woman paused, mid-crouch. She raised her hands and laced her fingers behind her head, rising to her full height. For a moment, the woman behind the mask came through and a single tear rolled down her cheek. "You can't stop him. It's too late. Look at what he's managed already."

A shockwave took her body, and her face hardened. That demonic grin appeared again, uttering only a single word. "Attack."

Roman and Triton wasted no time in pulling their triggers, although they still missed their mark. The woman rose into the air, avoiding the bullets by a hair's width. Roman's and Triton's bullets screamed past each other, narrowly avoiding hitting the two conduits.

The possessed crowd rioted, dividing and going for whoever was nearest to them. Tanya screamed as flashes of white light indicated the clawing hands of the possessed.

"Remain calm," Feng Mian soothed. "I can hold them off. Their energy is weak."

Roman and Triton tried for another shot at the woman, but she was gone. They were unsure if she had soared over the buildings or simply vanished into thin air.

Bodies flooded toward them. The conduits fought valiantly, their years of training conquering those who were being manipulated by the specter. They tactically avoided being cornered and surrounded and eventually made their way back to each other.

Tanya ran toward them, knocking the enemy out of the way as she did. The shield held them all at bay, and soon they were all reunited.

"Well, this has turned into a giant fustercluck," Triton commented.

"Later," Roman instructed. "Back to the car, we need to get away from this before the cops come."

Tanya balked. "Surely the cops won't think this was all our fault?"

"I don't know," Ula replied. "But I'm not sticking around to find out. Remember, the King's Court is young, still. We have no jurisdiction agreement with law enforcement around here."

They made it back to the car, but it was useless trying to drive. Abandoned cars littered the streets around them, and there was nowhere to go.

Roman waved for them to follow him, sprinting toward a side street that led off and away from the market square. Tanya and the others kept up, managing to outrun the possessed easily enough. As warped as their brains were, possession apparently didn't improve their stamina.

They ran three blocks before they lost sight of the possessed. Six blocks after that, Roman finally pulled them to a stop.

They gathered their breath. Even Ula and Triton, who maintained a healthy level of fitness, were panting. They listened for the cops. The sirens had stopped, but they didn't know what that meant.

"You think they're okay?" she asked the others.

"Who?" Ula replied.

Tanya clutched her heart, where a spiking pain indicated her stitch. "The cops."

"Oh," Ula replied.

Roman's face was set in a grim determination. "We need to find that poor woman. We need to expel that specter. We need to stop this before it goes any farther." He turned to Tanya. "Any word from the others?"

The last thing Tanya had been thinking about was her phone. She patted her pockets and realized that they were empty. She thought back to the scuffle, a sudden panic rising that she had dropped her phone somewhere in the crowd.

"Shit," she exclaimed.

"Don't worry," Ula reassured. "I'll take care of it." She fired off a text to Jennie. "Let's hope she sends assistance soon. Otherwise, we're going to have to find our own."

Triton laughed. "But who? Who is there in this town who could actually give us a hand?

Roman's eyes narrowed. "I've got an idea, but I'm not especially fond of it."

CHAPTER FORTY-FIVE

<u>Baltimore, Maryland, USA</u>

Jennie and her crew were back in Hannah Drampton's office, with the agent watching them expectantly. They had given her a brief overview of their situation, and Drampton had provided the equipment they needed to put a trace on Craig's phone.

They waited in tense silence as the phone began to ring.

Even though it wasn't on speakerphone, the dial tone carried around the room. Another note of silence followed a ring.

Jennie wondered if Craig was going to pick up at all. He'd be smart not to, although would he suspect anything at all? Would he believe that Cassie could have betrayed the Seven? Would he see this coming?

Just when the call was about to pass to voicemail, Craig picked up. His voice was rough and sharp. "What is it, Cass?"

Cassie hesitated, for a moment forgetting her role. She picked the phone off the desk and held it to her ear. "Craig. Zhao is dead. I was checking in to see if you'd heard the news?"

A beat of silence followed. "I know."

Jennie and Cassie exchanged a look. They hadn't told anyone that Zhao was gone, so how could he have known? The only people Jennie had told were Cassie, Daggro and her people, and Tanya back in Richmond. There was no way their news could have already spread to Craig and the others.

"You know?" Cassie nudged.

Craig grunted. "The Dragon has informed us. All of us. Were you not in that string of messages?"

Cassie held the phone away from her ear and saw numerous notifications at the top of the screen. In all honesty, she hadn't checked anything since she'd converted to Jennie's cause. Her cell phone had been off for the majority of the trip, wanting to conserve power.

"No," Cassie replied. "I must have missed them."

This seemed to raise alarm on Craig's side of the phone. He let out a slow breath. "They've got you, haven't they, Cass?"

Cassie's cheeks flushed. "I don't know what you're—"

"The Dragon said you'd be the first to break. She was right." He sighed. "Dammit, Cass, I liked you. More than your father. I thought you'd have something great to offer the Seven, but turns out you're nothing more than a traitorous—"

Jennie glanced at the technician tracking the call. He shook his head and tapped his wrist. They needed more time. On the screen in front of him, a map was slowly dialing in, reducing its circular perimeter to show the location of the call.

Jennie waved her hands, indicating for Cassie to stall him.

"Wait a minute," Cassie exclaimed. "I've been in hiding. How dare you accuse me of slipping over to the dark side?"

Craig cut across her. "I thought you were stronger than that, Cass. Enjoy life walking the straight and narrow. Lord knows you ain't going to have as much fun as we're going to have. Things get explosive on this side of the fence."

Before Cassie could respond, the line went dead. She was left with her mouth agape, her skin paling several shades.

"They know," Cassie declared. She placed the phone down and laced her fingers through her hair. "They know. Dear God, I'm in trouble. They're going to come for me, I know it. They know!"

Jennie did her best to calm Cassie, but it did little to comfort the woman. She made Cassie unlock her phone once more, then went through the notifications. There was a string of messages written in some kind of code between members of the Seven, their names saved under different aliases, but even these didn't seem to contain the mysterious new Dragon directly in the conversation.

Jennie's throat constricted. *Who the fuck was the new Dragon?* This mystery was killing her, and she needed answers. She was fairly certain that learning the new Dragon's identity would unlock this entire damn thing.

Baxter leaned over the back of the technician's chair and stared at the screen. "Did we get him?"

The technician's nose was nearly pressed to his monitor. He scratched his head, confusion written on his features. "I thought you said that Craig was going to be in Baltimore, no doubt planning to complete what he failed to do."

Cassie looked up, her brow creasing. "He is. That was the command. Baltimore was his."

The technician shook his head. "Well, either my equipment is fucked, or your man has been lying to you. I've narrowed him down to somewhere with a ten-mile radius, and it's certainly not in Baltimore."

Jennie crossed the room and joined Baxter. "Where is he, then?"

"A little place you may have heard of, called Washington DC." The technician tapped the screen. "According to this, he's somewhere in our great nation's capital."

Jennie turned to Cassie, who appeared just as confused as she was. She pushed out of the chair as a sudden inspiration hit her and advanced on Cassie so quickly that the woman recoiled a little. Jennie pushed her gently into a seat behind her and pulled up her own chair. They sat a foot apart from each other.

"Craig mentioned the new Dragon." Jennie spoke quickly, not wanting to lose the sudden clarity in her mind. "That means you've all been in contact with her, right?"

Cassie frowned. "No. I mean, all of our conversations have been with the Seven, Zhao taking up that seventh slot. He never released that information to us. I guess he believed it was critical to keep secrecy."

Baxter cottoned on to Jennie's thinking. "Surely if she contacted Craig, she contacted you all?"

"Weren't you listening?" Cassie asked. "I'm the traitor, okay? They know. And even if they didn't, Craig's no doubt going to tell her what's happened. I'm marked. There's a massive black X on my forehead, and my days are now limited. They're coming for me."

"No," Jennie reassured her. "They aren't. They know I'm here. They're not stupid enough to come for you under my protection. But tell me, why would Craig head to Washington? What would be there of note that would have him scarpering from Baltimore?"

Cassie blew a mouthful of air, eyes darting back and forth. "I don't know. Maybe…yes. Could it… I suppose the only thing I can think of is to complete the task that Ruben didn't? Washington is a high-profile spot, and Craig needs to prove his worth. Maybe he's gone there to accomplish that?"

Jennie sighed. "Fuck." She turned to her people. "I guess we're going to be heading to Washington."

Carolyn sat on a desk, her legs swinging. "You've gotta admit, this treasure hunt is rather fun." She smiled, somehow maintaining her air of excitement. "I've never seen so much of the country within such a short space of time."

Jennie chuckled. "I suppose there's always a bright side."

Drampton cocked an eyebrow. "How can you find levity at a time such as this? Shouldn't you be getting your asses moving? A *bomb* could be going off in Washington at any minute."

Jennie nodded but held her smile. "Without laughter, all we have is pain. Do me a favor, Drampton. Dial ahead and let Daggro know what's going on. Tell her to pull back her reinforcements, if necessary. Make it clear that Rogers needs to be in on this information, too. The President could be in trouble."

Drampton nodded, immediately moving to her phone to make the call.

"Er, Rogue?" The technician sat up straight in his chair and tapped the screen. "Is this of interest to you?"

"What is it?" Jennie asked.

The technician adjusted his glasses and ran his finger down a line of text on the screen. "I wasn't able to triangulate Craig's exact position, but I was able to pull up a history of his recent call activity. The man is old, right? No wonder he hasn't remembered how to use burn phones. Anyway, there are a few calls listed here, locations that may sound familiar to you: Harrisburg, Pennsylvania, Trenton, New Jersey, Hartford, Connecticut, and Washington, DC."

"Okay," Jennie replied. "Your point?"

The technician tapped a highlighted line on the screen. "You said you guys were currently stationed in Richmond, Virginia, correct?"

"Yeah?" Jennie's Spidey-senses began to tingle.

"Well," he continued. "There was a call placed around the time frame that Craig indicated the call from the Dragon would have been. The location is listed as somewhere in Richmond."

Jennie's skin went cold. The Dragon was near her new home base? *Renminbi...*

Richmond, Virginia, USA

Roman parked in the first available space on the street. They exited the car onto a quiet sub-section of Richmond. Storefronts sported colored awnings and took up the bottom floors while apartments took the upper levels.

Roman led the way, Tanya not far behind. They passed a Chinese restaurant, a Seven-Eleven, and an exchange bureau. Tanya's eyes were taken by the long list of numbers and foreign currencies that the dollar could be exchanged into. She had never understood why there wasn't just a universal currency for the planet. Wouldn't that make things easier for everyone?

She hesitated a moment, studying the digital list, a lightbulb flickering in the back of her mind. For some reason, there was something significant here, but she couldn't figure out what. It was as though her mind was several steps ahead of her, digesting information that she couldn't quite process.

"Tanya. Come on," Roman commanded.

"Coming," Tanya replied, pulling her mind away from the exchange list. They had bigger fish to fry, so why had that caught her attention?

A couple of buildings down, Roman stopped. The storefront was barred and looked like a prison cell. Firearms were displayed in the window. He pushed the door open, and the smell of gunpowder and sweat hit their nostrils.

A large man in a thick black t-shirt raised his eyebrows and called to them from behind a desk. "Not so many in the store at once. Read the sign. Three people policy. Choose your favorites."

Roman selected Tanya and Triton to join them. Feng Mian followed behind, undeterred. Roman strolled over to the desk.

The man smiled, only his lower lip visible thanks to his thick mustache. His stomach reached the desk, even though he was standing a few feet behind the counter. "How may I help you fine gentlemen?"

His eyes caught Tanya's as though he was trying to push her buttons. She refused to take the bait.

"I've been led to believe this is where the local GOA meetings occur," Roman stated. "Am I right? I'm in need of a favor."

"A favor?" The man chuckled, the sound a rattle in his throat. "You can't be from around here. A favor is earned, my friend. Something that one does for a neighbor they're familiar with. You won't be getting nothing expecting something for nothing."

Roman stood up straighter, easily a foot taller than the rotund man before him. "We're in need of…gunmen. We have a target that needs some attention, and my understanding is that other than firing your pistols into paper targets, your members don't get to see much action. Am I right?"

Despite Roman's facade, the man was not intimidated in any way at all. Tanya supposed he shouldn't be, given the profession he'd chosen.

They stared at each other for a moment, the man's eyes narrowing. After a beat, he moved out from behind the counter and flipped the sign on the door from OPEN to CLOSED. He locked it behind him, then motioned for them to follow out through the back door.

Tanya could just make out Ula's worried face before they trailed after the man.

He took them to a back corridor and down a set of concrete stairs. The light bulbs were exposed, and the lower they went, the more sounds of pistols firing could be heard.

They followed into a corridor, the windows on the left dirty and yellowed, but clear enough to showcase the gun enthusiasts honing their skills. The man didn't so much as blink or flinch with each deafening roar, and finally found his way to a door on his right.

They entered a large room with a circle of chairs in the center. Most of the chairs were accommodated. Twenty of so grimy men and a handful of women looked over to see who had entered.

One man stood and kicked back his chair. "What the fuck, Grimald? You brought the cops?"

Grimald furrowed his brow. "I'd be an idiot to bring a law enforcer down into our little slice of heaven." He turned to Roman. "You ain't cops, are you?"

Roman shook his head.

"See! No cops," Grimald exclaimed.

One of the women leaned forward in her chair, arms resting on her knees. She chewed gum as she spoke. "Then what are they? I thought strangers had to be initiated?" She studied Triton. "Not that I'm complaining. Could do with some fresh meat."

Grimald waved a hand toward the group. "Our pride and joy, the committee of Richmond's Gun Owner's Association. You chose the right day, fellas. Today's their weekly meeting."

Tanya scoffed. "What is there to talk about?"

The woman laughed and sat back in her chair. "You're kidding, ain't you, French Fry? We gots business. Members to look out for. Intel to manage. We gots to be ready to be called up into combat, able to blow our .45s into the heart of them goddam terrorists."

"We're always vigilant," a man with a deep voice and a rash of stubble added. "Always ready to put our skills to use."

Roman nodded, a pleased expression on his face.

"Isn't that the cops' job?" Tanya asked. "Why go through all this trouble when there are people hired to help? Can't you join the forces?"

Roman and Triton closed their eyes. The committee erupted into a chorus of laughs and admonishments.

Grimald turned to Tanya. "There ain't enough cops out there, and they sure as hell ain't as practiced with guns as we are. What's going to happen if the town suddenly gets overrun? They're going to need backup."

The deep-voiced man continued. "Who are they going to come crawling to when that happens? Damn liberals may not like us right now, but owning a gun is a goddam constitutional right. They can't stop us down here, and when we're called to duty, we'll sure as hell be ready to go."

Roman nodded. "Good. Because your time has come. We need you."

Grimald's eyes widened. A number of the committee shifted in their seats, their attention caught. Roman explained the situation at hand, ignoring the scoffs and chuckles he earned when he mentioned the involvement of spectral activity and possessed citizens.

A skinny man with bones for arms and clothes that were ill-fitted tsked. "Bullshit."

"We've got two of them back at our place," Tanya declared. "And, in case you haven't seen the news lately, shit is already going down across the city. Three unexplainable instances of disruption. A yoga studio attacked, a woman missing from her northside mansion with witnesses firmly in the belief that she flew out the window, and a marketplace shot up with fifty or so civilians in a trance and causing mayhem."

"Sounds like wherever you guys go, bad things happen," Grimald commented.

A few of the committee were less difficult to convince. The

woman chewed loudly, eyes narrowed at Roman. "So why come to us? Can't you guys go to the cops? Let them know what's going on?"

Triton took this one. "Can't risk it. We've not yet secured permission to operate in this city. We go to the cops, they're going to try and take us in. That can't happen. At the moment, there aren't enough of us to cover what's going on, and this new enemy is growing his forces at an alarming rate."

"We need you," Tanya finished.

They fell into a thoughtful silence, the members of the committee glancing at each other uncertainly. Grimald turned to the three. "Would you guys step outside for a minute while we discuss this? You've given us a lot to think about."

Twenty minutes they waited, standing in the corridor and covering their ears as shots fired behind the various booths. When the door eventually opened again, Grimald ushered them back inside.

The woman rose from her chair and folded her arms. "As President of the GOA of Richmond, I say we're in."

The rest of the committee stood simultaneously, each striking their heart three times with their fists before sitting back down.

Tanya glanced at Roman, uncertain of what to do next. His expression was as hard to read as ever.

"Good," he muttered. "Let's get moving."

Without another word, he turned and exited the room. The committee members followed without instruction.

CHAPTER FORTY-SIX

<u>Washington DC, USA</u>

Daggro couldn't remember the last time she had left her office. Her usually pristine desk had smudges on its varnished surface from the drool that had leaked from her mouth as she slept. Her eyes were red and her pupils so small they looked to have been swallowed.

There was a knock on the door.

Daggro grumbled. Would it ever end? This incessant non-stop activity of people wanting things, demanding things, needing, always needing things from her. Where the hell was Rogers? She needed him back. He had the experience. He was the one who had guided them this far, and all she was doing was bailing out the canoe while the President chewed his ear and talked strategy.

Another knock sounded.

"What is it?" Daggro grumbled, unable to recognize her own voice.

The door opened, and Daggro immediately sat straighter. The sudden movement made her head swim.

Special Agent in Charge Kurt Rogers swept into the room and stood by her desk. Compared to Daggro, this man was the pinnacle of health. How had he managed to keep in such great shape while she had been steadily declining since the moment he left?

He picked up a stained coffee cup, green stuff growing in the bottom. "Coffee is your problem." His words were flat, impossible to read his emotion. "Too much caffeine becomes a crutch you can't afford. That headache you're about to experience will fade over time, but don't feed the beast. Wean yourself off it, and you'll do just fine."

He took a seat. Daggro was suddenly aware of the stale scent of body odor in the air. When had she last changed her clothes?

"Sir… I… It's been…" Daggro stuttered.

Rogers stared at her levelly, silencing her with a look. It wasn't unkind, either. There was pity in his eyes. "It's a tall ask, I know. This department is too young to be sprinting into battle but needs must. The President is behind us and has just granted us a fresh injection of funding to ensure that we get to the bottom of this. I assume our operatives are in the field and Jennie is among them?"

Daggro's skin prickled. Jennie was nowhere near her men. She was on her way back to Washington, and the SIA were many steps behind. How would she explain this?

"Well?" Rogers nudged.

Daggro sighed and informed Rogers of the situation, right down to the latest intel fed to her by Jennie.

"And you didn't think to tell me?" Rogers asked, the first note of disapproval in his words. He pinched the bridge of his nose. "Holly, know that the minute this is all over, you will be instantly demoted to your old post."

Holly's eyes lowered, tears shimmering.

"It's not a punishment," Rogers continued, resting a hand on hers over the desk. "Sometimes we are asked to rise above our station before we are ready. This isn't your fault, it's mine. I threw you out of the nest before you were ready to fly. I'd rather you excel in a position that you can handle than fail in a position you can't."

"I…" Daggro stumbled over her words. "I can. I'm ready."

Rogers gave her a sympathetic smile. "No. You're not. But I'm back now and ready to take the helm. Fill me in on everything. The more I know, the more I can get to the bottom of this and help turn this all around. What do I need to know?"

Holly's heart quickened. There was so much she hadn't told him. Not only had she held back on letting him know that Jennie was coming to Washington, but how could she tell him about Lionus? About Rhone...

There was nothing for it. He would find out eventually. She told him everything, all the facts from the moment he had left for the White House. Her shoulders softened with each truth told, and after she was done, she had hardly any care left for the scolding expression on his face.

At least I can sleep soon, she thought. *I can sleep until my mind is fully rested, and the final weight will be off my shoulders.*

Jennie checked in with Sturgeon and Lionus on the way back to Washington. The journey wasn't long, but it gave her enough time to get an overview of the situation.

She drained one of Hendrick's solutions and offered more to her crew. She was nearly out. She'd have to visit Hendrick again soon. There was no time to sleep.

Sturgeon informed Jennie that they had come across an abandoned lot where operations for the detonations had clearly been planned. They found a few clues and had interrogated a number of specters, but the only information they had gotten from them was that their leader was gone. When pressed, they ascertained their head honchos had only left the city within the last twenty-four hours or so.

Lionus' information was similar. Jennie begrudgingly pulled the information from him. She was tired of having to threaten the junior. Soon Rogers would be informed of this and balance would hopefully be restored once more.

"Why have they all left?" Carolyn asked the crew in the Airbus. "Blow shit up and disappear? Is that what people normally do?"

"When they want to flee the scene of the crime," Cassie admitted. "I thought about it, but our initial instructions were to stay put. I wonder what changed."

"Everything has changed," Jennie muttered, an unsettled feeling in the pit of her stomach. "Everything."

***

Kurt Rogers exited Daggro's office and glanced up and down the empty corridors.

Most of the agents had been deployed by Daggro, and the SIA HQ was like a ghost town. He had only passed a couple of agents on the way down, and they had all looked as exhausted as she did.

I leave for five minutes, and this shit falls to pieces.

It had taken every ounce of his willpower to not rip Daggro a new asshole. She had shown such promise, but it turned out her ego had gotten in the way of her servitude. He would berate her soon. At that moment, there was little point. She was too tired to take any of it in.

At the end of the corridor, a group of agents shuffled quickly into and out of sight. There must have been half a dozen of them, carrying something between them.

Probably something for the labs, no doubt.

The hairs on the back of Roger's neck raised. He wasn't sure what it was, but something was registering as faulty.

He walked toward the T-junction. When he reached the end, he looked in either direction, surprised to see the agents were already out of sight. Should they have been moving so quickly? Actually, thinking about it now, had there been something off about their uniforms?

An itch clawed at the back of his mind, and without thinking, he reached for his pistol and followed in the direction they had headed.

***

Jennie was surprised by the number of agents awaiting them back at SIA HQ.

She only planned a brief visit to Daggro and check whether they had any further intelligence or scanning systems they could use to look for trouble.

Surely they must have some intelligence on potential bomb threats or criminal activity in the area? No criminal can just walk in undetected, right?

They must have come over in some kind of plane or helicopter. Jennie was almost certain she should be able to narrow down Craig's location based on that.

Two dozen SIA agents gathered in the reception area. She passed by them without a word, not wanting to draw attention or create another situation like she had with Lionus and his boys. The corridors inside were emptier, and Jennie wondered what they were all doing at the front.

She found Daggro's office and knocked loudly on the door. There was no answer. She shoved the door open and found Daggro lying on her desk, head resting on folded arms.

"Dead?" Baxter asked.

Jennie took the gross mug of mold and coffee and tipped it on Daggro. She shifted with a start and pushed herself up. Her eyes were red and bleary. "Wha… Oh! I was sleeping!"

"On the job?" Jennie asked.

Daggro pawed her eyes. "Rogers' orders. Says I need it. I'm inclined to agree."

Jennie's ears pricked up at Rogers' name. "You spoke to him? Is he with the President? We need to warn him—"

"He's here," Daggro interjected. "He came back to see how we're doing." Her words were slurred, so drunk with tiredness that she smiled while she spoke. "I'm being demoted. Can you believe it? Demoted. He's got some words left to spew at me, I can tell. Bless him, he's waiting until I'm rested enough to take it. I know these things." She tapped her nose, her head drooping.

"Where is he?" Jennie asked.

"Outside. Somewhere." Daggro yawned. "I'm surprised you didn't see him in the corridor."

Jennie turned to the others. "I didn't. Did you?"

They shook their heads.

"Aw, man," Jennie muttered as she detected a faint pulse of spectral energy from outside. "I think we've got a problem."

The farther Rogers went, the more concerned he became.

He had caught up with the agents, managing to hear their footsteps when they sprinted down the stairwell. He lingered far enough behind to remain undetected but struggled to find them again when he came to the multitude of doors leading to the different parts of the HQ building.

Nearing the basement—the location of the new rec room—he heard a disruption up ahead. There were shouts, and a handful of shots were fired. Rogers peeked through the small window of glass on the door and his heart dropped.

There were more of them there. At least two dozen men dressed similarly to his men, but clearly not agents. The bodies of the real agents lay on the floor, blood pooling around them as the intruders set up a large device in the center of the room. One man tapped buttons while the others kept lookout.

A bomb. Rogers gasped. He looked longingly back at the stairs, wishing that he had someone else with him.

But who was left? He had come into the facility expecting to speak to Daggro before putting himself back to work and contacting others to recall them to HQ. He hadn't even hooked himself up with a radio. His assistant was waiting in his office, likely setting up refreshments while Hopkins filled her in on his side of things.

There was nothing for it. Rogers was going to have to go in. These men looked set on causing destruction, and there was only one man available to stop them.

A flutter of excitement coursed through his veins. How long was it since he'd been on the sharp end? He cocked his gun, readied himself, and shoved the door open.

CHAPTER FORTY-SEVEN

Jennie went down the corridor, following the trail of spectral energy. The way ahead was quiet. Too quiet. She found herself at the staircase, and loud noises greeted her.

Shots were fired. A door slammed at the bottom of the stairwell. Jennie ran ahead, pausing as she got to the next floor down as dozens of SIA agents ran toward her.

"What's going…" was all she managed before someone took a shot at her.

She ducked out of the way and pushed back through the door. She had only glimpsed them for a moment, but the mass of SIA agents moving toward her was large. She couldn't get an accurate count, but the ones she had seen didn't seem too pleased to see her.

She ran back down the corridor, pausing only when she'd reached cover at a bend. She steadied her gun and took aim at the door, waiting for the agents to spill out.

The door slammed open so hard the glass window shattered. Agents flooded toward her. It was Jennie's turn to fire.

She sent two warning shots over the crowd and shouted, "Freeze, motherfuckers, before I open this baby up and splatter you on the walls."

The agents paid no heed. In fact, a few at the back pressed forward, sudden fear on their faces. Jennie didn't recognize any of the agents, but that didn't mean she hadn't met them, even if their clothes were rather ill-fitting.

They broke into a run, firing one after the other as Jennie backed once more down the corridor and ducked inside the open doorway to an office.

She waited there with Rhone, Baxter, Carolyn, Sandra, and Cassie. The agents didn't come for them, they fled down the corridor. After they had passed, Jennie stuck her head out, her brow creased in confusion.

"What the fuck is going on?" She turned her head and saw a specter trailing to catch up with the others. Jennie latched onto the specter and dragged her into the room with them.

She held the Big Bitch to her forehead. "Tell me why they're running. What's happening down there?" Jennie's teeth barely parted as she roared at the specter.

The specter grinned. "You'll find out soon enough."

Jennie punched her in the face and shook her. "Tell me!"

The specter's eyes rolled. She shook her head, but the smile stayed on her face. "You might want to run, Rogue. Your whole operation is about to blow."

A sudden dawning realization came over Jennie. "No. Not here. But... How?"

Jennie's mind flashed back to the moment she'd received the news of the break-in that had freed Zhao. Surely whoever had broken in the first time hadn't returned again? How had his passes and locks worked?

The specter laughed. "Time's ticking. It's too late to save your friend, but you can escape."

Jennie's eyes widened. *Rogers!*

Time moved in slow motion. Jennie latched onto her spectral energy cells and darted through the wall. Her muscles were tensed, her weapons clutched in a white-knuckled grip.

She melted through the stairwell door and allowed herself to fade through the floor. She plummeted through the stairs, making herself material only when she reached the bottom floor. Without hesitation, she dived through the final door and into the rec room.

The scene before her was pandemonium. Bodies littered the floor. It was impossible to tell who was friend and who was foe. Machines had broken, chairs were toppled, the whole thing looked like a bomb had already exploded.

The bomb...

Movement drew her eye to the bomb. A solitary figure dragged his body toward the device. One leg trailed behind, leaving red streaks, but it didn't slow him down. Not even that racking cough stopped him from his purpose.

"Rogers!" Jennie sprinted toward the Special Agent in Charge. His uniform was torn, one of his arms twisted at an unnatural angle. Holes in his trousers told of several bullet wounds, but he pressed on.

"Disarm...it." Rogers gasped for air. "Disarm...the bomb."

Jennie knelt by his side and relieved him of the colored wires he held in one hand. A knife was clutched in his palm. How was he going to cut the right wire with just one hand?

"Tell me how," Jennie instructed. She didn't want to look at him; judging by the glaze coming over his eyes, he was already fading. "Tell me which wire."

"Blue..." Rogers managed before his eyes closed and he slid onto his front.

Jennie's brow was peppered with sweat. She clutched the wire with shaking hands, praying that "blue" was the right instruction and not the ramblings of a dying man.

"Blue," Jennie repeated. She pulled the wire taut, brought the knife to it, and—

A blow from the side shoved Jennie back. The knife flew from her hand. She slid across the smooth floor and looked around for her attacker. There was no sign of anyone.

Another blow to her cheek. Then another to her stomach. Her attacker was invisible, which meant he was spectral. She hadn't been hit like that in some time.

A cackle echoed around the chamber. Jennie could make out footsteps on the metal staircase as her comrades came to her. She closed her eyes, and another blow caught her shoulder, then her waist. She was winded and gasped for air.

"Did you miss me?" The specter's voice came from all around. She clenched her jaw, knowing who she was dealing with but not quite believing the bastard was back.

"Rico?" Jennie called into the empty space. "Come out and fight me like a man!"

"Not a chance," came the probing reply. "Made that mistake last time, didn't I? Didn't move fast enough for you not to latch onto me. I'm not stopping now!" He let out an abrasive laugh.

Best change tack, then.

Jennie pushed herself to her feet and ran toward the bomb. She was knocked sideways again but managed to keep her footing. Another few feet forward and the blow came from the front, sending her sprawling on her ass.

"Sorry, Rogue. No luck for you. That bomb is going to blow if it's the last thing we do. No SIA means less chance of my employer getting caught. You're an additional bonus if I can make you burn in the flames."

Baxter and Carolyn appeared through the door with Sandra. Rhone followed them, gun poised and ready. When they saw Jennie getting knocked around by an invisible presence, they ran toward her.

"No!" Jennie shouted. She latched onto Carolyn, Baxter, and Sandra and shoved them back. Rhone stood where he was, watching them slide toward the wall. "Get out of here. It's too dangerous. This bomb is going to blow soon, and I don't want you here when it does."

"Don't you mean 'if?'" Baxter called, struggling against her power.

Jennie glanced at the bomb. There was no timer set, but she could hear the pieces inside starting to shift into place. "Go!" she repeated. "Clear the building. Save who you can."

She shoved the specters out of the room and pushed them as far as she could while they were within range. She couldn't see where they went but hoped it was up the stairwell, getting people out of the way.

Rhone stayed where he was.

"Rhone, leave!" Jennie cried, another blow taking her farther from the bomb. She clumsily rose to her feet and made a dash for it. The specter swooped in and pulled her back.

"No," Rhone stated. "Your powers don't work on me. I'm with you until the end."

Jennie's face grew dark. "This is not the time for heroics. Heroics killed Rogers, and you can't be next. They'll need you."

A force hit Jennie's throat and left her coughing.

"No," Rhone repeated. "They'll need *you*."

He waited for a second, calculating the regularity and rhythm of the blows Jennie was receiving from the invisible force. At the moment that the next one came, Rhone aimed the gun at her and unleashed the entire chamber of bullets. Jennie's head flew back from the punch of the specter, and she stayed on the floor as the bullets flew toward her.

Most of the bullets whizzed straight by, but at least two did their job.

A voice shouted in pain. Jennie focused her power and found Rico as he slowed down and crashed to the floor. The SI bullets had caught him in the thigh and chest.

Jennie latched onto him, and her spectral cells started filling. She dragged him into the air and choked him, draining his life force until he was unable to breathe.

Rhone dashed over to help Jennie, forced his eyes away from Rogers, and held the exposed wires. The knife was on the floor next to him.

Rico struggled, his face creased in pain. Jennie growled. "You've been a nuisance for the last time." Her face was red, eyes focused on the specter in front of her. How many times had he almost come between her and justice? A boiling fury overtook her.

"Which color?" Rhone asked, holding the knife to each in turn. Something inside the bomb clicked.

Jennie didn't hear him. "I don't take a lot of pleasure in eradicating people from this Earth, but I'm going to take a great deal of joy in destroying you." Her eyes widened as the words came unbidden to her tongue. *"Deus est; Et inimicos eorum dispersus est et eos, qui oderunt eum, a facie ejus..."*

Rhone shouted. "Jennie! Which color?"

If Jennie could hear him, she showed no sign. *"Ut impellere fumum, pulsi sunt..."*

Rhone shouted louder than ever, but there was still no response. The specter glowed white under her power, an orb of light taking him away. Rhone could see the irony as he imagined the bomb in front of him taking his life soon, too.

Jennie's eyes turned pale. Rico was all but lost in the light. *"...liquescit cera a facie ignis et peccatores coram Deo."*

With a final scream, Rico pulsed with holy light. Rhone was almost blinded. He shielded his eyes and looked down at the floor where Rogers lay with his head turned toward him. Rogers raised a weak hand and muttered a single word, "Blue."

Wasting no time, Rhone slashed the blue wire in his hand, catching the skin of his palm, too. The bomb shuddered, then was still. Rhone prayed he had cut the right wire, but he wouldn't be sure until they had gotten out of there and enough time had passed.

"Jennie! Let's go!" Rhone shouted.

The light vanished. Jennie's eyes snapped back into focus. She looked around as if remembering where she was.

"The bomb?" she asked.

Rhone nodded. "Taken care of, I think." He grabbed Rogers' arm and cradled it around his neck. "Here, help me get him back topside."

Jennie took Rogers' other arm, and they dashed from the rec room.

Neither of them uttered a word as with every step they took, they prepared for the inevitable explosion behind them.

When they reached the top floor and the bomb had still not detonated, they breathed a collective sigh of relief.

CHAPTER FORTY-EIGHT

Washington DC, USA

Jennie blinked as she stepped into the sunlight. Rogers was unconscious between her and Rhone and was the only one of the three who didn't look up in startled surprise as they exited the HQ.

Agent Sturgeon broke from her intense conversation with Baxter and stepped toward them. "Is it disarmed?"

Jennie could only give a small nod.

There were easily a hundred of them gathered outside the facility, half wearing SIA uniforms, the other half in SIS fatigues. Lionus stood beside Daggro, who had clearly been dragged out of the HQ by Carolyn, Baxter, and Sandra as they obeyed her wishes despite their personal feelings and rescued as many people as they could from the blast radius.

Clustered among them was the group of disheveled men and women who had masqueraded as SIA agents. Jennie glared at them. "You caught them all?"

Sturgeon nodded. "Anyone who left that building is with us now. It was lucky your friends came out when they did since we were all about to head inside to look for you."

Jennie glanced down at Rogers. Lucky didn't seem to be the right word for this occasion. "There'll be time to talk," she muttered. "Let's get Rogers to the hospital.

Ashton ferried them to the hospital in the Airbus. Jennie had handed over the reins to Sturgeon in her absence, much to Lionus' and Daggro's displeasure.

As agents from both sides interrogated the enemy, Jennie and Baxter waited for news on Rogers in the hallway of the hospital. Jennie had refused medical attention for her bruises and injuries, stating that they were nothing and would heal. They always did.

Jennie and Baxter were quiet, and time passed slowly. Jennie made an effort to catch up on her notifications and was alarmed to see that things had developed further in Richmond. Julia would need to catch her up fully when they were out of there, but for now, Jennie found Tanya's number and hit "Dial."

Tanya answered almost instantly. They were back at the manor, collecting together their forces to go against this new enemy—the Dreadnought. Tanya even spoke of trying to break the poltergeists out of their borders and bring them along for extra numbers as she knew how busy Jennie and the others were.

Jennie told her to slow down. Washington wasn't too far from Richmond, and they had the numbers to back them up. All Jennie needed to do was issue the command, and it would be likely many would follow. Especially given that she and Rhone—well, more Rhone —had saved Rogers' life.

"There is just one thing," Tanya added as they neared their good-bye. "We're not sure where Jiao has gotten to. She was supposed to be at the manor, but she's nowhere to be found. I wondered if she went for a walk into town, but that seems quite unlike her."

Jennie rubbed her eyes. "Seems to be the common thread at the minute—invisible friends and enemies." She thought back to Rico, still not quite believing he had reappeared yet again. "We've still got no clue who the Dragon is, and she seems to be the missing link in this mess. If we can find the Dragon, we can end this whole damn ordeal." Jennie sighed then muttered, "Renminbi…"

There was a pause on the other side of the phone.

"What?" Jennie asked. "Tanya, why have you gone quiet?"

Tanya stared at the wall, eyes unblinking. She held the phone loosely in her hand as a flood of memories came back to her. The gunmen were somewhere downstairs, waiting for the all-clear to attack the quarry. Jiao was missing.

Jiao…

It came back to her in crystal clarity, that niggling sensation she had experienced when staring at the exchange bureau sign. It was written right there in little red LEDs: *Renminbi.*

"Tanya, why have you gone quiet?" Jennie repeated.

"Jiao," Tanya mumbled, recalling the units of Chinese currency that had been listed. The Jiao was equivalent to one-tenth of a Chinese yuan. It had been in front of their faces all along.

Jennie's voice was sharp. "Tanya, speak up."

"Jiao," Tanya repeated. "Jiao is the Dragon. She's the one behind all this."

At that moment, the pieces of the puzzle clicked together. Why Jiao was so quiet, why she was so keen to learn about Jennie's operation, why she had been able to expunge the women of their specters.

Why she was gone at the pinnacle of their discoveries.

Jiao waited at the entrance to the quarry's cave. The sun was unrelenting, the sky a perfect azure. Surrounding her were the beginnings of the army of possessed, encircling her and standing like silent sentinels.

She stared into the dark mouth of the cave. Footsteps echoed around the large hole and reverberated out toward her. A moment later, two women stepped into view.

Madame Celestine looked awful. Her hair was a nest of tangles, and the bags beneath her eyes were dark. It seemed that in finding a new primary host, Rathbourne had left the husk of his former body behind, with only enough of him left inside to keep control over her.

The new woman, however, was in peak physical condition, older than she would have expected, but with the body of a soldier. She held an AK comfortably in her hands.

A man's voice leaked from the woman's mouth. "You come to us willingly?"

"I come with an offer," Jiao replied.

The woman cocked her head. "What can a puny excuse for a woman offer a god such as me? When I can enter who I may and control these lands, there is little of value to be had in negotiation."

Jiao held his stare. "I have dominion over a band of powerful mortals who will add sufficient sway to our discussions. You are the last king from your era, are you not?"

The woman grinned, the smile unnaturally wide for her face. "What use have I for you to shepherd more mortals my way? I can build my army alone."

"You're up against a challenge," Jiao declared. "A woman who is maybe more powerful even than you. You will need someone by your side. A power who can warn you of her approach. A woman who can govern at your side. Perhaps even a queen."

The woman narrowed her eyes, the Dreadnought's interest caught. "Or I could control you and *make* you tell me."

Her hands lashed out before her, dark shadows spreading from her fingertips. The smoke snaked toward Jiao, who took a step back and readied her stance. Three gold rings decorated her fingers, and as she circled her hands around her body and head, she created a forcefield that staved off the smoke and prevented it from touching her skin.

The smoke surrounded her, but with a final push, a flash of light extinguished it. The woman was lost for breath as a surge of power made its way toward her.

Jiao grinned. "You have no power or dominion here." She readjusted her stance and stared at the woman, able to just about see a hint of the spectral demon living inside of her. "So. Do we have a deal?"

CHAPTER FORTY-NINE

<u>Richmond, Virginia, USA</u>

The reception lounge of King Manor had never seen so many guests. The room was quiet as the assembled mix of SIA, SIS, King's Court, and Spectral Planes representatives waited for the last of their order to arrive.

Earlier that day, the Richmond sky had been buzzing with the humming drone of helicopters. Jennie summoned the leaders of each of the respective organizations to convene and discuss what lay ahead. The realization that the woman they had rescued from the clutches of Peter Zhao, the former Dragon, was linked to the madness currently taking place across Washington and its neighboring states had struck them like an ice pick to the heart.

It had been Tanya who had made the discovery, her memory triggered by the currency exchange bureau she had passed in Richmond. The only clue they had to go on had been "Renminbi," a word uttered several times by Zhao, but they hadn't known what it meant.

When Tanya had seen the denominations of the Chinese currency and her eyes had lingered on the "jiao"—a denomination of Chinese coin—she hadn't been sure why this stood out to her, until much later when she discovered that Jiao was missing from the manor.

She still couldn't believe it. No one could. Jiao was so quiet and innocent. It would, however, explain her strange behavior of late. The strange power she harnessed in freeing the two mortal women from their possession without telling anyone else. The sudden hanging up of her phone when Tanya had entered her chambers. Her curiosity and willingness to accompany Jennie and the others to their new headquarters without question or reserve.

Tanya's only *true* surprise was that Julia hadn't been the first to discover it all. Particularly with her massive brain and studious demeanor, Julia had been their go-to resource for research when it had come to the strange goings-on in Richmond. Julia had translated the text they found on the Dreadnought's sarcophagus and had since been trying to dive deeper into any mentions of his existence in the history books.

So far, nothing had shown up.

The front door opened, and all heads turned toward the lobby through a large open archway. Jennie walked inside, a paper bag in one hand, laden down by heavy items. She shut the door, then headed behind the makeshift bar she had created in the reception lounge.

Tanya caught the smiles of her friends: Carolyn, Lupe, Baxter, Sandra, and Feng Mian. They were the only ones among the gathered group who had grown accustomed to Jennie's obsession with cocktail-making.

The room remained silent as Jennie unloaded bottles, then quietly counted the number of heads in the room. It wasn't until she screwed up the paper bag and threw it into a wicker trash basket that someone actually spoke up.

Agent Sturgeon, of the Paranormal Court's SIS department, rose to her feet. "Excuse me, Rogue, I don't mean to cut into your recreational time, but I was under the impression that we had a crisis on our hands."

Jennie rested her hands on the bar and examined the bottles and cartons she had placed before her. She didn't bother to look up at Sturgeon. "We do. Doesn't mean we can't enjoy a little refreshment while we discuss the particulars of the operation, does it? Relax, it's just something to take the edge off."

Sturgeon turned to the spectral forms of Agent Clark and Agent Tiptry for help. They each shrugged their shoulders.

Before Sturgeon could say another word, Jennie unscrewed the lid from a bottle that contained a violently orange liquid. It was so bright that it was nearly neon. She started pouring. "Did you know that alcohol has been proven to lower stress and anxiety levels? Over the last few years, alcohol has gotten a bit of a bad rep, what with binge drinking and the associated health risks of chugging wine and whiskey on a regular basis, but when taken in moderation, alcohol can do a lot to lubricate social awkwardness, and limber up the mind."

Carolyn laughed. "Moderation? Is that what you call it?"

Jennie looked out from over her dark glasses. She smirked. "Yes. Moderation."

She filled five metallic shakers with a measure of the orange liquid, then started measuring out an array of white and brown liqueurs. Each of the drinks looked as though they shouldn't mix, but she added them with a confidence that couldn't be questioned. Despite the current situation, the newcomers to the manor watched on with interest.

The only person not taken by the demonstration was Tanya. "We should've seen it coming. Jiao. It's so obvious, now. We could have prevented this from happening."

Jennie started shaking each metallic container in turn. "It's not your fault. Hiding in plain sight is one of the oldest tricks in the book. Besides, you did what you could with the resources you had. The fact is that even if we hadn't been here, the Dreadnought would have found his way into existence, anyway. Jiao had nothing to do with his unleashing. We don't know that the two are connected, anyway, so let's keep optimistic and find a way to hunt down that bitch."

Jennie placed the last shaker down and wiped her brow with her forearm. "Orders are up. Get yours while they're cold."

She ducked under the desk and retrieved a number of glasses that she lined up on the counter. When she returned to standing, no one had moved a muscle.

"Oh, come on," she urged. "Don't make me beg. I made these for all of you."

Sturgeon's brow furrowed. Agent Lionus, who was the only member of the US Government's SIA currently in any kind of position to act as a representative, given SAiC Kurt Rogers' current incapacitation in the hospital, and Agent Daggro's much-needed hibernation, was the only one who leaped to his feet and took his drink.

He winked at Jennie as he took a sip. "How many of these until you and me finally end up in the sack?"

Jennie scratched her chin. "You're really still trying to go there?"

He grinned. "So, sue me."

Jennie sighed and leaned forward. His eyes trailed to her chest. "Hey, eyes up here. Good. That's better. I'm only going to say this once more, and you know me—I'm a woman of my word. The next time you try to come on to me, I'm going to take one of these corkscrews and find a way to uncork that little bean bag you've got dangling between your legs. I'll probably start while you're asleep. In case you haven't been informed yet, I can turn spectral and approach you when you least expect it."

The color drained from Lionus' face.

"Good," Jennie continued. "Now, tuck that little prick between your legs and sit down. Pray to God that I haven't poisoned your drink, too."

Lionus turned without a word and sat on one of the couches. Jennie clapped twice. "Order up! I'm not kidding. We need to be loose and limber for these discussions. Sturgeon, that means you, too. You never used to be this much of a prude in London. I remember you once drinking so much wine that you ended up snogging the deer head mounted on the wall of the White Lion. Just because you have a station now, doesn't mean you can't enjoy yourself."

Sturgeon glanced at Tiptry and Clark as if for permission. Clark, still bitter about losing his position as Queen Victoria's primary mortal agent and living life as a specter, shrugged. "It's up to you."

Sturgeon's shoulders softened. She rose and took her drink. After that, every mortal in the room followed suit.

Some of them drank faster than others. Jennie was glad to have Ruby and Jack in the room with her. Although they were currently employed by the SIA, she hoped it wouldn't be all that long before they joined her team in King's Court. Still, politics were a turbulent game, and she needed the SIA on her side. She didn't want to steal all of their best staff too quickly.

"You're a true alchemist," Lyla, one of the previously possessed women, commented as she drained half her drink in one.

Jennie hadn't met Lyla or Krissie until just then. She studied them both. They could not look more out of place in their yoga pants amongst the ranks of specters, secret agents, and studious mortals.

"Thanks," Jennie replied. "Really, Hendrick is the true alchemist, I just dabble in liquor."

Hendrick's ancient face wrinkled. "It's still a science." He raised his glass. "Thank you."

Lupe sat behind him and raised his glass, too.

"To the matter at hand," Sturgeon stated once more, trying to bring them to the present. "Rogue, I'm guessing you haven't brought us all here to break bread and get wobbly with alcohol, so can we get to the point, please? I still have men and women stationed out in Pennsylvania and New Jersey, and you're telling us that the threat has moved?"

Jennie raised her eyebrows. "Drink up, Sturgeon. Clearly, your cares haven't abated enough yet. I can feel your tension from here."

Sturgeon grumbled.

Baxter laughed and raised his eyebrows at Jennie.

"Fine!" Jennie resigned. "Firstly, I'm not saying that the threat has moved. The reason that I've gathered you all here is that in trying to bring ourselves together to address our problem, we have only gone and fractured ourselves further.

"Sturgeon, I want to thank you and your team once again for

coming to our aid in our time of need. Your agents and specters are a welcome addition to this operation. I believe we need to keep our eyes locked on the sites where the detonations have happened. We also need to round up the remaining Seven who are scattered and in hiding in order to end this."

"How many have we lost?" Jimmy Dean, a rotund specter with inflated cheeks asked. When Jennie had moved her attention to Washington to meet the SIA, it had been Jimmy who had stood in as a leader in their stead. "You said 'the remaining.'"

"There are only four mortals remaining," Jennie replied. "Tommy Vincenzo, Bobby Dalton, Craig Cowley, and Sammy Garcia. Ruben McAffey is now a specter and we've lost sight of him. Zhao is gone and destroyed."

Jennie's hand unconsciously moved to her temples, recalling how Zhao had implanted himself into her mind and memories and manipulated her on her a wild goose chase of New York.

"What about the last one?" Clark exclaimed. "You mentioned six."

Jennie pointed their attention toward a blonde woman on the couch beside Ashton, their helicopter pilot. She raised a hand and waved. "That would be me. Cassie Ferriss."

As a wave of mumbling rippled through the room, she added, "Please, I assure you I'm on your side. I never wanted to be a part of this. My father was the villain, I'm just another casualty in the collateral of his life. The sooner we rid the world of the Seven...well, the *Six*—"

"Actually, it's the Five, now," Carolyn interjected.

"The Five," Cassie continued. "The sooner I can be free to live a normal life."

Ruby let out a small laugh. Cassie turned to her.

"Oh, please," Ruby declared. "Nothing will be normal for you anymore. Nothing will be normal for any of us again, will it?"

"Depends what you mean by normal," Lupe replied.

Jennie waved her hands. "Let's not devolve into a philosophical debate, okay? Here's what needs to happen. Sturgeon, Jimmy, Lionus, I need to borrow some of your agents and specters to station at Richmond. I realize that we're all stretching our forces rather thin by trying to cover all the key cities that have been affected, but it's just what we need to do, okay? Times are tough, and they're about to get a whole lot tougher."

"Why should we?" Lionus replied. He had grown sulky since the news of Rogers' return had reached his ears. Who knew how long he'd have before Rogers revoked the powers Daggro had given him? "You've stolen some of our agents already. If we give you more, how do we know we'll get them back?"

Sturgeon sat up straighter, her ears pricking up.

Jennie rubbed a hand down her face. She pinched the bridge of her nose, nudging her glasses up for a second. "This isn't the time for getting petty, Lionus. I know you're yet to reach puberty with this kinda stuff, but understand that this is serious. Already we have a handful of terrorists out there causing havoc, and now we're introduced to a goddamn demon specter who's possessing this town? Not only that, but the latest in our line of Dragon suspects has taken off, and it's highly likely that she's gunning to find him. Put your ego aside and let's work on this together. This is bigger than all of us."

Sturgeon nodded her head slowly. "You're right. When I took this position, I didn't just vow to help Queen and Country. I vowed to protect the world from spectral disturbances and to let justice reign. We're with you, Jennie."

Tiptry let out a sudden, barking laugh. "Wait until the queen hears about this."

Sturgeon glared at him. He wilted into the sofa, vanishing from sight.

"Fine," Lionus added, lips barely moving.

Jennie turned to Julia and signaled to her with a nod. Julia leaned over the back of the couch and brought a folder into view. Inside was a series of neatly printed documents.

"What's this?" Sturgeon asked.

"A contract," Jennie replied. "Well, more of an agreement, really. If there's one thing I've learned working with you guys, it's that paper speaks louder than words. I'd like us all to sign on the dotted line before we break and get to work. You'll find my signature is already on there. We work as a team. A large team. For all intents and purposes, I'll act as commander-in-chief. That doesn't make me a dictator, that makes me a single point of contact for this operation. If you're with me, sign on the dotted line. If you're not, then my liquor clearly hasn't done the trick, and you should drink some more."

Jennie flashed a friendly smile to the group. "Come on, if we can't play nicely together, what's the point in calling us the good guys?"

Sturgeon's face broke into a smile. "She's got a point." She stepped forward and signed on the line.

Clark shook his head. "The queen is going to lose her shit when she hears about this."

"By then we'll be victorious," Sturgeon replied, letting Jimmy and Lionus step up to add their signatures. "Times are changing, guys. I trust Jennie. I've known her for years. Just because you couldn't check your egos at the door, doesn't mean I'm going to let the world suffer. Not on my watch."

Jennie beamed. For once, she had found a decent human being working for the paranormal court. Over a hundred years of service, and finally it had happened.

When everyone had signed and returned to their seats, Jennie closed the folder and handed it back to Julia. She poured herself another glass of her cocktail and raised it to the room. "Okay then, chaps. Shall we get to strategizing?"

CHAPTER FIFTY

<u>Richmond, Virginia, USA</u>

As the sun set in the west and the fleet of helicopters took off into the skies once again, Jennie stood on the manor's back lawn and watched them fade into the horizon.

She smiled. The weight that had been resting on her chest had lessened, and things were moving into action. Sturgeon had returned to Pennsylvania and would send a troop of agents to Richmond, and Lionus had followed. Within the next few hours, they might have enough of a mini-army to withstand the coming battle.

If there is *a battle to be had,* Jennie thought.

At this point, there were no guarantees. Hopefully, Jennie and her team could quell the coming flames before things really started to heat up. The worst-case scenario was that Jiao would be out there somewhere with the Dreadnought, but until that was confirmed, she'd remain optimistic.

What other explanation is there?

Jennie shook away the thoughts and ushered the rest of her team toward her. She assigned everyone their tasks and rolled out onto the street out front, piling her operative crew into a minibus she had managed to hire out on short notice from a local garage.

She only allowed her best and brightest on board, those who had training and combat experience. Carolyn, Feng Mian, Baxter, and Sandra represented the specters, while Jennie selected Triton, Roman, Ashton, and Rhone to join them. She was pleased to see that Ruby and Jack had been donated by Lionus as a gesture of goodwill. The only trained conduit to remain behind was Ula, given that Jennie was aware that they were leaving Cassie under the house's protection, and they would need someone to tackle any issues that arose in her absence.

They waved their goodbyes and sped into the city. Stars began to twinkle, and a haze of clouds left dark patches on the sky. The city had grown quieter since the incident at the marketplace, for which Jennie was thankful, and soon they left the houses and buildings behind them as the quarry came into view.

Roman leaned toward the window and looked out at the dark pit. Compared to the previous night when lights had been left on around the dig site, everything there was dark. The starlight did little to illuminate any activity down below.

"Are you sure they're going to be there?" Jennie asked Roman and Triton.

"No," Roman replied dryly.

Jack arched an eyebrow. "Then why are we going there?"

"That's not what he means," Triton clarified. "He means we'll have no idea what we'll find when we're there."

They fell into quiet as Ashton pulled the bus toward the pit's entrance.

They could make out no activity below. Each prepared with their weapons before them, they aimed into the darkness. The construction vehicles had all moved on, and now the quarry appeared even larger than before.

Jennie led the way, with Baxter only a step behind. They navigated their way toward the yawning mouth of the cave and paused before it. "You know, I had a dream about a tunnel like this…"

"And a train?" Baxter added.

A smile made its way onto the others' faces.

"Come on," Jennie instructed, passing into the tunnel without fear.

The darkness consumed them. After a dozen meters or so, Ruby, Jack, and Triton switched on the flashlights on their cell phones. It was just enough to make out a few feet before them. Every step echoed around them, giving the impression that an army was approaching, but other than the noise, Jennie could detect nothing of the specters who were possessing the mortals.

After some time, they reached the back of the cave. The room where Roman, Triton, and Ula had been waylaid and charged at was even smaller than they remembered.

Jennie searched in the dark. "Where is it?"

"What?" Baxter asked.

"The sarcophagus," Jennie replied. "It's not here. Look."

Where the sarcophagus had been, was nothing more than an empty space. A rectangular mark on the floor was the only sign that the tomb had once stood there.

"Well, that confirms it," Jennie muttered. "The sarcophagus is the key to this specter's undoing."

Carolyn appeared beside her. "Any idea what we're dealing with?"

Jennie was silent for a long time, buried in her own thoughts. Eventually, she took a deep breath and sighed. "There's a tenet of Ancient Egyptian religion known as *akh*. '*Akh*' represents the deceased, I have taken it to mean that a deceased person will become transfigured, that their spectral powers will reflect their deeds in life. At one point in history, Egyptians used to unlock the tombs of their forebears to insert the bodies of the recent dead within that bloodline. They were being economical with space and sparing resources."

"What does that have to do with our situation?" Carolyn asked.

Jennie shrugged. "When a specter is unsettled, no matter what its background it's going to look for a way to satisfy itself. I won't know without experiencing this specter myself, but my feeling is that *akh* is playing a big hand here. The ancient dead has an unfinished purpose, noble in its own beliefs, and until that purpose is settled, it will continue to wreak havoc."

Carolyn exhaled. "Damn. It's strong, then?"

Jennie nodded. "I'd say so. Given what we already know, we should prepare ourselves for the worst. Imagine the Mendlesons manifested into a single body, able to roam the city at will."

Baxter shuddered.

"Who are the Mendlesons?" Rhone asked.

"Irrelevant," Jennie replied. "All we need to focus on is where the hell this specter has gone. You said he has an army? Well, where are they all?"

Triton adjusted his rifle in his hands. "They do have an army. I've seen them. We were there. Must be at least a hundred of them now, at a minimum. What with the yoga studio, the marketplace, and that gun-happy woman, they should be easy to spot. How could they hide?"

Ruby tore her eyes away from where the sarcophagus had been. "Hiding in plain sight?"

"What do you mean?" Baxter asked.

"Same as Jiao," Ruby continued. "If all of those who had been possessed were just everyday citizens, then the best place to hide them would be in their normal, everyday lives, right? No uniforms, no markings, only that strange vacant stare you spoke about to distinguish them, it would be the perfect hiding place."

Jennie nodded, impressed. "You've got a good point there."

"We can't rule it out as a possibility," Roman agreed.

Jack grinned at Ruby. It was cute, there was almost something like sibling love between the pair. "So, where do we go from here?"

"On the hunt," Jennie replied. "We need to scour every inch of the city. Maybe we'll find Jiao, maybe we'll find the possessed army, we might even find the Dreadnought. Whatever we do, we have to prepare for the worst, keep our eyes open, and get ready to attack at any time."

"What about the missing sarcophagus?" Ruby asked.

Jennie turned back to the empty space. "I have a feeling that's going to be key to unlocking the Dreadnought's demise. From the tomb they rise, to the tomb they fall. Some specters, like the wraiths and the poltergeists, bind themselves to certain locales or trophies. The sarcophagus may just be this one's Achilles heel."

Empty-handed, they about-faced and retraced their footsteps through the tunnel. Halfway back to the fresh air, Jennie paused and held out an arm. "Someone's here."

"You can feel them?" Baxter asked.

Jennie didn't answer, instead choosing to move ahead with a slower pace.

The feeling grew stronger within her, the sense that nearby a specter was lurking. She replayed the incident with Rico in her head, remembering his final cry as he was exorcized and cast into the void. He couldn't be back. The signal didn't feel right. It felt…tainted.

They rounded a corner and the mouth of the cave came into sight. So did a figure standing in a floor-length cloak.

Jennie stopped the others. For a moment, they stood in silence.

"Move aside," Jennie finally instructed. "Whoever you are and whatever you want, we can deal with this peacefully. Move aside and let us talk like rational human beings."

The figure remained silent.

Jennie homed in on her signals, trying to determine what it was she was sensing. The being wasn't entirely spectral, that much was clear. That meant he or she was mortal and possessed.

Jennie took a step forward. "I can help you. You don't have to live like this."

The figure shuddered. A feminine gasp came from a mouth they couldn't see.

Jennie took another few steps. "We're on your side. Trust me. I can clear this demon from you."

When Jennie took her next step, the figure whirled on their heels and ran for the mouth of the cave. They didn't spare a glance at the small device they left on the tunnel's floor. A blinking LED light indicated that something was about to happen.

And Jennie knew exactly what it was.

"Get down!" she cried, throwing herself farther into the tunnel. High-pitched beeping came from the device, increasing in pace until it was a relentless shriek. They ran back into the darkness of the tunnel.

A moment later, the bomb exploded.

Julia stared at the screen, trying to make her eyes focus. The images and text were blurred, and she struggled to take in the information she was searching for.

She lay on the couch in the manor's brand-new library. Shelves had been installed along all of the walls, reaching from floor to ceiling, but only a handful of books accommodated the space. Julia hoped that Jennie would invest in enough books to fill this entire room, and then some. This could be her sanctuary, a place to while away the days and learn everything she ever wanted to know about specters.

For now, all she had to rely on was the tablet.

"Burning the midnight oil?" Tanya asked, appearing in the doorway.

Julia gave a weak grin, her head beginning to pound. "Something like that."

Tanya glanced around the bookshelves, taking it all in. "Not bad, huh? Well, maybe one day it will be filled. I've yet to ship over my library from New York. Throughout my time serving as the Spirit Mother, I managed to attain quite a collection of books and passages on specterdom."

"You were always a believer?" Julia sat up straighter, her bones groaning from the exertion.

"I was," Tanya continued. "Somehow, I always knew that something was out there, beyond the realms of mortal understanding. I'd spend days thinking that someone was standing just outside of the boundaries of my peripheral vision, only to find them gone when I turned to see. Graveyards would speak to me, and after a while, people started to learn my name," she scoffed. "I used to think I was an expert in all of this stuff."

"Then you experienced their world for yourself?" Julia murmured, reflecting on her own past.

Tanya took a seat across from Julia. The women looked worlds apart, Tanya with her flaming red hair and delicate contours of her cheeks, Julia with her hair as dark as night and an air of weariness that only came with age.

Tanya looked deep into her eyes. "I'm jealous of you, you know."

Julia looked surprised. "Oh? I can't imagine why you would ever waste your time with that."

"You've lived through it," Tanya explained. "You've fought on the frontlines and powered specters under your control. You've been able to contribute to a greater purpose and get your hands dirty…" She trailed away.

"You want to *control* specters?" Julia laughed. "I didn't have you pegged for a bad guy."

"I don't mean like that," Tanya clarified. "I mean, all I've managed to do is cause more trouble for Jennie. Without Sandra, I am powerless. All I have left are these books that I've abandoned. You know I haven't read a book in months? I used to read all the time. It was my life to dive into pages and learn the truths of the world."

Julia gave a knowing nod. "You've got time now, haven't you?"

Tanya considered this. "You don't mind me joining you?"

"Not at all," Julia replied. "We can compare notes." She tapped her chin. "Only, I do have three conditions."

Tanya smirked.

"One," Julia pressed on, "You wait for me while I fetch one of Hendrick's energy potions."

"Done," Tanya replied.

"Two, you get a move on and get those books over from NYC. If you like, I'll bring my collection over, too. We can start to stock this bibliotheque ourselves."

"And three?" Tanya asked.

"Three…" The humor left Julia's face, knowing that what she was about to ask would be a tall order, and she wasn't sure she'd earned the right yet. "Number three. I want to know what it's like to turn spectral. I want Sandra to show me."

Tanya pondered this for a moment. Her face straightened. Julia wondered if she'd pressed too far.

"Deal," Tanya replied at last. "Sort number one out, and I'll deal with number three."

Julia jumped up with renewed vigor in her step and ran to Hendrick's lab.

CHAPTER FIFTY-ONE

New York City, New York, USA, (one week earlier)

Zhao stared at Jiao, his eyes narrowed with the pain of carrying his mortal body. "United they stand, divided they fall."

He had grown more obese as the weeks and months had worn on. His internal organs had begun to falter. Lately, he hadn't been able to take a simple breath without the death rattle coming from his throat.

He was a sweaty mess, his naked torso covered with a shimmering coat of liquid. Small trails pooled in the folds of his fat before trickling down, a salty water feature that eventually soaked into his pants.

Jiao's heart beat faster. For months she had waited for this moment, and now that it had come, she was ready for it. Ready to carry the torch and take on the next stage of the Dragon's work.

Zhao wheezed and spluttered into the ring of his fist. "They are coming. My spies have spotted them out in the city, gathering their intel and sniffing out our trail. Soon they will burst through that door, and your time will come. Are you sure that you're prepared?"

Jiao said nothing, only nodded.

"I have moved the pieces into place," Zhao continued. "This plan is to be my magnum opus. I will buy you all the time that I can allow you in order to

give you the greatest chance of success possible. Immortality lies in the name of the Dragon, I am old. Weak. Unable to carry the flame any longer. You must ensure that the legacy continues. Do you understand?"

Jiao nodded, her lips a thin white line on her face. She had heard the plan a dozen times. As each of Zhao's henchmen knocked on the door and brought their reports on the whereabouts of those seeking Zhao, she had replayed it all over again in her mind. Zhao had spared no details, concocting his master plan out loud, asking for Jiao's input, and ensuring that she knew every single step as it came.

There were contingency plans baked in, alternatives for every eventuality. Even in the eventuality that he was exorcized, he had rolled the dice and found an answer.

"Do you think that likely?" Jiao asked. She knew enough about specters to understand their existence and how to rid them from the world, but even she doubted that anything could take down Zhao once he had begun his eternity as a ghost.

Zhao tried to adjust himself on his makeshift throne, the same place he made his bed and filled his bedpan. The same location Jiao had doted on him hand and foot, a faithful companion in his dying days, earning his trust as his successor.

Zhao coughed. "They have another. She is powerful. You must watch her closely. She may be the only one able to unravel our operation."

Zhao had preceded to tell Jiao all about the one they called Rogue. Though he had never met her personally, he had gathered enough intel from the faithful specters who roamed his castle, high up in the apartment building in Chinatown. Her name had spread like a chilly mist, seeping into the marrow of his bones, and he knew that he needed to be ready for her.

"I know not what gifts death will grant me," Zhao continued. "Yet I pray for a power that can help me execute our plan. Something that could challenge Rogue and bring her to her knees. Imagine it, the former-Dragon reaping the glory of being the one who removed the fabled Rogue."

"Very impressive," Jiao offered dryly.

Zhao choked with his whooping cough, and Jiao offered water. Somewhere far below them, gunfire rang out.

"They're coming," Zhao muttered. His eyes met Jiao's. "Are you ready?"

The truth was that Jiao had been ready for weeks. While silent in the company of her master, behind closed doors she had assembled her own task force, set forth her own spies. At the first mention of Rogue, who was known among her peers as Jennie, she had set out to discover as much as she could about her future opponent.

Layers of Jennie's past were cloaked in secrecy, but she had managed to pry information from specters in New York, and even some contacts abroad. While taking a nightly stroll through the city—something that Zhao had forbidden her from doing, but what he didn't know when he slept wouldn't hurt him—she had encountered a specter with slick-backed hair and a Tommy gun clutched tightly in his hands.

They had conversed, the specter happily detailing everything he knew about Rogue. She had been the reason that he was scouring the city, looking for the bitch so he may exact his revenge.

A chance meeting with a lot of potential. Jiao had brought Rico back to the apartment and introduced him to Zhao. Zhao had informed him of his plan to unite the Seven and bade him follow Ruben to Washington, knowing that he would likely be the one who got cold feet when it came to action. Not only that, but Zhao had heard rumor of an agency within Washington who were aiding Rogue and her comrades. Only a few weeks ago, social media footage had exposed the existence of a task force in Alexandria that had managed to suppress the amount of information leaked from an explosion at a former candy factory.

"This is bigger than we know." Zhao gasped, taking the water from Jiao and wetting his lips. "It will be a turbulent ride. Are you ready for your role?"

Jiao knelt before Zhao and kissed his feet. "Anything for you, my Dragon."

Zhao's lips peeled into a broad smile. His teeth were stained pink and yellow. "Good girl. Carry the mantle, but don't let them in on your true identity until it's time."

"I will serve the gold and red until my heart stills," Jiao replied, eyes locked on the floor, head bowed. When she raised them again, she took her place beside Zhao and waited.

The gunfire was increasing. People moved outside of their door. She bit her lip, unsure if that fluttering inside of her stomach was nervousness or excitement at what was to come.

She was ready to play the role she was given. She had been born for this. Trained and molded by the Dragon. No matter what happened next, she would play her part to the letter, discover the truth behind Rogue and her operation, and put herself in the greatest position possible to revolt the uprising and claim what was hers.

Her people would know her name. The US would know her name. Her long-lost ancestors would look down at her from the heavens and applaud her from the stars. A whole dynasty of infamy and glory coursed through her veins, and now it was time to act.

Richmond, Virginia, USA, (present day)

The community center had been abandoned over a decade ago. A large, red brick building on the edge of the city, the center was surrounded by an acre of overgrown foliage. A crooked mesh fence circled the perimeter, with plenty of holes cut into its side where kids and thugs had broken inside to leave their mark on the old building.

The building was basic. There was a large hall at the center of its fixtures, with a few smaller rooms leading off from broken doors that clung to their hinges. A large turret-like appendage poked out of the roof like a determined weed, and it was from here that Jiao looked out over the city.

The turret was a bell tower. The bell was rusty but large enough to hide her in its shadows. From up here, she could see a one-mile radius of the building. The suburbs of the city were spread out before her, oblivious to the Dragon in their midst. Richmond was not the ideal location for her to build her army, but it was good enough to hide their trail.

Her gown fluttered in the wind, a silk thing in shades of royal crimson. The edges of her gown were golden, and there was a large ornamental dragon stitched onto the left breast and trailing down toward her hip.

"I've waited so long to don the cloak of my people," Jiao muttered to the breeze. "To stand with my back straightened and stare upon the land that will soon be mine. One can only play the fool for so long before the real fools grow suspicious."

She smirked, her lips a vibrant red. She had masked herself in makeup, dolled herself into the queen that she would soon become. With an army at her side, she could rule these lands, and bring back the power of her forebears. A true dynasty that would carry indefinitely throughout time. Immortality belonged to the unforgettable.

Her reign would be larger than any of her predecessors since they'd migrated to the United States. Her face would be on currency, her name known to all across the land. If she played this right, then nothing would stand in her way. Mortals and specters would work under her command, and the great glories of the past would make their claim in the present day.

The past could rise again. She had living proof in the building below her. The possessed the Dreadnought had taken were standing in the hall, accommodating half of the space already. Like statues, they waited for a command, their eyes blank, their ears open.

Rathbourne was a wellspring of power. Each possession cost a tiny part of his entity, yet he had much to give. The woman he had taken as his primary host lay in the tomb they had pillaged from the quarry, the lid askew as they rested. He had been impressed by Jiao's display of power, and that had bought her his attention.

The rings glittered on her fingers, catching the rays of the dying sun. Heirlooms from her ancestors, pretty things whose potential had never been realized. For years her family had tracked the legacy of the Dragon, wormed its way into the system, and finally, she was sitting next to the throne, painfully close to her true position.

There was just one thing that stood in her way.

She stood at the bell tower, hands laced behind her back, and watched the sun set. Night fell, and yet she waited. When midnight neared, a faint boom told her of Madame Celestine's work.

Rogue knew the truth about her now, that much was clear. Though how much she truly knew was still a mystery. Still, buried deep beneath the packed earth of the outskirts of Richmond, she would be less likely to harm her operation. Maybe all Jiao had bought herself was time as she and Rathbourne laid their foundations, but at least it was progress.

Life was all about progress.

CHAPTER FIFTY-TWO

<u>**Richmond, Virginia, USA**</u>

The last of the falling rocks settled. Dust filled the air and filtered into Jennie's mouth. She brought her top to cover her face and used the white fabric as a filter.

The lights were gone, Jack, Ruby, and Triton's cell phones had been dropped in the scuffle, and they had no idea where they were. Around her, Jennie could sense the others. She could count the specters easily enough, her powers were designed for such an event, but it was the mortals she was concerned about.

"Roman? Triton?" Someone moved beside her. She patted her hands along the ground and touched a woman's chest.

"Jennie?" Ruby called out to her.

Jennie withdrew her hands. "Sorry."

"Do you really think now's the time to reveal your true feelings for me?" Ruby quipped before spitting out a mouthful of debris. "Honestly, romance can wait."

Jennie laughed weakly. People moved around her.

Triton's voice came from somewhere in the dark. "Jennie? Is that you?"

"Over here," Jennie replied. She helped Ruby to her feet and kept her close. "Hold onto my shoulder. Don't let go. We'll find everyone first."

Triton was about twenty feet away, standing with his back to the tunnel wall. The dark was all-encompassing. This deep underground, and with no access to natural light, it was like swimming through oil. Each step was considered and careful. Occasionally a boulder would block their way and they'd have to navigate around it.

Jennie's hand touched flesh.

"Ouch," Triton complained. "You should think about trimming your nails before you jab your fingers in the dark."

Jennie smiled. "Shut up and grab Ruby's shoulder. We're doing the Conga out of here."

Ruby started to hum the tune. She was stopped when Triton promptly replied with, "No."

Soon enough, they collected Ashton and Jack. Rhone was harder to find until Triton managed to fish out his IR glasses. The man showed up as a red flare in the dark, lying on the ground. Jennie and Triton worked to remove the debris that had fallen onto his stomach. He coughed out dust and spat on the floor. Jennie was almost certain that one of his ribs was broken.

"Shit," she muttered. "How did we not see this coming?"

"Because why would anyone do this?" Ruby replied. "Come on, who traps people in a mine? In the movies, they just straight-up shoot their enemy, not bury them underground." As if suddenly hearing her own words, her voice raised. "Oh, my God. We're buried under here, aren't we? We're going to die in here!"

Her voice echoed around the tunnel. Dust and loose rocks rained down on them. Jennie pulled them away from where it sounded like the cave-in was the worst. When it finally died down, she hissed, "No shouting. The integrity of the tunnel has already been compromised. If you don't want to die in here, then I suggest you shut up and don't disturb the tunnel anymore." She paused, thankful that the others couldn't see the contortions of her face.

"Hold on." Triton tapped Jennie's shoulder. "Have we picked up Roman?"

Jennie performed a roll call, listing everyone who had come into the tunnel with them. When she reached Roman, there was no response.

Jack sighed. "We probably passed him, thinking he was a boulder."

"Here." Triton took the IR glasses from Jennie and led them back the way they had come—although it was impossible to tell—where they found a faint flicker of red in the distance.

They increased their pace but found that the devastation was worse here. Rocks barred their passage, and it became clear that the reason they could see so little of Roman was because all the boulders were blocking the view.

Triton reached him and found that he was unconscious. Without being able to see him properly, there was no way to diagnose the issue.

"We need a light," Triton whispered. "Anything." He turned back to Roman. "Hey, buddy. Wake up, we need to get your ass out of there."

Jennie patted her various pockets and pouches. "Can I borrow someone's gun?"

Ruby donated her pistol. Jennie tore off her sleeve and wrapped it around the barrel of the gun after removing the magazine and clearing the chamber. From her pocket, she made her best judgment on the vial she was choosing and doused the material until it was covered.

She handed the butt of the gun to Triton. "Hold this. Keep it away from your face."

Triton obeyed.

"What are you going to do?" Jack asked.

"The impossible," Jennie replied. In the dark, she drew her two guns. The others heard the firearms drawn from their holsters and protested, knowing a gunshot could force another cave collapse.

Jennie ignored them and spread her arms wide. She cracked her neck, then rested the guns against each other in the shape of an X. With one swift, sharp movement, she pulled the guns apart, making the metal cylinders rub roughly against one another. The metal on metal created a spark that illuminated the tunnel for a split second.

She was too far away from the rag.

This time.

She brought the guns back and repeated the maneuver. This time, the rag caught one of the sparking embers and erupted into light and flames.

It was blinding, going from an abyss to the sight before them. They shielded their eyes, waiting for them to adjust. When their vision cleared, they saw Roman lying on the floor and their hearts fell.

His leg lay trapped under a boulder. Jennie and Triton ran to either side and tried to move it, but it held fast. They ushered Ashton and Rhone over, and between the four of them, they managed to remove the boulder from his leg, rolling it out of the way.

Triton knelt beside him. "It's a good thing he's out cold. That's going to be sore when he wakes up."

That was the understatement of the century. It looked as though Roman's knee had disappeared entirely. His lower leg hung limply as he and Jennie raised him from the floor and hooked his arms around their shoulders.

Baxter appeared from behind them, breathless and wild-eyed. "We've found something. Back there in the cave. It might be a way out."

Jennie looked at him incredulously. "Are you kidding?"

"It's true," Carolyn added. "When you lit that flame, it spread down the tunnel. It's amazing what a little light can do to pitch-black. There's a dark space that might be nothing, but it could be something. It's on the other side of the chamber where the tomb was."

"Lead the way," Jennie instructed.

Ruby was charged with looking after the flame. After a few minutes, it started to sputter and die, but before it could, Jennie ripped off her other sleeve and threw it onto the pistol.

Just keep it fed and it'll serve you well—advice her father had given her when Jennie was nearing her eighteenth birthday, not long after her mother had passed, and survival became a necessity. *Fire is hungry. It won't stop eating. Make sure you feed it sufficiently.*

The place the specters had found was no larger than a crawlspace, a jagged hole that had opened after the disturbance created by the bomb. Sandra appeared through the wall, an excited look on her face. "There's a tunnel in there. It's small, but I think it leads to the sewers."

"What do you mean, you think?" Ruby asked.

Sandra shrugged. "I've never seen sewers before. I think that's what's there. It doesn't smell great."

"That's the sewers," Ashton chuckled.

Feng Mian appeared next to Sandra. "The girl speaks true. The cave is narrow. You'll need to crawl through it. One loud noise could make the whole thing collapse, but it may be the only chance you have at getting the mortals out."

Jennie glanced back at the others. Feng Mian's words were directed at them, knowing that Jennie could turn spectral at any point and just waltz herself out of this predicament.

Not that I ever would leave these guys behind. Not in a million years.

Jennie and Triton gently eased Roman to the ground. He was still limp, but at least he was breathing. They could only hope that he would stay that way until they could clear everyone out and get to the other side.

God knew what would happen when he awoke. He was a strong man, but was anyone *that* strong?

"We'll wait behind," Jennie instructed the others. "Jack, Ruby, you go first. Ashton and Rhone, you follow after. Specters, get the hell out of here and see if you can find where to go once we reach the sewers. We're going to need a hospital, and fast."

"What about you guys?" Rhone asked. "We're not leaving without you."

"We'll go last," Jennie replied, fixing Triton with a concerned look. "We'll only slow you down."

Ruby was the first to head in. As the smallest among them, she was just about able to crawl on her hands and knees. The ceiling scraped her back, and at one point, she yelped when a jagged piece of rock scratched her shoulder.

Dust sprinkled down on her. She placed her hand over her mouth and apologized, the crawl space carrying her voice toward the others.

Jack had to take a different tack, dragging his feet behind as he rolled his forearms one over the other and Army-crawled out of there. Ashton was more graceful, lying on his back and using his feet to propel him onward.

When Rhone had disappeared through the hole, Jennie extinguished the flame on Ruby's pistol. They would have no need for fire in there.

"How are we going to do this?" Triton asked. "You on top, or me?"

A faint chuckle carried down the tunnel.

"Filthy minds," Jennie muttered. "You go first. You pull his arms and drag him backward. I'll stay at his tail end and keep an eye on that leg. If he gets stuck, I'll shove his good leg to unblock him, okay?"

Triton nodded but looked uncertain.

"Either way, this is going to be hard," Jennie soothed, resting a hand on Triton's shoulder. "He'll be okay, but we have to be quick. If he wakes and cries out in pain while he's in there, it might bring us all to ruin."

Triton's face hardened.

Although the trick was not to rush, they still had to try to move quickly. Jennie followed behind Triton as he exhausted himself by dragging Roman along the tunnel. Roman's body was only just narrow enough to fit, thanks to his ridiculously wide shoulders, and along the way, the tunnel narrowed enough that Jennie had to give an encouraging shove from her end to help him along.

At what Jennie guessed must be halfway through the tunnel, Roman grumbled. She was holding his left foot and felt his toes wiggle.

Not now, she thought. *Please, not yet.*

Triton must have felt it, too, because his movements became more jolting. Roman was dragged in quick bursts, their pace increasing. Jennie could hear Triton's exhausted panting.

Another narrow segment caused Roman's body to catch again. With a great effort, they pulled and shoved him ahead. This time his head lifted as he awoke, suddenly trying to raise himself off the ground.

"Fuck! What? Argh!" The syllables burst out his mouth rapid-fire. His arms, which were pinned above his head by Triton, tried to reach for his legs. Although they could not see, Jennie could sense the movements in his language and the movement of his body.

He cried out in pain. His voice was magnified in the crawl space, and rocks fell on Jennie's body. The cave behind her growled and protested, rumbling as Roman's sudden alarm triggered another rockfall.

Shit. Jennie had no other choice. They must be near the end of the tunnel by now since she could feel Baxter and Carolyn with Sandra some way ahead.

Jennie found one of the specters and latched onto them. She stood in the rock and moved past Roman and Triton. When she reached Triton, she lay down in the tunnel and turned material. She clutched his legs and pulled him toward her, hoping that would help him pull Roman. Roman kicked and yelled in pain, protesting the desecration of his broken leg. Jennie called to the others, and within seconds, they had a daisy chain of people dragging Roman out of the tunnel.

The walls shook around them. The others shouted out as rocks fell on their heads. They increased their speed, and finally Jennie popped out of the other side. She dragged Triton with her. Triton dragged Roman.

Just as they cleared the space, the tunnel collapsed. The small space they had just been in sealed without apology. Jennie and the others were left breathless with the smell of waste and sewage around them and a large muscular man wailing in pain.

Jennie looked at Baxter, who studied her with concern. She panted. "And you said that this would be a bad idea."

Despite himself, Baxter let out a soft laugh.

CHAPTER FIFTY-THREE

Richmond, Virginia, USA

Rhone couldn't believe that he was back in the sewers again.

Seriously, is this what my life has come to? A few weeks ago, I was a senior agent in the SIA, now I'm spending my life wasting away in shit-infested tunnels.

These tunnels weren't as generous as the New York sewers. They were crammed and less maintained, with slick stone pathways that ran parallel to the gutters. After they had managed to stifle Roman's cries of pain—thanks to another one of Jennie's array of vials—the group had allowed themselves a few minutes to recover and gather themselves.

"They're one step ahead of us," Ruby commented, brushing the dust off her front. Streams of silver moonlight came down from grates above them, but there was no way to climb up and take Roman out without causing him further damage.

"Always one step ahead," Carolyn repeated.

Jennie gave them an empathetic look. "Don't get disheartened. You know as well as I do that things get worse before they get better. That's just the way of Justice. The bad guys rise, but they reach their peak, and in that time, we catch up. We narrow in on them. We stop them before they go too far. This is just a part of the game."

"Seems like a shitty game to me," Jack sulked. His hair was flecked with dust, and he had faint scratches on his face. "I prefer Monopoly. Or Kerplunk."

Carolyn smirked. "That the one with the sticks and the marbles?"

"Yeah," Jack replied.

Jennie smiled at them. "See, even in the darkest moments, you can find humor. The light will never be extinguished by the dark. That's what we fight for, and that's what we're going to do here. Who cares if they're one step ahead, because all they have to do is slip up once, and we'll be on them like…"

"Roman on Julia?" Triton chuckled.

Jennie, who hadn't been around enough to understand the reference, raised an eyebrow.

Triton shook his head. "I'll explain later."

Rhone grinned.

They followed the sewer, eventually coming across an opening on their left that led into the outside world. The sludge trickled down a slight slope and past a large gray factory. Fresh air caressed their faces.

There were fields and trees around them. A few roads littered the landscape ahead. In the distance, they could just about make out the lights of the city a couple of miles from where they stood.

"Someone's going to have to find the bus," Rhone stated, eyes narrowed as he tried to get his bearings. "I'm thinking the quarry is in that direction somewhere. That's where the bus will be."

Ruby sighed. "It's not like we can call the others, is it? My cell phone is gone."

"Mine, too," Triton added.

Jack nodded. "And mine."

Jennie took hers from her pocket. She had already felt the tell-tale bend of her once-solid phone through her trousers and was prepared for the state that it was in. Tiny glass fragments jabbed her finger as she held the shattered phone. "Mine's out of commission, too."

Ashton walked up the grassy bank that ran either side of the sewer. "I'll volunteer, considering I'm your chauffeur. Ruby? Jack? You're young and sprightly. Want to keep me company? Who knows if that strange figure is still around? She might have blown all the tires on her trip out of the tunnel."

Jennie hadn't considered this. "Are you going to be okay?"

"Sure." Ashton grinned. "Just because I fly helicopters and planes, it doesn't mean I haven't been through the same basic training as Rhone, Jack, and Roobs."

Ruby glared. "It's Ruby."

"Whatever, princess." Ashton stuck out his tongue. "Shall we?"

Jennie watched them disappear over the verge before she slumped on the grass and took a long breath. Triton sat beside her, with Rhone lying peacefully at their feet.

Baxter paced around them, hands behind his back. He stared at the moon and began to sing. *"Stranded at the drive-in. Branded a fool..."*

"What are you doing?" Jennie asked, a smile creasing her cheeks.

Baxter continued, *"What will they say?"*

Rhone groaned. "Please don't."

"Monday at school," Baxter finished, his face breaking out into a huge grin. "I love that film."

"Grease?" Feng Mian asked, uncertain.

Sandra gave them all a strange look. "What are you talking about?"

Jennie waved a hand. "Forget about it. You're too young to understand."

"I'm older than you are," she retorted.

"True," Jennie replied. "But if you don't know what *Grease* is, you never watched the moon landing, and you have never heard of a Sloppy Joe, what life have you really lived to brag about?"

Sandra picked up a pebble and tossed it at Jennie. She batted it away, and it hit Roman in the chest. Roman grumbled.

Sandra and the others tried to stifle their laughs. Jennie playfully glared at Sandra. "Grow up, we've had enough rocks and dirt attacking us today."

When Sandra's eyes lowered, Jennie picked up her own pebble and chucked it through the specter. "Oh, what's one more?"

They arrived at the hospital a little past midnight. Roman still snoozed deeply, unaware of any time passing or the pain that would soon wrack his leg.

Jennie managed to coerce some nurses to rush out to the bus and take Roman on their stretcher. The nurses had a hard time hiding their confusion as they looked at the dirt-covered group, who looked as if they'd been playing in the dirt. The smell of the sewer wasn't kind to them either, and the nurses wrinkled their noses as they placed the injured man on a gurney and carted him away.

Triton was the first to volunteer to stay with Roman. When Jennie tried to argue, claiming they'd need Triton with them due to his skill set, Triton argued back, stating he wouldn't leave a fallen comrade behind. A few minutes later, Ashton put the bus in gear and they left Roman, Triton, and Rhone behind.

Baxter sat beside Jennie and played with his fingers. "We're falling apart. They're dividing us into smaller teams."

Jennie remained quiet.

"The more fractured we are, the more likely they are to win. It's in our constitution. 'United we stand, divided we fall.'"

Jennie knew the phrase very well, yet it was something she hadn't had to play with all that much over the years. In her experience, one person could put an end to injustice. It had only been the last few months that she had needed her team to help conquer the enemy.

Baxter continued, talking as if to himself. "We've been divided from the start. With the SIS in one state and the SIA in another, we're all over the place. We haven't been united since we started this whole thing. They're a clever bunch, really."

Jennie agreed. Ever since Zhao had split the Seven and created devastation amongst the separate states, they'd had to spread thinly to try to cover all possible outcomes. Even now, as they worked to find

Jiao and dispel the Dreadnought's army before it grew too large, their team was divided. Some in the manor, others in the hospital, the rest on this bus.

"You're right, Bax. We should unite," Jennie replied. "The problem is until we know where Jiao and the Dreadnought are, we can't zero in on anything. We *have* to find them first."

"How did they find us?" Carolyn asked. "That person was clearly ready for us at the tunnels, so how did they find us?"

Ashton answered, craning his neck over his shoulder. "They must have known we'd go and see the site ourselves. It's our only lead. After the fellas investigating the other day, it was obvious we'd be back."

Jennie stared out the window and put her brain into motion. Until she had confirmed evidence to the contrary, she had to assume that Jiao and the Dreadnought weren't united. In which case, where the hell would either of them go? Did Jiao have her own place in the city? Was the Dreadnought hiding underground, like every other goddamn spectral overlord she encountered?

As Ashton cruised along the streets toward King Manor, Jennie closed her eyes and allowed herself a few moments rest.

***

The manor was quiet when they returned. They stumbled through the door, all of them feeling the exhaustion of their adventure. They slumped on the nearby couches and closed their eyes.

Jennie moved straight over to the bar and busied herself in her favorite way, making cocktails for the wounded and tired.

"Not now," Ashton grumbled. "I don't think I could stomach any alcohol."

Baxter watched her carefully, unsurprised that Jennie hadn't pulled out anything alcoholic. She deftly added various juices and cordials to a pitcher until a neat purple liquid was produced. She disappeared from the room for a few minutes, then came back with Hendrick in tow. Hendrick dropped a couple of drops of something thick and black into the drink before Jennie poured the completed mixture into glasses.

"Drink up. I advise drinking in one go." Jennie drained her own in a heartbeat.

Ashton, Jack, and Ruby brought theirs to their noses and grimaced.

"Seriously," Jennie confirmed. "Just drink."

They did, with great effort.

Jack held back a gag. "Whatever is in that isn't your finest work."

Ruby wanted to speak but couldn't. She held her nose and swallowed down a mouthful of bile.

"What was that?" Ashton added.

"An old family recipe," Jennie explained. "Tweaked by Hendrick, of course. It's great for hangovers, but mostly it's designed to bring life to the parts of you that are hurting or sore. It may taste like shit right now, but give it a few minutes, and you'll feel ready to take on the world again."

Ashton furrowed his brow. "And is this FDA approved?"

Jennie didn't reply, but her amused stare told him everything he needed to know.

Footsteps on the stairs signaled the arrival of another. A moment later and Lupe appeared in the room. "Man, you guys look like shit. Rough night?"

They nodded.

He waved a finger around the room, counting the assembled. "Where are the others? Already hit the hay? Ula's been growing antsy without her two men around her. It's cute, really. They make quite a team. I'm not sure they're going to be able to get used to being separated so often."

Jennie took off her glasses and cleaned the lenses. Annoyance coursed through her as she noticed the scuff and crack at the top of the upper right-hand lens. All things considered, she had been lucky, but that scratch irritated her.

"Rhone and Roman are in the hospital," she explained. "Triton is with them."

She explained to Lupe what had happened in the tunnels and the journey they had gone through to get back to the manor. Lupe's face fell as she filled him in on the two men's injuries.

"Roman's our powerhouse," Lupe replied, stunned. "He can't be injured."

Jennie shrugged. "He's not immortal. Pain and injury are hazards of duty. He'll be okay, I'm sure. We should count ourselves lucky that we all managed to make it out alive. That explosion could have taken every single one of us."

Baxter, Carolyn, and Sandra gave each other sideways glances. "Yeah…super painful stuff…"

Jennie rolled her eyes and smiled. "Are the others around, or are they sleeping? I think we need to call another meeting to order. Things are escalating more quickly than I'd like, and I need to know we're moving forward. Where's Julia? Has she made any progress in finding out about this Dreadnought guy?"

Lupe glanced over his shoulder then shrugged. "I have literally no idea. Hendricks has been whipping me into shape, and this is the first time I've been outside that room since you guys left. Last time I saw her, she was upstairs in the library with Tanya. Want me to go get them?"

Jennie poured herself another drink, then drained it. She shook her head. "No need. I'll go to them."

As she swept out of the room and up the stairs, Ashton and the others sat on the couches staring at Lupe. After a few awkward moments, Lupe dismissed himself and returned to the lab.

Ashton yawned and stretched. "Well, I guess I should probably get some…" He paused, warmth running through his body. His eyes widened as his aches and pains melted away. From the looks of Jack and Ruby, they were experiencing the same thing.

"Actually," Ashton continued, a big grin on his face, "anyone up for a run?"

CHAPTER FIFTY-FOUR

<u>Richmond, Virginia, USA</u>

Tanya and Julia were sitting at a table, their faces only inches away from an iPad. Scattered around the pair of them were piles of papers with scribbles and sketches on them. A few bottles of Hendrick's energy potion lay on the floor.

"You guys have been productive." Jennie smirked and leaned against the doorframe.

They looked up at once, the same excited glint in their eyes. It was the same look she remembered Tanya giving her back in New York when they had first met and she had poured over her stacks of ancient tomes.

Tanya jumped out of her chair and hugged Jennie. "You have no idea how long I've waited to have a study buddy. Julia is amazing. Between us, we can divide and conquer the internet and share our knowledge of different realms of specterdom."

Jennie laughed. "Sounds like a productive pairing. Doesn't mean you keep tidy though, does it? I would have thought you'd have some kind of a filing system or something for all of this."

Julia, who was less bouncy than Tanya but by no means less alert, saluted Jennie and grinned. "We've made tremendous progress. All of this stuff, it's documentation on Rathbourne. Scattered through history have been..."

"Breadcrumbs," Tanya interjected. "Dozens of tiny clues. At first, we thought we were chasing a myth. Someone with such power should have left some kind of imprint on history, right?"

Julia picked up a stack of papers and pointed at various sections. "History is written by the victors, and Rathbourne is a loser. Well, not in a high school sense, but he wasn't victorious in his mission, that's how he found his way into a box in the first place. Someone stuffed him in there. They defeated him, and deliberately kept him out of history."

Jennie took a seat across from the pair. "If that's the case, then how have you got so many notes?"

"Because others remembered him," Tanya replied. "Over the years, there have been accounts of his whereabouts. Whispers and traces kept in old diaries and journals. We've pieced them together, tried to make some kind of logical sense of it all. I think we have it, Jennie. I think we're there."

Julia nodded eagerly.

Jennie waited patiently for them to continue.

Julia took the reins. "Rathbourne Valerius is the alias of one Richard Haybourne. Way back in the fifteenth century, Richard assembled himself a mighty army using tactics that were...less than favorable. His followers were loyal out of fear, rather than genuine affection, and over the span of a few months, he had swollen his army to triple the size and dominated a dozen nearby villages and towns."

"Born not far from this place," Tanya continued. "Richard had his sights set on a woman who lived in what would later become the city of Richmond. At the time, it was nothing more than a hamlet surrounded by fields. He set his eyes on the woman and, in an effort to win her affection, tried to win her over with a monstrous display of power."

Julia took over. "The village burned. Dozens of citizens died. Only one house remained. Richard knocked on the door and demanded to see his maiden, howling with laughter and drunk on destruction."

"The rest of the story is unclear, at that point," Tanya explained. "There are a few accounts of what may have happened at the time, but each one is as strange as the next. The overall theme we can find among the papers and documentation that we found accounts to magic, and on that doorstep, a spell was cast on Haybourne. He died on the spot. His men cursed. His army disbanded."

"Vague tracings of journals suggest that the woman he loved was a witch and knew of a world beyond mortal living. She was concerned that his specter would rise, and so enlisted the help of her family to find somewhere deep below the ground to bury him.

Julia's voice turned solemn. "They had built him a wooden casket, but it wouldn't contain him. It had only been a temporary measure, and already he escaped. When they found him again, they managed to lure him back, and a stone tomb was built to weigh him down and hold his power within."

"Time moved on," Tanya continued. "The years passed. His maiden died, but a few of his most loyal followers never forgot him. They hoped that one day their master would rise again, but were fearful enough that they didn't want to be around to experience the day his wrath was set free."

Julia nodded gently. "Lucky for us, we might get to witness the full extent of his power."

"Not on my watch," Jennie replied.

Tanya flicked through her notes. "The only thing I can't work out is what kind of specter he is. By all accounts, I can't find mention of a specter who can possess so many others and glide through the city as he does."

"I don't think that's the part you should be focusing on," Jennie commented, eyes deep in thought.

Throughout the entire story, one thing had leaped out to her. There was vagueness in that story that didn't make sense to her. If there had been a witch, and that witch was the suspected love of Richard Haybourne—later known as the Dreadnought—then shouldn't she be documented? Shouldn't this woman be in the history books with them?

Tanya raised an eyebrow. "Why not? Once we know the type of specter we're dealing with, we'll know how to kill it, right?"

Jennie's eyes met Julia's. "The woman. What was her name?"

"Who?" Julia replied.

"The Dreadnought's love. Who is she?" Jennie asked.

Julia rifled through her notes, running a finger along passages until she found the one she was looking for. "Susannah." When Jennie's face dropped, she added, "Why? Who is she?"

Jennie hadn't seen Susannah since that fateful day beneath the Lincoln Memorial when she had been under the ground with the specters, hiding from the experimental weapons of the Umbra.

She had confessed she was a witch of sorts. Hanged during the Salem Witch Trials at the end of the seventeenth century, Susannah had carried over her spells and magic into specterdom.

Susannah had not been present when the Washington specters had been met by the SIA and given a choice between representing their kind for the US government or going on their way to live life as they might.

Jennie hadn't thought about her since that day. There had been far too much going on at the time, and far too much going on since. Susannah had been friendly and had helped her find out the truth of the Umbra, and Jennie had never had the chance to say thank you.

Of course, the chances that the Susannah she knew would be the same one mentioned in the story were slim. Still, there was a niggling sensation in her stomach that they were on to something. How many cases of witch activity would there have been in that era? Was it just a coincidence that the woman the Dreadnought had fallen in love with went by the same name?

Jennie didn't know, but she sure as hell wanted to find out.

"Where in the world would she be?" Tanya asked after Jennie had finished filling them in on her thoughts. "Back in Washington?"

"I don't know," Jennie conceded. "I guess so. She'll likely be in hiding."

Julia scoffed. "That's going to make it easy to find her then, isn't it?"

Tanya and Julia laughed. Jennie narrowed her eyes. "I don't think I like you two working together. I may have to separate you into two different libraries. We still have a couple of spare rooms."

Their faces fell like two schoolgirls' who had just been told they would need to sit apart until the end of the semester. "You're kidding?" Tanya protested.

Jennie held her composure, then broke out into a grin. "Of course, I am. I'm not your mother." She scanned the pages. "You have done great work, but this has only left more questions to answer." She sighed. "At some point, this will all be over. It always is."

"But when?" Tanya asked.

"I don't know," Jennie admitted. "What with Rhone and Roman out of commission, we've lost two of our best—"

"Oh, goodness!" Julia interjected. "Roman? Is he okay? What happened?" She caught herself, regained her composure, then cleared her throat. "Are they okay?"

Jennie looked over the top of her glasses. "I think so. Triton is with them. Pretty sure Rhone has a busted rib." She stopped, wondering if there would be another outburst from Julia.

"Is Roman okay?" Julia repeated, trying to keep her cool. "What's wrong with him?"

Jennie let out a long breath. "His leg was crushed by a boulder. I'm not sure what they're going to be able to do to help him, but he was out cold when I left him there."

Julia put her hand to her mouth. "Concussion? Unconscious?"

"Maybe," Jennie replied. "We didn't allow him much chance to speak when he woke up in the cave-in. I put a little something special in his system to alleviate his pain by putting him into a temporary coma."

Julia's and Tanya's eyes widened.

"A cave-in?" Tanya asked.

Jennie waved a hand. "Details, lots of details. Look, we're reconvening in the lounge in ten minutes. Meet us down there and you'll hear the full story. Where's everyone else?"

Julia didn't answer, her mind was clearly elsewhere. Tanya pointed at the ceiling. "In the dorms, I believe. Haven't heard a peep from them since they went upstairs a few hours ago."

"Great," Jennie replied spritely. "Downstairs in ten. See you then."

Tanya placed a hand on Julia's leg. "Is everything okay?"

Julia started as if awoken from a dream. "Sure. Yeah. Everything's fine."

Jennie filled everyone in on the events that had occurred that night. When she was finished, she cast her gaze across the group.

"In light of these incidents," Jennie instructed, "We're going to have to rethink how we do this. I don't care whether or not you've had any battle experience, you're now on the front line of duty."

Krissie and Lyla raised their hands.

"Yes?" Jennie asked.

Lyla answered. "I'm sorry, but I'm not comfortable with this. To be honest, we stayed here for protection. Not to enlist in this strange army you're recruiting."

Jennie mentally counted the heads of those present. Hardly enough to be considered an army.

"I understand," Jennie replied. "But the truth is that we need all hands on deck. I'm not saying we'll all charge out there and slaughter the enemy. Clearly they're well-equipped, and it's all too dangerous for that. What we do need are analysts. People to monitor the news media, look online, help Julia and Tanya with their research. Krissie, Lyla, you're locals. That's useful to us. Keep your ears to the ground and your eyes glued to anything that might lead us to them. Tell us the places in the city where large groups of people can hide. Anything that you know could aid us in this mission."

Jennie addressed the rest of the room. "I've just had word from Sturgeon and Lionus that orders have been issued and our backup is on their way. Greet them kindly. Give them space. Ula, assign them rooms."

"Fuck that," Ula retorted, showing signs of rebellion for the first time. "I'm going to the hospital to see Roman and Triton. They're my comrades, and they're down."

Jennie straightened to her full height, her eyes taking on a terrible darkness. "Then they won't need you there, will they? I know times are hard, but we all need to contribute. Ula, you're one of our strongest. With Rhone and Roman out of commission, I need you to step up. Greet them when they come, settle them in, keep the peace."

Ula looked conflicted. She stamped one foot and saluted. "Yes, ma'am."

"What about you?" Carolyn asked. "What are you going to do?"

Jennie raised an eyebrow.

"Well, clearly you're heading off somewhere," Carolyn continued. "You've got that look on your face."

Jennie smirked. "Am I that predictable?"

"Yes." Carolyn sighed. "Where are you going? What aren't you telling us?"

Jennie side-eyed Baxter, the only other person apart from Tanya and Julia she had told her purpose. "I've got a lead. It may be of great relevance. It could be the key to unlocking this madness."

Jennie disbanded the group and set them into motion. Hendrick had been instructed to stock up on his energy elixir, with Jennie keen to ensure they maximized the output of everyone throughout this time. She answered questions from her team, gave Ula her specific instructions, and made her way through a few cocktails before she finally grabbed Baxter and headed out of the back door.

Ashton was waiting for them, his Airbus propellers already spinning. "Ready to go?" he shouted over the noise of the blades.

Jennie climbed inside with Baxter. "I think so."

She wouldn't let the others know she had never been more unsure in her life. For a short while, at least, she was going to have to command from long distance. Hopefully, with the overwhelming talent they had enlisted to join their cause, things would work out in their favor.

Jennie jumped on a call with the other factions, filling in Sturgeon and Jimmy Dean with her plan. She made them promise to keep quiet and listened to their updates from the other cities.

If there was one good thing to come out of that call, it was the knowledge that Tommy Vincenzo had been spotted by Sturgeon's men in Pennsylvania. They were closing in on his location, and soon they would have another one of the Seven out of the equation.

Jennie glanced back longingly at the manor as it shrank to a dot in the distance. She hoped to a god she didn't believe in that this wouldn't take too long and they'd be able to find her.

CHAPTER FIFTY-FIVE

<u>Richmond, Virginia, USA</u>

Julia waited until the excitement in the house had settled. She had never seen so many people at the manor, and soon there would be even more of them—suited and booted agents with expressionless faces and gadgets holstered around their waists, touching everything.

She needed to get out.

She hadn't told the others, but ever since Jennie had informed them of the cave-in, she had felt a pull toward the city. One thing was on her mind, and one thing only.

A half-hour later, she hung around the back door in the kitchen. She listened for any sign of company, waiting for the right moment to make her move.

She was alone.

Julia turned the door handle and exited the manor. The lawn was cloaked in shadow. She clung to the bushes around the edge of the building, keeping an eye out for the McFarlene brothers. This would be the trickiest part of her escape. Ever since they'd been freed from the basement, they had flown in endless loops around the property, never tiring of their race.

She made it to the corner before she heard them again. Ducking into a bush, she peeked out and watched them whizz by, leaving only their cackling behind. The minute they were gone, she ran to the next corner and hid again.

The stop-start felt endless and had her heart pumping like a piston. She made it to the front of the building, where she heard the chatter of the rest of the crew. Everyone in the manor was caught up in an expectant buzz while they awaited the arrival of their reinforcements.

Julia made out the whirring buzz of helicopters in the distance and knew her time was short. A bubble of guilt popped in her stomach, but she knew in her heart that what she was doing was right.

She was so preoccupied with her thoughts that she almost didn't catch the brothers until it was too late. She gasped and ducked, eliciting a response from one of the brothers as the other two sped by. One of them, either Don or Graham—she hadn't yet managed to differentiate between the two—paused and sniffed the air, an eyebrow cocked as he whirled and looked for something he could not see.

Julia's heart stopped.

"Lost your flow?" Jerry cackled. "Knew you'd be the first to surrender."

Don-or-Graham furrowed his brow. "I thought I heard something."

"The sound of you losing!" Graham-or-Don crowed before speeding around the corner.

Tugged by his pride, Don-or-Graham—Julia finally decided it was Don—shook his head and sped after his brothers. Julia exhaled once he was out of sight and made for the wrought iron gate that bordered the property. There was no cover on the way there; the lawn had been mowed, and there was nowhere to hide. She'd have to move fast.

She made a dash for it, her arms pumping by her side, hair flying behind her. She neared the gate, had it within reach, and managed to ease it open and close it behind her when Don's voice made her stop in her tracks.

"Hey! Where are you going?"

Julia spun and looked at the trio through the gate. "Out," she replied, trying to sound casual. "Is that a crime?"

Don scratched his head. "I mean, no, but you're *sneaking*. That means you're up to something."

Graham clapped his hands and chuckled. "I smell deviousness. What are you up to, little bird? Out to go find Jiao solo?"

"No! No!" Jerry cackled excitedly. "Out to find the bad guy by yourself, ain'tcha? *Or,* off like that other little bird flew. The one that escaped our clutches and hasn't come back. Jennie said to keep an eye out, yes, she did. Ooo, what will she think when we tell her about you?"

Julia's skin prickled. There was no way she'd allow these freaks to mark her as a traitor.

"I'm going out, okay?" she replied sharply. "It's not a crime, I've got something to do. Someone to see. Last I checked I wasn't a prisoner."

"We should bring her back inside, yes we should," Graham crooned. "Raise the alarm and let everyone know that there's *another* traitor in their midst."

Julia closed her eyes briefly. She had been rumbled, but she wouldn't allow her reputation to be tarnished. She had only just worked her way into Jennie's good books. "Raise an alarm if you want to, or you can trust me. I'm not Jiao. I'm not out to hurt anyone. I just want to see Roman, okay? I want to make sure he's okay, and I don't need everyone giving me shit about it."

Don clapped his hands to his cheeks. "Sweety-chicky is in *love*! Why didn't you say?"

Julia narrowed her eyes. "No, I'm not."

"Oh, how delicious," Jerry roared, slapping his thighs. "Lovey-love-love!"

Julia flinched at his noise. "Keep it down, please. I'm not wasting another minute here. I'm going, but I'll be back before dawn, I promise."

"We should stop her," Don declared. "Grab the birdy and make sure she can't fly away."

"Why?" Graham asked.

"What if she *is* a traitor?" Don replied.

Jerry nodded. "Good point. We don't want Jennie to punish us, do we?"

"No, we don't," Graham answered. "Getting thrown against a wall was not on my to-do today."

Jerry raised an eyebrow. "The only thing on your to-do is losing our race."

"She's leaving," Don told them.

Julia's eyes widened as the poltergeists rushed as one toward her. There was a flash of light when they hit the border of the property, unable to pass beyond their boundaries.

"Damn!" Jerry cursed.

Julia let out a relieved laugh. "Sorry, folks. Guess there's no capture for you." She moved as close to the gate as she dared. "I promise you, I'll be back. I just… I need to see him."

With that, she turned and dashed down the hill. Behind her, she heard the poltergeists raise the alarm. However, the sound of their wailing was lost as the helicopters closed in, staggering their arrival above the property as they came in to land on the back lawn.

Julia continued running down the hill toward the city. When she was under the sodium arcs of the nearest public street, she dialed a number on her cell phone. A cab arrived a few minutes later and took her to her destination.

She paid the fare and exited the cab. Difficult to miss, the hospital was an impressive building with a red brick square out front that had the large letters "VCU" announcing its purpose. Julia made her way inside and asked the receptionist where she would find him.

"We don't allow visitors this late," the receptionist told Julia when she asked to see Roman. She was tired, her hair a gray tangle and her eyes were bloodshot.

Julia informed the receptionist that she was a blood relative and would only be in town for the next couple of hours. She must have been convincing because she somehow managed to appeal to the woman's kind nature.

It was either that, or she was too tired to argue.

The corridor was dimly lit. Glass walls allowed Julia a glimpse inside each room as she was guided toward a room where a large man who barely fit the bed slept soundly. Roman's was one of six beds divided by pastel blue curtains. His leg was suspended in a traction sling and was wrapped entirely in a cast.

Roman had never looked frailer and more vulnerable to her.

Julia thanked the nurse, who emphasized that she'd only have a short amount of time. She took a seat beside Roman's bed, still uncertain why she had felt such a compulsion to come all of this way in secrecy to see him. Avoiding the teasing was only part of it.

A steady beep of monitors played a chorus in the room. Julia leaned forward and took Roman's hand in hers, stroking the back of his hand with her thumb.

"This is crazy," she whispered, conscious of how loud she sounded to the room. "I don't even know what I'm doing here, I just... For some reason, when I heard you were hurt, I couldn't help myself." She let out a soft chuckle. "You probably have no idea that I'm here, so hopped up on painkillers that this will all be a dream to you if you remember it at all. I guess...I think the others have got inside my head. I don't want to see you hurt. I want to see you well, and... Well, I know you probably don't feel the same way, but I..."

Someone coughed in the room and Julia trailed off, her face flushing. She imagined Roman waking and asking why the hell she was there. Scorning her emotions. He had no time for emotional affairs of any kind, being the honorable man that she knew him to be. He was cold, calculating, dedicated to his mission.

Yet she had felt *something*, she was sure.

She hadn't had much luck with relationships in the past, but she could tell when there was something between her and someone else. Something special, maybe.

Julia rose and stroked Roman's forehead. It was clammy and warm. He murmured gently.

A voice from behind made Julia jump. "He's been dreaming about you, you know?"

Julia spun sharply, surprised to see Triton's face appear around the curtain. He smiled warmly, but that didn't stop her heart from racing.

She stumbled for words. "How long have you been there?"

Triton drew back the curtain to reveal Rhone lying peacefully in his bed. His midsection was bound with white bandages, his face a mass of scratches and scrapes.

Triton ignored her question. "I've never known the man to talk in his sleep, but whatever drugs they've given him have amped up the visions he's seeing. Most of it was gibberish, but I heard your name pretty clearly. Quite a few times."

Julia's ears grew hot. She couldn't hide the grin appearing on her face. "Really? What was he saying?"

Triton's brow creased. "Something about calzone, I think. Then your name a few times in a short space of time, then he went quiet."

Julia hid her delight by turning back to Roman. "Is he going to be okay?"

Triton considered this. "I think so. The nurses seem hopeful, although they won't know how well his leg is going to heal until he wakes up and starts physio. That cave-in screwed him up pretty badly. Rhone too, to be honest. We were lucky enough to escape with the bare minimum of damage, but there were some casualties we can't afford along the way."

They fell quiet for a moment. The machines continued to beep their rhythmic music.

"I've never known Roman to show any interest in a woman," Triton confessed after a time. "He's always been dedicated to his work, a truly emotionless soldier. It wasn't until our powers as conduits became clear and we teamed up that he showed any sign of loyalty outside of his unit. If you're into him, just know that you'll have a rough journey ahead of you. He's tough to read and can be a real asshole at times, but his heart is in the right place."

Triton gave a small laugh. "God knows, maybe it's time for something to melt his stone-cold heart."

Julia couldn't stop smiling, the heat spread to her cheeks. She stroked his hair once more, and he moved beneath her hands as if nestling into them for comfort.

"I want to be here when he wakes up," Julia announced, turning to Triton. "How are you allowed to sit by Rhone's side outside of visiting hours?"

Triton tapped the side of his nose. "I'm a convincing liar. Plus, I arrived with both of them and showed them my military ID. I made a sob story about them both being brothers and promised not to kick up a fuss. I think the nurse has the hots for me, so as long as I stay out the way and be a good boy, I'm fine."

The nurse who had brought Julia returned to the entrance of the room. "Time to go, miss. You can come back in again at eight AM for morning visiting, okay?"

Julia spared one longing glance at Roman before conceding and following the woman out of the room. She waved at Triton as she left and let him know she'd wait downstairs until the morning came.

When she was gone, Triton shook his head in disbelief. "Can you believe it? All that kidding around, and it turns out she really does have the hots for him."

The curtain shifted a little more, revealing another woman who had been sitting out of sight and eavesdropping the entire time.

"I knew it," Ula boasted. "The minute I saw her leaving the manor, I knew where she was heading."

"How did you beat her?" Triton asked with a grin.

Ula smirked. "Do you really need to ask?"

Ula ducked out of sight as a nurse walked past the room. When she was gone, they both turned their attention to Roman.

"Do you think he heard any of that?" Triton asked.

"I hope so," Ula replied. "I think it's about time he made a connection. All these years of isolating himself and living a solitary life; it's about time he had a chance for love."

They fell into quiet discussion, their topics turning from Julia to Rhone and onto events at the manor. Ula confessed she couldn't stay long and had to return to the manor to take care of things for Jennie, but she admitted she had to at least see that Roman was okay first.

Soon enough, she left the hospital and sneaked back into the city. Triton turned back to Roman, noticing the smile that hadn't been on his face before the arrival of Julia.

"That's it, big guy," Triton whispered. "There's always light at the end of the tunnel."

CHAPTER FIFTY-SIX

Baxter followed Jennie closely as they rounded the corner into the shadow of the tall buildings surrounding them. "What are we doing here? You really think you're going to find a witch in the center of the city?"

Jennie marched ahead without slowing, latched onto Baxter in her spectral form so no one would see her coming or going. "We're taking a quick detour. It'd be wrong to come to Washington without seeing that he's okay."

Baxter knew instantly who Jennie was talking about and decided to let the matter drop. If there was one thing he'd learned over his time with Jennie, it was to trust the woman. Her methods were often strange and unorthodox, but had she ever failed to deliver?

No.

In spectral form, it was easy to enter the hospital. Little did the pair know that a few of their crew were doing exactly the same thing in Richmond at that moment. Jennie's face was emotionless as her mind ticked over thoughts that she'd rather leave behind in the dark. Her mind forced her to mentally count the number of people who had been injured and hurt because of her.

Not because of me. Because of the situation. Without you, these people would already be dead.

She told herself this repeatedly, but it did little to convince her. It worked even less when she managed to locate the man she'd come to see in the isolation ward. Two sides of Rogers' room were made of glass, which left him little privacy.

Jennie melted through the wall and stood at Kurt Rogers' bedside. He looked at peace, although his body was a messy painting of the pain he had endured in trying to defend the SIA HQ.

"Is he okay?" Baxter asked.

Jennie picked up his chart and flipped over the pages. "Vitals seem okay. He's had a couple of surgeries already to remove the bullets from his body. They've got him on OxyContin and morphine. That'll keep him out of it for a while."

Jennie placed the chart back just as a nurse came into sight. She did a double-take at the monitor she'd just seen changing screens by itself.

Jennie moved to stand beside Rogers. "I wish there was something more we could do for him."

Baxter nodded. "He's resting. That's what he needs right now. When do you think he last had a break?"

"Hard to say." Jennie cocked her head and looked at his tired face. It was the first time she'd seen him look truly at ease since she'd known him. "A man in his position, I bet he hardly gets time to sleep, let alone actually rest."

"You know that feeling, don't you?" Baxter stated.

Jennie smiled. "Yeah. Yeah, I do."

Rogers shuffled uncomfortably, his face tightened into a grimace as he moved. He gave a small snort then continued to breathe deeply and sleep.

Jennie drew a vial out of her pocket, this one smaller than the others. She eased it into Rogers' curled fingers and cupped them tightly around it.

"What's that?" Baxter asked.

"A little gift." Jennie smiled at Rogers. "Something to speed up his recovery. A gift from Hendrick."

Baxter nodded in understanding. While he didn't know the specifics of the formula, he had learned not to doubt Hendrick's tricks.

Baxter's brow creased. "What about the others in Richmond? Roman and Rhone?"

"Hendrick is working on it. He had time to concoct this batch for me while we were trapped underground. More will be made for the others in due time." Jennie sighed. "What a mess."

"Suck it up," Baxter declared.

Jennie looked at him quizzically.

"Double entendre." Baxter grinned. "One: we can be the vacuum cleaner that sucks up the mess. Two: get over it." He puffed out his chest proudly.

Jennie turned away from Rogers and gave Baxter a patronizing pat on the shoulder. "Sure. If you say so."

She spared one last glance at Rogers before heading back outside.

Jennie couldn't believe what she was seeing when they arrived at the Washington Monument. Only a few weeks ago, this had been a site of devastation. There was no sign of the damage caused by the bombs that the Shadows had set off to flush out Jennie, the conduits, and the specters from the hidden space beneath the memorials.

The bombs had obliterated this area. Dirt had blown in chunks, police had surrounded the area, putting up yellow tape kept journalists and civilians at a safe distance from the destruction.

The area was pristine, returned to its former glory. Only a few patches of juvenile grass showed that anything of significance had happened here at all.

"They wasted no time in clearing up the mess," Jennie observed. Moonlight shone silver on the grass, the water feature reflected the stars in the sky.

Baxter half-shrugged. "Are you surprised? This is one of the city's main attractions. Tourism would be slashed dramatically if people couldn't access this historic place." He glanced up at the stoic white statue of Abraham Lincoln. "Imagine if *he* had been blown up. That would've been a bitch to fix."

Jennie nodded. Luckily it had only been the side of the building where the hidden entrance to the underground caverns had existed. Where the door had been, was now nothing more than a plain white brick wall.

They crossed the grass to where they knew the tunnels lay beneath. Baxter crouched to one knee and touched the grass. "What do you think it's like down there? Can't be much left after what happened before? You were lucky to get the conduits out of there when you did."

Jennie's mind flashed back to that night, the devastation caused as they battled alongside the SIA against the Shadows and the SIS. A whole clusterfuck of allegiances fighting among each other. What a shitshow that had been.

She crouched by Baxter, something niggling at the back of her mind. There was still a residue from that battle, she could feel it in the air. "Only one way to find out," she replied. "The question is, how are we to best manage this? We don't have any equipment to scan and look for open pockets that have been left."

Baxter grinned. "We swim."

Without another word, he melted into the ground and disappeared into the dirt. Jennie laughed, her connection to Baxter remaining strong as she followed his signal. As long as she could feel him, he'd be safe.

He popped back up about thirty feet from her and shook his head. "Nothing yet. It's all just packed dirt."

"Keep looking," Jennie instructed.

Baxter obeyed, making a show of diving into the dirt as if it were a swimming pool. Jennie laughed as his fingers met over his head and he submerged himself in the earth. She once again followed until he resurfaced.

"Nothing." He wiped his brow.

"Keep searching," Jennie called, struggling to talk between laughing fits.

This time Baxter pretended he was walking down a staircase, his body descending into the dirt.

Jennie followed where he went, ensuring she was connected to him at all times. After twenty minutes of searching, Baxter's head poked up like a gopher from a burrow.

"I've found something," he informed her. "Some of the tunnel has held up. Come and see."

Jennie crossed to Baxter and allowed the earth to claim her. For a few seconds, all she could see was darkness, and all she could smell was earth. Then, a chamber came into sight. It was smaller than it had once been, but still somehow structurally sound. Torches were lit along the walls, although Jennie couldn't understand how or why. Someone was definitely living down here.

Baxter was already waiting at the entrance to a tunnel on the far side of the chamber. While Jennie had grown familiar with a lot of the tunnels and their direction during the time she'd spent down here, she never believed she'd seen the full extent of the tunnel system. Who knew how far the tunnels had stretched beneath this ancient site?

Not only did the tunnel extend far beyond what she'd believe to be possible, but there was still power here. Jennie sensed a spectral pulse around her. She didn't believe that this could solely be the residue of the battle, so she kept her hands poised to go for her weapons. She was ready for whoever made themselves known to her.

After a short while of ducking through the tunnels, they came across voices. The hairs on the back of Jennie's neck were already on end. She had sensed they would be here, but she didn't know who exactly *they* were yet.

Jennie met Baxter's eyes. She placed a finger on her lips and closed her eyes, trying to sense who was around. The signatures were strange, something she hadn't experienced before. They were definitely spectral, but she wasn't sure she'd met these particular specters.

The voices faded into the distance. They followed after them, sneaking through the tunnel until the voices grew louder.

Jennie reached a corner and poked her head around. Thanks to the firelight that edged the tunnels, she could make out around two dozen specters sitting around the room. Benches had been created from indentations in the earth, and if it hadn't been for the fact they were underground and worms were crawling through the walls, Jennie could easily have mistaken the room for a bar.

There were no drinks, but the patrons were clearly at ease. They spoke of old times, occasionally falling silent as conversation expired. Jennie watched them eagerly, not quite believing what she was seeing. All the specters wore the uniform of the SIS.

"Forgotten soldiers," Baxter whispered. "From the battle?"

Jennie supposed they were, although she had never seen this kind of behavior before. Why would they have confined themselves to the tunnels? They weren't poltergeists.

She broke away from cover and entered the room. All eyes turned to her, and immediately the smiles slipped from their faces.

"You," a man cried out, rising to his feet. His face showed a mixture of alarm, concern, and anger.

A woman who'd been in her mid-thirties when she died rose to her feet and glowered at them both. "You have a lot of nerve coming back here."

"We knew you would," added another. "We *knew* you'd be back."

Jennie placed her hands in the air, palms out in defense. "I'm not here to cause trouble. I didn't think any of you would still be here. Why are you hanging around in a filthy old tunnel?"

"What else is there to do?" the first man replied. His beard was dark, and a bullet wound showed the place where he had been shot. "The world has changed for us. We're too far from home, and a deranged maniac is out there laying waste to specters. You saw the machines we brought with us. You saw how those specters were exorcized. It's safer to stay here where no one can find us than risk going out there and ending it all."

Baxter appeared beside Jennie. A few of the spectral SIS agents flinched. "Brendan Koa is gone. We ended his tyranny weeks ago. He's no longer a threat."

"But *you* are," the woman growled through gritted teeth. She advanced on Jennie. "What do you want from us? To finish the job you started? Is that what you do? Clean up your mess weeks later and track down every last specter."

Jennie furrowed her brow. "Are you serious? I worked with the SIS for years. Are you telling me you don't know how I work?"

The bearded man barked. "All we know is you're a threat, and the queen wanted you removed. Since you've delivered yourself so eagerly into our laps, perhaps we can oblige."

Jennie sighed. She knew that look. Unfortunately, words were useless once a mind had been set and the rest of the group had fallen in line.

They closed in on her and raised their spectral weapons. Jennie drew her own guns, then tossed them behind her, eliciting raised eyebrows from the majority of the group.

"If you really want to do this, let's at least make it fair," Jennie declared. "Oh, who am I kidding? To make this fair, you'd have to cripple me, and there's no time for that. Go on, then. Bring me your worst."

To Jennie's surprise, it was the woman who was the first to attack.

CHAPTER FIFTY-SEVEN

Washington DC, USA

The woman caught Jennie by surprise, slamming her fist into her cheek.

Jennie was knocked backward, but Baxter caught her and nudged her back into the fray. Jennie returned the punch to the woman's face.

The woman yowled in pain and fell to the floor. The others rose around her, and everyone came at Jennie at once.

Jennie found a small gap to slip between them and twisted out of the way of their hands. She came out the other side and kicked a man close to her, causing him to bowl into three others. By the time her foot was back on the ground, another had recovered and came at her.

Jennie ducked out of the way of his fist, then twisted as she noticed another man firing at them. The gun boomed, but the shot found only air. Jennie raced toward him and aimed for the pistol.

Before she could get there, a body smashed into her side. Jennie was knocked off her feet, and three agents jumped on her. Her vision was filled with spectral agents as they attacked her body, throwing flurries of punches. Jennie sighed and closed her eyes, knowing that now was the time to use her powers. She gave an almighty shout and focused her attention on the three.

The cells on her waist glowed brightly from the collected power, and a moment later they shot off her, smacking into the ceiling. They fell on top of their comrades, giving Jennie a chance to push herself to her feet.

Baxter busied himself with four of his own opponents, throwing hammer-fisted punches and picking specters off the floor. With one hand, he threw a specter into the nearby wall, where he slid down and struggled to get back up.

"Keep it up, Bax!" Jennie shouted.

"Always do," he replied.

The woman launched from behind and grabbed Jennie around the neck. The specter with the pistol aimed as the women held her still. Jennie grimaced and fought against the woman who was surprisingly strong.

"A word of warning," Jennie gargled.

"What's that?" the specter replied, glee in her voice.

"I'd suggest you move out of the way," Jennie finished before disconnecting from the specters and becoming material.

The gun fired. The bullet sped through the chamber. A spectral bullet from a spectral pistol. The bullet passed straight through Jennie and entered the woman's stomach. She was knocked into the wall, a large hole decorating her gut.

Jennie turned spectral, crossed to her, and grabbed her by the throat. "I warned you."

Another shot fired. Jennie had planned it. She turned material once more and the bullet found the woman's head, exploding it like a cantaloupe dropped from a great height.

The man with the pistol gasped and dropped the weapon. "I'm so sorry!"

Jennie fixed him with a cold gaze. "It'll grow back. She'll be fine. You, however, won't be." She raised a hand and latched onto the specter. One moment he was standing, the next he was floating off the floor, his legs kicking wildly in the air. Jennie swept her hand to the side and he went flying with the movement, crashing into the wall on the far side of the chamber.

There were only a few left with the guts to fight. The nearest to Jennie was only further fueled by what he had seen.

So cute, Jennie thought. *No matter how much time mortals spend around specters, they still believe that they'll be the one who is different from all others when they die. Let's see how that plays out for you.*

"Baxter. Wrench," Jennie instructed.

The wrench flew through the air. Jennie caught it in one hand and thunked the man on the head. His eyes rolled up and he fell onto his back. When the next man came, Jennie used the momentum to catch him in the stomach on the backswing.

The weight of the wrench was impressive and dragged her around. As she turned, someone launched themselves onto her back again. Jennie threw herself back, using her attacker as a cushiony landing. When they were on the floor, she rolled sideways and climbed to her feet. She held the wrench over the specter and quickly examined the room.

This was the last specter with any fight in them.

"I think I've made my point," Jennie stated, the wrench still above the specter. "Thank you, Vegas, and good night."

She dropped the wrench the same way she'd seen celebrity stand-ups and musicians drop the mic on a thousand TV shows. The specter held out her hands before her but was unprepared and dazed from her encounter with the ground. The wrench slipped past her arms and found its bed on her face, sinking into the skin and leaving a dent.

Baxter threw one last punch to an agent he was caught with before that agent fell unconscious to the ground. Jennie picked up the wrench and tossed it back to him with some effort.

The bearded agent pushed himself to a sitting position. "I never believed you'd be as strong as they said you were. I thought it was all rumor and hearsay."

Jennie latched onto the specter and dragged him to his feet. She pulled him toward her and held him in her grasp, a few feet from her hands. "Be careful who you underestimate," she commanded. "That will be your undoing. Now, tell me the real reason you've been hiding in these tunnels."

"We've already told you," the woman on the floor replied. Her mouth was slightly caved in, so her words were slurred, but she managed around it okay. "We were afraid of what's happening outside. We heard the rumble of machines for days, weeks even, and remained hidden. We couldn't risk being vacuumed up by the Umbra's machines."

"Plus," the man took over, "We hoped you'd find your way back here. You left one of yours behind, didn't you?" He gave Jennie a knowing look.

Jennie's brows knitted together. "Where is she?"

The man didn't reply, he simply looked over his shoulder.

Jennie let him go. The man dropped to the floor and folded to his knees.

She strode past him and toward the end of the chamber, where a crude arch led further into the tunnels. With Baxter beside her, they took up the width of the space as they wandered toward the dark.

In this tunnel, no flames were lit. Jennie took a torch from the wall and carried it with her, ignoring the groans and complaints from the agents behind them.

Baxter turned over his shoulder. "What if they shoot us now our backs are turned?"

Jennie shook her head. "They wouldn't be dumb enough to try." She paused. "I hope."

The tunnel stretched farther than Jennie imagined it would. Impossibly, much of this structure had survived the blast. She guessed that they must be quite a distance from the memorial, trailing past the grasses and back into the city. After a few winding turns, she picked up a spectral signal ahead.

"Careful," she warned Baxter, extending an arm. They approached more slowly as a light flickered into existence ahead.

The smell of cooked meats and other strange aromas caressed their nostrils. The air held a strange mixture of bitter, sweet, and sour notes. Jennie and Baxter worked their way toward the light, and soon a small chamber came to light.

The firelight flickered in shades of green and purple beneath a large cauldron. The heat rose in ripples, distorting the air around the specter dancing around the cauldron with her eyes closed, deep in her own thoughts.

Jennie and Baxter watched from the mouth of the chamber, entranced. A wave of guilt washed over Jennie as she recalled the last time she had seen Susannah, standing beside Hendrick with her face set and stern as they prepared to take on the Umbra's army in the halls beneath Alexandria.

A lot had happened that day. There had been too many people to count. She could recall Susannah's face as she battled the possessed army but could not remember seeing her after the event. When all was said and done, Jennie was ushered onto her next project. Life moved so fast.

The cauldron bubbled and responded to her chants. Occasionally Susannah would wave her hands over the pot and add an ingredient— Lord only knew where she had gotten them—and the bubbles would grow and pop and roil.

After a few minutes of watching this strange dance, Jennie cleared her throat.

Baxter tensed beside her. While he had finally gotten used to Jennie's strain of spectral magic, he was clearly uncomfortable in the presence of this self-proclaimed witch.

Susannah froze on the far side of the cauldron. She opened her eyes and spun to face the pair with a knowing smile on her face.

"What are you making?" Jennie asked, as casually as if she were asking a neighbor the weather forecast.

Susannah's head tilted, the action twisting her face into a grotesque mask. She was considerably older than the pair of them or, at least, had been when she died. "Beef casserole."

Baxter's brow creased. "Specters can't eat."

Susannah grinned. "I know that. You know that. But those wretched agents out there don't know that. If you keep yourself busy brewing things and making it seem as though you have a nefarious purpose, they leave you be. Funny, isn't it? Those juvenile specters don't know the first thing about specterdom, even though they spent a good portion of their life fighting it. I guess you don't understand it until you're on the other side."

Baxter nodded his head in agreement.

Jennie took a cautious step into the room. "Why are you here, Susannah? Why did you stay in this hole?"

Susannah swiped a digit through the boiling concoction before sucking the mix off the end of her finger. Despite the heat pouring out of the cauldron, she showed no sign of pain.

Her eyes fixed on Jennie's. "Come on, dear. You're smarter than that. If you were going to waste time with stupid questions, I would've put out a lawn chair and relaxed. You know the answer. Otherwise, you wouldn't be here."

"I had a hunch," Jennie replied. "I didn't know for sure."

"You wanted to chase my trail," Susannah stated. "You hoped that enough of my spectral essence would remain behind, and you thought you could follow it like a bloodhound to find me." Her eyes narrowed. "But why?"

"I thought you knew?" Baxter commented innocently.

Jennie chuckled. "It's true that I went to the place where I thought your power might be strongest, and I hoped you'd be here, sure. But I didn't expect to find you here. Why did you come back? You spent months down here hiding. Why return to your place of confinement?"

Susannah's eyes drifted into a dreamy, far-off gaze. "It's funny, but 'prison' is defined by the mental state of the prisoner. When I had no choice but to exist down here, it was torture. Now that it's of my own volition, it's a comfort and a home."

She studied the pair of them standing in the entryway. "After the battle with the Shadows, I could already sense that there was going to be a rounding up of the specters. Any spectral force who had fought within that skirmish was to be rounded up and questioned by the SIA and logged in some notebook by someone or another. The moment I could sense the tide was turning, I fled, moving as fast as my spectral body would allow me until I was free on the surface again."

Her eyes were glassy. "There were camera crews and police and a thousand pairs of eyes watching that old factory. I slipped out the back and into the night, knowing that I couldn't be a statistic. Specters like me, those who have maintained their powers from their mortal bodies, we should exist in the shadows. I know the power that could be squeezed from me if I was caught by the enemy, so I went into hiding. I found the one place where I had existed in peace for the longest, and I made it my home."

Baxter forced his eyes away from the hypnotic bubbling pot. "And what a home you've made it. I love what you've done with the place."

Jennie elbowed him and laughed.

"It may be nothing to you," Susannah replied. "But after several centuries of moving from basements to abandoned churches and more, at least no one would think to look for me here."

"Except us," Jennie replied.

Susannah nodded. "Except you." She studied them once again. "The only thing I don't understand is why you're here. Your battle with the Shadows is ended. To what do I owe this unexpected pleasure?"

Baxter spoke before Jennie could. "If you knew the battle was over, why didn't you tell the agents out there? They've been in hiding for weeks, worried the Umbra would get them."

Susannah sighed. "I tried telling them, but they wouldn't listen. No one trusts an ancient witch like me." At the mention of "witch," Jennie's eyes met hers again. "What?"

"That's kind of why we wanted to find you," Jennie informed her. "We've run into a situation, and we want to ask you a few questions."

"Okay." Susannah threw another ingredient into the cauldron, causing the liquid to change color.

Jennie sighed, unsure of how best to approach this. Eventually, she settled on, "Have you ever lived in Richmond?"

Susannah flinched, and her lips tightened into a thin white line. Although it took her a while to answer, Jennie already had all the answers she needed.

CHAPTER FIFTY-EIGHT

Richmond, Virginia, USA

Jiao watched over the city as the sun climbed the horizon

She was patient, a skill she had picked up through years of observing others around her running around like headless chickens and realizing it didn't serve them. Winning was a short-term game. To dominate long-term required strategy and planning.

They lumbered toward her, the recruits from the previous night's mission. Rathbourne had been busy, stealing into houses in the middle of the night to perform his magic and cast his shadow on the city. He had to be selective. That was Jiao's advice worming its way into his ears. If Rathbourne was given his way, he would create one spectacle after another, until the entire city was alarmed and came for him.

"Take it easy, my love," Jiao had whispered into the woman's ear, feeling no strangeness at offering words of affection to a man who accommodated a female's body. "Secrecy is the key to your success. You've already stirred enough attention, now we play the quiet game. It's harder to detect a mouse than it is to catch an elephant."

Was that a proverb she had heard from somewhere? She could hardly remember. Rathbourne had given a simple nod and allowed

Jiao to reel out her plan. Times had changed. In Rathbourne's day, justice systems were still nascent, the population was a lot smaller, news spread slowly if at all. Jiao would act as his ticket to the twenty-first century, and together they would achieve both of their goals.

The new recruits milled around the abandoned community center like zombies—emotionless and with steady gaits. They'd been arriving through the night, and Jiao was almost certain they'd fill the building by afternoon.

What then? What comes next, when our forces need to grow and we can't expand without causing a scene?

They would cross that bridge when they came to it. Jiao still had her contacts in the other cities. Only an hour ago, she had come off a call with Tommy Vincenzo. It appeared that he had been more careless than she had desired, but he was trying his best to hide from law enforcement. It seemed specters showed little loyalty to mortals, particularly when the SIA or the SIS showed their faces and pinned them up against a wall.

What had Zhao been thinking, to center his plan almost entirely on mortals? This was the specters' game, and they would play it better than any mortal could. Mortals became spellbound by the revelation that something existed beyond the curtain, and because of that, they lost their focus. When you know you've got another life beyond mortality, you become careless. You take risks.

But not Jiao.

The helicopters had arrived sometime in the night. Jiao had watched the dark shapes appear over the horizon, their lights trailing like shooting stars. They'd passed over, heading in the direction of the manor, and disappeared from sight.

Were they backup for Jennie? Jiao couldn't tell from where she stood, although a bad feeling settled in her stomach. Although her army was growing, so was theirs. Maybe Jennie and the others hadn't worked out the full extent of her betrayal, but soon they would. There was only so much time she and Rathbourne could sit still.

Soon, they would make their attack and force the King's Court out of the picture.

Jiao took a steadying breath and calmed her mind. She already knew this to be her superpower: to see clearly despite adversity. On the long street below her, one figure moved faster than the others. Rathbourne sped along the street as though he were gliding.

Jiao waited until the figure had entered the building, then made her way downstairs. It was time to debrief with Rathbourne and figure the next part of their plan.

A large map of Richmond lay on the center table of the reception lounge. The heads of the various agencies using King Manor as a base of operations gathered around the table, while the remaining agents made themselves at home in the manor's facilities.

Krissie and Lyla leaned over the map, adding circles and scribbles with thick, red markers. Ula had already slipped back and was watching them closely, curious about the locations they were marking.

"You can get a good vantage point from here," Krissie explained when Ula queried a mark she made. "This is the tallest building around that quarter of Richmond. You should be able to see for a few kilometers in either direction."

Agent Sturgeon had returned with her men, leaving Tiptry and Clark in charge of the operations out in the other states. Standing beside her was SIA Agent Erik. On the other side of the table, Grimald stood with the GOA members, each shifting uncomfortably in the presence of the federal forces. Even Jimmy Dean had returned with a fleet of specters ready to lend a hand and scout the city.

Lyla pointed out a few more locations to recon, and the teams prepared to ship out from the manor and begin their search. An hour later, they set off into the city, after they had all been given their orders by Ula. They left the helicopters behind, knowing any disturbance in the sky would be witnessed and alert the city to their plight.

Once everyone had set off, Ula wandered up to Hendrick's lab and opened the door.

"You're just in time." Lupe was chipper, smiling brightly as he handed Ula two vials of a bright blue concoction. "Hendrick showed me how to make it. Consider this my first official creation in the laboratory."

Hendrick took his place beside him, a strange look of pride on his face. It didn't sit well on that wrinkled old visage.

Ula brought them up to eye level. "Are you sure these are okay? I'm not certain I'm comfortable that your first experiment is going to be tested on two of our finest agents."

Lupe looked hurt. "Hendrick watched every step. He inspected them himself."

"They're fine," Hendrick interjected. "Everything was done according to procedure. Do you think I'd allow a botched product to go out into the world? Please think before you speak such nonsense next time."

Ula couldn't help but grin. "Very well. I guess there's only one way to test that they'll work, then."

Hendrick grabbed her wrist to stop her from leaving. "They'll work. Do not doubt it."

Ula nodded and pulled herself free, leaving Lupe standing uncertainly behind.

"Are you sure it's fine?" he asked Hendrick.

Hendrick didn't reply. He simply went back to work.

Washington DC, USA

For the first time in days, Rogers was able to open his eyes without a piercing pain in his head.

The monitors he was hooked up to beeped discordantly around the head of his bed. He adjusted his position, surprised to find himself able to sit upright without a problem. The bandages wrapped around his body still showed the sites where the bullets had penetrated, but now there was no pain at all.

Nothing.

The small glass vial rested beneath his pillow. It all seemed so dreamlike, looking back. He had awoken in an opiate-induced spin and found the vial in his hand. The contents of the small bottle were easily identifiable as one of the signature potions that Jennie carried with her at all times. He wasn't sure when she had visited, but he was thankful that she had. All of his operatives were far too occupied to come and provide any company.

When a nurse walked by, he closed his eyes and hid the vial in his hand. She took his vitals, touched his head, then disappeared from the room.

The moment she was gone, he painstakingly raised the vial to his lips and drained the lot. Although he expected something to happen straight away, nothing did. After a few minutes, he found his head feeling heavy, and he fell back to sleep.

That had been one of the most fitful sleeps he'd ever had. Now that he was awake, he felt spritely. There was no trace of any of his pain, and he almost couldn't believe it. If he hadn't had spent the best part of the last year dealing with spectral matters and interacting with anomalies like Rogue, he wouldn't have believed it at all.

As it was, he was healed. He pulled the bandages away and inspected the sites of his wounds. The scars still remained, but as he prodded and tested the pain with shaking fingers, he found that nothing hurt at all.

How the hell is this even possible?

It wasn't his job to question it. It wasn't his job to doubt it or worry about what would come next. Kurt Rogers teased the various IV lines from his skin and removed the sticky pads connecting him to the machine that monitored his vitals. The beeping turned to a consistent squeal as he removed the final pad, and immediately three nurses rushed to his room.

He had already turned in the bed, his feet touching the floor. His hospital gown had fallen from his shoulders, revealing a ripped torso covered in dark scars.

The nurses were flummoxed, unable to take in what they were seeing.

"Before you say anything," Rogers declared, "Just know that I am leaving this hospital. I am well. There is nothing to concern yourself with. I have matters I must attend to."

He rose from his bed and stretched, enjoying each creak of his joints and the failure of pain to spike from any part of his body. He dropped his hands to cover his groin when the torn gown fell to the floor and revealed everything to the nurses. He sighed. "Before I go, could you tell me where my clothes are? I don't want to cause any more alarm than I already am at this moment."

Richmond, Virginia, USA

Ula didn't have to sneak into the hospital this time. Visiting hours were in session, and she expertly navigated to the room, while Jack and Ruby waited patiently with Cassie in the lobby.

Julia and Triton sat between the hospital cots of Rhone and Roman. They were deep in conversation, although Julia's eyes flicked to Roman every few seconds.

"How are they doing?" Ula asked, standing at the foot of Roman's bed.

"They haven't woken up," Julia replied, sadness in her voice. "They've moved a little, but they haven't opened their eyes."

"They just need rest to heal," Triton comforted. "The body goes into shutdown to recover."

Ula glanced over her shoulder to check that the coast was clear. When it was, she drew out the two vials of Lupe's concoction and handed them to Julia and Triton.

"What's this?" Julia asked.

"Something to help ease the pain," Ula replied. "Help them drink it. It should encourage the healing process."

Julia studied the solution doubtfully. "It looks like antifreeze. Are you sure it'll help?"

Triton had already risen and was pouring his vial between Rhone's lips. He held his chin up to ensure that none of the liquid dribbled back out. Rhone coughed but kept most of it in, his eyelids flickering as he woke up.

"What the…" He winced in pain as he tried to sit up, momentarily forgetting that his rib was broken. "Jesus Christ on a bike, what the hell was that stuff?"

Triton looked at Ula for help.

"Something to ease the pain," she answered.

"Ugh. It tasted like boiled licorice and dirt." He lowered his head and screwed his eyes shut as he tried to get comfortable again. "Was that prescribed? Not sure I've ever had a nurse administer something…like…" His voice trailed away, and instantly he was asleep again.

Ula grinned. "I guess it's safe to assume chloroform is one of the ingredients."

Julia's brow creased. "I'm not sure I should give it to him. The nurses know what they're doing. Shouldn't we check to make sure?"

Ula snatched the vial from Julia and unscrewed the top. Before Julia could protest, Ula put the vial to Roman's lips and emptied the contents into his mouth. In the same way that Rhone spluttered, so did Roman, and his eyes snapped open. He tried to sit up, then yelped in pain when the movement jarred his leg. He thrashed in the sheets like a creature disturbed from its slumber, pulling the wires attached to him until the machines screamed and drew the attention of the nurses.

"What the hell is going on in here?" a large woman in bright blue scrubs roared at them. "Out! Now!"

Julia, Triton, and Roman backed away to allow room for the nurses to work.

Ula's cheeks flushed. She hadn't expected that reaction from Roman, but he was in a frenzy. She wondered if different people reacted differently to the solution. If so, perhaps she should have eased it in slowly. Whatever *should* have been right, it was too late.

Roman continued to lash out, and the nurses couldn't get near him.

His eyes were bloodshot and wild. He searched the room frantically, only calming when his eyes locked onto Julia's. She balled her fists and clutched her heart, hating what she was seeing.

After a tense pause where they stared at each other, Roman's eyes grew heavy and closed again. A moment later, he was snoring loudly.

The nurses, flustered and adrenaline-pumped, started reconnecting the wires and machines. One of the monitors had fallen and smashed, and a nurse asked for a replacement. They shouted at the visitors and banished them from the room, issuing a word of caution that she did not want to see them back there again. Roman had a long road to recovery, and they hadn't helped.

Ula could feel Julia's eyes burning into the back of her head. She avoided meeting her eyes, hoping she had done the right thing. Somehow, deep down, she knew it had helped.

Just maybe not in the conventional way of modern medicine.

CHAPTER FIFTY-NINE

Washington DC, USA

Susannah was sitting at the side of the chamber with her back to the wall and Jennie and Baxter on either side of her.

The old witch pursed her lips, her eyes still shining with that far-off, dreamy look. "I haven't thought about Richmond in so long. That was years ago, a whole other lifetime. Several lifetimes, in fact. Things have changed a lot since then."

"We need to know what happened," Jennie pressed. "Every last detail, it could really help us."

Susannah shook her head and smiled. "Haybourne is back. And you called him, what? Rathbourne? Sounds about right. The man went by a thousand aliases at the time. I've never known someone so persistent, so twisted and deranged in their desire to leave their mark on the world. You know the easiest way to leave a mark? Scorch the earth. One small flame and that will spread and spread until everything is turned to ash. The only problem is that kind of legacy doesn't last. Over time, green will grow again, and you'll be forgotten."

Susannah handed Jennie a bowl filled with the contents from the cauldron. Jennie had thought Susannah was lying about the casserole, but it turned out that she was telling the truth. Where she had gotten the ingredients from Jennie had no idea, but it tasted amazing, none-theless. Baxter watched her enviously as she ate, the hot meal enriching her soul even as it nourished her body.

"I first met Haybourne when we were children," Susannah went on. "We can't have been more than eight years old. Every harvest, the town held a celebration at the town hall, and families from miles around would attend to get involved and socialize.

"Haybourne was handsome, I'll give him that. But he came from the outer reaches of town. His father raised and slaughtered cattle, and his mother died when he was born. Haybourne was raised by servants. He didn't stand a chance.

"When his father passed, it was thought he'd inherit the farm and continue trade, but Haybourne had other ideas. He used to write me letters and try to steal glances whenever his father brought his goods into the village. By the time he was a teen, he had made some friends, and they had a club of sorts. I don't know much about the specifics. All I know is that those became his first followers."

Susannah tilted her head back and looked at the ceiling. "People went missing. The local authorities hunted for a murderer, but what-ever Haybourne was doing seemed innocent enough. They had no evidence that it was him, but I always knew."

Jennie bowed her head. "Sometimes you can smell death on a person."

Susannah nodded. "It was around that time that my mother and aunties began to initiate me into their coven. Secret stuff, of course. No one around could ever know the true nature of our business in that cottage. I was receiving an education passed down from genera-tions, a way to retain the magic in our bloodline. I'd always known that magic existed within my heritage, but it was fun to learn and unleash. As the years went on, I withdrew from the public eye and practiced in the privacy of my mother's basement."

Outside the chamber, Jennie thought she could hear the agents regrouping and talking to one another. She felt no threat from them but kept an ear cocked, just in case.

"I don't know whether my disappearance fueled Haybourne's

insanity," Susannah continued. "Rumors began to fly about a dangerous force in the west—a man calling himself the 'Dreadnought.' Even back then I had an inkling that he was involved, though it wasn't until the fires started raging that I truly understood what was happening. He was coming for me. Other villagers warned me, their faces blackened and covered in ash. Haybourne was coming for me, thought that he could claim me for his own." She tucked a lock of hair behind her ear. "Some might find it flattering, all of this destruction for little old me."

"He must have really loved you," Baxter commented. "To go through all of that trouble to have you by his side."

Susannah's face straightened. "That's one word for it, though I would never believe that someone loved me after they killed my mother."

"He slew your mother?" Jennie repeated, shocked.

Susannah's eyes narrowed, the memory still painful. "She went out to try to stop him. The army was marching through the forest on their way to the village. She thought she could waylay them, sneak up and take them by surprise. Magic was as prohibited then as it is now, rumors of witches were growing in Massachusetts and women of a certain disposition were not being treated kindly. She created the first fire to be seen from the village and tried to smoke them out, destroy them before they could destroy us, but Haybourne was too fast. He shot into the dark with a musket and caught her. Whether by chance or with great skill, I'll never know, but he carried her body to my door."

Susannah rose to her feet and gave the cauldron a stir. "By that time, I knew the worst was coming. A few days later and no sign of my mother, I readied myself for him. The village burned, but I knew what my role was. I had to stop him. I had to end it."

"How?" Baxter asked. "What could possibly have brought him to his knees?"

"A curse," Jennie stated.

Susannah nodded. "A powerful curse, one that stilled his beating heart and disbanded his army." Her eyes grew glassy. "I've never felt so much anger and power running through my veins as I did that day. Haybourne entered my house, and I led him to my basement. When he was there, I hit him with all I had. He fought hard, but I managed to stop him. His men waited outside obediently, unknowing that their master was already entombed in the grave that I had built for him. A tomb that would lock him away for some time."

"And the men outside?" Baxter asked. "What happened to them?"

Susannah's face finally broke into a smile. There wasn't a great deal of pleasure in there, just a tickle of a familiar memory. "I became what they thought I was. A witch. I tangled my hair and cackled and donned a dark robe. I created the illusion of the thing they feared, and when I emerged from the house without their precious leader, they fled. I threw bottles of chemicals designed not to hurt but to create the illusion of power—what you would think of as smoke bombs— and scared them into the ether. After that, his reign was over."

Susannah fell silent. The only sound was the low chatter of the agents and the bubbling broth in the cauldron.

After a while, Jennie asked, "What happened to the tomb? What did you do next?"

Susannah met her eyes. "The tomb was too heavy to do anything with. It lay in the depths of my family's cottage, at least thirty feet below ground. I locked it away, gathered my things, and fled. What else was there to do? Those I scared had seen a witch that day, and I knew I was no longer safe. Even if I'd saved the town, no one would want to live anywhere near me. I gathered my things, found my aunts and cousins, and we fled to Massachusetts to find more of our kind."

Baxter scratched his head. "That doesn't make sense. If you fled and left the tomb, then who engraved the sides of it?"

"I don't know," Susannah admitted. "All I know is that, if you're telling me he's back, he's going to be pissed. He's a danger to everyone, and you need to stop him."

Jennie cocked an eyebrow. "Do you have any ideas as to where he might be? Somewhere that he could be hiding? Is there any place Haybourne would be desperate to get to in order to reconnect with the world he once knew?"

Susannah thought about this. "The world has changed dramatically. Little of what once was still remains."

Baxter nodded, unsurprised by her answer.

"I suppose," she continued. "There might be one place. I don't know if it still exists, but it could be worth a shot."

Jennie rose to her feet and patted down the dirt from her backside. "Come with us," she requested in earnest. "Show us around the city you once knew. We need you, now more than ever."

Susannah considered this, her face growing dark. "It's been so long since I've been back. I don't know how much help I'll be. All that I know is that ancient curses twist and bend over time. I may have stopped his heart, but I didn't still his destructive nature. There's no record of what happens to a specter under the conditions I used to bind him. You need to be prepared."

"Agreed," Jennie acknowledged. "So, are you in?"

Susannah snapped her fingers and the flames from beneath the cauldron hissed out of existence. She snapped them again, and the torches around the walls lit. "I'm in," she said, resigned. "One question. What's the SIA's attitude toward witches? I can't risk hanging again."

CHAPTER SIXTY

<u>Richmond, Virginia, USA</u>

Ula lay on the rooftop, her head dangerously close to the edge. A few more inches and she'd be looking at a twenty-story drop onto the street below.

She scanned the streets through her binoculars. A multitude of agents took the other four corners of the building as they searched for any strange activity below. Already pedestrians were making their way to work, cars drove lazily through the streets, and the sounds of the city coming alive met their ears.

Ula's earpiece buzzed with chatter. It felt like a real operation now that there were representatives from each of the major spectral groups keeping each other updated over the radio. They were stationed in twelve primary locations, and all things said, they had found nothing yet of note.

Julia sat a few feet away, scrolling through her cell phone and searching the city's news outlets. She hunted through tabloids, pouring past sensationalist media, looking for anything that mentioned anomalies in the city. Attacks on buildings or people roaming the streets with far-off looks in their eyes.

An article caught her eye. She clicked the link and found a piece titled *Sleepwalking incidents on the rise*.

She started to read the article, making it as far as the first few paragraphs when the door to the rooftop opened and two men arrived. Julia's attention was pulled away from her phone when she caught Roman's eyes and saw the trace of a smile on his lips.

"You've got to be kidding me," she declared, rising from the floor and running over to meet him. She jumped into his arms, and they wrapped around her instinctively. She buried her face in his neck, and he was left looking confused and a little out of his comfort zone. After a few seconds of her babbling into his neck, she pulled away and he put her gently down.

She glanced at his leg. There was no bandaging, no sign of a limp or a struggle to stand. "How…"

Roman shrugged. He lifted his leg off the floor and flexed his knee and foot. He looked past Julia to Ula. "My guess is that Hendrick threw something together?"

Ula crossed to them and stood beside Julia, who flushed bright red. "It seems so. Is there anything that man can't make?" She turned to Rhone. "And you?"

Rhone stretched his back out, flexing his hips forward before thumping his fist against his ribs. "Good as new. You may want to tell Hendrick to batch-produce that stuff. He could make millions selling a miracle cure to heal broken bones and damaged muscle."

Ula laughed. "I don't think he'd want the attention."

Rhone waved a hand. "I'll pitch it to him. We'll make it work."

Julia's eyes never left Roman's. "How are you feeling? I was worried about you."

Roman struggled for words. Ula and Rhone chuckled and left them to it. They walked over to Triton and took their place beside him at the roof's edge, filling Rhone in on their progress and the kind of things they were looking for.

Julia's eyes fell to the floor. She laced her fingers behind her back. Roman tried to find the words he wanted to say but couldn't.

Romance wasn't in his bank of knowledge. He couldn't remember the last time anyone had shown interest in him.

Julia waited for a response. The longer she waited, the more crestfallen she appeared. She looked into his eyes again and wasn't sure what was going on in the man's head. After a few seconds, she sighed. "It's good to have you back."

She turned and went to leave, suddenly finding that Roman had grabbed her wrist. He tugged gently and turned her back around before leaning down toward her and cupping a finger to her chin. He led her lips to his, and they kissed.

He was surprisingly tender for such a large man. Julia rose to the tips of her toes and took his cheeks in her hands. They lost themselves in the moment, their hearts racing as passion took over and they let their actions do the talking.

Ula and Triton exchanged a glance, eyebrows raised.

Ula's smile split her face from ear to ear. "When I'm right, I'm right." She chuckled. "Sexual tension from the moment they met."

Rhone, who had been staring into the street through the binoculars, turned and saw what they were seeing. He did a double-take, then grinned. "I was *not* expecting that."

"We were," Triton replied. "We were."

When Julia and Roman finally stepped apart from each other, they held each other's gaze, uncertain what to say next. They smiled and rested their foreheads against each other's.

"That was..." Roman started.

"Yeah," Julia added.

Roman pulled back, and he caught the others staring at them. He flushed and cleared his throat, rising once again to his full height. He whispered to Julia, "Maybe we can talk about this later?"

Julia nodded, unable to hide the pleasure from her face. "Sure." Her mind suddenly went back to the article she had been reading. "Oh!"

She pulled her phone out and found the page again. She studied the text and approached the others. "This looks like something."

They each read through the article, a small interest-piece which told the story of a number of sleepwalkers who had been seen through the window of an apartment on the west side of town. An old man, aged and possibly senile, had witnessed so-called "zombies" wandering through the city in the middle of the night.

For once, the journalist had added a layer of reason to the article and stated that perhaps it was all a dream. The source was unreliable, but it made for something that could make readers of that particular digest smile. Julia sensed there was more to it than that, though.

Ula tapped a finger to her ear and called out to the group nearest to the west end of town. Sturgeon picked up the call and proceeded to let them know that she'd not seen anything but would try to follow up the lead. She asked if there was a street mentioned, or any kind of address. They informed her where it was, and she promised to take her team to check it out.

Ula then tried to patch into Jennie but found no answer. She wondered if she was perhaps out of reach of signal, as she so often was, and left her a message.

They sat on the rooftop and waited. Each group had its mark and its position. Only once a target was confirmed would they all rush to take their places.

While Rhone, Julia, and Roman caught up with Triton and the others, they bided their time and waited for the signal from Sturgeon.

Sturgeon left her perch atop a high-rise block of apartments and made her way into the streets below. With her was a handful of SIS agents, a small group of specters donated by Jimmy Dean, Agent Erik, and a man who she already knew she hated and wished she'd never met who went by the name of Grimald.

She could understand the reasoning, but she wished they were never involved. Flailing for help and backup, the originators of this witch hunt had wanted to bulk their numbers and recruited a group of local gun enthusiasts. It might have seemed like a smart idea at the time, but they hadn't known that only a day or two later shit would truly hit the fan and the forces would be called in.

You know, the federal forces. The agency the GOA rebelled against.

Grimald had been a headache since the moment they had split into their groups and watched over the city. She wished he didn't have to follow her now, but there was safety in numbers.

Supposedly.

"I've got licenses, ain't I?" Grimald declared loudly, caught in a rant that Sturgeon had stopped paying attention to. "I've done my training. I've proven I'm responsible. I should be allowed out wherever the hell I want to hunt and play with these bad boys. The hoops you have to jump through, it's ridiculous."

"Will you keep your voice down?" Sturgeon asked, an edge to her voice. "How are we ever going to sneak up on the target if they can hear you coming from a mile off?"

Grimald threw his hands in the air. "Well, excuse me. I thought as an American, I had the right to free speech? If some federal force is trying to silence me—"

Sturgeon whirled on Grimald and he froze, taken aback by the sudden turn. "Here's the deal. You shut the fuck up for a few moments while we hunt for an enemy who is trying to sneak around the city, okay? If you can do that for more than a few moments, I'll give you a cookie later. Tax-free, no strings attached. I promise."

The man raised an eyebrow. "Is that supposed to be funny?"

Sturgeon advanced on him, staring him down. "Let's put this in terms you can understand. When you're hunting for game, do you shout and stomp and disturb nature around you to flush out the scared and vulnerable, or do you sneak and be quiet to try to catch the best prey? You ever tried to hunt deer by hollering and whooping like that?"

Grimald composed himself and shook his head. "No, ma'am."

"Then shut the fuck up," Sturgeon instructed. "I'm not sure if your issue is that I'm a federal agent, or because I'm a woman, but somewhere along this journey you're going to enter the twenty-first century and see what a real woman can do, okay?"

Grimald was quiet for a moment. Eventually, a smile appeared on his face. "I love your accent."

Sturgeon shook her head in disbelief. She addressed the others. "Follow me, and let's find this street. If he opens his mouth again, you have my permission to find a way to close it, got that?"

Grimald smirked and turned toward the empty space over his shoulder. As a mortal, the spectral addition to their group was lost from sight. "Who are you talking to?"

Sturgeon rolled her eyes and took the lead. Finally, she had been at a point where she believed she was ready to take charge and show the queen what she was capable of, and she got stuck with this guy.

They found the street mentioned in the article and looked out for any sign of the sleepwalkers. As she expected, there was nothing there at all. They made their way toward the apartment building where the old man lived and paused beneath its long shadow.

She scrolled to the forwarded article on her cell and studied the image. There was a shot of the old man in the window of his apartment, and it appeared as though he was level with the roof of the building opposite. She counted in her mind and took a stab at it, hoping she could find him and ask him a few additional questions.

The hallway of the tenth floor hosted half a dozen doors with nothing else on them but numbers. There were three on the side of the building where the old man had been, and she took a stab at each one. Inside the first apartment was a bitter old lady who instantly grew agitated at the sight of so many agents at her door. Clearly used to fighting off authority, she shouted out her rights then slammed the door when Sturgeon couldn't produce a warrant.

She breathed an internal sigh of relief when the old man appeared at the door of the second apartment. They had knocked three times and were almost certain no one was in when he finally answered.

"Yes?" His eyes drank them all in.

Sturgeon explained that she had a few additional questions for him. The old man nodded and allowed her inside but demanded that the others wait in the hall. He hadn't prepared for guests and was concerned about the state of his place.

Had he been this picky before the cops and papers had spoken to him?

After a long fifteen minutes of questioning him, she finally extracted the information that she needed. She managed to get him off his ass so that he could point which way down the street. Sitting in his chair and pointing at the general direction of the window was not helpful at all.

"That way," the old man declared, pointing out of the window. "They were walking that way."

She followed his finger, and from this high up, she could see that he was pointing toward the outer reaches of the west side of the city. In the distance, rolling hills and fields beaconed the start of Richmond's farming district. A little way beyond that was the quarry.

"Thanks," Sturgeon added before disappearing out of the apartment. She wasted no courtesy, wanting to get on with her quest. Even though the man called after her and offered her one of his butterscotch candies, she paid no heed.

When she arrived back in the street, she immediately headed in the direction he had told her. They walked straight for a few blocks and were on the verge of giving up when they came across a woman bellycrawling along the sidewalk.

Sturgeon swallowed her initial reaction to seeing the woman's struggle. She was clearly paralyzed. Her legs were thin and the muscle wasted. Still, she determinedly clawed her fingers and pushed them into the cracks of each flagstone and pulled herself onward.

"Excuse me, ma'am?" Grimald stood above the lady and looked down with eyebrows raised. "Are you okay?"

The woman stared ahead of her, unaware that anyone was nearby. She grunted as she pulled herself along, oblivious to anything around her.

Grimald exchanged a glance with Sturgeon.

Sturgeon moved closer and lowered to her knees. She waited in front of the woman and ducked her head, noticing the blank voids of her eyes.

Despite the horror of the woman's situation, a smile crept onto her face. They had the key to freeing all of the possessed. "Bingo."

CHAPTER SIXTY-ONE

<u>Richmond, Virginia, USA</u>

They followed the woman, moving at a pace that had Sturgeon impatient.

"Can't we pick her up or something?" Grimald asked. "Maybe she can be like a divining rod. She'll twitch when we're heading in the right direction."

Without much care, he scooped her into his arms from behind and held her in the air. She was lighter than he expected, although he hadn't believed she would flail so much. The instant he picked her up, she threw her arms in all directions, going into a frenzy until he eventually lowered her back to the floor and let her crawl.

"I guess not," Sturgeon confirmed.

The woman led them onward. Sturgeon followed a step behind her. After ten minutes or so, Grimald tutted beneath his breath and turned away from the group, running off into the street behind. Sturgeon didn't complain. She was tired of his company and believed that he would be more useful doing something else.

Another ten minutes passed, and the sound of wheels rolling on concrete met her ears. She turned and rolled her eyes. Grimald stood on a skateboard and sped toward them, a grin on his face.

"Thought it might speed up proceedings," he offered. "Try."

"You can pick her up," Sturgeon instructed. "After what I saw last time, I'm not even tempted."

"We don't have to. Look." Grimald placed the skateboard on the sidewalk in front of the woman. He tilted the far end into the air, and the woman's forward crawl made her mount the board. Once she was mobile, the wheels increased her speed. If it wasn't for her feet dragging behind causing friction, she would have shot ahead of them all.

"How does she know where she's going?" Grimald asked. "If the others are long gone, surely it should be over? Does this guy install a GPS in everyone?"

Sturgeon considered this. "I honestly don't know. There's little about this I understand. I have served Queen Victoria for only a decade, and this is out of my bank of knowledge. I think this is out of Jennie's, too."

"That weird chick from the manor?" Grimald asked. "The one with the tight corset and delicious tits?"

Sturgeon threw him a scalding look.

"What?" He defended himself with arms up. "Don't tell me she wears that because she doesn't want attention. Anyway, how would she know more than you guys? Aren't you the specials from Britain or something?"

Sturgeon narrowed her eyes. "I am. *We* are. There are a lot of things at play in this world you will never understand. Just because you think you have it all figured out, don't mistake that for truth or knowledge. What you know is nothing more than a drop in the goddamn ocean. You may learn a few things over the next couple of days. But even then, it won't be anything of significance."

Sturgeon increased her stride, speeding ahead of him and catching up with the woman. He turned to the handful of her agents and shrugged. "Women, huh?"

None of them met his eyes.

He had turned his attention to the old woman, when he suddenly seemed to take in what Sturgeon had said. "Wait a second, did you say Queen *Victoria?*"

The city grew quiet around them. In the distance tractors and combine harvesters turned the soil over acres of land.

The buildings grew more rustic, relics of things that once existed years ago. A bell tolled the hour and drew Sturgeon's eye to a bell tower in the near distance.

The old woman slowed at the sound of the bells. Her head lifted, and her eyes fixed to the tower.

Sturgeon could just about make out a solitary figure up at the bell tower, seemingly looking out at the approaching group. A strange sensation crept down her spine as she suddenly felt certain the figure was staring directly at them.

"Keep your guard up," she instructed the mortals and specters. She slowed and let the possessed woman take the lead. She beelined the skateboard for the large building, the rest of the city quiet as the wheels roared on the asphalt. She crossed into the road and a car screeched to a standstill. The driver shouted and raised her fists, then sped off as the woman cleared her path.

Sturgeon spoke into her radio and got Ula's request for a sit-rep in reply. "My team pursued a possessed individual to an old building with a bell tower on the west side of the city. There's a female standing at the top of the tower, but we've yet to confirm if she's a suspect or a prisoner."

Ula's voice came back to her. "What does she look like?"

"Hard to say without getting closer," Sturgeon replied.

"Then get closer," Ula commanded.

Sturgeon flushed. She was used to taking commands from superiors on her task force, but not from strangers. She took a deep breath to steady herself and tried to remember the agreement they had all signed in the manor: a contract to work together for the greater good. She was working for the good guys. Jennie was a good guy. Ula was her proxy.

"Hold on," she murmured. She wandered down the street, telling the others to stay behind her. When she reached the street corner, she could just about make out the shape of the person in the bell tower.

"An Asian woman, Chinese descent by the looks of things," she stated to Ula, finger pressed on her earpiece. "Short dark hair."

Ula described some additional features. "Could it be Jiao?"

"Maybe?" Sturgeon replied. "Honestly, I'm not sure from this distance." Yet a feeling in her gut told her that she was looking at the target Ula mentioned. Jiao was in the bell tower.

"What would you like me to do?" she asked. "It appears as though she's alone." Her eyes traced the woman skateboarding on her stomach toward the building. "Apart from one old woman."

"Wait there," Ula replied. "We're coming for you. Do *not* approach without backup. She may be armed and highly dangerous."

"She's definitely not armed," Sturgeon replied, unable to see any kind of weapon on her. In fact, it was strange that the woman was just standing there and not doing anything in particular.

Ula clicked off, and the earpiece was quiet. Sturgeon stared through narrowed eyes at the bell tower. Eventually, she turned to the others in her group, ready to dish an instruction to hold tight until backup came.

Only, when she turned, she was surprised to find that another group had appeared from out of nowhere. Her agents were frozen still, spellbound. The possessed grabbed them and held them from behind as their eyes turned to white blanks.

Sturgeon was at a loss as to how to react. The only ones free of the curse were the specters, who could do nothing to affect the mortals under the spell.

"Get marching," a disembodied voice demanded.

Sturgeon moved in front of her agents, meaning to stop them from obeying the strange voice. Where it had come from, she had no idea.

Although she stood in their way, they shoved past her indelicately, not caring one iota for her feelings. They pushed and marched toward the building, leaving Sturgeon breathless and confused. Grimald was among them, his firearm hanging from one clenched fist.

Sturgeon looked back at the specters with a pleading look but found a woman standing where her men had been.

She was older, retired, at least. She had a crop of blonde hair and kept in impressive shape for a woman her age. Her eyes were blanks, but where the other possessed individuals had seemed hollow, there was a definite power flowing from within this one.

"And you," a man's voice instructed from the woman's throat. "You get marching, too."

Sturgeon opened her mouth to protest, but something lunged out at her. A thick shadow leaked from the woman's throat and came for her.

It found its way into Sturgeon's mouth and entered her body. All of her worries, doubts, and fears dissipated in an instant. Her mind was clouded in a cotton ball of white. The only thing she cared about at that moment was making her way into the community center.

And finding a way—*any way*— to serve her master.

Washington DC, USA

Jennie ordered Ashton to hover over the Washington hospital before heading back to Richmond. She had an inkling in her stomach that, should her plan have succeeded, Rogers would be heading out of the hospital around this time, his bones healed and a spring in his step.

They waited for at least an hour and found no sign. Eventually, Jennie dialed his direct number, and he picked up on the second ring.

"Jennie! Long time, no speak." Rogers' voice was cheery and refreshed. He sounded as if she had called him after a perfect sleep and a hearty breakfast.

Jennie asked him where he was. Rogers told her that he was nearing the SIA HQ. He had some business to attend to and hated how out of the loop he was on things, considering he had been in hospital since a bomb had nearly blown up his base.

"We're coming to get you," Jennie informed him. "Wait out front. We'll update you on the way."

She had expected some resistance. Rogers was a busy man at the best of times, but he agreed to her without question. "See you soon."

Twenty minutes later, Rogers climbed into the chopper. He had returned to his usual self, his demeanor strong and authority oozing off him. He reminded her of the first time she had met him, commanding grace pouring out of every pore.

"I'm guessing this isn't a social flight," he asked as the chopper took off.

Jennie shook her head. "Afraid not. We've got business to attend to. The shit has hit the fan, figuratively speaking, and we need all hands on deck. How are you feeling?"

"Like I just returned from a three-week vacation in Maui." Rogers grinned. "What was in that potion?"

"Science," Jennie replied flatly, leaving no room for further explanation.

She filled him in on what he had missed while he was out of commission and in the hands of the President. He was particularly fascinated by Susannah's story, particularly since it involved events from over three hundred years ago.

"A witch, you say? How is that even possible? Magic isn't real?" He raised an eyebrow and gave Susannah an intense look. Specters had entered his zeitgeist, but witches clearly seemed out of his wheelhouse of belief.

"I don't proclaim to have the answers," she replied. "Maybe there's some kind of science in specterdom that can cross over to mortals? You could call conduits witches, I suppose. They can see things that others can't. My ability is to manipulate things others can't fathom." She turned to Jennie. "You say your friend Hendrick is able to manipulate chemicals that don't show themselves to mortals. Maybe witchcraft is just a further manipulation of that magic."

Jennie tilted her head and chewed her lip. She supposed that could be true. Hendrick and his masters before him had played with chemicals and substances beyond the realms of mortal-knowledge. Could magic just be an extension of that same logic?

When Richmond approached on the horizon, Ashton craned his head over his shoulder. "We're here, guys."

They were about to land on the lawn of the manor when Jennie received an update from Ula. It was a message to her cell phone. Ula and the others were in the heart of the city following a potential lead. According to Ula, Sturgeon had dropped off comms while pursuing a lead on Jiao on the west side of the city.

"The west side?" Susannah stated. "That's mostly farmland, right?"

Jennie confirmed that it was.

"That's out where I used to live," Susannah informed them. "The farmland used to be the heart of Richmond's trade. This is going back years, of course. I wonder if my old house is still there?"

"I doubt it," Baxter replied. "Unless you lived in a strip mall?"

Ashton touched down on the grass. The McFarlene brothers greeted them with cackles and laughs, and Tanya, Krissie, and Lyla ran out to meet them on the lawn.

Jennie waved at them from the Airbus. "We can't stay, more news has developed. We must be off."

Tanya nodded, her SI glasses slipping on her face. "Who's the specter?"

Jennie grinned. "You'll see later. She's kind of a big deal."

She commanded Ashton to take them back up into the air. The chopper soared, and they waved the others away. "Man, I hate it when meetings are brief." Jennie sighed. "At some point, it'll be nice just to have guests over and not have to worry about the end of humanity, you know?"

Baxter smirked.

Jennie directed Ashton toward a group of people running through the streets. She recognized them instantly and had him bring the chopper down on the building with the lowest roof. The minute they neared the roof, the group paused, knowing the Airbus by sight.

Jennie, Baxter, Ashton, and Susannah exited the chopper and ran down to the street. They found Ula and the others waiting for them, although they were jittery with impatience.

"What's the latest?" Jennie asked.

Ula informed her of Sturgeon's disappearance after a potential sighting of Jiao at the bell tower. They all broke into a run and headed toward the location, arriving within sight of the old community building only twenty minutes later.

Sturgeon appeared before them as they neared the road the building was on and made to cross. A long-manicured lawn led to the building where a solitary figure watched from above. Jennie recognized her instantly but held her cards to her chest.

"Sturgeon?" Jennie called between cupped hands. "What's the deal? You went silent, for what? Is everything okay?"

She asked for show, knowing that any sign she had figured things out would give away her advantage. "Get back over here, okay?"

Sturgeon stared blankly at her. She looked smart in her SIS uniform, her guns holstered to her hips. Behind her stood a handful of other SIS agents as well as a man that Jennie recognized as one of the frontrunners of the GOA.

Jennie moved her hand toward her weapons. "I'm not fucking around, Sturgeon. Get your arse over here. Now."

Sturgeon didn't move. Jennie looked over her shoulder toward where a troop of civilians was pouring from the community hall. There were people of every creed and denomination, but they all had one thing in common with Sturgeon. They filed out until they filled the lawn, their faces blank, their eyes nothing but whites.

Jennie leaned over to Baxter and sighed. "Get ready, I think shit might be about to go down." She scanned the group. "But where the hell is the Dreadnought?"

Susannah shuffled closer to her. "He'll be hiding. He can't afford to lead the pack. Without him, they all fall apart. He's the lead domino."

"So, who's going to take his place?" Baxter asked.

Jennie already knew. The woman had disappeared from the bell tower, and now walked from the back of the group, who parted like the Red Sea before Moses. She reached the front and stared levelly at Jennie.

"Jennie," Jiao stated.

"Jiao," Jennie returned. She narrowed her eyes. "I'll be honest, out of all of the twists and turns that have taken place during my hunt for the Dragon, I never expected you. We welcomed you. Gave you a home. Took you in when it looked like you had nowhere else to go, and this is how you repay us?"

Jiao cocked her head to the side. "You think that wasn't the plan? Do you think I wouldn't know every step along the way? Jennie, you've been in this game longer than I have, so I'm saddened by the fact you couldn't see through the ruse. It makes me think that you're not half the woman they say you are."

Jennie considered her words. "Jiao, step away from all this. The Dreadnought is not who you think he is. He will be your end. Call off your troops, and no one has to get hurt."

"Someone will," Jiao replied. "Someone always gets hurt in war. You know as well as I do that the game is bigger than you and me. You think it's all over in Washington, but you're wrong. If you think I don't have more men willing to die for me, you're wrong again. This is my time. The time of the Dragon has come, and you will not steal this from me."

Jennie sighed. "Very well. Have it your way."

Her hand moved to the Big Bitch. Without a moment's hesitation, she drew the chunky firearm and pulled the trigger.

CHAPTER SIXTY-TWO

For the first time since Jennie had met her, Jiao flinched.

The Big Bitch roared, smoke lazily curling up from the end of the barrel following the gunshot. The petite woman looked down in disbelief and patted her body, hunting for the wound.

But there was none. Jennie's aim had been true; the bullet had flown an inch above her head. Jiao's hair had wobbled beneath its trajectory.

"You missed," Jiao stated.

Jennie shook her head and looked at the hole that had been made in the roof of the community center. "I missed on purpose. Do you think I would make the same mistake I made with Zhao and kill you when we've got a number of other psychos on the loose? Oh, no, dear. Not today." She turned to Baxter, Ashton, and Susannah. "You guys ready?"

They all nodded.

"Fantastic." Jennie grinned. "Come on then, Jiao. Show us what a true Dragon is made of."

Jiao gave a solemn nod, then snapped her fingers. A spark of something flashed on the hand she wore three rings on.

The possessed gathered on the lawn started to run.

The gunshot tore through the city, sounding like a thunderclap. Outside the many windows of the houses and apartments in Richmond, faces appeared and looked at the sky.

For the first time in days, the clouds grew. The sun fought to be seen through the massing darkness caused by the thick gray clouds. In the east, a gentle drizzle began to fall.

Ula and her team were running through the streets when they heard the gunshot. A smile appeared on Ula's face. It was Jennie's signal.

She increased her pace and led the others onward. Roman, Rhone, and Triton weren't far behind, and even Julia was managing to keep up. There was something in her face that hadn't been there before, a grim determination that she must have sucked out of Roman's mouth and placed within her gut. Courage found in the presence of love.

They rounded the corner, and Ula could hardly believe they'd found them. A line of civilians with vacant stares stood swaying on the lawn, where Jennie was deep in conversation with Jiao.

Jiao…

The sight of her made Ula's rage burn. Although she hadn't freed the Dreadnought, she had betrayed those who had saved her. This was the final confirmation they needed of her betrayal.

The possessed broke into a run.

"Come on," Ula instructed. "Let's go."

Jiao remained where she was and let the possessed rush around her. Their number was large, and Jennie grouped her team nearby, creating a small island in the middle of the ocean of enemies.

Jennie hated fighting those who had been possessed. It wasn't their fault they were caught up in this, and the mortal shell that encapsulated the trace of specter would get battered and bruised along the way. It was the ultimate form of cowardice, to hide behind others and allow them to take the pain for you.

Still, if they didn't do something, *they* were going to get hurt.

Jennie holstered the Big Bitch and harnessed Baxter's power. The cells strapped to her waist throbbed with power, and she reached out with experimental fingers to ascertain what kind of spectral power she was dealing with in this batch of possessed.

The frequencies were murky. While the Shadows had taken whole specters and combined them with mortals, the Dreadnought had found a different way to possess his servants. All she could sense as she hurriedly tried to determine what they were dealing with was a strange darkness inside each person. Every possessed civilian was a tiny piece of the puzzle, too small to be able to create much significant change.

Jennie opened her eyes as the first punch was thrown. It caught her on the cheek and knocked her head back.

Jennie's lips thinned into a tight line. The man who had punched her closed the gap. "Okay, bozo. You want it that way, huh?"

Jennie balled her hands into fists and delivered a blow to his stomach. Even possessed, the man was winded. Jennie followed up when he doubled over to clutch his gut by raising her knee and delivering a hard blow to his head.

The man bowled backward, knocking over the possessed crowding behind him.

Ashton threw punches, catching the mortals who had now surrounded his side of the island. Although he was a pilot by trade, he hadn't forgotten his training and was able to hold his own. Baxter and Susannah found they were able to connect their blows with the spectral forces inside, each punch, kick, or headbutt sent their target to the ground.

Jennie let her training take over. Fighting had always felt like a dance to her, and she allowed her instincts to guide her. She kicked out when enemies came to close, ducked to avoid blows, and punched many a possessed in the face, wincing every time she felt the sickening crunch of bone against her knuckles.

She spun, and a break in the enemy afforded her a glance of a new group running to enter the fray. Jennie smiled at Ula as the conduit sprinted with a determined expression on her face. Her plan had worked. She hadn't been sure that Ula had received her message, but thankfully she had.

The conduits arrived and crashed into the enemy. Rhone was among them, wasting no time before getting stuck in. Rogers' face was determined as he added to their number. They found that if they hit the mortals hard enough, they fell unconscious, and there was little the spectral piece inside could do to pick them up.

"I see you've brought a friend back with you," Rhone commented as he swept out the legs of a woman in front and sent her sprawling to the floor. "Want to introduce us?"

Jennie grunted, just managing to avoid a punch that would have connected with her temple and potentially caused some real damage. "Maybe later. I'm a little busy right now."

Ula moved fast, lithe and nimble. Her body was a blur as she engaged with the possessed around her. She paused for the briefest of moments. "Jennie, can't you do something about this? They're specters inside, right?"

Jennie shook her head, then kicked the chest of the woman in front of her. "Not quite. Not from what I sensed anyway. I'm going to need more time to figure this out."

"Then get inside us," Ula shouted. Rhone shot her a strange look, a smirk on his face. "Really? Now? Now you want to play innuendo bingo?"

Jennie tucked herself into the middle of the circle the others formed around her. Her heart was racing. She closed her eyes and focused on what she was reading around her. While specters would usually appear as a bright white signature inside of her mind, the spectral energy inside of the possessed more resembled gray clouds. Jennie shot out a tendril of spectral energy and tested the connection.

The moment they connected, a wave of nausea swept over her. She held her connection tight, determined to figure this out.

The feeling was like waving a hand through fog. It was as though she *should* be able to touch it, but it just slipped through her fingers. Jennie sent out a second tendril and latched onto two at once.

She gagged, her body convulsing as it tried to repel the foreign feelings that were coursing through her. The Dreadnought was old, he had been cursed. Could it be that this had somehow tainted his spectral form?

Jennie attempted latching onto a third, but the sensation made her physically sick. She vomited on the ground.

Ula threw her a concerned look. "You okay?"

"I've been better," Jennie replied, wiping her mouth with the back of her hand.

The circle tightened as the enemy drew closer. Despite their best efforts to keep them at bay, there were just too many. Even Roman, who had been throwing his tree-trunk-sized arms in all directions, was now almost surrounded. Julia was tucked behind him, cowering from the reaching hands of those who were closing the gap.

Jennie hated to retreat, but she knew when to throw in the towel. If they were going to save as many of the possessed as possible, they'd need to change tack.

She forced her way back to the front line and scanned over the tops of the heads for Jiao. She couldn't see her anymore, though that didn't mean a lot. Jiao was tiny and could easily be lost in this crowd.

Jennie growled. "Fall back," she instructed. "Let's get the hell out of here."

The others didn't argue. As one, they about-faced and broke through the group, running for the other end of the street to put as much distance between themselves and their attackers as possible.

Jennie slowed after fifty meters or so and risked a look back. She found that the possessed weren't following them.

The two groups waited in a silent stand-off. The possessed had no need to pursue them. They had completed their objective. Bees don't continue to chase an invader when they've got a hive to protect.

Jennie took a step toward the possessed. As one, the possessed took a step forward.

"Interesting," she muttered. She narrowed her eyes and took another step.

The possessed copied her again.

"We need to get through to the others," Jennie instructed, glancing at Ula. "We've got the enemy in our sights, and it's about time we close in and finish this."

Ula was on it immediately, muttering into her earpiece to summon the others. She gave coordinates for their location and followed with the order to hurry.

Jennie tested her theory once more and took a larger step this time. The possessed, as one, took another step toward them.

"A predictable enemy is a removable enemy," Jennie muttered.

No sooner had she said this than movement at the back of the possessed caught her eye. A handful of figures worked their way through the crowd and took their place at the front of the throng.

Jennie's heart stopped when she recognized Sturgeon and one of the GOA guys.

Three other civilians holding firearms were beside them, and it was clear what they were about to do.

"Find cover!" Jennie shouted, already diving toward a parked car.

The others split up and found their own protection behind mailboxes, trees, and around the sides of buildings.

The possessed fired without hesitation, pumping their fingers against the triggers until their ammo was spent. Shots fired smashed windows, and bullets ricocheted off walls and car doors.

Jennie looked up at Baxter, who had found his hiding place beside her. Her face was a mixture of doubt and hurt. "I think we may have to hurt some people to win this one, Bax."

Baxter nodded solemnly. "I think so, too." He took a deep breath. "I think so, too."

The minute her horde surrounded the enemy, Jiao slipped out of sight.

Her usually calm demeanor had slipped, and a crazed expression masked her face. She walked speedily toward the community center, seeking the protection of inside the hall.

Jennie was here. Her group was small, that only meant reinforcements would come soon. Jiao and Rathbourne had built a decent-sized army so far, but they weren't ready at all. She'd thought they would have had more time to recruit. She had overruled Rathbourne and said her way was best. Recruit quietly, and soon the army would be ready to go.

She had underestimated Jennie.

Heart racing in her chest, Jiao strode through the community center and entered a room at the back of the building. Once this room may have hosted children's birthday parties, but now it was the holding place of Rathbourne's sarcophagus. Jiao was unsurprised to find the female mortal Rathbourne was possessing standing beside the tomb, one hand touching the stone.

"They're going to overrun us, aren't they?" His voice was calm and measured, that strange doubling effect like two people talking confusing Jiao's ears.

Jiao gave a curt nod. "They're summoning reinforcements as we speak. We need to move you. We need to get you out of here."

The woman turned to Jiao and met her eyes. The stare was so intense that a weaker woman might have withered, but Jiao held firm.

"You said you have kin?" Rathbourne didn't blink. "You said there were others."

"I do," Jiao replied, not bothering to correct the man that they weren't "kin" as such, but more devoted followers inherited by an ancient legacy. "Once we've gotten you out of here, I'll summon them to bolster our numbers. We need to grow much faster than we have been."

Rathbourne held Jiao's stare. It was a strange feeling, looking into the pits of those dark eyes. While the possessed had all lost their pupils and saw only from eyes of white, this woman's eyes had turned dark and were now swimming with the deep and ancient knowledge of magic that shouldn't have existed in this world. Jiao wondered what those eyes had seen on the other side of mortality.

"I agree," Rathbourne replied. The woman clapped her hands once, and eight possessed entered the room. They were muscular, part of the group Rathbourne had coordinated to shift the sarcophagus here in the first place. He issued the command and they got to work, raising the tomb onto a wheeled platform. Soon they were out of the door and rolling toward a white van.

Jiao made to follow them but found Rathbourne's hand holding her back. "No. We go our own way."

"Why?" Jiao asked.

"We must build our numbers," Rathbourne croaked. "Therefore, I must visit some old friends of mine. Soldiers who are willing to and have already died for me."

With an iron grip on her shoulder, Jiao was led out of the community center. In the distance behind them, gunfire broke the quiet of the city.

CHAPTER SIXTY-THREE

Richmond, Virginia, USA

Roman called to Jennie. They were separated by the width of the sidewalk, Jennie tucked behind the trunk of a car, Roman in the shadows of the alley.

"I'm making some cover. Get ready to run," Roman called.

Jennie looked at him curiously. Roman held up a smoke grenade and waved it.

Jennie grinned.

Roman pulled the pin and tossed the grenade as far as he could down the street. Bullets still ricocheted off walls and metal. He ducked back and waited for the explosion.

There was no cry of surprise when the grenade went off. Usually people would start in shock, but these weren't normal people; they were soulless drones.

Jennie looked around at the others. Ula and Triton were not too far from Roman. Julia was tucked next to Roman, shrunken as small as she could and flinching with every bullet fired. Across the way, Rogers' steeled expression stared into the growing mass of smoke. Rhone was not far from Rogers, his back to the wall of a florist's.

"Disarm and disband them!" Jennie cried. "Go!"

They broke cover and tore toward the smoke. The conduits had their IR goggles on, giving them the ability to see their enemies in the thickening fog. Jennie latched onto Baxter and rushed toward the group, keeping close to the edges of the street and doing her best to keep her bearings once they encountered the horde once more.

Jennie was heartened to hear helicopters whirring in the distance. Although it would draw more attention to them, it reassured Jennie to know she had her team coming to help her.

Birds are faster than cars.

Jennie issued an order into her radio to not kill where possible. She looked up and saw some of the helicopters landing on the nearby rooftops. Projectiles launched down and exploded in flashes of white and ear-piercing shouts—flash-bang grenades designed to scramble the possessed and confuse their circuits.

Pressing the advantage, Jennie slalomed through the group, occasionally kicking someone out of her way. She hoped that if she could make it through the crowd, she could find Jiao and the Dreadnought. With any luck, if she could find the ringleader, she could stop the followers all at once.

Susannah followed closely behind, keeping an impressive pace for an ancient witch. Baxter stayed by her side, knowing deep down that somehow Susannah was going to be the key to the Dreadnought's undoing, while Jennie would be Jiao's.

They were almost through the crowd when Jennie was taken by surprise by a woman who looked as if she had once been carved from stone. Her flat face showed Neanderthal features, and her body was twice as wide as it was tall. She bowled into Jennie and knocked her off her feet. Those immediately in the vicinity piled on top of her.

"Shit," Jennie grunted.

Baxter and Susannah tried to help, but there were just too many of them. The possessed piled on, squashing Jennie to the ground. She turned spectral, latching onto Susannah and Baxter, and tried to feel again for the signatures of the tainted ones nearby.

All she could see was darkness. Nausea immediately washed over her. She couldn't understand how something so corrupt could be living inside these people.

She rejected the possessed and focused on something else that presented itself to her. Another ancient kind of spectral power that flushed through her and brought with it a wash of memory and magic.

Susannah's energy signature was intoxicating. Where the possessed's was black and cloudy, Susannah's was white and throbbing with power. As Jennie explored her connection, memories that weren't her own flooded her. Years of running and moving and concocting potions and spells of all natures filled her head in a blink, but most of all, there was something that purified Jennie and ejected the corruption of those piled on top of her.

"Jennie!" Baxter exclaimed, tearing away at the bodies piling up on top of her. For every possessed that he picked up and threw into the crowd, another two jumped on. The large woman eyed him up and moved toward him.

Susannah narrowed her eyes and held out her hands. They glowed soft white and produced an orange-sized ball of light.

Jennie channeled Susannah's power and, following an instinct she didn't understand, kissed the face of the closest person to her. Her lips made contact with the sticky sheen of the man's face, and Susannah's power crept from her lips and worked its way into the man's system.

With her eyes closed, Jennie could make out the cloudy gray shape of corruption inside the man. Her kiss leaked a white power that made its way toward the corruption and immediately started its work.

Like an antibody to a virus, the power multiplied, growing and doubling in size until it was consuming the corruption. Jennie groaned under the weight of the specters on top but couldn't look away from what was happening in front of her. The man blinked and grimaced as the corruption was dispelled. He took a deep gulp of air, struggling under the mass of the others, and looked at Jennie in shock.

His eyes had returned to normal.

"Interesting," Jennie mouthed.

The man tried to talk but couldn't underneath the weight of everyone. She could hear Baxter still working away at clearing the pile, but it just continued to grow. Her mind was cast back to the tunnels of the abandoned New York subway tracks, where she had once repelled dozens of specters in a single glowing display of power. She wished she could try that here but knew that the corruption would only hurt her. She couldn't harness their powers the way she would like.

But she could harness Susannah's.

Jennie gasped for air, her lungs were nearing empty. Any more bodies on top and she'd be done. Even if she turned spectral, she wouldn't be able to escape, the corrupt power inside her enemies was a weight in the other world.

Jennie focused her energy on Susannah's power and her hands started to glow. She flailed her arms and reached for anyone she could, her heart racing fast as the power started leaking into them, repeating what it had done with the first man who grunted and complained in front of her, his hot breath on her face.

Susannah's power acted as a cure. One by one, those nearest to Jennie—those that she could physically touch—were cleared of their corruption. On the outside of the bundle of bodies, Susannah worked on her own targets, pushing her power into the others while Baxter fought on to remove the possessed.

As Jennie cleared people of possession, they began to struggle against the weight on top, pushing to try to free themselves from the tangle of bodies. Jennie was afforded a breath as the pressure eased. She flailed her arms, touching anyone and everyone she could, dispensing Susannah's healing powers into the remaining corrupt. After another minute the pain eased, and she was clear.

A hand reached in and helped Jennie up. Baxter gave a weak smile. The large woman was unconscious nearby. Baxter raised his wrench, and Jennie understood the large welt on the woman's forehead.

Jennie gasped for air. "Let's keep going. We're so close."

"What about those guys?" Baxter asked, pointing to the men and women they had freed from the spell. They were now fighting the corrupt, doing whatever they could to help, although their number was nothing compared to the enemy.

"We'll come back for them," Jennie replied. "That's all we can do."

They found their way through the remaining enemies and broke free on the other side. After the torture of wading through the bodies, the last few meters to the community center was a breeze.

Jennie barged through the door and scanned for any sign of Jiao and the Dreadnought.

She felt his power the minute she entered the building. A wave of corruption caused her to gag. She darted from room to room, hoping to find them, and it was only when they came to the final room off the back of the hall and saw the doors had been left wide open that she knew they'd escaped.

"Shit," Baxter cried. "So damn close."

Jennie couldn't help but smile.

"What have you got to be smiling about?" Baxter asked.

Susannah's face was stern as her eyes stared at the tire marks left on the asphalt by their speedy getaway. "They're on the run, and they've left their army behind."

Jennie, Susannah, and Baxter climbed the bell tower and took a stance where Jiao had been for most of the night before.

From there, they had a direct view of the battle. The smoke from the grenades had almost cleared. Their agents had disarmed the enemy and arrested those who had shot at them, including Agent Sturgeon and the ringleader of the GOA. While the other possessed civilians fought on, the battle was beginning to wind down.

Only a few had lost their lives, a better result than Jennie could have hoped for.

Jennie studied her hands then looked at Susannah. "What was that we did back there? What power lies within you?"

Susannah shrugged. "I don't proclaim to understand it; I just know that it can work. I'm able to manipulate dark magic and provide light in the darkness."

"Can you perform an exorcism?" Baxter asked.

Susannah shook her head. "Oh, no. That takes a great power that few possess. My power is limited and can only extend to the magic that I had in life."

"What do you mean?" Jennie replied.

Susannah looked at her own hands. "This mess is my fault. I put my curse on Haybourne, and now he has spread that curse to others. I didn't believe it to be possible when I removed him from the mortal realm, I only thought that I was binding him to his sarcophagus. Over time, magic can grow stronger and darker. As adversity strengthens the human condition, so too does it create fortified darkness. There is still so much we don't know about how magic acts beyond the grave."

"You're telling me," Jennie mused, remembering the Mendlesons and the bond they had made with the manor. Recalling the *sturmgeist* and the host of spectral creatures that had wandered alongside them in the forests of New Jersey.

"How do we clear all of those guys?" Baxter nodded toward the combat. "We need to help."

Jennie nodded. She leaned forward and rested her hands on the cold stone ledge, the action disturbing a pigeon that had nested below. Alarmed, the pigeon burst from its hiding in a mass of feathers and wings. Jennie jumped back and knocked into the bell, eliciting a chime that carried over to the battle.

Those nearest to them turned at the disturbance. The bell rocked gently back and forth. *Interesting*, Jennie thought. She took her pistol from its holster and whacked it against the metal. This time the chime was loud enough to carry over the entire horde, and they all turned their heads at once. A moment later, the possessed whirled on their heels and began marching back toward the community center.

"Summoned by the bell?" Jennie chuckled. "How Pavlovian."

They watched as the possessed crowd filed back inside the community center. Some remained unconscious on the battlefield. A few agents lay in bloody puddles, shot by those with firearms. The agents who had joined them worked their way after the crowd, guns trained on the group in case they took another sudden turn.

By the time Jennie made her way down the stairs, the hall was nearly full. The possessed civilians stood like statues, eyes all blanks and vacant. Jennie cautiously approached the nearest person and waved a hand in front of their face. They did not blink.

"What the hell?" Jennie muttered. "I've known certain sounds to trigger responses in primitive creatures, but this is just freaky."

She waved a hand again and gleaned no response. She poked the man's forehead with her finger, and he rocked gently on his heels.

Baxter chuckled. "When you're done playing, you might want to help free these poor folks from their trance."

Jennie smirked. "Of course. Come on, Susie. We've got work to do."

Susannah glared at Jennie. "It's Susannah."

"Sure," Jennie replied as she latched onto the witch and passed her power into the man. The shadow of corruption melted inside him. A few seconds later, he gasped as if he had been swimming and was surfacing for air. He blinked stupidly, flinching at how close Jennie was to him.

"What happened? Where am I?" he asked.

"It's a long story," Jennie replied. "Just wait until we've freed your brothers and sisters, and we'll do a mass announcement." She turned to Baxter. "Can you imagine explaining to each person individually?"

Baxter rolled his eyes and laughed.

CHAPTER SIXTY-FOUR

<u>Richmond, Virginia, USA</u>

Jennie found a folding table in a nearby cupboard and set it up at the far side of the room. She climbed on top and looked out over the confused faces of the possessed they had freed.

Jennie raised her arms and gained their silence. "I understand that you're all confused. We're confused as well, so I can imagine that this will be difficult for you all to take in. The best way I can explain it is this…"

It was a tough sell. Jennie, having lived around specters and mortals for years, knew that it was often best to keep the spectral realm hidden. As much as she wanted to explain the truth—that an ancient specter known as the Dreadnought had somehow infected everyone with pieces of himself and placed them under his spell—she knew that over a hundred people with the knowledge that specters were a real thing would only cause more trouble.

Instead, she concocted a master lie. It was something that she had used before, only with mixed results. Jennie explained that a crazed local who experimented with a trial drug had dropped a new form of hallucinogen into the water supply. Those who had drunk the water or been exposed in any way to this new drug had been instantly put into a collective daze that drove them from their houses and brought them into the open.

While Jennie spun her lie, her clean-up crew worked quickly outside, returning the street to normal, washing away the blood and mess and removing the dead bodies. Hands raised in the crowd, and people asked a multitude of questions. Many hadn't drunk any water from their taps in the hours before bed. Some had been under the influence longer than others. A few of the smarter among them questioned the government's role.

Jennie batted all of these away with the grace of a true diplomat, and soon the civilians filtered through the door to the community center and made their way home.

The only sign of the combat were the shells of smashed cars. A few eyes stared in confusion, unconvinced by the whole experience, but no one said anything further. Soon the crowd had dispersed and gone back to their homes, and Jennie found herself alone with the agents in the hall.

As they chatted among themselves, Jennie excused herself and found a side room she could get a moment of quiet. She needed a breather. From the moment the chopper had touched down in Richmond, things had been non-stop. She needed to compose her thoughts, try to understand just what exactly was happening. More than that, she needed to figure out where Jiao and the Dreadnought had fled to.

Jennie was so preoccupied in her own thoughts that she didn't even notice Agent Sturgeon balled up in the corner, her head resting against the wall. "Strange day, huh?"

"You could say that." Jennie sighed and took a seat beside her. "Are you okay? Can't have been fun to have that creepy darkness inside of you."

"You mean the tainted water?" Sturgeon smirked.

Jennie laughed.

Sturgeon continued. "Nah. It wasn't fun. It was like being trapped in a nightmare. One where I have no control over my body. You don't know who you are or what you're doing, but you know that it's wrong. I could see flashes of myself, moments where I raised the gun and aimed it at you all, but I was helpless to stop it. It was out of my hands."

Jennie thought back to the moment she had latched onto the corrupt, repressing the memory of the nausea that had brewed in her stomach. "Tell me, did you feel any nausea? Any kind of sickness ?"

Sturgeon shook her head. She was tired, the bags under her eyes telling the story. She fixed her gaze on the far corner of the wall. "No. Nothing like that. Only that I wasn't a part of my body. I was…"

Jennie waited expectantly. Sturgeon remained quiet. "Was what?"

Sturgeon opened her eyes as if suddenly picking her train of thought back up. "I was part of something bigger. I could feel my interconnectedness with all the others under the spell. Traces of their fears, their worries, their concerns. All of the negatives brewed inside me, and I just felt…"

"Miserable?" Jennie finished.

Sturgeon nodded.

Jennie heard the rest of the group in the other room, their voices rising and falling as they spoke animatedly among themselves. The door opened and Ula poked her head around the door. "Ah, that's where you went. We were looking for you."

Triton appeared behind her. "Rhone was worried."

"Was not," Rhone refuted, appearing behind him.

Jennie laughed. "Get your arses in here, we need to talk about what just happened."

They all filed in. It was a strange reunion as Jennie saw with joy that even Tanya and Sandra had answered the call she had put out over the radio. Rogers, Jack, and Ruby represented the SIA. Ula, Roman, Triton, Julia, Baxter, Carolyn, and Feng Mian represented the King's Court, and Sturgeon represented the SIS. The specters of the Spectral Plane held back, as did Grimald and his GOA members.

Jennie addressed them all. "We've built quite the congregation, but all of this means nothing if we can't trace down Jiao and the Dreadnought."

"We've finally got confirmation that Jiao is working with him?" Jack asked.

"We have," Baxter answered. "We still don't know how she's linked to all of this mess, but the only assumption we can make is that she's helping the Dreadnought."

"How do you know?" Ruby asked. "Was she here?"

Jennie nodded. "She set the possessed on us, commanding them into battle somehow." Her mind flashed back to that moment, Jiao's hands pulsing with power. The three rings had glinted on her hands. Her brow creased, and her mouth fell open.

"Jennie?" Carolyn asked. She had been bored on the other side of the city, looking out for the enemy and seemed relieved and eager to be back among the group. "Are you there?"

Jennie met her eyes. "The rings?"

"I'm sorry?" Carolyn replied.

"The rings!" Jennie exclaimed. "When Jiao snapped her fingers and commanded the possessed, something sparked between the rings—a pulsing light. They must be the reason she's able to command them."

Julia and Tanya exchanged glances. Julia spoke up. "I suppose that's possible. There are thousands of records from history detailing items possessing strange abilities or unexplainable powers that have aided leaders and rulers over time."

Tanya nodded in agreement. "Tokens, talismans, usually objects made of precious metals. The more expensive objects were the ones that were used to contain the power, adding further value beyond the magic they were chosen to contain. I've got ledgers and books full of that kind of thing back in NYC. All hearsay, though. None of it is proven."

Jennie touched her chin. "I've seen a few objects of power over the years, but they're rarer and rarer with each passing year. Most of these objects are buried with their owners, now hidden beneath the earth, yet when they do come to light, they're a real pain in the ass."

"What about that sword you took from London?" Carolyn asked. "That's one, right?"

"It was." Jennie thought back to the sword, tucked away safely in a hidden nest at the manor. "One of the few items that had found its way into the hands of a clueless mortal. If he truly knew the power he held with that possession, there would have been some trouble."

"What sword?" Julia asked, her curiosity piqued.

Tanya grinned. "The Holy Saber of the Divinity. It's a sword that instantly exorcizes a specter on contact."

A few eyes around the room widened.

"You're kidding?" Julia breathed.

Jennie smiled, turning the conversation back in the right direction. "The rings must be imbued with some kind of power. Something that allows Jiao to work with the specters and hold influence over them."

"But how?" Rogers asked. "Where would she find those?"

"None of that matters right now," Jennie replied. "All that matters is we find the pair of them before they can do any further damage. I have a feeling we've just flushed the hornets from their nest, and now they're going to be pissed."

Sturgeon ran a hand through her hair. "Which brings us back to the big question. How the hell are we going to find them before they attack?"

Jennie looked around and motioned to the old female specter looking behind the group. She waved her toward the front and the others fell silent.

Jennie put a hand on her shoulder. She introduced Susannah and told them of Susannah's history in Richmond, of the approach of Richard Haybourne and his men. She told them of the curse and the burial place of the monster before she had to uproot and leave the city.

When she was done, she turned to Susannah. "You must know of somewhere the Dreadnought would want to hide. My experience tells me that specters cling to places that hold great personal memory and value. Does anything spring to mind for you?"

Susannah nodded. "It does. A few places. The world has changed much since I last visited, though, so I can only give you approximations of their locations."

"That's fine," Jennie replied. "We're not averse to splitting up and covering ground again."

Carolyn's eyes lowered.

"What?" Jennie asked.

"Can I come with you this time?" Carolyn pleaded.

Jennie chuckled. "Sure. Of course, you can.

CHAPTER SIXTY-FIVE

<u>**Richmond, Virginia, USA**</u>

The rain came down in sheets, slickening the mud beneath their feet. The sky was dark, and the cemetery was empty.

Tombstones littered the ground like fallen giant's teeth. Many were cracked, most were faded. This far into the cemetery weeds were overgrown, and trees hung low above them.

The man of many names, Rathbourne, soaked it all in. From inside the woman, he could feel her skin prickle. He had gotten used to riding around in this vessel, although he wondered how long it would be before he could finally take his true form once again.

The little woman, his future queen, stood beside him silently.

Rathbourne crouched down and pressed his fingers into the soil. The damp earth gave way to him easily and covered his nails. He closed his eyes and felt for their vibrations, sensing and hunting those for whom he searched.

He could feel the woman's eyes on him, studious, unconvinced. She knew nothing of the power that emanated from his body. For years he had lain awake in that tomb, brewing, simmering, harnessing every piece of spectral power he could until all he could see was black.

Waiting for the moment he'd be found, and revenge would at last be his.

They had suffered a small setback by losing their mortals to the enemy. But Rathbourne should have known better, it was the specters who would be his ticket to domination.

Jiao's eyes widened as the ground rumbled. Nearby, half a dozen tombs cracked. The dirt seemed to shift, and from out of the soil came hands and feet and bodies and heads. Jiao flinched, ever so slightly, but it was enough for him to notice. Rathbourne grinned.

The specters rose from the grave. They weren't the color and tone of the specters that roamed the world but appeared as manifestations of the gray darkness that poured from Rathbourne. Their eyes were black and their bodies gaseous, as though the storm clouds had fallen and taken the shape of specters.

They limped toward Rathbourne, the figures clothed in strange attire. Rathbourne stood straight and awaited their presence. They gathered close to him, then knelt.

"My King," one of them declared, his voice like rocks thrown down a wind tunnel.

Rathbourne allowed himself a slight smile. He moved to each in turn and touched their shoulder, an ancient form of greeting. He asked them to rise.

"We have work to do," Rathbourne stated. "For years, we have lain dormant in our slumber, but our time has come to rise. Stand with me, brothers, as we claim what should have been ours long ago."

They nodded curtly and followed Rathbourne as he turned from the cemetery. They loaded into the van, gathered around Rathbourne's tomb, and set off to their next destination.

Jiao checked her cell phone, knowing that if she didn't hold up her end of the bargain, the Dreadnought would be pissed. To her relief, her men had replied, and would soon reunite with their Dragon.

She smiled. A Dragon and a Dreadnought, ruling from on high. Mortal and specter. Oh, how the world would soon bow before them.

The house stood alone on the top of a small rise. It was a dilapidated thing, the windows bare of glass and the door standing crookedly on rusted hinges.

At one point in time, it had been a family home. Susannah told them of her aunts and uncles, her mother and father, the brothers and sisters who had once run around the hallways and rooms and breathed life into the place.

"It must have been beautiful," Jennie commented, withholding the word she wanted to add, *once.*

The city had turned the house into a monument to the past. The lawns were neatly kept, but the house and all inside it had been left untouched. Jennie and her team strode up to the house and nudged the door open. It was dark, the thick layers of dust absorbing what little light made it through the grimy windows.

Tanya shook off the rain that had drizzled onto her. Far off in the distance, the sky rumbled.

A thoughtful look crossed Susannah's face as she breathed in her childhood home.

"What are we looking for?" Baxter asked.

Susannah ran a hand through her hair. "A sign that they have been here. Beneath this house is the original burial site of Richard Haybourne. Rathbourne Valerius. The Dreadnought."

Carolyn scoffed. "We should start calling him 'The Artist Formerly Known as the Specter Now Known as The Dreadnought.'"

Jennie and Baxter chuckled. Tanya rolled her eyes, her careworn expression lifted ever since she had reunited with Sandra, who currently clutched her leg.

Jennie examined the floor, surely if anyone had been here, their footsteps would be the first tell-tale signs. There was no way someone could walk in here without leaving some kind of trail.

Still, what if they were all specters?

They divided and explored the house. Jennie took in the rusted pots and pans left by a sink overgrown with weeds and ivy. Most of the doors had fallen and were now bent and bowed, slumped against the jams like drunken sailors. The stairs creaked as they explored the upper floor, wandering around the empty bedrooms with linens that may once have been white but were now a mottled shade of brown and gray.

Then they came to the basement.

Susannah led the way, finding the entryway hidden in a cupboard under the stairs. At the back, cast entirely in darkness until lit by Tanya's phone, was a concrete slab with a thick metal ring set into it. "There's another sub-level below the basement."

Jennie tugged at the slab, but it didn't move at first. A second tug cracked the dirt seal around the edges. A third tug brought the slab away from the wall and revealed a doorway beyond.

The stairs went lower than Jennie had anticipated. They had already descended ten to fifteen feet into the basement. The stairs into the sub-basement went down for almost triple that. The stairs curved into the earth beneath the house and finally opened into a large chamber with smooth stone walls.

A chill lingered down here that prickled the skin of the mortals. Tanya shivered as she shone her light, casting shaky shadows as she swept it over bookshelves, cupboards, desks, hanging hooks, and other paraphernalia that told of only one possible reason: witches.

Susannah's eyes turned glassy as she floated into the center of the room, a nostalgic smile on her face. "I spent the formative years of my life down here, learning, studying, playing. Being a witch is nothing like they make it out in the movies or books. It's a science, it's art. Delicate balances must be assumed to create the perfect concoction."

She crossed over to a shelf where thick tomes were almost lost in dust and webs. The pages were yellowed. Jennie brought one down and placed it on the side, opening the book to a random page where handwritten scrawls in penmanship she could hardly understand decorated the page.

"A potion to lengthen your lifespan," Susannah stated. "The body is nothing more than a biological machine. Feed it the right ingredients, and you can keep that ticker going far beyond what anyone thinks is possible."

Carolyn studied the far wall where an array of neatly-labeled animal skeletons were displayed. "You make it sound like a general science. Something that anyone can learn. Like it's not even magic."

"Magic is just a word people use to explain what they can't comprehend," Susannah replied. "Most of our work centered around medical practices that would be recognized today by science. It was only our work playing with the borders of the spectral realm that could be called real magic." She scanned the room, her eyes wide with wonder. "We didn't know what we were playing with, but there are forces greater than those known to man. Jennie is a prime example of the mysteries that still exist in this world. If one can draw on the unknown and harness the secrets of this world, then many who remain blind may call it magic, but we just call it life."

Susannah turned to Jennie. "Do you not agree? Are you not also a witch yourself?"

Jennie considered this. She had never thought of herself in that light, but she supposed that mortals who didn't understand what she was capable of or the powers she drew from might call what she did magic.

"Magic is nothing more than a cop-out to explain that which people do not understand," Jennie replied. "In the same way that ancient cultures used to explain patterns of nature by attributing them to gods, magic is used to explain the impossible."

Susannah nodded. "The impossible that *is* possible. So, I ask again, are you not one of my coven?"

Jennie grinned. There was a playfulness on Susannah's face she hadn't seen before. "I suppose."

Carolyn looked between the pair. "I suppose that could explain some of my gifts."

Susannah cocked an eyebrow.

Carolyn continued. "Oh. Yeah, I can draw on spectral frequencies and draw items to me from afar. A kind of telekinesis. Feng Mian can draw shields around himself, too. Bax...Well, I'm not sure what your skill is, Bax."

Bax held up his wrench. "Being able to interact with the mortal world isn't too shabby as an ability. I can bludgeon with this. Also, I'm good with technology."

Carolyn looked unimpressed. "Yeah, that too…"

Susannah nodded. "And yet, there is nothing to explain *you*, Jennie. If anyone here could be considered a witch, it's you."

Jennie grinned. "Just show us where you buried The Artist Formerly Known as The Dreadnought."

The sub-basement had more rooms than Jennie had anticipated. A whole family could easily have lived down here without anyone knowing. Susannah led them through a doorway, then down another set of stairs.

Jennie looked around when they arrived at the bottom. The room was smaller than the others, and a long rectangular mark on the floor signaled where the tomb had once lain.

"I put him there," Susannah explained. "The tomb we carved from the rock down here, and once he was dead and cursed, we carried him down into the darkness and sealed this level away from prying eyes. Unfortunately, it was only a day or two later we had to abandon our place here and find new pastures. Rumors of our deeds had already spread too far."

Jennie crouched and ran a hand along the dusty floor. Drag marks were scored into the floor by the weight of the tomb. "They must have had a hell of a job carrying the sarcophagus all the way back to the surface."

"I reckon so," Baxter replied.

Jennie placed a hand flat on the stone and felt for the residue of spectral energy. After a few moments of searching, nothing came to her. "It's a dead end."

Voices filtered down to them from somewhere in the rooms above. The faint whispers echoed around the room, magnified by the rock. A second later and a scraping sound reached them.

Jennie's eyes widened. She sprinted back up the stairs and made her way through the rooms. When she reached the stairs leading to the surface, she was afforded enough of a glance to find a man dragging the stone slab back into place in the under stairs cupboard.

Jennie raced up the stairs and barged shoulder-first against the stone. It jolted, but the man held fast and pushed back. The remaining sliver of light raised Jennie's alarm. As it closed, she realized she was all that stood between the men getting their way and her team avoiding being trapped once again.

"Help me out, will you?" the man called. The rock was pushed toward Jennie again, and the final gap closed.

Jennie shouldered the rock again but felt no give. Tanya came up to join her and added to the push on their side, but whatever they'd done on the other side of the rock held it securely in place.

"Wait here," Jennie told Tanya.

Tanya looked disheveled, already concerned about being trapped under the ground in a secret basement once inhabited by witches.

Jennie latched onto Baxter, and together they melted through the rock. They made their way out of the cupboard and stopped in the hallway, no more than a couple feet away from a handful of men who were grinning triumphantly.

"That oughta hold them in place," a burly man declared, clapping his hands to clear the dirt from his palms. "The Dragon was right, straight back to the witch's house. So predictable."

Another man, this one more slight with a receding hairline, nodded. "Thought she'd put up more of a fight, given what the boss said about her. She was supposed to be stronger than that?"

"Nah, not strong," the third commented. "Just good at communicating with specters."

The first thug shuddered. "Creepy things. Ain't no difference between them and ghosts, I reckon."

The third man cocked an ear toward the rock. "Awfully quiet, ain't they?"

"Thick rock," the balding man explained. "Come on, let's go give Vincenzo the good news. They'll want some of that with their reunion tour coming up, won't they?"

"Think we'll get a reward for this?" the first man asked.

A woman whose hair was cut into a short bob and had a face like a stone gargoyle walked in. "I fucking hope so. If she is as dangerous as they say she is, we just put our necks on the line." She bumped into a sideboard, and an ancient vase toppled and smashed. "Oh, shit. Let's get out of this place. It's dirty, and it's giving me the creeps."

The first man grinned. "I thought you liked it dirty."

"Not now," the woman replied, rolling her eyes.

Jennie exchanged a look with Baxter as Feng Mian and Carolyn came out from a cupboard under the stairs.

"Vincenzo?" Jennie asked Baxter, aware the mortals wouldn't hear her as a specter. "He's one of the Seven, right?"

Baxter and Carolyn shrugged.

"I think so," Baxter replied.

Feng Mian nodded. "He is. Last seen in Pennsylvania, Cassie informed us. Your SIS friends are there hunting for him right now."

Jennie cocked an eyebrow. "Then how the hell is he ordering these guys around Richmond so effectively?" A dawning realization crossed her mind and made her blood run cold. She needed confirmation, and she needed it fast.

Jennie ran through the thugs and reached the doorway before they did. As she passed through them, the woman shuddered. "Jesus, freezing in here. Did you feel that?"

The balding man, trying to maintain his bravado, shook his head. "No. Don't know what you're talking about. Got the spooks, have you?"

A moment before they reached the door, they froze as Jennie disconnected from Baxter and turned material before them. She appeared in the blink of an eye, casually leaning one arm against the rotting door jamb as she inspected the nails on her other hand. "Oh, dear. Oh, dear. You *are* in trouble, aren't you?"

CHAPTER SIXTY-SIX

<u>Richmond, Virginia, USA</u>

"I hate to say this, but your boss might have allowed you to enter combat ill-prepared." Jennie aimed the Big Bitch in their direction, causing them to freeze. "It's not his fault. I can't imagine he would believe the stories since he hasn't met me in person. Most people who hear about a woman who can tread the line between specter and mortal brush it aside and think it's BS. But now that you know better, you'll be able to tell your boss, won't you?"

The thugs remained tight-lipped. A couple of them growled, but none of them moved.

"The problem is," Jennie continued, "that I'm a big fan of balance. Karma. The world exists on the edge of a knife. Tilt too far one way and...poof. You've fallen to your doom. You people came in here with the intention of trapping me in a basement for God knows how long. I could've died in there. Suffocated. No one would have found my body."

The woman boldly stepped forward. The man to her right grabbed her wrist. "But you didn't, did you? You're here holding us at gunpoint. Think that makes us even, don't you?"

Jennie grinned. "Nice try, bitch. The problem is, you didn't expect this to happen. I escaped without incident, but it doesn't mean you get away scot-free. We need to balance the tables, don't we?"

"What do you suggest?" the man nearest to Jennie asked.

"Good question." Jennie held the Big Bitch on the group and touched her lip. "How about an eye for an eye? You thought you'd killed me, so I'll kill one of you."

They looked uneasily at each other.

"I'm serious," Jennie confirmed. "Four of you can live. The other will die. Pick one."

When they remained silent, Jennie tapped her wrist. "You've got sixty seconds. Go."

The group fell into a sudden and urgent debate that quickly devolved into a cacophony of shouts. In the confines of the corridor, they screamed at each other, shoving each other into the walls as they punched, clawed, and kicked.

Jennie waited patiently, with Baxter on the other end of the hallway by the door to the basement. He smirked as he watched them fight like animals, each one desperate to not be the sacrifice for the rest.

When sixty seconds had passed, Jennie shouted to draw their attention. They slowed down, faces flushed and breathing heavily. Jennie bounced her eyebrows. "Well?"

They started shouting over one another again, each stating their case for survival. Jennie shook her head and aimed at the balding man near the back. "Enough! You'll do. Say goodbye, friend. I'm sorry it had to end this way."

The man's eyes widened and he waved his hands in front of his face. "No! No! Please, I swear… No!"

He ducked behind one of the other men, who immediately shoved him back to the foreground. As a team, they grabbed him and held him before Jennie. He was inches away from the barrel of the gun.

Jennie held his gaze for a few seconds before shaking her head and sighing. "I expected no better from you than to cower and let someone else make the decision for you. Where I'm from, it would be an honor to die protecting those you care about. But that's not what this is, is it? None of you gives a shit about the others. You're all in this for yourselves."

Jennie holstered the Big Bitch. The man breathed a sigh of relief.

Jennie continued. "You tell me where I can find this Vincenzo motherfucker, and I'll let you all go. How's that?"

Their faces contorted in a mixture of emotions. Many of them wanted to save their own lives, but none of them wanted to be known as the rat who snitched on their boss. Jennie was unsurprised to find it was the balding man before her that gave up the answers.

"I'll tell you where he is," he grumbled. "He's at—"

The woman grabbed the back of his head and was about to ram his skull against the wall when a shot exploded in the hallway.

The woman's head disappeared in a fountain of crimson as the bullet passed through her skull and embedded itself in the wall.

The other thugs froze, holding their breath.

Jennie growled and lowered the pistol. "I warned you. Don't fuck with me. I'm really not in the mood." She turned to the balding man. "You were saying?"

"Hotel Snyder," the man answered, his voice dropping a level in volume. "We arrived this morning and were set straight to work by the Dragon. Vincenzo is leaving for some meeting later today, but I don't know when."

"Hotel Snyder?" Jennie confirmed.

The man nodded his head.

Jennie chewed her lip in thought, eyes narrowed at the remaining men. The one at the back couldn't look away from the bloody mess before him.

"Relax," Jennie scolded. "She was always going to be a problem. I've come across a million women like her in my lifetime. You're better off without her. Now, wait right here while I get my friends out of the basement."

She moved toward the men, who were so taken aback by her brazenness that the idea of grabbing her didn't even cross their mind. She kept the pistol on them, warning them not to move a muscle, and beckoned them over to the cupboard beneath the stairs.

"Get it open. Stay where I can see you," she instructed. "I'm fast. Don't test me."

Jennie kept the Big Bitch trained on the men as they ducked beneath the stairs and pulled the slab free. "Now move," she told them in an icy tone.

Tanya coughed, then breathed in the clean air when she made it into the light. She froze as she saw the men.

"Interrupting a party?" she asked. Her eyes landed on the dead woman. "I guess not."

Jennie waited until Tanya and the specters who had been accompanying her were out of the basement before addressing the men once more. "Go on, then. Your turn."

The men stared at her blankly.

"What?" she continued. "You think after all you've seen of me that I'm the kind of person that would kid about this shit? Get your traitorous arses inside. Now."

They slowly advanced, confused looks on their faces. One by one, they made their way into the cupboard and started down the stairs.

Jennie stopped the balding man when he reached her. "Not you. Stay here."

She ushered the remaining two into the dark, then when they were far enough down that they would be no issue, she grabbed the stone slab. "Let's see how you guys like it when the tables are turned, eh?"

With one strong push, she shut them inside.

Their footsteps echoed on the stairs, and soon their fists pounded on the rock. Jennie moved various items of furniture into the cupboard in front of the slab to block it in case they broke free.

Tanya raised an eyebrow. "Are you really going to leave them there?"

"For a while." Jennie cleared her throat from the dust that had found its way inside. "At least let them learn their lesson before we free them." She turned to the balding man who had gone a strange shade of white. "As for you, you're coming with us. I want to know as much as I can about Vincenzo before we meet him, and if there's anything I've learned in my years of playing this game is that when a bird sings once, they never shut up."

She grabbed the back of his collar, stepped over the woman's corpse, and dragged him outside.

The rain beat down on them as they drove toward the hotel. They didn't have far to travel. It was located on the edge of the city, only around a twenty-minute drive from Susannah's former residence.

The car journey was oddly quiet; the only sound was Jennie summoning the rest of her squad to come and meet her near the hotel. The wipers fought the rain on the windshield, allowing them visibility, and soon the hotel loomed before them.

It was a cute building. Wider than it was tall, it looked more like a retirement home than a hotel to Jennie. She parked far enough away to keep the hotel in view without drawing attention and cut the lights. From here, she could make out the car park and would be able to monitor anyone heading in or out.

"That's Vincenzo's car," the balding man commented, pointing to a sleek silver Rolls Royce.

"I thought you said you flew in this morning?" Carolyn quizzed.

The balding man didn't hear her.

Tanya repeated the question.

The man shrugged. "Vincenzo has money. He doesn't go anywhere without his baby. I don't question his methods, I just do what he tells me."

"The blind leading the blind," Baxter remarked.

Jennie narrowed her eyes and studied the hotel. It seemed a strange place for a gangster to be hiding. The hotel was upmarket, one of the places where senior citizens might go for a weekend retreat. She wanted nothing more than to storm the building and grab Vincenzo by the collar, but she didn't want to risk any casualties. They'd already lost innocents in the skirmish outside the community center. More innocent blood on her hands would count as a failure to her.

They waited patiently. Nothing came in or out of the hotel. After another ten minutes, Jennie grew bored of the silence and put her phone's music on shuffle. The low-volume dance tunes were a stark contrast to their situation and drew a curious stare from the balding man.

Ten minutes later, Jennie looked over her shoulder and studied the man. He shrank beneath her stare. "What's your name?"

"Tim," he replied.

Jennie smirked. "Scary name."

"You don't need a scary name to do scary things," Tim replied, growing defensive.

Jennie considered this and nodded curtly.

"Think I can hop out in the rain for a sec?" Tim asked, hands moving to his crotch. "I got to go."

Jennie was silent for a moment before reaching into the glove compartment and taking out a pair of SI goggles. She handed them to the confused man. "Put them on," she commanded.

He did, immediately jumping back into his seat. He turned from left to right, taking in the spectral forms of Feng Mian, Tanya, Sandra, Baxter, Carolyn, and Susannah, all crammed in the car around him.

"What the…" His respiration increased rapidly, and he wasn't sure where to put his hands. Carolyn had taken the place on his lap.

"These are specters," Jennie informed him. "Ghosts. Dead people. They are my friends, and we protect each other. Here's the deal: if you go out there to piss, one of my friends is coming with you. If you try to run, you will be haunted for the rest of your days. You got that?"

Tim nodded emphatically, turning as pale as the specters. "Y-yes. Of course!"

Jennie grinned. "Okay. Go."

If the rain wasn't reason enough to get back into the car as quickly as possible, having a specter studying him as he did his business did the trick. He launched back into the car, his head gleaming with rain and his clothing sodden. Instantly, the water began to evaporate and steam up the car.

Jennie switched the engine on and pumped the heat to clear the condensation from the windows. "Better?" she asked.

Tim didn't answer, instead choosing to take the SI glasses on and off as if investigating their effects. "It's like VR," he commented. "One minute they're there, the next minute they're not."

Jennie turned back to the front as a pair of headlights caught her attention. "Kind of. Except they're always there, let me assure you."

Baxter laughed from the passenger seat.

Jennie didn't recognize the approaching car, but when another dozen turned up and parked nearby, she guessed they were her people. A quick call to Roman confirmed they were indeed parked out front.

They waited for hours, wondering when Vincenzo was going to make his move, or if the rain had put him off going to this meeting that Tim had informed them of when finally the doors to the hotel opened and a group of suited men emerged into the protection of the canopy.

Tim shifted in his seat and muttered, "That's him."

Vincenzo looked exactly as Jennie had pictured him, a least a foot shorter than the men around him, with black, slicked-back hair like she'd seen in Italian gangster movies. The men protected him from the rain with a mass of black umbrellas as they left the awning and crossed the parking lot toward the Rolls. One man held the door open for him, while the others climbed inside. Vincenzo took the driver's seat.

"Funny," Jennie mused.

"What?" Baxter asked.

"Most head honchos let others do their driving," Jennie replied. "It's a power thing with crime bosses. You don't do anything someone else can do for you."

Carolyn chuckled. "So, the complete opposite of you?"

Jennie blushed.

Tim leaned between the seats. "Vincenzo loves his precious baby too much to let someone else handle it. This is his third Rolls."

"His men crashed the car?" Baxter asked.

Tim looked at him through the SI goggles. "No. That's the worst part. Minor scratches. Country roads and bramble branches left the tiniest of scrapes, so he fired them. Well…"

"No need to say it," Jennie remarked, knowing what gangsters often did with the men they wanted to get rid of.

Vincenzo started the car, and the headlights bloomed. The rain could be seen in their beams, pounding into the ground as the downpour increased. Far off, the rumble of thunder came again.

"What's he waiting for?" Jennie asked after a few minutes when the car hadn't moved.

Her answer came when another group of men—and women this time—emerged from the hotel. They made their way to another car. A few minutes later, another group came.

A strange feeling settled in Jennie's stomach.

After another group emerged, Vincenzo finally kicked the Rolls into gear and accelerated out of the parking lot. He turned right at the main road. Jennie shot a message to the others and drove silently behind the other cars leaking onto the road. She kept her headlights off, following like a silent specter in the night.

To wherever the cars might lead.

CHAPTER SIXTY-SEVEN

<u>Richmond, Virginia, USA</u>

Sturgeon watched from the passenger seat of the car as they crawled through the rain, following the line of cars. The only light inside the car was made by her phone screen as she scanned the mountain of messages and checked in with her team.

Updates from Clark and Tiptry gave a step-by-step report of their mission to catch the Seven. After following a number of leads, they had turned up empty-handed. The good news was that no further bombs had exploded, the bad news was that they had no idea where to turn.

Sturgeon checked the subject line of each message, doing her best to absorb the information and decide its importance. There were other messages mixed among the rest, updates from her fiancé in London, a few forwarded messages about ongoing cases in the UK.

She wondered where the missing members of the Seven could have gone. As far as she was aware, there had been no updates about them from the teams who had been sent to explore the neighboring states. They couldn't have just vanished into thin air, could they? The cities were large enough to make hiding easy, but with the mass of cameras and the combined expertise of the people looking for them, something should have turned up by now.

So far, only this Vincenzo figure had arrived in Richmond. Sturgeon had been too far down the line to see anything happening at the hotel, but she wondered where they were heading. Nothing in the world outside the window looked familiar thanks to the hammering rain. It was as though a great cloud had descended upon them and cloaked them in its mist.

Sturgeon stared out the window and took a deep breath. When she exhaled, she misted up the glass. She missed the UK terribly, but she knew that this was important for everyone involved. Agreements made by opposing parties only led to aggravations if either side didn't make the effort to uphold their end. It was humbling for Jennie to ask for help and magnanimous for Victoria to offer it when called on.

Sturgeon just hoped that soon they would wrap up this never-ending mystery and finally get into a position where she could go home victorious. The last thing she wanted was to end up in the same way as Agents Clark and Tiptry.

The SIS was a place run by mortals.

Jennie kept her map open on her phone screen, tracking their progress along the edges of the city.

The rain beat down hard, drumming against the metal skeleton of the vehicle and making it near-impossible to see much beyond the car ahead. The world around them looked like an alien landscape. The road was slick with puddles, and drains were threatening to overflow. Lightning flashed in the distance and thunder followed as they journeyed ever west.

"What is it with these guys and the west side of town?" Jennie asked, craning her neck to catch Susannah's eye in the rearview.

"That's where it all happened," Susannah replied. "Haybourne came in from the west and crossed east into the city. That was the route of his destruction."

"Haybourne?" Tim asked, emboldened by his entry into the world of specters. "I thought he was called Wraithbourne, or something?"

"Rathbourne," Carolyn corrected. "Or The Dreadnought when he enters the ring."

Susannah raised an eyebrow. "What ring?"

Baxter smiled. "The wrestling ring, of course. All the greats have stage names and aliases. Names like The Rock or Stone Cold Steve Austin."

Carolyn raised an eyebrow. "You didn't think to mention The Undertaker, Big Show, or The Ultimate Warrior? I'm revoking your man card, Bax."

Baxter had the grace to blush. "I was always more of a football fan," he mumbled.

Susannah looked unimpressed by the exchange. "They say he had a hideout. I'm not sure where he would meet with his advisors to plan his operations., but it had to be somewhere beyond the city limits."

An idea came to Jennie. She envisioned Haybourne and his men marching over the fertile hills on the west side of the city to the only place nearby that could have acted as the perfect meeting point for a secret organization to plan their domination.

Her eyes flicked to the map. She only hoped that her hunch was wrong. Still, when the cars ahead found their way into the rolling hills, Jennie knew that that wouldn't be the case.

They were heading back to the quarry.

The map showed the quarry nearby, although it was impossible to see it from inside the car. The clouds rumbled and rolled overhead, and the cars in front of them started to slow as they came up on the turn for the dirt access road.

Jennie leaned toward the windshield, doing her best to track the cars through the misty glass. When they finally pulled to a stop, she turned and found a place to park. The line of cars following her swept in a circle around her and came to a halt.

Jennie rested a hand on the door, wishing she wouldn't have to go into the rain. Roman's voice came through her earpiece. "Back where it all began, huh?"

"Well, this part of the journey," Jennie replied. "But what's Vincenzo doing here?"

This time, Rhone's voice came over the radio. The former SIA agent was stationed in another vehicle. "I think you know the answer to that question."

Jennie did. *The Dragon has summoned them.*

"I thought the tunnels collapsed?" Carolyn muttered. "This doesn't make sense. Where are they all going?"

Susannah answered. "Where there's one tunnel, there's normally a network." She stared determinedly from the car, then rose and melted through the door.

Jennie turned in her seat. "You guys stay here. We're going to scout ahead."

"Really?" Carolyn complained. "Or are you going to run into action and complete the mission without us?"

Jennie laughed. "Whatever it takes. Although, I'm going to go out on a limb and say that this one might need all of us. Okay?"

Carolyn nodded but folded her arms and slumped back in the seat. Tim gave a shocked look when she disappeared into the trunk.

Jennie latched onto Susannah and melted out of the car. While she could still feel the rain, it didn't soak into her clothes the way it would if she was mortal. She took a step toward the waiting Susannah, then turned back, confusion on her face.

She poked her head back inside the car. "Are you coming, Bax?"

"Right!" Baxter disappeared through his door and emerged on the outside.

The three of them stalked toward the other cars. At first, Jennie worried that they had continued driving because there was no sign of them through the rain. After a moment, they came into view as dark shapes through the downpour.

They sneaked toward the cars, wary that people may still be inside them despite being spectral. The procession contained nine vehicles in total. The windows were all blacked out. Jennie edged around the nearest car and allowed her head to melt through the door into the inside.

It was bare. All she found was the lingering smell of cigarette smoke and something malty like bourbon or beer.

They approached the next car and found the same thing again, only this time the car smelled brand new. They worked their way along the line until they found themselves at the Rolls Royce.

Jennie ran a hand along its side. "God, it's a beautiful piece of craftsmanship, isn't it?"

Baxter nodded and melted inside, examining the dashboard and the circuitry contained within. Jennie joined him inside and took a spot in the driver's seat, made herself comfortable and imagined that she was driving the car. "Maybe this will be my next car," she mused. "Something beefy with some edge that'll draw people's eyes."

Baxter laughed, his head down by the footwell of the passenger side. "What's wrong with the Mustang? That not beefy enough for you?"

Jennie chewed her lip. "I guess so. Just always nice to have something new, isn't it?"

"And why would you want to *draw* the eye?" Baxter chuckled. "Our line of business is hiding from sight, isn't it? You don't want the extra attention."

A smile appeared on Jennie's face as she glanced down at Baxter. He noticed the look and added, "What?"

"I think it's the first time you've ever said 'our' business, instead of 'yours,'" she explained. "Nice to see you're finally admitting that you're on my side."

Baxter pushed himself to an upright position. "You know I've always got your back, Jen."

Jennie shuddered.

"What?" Baxter asked.

"Jen?" Jennie replied. "That's pushing it a little, okay? Stick with Jennie."

Baxter told her he would.

Jennie reluctantly pulled herself away from the Rolls Royce and emerged back into the rain. She looked around for Susannah and was alarmed to find that the witch was missing. No matter which way she looked, she couldn't see her anywhere.

"Shit," Jennie hissed. She took a few cautious steps toward where she imagined the quarry to be and found the lip of the pit below her. The muddied edge was slick and seemed determined to drag her in, but she managed to backpedal before gravity could pull her over.

When she was confident that she was safe again, she found a specter walking up the haul road toward her. It took a few seconds to realize that it was Susannah.

"Where did you go?" Jennie scalded. "We're supposed to be a team."

Susannah was unabashed. "While you two were playing with toys, I scouted ahead. All I can see is a cave mouth filled with rubble. There's nowhere else around that a group of mortals could have disappeared."

"You're sure?" Jennie asked.

Susannah nodded.

"Come on," Jennie instructed. "Sometimes a second set of eyes can help."

She strode down the access road, which the rain had almost turned into a natural slip 'n' slide. Giving in to the momentum, Jennie turned mortal and allowed herself to slide down until they were at the bottom of the pit.

The floor had trapped the rain, and she turned spectral once more as they trudged through six-inch-deep puddles. They found the mouth of the cave, and it was as Susannah had said—there was no way mortals could have entered.

"You mentioned other tunnels," Baxter called, raising his voice to be heard over the rain.

Susannah nodded. "That's usually the case. I wouldn't know where to start looking, though."

"The same method we used to find you," Jennie called back. "Or we could use my trusted method."

Jennie closed her eyes and picked up a faint trace of spectral energy to her right. She followed the signal until she found herself at a dirt wall that easily exceeded forty feet in height.

Susannah gave her a strange look. "It's just dirt."

Jennie smiled and traced the mud with her hands. She allowed herself to become material, and as her hand slid over the mud, it revealed a rusted door behind it, the orange-brown color an almost perfect match of the muddy water dripping down over it.

"Bingo." Jennie smirked. "Let's assemble the troops. Whatever is going on is on the other side of this door. I can just feel it."

CHAPTER SIXTY-EIGHT

<u>Richmond, Virginia, USA</u>

The rusted door looked to have been a makeshift barrier. There were no hinges, and when they entered the tunnel, the walls were crudely carved into the side of the hill and supported by haphazardly-placed timbers.

Jennie ushered the others inside, out of the attack of the rain. The tunnel stretched ahead and widened into a round chamber where they could stand comfortably together. After the initial sound of shuffling feet and people jostling for positions while they got their bearings, they waited in tense silence while Jennie took a headcount.

They listened closely but heard no one nearby, although Jennie could still feel the buzz of spectral energy somewhere in the tunnels.

There were three tunnels leading off the main chamber, but no signage to indicate what lay down any of them. Jennie had sudden flashbacks to the previous cave-in and exchanged glances with Ashton, Rhone, Roman, Triton, and the others who had accompanied her and somehow survived. "Stay alert," she instructed quietly. "Stick together, so you don't get separated if anything goes down."

She coordinated the assembly, splitting them into three groups. Roman led his group, which included Triton, Ula, Rogers, Feng Mian, and Carolyn, into the tunnel on the left-hand side. Sturgeon led Jack, Ruby, and Ashton into the right tunnel. Jennie took a group that consisted mostly of specters and started her trek down the center tunnel. Before she continued, she sent a message to Julia and the others waiting back at base, instructing them to conduct some research and see if they could turn up a plan of the tunnels.

Jennie turned spectral. Sandra latched onto Tanya and brought her into the spectral world. They crept through their tunnel, grateful for the spectral glow coming from their bodies since torchlight would give them away. At one point, the wall opened to the right and revealed another tunnel, but Jennie pushed them onward, following the places where the spectral trail felt strongest.

The tunnel grew wider, and a fresh breeze came to meet them. Jennie wasn't sure how long they'd been walking, but a strange sight met them as they rounded a corner.

There was a door, its shape neatly defined by a thin line of light leaking around its edges. The light was warm and flickered beyond the door.

Jennie cocked her head to the side. From here, she could feel the spectral signals stronger than ever.

She placed a finger on her lips and approached the door. She leaned in and could just about make out the sound of people talking. She pressed her face through the door and then went all the way through.

The tunnel was brightly lit by torches lining the walls. The way ahead split into several directions, but it was clear where the voices were coming from.

Jennie found herself at a place where the floor fell away beneath her. She was standing by a balcony overlooking a large, neatly cut arena of rock, mud, and stone. In the center of the chamber were a long stone table and a number of chairs. Plates and goblets had been set in place, although they looked as if they had been left from a party that had been held two hundred years ago.

Or three hundred...

Jiao and the woman the Dreadnought had possessed were sitting at one end of the table. In the seats surrounding them on either side was a gaggle of men Jennie had never seen before, except for one: Vincenzo. She could guess their names, however. The remaining members of the Seven had a particular look about them, the easy arrogance that spoke of a life of privilege and corruption.

The men sat straight-backed in their seats. Vincenzo was busy talking while Jiao and the Dreadnought looked on dispassionately.

Jennie's blood boiled at the pompous expression on Jiao's face. How regal she appeared as she stared down her nose at her subjects.

"They took care of the problem. There should be no more concern regarding this…Rogue," Vincenzo finished. "To be honest, I don't know what all the fuss was about. If the idiot is stupid enough to climb into a trap, then she's stupid enough to get stuck down there indefinitely."

Jiao's nostrils flared. "You absolute buffoon."

The cocky expression on Vincenzo's face fell. "I'm sorry."

"Rogue has the ability to turn spectral, you idiot. She'll be able to crawl out of that hole in seconds. I'd wager that your men are already either dead where they stood, or trapped down in that basement themselves." She picked up a goblet and hurled it at him. "Zhao told me you'd be one of the smart ones. It didn't take you long to prove him wrong. Then again, he was never too smart himself."

Jennie's fists trembled. She did everything she could to hold herself back from jumping down there and taking care of Jiao herself.

The woman beside her cleared her throat and placed a hand on Jiao's arm to calm her. The other men watched her warily. When the woman spoke, her voice was masculine and aged. "Please do forgive my bride-to-be. While mistakes have been made, we are thankful for your presence and assistance in the matters at hand. From the accounts I hear, you've done a tremendous job at disbanding the opposition and laying false trails for them to follow."

"It wasn't easy," a podgy older man spoke up. "They were quick. If I were a few years younger, this would have been a breeze. But following instructions, setting off bombs, and finding places to hide is a young person's game."

"You had specters to help you!" another man exclaimed.

"So did you," the pudgy man retorted.

"Barely!" the man replied. "A handful of weak-ass specters who gave up the instant that Zhao was pronounced dead? I barely scraped through by the skin of my teeth, and I thought about just handing myself in."

"Yet you didn't," Jiao remarked, trying to reinstate composure. "That's commendable, and we admire your loyalty."

"Be honest," the pudgy man began. "What the hell is going on here? Zhao promised us great wealth and power, and so far, all we've done is scramble around and confuse the feds. You told us you had some kind of spectral update to give, and all we see is this woman who, no offense, sounds like Louis Armstrong after a packet of Camels."

"Yeah," the other man added. "Are you telling us the order of the Golden Dragon is getting with the times? Growing more progressive? Are we going to have our first lesbian dynasty? Is that it?"

"How PC of you," a third man commented.

Jiao grinned. "You should be careful how you speak to your new king," she stated, enjoying the wave of confusion that came over the older men's faces.

"King?" the fourth man grumbled. "All I see are two women sitting side by side. The only men in this room are us."

At that, the woman grabbed the table and rose to her feet. Her chair fell over behind her, and her body began jerking spasmodically. Her limbs flailed, and a strange choking sound came from the back of her throat.

The men recoiled in their chairs, disgusted by the sight in front of them. After a few seconds, she stopped and fell limply into her chair, unconscious.

The men couldn't see what Jennie was seeing. If they had SI glasses, they'd chosen not to wear them just then. The dark, haunting shape of the Dreadnought strode through the table and deliberated for a while before choosing one of the men to enter.

The pudgy man choked and spluttered in imitation of the woman. He sat up straighter in his chair, his eyes growing wide before they turned into dark pools. He finally settled, then he stretched. "That's better."

The man next to him gasped and half-pushed himself from his chair. "What the fuck is going on?"

The Dreadnought's new vessel grinned. He turned his head at an unnatural angle, keeping his body fixed and twisting his neck until he was staring at the other man. A second later, the pudgy man spasmed and fell limp, and the Dreadnought left him.

Jennie watched the Dreadnought jump across the table and inhabit the other man as the first recovered and looked around in shock.

"Fuck," she whispered to Bax. "It's like *Return of the Body Snatchers.*" She thought back to what it felt like to latch onto the possessed and wondered how it would feel to be inhabited by such a corrupt specter. That nauseated feeling in her stomach returned.

The older man repeated the same process as the other, twisting his head around to the point it looked like it should snap. The Dreadnought then worked his way around the group until each had had a turn, before settling back in place inside the woman.

"I wonder why he's so comfortable in the woman," Baxter commented. "Everyone else he's only remained inside for a few seconds, but he seems to favor her."

Jennie nodded gently, unable to tear her eyes away from the goings-on below them. She shifted her attention to the rings on Jiao's hand and once again grew curious about the power they held.

The men were shaken, shrinking back in fear the moment the Dreadnought exited their bodies. They had all gone an unhealthy shade of white, and two of them clutched their stomachs as they dry-heaved.

"Is that better for you?" Jiao smiled. It was the same smile that she had given Jennie on a dozen occasions, an unreadable smile that gave away none of the thoughts that ran through her head. "You have been blessed by your new king, so will you kneel, or will you die?"

The men looked at each other, their brows creased. Caught in the dilemma presented to them, it was obvious they hardly enjoyed obeying a woman who had taken the role of Dragon, let alone an unknown entity masquerading inside of a human suit.

The podgy man's face grew hard. He pushed himself to his feet and puffed out his chest. "I swore my loyalty to the Seven a long time ago. Long before the Dragon presented itself as a possible ally. Over the years, I've seen a mountain of change. I've conquered my adversities and come out the other side a better man. I was dubious about following Zhao's rule, and I'm much more so under the thumb of a female oppressor. We Daltons are proud people, and I would rather die than go along with this charade any longer."

Without looking back, he turned and marched toward the tunnel leading out of the room. "I'll grab my men and be on my way. This attempt at subduing the crime families of New York is farcical."

Jiao's lips tightened. She placed her hand over the woman's, and the rings flashed in tiny bursts of white. The woman rose to her feet again and held out a hand.

A pulse of darkness sprang from her fingers, invisible to the naked eye but visible to Baxter, Susannah, and Jennie. The dark cloud streamed toward the pudgy man, and before he could reach the tunnel, he stopped in place.

He spun as if tugged on an invisible wire, his face a mask of pain. His mouth opened in a wide scream, but no sound came. The woman scrunched her fingers into her fist, and the man collapsed to his knees. His eyes turned completely white, and his face turned blue. He slumped to the floor and remained still.

Jesus Christ, Jennie thought. *We've only seen a glimpse of this guy's power.* She turned to Susannah, who stared forlornly below her.

Susannah caught Jennie's eyes and mouthed, "What have I done?"

CHAPTER SIXTY-NINE

<u>Richmond, Virginia, USA</u>

For a big guy, Roman knew how to stay quiet.

He led the exploration group, his head almost scraping the ceiling as he went along. Ula and Triton behind him were just as silent. Rogers kept pace between them, and Feng Mian and Carolyn followed at the rear.

Ula watched Rogers with a curious eye. She knew little about the man, but she knew an ex-soldier when she saw one. From what she did know, Rogers had been heading the SIA since its inception almost two years ago. Their progress had been slow to begin with, but Jennie had acted like a catalyst for the organization.

Bound to a desk for the most part, Rogers was a strategist. Ula had considered the idea of dedicating herself to the roles away from the frontline, but always found she couldn't stand the idea of not getting her hands dirty. From the way Rogers carried himself through the tunnel, she wondered if the same couldn't be said for him.

Even the longest-serving desk jockeys must hear the call of duty.

The tunnels curved in directions without order. After taking a few turns, they came across the echoing sound of voices ahead. Roman raised a fist to halt them. The others obeyed instantly, a well-oiled machine.

There were a lot of voices, that much was clear. Whether they belonged to mortals or specters was another question entirely. They were clearly trying to remain quiet, but all of them were failing. The tunnels carried sound easily, and if there hadn't been so many people speaking, they might have picked up individual conversations.

Roman ushered them carefully forward. They found a nook at the side of the tunnel where they could see the way ahead, a mouth to another room that was lit in torch flames.

Even from this far back, they could see that the room was filled with people.

"Shit," Roman muttered.

Rogers peeked out from behind him. They looked at each other then retreated back down the tunnel a stretch, minimizing their own voices as they discussed the unexpected discovery.

"Who are they all?" Ula asked.

"Don't know," Roman replied. "There's a lot of them, though." He turned to Feng Mian and Carolyn. "Time for some reconnaissance."

Feng Mian nodded.

Carolyn breathed deeply. "What if there are conduits in there? They might not be able to hurt us, but you'll all be in danger."

Roman and Ula shrugged. "That's a risk we'll have to take."

Carolyn gave up and walked alongside Feng Mian toward the group.

Although Sturgeon had seen some strange sights in her lifetime, she had never encountered anything like this.

Most of the time, her job was to keep specters in line, to patrol the streets of London and the wider counties to ensure that specters behaved and remained in line with Queen Victoria's rules. Sure, she had encountered some strange types of spectral activity over the years, but this Dreadnought behaved in a way that she had never come across before.

And these tunnels… Where the hell were they right now? She had never come across subterranean specters. Surely, if these tunnels had been here the whole time, there was no need for the focus on drilling the tunnels from the quarry to the sarcophagus? More than that, why didn't the Dreadnought and his followers seek shelter in these tunnels in the first place?

A lot of questions rolled around in her head, things that needed answers. There was something fishy about this whole situation, and she hoped to get to the bottom of it soon.

The agents that had been assigned to her team walked behind her. She missed her SIS unit. She had been tempted to pull them all back once they had found Vincenzo, but without confirmation about the location of the rest of the Seven, they needed to be protecting the other states. So far, all was quiet on that front, which in SIS land meant that either they were doing a good job, or something big was coming soon.

Often it meant both.

The air in the tunnels was cloying. The young agents walked behind, accompanied by Sandra and Tanya. Sturgeon wished again that this would be over soon. Everything that was meant to be simple had turned out the exact opposite. All she'd been asked to do was establish a rapport with Rogue and the King's Court, give the support they needed, and leave. This had been meant to be an in and out job. It hadn't worked out that way whatsoever.

The tunnel finally opened onto a small room and her heart stopped. There was nothing in the room beside a large stone object, and Sturgeon instantly knew what it was without having seen it before.

"The sarcophagus," she exclaimed as she broke cover and moved toward it. The chamber was empty of people and clutter, nothing more than a pocket within the tunnels. The walls opened to reveal more tunnels around them.

Jack placed his hands on the edge of the sarcophagus and peered inside. "Not a very comfortable bed, is it? No wonder he refuses to go back."

Tanya scoffed. "Why would they bother making a tomb comfortable?"

"Seems contradictory, doesn't it?" Jack replied. "We say 'Rest In Peace,' but can you rest comfortably if there's a slab of rock sticking into your back? The bottom of this is rougher than my face when I had acne in high school."

"The point is that no one will rise again," Sturgeon stated. "I don't know if they had it in mind that Rathbourne would find his way back into the real world again?"

"Then why make the tomb from stone?" Ruby asked. "Whoever tucked him into this oversized shoebox knew what they were doing. Why else would they weigh him down in here?"

Sturgeon considered this. "You have a good point. That witch has a lot to answer for." She turned to Sandra. "Do you think you could climb inside?"

Tanya went to her defense. "Oh, no. We're not locking her away just to test a theory."

Sturgeon rolled her eyes. "Fine, but can you at least come here and try something for me?"

Sturgeon asked Sandra to try to push her hand through the stone. "There must be some power in the stone to stop specters from getting in or out, considering the guy was buried in it for almost half a millennium."

Sandra touched the stone and immediately pulled her hand back with a cry of shock.

"What is it?" Tanya exclaimed, going to Sandra's side and nursing her hand. The usual white pallor of her spectral skin had darkened.

"That... It *hurt*," Sandra replied, her brows knitting together. "I couldn't push through. If anything, it pushed me back."

"What kind of curse did the witch put on this guy?" Jack mused. "We should find Jennie and let her know what we found." He moved to the tomb and tried to lift it.

"What are you doing?" Ruby asked.

"Seeing if we can bring it back with us." Jack grunted from the effort. "Damn, that must've taken some manpower to bring all the way in here. I wonder why no one's guarding it."

Ruby smirked. "Because no one can lift it, idiot."

"Then how did it get down here?" Jack retorted.

"Enough," Sturgeon exclaimed. "It's like dealing with children. You're worse than Sandra. No, I take that back. Sandra's actually reasonable."

Sandra grinned.

Ashton had been busy ignoring the petty dispute. He neared the mouth of one of the other tunnels. "There's something down there," he informed them. "In the distance. This tunnel is straighter than any others, and there's a light flickering down there."

Sturgeon hushed the others and joined Ashton. "A light?" She narrowed her eyes and confirmed Ashton's observation. "Where there's a light, there are likely people."

"You mean, like here?" Jack replied.

Sturgeon stared daggers his way. She motioned them toward her and tiptoed down the tunnel toward the light.

Carolyn and Feng Mian strode side by side toward the mass of people.

Roman had been right, there were dozens of men and women gathered in one of the largest chambers they'd yet encountered. There were a number of small wooden tables and benches, and the people milling around the room could not have looked like they belonged in the torch-lit tunnels any less.

Many of them wore suits. They were dust-coated, and the white shirts had stained brown collars and cuffs. Many of them had guns at their side, and a few of those roaming between the aisles of the crowd wore black jackets with the golden emblem of the dragon on them.

But that wasn't where Carolyn's and Feng Mian's eyes were drawn.

At the very back of the hall, they spied a pair of specters. These looked as though they had become spectral after at least a hundred years of rotting in the grave. While most specters' bodies kept their mortal appearance and still looked mostly human, these gazed over the crowd with furrowed brows, their skin flaky and lumpy. Their spectral auras were sepia rather than the usual bluish-white.

Carolyn and Feng Mian ducked to the side and out of sight of the specters. "What *are* they?" Carolyn asked. "I've never seen anything like that."

"Me either," Feng Mian replied. "I don't like the look of that."

"What do we do?" Carolyn asked, counting the heads in the room. She easily reached one hundred before she stopped counting.

"We find another way," Feng Mian whispered. "If we start an attack in here, the only possible outcome is our mortals get obliterated." He looked at the ceiling. "We also know how fragile these tunnels are. We have to approach with caution. I'm not sure how useful guns will be."

Carolyn sighed. "Why is it never easy?"

"Because easy doesn't make heroes," Feng Mian replied.

Jennie watched the group for a moment longer before she knew that action had to be taken.

They slunk back far enough down the tunnel that they wouldn't draw attention to themselves. She tapped her earpiece and tried to reach the others. "Update report, check in."

There was no reply. She hadn't expected one this far underground, with thick earth walls blocking the signals.

"What's the plan?" Baxter asked. "Jump down there and cut them off at the source?"

Jennie shook her head. "Not this time, Bax. We need all hands on deck for this one. We don't know what the Dreadnought is capable of, and judging by his display of power there, we'll need to bolster our numbers to take him down." Her mind went once more to the nausea she'd felt when attaching to the corrupt and couldn't imagine what it would feel like latching onto the primary source of that discomfort. "We need to go back and see what the others have found. With any luck, they haven't found themselves in too much trouble."

As they turned to leave, the tunnel echoed with a fit of the Dreadnought's rage. His voice shook the earth around them as he roared, "You will bow down to your new emperor and empress, or you and your followers will die!"

Chunks of dirt fell around them. Somewhere down a distant tunnel, the sounds of a cave-in came. Jennie listened until the dust settled, an idea coming to her. It would be risky, but dammit, it just might work.

CHAPTER SEVENTY

Agents from all sides waited patiently in the first chamber as Jennie and her team made their way back. A short while after arriving, they heard footsteps from one of the other tunnels, and Roman and his team emerged.

"Where's Sturgeon?" Jennie asked.

No one had seen her return. "Damn, we need her to come back," Jennie complained. She looked longingly down the tunnel they had disappeared into. "Don't tell me we'll have to arrange a rescue mission for them?"

"They'll be fine," Baxter replied. "Surely if they were in any trouble, we'd know."

Jennie understood his logic, but she still had her doubts. While they waited a little longer for them to return, she asked Roman what his group had discovered.

Jennie's eyebrows lifted as they described the mass of men and women at the end of their tunnel. Armed and dangerous, their force outnumbered Jennie's by the sounds of it. She allowed her mind to process their situation, even as Carolyn informed her of the spectral anomalies they had come across in the back of the chamber.

Jennie's face grew hard. "Ghouls?"

The word sent a wave of apprehension around the room. "What exactly are ghouls?" someone in the crowd of agents asked.

"Corrupt specters, risen from the dead." Jennie sighed. "It's been years since I've had to deal with those bastards. I haven't come across them since the great Zombie Revolt of 1902."

Baxter stared at her inquisitively. "Zombie revolt?"

"It's exactly what it sounds like," Jennie commented, providing no further explanation.

"But I thought that specters came out of their bodies immediately after death and had a choice between life as a specter or an end in the abyss," Carolyn asked. "That's the choice that was presented to me."

"And that's often the case," Jennie replied. "Although you of all people should know by now that it's not always that simple. Ghouls are specters who delayed their choice by remaining inside their bodies for tens, sometimes hundreds, of years. They think that they haven't made a choice, but really, they have. Some people can't face not following the way that they believed they would die and think that remaining inside their corpse while it rots away will be a proper end, little realizing that the degradation process affects the specter, too."

"Thus rise ghouls," Jennie stated. "Specters with corrupted energy that makes it more difficult for me to affect them, and for them to die. I've only ever exorcized a handful of ghouls in my lifetime, and even then, it was at a great cost."

Ula shook her head. "If there are more ghouls in there, that means they're under the Dreadnought's power. More than that, Sturgeon and the others might be in real danger alone in the tunnels."

"I thought you said the Dreadnought was an Akh?" Baxter questioned.

Jennie furrowed her brow and touched her chin. "*He* may be, but those who he has returned from the grave, they're something else entirely. To be fair, the Dreadnought may not be, either. I just don't know at this point."

Ula looked to Jennie. "Hello? Are we going in there after them or not?"

Jennie grew resolute. "Rescue party time. Bax, you're with me."

Baxter nodded.

"The rest of you, I've got a plan, and it's going to be a risky one. I need all of you to listen closely and obey to the letter. We've only got one chance to get this right. Otherwise, a *lot* of lives are going to be lost."

The agents listened closely as Jennie detailed the specifics of the plan. A few of them looked downcast but remained silent nonetheless. When Jennie was finished, she summoned Rogers to her side.

"There's an extra job I need you to do for me," Jennie whispered, making sure no one else could hear as the agents started filing out of the tunnels.

Rogers grinned. "Feels weird taking orders from you," he stated.

"Weird-bad?" Jennie asked.

"Actually, no," Rogers replied. "Weird-good."

Jennie grinned. "That's good news. Maybe when this is all over, we can discuss a closer partnership. Until then, here's what I need, and it's in relation to the remaining members of the Seven, who I'm ninety percent sure are in these tunnels with us."

Rogers nodded as Jennie spoke. When she was finished, he raised a hand in salute. "Consider it done, Rogue."

"Oh, come on," Jennie moaned. "After all this, you still can't call me Jennie?"

Rogers smirked. "Get this mess sorted out, and I'll call you whatever you want."

Jennie winked. "I'll take you up on that offer."

They separated and headed in different directions.

Sturgeon's eyes narrowed at the light down the tunnel. They had moved painfully slowly closer as the sounds of their enemies grew louder, and when she reached the lip of the shelf that looked over the inner room, her skin had broken out in gooseflesh.

There were dozens of specters, the likes of which she had never seen before. They stood in place, swaying like seaweed caught by a gentle current. Their skin was moldering and rotted as though they had recently risen from the grave.

Which, by all accounts, was a possibility she wouldn't discount.

Fuck, she thought, leaning as far as she dared to look below. She counted at least thirty of them but could make out more bodies disappearing in a tunnel off the main room.

I wonder if Jennie knows anything about this yet.

She controlled her breath, ensuring she remained quiet. She heard movement from Jack and Ruby behind her. Jack came up beside her and shot a glance at the strange specters.

He didn't try to hide his dismay. "What are they?" he mouthed, the color draining from his face.

Sturgeon shook her head.

Ruby, keen to get a look as well, stepped up to the lip and held back a gasp. She shrank away, worried that even the tiny exhalation might be enough to draw their attention when the cave magnified their noise.

Sturgeon waved for the others to back out of sight. One of the specters slowly turned their head toward the ledge.

Sturgeon's heart stopped when Jack's foot kicked a pebble, which rolled off the edge of the ledge and landed below with a gentle click.

The specters grumbled, aware of the disturbance.

Sturgeon commanded her team to remain still, painfully afraid they'd make more noise in hurrying their escape.

She wasn't sure how long they remained still, but after a beat, she braved a peek over the edge once more.

Two of the specters were gone.

Dammit. Sturgeon crept back and waved the others with her. They had to be as quiet as possible while working their way the hell out of there.

Jennie's heart thumped as she stalked the tunnels once more. There was trepidation in her step, knowing what at least two of them contained but not knowing what was down the third.

She and Baxter roamed in relative silence, following the trailing darkness until they came to a small pocket chamber with a stone tomb in the center.

Jennie sighed. "Well, this screws up my plan somewhat."

"Just what is your plan?" Baxter asked. "Speaking as someone who's boldly following you into the dark without question."

"Without question?" Jennie retorted. "You're asking a question right now."

Baxter stared at her.

Jennie chuckled. "We need to draw the enemy out. If we attack in the tunnels, we've got no hope of winning. These tunnels are unlike the ones in Alexandria, and there's not enough space to attack. More than that, they're spread out in separate places along the way. We have no clue what we're getting into, and any direct attack will likely cause the walls to collapse. If we can flush them out of the tunnels, we can battle them on our own terms."

Baxter nodded. "Okay, good plan. What about the tomb?"

Jennie sighed. "We need that out there with us. We don't know if the tomb will be the only way to trap the Dreadnought again. We can't bury it in here, or we'll be screwed."

Baxter narrowed his eyes and thought. The tomb was a weighty piece of stone, and it would take a number of people to shift it. He skirted its edge and tapped his chin. "We can use physics to our advantage, but we will need more bodies." He chewed his lip. "The only way we'll be able to do this is to bring some of our strongest backs and make a quick escape."

Jennie grinned at him.

"I thought that was coming," Baxter resigned. "Good luck finding them, Jennie. You can count on me to sort this out for you."

"Bring Roman," Jennie instructed. "He's as strong as three. Anyone else with an ounce of muscle can come back. The good news is that we know this route is empty." A sudden thought came to her. "But why? If this thing is so important, why would he abandon it without a guard?"

Baxter shrugged. "No idea, but if I move quickly, I can have people carrying this out in a jiffy."

Jennie cocked an eyebrow. "A jiffy?"

"That's a British term, right?" Baxter laughed. "I'm sure I've heard it somewhere."

Jennie grinned. "Chop-chop, Bax. We haven't got all bloody day."

Baxter smiled and dashed back the way they had come.

Jennie eyed the remaining tunnels, realizing that her choices to go or seek her missing comrades had annoyingly multiplied.

"How do moles live like this?" she mused. "Do they remember all their tunnels?" She closed her eyes, and a slight bubble of nausea found its way to her, its dry sickness sticking to her throat.

"They're nearby," she muttered, sensing the tunnel where the signal was strongest. "Knowing my luck, they're down there."

Jennie chose a tunnel and left the sarcophagus behind, her focus fixed on bringing her comrades back to the outside world.

***

Sturgeon crept along the passages, flinching at every scuffle that came from their feet. It was impossible to remain silent, but it was possible to remain quiet. Still, the more they hurried, the more they failed at both.

The way back was more confusing than the way forward, and the urgency that filled her also cost her her bearings. Every tunnel looked the same. More routes opened around her, and down those tunnels were more tunnels. Sturgeon continued in the direction she believed she should be heading, but it seemed as though they were taking a lot longer to get out than they had getting in. Since they were moving faster to get out, that shouldn't have been the case.

Sturgeon paused at a crossroads and studied each direction. All the tunnels were dark, only the faint light from the previous chamber providing any luminosity. Jack drew up beside her. "It's left."

Sturgeon shook her head. "That doesn't seem right."

Ruby scratched her head. "Right?"

Ashton pointed straight ahead. "That way."

Sturgeon felt a flush of frustration. As the leader of the expedition, it was on her to ensure the others were safe. She didn't need their input, she just needed quiet.

She waved her hands and shushed them. After a second, she took Ashton's suggestion. Out of all of them, Ashton seemed to have a better sense of direction. She hoped that he was right.

A few minutes later, they came to another crossroads. There was light leaking around the bend of one of the tunnels, and Sturgeon could see someone coming toward them. Backlit by the torchlight, it was hard to make out, but the figure looked familiar.

She took a few steps forward, then slumped her shoulders when a second figure appeared, then a third, all of them limping clumsily toward the group.

Sturgeon sighed. *Aw, shit.*

CHAPTER SEVENTY-ONE

<u>**Richmond, Virginia, USA**</u>

The sound of a scuffle hit Jennie's ears. She slowed her pace and kept to the wall, able to pick out figures ahead of her. That nauseated feeling in the pit of her stomach increased, and she nearly doubled over as a wave attacked her.

Maybe this is the ghost of all of my hangovers hitting me at once. I told Hendrick his formula wouldn't last forever.

She knew the truth, of course. The limping figures told her enough that this was no mere hangover. She crept forward, drawing on the spectral power cells to reduce her noise and provide her with some cover as she closed the gap on the ghouls ahead.

After a minute, the ghouls paused and tensed. Jennie could make out something else down the tunnel. Four figures who had also frozen and were staring at the ghouls.

Shit. It's them.

Jennie broke forward as the ghouls ran at them. The agents raised their weapons but were reluctant to use them in the tunnels, knowing any sharp noise might cause the walls to crumble around them.

Though they could see the threat, they could do nothing to halt it. Jennie doubled over and increased her pace, wanting to get it over with. Not only would the tunnels collapse, but they also risked alerting the others, and that was something she wasn't willing to do yet.

The agents sprinted away, looking over their shoulders as they did. Jennie wondered if Sturgeon was pinning her hopes on being able to find another way out of there. The ghouls groaned, the sound echoing down the tunnels, and Jennie knew she had to do the very thing she feared the most.

"Here goes nothing," she muttered.

She stretched out her tendrils of power and connected to one of the ghouls. The moment her power latched on, she gagged as the sickening corruption slithered through her veins. Her head was filled with visions of dirt and worms and rotting food. She focused on trying to see the light and pulled the ghoul toward her.

The ghoul fell on its ass and slid along the floor. When it reached Jennie, it snapped its neck sickeningly toward her. Jennie threw a haymaker to the ghoul's jaw and its eyes rolled back. A swift kick to its mid-section threw it back against the wall and caused it to lie still.

"One down." Jennie disconnected from the first ghoul and dry-heaved. The sudden influx of clean energy through her body was refreshing, but it only magnified the miasma she had just experienced. She was hesitant to chase the second ghoul but knew she had to do something.

She left the first ghoul behind. The agents had stopped midway down the next tunnel, having seen Jennie approach. The ghoul now advanced on the group, lumbering toward them with mismatched steps.

Jennie took a deep breath before latching onto the ghoul. This time, the effect was so overwhelming that she was forced to her knees. She tried to focus on pulling the ghoul toward her, but her vision went blurry, and she struggled to maintain her grip.

Come on, Jennie. Just a little bit more. You can do this.

She gritted her teeth and tugged the ghoul away from her comrades. Her *friends.*

The ghoul stumbled over its own feet and crashed on the floor in front of her. Though spectral, a fetid smell came from its skin. Jennie had to use every bit of reserve in her to punch this ghoul and incapacitate it.

A punch to the throat. Another to the cheek. A third to the temple.

The ghoul lay still, its eyes pure white. Jennie disconnected, and this time emptied the contents of her stomach. The others rushed to her and crowded around her, speaking quietly as they thanked her and tried to soothe her.

"That doesn't look like fun," Jack muttered. "First point of order when we get out of this tube: spectrally-imbued knives."

Jennie nodded and took deep, clean breaths.

Ruby continued, "And baseball bats, and riot shields, and switchblades, and swords."

"Speaking of which," Jack commented. "Where's the Holy Saber Whoosit?"

Jennie gasped in lungfuls of air, her forehead peppered with sweat. "At the manor. It is too unwieldy to carry it in spaces where I have to be nimble."

Jack nodded in understanding. "Would have been useful around now, wouldn't it?"

Jennie glared at him. "You think?"

They helped her up. After a minute, she was able to walk without heaving.

Jennie looked down at the ghoul. "Things are really taking a turn, aren't they?"

Sturgeon bit her lip. "If the Dreadnought is supplying the power to these guys, what's it going to be like if you latch onto the primary power source? Can you handle that much corruption?"

Jennie struggled to answer. The thought had crossed her mind. She supposed she wouldn't know until the moment came and she was called on to try.

"Come," she commanded, ignoring the question. "We need to get this party started, but the first priority is getting you guys the hell out of here."

They started down the tunnel, Jennie's sense of direction considerably better than the others. They passed the second ghoul and headed back toward the entry chamber.

A few minutes after they left, the two ghouls rose once more and stumbled back toward their master to raise the alarm.

The Dreadnought eyed the remaining three men through eyes that weren't his.

He reveled in their cowardice. They shuddered and trembled beneath his power. His promised queen had informed him that these were some of the most powerful men in New York City, yet he could smell the tang of urine emanating from their trousers.

Fear was the great equalizer. Under the oppressor's thumb, all became equal, ground down to nothing, no more threat than worms. He and his bride would use these new puppets to command their mortal army, and they would rise from these tunnels anew, ready to resume his work and dominate the sleepy city.

He grinned, although the smile didn't reach the lips of the woman he inhabited. He enjoyed her body, the powerful flexing of her muscles, and the sweet aroma of her skin. Out of all of his vessels, he had fit most comfortably inside of her, although he longed to be reunited with his own body and roam the world in the image God meant for him.

Jiao explained the deal to the trembling men, and they nodded eagerly. The man he had destroyed earlier had risen in his spectral form and was sitting sullenly beside them, a lot quieter than he had been before.

The great equalizer.

The Dreadnought relaxed in his chair, excitement buzzing inside him as Jiao—his Dragon bride—drew close to the end of her orders. It was about to begin. The great unity would ignite the massacre, and all would bow before—

The Dreadnought stiffened and sat up straight in his chair. His eyes widened as a tingling sensation ran down his spine. He was vaguely aware of Jiao speaking to him, asking questions he couldn't hear. His mind wasn't with them in the chamber at that moment. It was responding to the connection he shared with his former prison.

Someone was touching his sarcophagus. Someone was *moving* what was his. The curse that bound him to the stone left the threads of communication, and like a spider responding to the vibrations in its web, the Dreadnought rose from his seat in fury.

"They're here," he growled. "They're invading."

Jiao raised an eyebrow. "But how? How have they found us?"

The Dreadnought scanned the men in turn, his eyes locking onto Vincenzo's as if he could read the thoughts rattling around in his brain. "Did you lead them here?"

Vincenzo was able to get out a single syllable before the Dreadnought poured his being into him and ripped him open from the inside. When Vincenzo fell to the floor, he returned to the woman's shell and glared at Jiao, eyes blazing. "You said they'd aid our cause, not reveal us to our enemy."

For the first time since he had met her, Jiao cast a doubtful look at the floor. "I..."

The Dreadnought raised a hand. "Enough. We must move and quickly." He turned from the tunnels even as two of his ghouls limped into the chamber. "I know!" he roared before they could open their mouths.

He waved his hand and threw them both into the wall, where they collapsed and laid still.

Jennie was impressed to find that the chamber in which the tomb was located had been emptied. As they marched swiftly to the entrance, they caught up with Roman and his team of agents, who were struggling to lift the damn sarcophagus even though they had eight people working together to carry the thing.

Jennie gave them a hand, glancing over her shoulder as creeping dread spread inside her. They were running out of time and needed to get a move on.

When at last they'd dragged the tomb out of the tunnels, Jennie ensured everyone was clear before returning to the entrance. She spared a glance over her shoulder as she latched onto Baxter and recharged her power cells before diving back inside.

The moment she entered the tunnel, she knew that something was wrong.

CHAPTER SEVENTY-TWO

<u>Richmond, Virginia, USA</u>

Despite the quietness of the tunnels, Jennie couldn't shake off her feeling of unease. It was becoming a permanent chill creeping down the back of her neck and trailing her spine. Something was happening ahead, but she wasn't sure what.

It doesn't matter. Do what you need to do, and get the hell out of there.

Jennie took the tunnel that she had sent the conduits down, knowing that somewhere ahead lay the bulk of the enemy's army. A collected group of mortal thugs who were doggedly obedient to their masters.

She crept onward, caring a little less about the noise she made since it wouldn't matter soon. Soon the tunnels would be filled with sound.

The light came ahead. She ran toward it, turning the heads of the gathered mortals as she boldly entered the room. The crowd fell into silence as they tried to work out if what they were seeing was real.

"I know," Jennie announced. "Hard to take it in when you've got a celebrity in the house, eh? Stare at me all you want, I'm here to tell you one thing, and one thing only. You best get your arses in gear because this whole tunnel is about to collapse."

The silence continued as they stared at Jennie. She sighed and drew the Big Bitch. "I'm serious. Get your arses in gear and *go*. Before it's too late."

A man in a thousand-dollar suit encrusted with dirt stood up and cocked his head to the side. "You think we can't take you, bitch? We know about you. Our boss told us the stories." He spat on the floor. "Bunch of bullshit if you ask me."

The man beside him muttered, "Who is it?"

"That's that Rogue chick," he replied. "The ghost-tamer, or whatever it is she does." He leaned forward, a cocky expression on his face. "We don't believe the stories, sugar tits. Ain't no one can do what they say you can do. Now put your pretty gun away before we all blow you to a thousand pieces. We outnumber you a hundred to one."

Jennie didn't feel the need to correct him as the ghouls started leaking into the room, drawn by the disturbance. They significantly raised the number.

"You've got until the count of five to get your feet in motion," Jennie instructed. "Five…"

"Screw this!" the man cried. "Let's fucking take her."

He raised his pistol, but the man next to him knocked his hand away. A few men and women ducked out of his trajectory. "What are you doing? One shot will send this tunnel into collapse. You'll be doing her work for her."

"Four," Jennie continued.

The man furrowed his brow. "Fine." He threw the gun on the floor and ran for Jennie.

"Three," she stated.

There was a movement from behind, and Jennie knew that they were trying to gang up on her. Little did they know that they could not get their hands on her.

"Two." Jennie readied the Big Bitch.

The man dived at her. At that same moment, Jennie latched onto her power cells and became spectral. He lost his balance and faceplanted on the floor when she vanished.

Jennie reappeared five feet from where she had been and smirked. "One."

The man's eyes widened in alarm as Jennie aimed the Big Bitch at the ceiling. The men and women started to babble and run in a panic, stunned by what they had just seen. They crashed into each other, many of them filing toward the tunnels to get out of there.

Jennie had enough time to look toward the far tunnel, where a pair of figures stood in the shadows. Though she couldn't make out their features, she knew who they were: Jiao and the Dreadnought, ready to join the party.

"Go," Jennie finished.

She pulled the trigger. The bullet lodged into the ceiling above and sent chunks of dirt crashing into the tunnel. The sound reverberated around them, magnified in the chamber and tunnels. The ceiling shook and started falling inward, landing heavily on some of those less willing to accept what they had seen Jennie do, while the rest sprinted for the entrance.

The tunnel rained debris. Jennie looked again for the Dreadnought and found with alarm that he had gone. She had thought he would follow his men out of the tunnel, but that wasn't the case. He had dashed farther into the darkness.

Against her better instincts, Jennie gave chase, latching onto her power cells and sprinting against the tide of bodies. If the Dreadnought found another way out, they'd be back at square one. She needed to follow them and get them to where she wanted them to go.

The tunnels collapsed at a more rapid pace than Jennie had anticipated. Her immaterial body passed through falling boulders and earth as she ran. She finally found the tunnel and followed along its path, already feeling nauseated as she ran in the wake of the Dreadnought.

What about Jiao? she thought. *Wouldn't the Dreadnought want her to escape as well? Why would he lead her toward destruction?*

Jennie tried to keep her mind off the urge to vomit she was feeling as she ran. The tunnels twisted on her, squeezing like the digestive tract of some great monster and forcing her onward. She disconnected from her cells when she was far enough away that she felt safe to run as a mortal, realizing that she only had one cell of power left with her.

For emergencies.

Jennie followed the corrupt energy trace and took a sharp left. The tunnel floor was uneven. Up ahead, it appeared as though the tunnel had already been closed off from an earlier collapse. Jennie latched on to her cell, dashed through in spectral form, and then turned material on the other side.

It was quiet here. The blockade acted as a barricade from the crumbling of the tunnels. She was about to continue ahead when something caught her attention.

Someone was trapped under the boulders. Only her head and torso were clear and free from harm. Jennie's heart sank as she recognized the woman's face. The Dreadnought had abandoned her body when she had been caught and destroyed as he fled.

The woman groaned.

Jennie knelt beside her. "Ma'am?"

The woman didn't open her eyes. She tried to move her fingers, but when her final breath came, she lay still.

Jennie's anger grew. Another innocent to add to the list. An honorable woman killed, and for what? No other reason than unbridled destruction.

Jennie narrowed her eyes and continued her pursuit. The combined force of the Dreadnought and the Dragon had taken enough victims.

It was time for them to pay.

***

Roman, Rogers, Sturgeon, and Baxter stood side-by-side in the center of the quarry and waited.

Behind them, the SIA agents were waiting, guns poised and ready to take down any enemy who emerged from the tunnel. Baxter waited for Jennie to appear, narrowing his eyes to peer through the curtain of rain. She would be the beacon that would light the action. She was the mouse leading the cats out into the open.

The clouds roiled above them. Thunder rumbled nearby. The agents waited dutifully in silence for the order to act. One word from their commanding officer and the tunnel entrance would be hit with a hail of bullets.

Baxter only hoped it wouldn't come to that.

The rumble of something deep inside the cave burped out at them. Jennie had delivered the first shot, and the enemy was awakening. A few minutes later, they started pouring out into the quarry, blinking stupidly in the rain as the water soaked their clothing and stung their eyes. They couldn't believe what they were seeing as they stared at the mass gathering of agents pointing firearms their way.

Baxter looked in the crowd for Jennie but could not find her. He leaned toward Roman and muttered, "Where is she?"

Roman gave no response.

One after the other, the thugs filed out, their shirts turning see-through in the rain. With them were the ghouls, scattered amongst the crowd. Behind them, the great mound of dirt shook as the tunnels within collapsed.

Baxter's anxiety spiked. *Where the hell is Jennie?*

The two sides faced off, a clear dividing line drawn between them. The agents held their fire, ready to act if it came to it. They were more prepared. They had the enemy at a disadvantage; even they could see that. Still, tension permeated the quarry floor, the only sound the relentless rain.

An elderly man made his way to the front of the crowd. His eyes were almost lost in the folds of his face. He tracked down Rogers, Roman, and Sturgeon and shook his head dispiritedly. "You'll never win," he declared. "He's too powerful. He has abilities beyond anything you could imagine."

Rogers, Roman, Sturgeon, and Baxter looked at each other and smiled.

"Oh, I'm sure that's not true," Rogers returned.

There was a disruption from their side as someone muscled their way to the front. Cassie Ferriss had answered Rogers' call and stood beside the four. "Give it up, Sammy. It's over."

Sammy Garcia's face contorted in anger. "The traitor."

"I might be a traitor to the Seven, but I'm not a traitor to my country," Cassie bellowed. "I had enough of your politics, and I took an out. You need to break away from this darkness. You need to remember what you're in this for. The Dragon is losing her grip on the situation, and she's on the losing side. Is that where you want to be?"

Sammy struggled to reply, a whirlwind of emotions passing over his face. "You don't understand. He killed Vincenzo. He killed Dalton. Like they were *nothing*. He is the future."

Cassie's eyes widened as she was jarred by an impact.

She glanced down in disbelief. Blood blossomed from the hole in her chest. She lifted her fingers and dabbed the wound, looking at the blood on her fingers for a few seconds before the rain washed it away. "Why?"

Cassie collapsed into the mud and lay still.

There was a beat of charged silence before both sides started firing and the battle began.

Baxter ran straight at the closest ghoul, his wrench raised and his pistol already firing. The ghoul jerked back with each shot, then fell to the ground when the wrench smacked his skull.

Baxter readied himself for the next ghoul when a strong hand grabbed his wrist. Susannah tugged him out of the way of harm and toward the clear edge of the fight. "Forget them," she urged. "Don't take out the pawns when you need to kill the queen."

Baxter turned back to the crowd, then nodded and followed Susannah. They skirted the battle, cleared the path as a handful of ghouls blocked their way, and darted back into the tunnels, unable to recognize the interior after the collapse.

CHAPTER SEVENTY-THREE

<u>Richmond, Virginia, USA</u>

Every step closer brought Jennie more pain.

She was swimming in her nausea, swirling in the eddies of the Dreadnought's filth. If she'd thought that latching onto ghouls was bad, it was nothing compared to being in the presence of the vile creature.

What had Susannah done to him?

She slowed as she neared the end of a tunnel, her bearings lost. She had been running and focusing on not throwing up, and she'd had no energy to spare to keep her direction. She gasped for air, hoping each breath would bring her relief, but the opposite happened.

She was getting close, she knew that much. They were ahead of her in the tunnels. She could hear them arguing. Their shadows flickered in the light from an abandoned torch on the ground. They were fighting, the great dark shape of the Dreadnought in combat with Jiao. She screamed, the sound traveling to Jennie and disturbing the ceiling.

No more screaming. No more collapses.

Jennie clutched her stomach with both hands, hugging herself to try to ease the pain. She raised heavy feet as she pressed onward, hoping she could use this moment of distraction to get the drop on them both.

She peered around the corner and found Jiao and the Dreadnought facing off against each other. The Dreadnought's eyes flashed, his spectral body a gaseous cloud of darkness and corruption. He was taller than Jiao and towered over her, but he could not get what he was after.

"Yield your body to me," the Dreadnought barked. "You are *mine*."

"I belong to no one," Jiao returned, scowling. Her face looked nothing like the sweet angelic woman Jennie's comrades had rescued from the Dragon's tower. She held out her hand and her rings flashed, keeping the Dreadnought at bay. "You promised a partnership, yet what value have you added to this arrangement? None. I've got bands of followers in New York, the Seven were mine to command, and you've destroyed all chances of domination with your petty ego. Couldn't handle them arguing back, so you squashed them—"

"Like the bugs they are!" The Dreadnought glowered. "Now, give me your power and allow us to join in union. Together we can rule as one solid entity. A demon and a Dragon, combined to give us power like no other."

Jiao smirked. "You think I'm stupid enough to believe that? Do you really think I will fall to your whimsy like that bitch you left hollow and dead? No. Show me the way out of here and we are done. Our arrangement is off."

The Dreadnought's nostrils flared. "Then you are no more use to me."

He roared, the sound rocking the tunnels. Then he glanced upward and tore into the earthen ceiling above.

Jennie ran into the sight of Jiao, catching her gaze for the merest of moments before she latched onto the Dreadnought and became immaterial. She rode his coattails, driving through the mud and dirt, her body whipped from sight. Her stomach flipped over and she struggled to hold in her vomit. Everything around her went black, and she wondered then if she had made the biggest mistake of her life.

Kurt Rogers couldn't remember the last time he had felt so alive.

The two sides clashed, and he was in the center of the skirmish. The thug in front raised his weapon, but Rogers was too quick. Even with the rain dripping down his face, he was focused and his aim was true. The bullet found the center of his target's forehead, then exploded out the back and hit the man behind.

He skirted the fallen enemy and took another shot, hyperaware that in a few seconds, firearms would be useless. When the two crowds collided and close-range combat ensued, it would be too risky to fire aimlessly into the crowd.

His reflexes were fast, and he dodged a blow from a suited woman. He twisted around her arm and retaliated with a headbutt to her temple. Her eyes rolled and she wobbled sideways, receiving a second blow from an agent to his right.

A fist caught his shoulder, and he spun and hooked a right. Someone tried to grab his throat from behind, but he wedged his free hand between the crook of the guy's elbow and the flesh of his neck. With a quick twist, he doubled over and threw the man over him, finishing him off with a stomp to the face.

It was amazing how it had all stayed with him. Years of sitting in the office had done little to degrade his combat skills. Like a pianist remembering the finger work to his favorite concerto decades after he last played it, his muscle memory did the job for him. There was a gleam in his eyes, a gleeful smirk on his face. He didn't care about the bruises he received; it felt good to be back on the front line again.

Fighting for justice.

Sturgeon was tired, but the second wave of adrenaline pushed her on.

The rain made things more difficult. The wet ground was slippery, and they had to be careful to keep their footing. She was acutely aware of agents wrestling with enemies and falling into the mud around her. The rain was a relentless force, and she wasn't sure if the weather was working in their favor or not. She could only see in a ten-foot radius around her, which made the numbers of both good and bad feel endless.

The enemy fired a shot and caught the man in front of her in the back of the head. She jerked out of reach of his fist and he flopped forward, landing in the mud with a wet slap. She relieved him of his weapon and returned fire, knowing she wouldn't escape again so easily. It was easy to identify the person who'd fired the shot since he was lining up again for round two.

Sturgeon took aim, strafed left, then fired. The bullet flew into the man's open mouth and his head exploded. Sturgeon sensed the woman to her left about to strike and whipped around, using the butt of the gun as a bludgeon. She caught the woman on the nose but was unable to avoid her left hook.

The punch turned her face, but the woman was also knocked back. By the time Sturgeon came back around, the woman was nowhere to be seen. The mammoth figure of Roman was blocking the way, a trunk-like arm swinging to take out the advancing enemies.

"Thanks, big guy," Sturgeon stated.

Roman didn't bother to acknowledge her statement. He barreled into the crowd, wading through as though the enemy were ants.

Sturgeon blocked a punch and delivered an uppercut to a scrawny man, her mind still on Roman. At his height, he was an easy target. She only hoped the enemy wouldn't take advantage of that and fire when the opportunity presented itself.

The tunnels did not exist anymore. All that was left for Baxter and Susannah to follow was the debris left following the devastation.

There was a slight difference between the undisturbed packed earth and the collapsed tunnels. Pockets of air space gave some indication of where they were going, although it was tough since they could only see a foot in front of them.

"This way, I think," Baxter commented. "Was this the first chamber?"

Susannah remained close, holding his wrist as she determinedly drove forward. While Baxter second-guessed every turn, Susannah didn't look back once. The expression on her face was one of determination, and Baxter knew better than to argue with that level of focus.

The journey seemed to take forever. This far into the darkness and underground, Baxter wondered if Jennie was even alive. The farther they went, the more he expected to come across her body trapped under a rock. Or maybe she would be eviscerated by the Dreadnought's powers. He had seen what the Dreadnought could do to mortals. How he could inhabit them and destroy them from the inside. How easy would it be to...

Baxter pushed the traitorous thoughts away. *Jennie's* not *mortal. Jennie's a whole other breed.*

Still, he couldn't shake off that lingering sense of dread that she was already gone, either a victim to the Dreadnought or buried under rock. After all, her spectral power cells could only last so long, and he was almost certain she wouldn't be stupid enough to latch onto the Dreadnought.

Jennie opened her eyes and felt the world spinning around her. The sky was dark, the rain pelting her as if it held a grudge. While the water was somewhat soothing, her stomach felt as though someone had folded it into the shape of a crane.

She was lying in an inch-deep puddle of mud, her hearing muted by the filthy water. At some point on her journey to the surface, she had blacked out, unable to take the dizzying pain of holding onto the Dreadnought.

But now she was...where? On the surface? Miles from her friends?

She pushed herself uneasily to her feet and discovered she was in the center of a field. Deep grooves in the dirt told of the tractors and machines that cultivated the land. She couldn't see beyond the sheet of torrential rain. The only thing of note came in the form of the darkened figure sitting patiently on a large boulder six feet away from where she lay.

The Dreadnought.

In spectral form, the Dreadnought reflected no shimmer from the rain. He stared at her with ink-black eyes, his body a thick arrangement of dense gray smog. A dizzy spell came over Jennie just from looking at him, and the whole world rocked like a ship in stormy seas.

"You are powerful, yes?" the Dreadnought spoke in a neutral tone.

Jennie pushed herself uneasily to her feet. It took everything within her to stand up straight and fight her legs, which seemed determined to wobble beneath her. "I am."

The Dreadnought cocked his head, losing himself in his thoughts. "I've never met anyone like you, a person who can tread the thin line between life and death. I would be doing myself a disservice not to question whether someone with your talents would be interested in joining me." He grinned. "We could do great things together."

Jennie glanced at the ground beneath them. Somewhere down there, Jiao was trapped. A mortal lost in the tunnels beneath the earth, already in her grave. "I've seen what you do to your friends."

The Dreadnought's eyes were unblinking. "I don't have friends."

Lightning struck in the distance, the sky pulsing with white-hot light. Thunder crashed.

"You know, I think I'm going to have to take the alternative," Jennie replied. "Considering all the problems you've caused for this city."

That predatory grin returned. "What is that alternative?"

Jennie drew the Big Bitch. "I'm going to have to destroy you."

The Dreadnought lowered his head. "I thought you might say that. Very well. Have it your way."

In the blink of an eye, he attacked.

CHAPTER SEVENTY-FOUR

The gaseous cloud of corruption streamed toward Jennie. She had no time to think, no time to react. It flooded her vision and dived straight at her. One minute all she could see was gray; the next it was gone.

A beat of quiet passed; even the pummeling rain was muted. Then almighty pain came from inside Jennie.

She closed her eyes and fell to her knees. All she could see was the Dreadnought as he writhed inside her and wrestled for control. If the nausea she had felt before was dizzying, it was nothing to how she felt now. She had never experienced anything like this—a constant sickening swirl of pain as the world revolved around her.

She fought for control, sensing him doing things to her that she wouldn't have dreamed were possible. Her arm belonged to him, and it stretched out and wriggled its fingers, testing the flex of the muscles. The fingers on her other hand did the same shortly after, and with a growing sense of panic, Jennie realized he was winning.

He was taking control.

Jennie's mouth was a permanent O as she struggled to take in air. She turned inward and looked for the power inside her, focusing her attention on identifying what he was doing and looking for a way to fix it. To stop him.

One eye opened with no trace of white, only the permeating darkness of the Dreadnought. She fought for control of the other while staving off the urge to vomit. She was beyond that now. Her throat was dry and raspy, her stomach a bag of needles rocked and disturbed on the back of a pickup truck speeding down an uneven road.

Jennie gasped at the surge of power from the Dreadnought, and her vision went black.

She waited for a few seconds, afraid to move in case more pain came. When she opened her eyes, she was not in this world, but on a plane that was entirely white. She stood upright, staring at a projection of herself. The Dreadnought examined the fingers and legs of his new body, exploring and playing with Jennie's power.

She stood two feet behind him, frozen to the spot. She had never had an out-of-body experience and had wondered what it would be like. Not in a million years had she envisioned something like this.

"You have a gift," a voice called from somewhere in the room.

Jennie studied the Dreadnought, wondering if it was him, then sensed someone moving behind her. She pivoted on the spot and looked into the faces of two people she hadn't seen in years.

"Dad?" Jennie breathed.

Jennie's father smiled, his face creasing as he did. Beside him stood Jennie's mother, the pair of them wearing clothes of brilliant white, their auras serene.

Her father continued. "You have a gift, Genevieve. Something you have been blessed with since birth."

"We've always known you were special," her mother added. "We just didn't know how special." She reached forward and cupped Jennie's cheek in her hand. Her skin was soft. "You've done amazing things. More than we ever could have imagined. This is not where your journey has to end."

Jennie's brows knitted, her eyes shimmering with tears. "Isn't this the end? Isn't this death? Life beyond the abyss? The great white light so many people have spoken about throughout history? I mean…" She let out a small chuckle. "You're both here."

Her father looked at her mother in the way he used to when Jennie was a child and had said something both ignorant and adorable.

"We're here because we live inside you," her father replied. "Where do you think all your power is drawn from? You think we vanished without a trace and wouldn't watch you on your journey?"

Jennie's mouth fluttered open and closed. "How…"

"A story for another time." Her mother nodded toward the Dreadnought. "You know what you've got to do."

Jennie turned back to the Dreadnought, who was now moving in slow motion. One hand reached for the sky, the other flexed her fingers and slowly began to beat her chest.

"It's too much," Jennie managed at last. "It hurts. I can't…"

When she turned back to her parents, they were gone.

Jennie looked at the Dreadnought and took a steadying breath. She had never felt so violated, having someone block her from controlling her own body. She recovered, savoring the moments she had when the poison had been expelled from her body and she felt okay once more.

Soon that would fade, and she would enter one of the toughest battles she had ever faced.

Hendrick had given up on his glasses ages ago.

The rain created a never-ending veil of liquid over the lenses. Despite his persistent wiping, he couldn't fight off the downpour. His clothes were soaked and clung to his skin, and every footstep had been heavy since he'd climbed out of the cab and walked the remainder of the way out of the city.

He squinted down at the object in his hands. It didn't matter which way he thought he should go, this object would guide him. All he needed to focus on was the direction the tiny spectral fish was swimming as it pulled him onward toward the source of spectral power.

The rain beat down, an endless drone of sloshing liquid around him. On a few occasions his feet had caught in the muddy puddles around him, and he had lost one of his shoes along the way. A lone figure, shuffling through the curtain of rain, drawn by the instinctual sense that something was happening out there, and Jennie needed him.

Was he afraid to be walking into a potential war zone? Not really. Anything is survivable when you have a weapon to use.

And that weapon glowed neatly at his side.

From the moment Jennie latched onto the Dreadnought, her whole world rocked.

The white-washed world vanished in an instant, replaced with the reality that she was trapped inside her own body, and she had no control over it whatsoever. She felt like an invader in her own skin, a parasite or leech trying to wrestle control from a much stronger soul.

The Dreadnought's voice came from her lips. "I see you've grown bold. That should make victory all the sweeter."

A pulsing wave of nausea hit her, and in the absence of a physical mouth to throw up from, Jennie's head pounded with pain. Her skull felt fit to split, the Dreadnought's laughter echoing inside of her as though she were standing next to the speakers at the world's loudest concert.

Jennie gritted her spectral teeth and a growling roar came from her throat. It grew until she was screaming, an endless stream of rage coming from her mouth. She closed her eyes and explored the connection she held with the Dreadnought, unearthing years of darkness within his memory banks. She saw glimpses of his past, his treading across the city and burning everything in his path, the destruction of the townsfolk after he'd forced them to bow to him.

Her head echoed with a thousand poisonous sentiments, the evil thoughts and feelings that had stewed in his mind while he lay in the darkness. Jennie felt them all like a bubbling cauldron of pain. She sought the one she was after, the one weakness she knew the Dreadnought to have, and pushed it to the forefront of his mind.

Susannah opened the door to her house, surprise on her face. The Dreadnought offering a place by his side as he knelt before her and asked for her hand.

The rejection from Susannah. The toxic pain that flooded his body, and the fear as she cast her spell, flicking her potion his way before closing her eyes and freezing him on the spot, stilling his heart until his mind was starved of oxygen.

Susannah rapidly dragging his body to the basement and hurling it into the tomb, sealing the lid with great effort and plunging him into eternal darkness.

The Dreadnought fell to his knees, for the first time allowing Jennie to feel something inside her body. She used this moment of distraction to wrestle back one arm, then the other. It was working! She forced open one eye and wasn't sure if what she was seeing was a hallucination.

Her eye slammed shut, and the Dreadnought growled within her. "No. This vessel is mine!"

Jennie fought to regain her sight once more, and as the voices came to her, she knew that she had not been hallucinating.

"Go!" Baxter shouted from somewhere in the darkness she couldn't break.

"Richard Haybourne…" Susannah's voice was soft. The Dreadnought opened his eyes, and Jennie was allowed a glance at the spectral woman kneeling before them.

A flurry of emotion raced through Haybourne, and Jennie felt all of it. A mixture of confusion, hatred, and love overwhelmed him, and he rooted himself to the spot as he stared into Susannah's eyes.

"It's been so long," he muttered.

Susannah nodded, reached out a hand to his cheek. He fell into her palm like a dog stroked by its owner. Susannah smiled softly.

"You've been causing trouble," she whispered.

The Dreadnought nodded. "It's all for you, my love. I never thought I'd see you again." Suddenly, his demeanor changed as the realization of what had happened during their last encounter sprang to the foreground of his mind. "You killed me."

"I helped you," Susannah corrected. "And I'm here to do so again. Jennie, now."

Jennie moved her focus from the Dreadnought to Susannah, a wave of clean energy spiking through her. Where before she had felt like she was trying to breathe smoke, now she was rejuvenated and refreshed. She was still fighting the affliction of being so close to the Dreadnought's corruption, but now pure power surged through her.

Susannah's power.

Jennie wrapped her arms around the spectral form of the Dreadnought and held on tight. She channeled Susannah's healing power through her own body and felt it seeping into the very fiber of the Dreadnought's being. Her mortal body jerked and spasmed as the fight raged within, and the Dreadnought began to scream and protest, shaking in an effort to rid himself of Jennie.

Jennie shifted her attention to her body, letting the Dreadnought fight his battle against the white light cleansing him. She took control of her arms, then her legs, and with a final surge of effort, she leaped into her material body and ejected the Dreadnought.

The sudden release forced Jennie to her hands and knees. Mud splashed onto her clothes, and a tingling sensation was left in the aftermath of what had just happened.

She pushed herself uncertainly to her feet, her energy expended, and spun to face the Dreadnought.

He was fighting with himself. White strains of the healing power Jennie had cast appeared on his skin like an infection trying to multiply and grow and swallow him whole. He fought it off, the white fading in and out of existence until at last there was no more left.

The Dreadnought fixed his eyes on Jennie. "You…"

Jennie glanced beyond the Dreadnought to where a figure was emerging through the rain, appearing like a lighthouse through the fog. She recognized that squat limp, the short stature, the beady eyes.

The Dreadnought paid no attention, thinking that Jennie was staring at him. He rose to his feet and lumbered toward her, each step an effort. Baxter and Susannah retreated several steps, but Jennie remained where she stood.

"Duck," she warned.

The Dreadnought ducked in time to avoid the sword spinning toward him. It missed him by a hair's breadth, eliciting a raucous laugh from the specter. "You missed."

Jennie grinned when she caught the handle of the saber in her palm. She shook her head. "No. He didn't."

The Dreadnought had just enough time to scream in fury as Jennie plunged the Saber of Holy Divinity into the center of his gaseous stomach. The moment the blade connected with his matter, white light exploded and burned their eyes.

The Dreadnought clutched his stomach, but it was pointless; the blade was doing its work, and there was nothing left to do but watch it happen.

The light beamed brightly, illuminating the field around them for the merest of moments before it faded into nothing.

When Jennie was able to see clearly again, the Dreadnought was gone.

All that was left was the rain.

Susannah moved to stand beside Jennie. "Are you sure he's not coming back?"

Jennie and Baxter exchanged glances and laughed.

A moment later, she threw up.

CHAPTER SEVENTY-FIVE

<u>Richmond, Virginia, USA</u>

"What about Jiao?" Baxter asked as they ran back toward the fight.

"She'll be fine for a while," Jennie replied, picturing the petite woman stuck in the tunnels. Where could she go? There was no way out.

By the time they got back to the skirmish, the fight was dying down. A few agents remained engaged in detaining the enemy, but most were lying in the mud, unconscious or exhausted.

Jennie latched onto Baxter and jumped over the edge of the quarry and into the center of the battle. She held the sword in her hand, its blade pulsing with a faint glow of energy. She was pleased to see that her comrades were still fighting.

Ula, Triton, Rhone, Rogers, Sturgeon, and the rest of the mortals were doing their piece. Sandra, Feng Mian, and Carolyn fought the remaining ghouls.

Jennie turned as a ghoul grabbed her ankle. The specter was lying in the mud, its body in pieces. Jennie sighed and drove the saber into its back.

The flash of blinding light was enough to draw the attention of everyone else in the quarry. Jennie furrowed her brow and raised her voice. "The Dreadnought is dead, and your Dragon has been captured. The time to surrender is now. No more lives need be lost this night."

There was a moment of hesitation. Agents glared at the enemy, and the enemy glared at the agents. Some still had hold of each other, and it looked as though they would not obey.

Sammy Garcia was the first one to throw down his weapon. He tossed his pistol to the mud and fell to his knees. One by one, his men, and the men of the Seven followed suit.

Jennie nodded at Rogers and Sturgeon, who set their men to arresting those who remained conscious.

Baxter stood beside Jennie as she watched the agents clear up the mess. She had grown cold, her skin prickling from the constant exposure to the elements. "Is it time to get Jiao, now?"

Jennie examined the scene for a few moments before finally feeling satisfied. She could just about make out Hendrick sitting at the lip of the quarry, his legs hanging over the edge, reminding Jennie that she would need some extra help to get Jiao free from her tomb.

Jennie crossed over to the edge of the quarry and found Tanya holding Sandra tightly. Apparently, while the fight had ensued, Sandra had insisted that Tanya hide out of sight while she helped the other specters with the ghouls.

"I don't know how you dealt with them," Sandra explained. "The ghouls were filthy and dirty. They hurt to touch."

Jennie smiled in agreement and asked Sandra to accompany her. It took some convincing of Tanya on Jennie's part. Tanya watched Sandra leave like a mother watching her baby go to college. Maybe she was finally getting used to the idea that as a specter, Sandra could handle herself and wasn't the innocent child she seemed on the surface.

"Where are we going?" Sandra asked.

"Digging," Jennie replied. She wrapped an arm around Sandra's shoulder and walked into the earthen walls of the quarry.

"I don't wanna." Sandra folded her arms and stared daggers at Jiao.

The tunnel was smaller than Jennie remembered. Jiao had been sitting with her back against the wall when they melted through and appeared before her. She had been so startled she pressed herself against the wall as though it would swallow her up and hide her.

Jiao returned Sandra's stare. "To tell you the truth, I'm not thrilled about this either." She threw her hand in front of her and her rings flashed.

There was a slight change in Sandra's demeanor, her shoulders slumping, and a goofy smile on her face before Jennie drew the sword and touched it to the skin on Jiao's wrist. "You try, you die. Simple as that."

Jiao growled, then lowered her hand. Jennie held the sword on her and crouched, relieving Jiao of her three gold rings.

Jennie weighed them in her hand, surprised by how heavy they were. "What are these?"

"Family heirlooms," Jiao replied.

"Fine. Keep your secrets." Jennie pocketed the rings. "We have ways of making you talk, but maybe our priority should be getting you out of here." She looked down at Sandra. "Ready?"

Sandra folded her arms.

Jennie looked over the top of her glasses and gave the specter a stern smile. "Sandra, don't make me tell your mother."

Sandra rolled her eyes. "Fine." She grabbed Jiao's wrist and turned spectral. Then she took a few steps toward the earthen walls, turned her face upward, and started climbing to the surface.

Jennie waited until they were gone before she examined the three rings in her pocket. They each bore an insignia on their golden faces. One showed a picture of a dragon—the same dragon Jiao had stitched onto her gown. Another showed an image of a crown, and the third one had a symbol she couldn't quite make out but was almost certain that she had seen it somewhere before.

Jennie shrugged and pocketed the rings. Without wasting any more time, she activated her power cells to turn spectral and left the tunnels behind.

The rainstorm had masked almost the entirety of the event. The storm had been the worst the city had seen in a decade. The rain came down so hard that most civilians remained indoors, and those who ventured outside were brave weather people and the emergency services.

The streets were flooded, a few homes had valuables water-soaked and ruined. A single lightning strike had hit a transformer and blown it, leaving an entire quarter of the city without power.

All told, there were no eyes on the quarry that night. The only sign that anything had happened was the procession of vehicles that carted away those who had been arrested. The convoy skirted the city's edge and found their way toward the King's Manor. Detainees were held in cells on the second floor until such a time that the weather abated and they could be shipped to Washington.

That night, members of the King's Court, the SIS, the SIA, the Spectral Plane, and even the few remaining brave souls of the GOA celebrated in the isolated manor. The rooms were full, the windows steamed from the heat and mixture of rain still soaking people's clothes, and the music was loud.

Jennie worked the bar, enjoying the feeling of peace. For the first time since the spectral realm had come into the knowledge of the United States federal government, all sides were at peace with one another. Differences were resolved, agents let loose and allowed to celebrate a job well done.

Even she knew that it wouldn't last long. There was one thing she needed to do, and it was certain to ruffle some feathers. While she shook the metallic shakers and beamed at the crowded room, she was counting down the seconds toward the next stage of her journey.

A stage that was necessary but tough.

CHAPTER SEVENTY-SIX

The lights were out, clothing the house in darkness. Jennie padded along the corridor and down the stairs, hunting through the manor's endless corridors for the person she wanted to talk to more than anything else in the world.

She wasn't sure why she wanted to speak to her so badly. There was a feeling in her gut that wouldn't settle. To be fair, since Jennie had latched onto the Dreadnought, she had struggled to shift the nauseated feeling deep within her. She felt as if she had just come off a rollercoaster all the time.

The second floor was nearly silent. On the floor below, there were still some partygoers, but the music had been turned down. Jennie found the holding cell and opened the slit in the door.

"Mind if I join you?" she asked.

Jiao shrugged. "It's your house."

Jennie unlocked the door and let herself in.

Jiao remained sitting on her bed, her knees tucked to her chest and her head resting against the wall.

"Thought you'd be asleep," Jennie remarked.

Jiao fixed her with a neutral stare. "No, you didn't. You wouldn't have come if you had."

Jennie supposed that was true. She took a seat against the opposite wall. "Why did you do it?"

Her question hung in the air, unanswered for a few minutes. Eventually, Jiao lowered her legs and crossed them beneath her. Her face was earnest, although Jennie had believed her before and had been proven wrong.

"It's in my blood," Jiao answered. "My family stretches back centuries, each one awaiting their turn in line for the throne. I cannot reject the call. It is a part of my very fabric. You of all people should understand that."

Jennie raised an eyebrow.

"Oh, come on," Jiao continued. "You're telling me that you don't know the plight of the Dragon? That innate desire to rise to the top and be crowned the victor?"

She leaned forward. "Jennie, you're already engaged in a battle of your own. You may not entirely see it, but all of this," she indicated the manor around them, "Is your castle, and you are fighting for dominance. We want the same things, we just approach them in different ways."

"I'm not in a battle with the forces of good," Jennie replied sharply. They quieted as someone walked down the corridor and past the cell.

Jiao grinned. "Oh, but you are. You may think that the path you're treading down is going to bring peace, but whether you feel you're fighting for good or bad, there'll always be someone gunning for your seat. Power corrupts, even on the side of justice, and it's obvious that one day your biggest battle will come, and you'll be forced to make decisions you've never thought to make."

Jennie shook her head. "No."

Yet, although she denied it, she didn't entirely believe it. No matter what level of Justice she had played at, there had always been some kind of battle. When working for the queen, there were those who were jealous of her, who tried to bring her down while claiming to be on the side of "good." Now she was in the US, and the SIA was battling to become the dominant organization that dealt with spectral forces. That was Jennie's goal as well.

"It doesn't matter what strategy you formulate," Jiao continued as if reading her thoughts. "The end result is the same. Others have to bow out to allow you to take your rightful place as ruler."

"We're not a dictatorship, we're a democracy," Jennie retorted.

Jiao shuffled toward the edge of the bed and sat down, her brow furrowed, eyes dark. "The choice you are about to make is going to aggravate people on all sides. What you are thinking about is poaching. Stealing. Let me ask you: is that moral?"

Jennie lowered her eyes to the floor. Her head was already clouded with the oncoming conversation she was going to have, only, the difference between hers and Jiao's way of thinking, is that Jennie wasn't going to *steal*. She was going to *ask*. She was going to *offer*. Her perfect world respected free choice, and that was what she would give them.

The other key players may not see it that way.

Jennie looked at Jiao in earnest. "You're a great liar, you know that?"

Jiao shrugged and turned away. "A lifetime of lessons taught me how to be." She was silent a moment. "You're truly special, Jennie. Maybe one day when I'm free, you'll find a place for me by your side. I have powerful connections, I can help you. We can rule together."

This elicited a laugh from Jennie. She clutched her stomach and tried to contain it, aware that she didn't want others to know where she was. "You're kidding, right? You think I'd ever trust you again?"

Jiao grinned. "It was worth a shot."

Jennie climbed to her feet. "Well, this was a pleasure."

"Your sarcasm is unwarranted," Jiao replied. "And give me back my rings."

"Tell me what they do." Jennie's face straightened.

Jiao turned away and laid down. "No."

Jennie exited the cell and didn't look back.

Jennie paused outside her bedroom door. She could hear the others inside, chattering. She placed her hand flat on the door and took a deep breath, preparing herself for what came next.

"That's not the Jennie you let the world see," Baxter whispered, appearing at her side.

Jennie looked up and down the corridor. "How did you sneak up on me?"

Baxter nodded over his shoulder. "I'm in the room down the hall. You think I wouldn't know when you returned. How come I wasn't invited to your party?"

"You knew I was here? You were in your room," Jennie questioned.

Baxter smirked. "After all that time you've spent latching onto me, I'm starting to sense when *you're* nearby. Didn't think you could spend this much time with someone and not grow some kind of bond, did you?"

Jennie smiled. "Well, if there's anyone I'm happy to see right now, it's you."

Baxter returned the smile, then cocked his head at the solemn expression on Jennie's face. "What's eating you?"

Jennie frowned. "I want to protect people, and for that I need help. The spectral world is still a mystery for most mortals, and I need experts." Her eyes flickered to the door. "I need the best."

Baxter nodded in understanding. "You need to employ mortal experts in the field of spectral relations, but you're worried about upsetting the other key players in the game? Pissing the queen off? Going against your agreement?"

Jennie raised a finger. "The agreement didn't state that our agents couldn't switch teams."

Baxter chuckled. "There's a reason I chose technology over politics. I don't envy you, Genevieve King. You're playing the impossible game, and no matter how you play it, it's going to piss people off. The real question is, are you playing it for the side of good?"

Jennie chewed her lip. For years she had avoided this moment, knowing that it was easy to keep her head down and stay quiet. But now, things were accelerating at an alarming rate, and the manor she had purchased as a base of operations was going to need the world's best in order to achieve the vision she saw in her mind.

She didn't belong to the federal government, she didn't belong to the Paranormal Court. Jennie's mission was to remain a neutral force that could support any and all bodies that dealt with spectral relations and problems. She would learn from the Paranormal Court, she would learn from the SIS, she would learn from the SIA.

She had created the King's Court, and they would be a force to be reckoned with. Jennie had Justice on her side, and that was the only thing that mattered.

"Jennie?" Baxter nudged, a concerned expression on his face. "Well?"

Jennie took a deep breath and gave a resolute nod. "Yes, Bax. I'm playing on the side of good."

She pushed open the door and entered, looking into the faces of Rogers, Sturgeon, Jack, Ruby, and a host of other agents she had hand-selected from the previous operation. At the back of the room, Roman and Julia sat sharing the half-eaten remains of a steaming calzone.

Jennie clapped her hands and addressed the rooms. "Thank you for joining me, everyone. I've got an important question for you all." She grinned at Baxter. "Shall we begin?"

The End

AUTHOR NOTES MICHAEL ANDERLE
MAY 22, 2020

Hello! I appreciate you making it all the way to the back of the book, and here to these author notes before you head on to the next fantastically fun series in your future.

If you have enjoyed the drinks (or the idea of the drinks with Rogue) in this series then we do have a fun book coming that I've done with Dan Willcocks related to Rogue and her stories about drinking concoctions.

The funny thing is that I have never personally been drunk. The reason isn't what you might think, although there might be a little of it, but rather I really hate the flavor of alcohol. So, when I was working my way up post parents and living the dream of a late teenager I never found any drinks worth drinking.

For me, alcohol tasted horrible.

Coke was where it was at, why add additional horrible flavors just to become stupid? It didn't make any sense to me at 18 and while I understand it at 50...plus... It is very rare that I have anything with alcohol.

Still, 30 years later, because of the taste.

But, when I conceived of this character, I thought about a person who was world-weary at one point and (unlike today) she was a party animal from way back. Would she have some stories to tell? Would she have known famous people and been a part of famous (or infamous) parties in the past?

Would she have partied enough to make the church blush?

Then, Prince's song Party Like It's 1999 came to mind and that sealed the deal. Our protagonist (brought to life by the amazing artist Mihaela who lives in Romania) was complete.

I hope you have enjoyed Rogues story, and seen a bit of a different side of history. Who said that history was written by the winners? As a fiction writer, we get to change history all of the time!

Ad Aeternitatem,

Michael Anderle

CONNECT WITH THE AUTHOR

Connect with Michael Anderle and sign up for his email list here:

Website: http://lmbpn.com

Email List: http://lmbpn.com/email/

Facebook:
www.facebook.com/TheKurtherianGambitBooks